Khushwant Singh was born in 1915 in Hadali, Punjab. He was educ...
Government College, Lahore and at King's College and the Inner Temple in London. He practised at the Lahore High Court for several years before joining the Indian Ministry of External Affairs in 1947. He was sent on diplomatic postings to Canada and London and later went to Paris with UNESCO.

He began a distinguished career as a journalist with All India Radio in 1951. Since then he has been founder-editor of *Yojna* (1951-53), editor of the *Illustrated Weekly of India* (1969-79), editor of the *National Herald* (1978-79), and the editor of the *Hindustan Times* (1980-83). Today he is India's best-known columnist and journalist.

Khushwant Singh has also had an extremely successful career as a writer. Among the works published are a classic two-volume history of the Sikhs, several novels—including *Train to Pakistan*, which won the Grove Press Award for the best work of fiction in 1954, *I Shall Not Hear the Nightingale* and *Delhi*—and a number of translated works and non-fiction books on Delhi, nature and current affairs. His latest novel, *The Company of Women*, has been published by Penguin Books.

Khushwant Singh was a Member of Parliament from 1980 to 1986. Among other honours he was awarded the Padma Bhushan in 1974 by the President of India (he returned the decoration in 1984 in protest against the Union Government's siege of the Golden Temple, Amritsar).

Books by the same author

Fiction
Mark of Vishnu
Train to Pakistan
I Shall Not Hear the Nightingale
Many Moods and Many Faces

Non-Fiction
History of the Sikhs: Two Volumes
Ranjit Singh: Maharaja of the Punjab
Fall of the Sikh Kingdom
Indira Gandhi Returns
Nature Watch

Translations
Umrao Jan Ada—Courtesan of Lucknow
The Skeleton
Land of the Five Rivers
Iqbal's Dialogue with Allah

Essays
Khushwant Singh's India
Editor's Page

Khushwant Singh

The Collected Novels

Train to Pakistan
I Shall Not Hear the Nightingale
Delhi

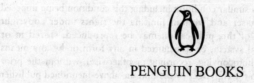

PENGUIN BOOKS

PENGUIN BOOKS

Published by the Penguin Group

Penguin Books India Pvt Ltd, 11 Community Centre, Panchsheel Park, New Delhi 110 017, India

Penguin Group (USA) Inc., 375 Hudson Street, New York, New York 10014, USA

Penguin Group (Canada), 90 Eglinton Avenue East, Suite 700, Toronto, Ontario, M4P 2Y3, Canada (a division of Pearson Penguin Canada Inc.)

Penguin Books Ltd, 80 Strand, London WC2R 0RL, England

Penguin Ireland, 25 St Stephen's Green, Dublin 2, Ireland (a division of Penguin Books Ltd)

Penguin Group (Australia), 250 Camberwell Road, Camberwell, Victoria 3124, Australia (a division of Pearson Australia Group Pty Ltd)

Penguin Group (NZ), cnr Airborne and Rosedale Roads, Albany, Auckland 1310, New Zealand (a division of Pearson New Zealand Ltd)

Penguin Group (South Africa) (Pty) Ltd, 24 Sturdee Avenue, Rosebank, Johannesburg 2196, South Africa

Penguin Books Ltd, Registered Offices: 80 Strand, London WC2R 0RL, England

First published in Viking by Penguin Books India 1996
Pubilshed in Penguin Books 1999

Train to Pakistan and *I Shall Not Hear the Nightingale* copyright © Ravi Dayal Publisher
Delhi copyright © Khushwant Singh
This omnibus edition copyright © Penguin Books India 1996, 1999

Typeset in Palatino by Digital Technologies and Printing Solutions, New Delhi
Printed at Baba Barkhanath Printers, New Delhi

Contents

Introduction   vii

Train to Pakistan   1

I Shall Not Hear the Nightingale   159

Delhi   361

Introduction

I had written a lot of short stories before I embarked on writing my first novel *Mano Majra*, better known by its later title, *Train to Pakistan*. I had no idea how one wrote a novel. I did not think I had the stamina to write one. But I did have the theme. I had lived through the civil strife that engulfed the whole of northern India. Almost every other day of the spring to summer of 1947, we heard stories of massacres of Sikhs and Hindus in the villages of the Northwest Frontier Province and Rawalpindi and Campbellpur districts; and of thousands of refugees trekking eastwards to areas where Hindus and Sikhs were in preponderance. When communal violence broke out in Lahore there was hardly a night when we were not woken up by the sounds of gunfire and mobs yelling: *Allah-o-Akbar* from the one side and *Har Har Mahadev* and *Sat Sri Akal* from the other. The spreading communal violence did not affect our small circle of friends: Muslims, Hindus, Sikhs and Christians continued to meet as usual and enjoy their sundowners. Of course we developed a sense of guilt. There was so much violence and wickedness going on around us and we did nothing about it except talk and drown our consciences in drink. It was after the Partition of the country was over, after ten million people had been rendered homeless and one million slain, that I felt I had to purge myself of the guilt I bore by writing about it.

At the time the novel was taking nebulous shape in my mind, I was in London. I decided to throw up my job and try to live by writing. I took myself off to the Italian lakes to put my ideas on paper. I chose the location for my novel, a hamlet along the river Sutlej. I chose models on which I would base my characters. In the initial draft I picked three, representing the trinity of Hindu gods: Brahma the Creator, Vishnu the Preserver and Shiva the Destroyer. The characters of my novels would be a poor farmer symbolizing the Creator; a magistrate whose duty was to maintain peace in this district as the Preserver; a communist as the Destroyer. However, I soon realized that every human being has all the three aspects of the trinity in him in different proportions.

When I actually started writing the novel, I was in Bhopal living alone in a large bungalow overlooking the lake. I made a synopsis of all the chapters before getting down to writing. It was when I started writing the chapters that I discovered, to my dismay, that instead of my dictating to my characters how they should behave and what they should say in a particular situation, they began to evolve independent personalities of their own and dictate their actions and speeches to me. Most writers agree that they have had similar experiences of characters created by them. However, I persisted as best as I could and finished the draft of my novel. I sent it as an entry to the Grove Press competition for the best work of fiction from India. An American friend, Mrs Tatty Bell, wife of a British diplomat, who typed the manuscript for me told me bluntly one day: 'It's no good. It won't get you anywhere.' A few months later, when I was with UNESCO in Paris, came an announcement that *Mano Majra* had won the award. It was published under this title in the United States and the Commonwealth rights were sold to Chatto and Windus of London. It was my hunch that if the title was changed to *Train to Pakistan*, it would sell better. And so it did. It was published in most European and Indian languages. It has been reprinted over thirty times. And goes on selling.

The success of *Train to Pakistan* emboldened me to try my hand at a second novel. All said and done, *Train to Pakistan* was more a documentary than a novel. This time it would be a simple story of a close-knit family divided by conflicting political loyalties. I chose to set it around the time when the 'Quit India' movement was launched by Mahatma Gandhi during World War II. The main characters were the father who after years of loyal service to the British Raj, expected to be honoured with a title in the King's Birthday Honours list and his young son who, undetected by anyone in the family, had joined a band of terrorists to disrupt arms supplies traffic on road and rail, and perhaps kill an Englishman or two. The story was built around my own family. I located it in Amritsar. This too was published in the States, England and India. I gave it the title (I have a fetish for giving titles to my books after I have written the last word) *I Shall Not Hear the Nightingale*. I think it is a better novel than *Train to Pakistan*. Not many people agree with me. It did not do as well as my first novel. Now you have the two together. I leave the judgement to you.

My third novel, *Delhi*, had a prolonged gestation. The idea of telling the story of my city, in which I had spent most of my life, came after I had read Ivo Andric's *The Bridge on the Drina*, which tells the story of Yugoslavia through events that occurred on a bridge. (Andric won the Nobel prize for Literature.) First I read all I could find of contemporary accounts of different periods: *Prithvi Raj Raso* for the Rajput rule in India, the life of Hazrat Nizamuddin and the writings of Amir Khusro for the Sultanate, Taimur's memoirs, volumes on the life of Emperor Aurangzeb, the poet Mir Taqi Meer, of Delhi devastated by Ahmad Shah Abdali, the later Mughals and the trial of the last Emperor, Bahadur Shah Zafar. For the British period, I relied largely on my ancestors; my father and grandfather had taken the lion's share in the construction of New Delhi. Likewise for the impact of Partition and the assassination of Mahatma Gandhi. I examined Pyare Lal's documentation of the last day of the Mahatma. The final chapter, the murder of Mrs Gandhi and the massacre of Sikhs that followed, were deeply imprinted in my mind. The daunting task was to string these episodes together and make them read like one continuous story. Over twenty years I tried many methods of linkage and admitted failure to find a satisfactory one. At one stage, I decided to give up the project. I let my colleague, David Davidar, have a look at it. He suggested inserting a few more chapter links. I did so. Even so I was not happy with the final product. However, three editions of the novel sold out before the first copy was available in the bookstores. Despite being panned by the literary critics, it remained at the top of best-seller lists for some months. There is no accounting for the tastes of readers!

New Delhi   *Khushwant Singh*
October 1995

Train to Pakistan

For My Daughter
Mala

Dacoity

The summer of 1947 was not like other Indian summers. Even the weather had a different feel in India that year. It was hotter than usual, and drier and dustier. And the summer was longer. No one could remember when the monsoon had been so late. For weeks, the sparse clouds cast only shadows. There was no rain. People began to say that God was punishing them for their sins.

Some of them had good reason to feel that they had sinned. The summer before, communal riots, precipitated by reports of the proposed division of the country into a Hindu India and a Muslim Pakistan, had broken out in Calcutta, and within a few months the death toll had mounted to several thousand. Muslims said the Hindus had planned and started the killing. According to the Hindus, the Muslims were to blame. The fact is, both sides killed. Both shot and stabbed and speared and clubbed. Both tortured. Both raped. From Calcutta, the riots spread north and east and west: To Noakhali in East Bengal, where Muslims massacred Hindus; to Bihar, where Hindus massacred Muslims. Mullahs roamed the Punjab and the Frontier Province with boxes of human skulls said to be those of Muslims killed in Bihar. Hundreds of thousands of Hindus and Sikhs who had lived for centuries on the Northwest Frontier abandoned their homes and fled toward the protection of the predominantly Sikh and Hindu communities in the east. They travelled on foot, in bullock carts, crammed into lorries, clinging to the sides and roofs of trains. Along the way—at fords, at crossroads, at railroad stations—they collided with panicky swarms of Muslims fleeing to safety in the west. The riots had become a rout. By the summer of 1947, when the creation of the new state of Pakistan was formally announced, ten million people—Muslims and Hindus and Sikhs—were in flight. By the time the monsoon broke, almost a million of them were dead, and all of northern India was in arms, in terror, or in hiding. The only remaining oases of peace were a scatter of little villages lost in the remote reaches of the frontier. One of these villages was Mano Majra.

Mano Majra is a tiny place. It has only three brick buildings, one of which is the home of the moneylender Lala Ram Lal. The other two are the Sikh temple and the mosque. The three brick buildings enclose a triangular common with a large peepul tree in the middle. The rest of the village is a cluster of flat-roofed mud huts and low-walled courtyards, which front on narrow lanes that radiate from the centre. Soon the lanes dwindle into footpaths and get lost in the surrounding fields. At the western end of the village there is a pond ringed round by keekar trees. There are only about seventy families in Mano Majra, and Lala Ram Lal's is the only Hindu family. The others are Sikhs or Muslims, about equal in number. The Sikhs own all the land around the village; the Muslims are tenants and share the tilling with the owners. There are a few families of sweepers whose religion is uncertain. The Muslims claim them as their own, yet when American missionaries visit Mano Majra the sweepers wear khaki sola topees and join their womenfolk in singing hymns to the accompaniment of a harmonium. Sometimes they visit the Sikh temple, too. But there is one object that all Mano Majrans—even Lala Ram Lal—venerate. This is a three-foot slab of sandstone that stands upright under a keekar tree beside the pond. It is the local deity, the *deo* to which all the villagers—Hindu, Sikh, Muslim or pseudo-Christian—repair secretly whenever they are in a special need of blessing.

Although Mano Majra is said to be on the banks of the Sutlej River, it is actually half a mile away from it. In India villages cannot afford to be too close to the banks of rivers. Rivers change their moods with the seasons and alter their courses without warning. The Sutlej is the largest river in the Punjab. After the monsoon its waters rise and spread across its vast sandy bed, lapping high up the mud embankments on either side. It becomes an expanse of muddy turbulence more than a mile in breadth. When the flood

4

subsides, the river breaks up into a thousand shallow streams that wind sluggishly between little marshy islands. About a mile north of Mano Majra the Sutlej is spanned by a railroad bridge. It is a magnificent bridge—its eighteen enormous spans sweep like waves from one pier to another, and at each end of it there is a stone embankment to buttress the railway line. On the eastern end the embankment extends all the way to the village railroad station.

Mano Majra has always been known for its railway station. Since the bridge has only one track, the station has several sidings where less important trains can wait, to make way for the more important.

A small colony of shopkeepers and hawkers has grown up around the station to supply travellers with food, betel leaves, cigarettes, tea, biscuits and sweetmeats. This gives the station an appearance of constant activity and its staff a somewhat exaggerated sense of importance. Actually the stationmaster himself sells tickets through the pigeonhole in his office, collects them at the exit beside the door, and sends and receives messages over the telegraph ticker on the table. When there are people to notice him, he comes out on the platform and waves a green flag for trains which do not stop. His only assistant manipulates the levers in the glass cabin on the platform which control the signals on either side, and helps shunting engines by changing hand points on the tracks to get them onto the sidings. In the evenings, he lights the long line of lamps on the platform. He takes heavy aluminum lamps to the signals and sticks them in the clamps behind the red and green glass. In the mornings, he brings them back and puts out the lights on the platform.

Not many trains stop at Mano Majra. Express trains do not stop at all. Of the many slow passenger trains, only two, one from Delhi to Lahore in the mornings and the other from Lahore to Delhi in the evenings, are scheduled to stop for a few minutes. The others stop only when they are held up. The only regular customers are the goods trains. Although Mano Majra seldom has any goods to send or receive, its station sidings are usually occupied by long rows of wagons. Each passing goods train spends hours shedding wagons and collecting others. After dark, when the countryside is steeped in silence, the whistling and puffing of engines, the banging of buffers, and the clanking of iron couplings can be heard all through the night.

All this has made Mano Majra very conscious of trains. Before daybreak, the mail train rushes through on its way to Lahore, and as it approaches tne bridge, the driver invariably blows two long blasts of the whistle. In an instant, all Mano Majra comes awake. Crows begin to caw in the keekar trees. Bats fly back in long silent relays and begin to quarrel for their perches in the peepul. The mullah at the mosque knows that it is time for the morning prayer. He has a quick wash, stands facing west toward Mecca and with his fingers in his ears cries in long sonorous notes, '*Allah-o-Akbar*'. The priest at the Sikh temple lies in bed till the mullah has called. Then he too gets up, draws a bucket of water from the well in the temple courtyard, pours it over himself, and intones his prayer in monotonous singsong to the sound of splashing water.

By the time the 10:30 morning passenger train from Delhi comes in, life in Mano Majra has settled down to its dull daily routine. Men are in the fields. Women are busy with their daily chores. Children are out grazing cattle by the river. Persian wheels squeak and groan as bullocks go round and round, prodded on by curses and the jabs of goads in their hindquarters. Sparrows fly about the roofs, trailing straw in their beaks. Pye-dogs seek the shade of the long mud walls. Bats settle their arguments, fold their wings, and suspend themselves in sleep.

As the midday express goes by, Mano Majra stops to rest. Men and children come home for dinner and the siesta hour. When they have eaten, the men gather in the shade of the peepul tree and sit on the wooden platforms and talk and doze. Boys ride their buffaloes into the pond, jump off their backs, and splash about in the muddy water. Girls play under the trees. Women rub clarified butter into each other's hair, pick lice from their children's heads, and discuss births, marriages and deaths.

When the evening passenger from Lahore comes in, everyone gets to work again. The cattle are rounded up and driven back home to be milked and locked in for the night. The women cook the evening meal. Then the families foregather on their rooftops where most of them sleep during the summer. Sitting on their charpoys, they eat their supper of vegetables and chapatties and sip hot creamy milk out of large copper tumblers and idle away the time until the signal for sleep. When the goods train steams in, they say to each other, 'There is the goods train.' It is like saying goodnight. The mullah again calls the faithful to prayer by shouting at the top of his voice, 'God is great.' The faithful nod their amens from their rooftops. The Sikh priest murmurs the evening prayer to a semicircle of drowsy old men and women. Crows caw softly from the keekar trees. Little bats go flitting about in the dusk and large ones soar with slow graceful sweeps. The goods train takes a long time at the station, with the engine running up and down the sidings exchanging wagons. By the time it leaves, the children are asleep. The older people wait for its rumble over the bridge to lull them to slumber. Then life in Mano Majra is stilled, save for the dogs barking at the trains that pass in the night.

It had always been so, until the summer of 1947.

One heavy night in August of that year, five men emerged from a keekar grove not far from Mano Majra, and moved silently toward the river. They were dacoits, or professional robbers, and all but one of them were armed. Two of the armed men carried spears. The others had carbines slung over their shoulders. The fifth man carried a chromium-plated electric torch. When they came to the embankment, he flicked the torch alight. Then he grunted and snapped it off.

'We will wait here,' he said.

He dropped down on the sand. The others crouched around him, leaning on their weapons. The man with the torch looked at one of the spearmen.

'You have the bangles for Jugga?'

'Yes. A dozen of red and blue glass. They would please any village wench.'

'They will not please Jugga,' one of the gunmen said.

The leader laughed. He tossed the torch in the air and caught it. He laughed again and raised the torch to his mouth and touched the switch. His cheeks glowed pink from the light inside.

'Jugga could give the bangles to that weaver's daughter of his,' the other spearman said. 'They would look well with those large gazelle eyes and the little mango breasts. What is her name?'

The leader turned off the torch and took it from his mouth. 'Nooran,' he said.

7

'Aho,' the spearman said. 'Nooran. Did you see her at the spring fair? Did you see that tight shirt showing off her breasts and the bells tinkling in her plaits and the swish-swish of silk? Hai!'

'Hai!' the spearman with the bangles cried. 'Hai! Hai!'

'She must give Jugga a good time,' said the gunman who had not yet spoken. 'During the day, she looks so innocent you would think she had not shed her milk teeth.' He sighed. 'But at night, she puts black antimony in her eyes.'

'Antimony is good for the eyes,' one of the others said. 'It is cooling.'

'It is good for other people's eyes as well,' the gunman said.

'And cooling to their passions, too.'

'Jugga?' the leader said.

The others laughed. One of them suddenly sat erect.

'Listen!' he said. 'There is the goods train.'

The others stopped laughing. They all listened in silence to the approaching train. It came to a halt with a rumble, and the wagons groaned and creaked. After a time, the engine could be heard moving up and down, releasing wagons. There were loud explosions as the released wagons collided with the ones on the sidings. The engine chuffed back to the train.

'It is time to call on Ram Lal,' the leader said, and got to his feet.

His companions rose and brushed the sand off their clothes. They formed a line with their hands joined in prayer. One of the gunmen stepped in front and began to mumble. When he stopped, they all went down on their knees and rubbed their foreheads on the ground. Then they stood up and drew the loose ends of their turbans across their faces. Only their eyes were uncovered. The engine gave two long whistle blasts, and the train moved off toward the bridge.

'Now,' the leader said.

The others followed him up the embankment and across the fields. By the time the train had reached the bridge, the men had skirted the pond and were walking up a lane that led to the centre of the village. They came to the house of Lala Ram Lal. The leader nodded to one of the gunmen. He stepped forward and began to pound on the door with the butt of his gun.

'Oi!' he shouted. 'Lala!'

8

There was no reply. Village dogs gathered round the vis... and began to bark. One of the men hit a dog with the flat side of his spear blade. Another fired his gun into the air. The dogs ran away whimpering and started to bark louder from a safer distance.

The men began to hammer at the door with their weapons. One struck it with his spear which went through to the other side.

'Open, you son of fornication, or we will kill the lot of you,' he shouted.

A woman's voice answered. 'Who is it who calls at this hour? Lalaji has gone to the city.'

'Open and we will tell you who we are or we will smash the door,' the leader said.

'I tell you Lalaji is not in. He has taken the keys with him. We have nothing in the house.'

The men put their shoulders to the door, pressed, pulled back and butted into it like battering-rams. The wooden bolt on the other side cracked and the doors flew open. One of the men with a gun waited at the door; the other four went in. In one corner of the room two women sat crouching. A boy of seven with large black eyes clung to the older of the two.

'In the name of God, take what we have, all our jewellery, everything,' implored the older woman. She held out a handful of gold and silver bracelets, anklets and earrings.

One of the men snatched them from her hands.

'Where is the Lala?'

'I swear by the Guru he is out. You have taken all we have. Lalaji has nothing more to give.'

In the courtyard four beds were laid out in a row.

The man with the carbine tore the little boy from his grandmother's lap and held the muzzle of the gun to the child's face. The women fell at his feet imploring.

'Do not kill, brother. In the name of the Guru—don't.'

The gunman kicked the women away.

'Where is you father?'

The boy shook with fear and stuttered, 'Upstairs.'

The gunman thrust the boy back into the woman's lap, and the men went out into the courtyard and climbed the staircase. There was only one room on the roof. Without pausing they put their shoulders to the door and pushed it in, tearing it off its hinges.

The room was cluttered with steel trunks piled one on top of the other. There were two charpoys with several quilts rolled up on them. The white beam of the torch searched the room and caught the moneylender crouching under one of the charpoys.

'In the name of the Guru, the Lalaji is out,' one of the men said, mimicking the woman's voice. He dragged Ram Lal out by his legs.

The leader slapped the moneylender with the back of his hand. 'Is this the way you treat your guests? We come and you hide under a charpoy.'

Ram Lal covered his face with his arms and began to whimper.

'Where are the keys of the safe?' asked the leader, kicking him on the behind.

'You can take all—jewellery, cash, account books. Don't kill anyone,' implored the moneylender, grasping the leader's feet with both his hands.

'Where are the keys of your safe?' repeated the leader. He knocked the moneylender sprawling on the floor. Ram Lal sat up, shaking with fear.

He produced a wad of notes from his pocket. 'Take these,' he said, distributing the money to the five men. 'It is all I have in the house. All is yours.'

'Where are the keys of your safe?'

'There is nothing left in the safe; only my account books. I have given you all I have. All I have is yours. In the name of the Guru, let me be.' Ram Lal clasped the leader's legs above the knees and began to sob. 'In the name of the Guru! In the name of the Guru!'

One of the men tore the moneylender away from the leader and hit him full in the face with the butt of his gun.

'Hai!' yelled Ram Lal at the top of his voice, and spat out blood.

The women in the courtyard heard the cry and started shrieking, '*Dakoo! dakoo!*'

The dogs barked all round. But not a villager stirred from his house.

On the roof of his house, the moneylender was beaten with butts of guns and spear handles and kicked and punched. He sat on his haunches, crying and spitting blood. Two of his teeth were smashed. But he would not hand over the keys of his safe. In sheer exasperation, one of the men lunged at the crouching figure with his spear. Ram Lal uttered a loud yell and collapsed on the floor with blood spurting from his belly. The men came out. One of them fired two shots in the air. Women stopped wailing. Dogs stopped barking. The village was silenced.

The dacoits jumped off the roof to the lane below. They yelled defiance to the world as they went out toward the river.

'Come!' they yelled. 'Come out, if you have the courage! Come out, if you want your mothers and sisters raped! Come out, brave men!'

No one answered them. There was not a sound in Mano Majra. The men continued along the lane, shouting and laughing, until they came to a small hut on the edge of the village. The leader halted and motioned to one of the spearmen.

'This is the house of the great Jugga,' he said. 'Do not forget our gift. Give him his bangles.'

The spearman dug a package from his clothes and tossed it over the wall. There was a muffled sound of breaking glass in the courtyard.

'O Juggia,' he called in a falsetto voice, 'Juggia!' He winked at his companions. 'Wear these bangles, Juggia. Wear these bangles and put henna on your palms.'

'Or give them to the weaver's daughter,' one of the gunmen yelled.

'*Hai*,' the others shouted. They smacked their lips, making the sound of long, lecherous kisses. '*Hai! Hai!*'

They moved on down the lane, still laughing and blowing kisses, toward the river. Juggut Singh did not answer them. He didn't hear them. He was not at home.

Juggut Singh had been gone from his home about an hour. He had only left when the sound of the night goods train told him that it would now be safe to go. For him, as for the dacoits, the arrival of the train that night was a signal. At the first distant rumble, he slipped quietly off his charpoy and picked up his turban and wrapped it round his head. Then he tiptoed across the courtyard to the haystack and fished out a spear. He tiptoed back to his bed, picked up his shoes, and crept toward the door.

'Where are you going?'

Juggut Singh stopped. It was his mother.

11

'To the fields,' he said. 'Last night wild pigs did a lot of damage.'

'Pigs!' his mother said. 'Don't try to be clever. Have you forgotten already that you are on probation—that it is forbidden for you to leave the village after sunset? And with a spear! Enemies will see you. They will report you. They will send you back to jail.' Her voice rose to a wail. 'Then who will look after the crops and the cattle?'

'I will be back soon,' Juggut Singh said. 'There is nothing to worry about. Everyone in the village is asleep.'

'No,' his mother said. She wailed again.

'Shut up,' he said. 'It is you who will wake the neighbours. Be quiet and there will be no trouble.'

'Go! Go wherever you want to go. If you want to jump in a well, jump. If you want to hang like your father, go and hang. It is my lot to weep. My kismet,' she added, slapping her forehead, 'it is all written there.'

Juggut Singh opened the door and looked on both sides. There was no one about. He walked along the walls till he got to the end of the lane near the pond. He could see the gray forms of a couple of adjutant storks slowly pacing up and down in the mud looking for frogs. They paused in their search. Juggut Singh stood still against the wall till the storks were reassured, then went off the footpath across the fields toward the river. He crossed the dry sand bed till he got to the stream. He stuck his spear in the ground with the blade pointing upward, then stretched out on the sand. He lay on his back and gazed at the stars. A meteor shot across the Milky Way, trailing a silver path down the blue-black sky. Suddenly a hand was on his eyes.

'Guess who?'

Juggut Singh stretched out his hands over his head and behind him, groping; the girl dodged them. Juggut Singh started with the hand on his eyes and felt his way up from the arm to the shoulder and then on to the face. He caressed her cheeks, eyes and nose that his hands knew so well. He tried to play with her lips to induce them to kiss his fingers. The girl opened her mouth and bit him fiercely. Juggut Singh jerked his hand away. With a quick movement he caught the girl's head in both his hands and brought her face over to his. Then he slipped his arms under her waist and

12

hoisted her into the air above him with her arms and legs kicking about like a crab. He turned her about till his arms ached. He brought her down flat upon him limb to limb.

The girl slapped him on the face.

'You put your hands on the person of a strange woman. Have you no mother or sister in your home? Have you no shame? No wonder the police have got you on their register as a bad character. I will also tell the Inspector Sahib that you are a budmash.'

'I am only budmash with you, Nooro. We should both be locked up in the same cell.'

'You have learned to talk too much. I will have to look for another man.'

Juggut Singh crossed his arms behind the girl's back and crushed her till she could not talk or breathe. Every time she started to speak he tightened his arms round her and her words got stuck in her throat. She gave up and put her exhausted face against his. He laid her beside him with her head nestling in the hollow of his left arm. With his right hand he stroked her hair and face.

The goods train engine whistled twice and with a lot of groaning and creaking began to puff its way toward the bridge. The storks flew up from the pond with shrill cries of 'kraak, kraak' and came toward the river. From the river they flew back to the pond, calling alternately long after the train had gone over the bridge and its puff-puffs had died into silence.

Juggut Singh's caresses became lustful. His hand strayed from the girl's face to her breasts and her waist. She caught it and put it back on her face. His breathing became slow and sensuous. His hand wandered again and brushed against her breasts as if by mistake. The girl slapped it and put it away. Juggut Singh stretched his left arm that lay under the girl's head and caught her reproving hand. Her other arm was already under him. She was defenceless.

'No! No! No! Let go my hand! No! I will never speak to you again.' She shook her head violently from side to side, trying to avoid his hungry mouth.

Juggut Singh slipped his hand inside her shirt and felt the contours of her unguarded breasts. They became taut. The nipples became hard and leathery. His rough hands gently moved up and down from her breasts to her navel. The skin on her belly came up in goose flesh.

The girl continued to wriggle and protest.

'No! No! No! Please. May Allah's curse fall on you. Let go my hand. I will never meet you again if you behave like this.'

Juggut Singh's searching hand found one end of the cord of her trousers. He pulled it with a jerk.

'No,' cried the girl hoarsely.

A shot rang through the night. The storks flew up from the pond calling to each other. Crows started cawing in the keekar trees. Juggut Singh paused and looked up into the darkness toward the village. The girl quietly extricated herself from his hold and adjusted her dress. The crows settled back on the trees. The storks flew away across the river. Only the dogs barked.

'It sounded like a gunshot,' she said nervously, trying to keep Juggut Singh from renewing his love-making. 'Wasn't it from the village?'

'I don't know. Why are you trying to run away? It is all quiet now.' Juggut Singh pulled her down beside him.

'This is no time for jesting. There is murder in the village. My father will get up and want to know where I have gone. I must get back at once.'

'No, you will not. I won't let you. You can say you were with a girl friend.'

'Don't talk like a stupid peasant. How . . . ' Juggut Singh shut her mouth with his. He bore upon her with his enormous weight. Before she could free her arms he ripped open the cord of her trousers once again.

'Let me go. Let me . . . '

She could not struggle against Juggut Singh's brute force. She did not particularly want to. Her world was narrowed to the rhythmic sound of breathing and the warm smell of dusky skins raised to fever heat. His lips slubbered over her eyes and cheeks. His tongue sought the inside of her ears. In a state of frenzy she dug her nails into his thinly bearded cheeks and bit his nose. The stars above her went into a mad whirl and then came back to their places like a merry-go-round slowly coming to a stop. Life came back to its cooler, lower level. She felt the dead weight of the lifeless man; the sand gritting in her hair; the breeze trespassing on her naked limbs; the censorious stare of the myriads of stars. She pushed Juggut Singh away. He lay down beside her.

14

'That is all you want. And you get it. You are just a peasant. Always wanting to sow your seed. Even if the world were going to hell you would want to do that. Even when guns are being fired in the village. Wouldn't you?' she nagged.

'Nobody is firing any guns. Just your imagination,' answered Juggut Singh wearily, without looking at her.

Faint cries of wailing wafted across to the riverside. The couple sat up to listen. Two shots rang out in quick succession. The crows flew out of the keekars, cawing furiously.

The girl began to cry.

'Something is happening in the village. My father will wake up and know I have gone out. He will kill me.'

Juggut Singh was not listening to her. He did not know what to do. If his absence from the village was discovered, he would be in trouble with the police. That did not bother him as much as the trouble the girl would be in. She might not come again. She was saying so: 'I will never come to see you again. If Allah forgives me this time, I will never do it again.'

'Will you shut up or do I have to smack your face?'

The girl began to sob. She found it hard to believe this was the same man who had been making love to her a moment ago.

'Quiet! There is someone coming,' whispered Juggut Singh, putting his heavy hand on her mouth.

The couple lay still, peering into the dark. The five men carrying guns and spears passed within a few yards of them. They had uncovered their faces and were talking.

'*Dakoo!* Do you know them?' the girl asked in a whisper.

'Yes,' Juggut said, 'The one with the torch is Malli.' His face went tight. 'That incestuous lover of his sister! I've told him a thousand times this was no time for dacoities. And now he has brought his gang to my village! I will settle this with him.'

The dacoits went up to the river and then downstream toward the ford a couple of miles to the south. A pair of lapwings pierced the still night with startled cries: Teet-tittee-tittee-whoot, tee-tee-whoot, tee-tee-whoot, tit-tit-tee-whoot.

'Will you report them to the police?'

Juggut Singh sniggered. 'Let us get back before they miss me in the village.'

The pair walked back toward Mano Majra, the man in front,

15

the girl a few paces behind him. They could hear the sound of wailing and the barking of dogs. Women were shouting to each other across the roofs. The whole village seemed to be awake. Juggut Singh stopped near the pond and turned round to speak to the girl.

'Nooro, will you come tomorrow?' he asked, pleading.

'You think of tomorrow and I am bothered about my life. You have your good time even if I am murdered.'

'No one can harm you while I live. No one in Mano Majra can raise his eyebrows at you and get away from Jugga. I am not a budmash for nothing,' said he haughtily. 'You tell me tomorrow what happens or the day after tomorrow when all this—whatever it is—is over. After the goods train?'

'No! No! No!' answered the girl. 'What will I say to my father now? This noise is bound to have woken him up.'

'Just say you had gone out. Your stomach was upset or something like that. You heard the firing and were hiding till the dacoits had left. Will you come the day after tomorrow then?'

'No,' she repeated, this time a little less emphatically. The excuse might work. Just as well her father was almost blind. He would not see her silk shirt, nor the antimony in her eyes. Nooran walked away into the darkness, swearing she would never come again.

Juggut Singh went up the lane to his house. The door was open. Several villagers were in the courtyard talking to his mother. He turned around quietly and made his way back to the river.

In bureaucratic circles Mano Majra has some importance because of an officers' rest house just north of the railway bridge. It is a flat-roofed bungalow made of khaki bricks with a verandah in front facing the river. It stands in the middle of a squarish plot enclosed by a low wall. From the gate to the verandah runs a road with a row of bricks to deckle-edge each side and mark it off from the garden. The garden is a pancake of plastered mud without a blade of grass to break its flat, even surface, but a few scraggy bushes of jasmine grow beside the columns of the verandah and near the row of servants' quarters at the rear of the house. The rest house was originally built for the engineer in charge of the construction of the bridge. After the completion of the bridge, it became the common property of all senior officers. Its popularity is due to its proximity to the river. All about it are wild wastes of pampas grass and dhak, or flame of the forest, and here partridges call to their mates from sunrise to sundown. When the river has receded to its winter channel, bulrushes grow in the marshes and ponds left behind. Geese, mallard, widgeon, teal, and many other kinds of waterfowl frequent these places, and the larger pools abound with rahu and malli and mahseer.

Throughout the winter months, officers arrange tours that involve a short halt at the Mano Majra rest house. They go for waterfowl at sunrise, for partridges during the day, fish in the afternoons, and once more for ducks when they come back in their evening flight. In spring the romantic come to ruminate—to sip their whisky and see the bright orange of the dhak shame the rich red hues of the sun setting over the river; to hear the soothing snore of frogs in the marshes and the rumble of trains that go by; to watch fireflies flitting among the reeds as the moon comes up from under the arches of the bridge. During the early months of summer, only those who are looking for solitude come to the Mano Majra rest house. But once the monsoon breaks, the visitors multiply, for the swollen waters of the Sutlej are a grand and terrifying sight.

On the morning before the dacoity in Mano Majra, the rest house had been done up to receive an important guest. The sweeper had washed the bathrooms, swept the rooms, and sprinkled water on the road. The bearer and his wife had dusted and rearranged the furniture. The sweeper's boy had unwound the rope on the punkah which hung from the ceiling and put it through the hole in the wall so that he could pull it from the verandah. He had put on a new red loincloth and was sitting on the verandah tying and untying knots in the punkah rope. From the kitchen came the smell of currying chicken.

At eleven o'clock a subinspector of police and two constables turned up on bicycles to inspect the arrangements. Then two orderlies arrived. They wore white uniforms with red sashes round their waists and white turbans with broad bands in front. On the bands were pinned brass emblems of the government of the Punjab—the sun rising over five wavy lines representing the rivers of the province. With them were several villagers who carried the

17

baggage and the glossy black official dispatch cases.

An hour later a large gray American car rolled in. An orderly stepped out of the front seat and opened the rear door for his master. The subinspector and the policemen came to attention and saluted. The villagers moved away to a respectful distance. The bearer opened the wire gauze door leading to the main bed-sitting room. Mr Hukum Chand, magistrate and deputy commissioner of the district, heaved his corpulent frame out of the car. He had been travelling all morning and was somewhat tired and stiff. A cigarette perched on his lower lip sent a thin stream of smoke into his eyes. In his right hand he held a cigarette tin and a box of matches. He ambled up to the subinspector and gave him a friendly slap on the back while the other still stood at attention.

'Come along, Inspector Sahib, come in,' said Hukum Chand. He took the inspector's right hand and led him into the room. The bearer and the deputy commissioner's personal servant followed. The constables helped the chauffeur to take the luggage out of the car.

Hukum Chand went straight into the bathroom and washed the dust off his face. He came back still wiping his face with a towel. The subinspector stood up again.

'Sit down, sit down,' he commanded.

He flung the towel on his bed and sank into an armchair. The punkah began to flap forward and backward to the grating sound of the rope moving in the hole in the wall. One of the orderlies undid the magistrate's shoes and took off his socks and began to rub his feet. Hukum Chand opened the cigarette tin and held it out to the subinspector. The subinspector lit the magistrate's cigarette and then his own. Hukum Chand's style of smoking betrayed his lower-middle-class origin. He sucked noisily, his mouth glued to his clenched fist. He dropped cigarette ash by snapping his fingers with a flourish. The subinspector, who was a younger man, had a more sophisticated manner.

'Well, Inspector Sahib, how are things?'

The subinspector joined his hands. 'God is merciful. We only pray for your kindness.'

'No communal trouble in this area?'

'We have escaped it so far, sir. Convoys of Sikh and Hindu refugees from Pakistan have come through and some Muslims

18

have gone out, but we have had no incidents.'

'You haven't had convoys of dead Sikhs this side of the frontier. They have been coming through at Amritsar. Not one person living! There has been killing over there.' Hukum Chand held up both his hands and let them drop heavily on his thighs in a gesture of resignation. Sparks flew off his cigarette and fell on his trousers. The subinspector slapped them to extinction with obsequious haste.

'Do you know,' continued the magistrate, 'the Sikhs retaliated by attacking a Muslim refugee train and sending it across the border with over a thousand corpses? They wrote on the engine 'Gift to Pakistan'!'

The subinspector looked down thoughtfully and answered: 'They say that is the only way to stop killings on the other side. Man for man, woman for woman, child for child. But we Hindus are not like that. We cannot really play this stabbing game. When it comes to an open fight, we can be a match for any people. I believe our R.S.S. boys beat up Muslim gangs in all the cities. The Sikhs are not doing their share. They have lost their manliness. They just talk big. Here we are on the border with Muslims living in Sikh villages as if nothing had happened. Every morning and evening the muezzin calls for prayer in the heart of a village like Mano Majra. You ask the Sikhs why they allow it and they answer that the Muslims are their brothers. I am sure they are getting money from them.'

Hukum Chand ran his fingers across his receding forehead into his hair.

'Any of the Muslims in this area well-to-do?'

'Not many, sir. Most of them are weavers or potters.'

'But Chundunnugger is said to be a good police station. There are so many murders, so much illicit distilling, and the Sikh peasants are prosperous. Your predecessors have built themselves houses in the city.'

'Your honour is making fun of me.'

'I don't mind your taking whatever you do take, within reason of course—everyone does that—only, be careful. This new government is talking very loudly of stamping out all this. After a few months in office their enthusiasm will cool and things will go on as before. It is no use trying to change things overnight.'

19

'They are not the ones to talk. Ask anyone coming from Delhi and he will tell you that all these Gandhi disciples are minting money. They are as good saints as the crane. They shut their eyes piously and stand on one leg like a yogi doing penance; as soon as a fish comes near—hurrup.'

Hukum Chand ordered the servant rubbing his feet to get some beer. As soon as they were alone, he put a friendly hand on the subinspector's knee.

'You talk rashly like a child. It will get you into trouble one day. Your principle should be to see everything and say nothing. The world changes so rapidly that if you want to get on you cannot afford to align yourself with any person or point of view. Even if you feel strongly about something, learn to keep silent.'

The subinspector's heart warmed with gratitude. He wanted to provoke more paternal advice by irresponsible criticism. He knew that Hukum Chand agreed with him.

'Sometimes, sir, one cannot restrain oneself. What do the Gandhi-caps in Delhi know about the Punjab? What is happening on the other side in Pakistan does not matter to them. They have not lost their homes and belongings; they haven't had their mothers, wives, sisters and daughters raped and murdered in the streets. Did your honour hear what the Muslim mobs did to Hindu and Sikh refugees in the market places at Sheikhupura and Gujranwala? Pakistan police and the army took part in the killings. Not a soul was left alive. Women killed their own children and jumped into wells that filled to the brim with corpses.'

'Harey Ram, Harey Ram,' rejoined Hukum Chand with a deep sigh. 'I know it all. Our Hindu women are like that: so pure that they would rather commit suicide than let a stranger touch them. We Hindus never raise our hands to strike women, but these Muslims have no respect for the weaker sex. But what are we to do about it? How long will it be before it starts here?'

'I hope we do not get trains with corpses coming through Mano Majra. It will be impossible to prevent retaliation. We have hundreds of small Muslim villages all around, and there are some Muslim families in every Sikh village like Mano Majra,' said the subinspector, throwing a feeler.

Hukum Chand sucked his cigarette noisily and snapped his fingers.

'We must maintain law and order,' he answered after a pause. 'If possible, get the Muslims to go out peacefully. Nobody really benefits by bloodshed. Bad characters will get all the loot and the government will blame us for the killing. No, Inspector Sahib, whatever our views—and God alone knows what I would have done to these Pakistanis if I were not a government servant—we must not let there be any killing or destruction of property. Let them get out, but be careful they do not take too much with them. Hindus from Pakistan were stripped of all their belongings before they were allowed to leave. Pakistani magistrates have become millionaires overnight. Some on our side have not done too badly either. Only where there was killing or burning the government suspended or transferred them. There must be no killing. Just peaceful evacuation.'

The bearer brought a bottle of beer and put two glasses before Mr Hukum Chand and the subinspector. The subinspector picked up his glass and put his hand over it, protesting, 'No, sir, I could not be impertinent and drink in your presence.'

The magistrate dismissed the protest peremptorily. 'You will have to join me. It is an order. Bearer, fill the Inspector Sahib's glass and lay out lunch for him.'

The subinspector held out his glass for the bearer to fill. 'If you order me to, I cannot disobey.' He began to relax. He took off his turban and put it on the table. It was not like a Sikh turban which needed re-tying each time it was taken off; it was just three yards of starched khaki muslin wrapped round a blue skullcap which could be put on and off like a hat.

'What is the situation in Mano Majra?'

'All is well so far. The lambardar reports regularly. No refugees have come through the village yet. I am sure no one in Mano Majra even knows that the British have left and the country is divided into Pakistan and Hindustan. Some of them know about Gandhi but I doubt if anyone has ever heard of Jinnah.'

'That is good. You must keep an eye on Mano Majra. It is the most important village on the border here. It is so close to the bridge. Are there any bad characters in the village?'

'Only one, sir. His name is Jugga. Your honour confined him to the village. He reports himself to the lambardar every day and comes to the police station once every week.'

'Jugga? Which one is he?'

'You must remember Juggut Singh, son of the dacoit Alam Singh who was hanged two years ago. He is that very big fellow. He is the tallest man in this area. He must be six foot four—and broad. He is like a stud bull.'

'Oh yes, I remember. What does he do to keep himself out of mischief? He used to come up before me in some case or other every month.'

The subinspector smiled broadly. 'Sir, what the police of the Punjab has failed to do, the magic of the eyes of a girl of sixteen has done.'

Hukum Chand's interest was aroused.

'He has a liaison?' he asked.

'With a Muslim weaver's daughter. She is dark, but her eyes are darker. She certainly keeps Jugga in the village. And no one dares say a word against the Muslims. Her blind father is the mullah of the mosque.'

The two drank their beer and smoked till the bearer brought in lunch. They continued drinking and eating and discussing the situation in the district till late in the afternoon. Beer and rich food made Hukum Chand heavy with sleep. Chicks on the verandah had been lowered to keep out the glare of the noonday sun. The punkah flapped gently to and fro with a weary plaintive creak. A feeling of numb drowsiness came over Hukum Chand. He got out his silver toothpick, picked his teeth and rubbed the toothpick on the tablecloth. Even that did not help him ward off sleep. The subinspector noticed the magistrate nodding and stood up to take leave.

'Have I your permission to leave, sir?'

'If you want to rest, you can find a bed here.'

'You are very kind, sir, but I have a few things to attend to at the station. I will leave two constables here. If your honour desires my presence, they will inform me.'

'Well,' said the magistrate hesitantly, 'have you made any arrangements for the evening?'

'Is it possible for me to have overlooked that? If she does not please you, you can have me dismissed from service. I will tell the driver where to go and collect the party.'

The subinspector saluted and left. The magistrate stretched

himself on the bed for a late afternoon siesta.

The sound of the car leaving the bungalow woke Hukum Chand from his sleep. Pampas-stalk chicks which hung on the verandah had been folded into large Swiss rolls and tied between the columns. The stark white of the verandah was mellowed in the soft amber of the setting sun. The sweeper boy lay curled on the brick floor clutching the punkah rope in his hand. His father was sprinkling water all around the rest house. The damp smell of earth mixed with the sweet odor of jasmines came through the wire gauze door. In front of the house, the servants had spread a large coir mat with a carpet on it. At one end of the carpet was a big cane chair, a table with a bottle of whisky, a couple of tumblers and plates of savouries. Several bottles of soda water stood in a row beneath the table.

Hukum Chand shouted for his servant to get his bath ready and bring in hot water for shaving. He lit a cigarette and lay in bed staring at the ceiling. Just above his head two geckos were getting ready for a fight. They crawled toward each other emitting little rasping noises. They paused with half an inch between them and moved their tails with slow, menacing deliberation, then came to a head-on collision. Before Hukum Chand could move away they fell with a loud plop just beside his pillow. A cold clammy feeling came over him. He jumped out of bed and stared at the geckos. The geckos stared back at him, still holding onto each other by the teeth as if they were kissing. The bearer's footsteps broke the hypnotic stare with which the magistrate and the geckos had been regarding each other. The geckos ran down the bed and up the wall back to the ceiling. Hukum Chand felt as if he had touched the lizards and they had made his hands dirty. He rubbed his hands on the hem of his shirt. It was not the sort of dirt which could be wiped off or washed clean.

The bearer brought a mug of hot water and laid out the shaving gear on the dressing table. He put on a chair his master's clothes—a thin muslin shirt, a pair of baggy trousers strung with a peacock-blue silken cord interwoven with silver thread. He brushed the magistrate's black pumps till they shone and put them beside the chair.

Hukum Chand shaved and bathed with great care. After bathing he rubbed skin-lotion on his face and arms and dusted himself with perfumed talcum powder. He dabbed his fingers with eau de cologne. Brilliantine made his hair smooth and soggy and showed the white at the roots of it. He had not dyed it for a fortnight. He waxed his thick moustache and twirled it till the ends stiffly pointed to his eyes; the roots of his moustache also showed purple and white. He put on his thin muslin shirt through which his aertex vest showed clearly. The trousers fell in ordered starchy folds. He dabbed his clothes with a swab of cotton dipped in scent of musk rose. When he was ready he looked up at the ceiling. The geckos were there staring at him with their bright, black, pin-point eyes.

The American car drove back into the driveway. Hukum Chand went up to the wire gauze door still waxing his moustache. Two men and two women stepped out. One of the men carried a harmonium and the other a pair of drums. One of the women was old, with white hair dyed a rich henna-orange. The other was a young girl whose mouth was bloated with betel leaf and who wore a diamond glistening on one side of her flat nose. She carried a small bundle which jingled as she stepped out of the car. The party went and squatted on the carpet.

Hukum Chand carefully examined himself in the mirror. He noticed the white at the roots of his hair and smoothed it back again. He lit a cigarette and in his customary manner carried the tin of cigarettes with a matchbox on it. He half opened the wire gauze door and shouted for his bearer to bring the whisky, which he knew had already been put on the table. It was to warn the people outside of his coming. As he came out he let the door slam noisily. With slow deliberate steps punctuated by the creaking of his glossy pumps he walked up to the cane chair.

The party stood up to greet the magistrate. The two musicians salaamed, bowing their heads low. The old toothless woman broke into a sonorous singsong of praise: 'May your fame and honour increase. May your pen write figures of thousands and hundreds of thousands.' The young girl just stared at him with her large eyes lined with antimony and lampblack. The magistrate made a gesture with his hand ordering them to sit down. The old woman's voice came down to a whimper. All four sat down on the carpet.

The bearer poured out the whisky and soda for his master. Hukum Chand took a large gulp and wiped his moustache with

the back of his hand. He twirled the pointed ends nervously. The
girl opened her bundle and tied the ankle-bells round her ankles.
The harmonium player played a single note. His companion beat
the drums all round the edges with a tiny mallet and tightened and
loosened the leather thongs by hammering the ring of wooden
blocks wedged between them. He beat the taut white skin with his
fingers till the drums were in key with the harmonium. The
accompaniment was ready.

The young girl spat out the betel saliva and cleared her throat
with a series of deep chesty coughs that brought up phlegm. The
old woman spoke:

'Cherisher of the poor. What does your honour fancy?
Something classical—pukka—or a love song?'

'No, nothing pukka. Something from the films. Some good
film song—preferably Punjabi.'

The young girl salaamed. 'As you order.'

The musicians put their heads together and after a brief
consultation with the girl they began to play. The drums beat a
preliminary tattoo and then softened down for the harmonium to
join in. The two played for some time while the girl sat silently,
looking bored and indifferent. When they finished the
introductory piece, she blew her nose and cleared her throat again.
She put her left hand on her ear and stretched the other toward the
magistrate, addressing him in a shrill falsetto:

> *O lover mine, O lover that art gone,*
> *I live but would rather die,*
> *I see not for the tears that flow,*
> *I breathe not, for I sigh.*
> *As a moth that loves the flame,*
> *By that flame is done to death,*
> *Within myself have I lit a fire*
> *That now robs me of my breath.*
> *The nights I spend in counting stars,*
> *The days in dreams of days to be*
> *When homewards thou thy reins shall turn*
> *Thy moon-fair face I again shall see.*

The girl paused. The musicians started to play again for her to sing the refrain:

> *O letter, let my lover learn*
> *How the fires of separation burn.*

When the girl had finished her song, Hukum Chand flung a five-rupee note on the carpet. The girl and the musicians bowed their heads. The hag picked up the money and put it in her wallet, proclaiming: 'May you ever rule. May your pen write hundreds of thousands. May . . .'

The singing began again. Hukum Chand poured himself a stiff whisky and drank it in one gulp. He wiped his moustache with his hand. He did not have the nerve to take a good look at the girl. She was singing a song he knew well; he had heard his daughter humming it:

> *In the breeze is flying*
> *My veil of red muslin*
> *Ho Sir, Ho Sir.*

Hukum Chand felt uneasy. He took another whisky and dismissed his conscience. Life was too short for people to have consciences. He started to beat time to the song by snapping his fingers and slapping his thighs to each 'Ho Sir. Ho Sir.'

Twilight gave way to the dark of a moonless night. In the swamps by the river, frogs croaked. Cicadas chirped in the reeds. The bearer brought out a hissing paraffin lamp which cast a bright bluish light. The frame of the lamp threw a shadow over Hukum Chand. He stared at the girl who sat sheltered from the light. She was only a child and not very pretty, just young and unexploited. Her breasts barely filled her bodice. They could not have known the touch of a male hand. The thought that she was perhaps younger than his own daughter flashed across his mind. He drowned it quickly with another whisky. Life was like that. You took it as it came, shorn of silly conventions and values which deserved only lip worship. She wanted his money, and he . . . well. When all was said and done she was a prostitute and looked it. The silver sequins on her black sari sparkled. The diamond in her nose glittered like a star. Hukum Chand took another drink to dispel his remaining doubts. This time he wiped his moustache with his silk handkerchief. He began to hum louder and snapped his fingers with a flourish.

One film song followed another till all the Indian songs set to tunes of tangos and sambas that Hukum Chand knew were exhausted.

'Sing anything else you know,' ordered the magistrate with lordly condescension. 'Something new and gay.'

The girl started to sing a song which had several English words in it:

Sunday after Sunday, O my life.

Hukum Chand exploded with an appreciative 'wah, wah.' When the girl finished her song, he did not throw the five-rupee note at her but asked her to come and take it from his hand. The old woman pushed the girl ahead.

'Go, the Government sends for you.'

The girl got up and went to the table. She stretched out her hand to take the money; Hukum Chand withdrew his and put the note on his heart. He grinned lecherously. The girl looked at her companions for help. Hukum Chand put the note on the table. Before she could reach it he picked it up and again put it on his chest. The grin on his face became broader. The girl turned back to join the others. Hukum Chand held out the note for the third time.

'Go to the Government,' pleaded the old woman. The girl turned round obediently and went to the magistrate. Hukum Chand put his arm round her waist.

'You sing well.'

The girl gaped wide-eyed at her companions.

'The Government is talking to you. Why don't you answer him?' scolded the old woman. 'Government, the girl is young and very shy. She will learn,' she exclaimed.

Hukum Chand put a glass of whisky to the girl's lips. 'Drink a little. Just a sip for my sake,' he pleaded.

The girl stood impassively without opening her mouth. The old woman spoke again.

'Government, she knows nothing about drink. She is hardly sixteen and completely innocent. She has never been near a man before. I have reared her for your honour's pleasure.'

'Then she will eat something even if she does not drink,' said Hukum Chand. He preferred to ignore the rest of the woman's speech. He picked up a meatball from a plate and tried to put it in the girl's mouth. She took it from him and ate it.

Hukum Chand pulled her onto his lap and began to play with her hair. It was heavily oiled and fixed in waves by gaudy celluloid hair-clips. He took out a couple of hairpins and loosened the bun at the back. The hair fell about her shoulders. The musicians and the old woman got up.

'Have we permission to leave?'

'Yes, go. The driver will take you home.'

The old woman again set up a loud singsong: 'May your fame and honour increase. May your pen write figures of thousands—nay, hundreds of thousands.'

Hukum Chand produced a wad of notes and put it on the table for her. Then the party went to the car, leaving the magistrate with the girl in his lap and the bearer waiting for orders.

'Shall I serve dinner, sir?'

'No, just leave the food on the table. We will serve ourselves. You can go.' The bearer laid out the dinner and retired to his quarters.

Hukum Chand stretched out his hand and put out the paraffin lamp. It went out with a loud hiss, leaving the two in utter darkness save for a pale yellow light that flickered from the bedroom. Hukum Chand decided to stay out of doors.

The goods train had dropped the Mano Majra wagons and was leaving the station for the bridge. It came up noisily, its progress marked by the embers which flew out of the funnel of the engine. They were stoking coal in the firebox. A bright red-and-yellow light travelled through the spans of the bridge and was lost behind the jungle on the other side. The train's rumble got fainter and fainter. Its passing brought a feeling of privacy.

Hukum Chand helped himself to another whisky. The girl in his lap sat stiff and frigid.

'Are you angry with me? You don't want to talk to me?' asked Hukum Chand, pressing her closer to him. The girl did not answer or look back at him.

The magistrate was not particularly concerned with her

28

reactions. He had paid for all that. He brought the girl's face nearer his own and began kissing her on the back of her neck and on her ears. He could not hear the goods train any more. It had left the countryside in utter solitude. Hukum Chand could hear his breathing quicken. He undid the strap of the girl's bodice.

The sound of a shot shattered the stillness of the night. The girl broke loose and stood up.

'Did you hear a shot?'

The girl nodded. 'May be a shikari,' she answered, speaking to him for the first time. She refastened her bodice.

'There can't be any shikar on a dark night.'

The two stood in silence for some time—the man a little apprehensive; the girl relieved of the attentions of a lover whose breath smelled of whisky, tobacco and pyorrhea. But the silence told Hukum Chand that all was well. He took another whisky to make assurance doubly sure. The girl realized that there was no escape.

'Must be a cracker. Somebody getting married or something,' said Hukum Chand, putting his arms round the girl. He kissed her on the nose. 'Let us get married too,' he added with a leer.

The girl did not answer. She allowed herself to be dragged onto the table amongst plates covered with stale meatballs and cigarette ash. Hukum Chand swept them off the table with his hand and went on with his love-making. The girl suffered his pawing without a protest. He picked her up from the table and laid her on the carpet amongst the litter of tumblers, plates and bottles. She covered her face with the loose end of her sari and turned it sideways to avoid his breath. Hukum Chand began fumbling with her dress.

From Mano Majra came sounds of people shouting and the agitated barking of dogs. Hukum Chand looked up. Two shots rang out and silenced the barking and shouting. With a loud oath Hukum Chand left the girl. She got up, brushing and adjusting her sari. From the servants' quarters the bearer and the sweeper came out carrying lanterns and talking excitedly. A little later the chauffeur drove the car into the driveway, its headlights lighting up the front of the bungalow.

The morning after the dacoity the railway station was more crowded than usual. Some Mano Majrans made a habit of being there to watch the 10:30 slow passenger train from Delhi to Lahore come in. They liked to see the few passengers who might get on or off at Mano Majra, and they also enjoyed endless arguments about how late the train was on a given day and when it had last been on time. Since partition of the country there had been an additional inteiest. Now the trains were often four or five hours late and sometimes as many as twenty. When they came, they were crowded with Sikh and Hindu refugees from Pakistan or with Muslims from India. People perched on the roofs with their legs dangling, or on bedsteads wedged in between the bogies. Some of them rode precariously on the buffers.

The train this morning was only an hour late—almost like pre-war days. When it steamed in, the crying of hawkers on the platform and the passengers rushing about and shouting to each other gave the impression that many people would be getting off. But when the guard blew his whistle for departure, most of them were back on the train. Only a solitary Sikh peasant carrying an ironshod bamboo staff and followed by his wife with an infant resting on her hip remained with the hawkers on the platform. The man hoisted their rolled bedding onto his head and held it there with one hand. In the other he carried a large tin of clarified butter. The bamboo staff he held in his armpit, with one end trailing on the ground. Two green tickets stuck out beneath his moustache, which billowed from his upper lip onto his beard. The woman saw the line of faces peering through the iron railing of the station and drew her veil across her face. She followed her husband, her slippers sloshing on the gravel and her silver ornaments all ajingle. The stationmaster plucked the tickets from the peasant's mouth and let the couple out of the gate, where they were lost in a tumult of greetings and embraces.

The guard blew his whistle a second time and waved the green flag. Then, from the compartment just behind the engine, armed policemen emerged. There were twelve of them, and a subinspector. They carried rifles and their Sam Browne belts were charged with bullets. Two carried chains and handcuffs. From the other end of the train, near the guard's van, a young man stepped down. He wore a long white shirt, a brown waistcoat of coarse

cotton, and loose pajamas, and he carried a holdall. He stepped
gingerly off the train, pressing his tousled hair and looking all
round. He was a small slight man, somewhat effeminate in
appearance. The sight of the policemen emboldened him. He
hoisted the holdall onto his left shoulder and moved jauntily
toward the exit. The villagers watched the young man and the
police party move from opposite directions toward the
stationmaster who stood beside the gate. He had opened it wide
for the police and was bowing obsequiously to the subinspector.
The young man reached the gate first and stopped between the
stationmaster and the police. The stationmaster quickly took the
ticket from him, but the young man did not move on or make way
for the subinspector.

'Can you tell me, Stationmaster Sahib, if there is a place I can
stay in this village?'

The stationmaster was irritated. The visitor's urban accent, his
appearance, dress and holdall had the stationmaster holding back
his temper.

'There are no hotels or inns in Mano Majra,' he answered with
polite sarcasm. 'There is only the Sikh temple. You will see the
yellow flag-mast in the centre of the village.'

'Thank you, sir.'

The police party and the stationmaster scrutinized the youth
with a little diffidence. Not many people said 'thank you' in these
parts. Most of the 'thank you' crowd were foreign-educated. They
had heard of several well-to-do young men, educated in England,
donning peasant garb to do rural uplift work. Some were known
to be Communist agents. Some were sons of millionaires, some
sons of high government officials. All were looking for trouble, and
capable of making a lot of noise. One had to be careful.

The young man went out of the station toward the village. He
walked with a consciously erect gait, a few yards in front of the
policemen. He was uneasily aware of their attention. The itch on
the back of his neck told him that they were looking at him and
talking about him. He did not scratch or look back—he just walked
on like a soldier. He saw the flag-mast draped in yellow cloth with
a triangular flag above the conglomeration of mud huts. On the
flag was the Sikh symbol in black, a quoit with a dagger running
through and two swords crossed beneath. He went along the dusty

path lined on either side by scraggy bushes of prickly pear which fenced it off from the fields. The path wound its narrow way past the mud huts to the opening in the centre where the moneylender's house, the mosque and the temple faced each other. Underneath the peepul tree half a dozen villagers were sitting on a low wooden platform talking to each other. They got up as soon as they saw the policemen and followed them into Ram Lal's house. No one took any notice of the stranger.

He stepped into the open door of the temple courtyard. At the end opposite the entrance was a large hall in which the scripture, the Granth, lay wrapped in gaudy silks under a velvet awning. On one side were two rooms. A brick stairway ran along the wall to the roof of the rooms. Across the courtyard was a well with a high parapet. Beside the well stood a four-foot brick column supporting the long flag-mast with the yellow cloth covering it like a stocking.

The young man did not see anyone about. He could hear the sound of wet clothes being beaten on a slab of stone. He walked timidly to the other side of the well. An old Sikh got up with water dripping from his beard and white shorts.

'Sat Sri Akal.'

'Sat Sri Akal.'

'Can I stay for two or three days?'

'This is a gurudwara, the Guru's house—anyone may stay here. But you must have your head covered and you must not bring in any cigarettes or tobacco, nor smoke.'

'I do not smoke,' said the young man putting the holdall on the ground and spreading his handkerchief on his head.

'No, Babu Sahib, only when you go in near the Book, the Granth Sahib, you take your shoes off and cover your head. Put your luggage in that room and make yourself comfortable. Will you have something to eat?'

'That is very kind of you. But I have brought my own food.'

The old man showed the visitor to the spare room and then went back to the well. The young man went into the room. Its only furniture was a charpoy lying in the middle. There was a large colored calender on one wall. It had a picture of the Guru on horseback with a hawk on one hand. Alongside the calendar were nails to hang clothes.

The visitor emptied his holdall. He took out his air mattress and blew it up on the charpoy. He laid out pajamas and a silk dressing gown on the mattress. He got out a tin of sardines, a tin of Australian butter and a packet of dry biscuits. He shook his water bottle. It was empty.

The old Sikh came to him, combing his long beard with his fingers.

'What is your name?' he asked, sitting down on the threshold.

'Iqbal. What is yours?'

'Iqbal Singh?' queried the old man. Without waiting for an answer, he continued. 'I am the bhai of the temple. Bhai Meet Singh. What is your business in Mano Majra, Iqbal Singhji?'

The young man was relieved that the other had not gone on with his first question. He did not have to say what Iqbal he was. He could be a Muslim, Iqbal Mohammed. He could be a Hindu, Iqbal Chand, or a Sikh, Iqbal Singh. It was one of the few names common to the three communities. In a Sikh village, an Iqbal Singh would no doubt get a better deal, even if his hair was shorn and his beard shaved, than an Iqbal Mohammed or an Iqbal Chand. He himself had few religious feelings.

'I am a social worker, Bhaiji. There is much to be done in our villages. Now with this partition there is so much bloodshed going on, someone must do something to stop it. My party has sent me here, since this place is a vital point for refugee movements. Trouble here would be disastrous.'

The bhai did not seem interested in Iqbal's occupation.

'Where are you from, Iqbal Singhji?'

Iqbal knew that meant his ancestors and not himself.

'I belong to district Jhelum—now in Pakistan—but I have been in foreign countries a long time. It is after seeing the world that one feels how backward we are and one wants to do things about it. So I do social work.'

'How much do they pay you?'

Iqbal had learned not to resent these questions.

'I don't get paid very much. Just my expenses.'

'Do they pay the expenses of your wife and children also?'

'No, Bhaiji. I am not married. I really . . .'

'How old are you?'

'Twenty-seven. Tell me, do other social workers come to this village?' Iqbal decided to ask questions to stop Meet Singh's interrogation.

'Sometimes the American padres come.'

'Do you like their preaching Christianity in your village?'

'Everyone is welcome to his religion. Here next door is a Muslim mosque. When I pray to my Guru, Uncle Imam Baksh calls to Allah. How many religions do they have in Europe?'

'They are all Christians of one kind or other. They do not quarrel about their religions as we do here. They do not really bother very much about religion.'

'So I have heard,' said Meet Singh ponderously. 'That is why they have no morals. The sahibs and their wives go about with other sahibs and their wives. That is not good, is it?'

'But they do not tell lies like we do and they are not corrupt and dishonest as so many of us are,' answered Iqbal.

He got out his tin opener and opened the tin of sardines. He spread the fish on a biscuit and continued to talk while he ate.

'Morality, Meet Singhji, is a matter of money. Poor people cannot afford to have morals. So they have religion. Our first problem is to get people more food, clothing, comfort. That can only be done by stopping exploitation by the rich, and abolishing landlords. And that can only be done by changing the government.'

Meet Singh, with disgusted fascination, watched the young man eating fish complete with head, eyes and tail. He did not pay much attention to the lecture on rural indebtedness, the average national income, and capitalist exploitation which the other poured forth with flakes of dry biscuits. When Iqbal had finished eating Meet Singh got up and brought him a tumbler of water from his pitcher. Iqbal did not stop talking. He only raised his voice when the bhai went out.

Iqbal produced a little packet of cellophane paper from his pocket, took a white pill from it and dropped it in the tumbler. He had seen Meet Singh's thumb, with its black crescent of dirt under the nail, dipping into the water. In any case it was out of a well which could never have been chlorinated.

'Are you ill?' asked the old man, seeing the other wait for the pill to dissolve.

'No, it helps me to digest my food. We city-dwellers need this sort of thing after meals.'

Iqbal resumed his speech. 'To add to it all,' he continued, 'there is the police system which, instead of safeguarding the citizen, maltreats him and lives on corruption and bribery. You know all about that, I am sure.'

The old man nodded his head in agreement. Before he could comment, the young man spoke again. 'A party of policemen with an inspector came over on the same train with me. They will no doubt eat up all the chickens, the inspector will make a little money in bribes, and they will move on to the next village. One would think they had nothing else to do but fleece people.'

Reference to the police awakened the old man from his absent-minded listening. 'So the police have come after all. I must go and see what they are doing. They must be at the moneylender's house. He was murdered last night, just across from the gurudwara. The dacoits took a lot of cash and they say over five thousand rupees in silver and gold ornaments from his women.'

Meet Singh realized the interest he had created and slowly got up, repeating, 'I should be going. All the village will be there. They will be taking the corpse for medical examination. If a man is killed he cannot be cremated till the doctor certifies him dead.' The old man gave a wry smile.

'A murder! Why, why was he murdered?' stammered Iqbal, somewhat bewildered. He was surprised that Meet Singh had not mentioned the murder of a next-door neighbour all this time. 'Was it communal? Is it all right for me to be here? I do not suppose I can do much if the village is all excited about a murder.'

'Why, Babu Sahib, you have come to stop killing and you are upset by one murder?' asked Meet Singh, smiling. 'I thought you had come to stop such things, Babu Sahib. But you are quite safe in Mano Majra,' he added. 'Dacoits do not come to the same village more than once a year. There will be another dacoity in another village in a few days and people will forget about this one. We can have a meeting here one night after the evening prayer and you can tell them all you want. You had better rest. I will come back and tell you what happens.'

The old man hobbled out of the courtyard. Iqbal collected the empty tin, his knife and fork and tin plate, and took them to the well to wash.

In the afternoon, Iqbal stretched himself on the coarse string charpoy and tried to get some sleep. He had spent the night sitting on his bedroll in a crowded third-class compartment. Every time he had dozed off, the train had come to a halt at some wayside station and the door was forced open and more peasants poured in with their wives, bedding and tin trunks. Some child sleeping in its mother's lap would start howling till its wails were smothered by a breast thrust into its mouth. The shouting and clamour would continue until long after the train had left the station. The same thing was repeated again and again, till the compartment meant for fifty had almost two hundred people in it, sitting on the floor, on seats, on luggage racks, on trunks, on bedrolls, and on each other, or standing in the corners. There were dozens outside perched precariously on footboards, holding onto the door handles. There were several people on the roof. The heat and smell were oppressive. Tempers were frayed and every few minutes an argument would start because someone had spread himself out too much or had trod on another's foot on his way to the lavatory. The argument would be joined on either side by friends or relatives and then by all the others trying to patch it up. Iqbal had tried to read in the dim light speckled with shadows of moths that fluttered round the globe. He had hardly read a paragraph before his neighbour had observed:

'You are reading.'

'Yes, I am reading.'

'What are you reading?'

'A book.'

It had not worked. The man had simply taken the book out of Iqbal's hand and turned over its pages.

'English.'

'You must be educated.'

Iqbal did not comment.

The book had gone round the compartment for scrutiny. They had all looked at him. He was educated, therefore belonged to a different class. He was a babu.

'What honourable noun does your honour bear?'

'My name is Iqbal.'

'May your Iqbal [fame] ever increase.'

The man had obviously taken him to be a Muslim. Just as well.

All the passengers appeared to be Muslims on their way to Pakistan.

'Where does your wealth reside, Babu Sahib?'

'My poor home is in Jhelum district,' Iqbal had answered without irritation. The answer confirmed the likelihood of his being Muslim: Jhelum was in Pakistan.

Thereafter other passengers had joined in the cross-examination. Iqbal had to tell them what he did, what his source of income was, how much he was worth, where he had studied, why he had not married, all the illnesses he had ever suffered from. They had discussed their own domestic problems and diseases and had sought his advice. Did Iqbal know of any secret prescriptions or herbs that the English used when they were 'run down'? Iqbal had given up the attempt to sleep or read.They had kept up the conversation till the early hours of the morning. He would have described the journey as insufferable except that the limits to which human endurance could be stretched in India made the word meaningless. He got off at Mano Majra with a sigh of relief. He could breathe the fresh air. He was looking forward to a long siesta.

But sleep would not come to Iqbal. There was no ventilation in the room. It had a musty earthy smell. A pile of clothes in the corner stank of stale clarified butter, and there were flies buzzing all round. Iqbal spread a handkerchief on his face. He could hardly breathe. With all that, just as he had managed to doze off, Meet Singh came in exclaiming philosophically:

'Robbing a fellow villager is like stealing from one's mother. Iqbal Singhji, this is Kalyug—the dark age. Have you ever heard of dacoits looting their neighbour's homes? Now all morality has left the world.'

Iqbal removed the handkerchief from his face.

'What has happened?'

'What has happened?' repeated Meet Singh, feigning surprise. 'Ask me what has not happened! The police sent for Jugga—Jugga is a budmash number ten [from the number of the police register in which names of bad characters are listed]. But Jugga had run away, absconded. Also, some of the loot—a bag of bangles—was found in his courtyard. So we know who did it. This is not the first murder he has committed—he has it in his blood. His father and grandfather were also dacoits and were hanged for murder. But they never robbed their own village folk. As a matter of fact, when they were at home, no dacoit dared come to Mano Majra. Juggut Singh has disgraced his family.'

Iqbal sat up rubbing his forehead. His countrymen's code of morals had always puzzled him, with his anglicized way of looking at things. The Punjabi's code was even more baffling. For them truth, honour, financial integrity were 'all right', but these were placed lower down the scale of values than being true to one's salt, to one's friends and fellow villagers. For friends you could lie in court or cheat, and no one would blame you. On the contrary, you became a *nar admi*—a he-man who had defied authority (magistrates and police) and religion (oath on the scripture) but proved true to friendship. It was the projection of rural society where everyone in the village was a relation and loyalty to the village was the supreme test. What bothered Meet Singh, a priest, was not that Jugga had committed murder but that his hands were soiled with the blood of a fellow villager. If Jugga had done the same thing in the neighbouring village, Meet Singh would gladly have appeared in his defence and sworn on the holy Granth that Jugga had been praying in the gurudwara at the time of the murder. Iqbal had wearied of talking to people like Meet Singh. They did not understand. He had come to the conclusion that he did not belong.

Meet Singh was disappointed that he had failed to arouse Iqbal's interest.

'You have seen the world and read many books, but take it from me that a snake can cast its slough but not its poison. This saying is worth a hundred thousand rupees.'

Iqbal did not register appreciation of the valuable saying. Meet Singh explained: 'Jugga had been going straight for some time. He ploughed his land and looked after his cattle. He never left the village, and reported himself to the lambardar every day. But how long can a snake keep straight? There is crime in his blood.'

'There is no crime in anyone's blood any more than there is goodness in the blood of others,' answered Iqbal waking up. This was one of his pet theories. 'Does anyone ever bother to find out why people steal and rob and kill? No! They put them in jail or hang them. It is easier. If the fear of the gallows or the cell had stopped people from killing or stealing, there would be no murdering or stealing. It does not. They hang a man every day in this province. Yet ten get murdered every twenty-four hours. No, Bhaiji, criminals are not born. They are made by hunger, want and injustice.'

Iqbal felt a little silly for coming out with these platitudes. He must check this habit of turning a conversation into a sermon. He returned to the subject.

'I suppose they will get Jugga easily if he is such a well-known character.'

'Jugga cannot go very far. He can be recognized from a kos. He is an arm's length taller than anyone else. The Deputy Sahib has already sent orders to all police stations to keep a lookout for Jugga.'

'Who is the Deputy Sahib?' asked Iqbal.

'You do not know the Deputy?' Meet Singh was surprised. 'It's Hukum Chand. He is staying at the dak bungalow north of the bridge. Now Hukum Chand is a *nar admi*. He started as a foot-constable and see where he is now! He always kept the sahibs pleased and they gave him one promotion after another. The last one gave him his own place and made him Deputy. Yes, Iqbal Singhji, Hukum Chand is a *nar admi*—and clever. He is true to his friends and always gets things done for them. He has had dozens of relatives given good jobs. He is one of a hundred. Nothing counterfeit about Hukum Chand.'

'Is he a friend of yours?'

'Friend? No,no,' protested Meet Singh. 'I am a humble bhai of the gurudwara and he is an emperor. He is the government and we are his subjects. If he comes to Mano Majra, you will see him.'

There was a pause in the conversation. Iqbal slipped his feet into his sandals and stood up.

'I must take a walk. Which way do you suggest I should go?'

'Go in any direction you like. It is all the same open country. Go to the river. You will see the trains coming and going. If you cross the railroad track you will see the dak bungalow. Don't be too late. These are bad times and it is best to be indoors before dark. Besides, I have told the lambardar and Uncle Imam Baksh—he is mullah of the mosque—that you are here. They may be coming in to talk to you.'

39

'No, I won't be late.'

Iqbal stepped out of the gurudwara. There was no sign of activity now. The police had apparently finished investigating. Half a dozen constables lay sprawled on charpoys under the peepul tree. The door of Ram Lal's house was open. Some villagers sat on the floor in the courtyard. A woman wailed in a singsong which ended up in convulsions of crying in which other women joined. It was hot and still. The sun blazed on the mud walls.

Iqbal walked in the shade of the wall of the gurudwara. Children had relieved themselves all along it. Men had used it as a urinal. A mangy bitch lay on her side with a litter of eight skinny pups yapping and tugging at her sagging udders.

The lane ended abruptly at the village pond—a small patch of muddy water full of buffaloes with their heads sticking out.

A footpath skirted the pond and went along a dry watercourse through the wheat fields toward the river. Iqbal went along the watercourse watching his steps carefully. He reached the riverside just as the express from Lahore came up on the bridge. He watched its progress through the crisscross of steel. Like all the trains, it was full. From the roof, legs dangled down the sides onto the doors and windows. The doors and windows were jammed with heads and arms. There were people on buffers between the bogies. The two on the buffers on the tail end of the train were merrily kicking their legs and gesticulating. The train picked up speed after crossing the bridge. The engine driver started blowing the whistle and continued blowing till he had passed Mano Majra station. It was an expression of relief that they were out of Pakistan and into India.

Iqbal went up the riverbank toward the bridge. He was planning to go under it toward the dak bungalow when he noticed a Sikh soldier watching him from the sentry box at the end of the bridge. Iqbal changed his mind and walked boldly up to the rail embankment and turned toward Mano Majra station. The manoeuvre allayed the sentry's suspicion. Iqbal went a hundred yards up and then casually sat down on the railway line.

The passing express had woken Mano Majra from its late siesta. Boys threw stones at the buffaloes in the pond and drove them home. Groups of women went out in the fields and scattered themselves behind the bushes. A bullock cart carrying Ram Lal's corpse left the village and went toward the station. It was guarded by policemen. Several villagers went a little distance with it and them returned along with the relatives.

Iqbal stood up and looked all round. From the railway station to the roof of the rest house showing above the plumes of pampas, from the bridge to the village and back to the railway station, the whole place was littered with men, women, children, cattle, and dogs. There were kites wheeling high up in the sky, long lines of crows were flying from somewhere to somewhere, and millions of sparrows twittered about the trees. Where in India could one find a place which did not teem with life? Iqbal thought of his first reaction on reaching Bombay. Milling crowds—millions of them—on the quayside, in the streets, on railway platforms; even at night the pavements were full of people. The whole country was like an overcrowded room. What could you expect when the population went up by six every minute—five millions every year! It made all planning in industry or agriculture a mockery. Why not spend the same amount of effort in checking the increase in population? But how could you, in the land of the *Kama Sutra*, the home of phallic worship and the son cult?

Iqbal was woken from his angry daydreaming by a shimmering sound along the steel wires which ran parallel to the railway lines. The signal above the sentry's box near the bridge came down. Iqbal stood up and brushed his clothes. The sun had gone down beyond the river. The russet sky turned gray as shades of twilight spread across the plain. A new moon looking like a finely pared finger nail appeared beside the evening star. The muezzin's call to prayer rose above the rumble of the approaching train.

Iqbal found his way back easily. All lanes met in the temple–mosque–moneylender's–house triangle with the peepul tree in the centre. Sounds of wailing still came from Ram Lal's house. In the mosque, a dozen men stood in two rows silently going through their genuflections. In the gurudwara, Meet Singh, sitting beside the Book which was folded up in muslin on a cot, was reciting the evening prayer. Five or six men and women sat in a semicircle around a hurricane lantern and listened to him.

Iqbal went straight to his room and lay down on his charpoy in the dark. He had barely shut his eyes when the worshippers

41

began to chant. The chanting stopped for a couple of minutes, only to start again. The ceremony ended with shouts of '*Sat Sri Akal*' and the beating of a drum. The men and women came out. Meet Singh held the lantern and helped them find their shoes. They started talking loudly. In the babel the only word Iqbal could make out was 'babu'. Somebody who had noticed Iqbal come in, had told the others. There was some whispering and shuffling of feet and then silence.

Iqbal shut his eyes once more. A minute later Meet Singh stood on the threshold, holding the lantern.

'Iqbal Singhji, have you gone to bed without food? Would you like some spinach? I have also curd and buttermilk.'

'No, thank you, Bhaiji. I have the food I want.'

'Our poor food . . .' started Meet Singh.

'No, no, it is not that,' interrupted Iqbal sitting up, 'it is just that I have it and it may be wasted if I don't eat it. I am a little tired and would like to sleep.'

'Then you must have some milk. Banta Singh, the lambardar, is bringing you some. I will tell him to hurry up if you want to sleep early. I have another charpoy for you on the roof. It is too hot to sleep in here.' Meet Singh left the hurricane lantern in the room and disappeared in the dark.

The prospect of having to talk to the lambardar was not very exciting. Iqbal fished out his silver hip flask from underneath the pillow and took a long swig of whisky. He ate a few dry biscuits that were in the paper packet. He took his mattress and pillow to the roof where a charpoy had been laid for him. Meet Singh apparently slept in the courtyard to guard the gurudwara.

Iqbal lay on his charpoy and watched the stars in the teeming sky until he heard several voices entering the gurudwara and coming up the stairs. Then he got up to greet the visitors.

'*Sat Sri Akal*, Babu Sahib.'

'Salaam to you, Babu Sahib.'

They shook hands. Meet Singh did not bother to introduce them. Iqbal pushed the air mattress aside to make room on the charpoy for the visitors. He sat down on the floor himself.

'I am ashamed for not having presented myself earlier,' said the Sikh. 'Please forgive me. I have brought some milk for you.'

'Yes, Sahib, we are ashamed of ourselves. You are our guest

and we have not rendered you any service. Drink the milk before it gets cold,' added the other visitor. He was a tall lean man with a clipped beard.

'It is very kind of you. . . I know you have been busy with the police . . . I don't drink milk. Really I do not. We city-dwellers . . .'

The lambardar ignored Iqbal's well-mannered protests. He removed his dirty handkerchief from a large brass tumbler and began to stir the milk with his forefinger. 'It is fresh. I milked the buffalo only an hour back and got the wife to boil it. I know you educated people only drink boiled milk. There is quite a lot of sugar in it; it has settled at the bottom,' he added with a final stir. To emphasize the quality of the milk, he picked up a slab of clotted cream on his forefinger and slapped it back in the milk.

'Here, Babuji, drink it before it gets cold.'

'No! No! No, thank you, no!' protested Iqbal. He did not know how to get out of his predicament without offending the visitors. 'I don't ever drink milk. But if you insist, I will drink it later. I like it cold.'

'Yes, you drink it as you like, Babuji,' said the Muslim, coming to his rescue. 'Banta Singh, leave the tumbler here. Bhai will bring it back in the morning.'

The lambardar covered the tumbler with his handkerchief and put it under Iqbal's charpoy. There was a long pause. Iqbal had pleasant visions of pouring the milk with all its clotted cream down the drain.

'Well, Babuji,' began the Muslim. 'Tell us something. What is happening in the world? What is all this about Pakistan and Hindustan?'

'We live in this little village and know nothing,' the lambardar put in. 'Babuji, tell us, why did the English leave?'

Iqbal did not know how to answer simple questions like these. Independence meant little or nothing to these people. They did not even realize that it was a step forward and that all they needed to do was to take the next step and turn the make-believe political freedom into a real economic one.

'They left because they had to. We had hundreds of thousands of young men trained to fight in the war. This time they had the arms too. Haven't you heard of the mutiny of the Indian sailors? The soldiers would have done the same thing. The English were frightened. They did not shoot any of the Indians who joined the Indian National Army set up by the Japanese, because they thought the whole country would turn against them.'

Iqbal's thesis did not cut much ice.

'Babuji, what you say may be right,' said the lambardar hesitantly. 'But I was in the last war and fought in Mesopotamia and Gallipoli. We liked English officers. They were better than the Indian.'

'Yes,' added Meet Singh, 'my brother who is a havildar says all sepoys are happier with English officers than with Indian. My brother's colonel's mem-sahib still sends my niece things from London. You know, Lambardar Sahib, she even sent money at her wedding. What Indian officers' wives will do that?'

Iqbal tried to take the offensive. 'Why, don't you people want to be free? Do you want to remain slaves all your lives?'

After a long silence the lambardar answered: 'Freedom must be a good thing. But what will we get out of it? Educated people like you, Babu Sahib, will get the jobs the English had. Will we get more lands or more buffaloes?'

'No,' the Muslim said. 'Freedom is for the educated people who fought for it. We were slaves of the English, now we will be slaves of the educated Indians—or the Pakistanis.'

Iqbal was startled at the analysis.

'What you say is absolutely right,' he agreed warmly. 'If you want freedom to mean something for you—the peasants and workers—you have to get together and fight. Get the bania Congress government out. Get rid of the princes and the landlords and freedom will mean for you just what you think it should. More land, more buffaloes, no debts.'

'That is what that fellow told us,' interrupted Meet Singh, 'that fellow . . . Lambardara, what was his name? Comrade Something-or-other. Are you a comrade, Babu Sahib?'

'No.'

'I am glad. That comrade did not believe in God. He said when his party came into power they would drain the sacred pool round the temple at Turun Tarun and plant rice in it. He said it would be more useful.'

'That is foolish talk,' protested Iqbal. He wished Meet Singh had remembered the comrade's name. The man should be reported to headquarters and taken to task.

'If we have no faith in God then we are like animals,' said the Muslim gravely. 'All the world respects a religious man. Look at Gandhi! I hear he reads the Koran Sharif and the Unjeel along with his Vedas and Shastras. People sing his praise in the four corners of the earth. I have seen a picture in a newspaper of Gandhi's prayer meeting. It showed a lot of white men and women sitting cross-legged. One white girl had her eyes shut. They said she was the Big Lord's daughter. You see, Meet Singh, even the English respect a man of religion.'

'Of course, Chacha. Whatever you say is right to the sixteenth anna of the rupee,' agreed Meet Singh, rubbing his belly.

Iqbal felt his temper rise. 'They are a race of four-twenties,' he said vehemently. [Section 420 of the Indian Penal Code defines the offence of cheating.] 'Do not believe what they say.'

Once again he felt his venom had missed its mark. But the Big Lord's daughter sitting cross-legged with her eyes shut for the benefit of press photographers, and the Big Lord himself—the handsome, Hindustani-speaking cousin of the King, who loved India like the missionaries—was always too much for Iqbal.

'I have lived in their country many years. They are nice as human beings. Politically they are the world's biggest four-twenties. They would not have spread their domain all over the world if they had been honest. That, however, is irrelevant,' added Iqbal. It was time to change the subject. 'What is important is: what is going to happen now?'

'We know what is happening,' the lambardar answered with some heat. 'The winds of destruction are blowing across the land. All we hear is kill, kill. The only ones who enjoy freedom are thieves, robbers and cutthroats.' Then he added calmly: 'We were better off under the British. At least there was security.'

There was an uneasy silence. An engine was shunting up and down the railway line rearranging its load of goods wagons. The Muslim changed the subject.

'That is the goods train. It must be late. Babu Sahib, you are tired; we must let you rest. If you need us, we will be always at your service.'

They all got up. Iqbal shook hands with his visitors without showing any trace of anger. Meet Singh conducted the lambardar

45

and the Muslim down to the courtyard. He then retired to his charpoy there.

Iqbal lay down once more and gazed at the stars. The wail of the engine in the still vast plain made him feel lonely and depressed. What could he—one little man—do in this enormous impersonal land of four hundred million? Could he stop the killing? Obviously not. Everyone—Hindu, Muslim, Sikh, Congressite, Leaguer, Akali, or Communist—was deep in it. It was fatuous to suggest that the bourgeois revolution could be turned into a proletarian one. The stage had not arrived. The proletariat was indifferent to political freedom for Hindustan or Pakistan, except when it could be given an economic significance like grabbing land by killing an owner who was of a different religious denomination. All that could be done was to divert the kill-and-grab instinct from communal channels and turn it against the propertied class. That was the proletarian revolution the easy way. His party bosses would not see it.

Iqbal wished they had sent someone else to Mano Majra. He would be so much more useful directing policy and clearing the cobwebs from their minds. But he was not a leader. He lacked the qualifications. He had not fasted. He had never been in jail. He had made none of the necessary 'sacrifices'. So, naturally, nobody would listen to him. He should have started his political career by finding an excuse to court imprisonment. But there was still time. He would do that as soon as he got back to Delhi. By then, the massacres would be over. It would be quite safe.

The goods train had left the station and was rumbling over the bridge. Iqbal fell asleep, dreaming of a peaceful life in jail.

Early next morning, Iqbal was arrested.

Meet Singh had gone out to the fields carrying his brass mug of water and chewing a keekar twig he used as a toothbrush. Iqbal had slept through the rumble of passing trains, the muezzin's call, and the other village noises. Two constables came into the gurudwara, looking in his room, examined his celluloid cups and saucers, shining aluminum spoons, forks and knives, his thermos, and then came up onto the roof. They shook Iqbal rudely. He sat up rubbing his eyes, somewhat bewildered. Before he could size

46

up the situation and formulate the curt replies he would like to have given, he had told the policemen his name and occupation. One of them filled in the blank spaces on a yellow piece of printed paper and held it in front of Iqbal's blinking eyes.

'Here is warrant for your arrest. Get up.'

The other slipped the ring at one end of a pair of handcuffs in his belt and unlocked the links to put round Iqbal's wrists. The sight of the handcuffs brought Iqbal wide awake. He jumped out of bed and faced the policemen.

'You have no right to arrest me like this,' he shouted. 'You made up the warrant in front of me. This is not going to end here. The days of police rule are over. If you dare put your hands on me, the world will hear about it. I will see that the papers tell the people how you chaps do your duty.'

The policemen were taken aback. The young man's accent, the rubber pillows and mattress and all the other things they had seen in the room, and above all, his aggressive attitude, made them uneasy. They felt that perhaps they had made a mistake.

'Babu Sahib, we are only doing our duty. You settle this with the magistrate,' one of them answered politely. The other fumbled uneasily with the handcuffs.

'I will settle it with the whole lot of you—police and magistrates! Come and disturb people in sleep! You will regret this mistake.' Iqbal waited for the policemen to say something so that he could go on with his tirade against law and order. But they had been subdued.

'You will have to wait. I have to wash and change and leave my things in somebody's care,' said Iqbal aggressively, giving them another chance to say something.

'All right, Babu Sahib. Take as long as you like.'

The policemen's civil attitude deflated Iqbal's anger. He collected his things and went down the stairs to his room. He went to the well, pulled up a bucket of water and began to wash. He was in no hurry.

Bhai Meet Singh came back vigorously brushing his teeth with the end of the keekar twig which he had chewed into a fibrous brush. The presence of policemen in the gurudwara did not surprise him. Whenever they came to the village and could not find accommodation at the lambardar's house they came to the temple.

He had been expecting them after the moneylender's murder.

'*Sat Sri Akal,*' said Meet Singh, throwing away his keekar toothbrush.

'*Sat Sri Akal,*' replied the policemen.

'Would you like some tea or something? Some buttermilk?'

'We are waiting for the Babu Sahib,' the policemen said. 'If you can give us something while he is getting ready, it will be very kind.'

Meet Singh maintained a casual indifference. It was not up to him to argue with the police or be nosy about their business. Iqbal Singh was probably a 'comrade'. He certainly talked like one.

'I will make some tea for him, too,' replied Meet Singh. He looked at Iqbal. 'Or will you have your own out of the big bottle?'

'Thank you very much,' answered Iqbal through the tooth paste froth in his mouth. He spat it out. 'The tea in the bottle must be cold by now. I would be grateful for a hot cup. And would you mind looking after my things while I am away? They are arresting me for something. They do not know themselves for what.'

Meet Singh pretended he had not heard. The policemen looked a little sheepish.

'It is not our fault, Babu Sahib,' one of them said. 'Why are you getting angry with us? Get angry with the magistrate.'

Iqbal ignored their protest by more brushing of his teeth. He washed his face and came back to the room rubbing himself with a towel. He let the air out of the mattress and the pillow and rolled them up. He emptied the holdall of its contents: books, clothes, torch, a large silver hip flask. He made a list of his things and put them back. When Meet Singh brought tea, Iqbal handed him the holdall.

'Bhaiji, I have put all my things in the holdall. I hope it will not be too much trouble looking after them. I would rather trust you than the police in this free country of ours.'

The policemen looked away. Meet Singh was embarrassed.

'Certainly, Babu Sahib,' he said meekly. 'I am your servant as well as that of the police. Here everyone is welcome. You like tea in your own cup?'

Iqbal got out his celluloid teacup and spoon. The constables took brass tumblers from Meet Singh. They wrapped the loose ends of their turbans round the tumblers to protect their hands from the hot brass. To reassure themselves they sipped noisily. But Iqbal was in complete possession of the situation. He sat on the string cot while they sat on the threshold and Meet Singh on the floor outside. They did not dare to speak to him for fear of rudeness. The constable with the handcuffs had quietly taken them off his belt and thrust them in his pocket. They finished their tea and looked up uneasily. Iqbal sat sullenly staring over their heads with an intensity charged with importance. He glared vacantly into space, occasionally taking a spinsterish sip of his tea. When he had finished, he stood up abruptly.

'I am ready,' he announced, dramatically holding out his hands. 'Put on the handcuffs.'

'There is no need for handcuffs, Babuji,' answered one of the constables. 'You had better cover your face or you will be recognized at the identification parade.'

Iqbal pounced on the opportunity. 'Is this how you do your duty? If the rule is that I have to be handcuffed, then handcuffed I shall be. I am not afraid of being recognized. I am not a thief or a dacoit. I am a political worker. I will go through the village as I am so that people can see what the police do to people they do not like.'

This outburst was too much for one of the constables. He spoke sharply:

'Babuji, we are being polite to you. We keep saying "ji", "ji" to you all the time, but you want to sit on our heads. We have told you a hundred times we are doing our duty, but you insist on believing that we have a personal grudge.' He turned to his colleague. 'Put the handcuffs on the fellow. He can do what he likes with his face. If I had a face like his, I would want to hide it. We will report that he refused to cover it.'

Iqbal did not have a ready answer to the sarcasm. He had a Semitic consciousness of his hooked nose. Quite involuntarily he brushed it with the back of his hand. Reference to his physical appearance always put him off. The handcuffs were fastened round his wrists and chained onto the policeman's belt.

'*Sat Sri Akal*, Bhaiji. I will be back soon.'

'*Sat Sri Akal*, Iqbal Singhji, and may the Guru protect you. *Sat Sri Akal*, Sentryji.'

'*Sat Sri Akal.*'

49

The party marched out of the temple courtyard, leaving Meet Singh standing with the kettle of tea in his hand.

At the time the two constables were sent to arrest Iqbal, a posse of ten men was sent to arrest Juggut Singh. Policemen surrounded his house at all points. Constables armed with rifles were posted on neighbouring roofs and in the front and rear of the house. Then six others armed with revolvers rushed into the courtyard. Juggut Singh lay on his charpoy, wrapped from head to foot in a dirty white sheet and snoring lustily. He had spent two nights and a day in the jungle without food or shelter. He had come home in the early hours of the morning when he believed everyone in the village would be asleep. The neighbours had been vigilant and the police were informed immediately. They waited till he had filled himself with food and was sound asleep. His mother had gone out, bolting the door from the outside.

Juggut Singh's feet were put in fetters and handcuffs were fastened on his right wrist while he slept. Policemen put their revolvers in their holsters. Men with rifles joined them in the courtyard. They prodded Juggut Singh with the butt ends of their guns.

'O Jugga, get up, it is almost afternoon.'

'See how he sleeps like a pig without a care in the world.'

Jugga sat up wearily, blinking his eyes. He gazed at the handcuffs and the fetters with philosophic detachment, then stretched his arms wide and yawned loudly. Sleep came on him again and he began to nod.

Juggut Singh's mother came in and saw her courtyard full of armed policemen. Her son sat on the charpoy with his head resting on his manacled hands. His eyes were shut. She ran up to him and clasped him by the knees. She put her head in his lap and started to cry.

Juggut Singh woke up from his reverie. He pushed his mother back rudely.

'Why are you crying?' he said. 'You know I had nothing to do with the dacoity.'

She began to wail. 'He did not do it. He did nothing. In the name of God, I swear he did nothing.'

'Then where was he on the night of the murder?' the head constable said.

'He was out in his fields. He was not with the dacoits. I swear he was not.'

'He is a *budmash* under orders not to go out of the village after sunset. We have to arrest him for that in any case.' He motioned to his men. 'Search the rooms and the barn.' The head constable had his doubts about Juggut Singh partaking in a dacoity in his own village. It was most unusual.

Four constables busied themselves looking around the house, emptying steel trunks and tin cans. The haystack was pulled down and the hay scattered in the yard. The spear was found without difficulty.

'I suppose this has been put here by your uncle?' said the head constable addressing the mother sourly. 'Wrap the blade in a piece of cloth, it may have blood stains on it.'

'There is nothing on it,' cried the mother, 'nothing. He keeps it to kill wild pigs that come to destroy the crops. I swear he is innocent.'

'We will see. We will see,' the head constable dismissed her. 'You better get proof of his innocence ready for the magistrate.'

The old woman stopped moaning. She did have proof—the packet of broken bangles. She had not told Jugga about it. If she had, he would certainly have gone mad at the insult and been violent to someone. Now he was in fetters and handcuffs, he could only lose his temper.

'Wait, brother policemen. I have the evidence.'

The policemen watched the woman go in and bring out a packet from the bottom of her steel trunk. She unwrapped the brown paper. There were broken pieces of blue and red glass bangles with tiny gold spots. Two of them were intact. The head constable took them.

'What sort of proofs are these?'

'The dacoits threw them in the courtyard after the murder. They wanted to insult Jugga for not coming with them. Look!' She held out her hands. 'I am too old to wear glass bangles and they are too small for my wrists.'

'Then Jugga must know who the dacoits were. What did they say when they threw them?' asked the head constable.

'Nothing, they said nothing. They abused Jugga . . .'

'Can't you keep your mouth shut?' interrupted Jugga angrily. 'I do not know who the dacoits were. All I know is that I was not with them.'

'Who leaves you bangles?' asked the head constable. He smiled and held up the bits of glass in his hands.

Jugga lost his temper. He raised his manacled fists and brought them heavily down on the head constable's palms. 'What seducer of his mother can throw bangles at me? What . . .'

The constables closed round Juggut Singh and started slapping him and kicking him with their thick boots. Jugga sat down on his haunches, covering his head with his arms. His mother began to beat her forehead and started crying again. She broke into the cordon of policemen and threw herself on her son.

'Don't hit him. The Guru's curse be on you. He is innocent. It is all my fault. You can beat me.'

The beating stopped. The head constable picked pieces of glass out of his palm, pressed out blood, and wiped it with his handkerchief.

'You keep the evidence of your son's innocence,' he said bitterly. 'We will get the story out of this son of a bitch of yours in our own way. When he gets a few lashes on his buttocks, he will talk. Take him out.'

Juggut Singh was led out of the house in handcuffs and fetters. He left without showing a trace of emotion for his mother, who continued to wail and beat her forehead and breasts. His parting words wore:

'I will be back soon. They cannot give me more than a few months for having a spear and going out of the village. *Sat Sri Akal.*'

Jugga recovered his temper as quickly as he had lost it. He forgot the incident of the bangles and the beating as soon as he stepped across his threshold. He had no malice or ill will toward the policemen: they were not human like other human beings. They had no affections, no loyalties or enmities. They were just men in uniform you tried to avoid.

There was not much point in Juggut Singh covering his face. The whole village knew him. He went past the villagers, smiling and raising his manacled hands in a greeting to everyone. The fetters around his feet forced him to walk slowly with his legs apart.

He had a devil-may-care jauntiness in his step. He showed his unconcern by twirling his thin brown moustache and cracking obscene jokes with the policemen.

Iqbal and the two constables joined Juggut Singh's party by the river. They all proceeded upstream toward the bridge. The head constable walked in front. Armed policemen marched on the sides and at the rear of the prisoners. Iqbal was lost in the khaki and red of their uniforms. Juggut Singh's head and shoulders showed above the turbans of the policemen. It was like a procession of horses with an elephant in their midst—taller, broader, slower, with his chains clanking like ceremonial trappings.

No one seemed to be in the mood to talk. The policemen were uneasy. They knew that they had made a mistake, or rather, two mistakes. Arresting the social worker was a blunder and a likely source of trouble. His belligerent attitude confirmed his innocence. Some sort of case would have to be made up against him. That was always a tricky thing to do to educated people. Juggut Singh was too obvious a victim to be the correct one. He had undoubtedly broken the law in leaving the village at night, but he was not likely to have joined in a dacoity in his own village. He would be too easily recognized by his enormous size. Also, it was quite clear that these two had met for the first time.

Iqbal's pride had been injured. Up to the time he met Juggut Singh, he was under the impression that he had been arrested for his politics. He had insisted on being handcuffed so that the villagers could see with what dignity he bore himself. They would be angered at such an outrage to civil liberties. But the men had gaped stupidly and the women peered through their veils and asked each other in whispers, 'Who is this?' When he joined the group that escorted Juggut Singh, the point of the policeman's advice, 'Cover your face, otherwise you may be recognized at the identification parade,' came home to him. He was under arrest in connection with the murder of Ram Lal. It was so stupid he could hardly believe it. Everyone knew that he had come to Mano Majra after the murder. On the same train as the policemen, in fact. They could be witness of his alibi. The situation was too ludicrous for words. But Punjabi policemen were not the sort who admitted making mistakes. They would trump up some sort of charge: vagrancy, obstructing officers in doing their duty, or some such thing. He would fight them tooth and nail.

The only one in the party who did not seem to mind was Juggut Singh. He had been arrested before. He had spent quite as much time in jail as at home. His association with the police was an inheritance. Register number ten at the police station, which gave the record of the activities of the bad characters of the locality, had carried his father Alam Singh's name while he lived. Alam Singh had been convicted of dacoity with murder, and hanged. Juggut Singh's mother had to mortgage all their land to pay lawyers. Juggut Singh had to find money to redeem the land, and he had done that within the year. No one could prove how he had raised the money, but at the end of the year the police had taken him. His name was entered in register number ten and he was officially declared a man of bad character. Behind his back everyone referred to him as a 'number ten'.

Juggut Singh looked at the prisoner beside him several times. He wanted to start a conversation. Iqbal had his eyes fixed in front of him and walked with the camera-consciousness of an actor facing the lens. Juggut Singh lost patience.

'Listen. What village are you from?' he asked and grinned, baring a set of even teeth studded with gold points in the centres.

Iqbal looked up, but did not return the smile.

'I am not a villager. I come from Delhi. I was sent to organize peasants, but the government does not like the people to be organized.'

Juggut Singh became polite. He gave up the tone of familiarity. 'I hear we have our own rule now,' he said. 'It is Mahatma Gandhi's government in Delhi, isn't it? They say so in our village.'

'Yes, the Englishmen have gone but the rich Indians have taken their place. What have you or your fellow villagers got out of independence? More bread or more clothes? You are in the same handcuffs and fetters which the English put on you. We have to get together and rise. We have nothing to lose but these chains. Iqbal emphasized the last sentence by raising his hands up to his face and jerking them as if the movement would break the handcuffs.

The policemen looked at each other.

Juggut Singh looked down at the fetters round his ankles and the iron bars which linked them to the handcuffs.

'I am a budmash. All governments put me in jail.'

'But,' interrupted Iqbal angrily, 'what makes you budmash? The government! It makes regulations and keeps registers, policemen and jailers to enforce them. For anyone they do not like, they have a rule which makes him a bad character and a criminal. What have I . . .'

'No, Babu Sahib,' broke in Juggut Singh good-humouredly, 'it is our fate. It is written on our foreheads and on the lines of our hands. I am always wanting to do something. When there is ploughing to be done or the harvest to be gathered, then I am busy. When there is no work, my hands still itch to do something. So I do something, and it is always wrong.'

The party passed under the bridge and approached the rest house. Juggut Singh's complacency had put Iqbal off. He did not want to waste his breath arguing with a village bad character. He wanted to save his words for the magistrate. He would let him have it in English—the accent would make him squirm.

When the police brought in the prisoners the subinspector ordered them to be taken to the servants' quarters. The magistrate was in his room dressing. The head constable left the prisoners with his men and came back to the bungalow.

'Who is this small chap you have brought?' asked the subinspector, looking a little worried.

'I arrested him on your orders. He was the stranger staying at the Sikh temple.'

The answer irritated the subinspector. 'I do not suppose you have any brains of your own! I leave a little job to you and you go and make a fool of yourself. You should have seen him before arresting him Isn't he the same man who got off the train with us yesterday?'

'The train?' queried the head constable, feigning ignorance. 'I did not see him on the train, cherisher of the poor. I only carried out your orders and arrested the stranger loitering about the village under suspicious circumstances.'

The subinspector's temper shot up.

'Ass!'

The head constable avoided his officer's gaze.

'You are an ass of some place,' he repeated with greater vehemence. 'Have you no brains at all?'

'Cherisher of the poor, what fault have I . . .'

'Shut up!'

The head constable started looking at his feet. The subinspector let his temper cool. He had to face Hukum Chand, who relied on him and did not expect to be let down. After some thought, the subinspector peered through the wire gauze door.

'Have I permission to enter?'

'Come in. Come in, Inspector Sahib,' Hukum Chand replied. 'Do not wait on formalities.'

The subinspector went in, and saluted.

'Well, what have you been doing?' asked the magistrate. He was rubbing cream on his freshly shaven chin. In a tumbler on the dressing table a flat white tablet danced about the bottom, sending up a stream of bubbles.

'Sir, we have made two arrests this morning. One is Jugga budmash. He was out of his house on the night of the dacoity. We are bound to get some information out of him. The other is the stranger whose presence had been reported by the headman and you ordered him to be arrested.'

Hukum Chand stopped rubbing his chin. He detected the attempt to pass off the second arrest onto him.

'Who is he?'

The inspector shouted to the head constable outside.

'What is the name of the fellow you arrested at the Sikh temple?'

'Iqbal.'

'Iqbal what?' questioned the magistrate loudly.

'I will just find out, sir.' The head constable ran across to the servants' quarters before the magistrate could let fly at him. Hukum Chand felt his temper rising. He took a sip out of his glass. The subinspector shuffled uneasily. The head constable came back a few minutes later and coughed to announce his return.

'Sir,' he coughed again. 'Sir, he can read and write. He is educated.'

The magistrate turned to the door angrily.

'Has he a father and mother, a faith, or not? Educated!'

'Sir,' faltered the head constable, 'he refuses to tell us his father's name and says he has no religion. He says he will speak to you himself.'

56

'Go and find out,' roared the magistrate. 'Whip him on his buttocks till he talks. Go . . . no, wait, the Subinspector Sahib will handle this.'

Hukum Chand was in a rage. He gulped down the fizzing water in the tumbler and mopped his head with the shaving towel. A belch relieved him of his mounting wrath.

'Nice fellows, you and your policemen! You go and arrest people without finding out their names, parentage or caste. You make me sign blank warrants of arrest. Some day you will arrest the Governor and say Hukum Chand ordered you to do so. You will have me dismissed.'

'Cherisher of the poor, I will go and look into this. This man came to Mano Majra yesterday. I will find out his antecedents and business.'

'Well, then, go and find out, and do not just stand and stare,' barked Hukum Chand. He was not in the habit of losing his temper or of being rude. After the subinspector had left, he examined his tongue in the mirror and put another tablet of seltzer in the tumbler.

The subinspector went out and stopped on the verandah to take a few deep breaths. The magistrate's wrath decided his attitude. He would have to take a strong line and finish the shilly-shallying. He went to the servants' quarters. Iqbal and his escort stood apart from Juggut Singh's crowd. The young man had a look of injured dignity. The subinspector thought it best not to speak to him.

'Search this man's clothes. Take him inside one of the quarters and strip him. I will examine them myself.'

Iqbal's planned speech remained undelivered. The constable almost dragged him by the handcuffs into a room. His resistance had gone. He took off his shirt and handed it to the policeman. The subinspector came in and without bothering to examine the shirt ordered:

'Take off your pajamas!'

Iqbal felt humiliated. There was no fight left in him. 'There are no pockets to the pajamas. I cannot hide anything in them.'

'Take them off and do not argue.' The subinspector slapped his khaki trousers with his swagger stick to emphasize the order.

Iqbal loosened the knot in the cord. The pajamas fell in a heap around his ankles. He was naked save for the handcuffs on his wrists. He stepped out of the pajamas to let the policemen examine them.

'No, that is not necessary,' broke in the subinspector. 'I have seen all I wanted to see. You can put on your clothes. You say you are a social worker. What was your business in Mano Majra?'

'I was sent by my party,' answered Iqbal, re-tying the knot in the cord of his pajamas.

'What party?'

'People's Party of India.'

The subinspector looked at Iqbal with a sinister smile. 'The People's Party of India,' he repeated slowly, pronouncing each word distinctly. 'You are sure it was not the Muslim League?'

Iqbal did not catch the significance of the question.

'No, why should I be a member of the Muslim League? I . . .'

The subinspector walked out of the room before Iqbal had finished his sentence. He ordered the constables to take the prisoners to the police station. He went back to the rest house to report his discovery to the magistrate. There was an obsequious smile on his face.

'Cherisher of the poor, it is all right. He says he has been sent by the People's Party. But I am sure he is a Muslim Leaguer. They are much the same. We would have had to arrest him in any case if he was up to mischief so near the border. We can charge him with something or other later.'

'How do you know he is a Muslim Leaguer?'

The subinspector smiled confidently. 'I had him stripped.'

Hukum Chand shook his glass to churn the dregs of chalk at the bottom, and slowly drank up the remaining portion of the seltzer. He looked thoughtfully into the empty tumbler and added:

'Fill in the warrant of arrest correctly. Name: Mohammed Iqbal, son of Mohammed Something-or-other, or just father unknown. Caste: Mussulman. Occupation: Muslim League worker.'

The subinspector saluted dramatically.

'Wait, wait. Do not leave things half done. Enter in your police diary words to the effect that Ram Lal's murderers have not yet been traced but that information about them is expected soon. Didn't you say Jugga has something to do with it?'

'Yes, sir. The dacoits threw glass bangles in his courtyard

before leaving. Apparently he had refused to join them in their venture.'

'Well, get the names out of him quickly. Beat him if necessary.'

The subinspector smiled. 'I will get the names of the dacoits out of him in twenty-four hours and without any beating.'

'Yes, yes, get them in any way you like,' answered Hukum Chand impatiently. 'Also, enter today's two arrests on separate pages of the police station diary with other items in between. Do not let there be any more bungling.'

The subinspector saluted again.

'I will take good care, sir.'

Iqbal and Jugga were taken to Chundunnugger police station in a tonga. Iqbal was given the place of honour in the middle of the front seat. The driver perched himself on the wooden shaft alongside the horse's flank, leaving his seat empty. Juggut Singh sat on the rear seat between two policemen. It was a long and dusty drive on an unmetalled road which ran parallel to the railway track. The only person at ease was Jugga. He knew the policemen and they knew him. Nor was the situation unfamiliar to him.

'You must have many prisoners in the police station these days,' he stated.

'No, not one,' answered one of the constables. 'We do not arrest rioters. We only disperse them. And there is no time to deal with other crimes. Yours are the first arrests we have made in the last seven days. Both cells are vacant. You can have one all to yourself.'

'Babuji will like that,' Jugga said. 'Won't you, Babuji?'

Iqbal did not answer. Jugga felt slightly snubbed, and tried to change the subject quickly.

'You must have a lot of work to do with this Hindustan-Pakistan business going on,' he remarked to the constable.

'Yes. There is all this killing and the police force has been reduced to less than half.'

'Why, have they joined up with Pakistan?'

'We do not know whether they have joined up on the other side—they kept protesting that they did not want to go at all. On the day of independence, the Superintendent Sahib disarmed all Muslim policemen and they fled. Their intentions were evil. Muslims are like that. You can never trust them.'

'Yes,' added another policeman, 'it was the Muslim police taking sides which made the difference in the riots. Hindu boys of Lahore would have given the Muslims hell if it had not been for their police. They did a lot of *zulum*.'

'Their army is like that, too. Baluch soldiers have been shooting people whenever they were sure there was no chance of running into Sikh or Gurkha troops.'

'They cannot escape from God. No one can escape from God,' said Juggut Singh vehemently. Everyone looked a little surprised. Even Iqbal tuned round to make sure that the voice was Juggut Singh's.

'Isn't that right, Babuji? You are a clever man, you tell me, can one escape the wrath of God?'

Iqbal said nothing.

'No, of course not,' Jugga answered himself. 'I tell you something which Bhai Meet Singh told me. It is worth listening to, Babuji. It is absolutely sixteen annas' worth in the rupee.'

Every rupee is worth sixteen annas, thought Iqbal. He refused to take interest. Jugga went on.

'The Bhai told me of a truckful of Baluch soldiers who were going from Amritsar to Lahore. When they were getting near the Pakistan border, the soldiers began to stick bayonets into Sikhs going along the road. The driver would slow down near a cyclist or a pedestrian, the soldiers on the footboard would stab him in the back and then the driver would accelerate away fast. They killed many people like this and were feeling happier and happier as they got nearer Pakistan. They were within a mile of the border and were travelling at great speed. What do you think happened then?'

'What?' asked an obliging policeman. They all listened intently—all except Iqbal. Even the driver stopped flogging the horse and looked back.

'Listen, Babuji, this is worth listening to. A pariah dog ran across the road. The very same driver of the truck who had been responsible for killing so many people swerved sharply to the right to avoid the dog, a mangy pariah dog. He crashed into a tree. The driver and two of the soldiers were killed. All the others seriously wounded. What do you say to that?'

Policemen murmured approval. Iqbal felt irritated.

'Who caused the crash, the dog or God?' he asked cynically.

'God, of course,' answered one of the policemen. 'Why should one who enjoyed killing human beings be bothered by a stray dog getting under his wheels?'

'You tell me,' said Iqbal coldly. He squashed everyone except Jugga, who was irrepressible. Jugga turned to the tonga driver. The man had started whipping his horse again.

'Bhola, have you no fear of God that you beat your animal so mercilessly?'

Bhola stopped beating the horse. The expression on his face was resentful: it was his horse and he could do what he liked to it.

'Bholeya, how is business these days?' asked Jugga, trying to make up.

'God is merciful,' answered the driver pointing to the sky with his whip, then added quickly, 'Inspector Sahib is also merciful. We are alive and manage to fill our bellies.'

'Don't you make money off these refugees who are wanting to go to Pakistan?'

'And lose my life for money?' asked Bhola angrily. 'No, thank you, brother, you keep your advice to yourself. When the mobs attack they do not wait to find out who you are, Hindu or Muslim; they kill. The other day four Sikh Sardars in a jeep drove alongside a mile-long column of Muslim refugees walking on the road. Without warning they opened fire with their sten guns. Four sten guns! God alone knows how many they killed. What would happen if a mob got hold of my tonga full of Muslims? They would kill me first and ask afterwards.'

'Why didn't a dog get under the jeep and upset it?' asked Iqbal sarcastically.

There was an awkward pause. No one knew what to say to this sour-tempered babu. Jugga asked naïvely:

'Babuji, don't you believe that bad acts yield a bitter harvest? It is the law of karma. So the bhai is always saying. The Guru has also said the same in the Book.'

'Yes, absolutely, sixteen annas in the rupee,' sneered Iqbal.

'*Achhaji*, have it your own way,' said Jugga, still smiling. 'You

will never agree with ordinary people.' He turned to the driver
again.

'Bholeya, I hear a lot of women are being abducted and sold
cheap. You could find a wife for yourself.'

'Why, Sardara, if you can find a Mussulmanni without paying
for her, am I impotent that I should have to buy an abducted
woman?' replied Bhola.

Jugga was taken aback. His temper began to rise. The
policemen, who had started to snigger, looked nervously at Juggut
Singh. Bhola regretted his mistake.

'Why, Juggia,' he said, changing his tone. 'You make fun of
others, but get angry when someone retorts.'

'If these handcuffs and fetters had not been on me, I would
have broken every bone in your body,' said Jugga fiercely. 'You are
lucky to have escaped today, but if I hear you repeat this thing
again I will tear your tongue out of your mouth.' Jugga spat loudly.

Bhola was thoroughly frightened. 'Do not lose your temper.
What have I . . .'

'Bastard.'

That was the end of the conversations. The uneasy silence in
the tonga was broken only by Bhola swearing at his horse. Jugga
was lost in angry thoughts. He was surprised that his clandestine
meetings were public knowledge. Somebody had probably seen
him and Nooran talking to each other. That must have started the
gossip. If a tonga driver from Chundunnugger knew, everyone in
Mano Majra would have been talking about if for some time. The
last to learn of gossip are the parties concerned. Perhaps Imam
Baksh and his daughter Nooran were the only ones in the village
who knew nothing of what was being said.

The party reached Chundunnugger after noon. The tonga
came to a halt outside the police station, which was a couple of
furlongs distant from the town. The prisoners were escorted
through an arched gateway which had WELCOME painted on it
in large letters. They were first taken to the reporting room. The
head constable opened a large register and made the entries of the
day's events on separate pages. Just above the table was an old
framed picture of King George VI with a placard stating in Urdu,
BRIBERY IS A CRIME. On another wall was pasted a coloured
portrait of Gandhi torn from a calendar. Beneath it was a motto

written in English, HONESTY IS THE BEST POLICY. Other portraits in the room were those of absconders, bad characters, and missing persons.

After the daily diary entries had been made, the prisoners were taken across the courtyard to their cells. There were only two cells in the police station. These were on one side of the courtyard facing the policemen's barracks. The wall of the farther end of the square was covered by a railway creeper.

Jugga's arrival was the subject of much hilarity.

'Oye, you are back again. You think it is your father-in-law's house,' shouted one of the constables from his barrack.

'It is, seeing the number of policemen's daughters I have seduced,' answered Juggut Singh at the top of his voice. He had forgotten the unpleasantness in the tonga.

'Oye, Budmasha, you will not desist from your budmashi. Wait till the Inspector Sahib hears of what you said and he will put ·hot chillies up your bottom.'

'You cannot do that to your son-in-law!'

With Iqbal it was different. His handcuffs were removed with apologies. A chair, a table, and a charpoy were put in his cell. The head constable collected all the daily newspapers and magazines, English and Urdu, that he could find and left them in the cell. Iqbal's food was served on a brass plate and a small pitcher and a glass tumbler were put on the table beside his charpoy. Jugga was given no furniture in his cell. His food was literally flung at him and he ate his chapatties out of his hand. A constable poured water onto his cupped palm through the iron bars. Jugga's bed was the hard cement floor.

The difference in treatment did not surprise Iqbal. In a country which had accepted caste distinctions for many centuries, inequality had become an inborn mental concept. If caste was abolished by legislation, it came up in other forms of class distinction. In thoroughly westernized circles like that of the civil servants in the government secretariat in Delhi, places for parking cars were marked according to seniority, and certain entrances to offices were reserved for higher officials. Lavatories were graded according to rank and labelled SENIOR OFFICERS, JUNIOR OFFICERS, CLERKS AND STENOGRAPHERS and OTHER RANKS. With a mental make-up so thoroughly sectionalized, grading according to their social status people who were charged or convicted of the same offence did not appear incongruous. Iqbal was A-class. Jugga was the rock-bottom C.

After his midday meal, Iqbal lay down on the charpoy. He heard snoring from Jugga's cell. But he himself was far too disturbed to sleep. His mind was like the delicate spring of a watch, which quivers for several hours after it has been touched. He sat up and began to turn over the pile of newspapers the head constable had left him. They were all alike: the same news, the same statements, the same editorials. Except for the wording of the headlines, they might all have been written by the same hand. Even the photographs were the same. In disgust, he turned to the matrimonial ads. There was sometimes entertainment there. But the youth of the Punjab were as alike as the news. The qualities they required in a wife were identical. All wanted virgins. A few, more broad-minded than the rest, were willing to consider widows, but only if they had not been deflowered. All demanded women who were good at h. h. a., or household affairs. To the advanced and charitable, c. & d. [caste and dowry] were no bar. Not many asked for photographs of their prospective wives. Beauty, they recognized, was only skin-deep. Most wanted to 'correspond with horoscopes'. Astronomical harmony was the one guarantee of happiness. Iqbal threw the papers away, and rummaged through the magazines. If anything, they were worse than the newspapers. There was the inevitable article on the Ajanta cave frescoes. There was the article on Indian ballet. There was the article on Tagore. There was the article on the stories of Prem Chand. There were the articles on the private lives of film stars. Iqbal gave up, and lay down again. He felt depressed about everything. It occurred to him that he had hardly slept for three days. He wondered if this would be considered a 'sacrifice'. It was possible. He must find some way of sending word to the party. Then, perhaps . . . He fell asleep with visions of banner headlines announcing his arrest, his release, his triumphant emergence as a leader.

In the evening a policeman came to Iqbal's cell, carrying another chair.

'Is somebody going to share my cell?' asked Iqbal a little apprehensively.

'No, Babuji. Only the Inspector Sahib. He wishes to have a word with you. He is coming now.'

Iqbal did not answer. The policeman studied the position of the chair for a moment. Then he withdrew. There was a sound of voices in the corridor, and the subinspector appeared.

'Have I your permission to enter?'

Iqbal nodded. 'What can I do for you, Inspector Sahib?'

'We are your slaves, Mr Iqbal. You should command us and we will serve you,' the subinspector answered with a smile. He was proud of his ability to change his tone and manner as the circumstances required. That was diplomacy.

'I did not know you were so kind to people you arrested for murder. It is on a charge of murder that you have brought me here, isn't it? I do not suppose your policemen told you I came to Mano Majra yesterday on the same train as they did.'

'We have framed no charge. That is for the court. We are only detaining you on suspicion. We cannot allow political agitators in the border areas.' The subinspector continued to smile. 'Why don't you go and do your propaganda in Pakistan where you belong?'

Iqbal was stung to fury, but he tried to suppress any sign of his anger.

'What exactly do you mean by "belonging to Pakistan", Inspector Sahib?'

'You are a Muslim. You go to Pakistan.'

'That is a bloody lie,' exploded Iqbal. 'What is more, you know it is a bloody lie. You just want to cover up your stupidity by trumping up a false case.'

The Inspector spoke back sourly.

'You should use your tongue with some discrimination, Mr Iqbal. I am not in your father's pay to have to put up with your "bloodys". Your name is Iqbal and you are circumcised. I have examined you myself. Also, you cannot give any explanation for your presence in Mano Majra. That is enough.'

'It will not be enough when it comes up in court, and in the newspapers. I am not a Muslim—not that that matters—and what I came to Mano Majra for is none of your business. If you do not release me within twenty-four hours I will move a habeas corpus petition and tell the court the way you go about your duties.'

'Habeas corpus petition?' The subinspector roared with laughter. 'It seems you have been living in foreign lands too long, Mr Iqbal. Even now you live in a fool's paradise. You will live and learn.'

The subinspector left the cell abruptly, and locked the steel bar gate. He opened the adjoining one behind which Jugga was locked.

'*Sat Sri Akal*, Inspector Sahib.'

The subinspector did not acknowledge the greeting.

'Will you ever give up being a budmash?'

'King of pearls, you can say what you like, but this time I am innocent. I swear by the Guru I am innocent.'

Jugga remained seated on the floor. The subinspector stood leaning against the wall.

'Where were you on the night of the dacoity?'

'I had nothing to do with the dacoity,' answered Jugga evasively.

'Where were you on the night of the dacoity?' repeated the subinspector.

Jugga looked down at the floor. 'I had gone to my fields. It was my turn of water.'

The subinspector knew he was lying. 'I can check up the turn of water with the canal man. Did you inform the lambardar that you were going out of the village?'

Jugga only shuffled his feet and kept on looking at the floor.

'Your mother said you had gone to drive away wild pigs.'

Jugga continued to shuffle his feet. After a long pause he said again, 'I had nothing to do with the dacoity. I am innocent.'

'Who were the dacoits?'

'King of pearls, how should I know who the dacoits were? I was out of the village at the time, otherwise you think anyone would have dared to rob and kill in Mano Majra?'

'Who were the dacoits?' repeated the subinspector menacingly. 'I know you know them. They certainly know you. They left a gift of glass bangles for you.'

Jugga did not reply.

'You want to be whipped on your buttocks or have red chillies put up your rectum before you talk?'

Jugga winced. He knew what the subinspector meant. He had

been through it—once. Hands and feet pinned under legs of charpoys with half a dozen policemen sitting on them. Testicles twisted and squeezed till one became senseless with pain. Powdered red chillies thrust up the rectum by rough hands, and the sensation of having the tail on fire for several days. All this, and no food or water, or hot spicy food with a bowl of shimmering cool water put outside the cell just beyond one's reach. The memory shook him.

'No,' he said. 'For God's sake, no.' He flung himself on the floor and clasped the subinspector's shoes with both his hands. 'Please, O king of pearls.' He was ashamed of himself, but he knew he could never endure such torture again. 'I am innocent. By the name of the Guru, I had nothing to do with the dacoity.'

Seeing six foot four of muscle cringing at his feet gave the subinspector a feeling of elation. He had never known anyone to hold out against physical pain, not one. The pattern of torture had to be carefully chosen. Some succumbed to hunger, others—of the Iqbal type—to the inconvenience of having to defecate in front of the policemen. Some to flies sitting on their faces smeared with treacle, with their hands tied behind them. Some to lack of sleep In the end they all gave in.

'I will give you two days to tell me the names of the dacoits,' he said. 'Otherwise, I will beat your behind till it looks like the tail of a ram.'

The subinspector freed his feet from Jugga's hands and walked out. His visits had been a failure. He would have to change his tactics. It was frustrating to deal with two people so utterly different.

Kalyug

Early in September the time schedule in Mano Majra started going wrong. Trains became less punctual than ever before and many more started to run through at night. Some days it seemed as though the alarm clock had been set for the wrong hour. On others, it was as if no one had remembered to wind it. Imam Baksh waited for Meet Singh to make the first start. Meet Singh waited for the mullah's call to prayer before getting up. People stayed in bed late without realizing that times had changed and the mail train might not run through at all. Children did not know when to be hungry, and clamoured for food all the time. In the evenings, everyone was indoors before sunset and in bed before the express came by—if it did come by. Goods trains had stopped running altogether, so there was no lullaby to lull them to sleep. Instead, ghost trains went past at odd hours between midnight and dawn, disturbing the dreams of Mano Majra.

This was not all that changed the life of the village. A unit of Sikh soldiers arrived and put up tents near the railway station. They built a six-foot-high square of sandbags about the base of the signal near the bridge, and mounted a machine gun in each face. Armed sentries began to patrol the platform and no villagers were allowed near the railings. All trains coming from Delhi stopped and changed their drivers and guards before moving on to Pakistan. Those coming from Pakistan ran through with their engines screaming with release and relief.

One morning, a train from Pakistan halted at Mano Majra railway station. At first glance, it had the look of the trains in the days of peace. No one sat on the roof. No one clung between the bogies. No one was balanced on the footboards. But somehow it was different. There was something uneasy about it. It had a ghostly quality. As soon as it pulled up to the platform, the guard emerged from the tail end of the train and went into the stationmaster's office. Then the two went to the soldiers' tents and spoke to the officer in charge. The soldiers were called out and the villagers loitering about were ordered back to Mano Majra. One man was sent off on a motorcycle to Chundunnugger. An hour later, the subinspector with about fifty armed policemen turned up at the station. Immediately after them, Mr Hukum Chand drove up in his American car.

The arrival of the ghost train in broad daylight created a commotion in Mano Majra. People stood on their roofs to see what was happening at the station. All they could see was the black top of the train stretching from one end of the platform to the other. The station building and the railings blocked the rest of the train from view. Occasionally a soldier or a policeman came out of the station and then went back again.

In the afternoon, men gathered in little groups, discussing the train. The groups merged with each other under the peepul tree, and then everyone went into the gurudwara. Women, who had gone from door to door collecting and dropping bits of gossip, assembled in the headman's house and waited for their menfolk to come home and tell them what they had learned about the train.

This was the pattern of things at Mano Majra when anything of consequence happened. The women went to the headman's house, the men to the temple. There was no recognized leader of the village. Banta Singh, the headman, was really only a collector of revenue—a lambardar. The post had been in his family for several generations. He did not own any more land than the others. Nor was he a head in any other way. He had no airs about him: he was a modest hard-working peasant like the rest of his fellow villagers. But since government officials and the police dealt with him, he had an official status. Nobody called him by his name. He was 'O Lambardara', as his father, his father's father, and his father's father's father had been before him.

The only men who voiced their opinions at village meetings were Imam Baksh, the mullah of the mosque, and Bhai Meet Singh.

Imam Baksh was a weaver, and weavers are traditionally the butts of jokes in the Punjab. They are considered effeminate and cowardly—a race of cuckolds whose women are always having liaisons with others. A series of tragedies in his family had made him an object of pity, and then of affection. The Punjabis love people they can pity. His wife and only son had died within a few days of each other. His eyes, which had never been very good, suddenly became worse and he could not work his looms any more. He was reduced to beggary, with a baby girl, Nooran, to look after. He began living in the mosque and teaching Muslim children the Quran. He wrote out verses from the Quran for the village folk to wear as charms or for the sick to swallow as medicine. Small offerings of flour, vegetables, food, and castoff clothes kept him and his daughter alive. He had an amazing fund of anecdotes and proverbs which the peasants loved to hear. His appearance commanded respect. He was a tall, lean man, bald save for a line of white hair which ran round the back of his head from ear to ear, and he had a neatly trimmed silky white beard that he occasionally dyed with henna to a deep orange-red. The cataract in his eyes gave them a misty philosophical look. Despite his sixty years, he held himself erect. All this gave his bearing a dignity and an aura of righteousness. He was known to the villagers not as Imam Baksh or the mullah but a *chacha*, or 'Uncle.'

Meet Singh inspired no such affection and respect. He was only a peasant who had taken to religion as an escape from work. He had a little land of his own which he had leased out, and this, with the offerings at the temple, gave him a comfortable living. He had no wife or children. He was not learned in the scriptures, nor had he any faculty for conversation. Even his appearance was against him. He was short, fat, and hairy. He was the same age as Imam Baksh, but his beard had none of the serenity of the other's. It was black, with streaks of gray. And he was untidy. He wore his turban only when reading the scripture. Otherwise, he went about with his long hair tied in a loose knot held by a little wooden comb. Almost half of the hair was scattered on the nape of his neck. He seldom wore a shirt and his only garment—a pair of shorts—was always greasy with dirt. But Meet Singh was a man of peace. Envy had never poisoned his affection for Imam Baksh. He only felt that he owed it to his own community to say something when Imam

Baksh made any suggestions. Their conversation always had an undercurrent of friendly rivalry.

The meeting in the gurudwara had a melancholic atmosphere. People had little to say, and those who did spoke slowly, like prophets.

Imam Baksh opened the discussion. 'May Allah be merciful. We are living in bad times.'

A few people sighed solemnly, 'Yes, bad days.'

Meet Singh added, 'Yes, Chacha—this is Kalyug, the dark age.'

There was a long silence and people shuffled uneasily on their haunches. Some yawned, closing their mouths with loud invocations to God: '*Ya Allah. Wah Guru, wah Guru.*'

'Lambaradara,' started Imam Baksh again, 'you should know what is happening. Why has not the Deputy Sahib sent for you?'

'How am I to know, Chacha? When he sends for me I will go. He is also at the station and no one is allowed near it.'

A young villager interjected in a loud cheery voice: 'We are not going to die just yet. We will soon know what is going on. It is a train after all. It may be carrying government treasures or arms. So they guard it. Haven't you heard, many have been looted?'

'Shut up,' rebuked his bearded father angrily. 'Where there are elders, what need have you to talk?'

'I only . . .'

'That is all,' said the father sternly. No one spoke for some time.

'I have heard,' said Imam Baksh, slowly combing his beard with his fingers, 'that there have been many incidents with trains.'

The word 'incident' aroused an uneasy feeling in the audience. 'Yes, lots of incidents have been heard of,' Meet Singh agreed after a while.

'We only ask for Allah's mercy,' said Imam Baksh, closing the subject he had himself opened.

Meet Singh, not meaning to be outdone in the invocation to God, added, '*Wah Guru, wah Guru.*'

They sat on in silence punctuated by yawns and murmurs of '*Ya Allah*' and '*Hey wah Guru.*' Several people, on the outer fringe of the assembly, stretched themselves on the floor and went to sleep.

Suddenly a policeman appeared in the doorway of the

gurudwara. The lambardar and three or four villagers stood up. People who were asleep were prodded into getting up. Those who had been dozing sat up in a daze, exclaiming, 'What is it? What's up?', then hurriedly wrapped their turbans round their heads.

'Who is the lambardar of the village?'

Banta Singh walked up to the door. The policeman took him aside and whispered something. Then as Banta Singh turned back, he said loudly: 'Quickly, within half an hour. There are two military trucks waiting on the station side. I will be there.'

The policeman walked away briskly.

The villagers crowded round Banta Singh. The possession of a secret had lent him an air of importance. His voice had a tone of authority.

'Everyone get all the wood there is in his house and all the kerosene oil he can spare and bring these to the motor trucks on the station side. You will be paid.'

The villagers waited for him to tell them why. He ordered them off brusquely. 'Are you deaf? Haven't you heard? Or do you want the police to whip your buttocks before you move? Come along quickly.'

People dispersed into the village lanes whispering to each other. The lambardar went to his own house.

A few minutes later, villagers with bundles of wood and bottles of oil started assembling outside the village on the station side. Two large mud-green army trucks were parked alongside each other. A row of empty petrol cans stood against a mud wall. A Sikh soldier with a sten gun stood on guard. Another Sikh, an officer with his beard neatly rolled in a hair net, sat on the back of one of the trucks with his feet dangling. He watched the wood being stacked in the other truck and nodded his head in reply to the villagers' greetings. The lambardar stood beside him, taking down the names of the villagers and the quantities they brought. After dumping their bundles of wood on the truck and emptying bottles of kerosene into the petrol cans, the villagers collected in a little group at a respectful distance from the officer.

Imam Baksh put down on the truck the wood he had carried on his head and handed his bottle of oil to the lambardar. He re-tied his turban, then greeted the officer loudly, 'Salaam, Sardar Sahib.'

The officer looked away.

Iman Baksh started again, 'Everything is all right, isn't it, Sardar Sahib?'

The officer turned around abruptly and snapped, 'Get along. Don't you see I am busy?'

Imam Baksh, still adjusting his turban, meekly joined the villagers.

When both the trucks were loaded, the officer told Banta Singh to come to the camp next morning for the money. The trucks rumbled off toward the station.

Banta Singh was surrounded by eager villagers. He felt that he was somehow responsible for the insult to Imam Baksh. The villagers were impatient with him.

'O Lambardara, why don't you tell us something? What is all this big secret you are carrying about? You seem to think you have become someone very important and don't need to talk to us any more,' said Meet Singh angrily.

'No, Bhai, no. If I knew, why would I not tell you? You talk like children. How can I argue with soldiers and policemen? They told me nothing. And didn't you see how that pig's penis spoke to Chacha? One's self-respect is in one's own hands. Why should I have myself insulted by having my turban taken off?'

Imam Baksh acknowledged the gesture gracefully. 'Lambardar is right. It somebody barks when you speak to him, it is best to keep quiet. Let us all go to our homes. You can see what they are doing from the tops of your roofs.'

The villagers dispersed to their rooftops. From there the trucks could be seen at the camp near the station. They started off again and went east along the railway track till they were beyond the signal. Then they turned sharp left and bumped across the rails. They turned left again, came back along the line toward the station, and disappeared behind the train.

All afternoon, the villagers stood on their roofs shouting to each other, asking whether anyone had seen anything. In their excitement they had forgotten to prepare the midday meal. Mothers fed their children on stale leftovers from the day before. They did not have time to light their hearths. The men did not give fodder to their cattle nor remember to milk them as evening drew near. When the sun was already under the arches of the bridge everyone became conscious of having overlooked the daily chores.

It would be dark soon and the children would clamour for food, but still the women watched, their eyes glued to the station. The cows and buffaloes lowed in the barns, but still the men stayed on the roofs looking toward the station. Everyone expected something to happen.

The sun sank behind the bridge, lighting the white clouds which had appeared in the sky with hues of russet, copper, and orange. Then shades of gray blended with the glow as evening gave way to twilight and twilight sank into darkness. The station became a black wall. Wearily, the men and women went down to their courtyards, beckoning the others to do the same. They did not want to be alone in missing anything.

The northern horizon, which had turned a bluish gray, showed orange again. The orange turned into copper and then into a luminous russet. Red tongues of flame leaped into the black sky. A soft breeze began to blow toward the village. It brought the smell of burning kerosene, then of wood. And then—a faint acrid smell of searing flesh.

The village was stilled in a deathly silence. No one asked anyone else what the odour was. They all knew. They had known it all the time. The answer was implicit in the fact that the train had come from Pakistan.

That evening, for the first time in the memory of Mano Majra, Imam Baksh's sonorous cry did not rise to the heavens to proclaim the glory of God.

The day's happenings cast their gloom on the rest house. Mr Hukum Chand had been out since the morning. When his orderly came from the station at midday for a thermos flask of tea and sandwiches, he told the bearer and the sweeper about the train. In the evening, the servants and their families saw the flames shooting up above the line of trees. The fire cast a melancholy amber light on the khaki walls of the bungalow.

The day's work had taken a lot out of Hukum Chand. His fatigue was not physical. The sight of so many dead had at first produced a cold numbness. Within a couple of hours, all his emotions were dead, and he watched corpses of men and women and children being dragged out, with as little interest as if they had been trunks or bedding. But by evening, he began to feel forlorn and sorry for himself. He looked weary and haggard when he stepped out of the car. The bearer, the sweeper, and their families were on the roof looking at the flames. He had to wait for them to come down and open the doors. His bath had not been drawn. Hukum Chand felt neglected and more depressed. He lay on his bed, ignoring the servants' attentions. One unlaced and took off his shoes and began to rub his feet. The other brought in buckets of water and filled the bathtub. The magistrate got up abruptly, almost kicking the servant, and went into the bathroom.

After a bath and a change of clothes, Hukum Chand felt somewhat refreshed. The punkah breeze was cool and soothing. He lay down again with his hands over his eyes. Within the dark chambers of his closed eyes, scenes of the day started coming back in panoramic succession. He tried to squash them by pressing his fingers into his eyes. The images only went blacker and redder and then came back. There was a man holding his intestines, with an expression in his eyes which said: 'Look what I have got!' There were women and children huddled in a corner, their eyes dilated with horror, their mouths still open as if their shrieks had just then become voiceless. Some of them did not have a scratch on their bodies. There were bodies crammed against the far end wall of the compartment, looking in terror at the empty windows through which must have come shots, spears and spikes. There were lavatories, jammed with corpses of young men who had muscled their way to comparative safety. And all the nauseating smell of putrefying flesh, faeces and urine. The very thought brought vomit to Hukum Chand's mouth. The most vivid picture was that of an old peasant with a long white beard; he did not look dead at all. He sat jammed between rolls of bedding on the upper rack meant for luggage, looking pensively at the scene below him. A thin crimson line of coagulated blood ran from his ear onto his heard. Hukum Chand had shaken him by the shoulder, saying 'Baba, Baba!' believing he was alive. He was alive. His cold hand stretched itself grotesquely and gripped the magistrate's right foot. Cold sweat came out all over Hukum Chand's body. He tried to shout but could only open his mouth. The hand moved up slowly from the ankle to the calf, from the calf to the knee, gripping its way all along. Hukum Chand tried to shout again. His voice stuck in his throat. The hand kept moving upwards. As it touched the fleshy part of his thigh, its grip loosened. Hukum Chand began to moan and then with a final effort broke out of the nightmare with an agonized shriek. He sat up with a look of terror in his eyes.

The bearer was standing beside him looking equally frightened.

'I thought the Sahib was tired and would like his feet pressed.'

Hukum Chand could not speak. He wiped the sweat off his forehead and sank back on the pillow, exclaiming 'Hai Ram, hai Ram.' The nervous outburst purged him of fear. He felt weak and foolish. After some time a sense of calm descended on him.

'Get me some whisky.'

The bearer brought him a tray with whisky, soda, and a tumbler. Hukum Chand filled a quarter of the glass with the honey-colored liquid. The bearer filled the rest with soda. The magistrate drank half of the glass in a gulp and lay back. The alcohol poured into his system, warming his jaded nerves to life. The servant started pressing his feet again. He looked up at the ceiling, feeling relaxed and just pleasantly tired. The sweeper started lighting lamps in the rooms. He put one on the table beside Hukum Chand's bed. A moth fluttered round the chimney and flew up in spirals to the ceiling. The geckos darted across from the wall. The moth hit the ceiling well out of the geckos' reach and spiralled back to the lamp. The lizards watched with their shining black eyes. The moth flew up again and down again. Hukum Chand knew that if it alighted on the ceiling for a second, one of the geckos would get it fluttering between its little crocodile jaws. Perhaps that was its destiny. It was everyone's destiny. Whether it was in hospitals, trains, or in the jaws of reptiles, it was all the same. One could even die in bed alone and no one would discover until the stench spread all round and maggots moved in and out of the sockets of the eyes and geckos ran over the face with their slimy clammy bellies. Hukum Chand wiped his face with his hands. How could one escape one's own mind! He gulped the rest of the whisky and poured himself another.

Death had always been an obsession with Hukum Chand. As a child, he had seen his aunt die after the birth of a dead child. Her whole system had been poisoned. For days she had had hallucinations and had waved her arms about frantically to ward off the spirit of death which stood at the foot of her bed. She had died shrieking with terror, staring and pointing at the wall. The scene had never left Hukum Chand's mind. Later in his youth, he had fought the fear of death by spending many hours at a cremation ground near the university. He had watched young and old brought on crude bamboo stretchers, lamented for, and then burned. Visits to the cremation ground left him with a sense of tranquillity. He had got over the immediate terror of death, but the idea of ultimate dissolution was always present in his mind. It made him kind, charitable and tolerant. It even made him cheerful in adversity. He had taken the loss of his children with phlegmatic resignation. He had borne with an illiterate, unattractive wife, without complaint. It all came from his belief that the only absolute truth was death. The rest—love, ambition, pride, values of all kinds—was to be taken with a pinch of salt. He did so with a clear conscience. Although he accepted gifts and obliged friends when they got into trouble, he was not corrupt. He occasionally joined in parties, arranged for singing and dancing—and sometimes sex—but he was not immoral. What did it really matter in the end? That was the core of Hukum Chand's philosophy of life, and he lived well.

But a trainload of dead was too much for even Hukum Chand's fatalism. He could not square a massacre with a philosophical belief in the inevitability of death. It bewildered and frightened him by its violence and its magnitude. The picture of his aunt biting her tongue and bleeding at the mouth, her eyes staring at space, came back to him in all its vivid horror. Whisky did not help to take it away.

The room was lit by the headlights of the car and then left darker than before; the car had probably been put into the garage. Hukum Chand grew conscious of the coming night. The servants would soon be retiring to their quarters to sleep snugly surrounded by their women and children. He would be left alone in the bungalow with its empty rooms peopled by phantoms of his own creation. No! No! He must get the orderlies to sleep somewhere nearby. On the verandah perhaps? Or would they suspect he was scared? He would tell them that he might be wanted during the night and must have them at hand; that would pass unnoticed.

'Bairah.'

'Sahib.' The bearer came in through the wire gauze door.

'Where have you put my charpoy for the night?'

'Sahib's bed has not been laid yet. It is clouded and there might be rain. Would *Huzoor* like to sleep on the verandah?'

'No, I will stay in my room. The boy can pull the punkah for an hour or two till it gets cool. Tell the orderlies to sleep on the verandah. I may want them for urgent work tonight,' he added, without looking up at the man.

'Yes, Sahib. I will tell them straightaway before they go to bed. Should I bring the Sahib's dinner?'

Hukum Chand had forgotten about dinner.

'No, I do not want any dinner. Just tell the orderlies to put their beds on the verandah. Tell the driver to be there too. If there is not enough space on the verandah, tell him to sleep in the next room.'

The bearer went out. Hukum Chand felt relieved. He had saved face. He could sleep peacefully with all these people about him. He listened to the reassuring sounds of human activity—the servants arguing about places on the verandah, beds being laid just outside his door, a lamp being brought in the next room, and furniture being moved to make place for charpoys.

The headlights of the car coming in, lit the room once more. The car stopped outside the verandah. Hukum Chand heard voices of men and women, then the jingle of bells. He sat up and looked through the wire gauze door. It was the party of musicians, the old woman and the girl prostitute. He had forgotten about them.

'Bairah.'

'Huzoor.'

'Tell the driver to take the musicians and the old woman back. And ... let the servants sleep in their quarters. If I need them, I will send for them.'

Hukum Chand felt a little stupid being caught like that. The servants would certainly laugh about it. But he did not care. He poured himself another whisky.

The servants started moving out before the bearer came to speak to them. The lamp in the next room was removed. The driver started the car again. He switched on the headlights and switched them off again. The old woman would not get in the car and began to argue with the bearer. Her voice rose higher and higher till it passed the bounds of argument and addressed itself to the magistrate inside the room.

'May your government go on forever. May your pen inscribe figures of thousands—nay, hundreds of thousands.'

Hukum Chand lost his temper. 'Go!' he shouted. 'You have to pay my debt of the other day. Go! Bearer, send her away!'

The woman's voice came down. She was quickly hustled into the car. The car went out, leaving only the flickering yellow light of the oil lamp beside Hukum Chand's bed. He rose, picked up the lamp and the table, and put them in the corner by the door. The moth circled round the glass chimney, hitting the wall on either side. the geckos crawled down from the ceiling to the wall near the lamp. As the moth alighted on the wall, one of the geckos crept up stealthily behind it, pounced, and caught it fluttering in its jaws. Hukum Chand watched the whole thing with bland indifference.

The door opened and shut gently. A small dark figure slid into the room. The silver sequins on the girl's sari twinkled in the lamplight and sent a hundred spots of light playing on the walls and the ceiling. Hukum Chand turned around. The girl stood staring at him with her large black eyes. The diamond in her nose glittered brightly. She looked thoroughly frightened.

'Come,' said the magistrate, making room for her beside him and holding out his hand.

The girl came and sat down on the edge of the bed, looking away. Hukum Chand put his arm round her waist. He stroked her thighs and belly and played with her little unformed breasts. She sat impassive and rigid. Hukum Chand shuffled further away and mumbled drowsily, 'Come and lie down.' The girl stretched herself beside the magistrate. The sequins on her sari tickled his face. She wore perfume made of khas; it had the fresh odour of dry earth when water has been sprinkled on it. Her breath smelled of cardamom, her bosom of honey. Hukum Chand snuggled against her like a child and fell fast asleep.

Monsoon is not another word for rain. As its original Arabic name indicates, it is a season. There is a summer monsoon as well as a winter monsoon, but it is only the nimbused southwest winds of summer that make a *mausem*—the season of the rains. The winter monsoon is simply rain in winter. Is it like a cold shower on a frosty morning. It leaves one chilled and shivering. Although it is good for the crops, people pray for it to end. Fortunately, it does not last very long.

The summer monsoon is quite another affair. It is preceded by several months of working up a thirst so that when the waters come they are drunk deep and with relish. From the end of February, the sun starts getting hotter and spring gives way to summer. Flowers wither. Then flowering trees take their place. First come the orange showers of the flame of the forest, the vermilion of the coral tree, and the virginal white of the champak. They are followed by the mauve Jacaranda, the flamboyant gul mohur, and the soft gold cascades of the laburnum. Then the trees also lose their flowers. Their leaves fall. Their bare branches stretch up to the sky begging for water, but there is no water. The sun comes up earlier than before and licks up the drops of dew before the fevered earth can moisten its lips. It blazes away all day long in a cloudless gray sky, drying up wells, streams and lakes. It sears the grass and thorny scrub till they catch fire. The fires spread and dry jungles burn like matchwood.

The sun goes on, day after day, from east to west, scorching relentlessly. The earth cracks up and deep fissures open their gaping mouths asking for water; but there is no water—only the shimmering haze at noon making mirage lakes of quicksilver. Poor villagers take their thirsty cattle out to drink and are struck dead. The rich wear sunglasses and hide behind chicks of khus fibre on which their servants pour water.

The sun makes an ally of the breeze. It heats the air till it becomes the loo and then sends it on its errand. Even in the intense heat, the loo's warm caresses are sensuous and pleasant. It brings up the prickly heat. It produces a numbness which makes the head nod and the eyes heavy with sleep. It brings on a stroke which takes its victim as gently as breeze bears a fluff of thistledown.

Then comes a period of false hopes. The loo drops. The air becomes still. From the southern horizon a black wall begins to advance. Hundreds of kites and crows fly ahead. Can it be . . . ? No, it is a dust storm. A fine powder begins to fall. A solid mass of locusts covers the sun. They devour whatever is left on the trees and in the fields. Then comes the storm itself. In furious sweeps it smacks open doors and windows, banging them forward and backward, smashing their glass panes. Thatched roofs and corrugated iron sheets are borne aloft into the sky like bits of paper. Trees are torn up by the roots and fall across power lines. The tangled wires electrocute people and start fires in houses. The storm carries the flames to other houses till there is a conflagration. All this happens in a few seconds. Before you can say *Chakravartyrajagopalachari,* the gale is gone. The dust hanging in the air settles on your books, furniture and food; it gets in your eyes and ears and throat and nose.

This happens over and over again until the people have lost all hope. They are disillusioned, dejected, thirsty and sweating. The prickly heat on the back of their necks is like emery paper. There is another lull. A hot petrified silence prevails. Then comes the shrill, strange call of a bird. Why has it left its cool bosky shade and come out in the sun? People look up wearily at the lifeless sky. Yes, there it is with its mate! They are like large black-and-white bulbuls with perky crests and long tails. They are pie-crested cuckoos who have flown all the way from Africa ahead of the monsoon. Isn't there a gentle breeze blowing? And hasn't it a damp smell? And wasn't the rumble which drowned the birds' anguished cry the sound of thunder? The people hurry to the roofs to see. The same ebony wall is coming up from the east. A flock of herons fly across. There is a flash of lighting which outlines the daylight. The wind fills the black sails of the clouds and they billow out across the sun. A profound shadow falls on the earth. There is another clap of thunder. Big drops of rain fall and dry up in the dust. A fragrant smell rises from the earth. Another flash of lightning and another crack of thunder like the roar of a hungry tiger. It has come! Sheets of water, wave after wave. The people lift their faces to the clouds and let the abundance of water cover them. Schools and offices close. All work stops. Men, women, and children run madly about the streets, waving their arms and shouting 'Ho, Ho,'—hosannas to the miracle of the monsoon.

The monsoon is not like ordinary rain which comes and goes. Once it is on, it stays for two months or more. Its advent is greeted with joy. Parties set out for picnics and litter the countryside with the skins and stones of mangoes. Women and children make swings on branches of trees and spend the day in sport and song. Peacocks spread their tails and strut about with their mates; the woods echo with their shrill cries.

But after a few days the flush of enthusiasm is gone. The earth becomes a big stretch of swamp and mud. Wells and lakes fill up and burst their bounds. In towns, gutters get clogged and streets become turbid streams. In villages, mud walls of huts melt in the water and thatched roofs sag and descend on the inmates. Rivers which keep rising steadily from the time the summer's heat starts melting the snows, suddenly turn to floods as the monsoon spends itself on the mountains. Roads, railway tracks and bridges go under water. Houses near the riverbanks are swept down to the sea.

With the monsoon, the tempo of life and death increases. Almost overnight, grass begins to grow and leafless trees turn green. Snakes, centipedes and scorpions are born out of nothing. The ground is strewn with earthworms, ladybirds and tiny frogs. At night, myriads of moths flutter around the lamps. They fall in everybody's food and water. Geckos dart about filling themselves with insects till they get heavy and fall off ceilings. Inside rooms, the hum of mosquitoes is maddening. People spray clouds of insecticide, and the floor becomes a layer of wriggling bodies and wings. Next evening, there are many more fluttering around the lamp shades and burning themselves in the flames.

While the monsoon lasts, the showers start and stop without warning. The clouds fly across, dropping their rain on the plains as it pleases them, till they reach the Himalayas. They climb up the mountainsides. Then the cold squeezes the last drops of water out of them. Lightning and thunder never cease. All this happens in late August or early September. Then the season of the rains gives way to autumn.

A roll of the thunder woke Hukum Chand. He opened his eyes. There was a gray light in the room. In the corner, a weary yellow flame flickered through the soot of the lamp chimney. There was a flash of lightning followed by another peal of thunder. A gust of cool, damp breeze blew across the room. The lamp fluttered and went out. Raindrops began to fall in a gentle patter.

Rain! At long last the rain, thought the magistrate. The monsoon had been a poor one. Clouds had come, but they were high and fleecy and floated by, leaving the land thirstier than before. September was very late for the rain, but that only made it more welcome. It smelled good, it sounded good, it looked good—and above all, it did good. Ah, but did it? Hukum Chand felt feverish. The corpses! A thousand charred corpses sizzling and smoking while the rain put out the fire. A hundred yards of charred corpses! Beads of sweat broke out on his temples. He felt cold and frightened. He reached across the bed. The girl had left. He was all alone in the bungalow. He got his wrist watch from under the pillow and cupped his hands round the dial. The glow-worn green of the radium hands pointed to 6:30. He felt comforted. It was fairly late in the morning. The sky must be heavily overcast. Then he heard the sound of coughing on the verandah, and felt reassured. He sat up with a jerk.

A dull pain rocked his forehead. He shut his eyes and held his head between his hands. The throbbing ebbed away. After a few minutes, he opened his eyes, looked around the room—and saw the girl. She hadn't left. She was asleep on the big cane armchair, wrapped in her black sequined sari. Hukum Chand felt a little foolish. The girl had been there two nights, and there she was sleeping all by herself in a chair. She was still, save for the gentle heaving of her bosom. He felt old and unclean. How could he have done anything to this child? If his daughter had lived, she would have been about the same age. He felt a pang or remorse. He also knew that his remorse and good resolutions went with the hangover. They always did. He would probably drink again and get the same girl over and sleep with her—and feel badly about it. That was life, and it was depressing.

He got up slowly and opened the attaché case that lay on the table. He looked at himself in the mirror on the inside of the lid. There was a yellow rheum in the corners of his eyes. The roots of his hair were showing white and purple. There were several folds of flesh under his unshaven jaw. He was old and ugly. He stuck out his tongue. It was coated with a smooth pale yellow from the middle to the back. Dribble ran down the tip onto the table. He could smell his own breath. It must have been nauseating for the girl! No wonder she spent the night in an uncomfortable chair. Hukum Chand took out a bottle of liver salts and put several large teaspoonfuls into a glass. He unscrewed the thermos flask and poured in the water. The effervescence bubbled over from all sides of the tumbler onto the table. He stirred the water till the fizz died down, then drank it quickly. For some time he stood with his head bent and his hands resting on the table.

The dose of salts gurgled down pleasantly. An airy fullness rose from the pit of his stomach up to his throat and burped out in a long satisfying belch. The throbbing ebbed away and the ache receded into the back of his head. A few cups of strong hot tea and he would be himself again. Hukum Chand went to the bathroom. From the door opening out toward the servants' quarters he shouted for his bearer.

'Bring shaving water and bring my tea. Bring it here. I will take it in myself.'

When the bearer came, Hukum Chand took the tea tray and the mug of hot shaving water into the bedroom and put them on the table. He poured himself a cup of tea and laid out his shaving things. He lathered his chin and shaved and sipped his tea. The tinkle of the china and silver did not disturb the girl. She slept with her mouth slightly open. She looked dead except for the periodic upward movement of her breasts vainly trying to fill her bodice. Her hair was scattered all over her face. A pink celluloid clip made in the shape of a butterfly dangled by the leg of the chair. Her sari was crushed and creased, and bits of sequins glistened on the floor. Hukum Chand could not take his eyes off her while he sipped his tea and shaved. He could not analyze his feelings except that he wanted to make up to her. If she wanted to be slept with, he would sleep with her. The thought made him uneasy. He would have to drink hard to do that to her now.

The noise of shuffling feet and coughing on the verandah disturbed Hukum Chand's thoughts. It was a cough intended to draw attention. That meant the subinspector. Hukum Chand finished his tea and took his clothes into the bathroom to change. Afterwards, he went out of the door which opened toward the quarters and stepped onto the verandah. The subinspector was reading a newspaper. He jumped up from his chair and saluted.

'Has your honour been out walking in the rain?'

'No, no. I just went round the servants' quarters. You are early. I hope all is well.'

'These days one should be grateful for being alive. There is no peace anywhere. One trouble after another . . .'

The magistrate suddenly thought of the corpses. 'Did it rain in the night? How is it going near the railway station?'

'I went by this morning when the rain had just started. There wasn't very much left—just a big heap of ashes and bones. There are many skulls lying about. I do not know what we can do about them. I have sent word to the lambardar that no one is to be allowed near the bridge or the railway station.'

'How many were there? Did you count?'

'No, sir. The Sikh officer said there were more than a thousand. I think he just calculated how many people could get into a bogie and multiplied it by the number of bogies. He said that another four or five hundred must have been killed on the roofs, on footboards and between buffers. They must have fallen off when they were attacked. The roof was certainly covered with dried-up blood.'

'*Harey Ram, Harey Ram.* Fifteen hundred innocent people! What else is a Kalyug? There is darkness over the land. This is only one spot on the frontier. I suppose similar things are happening at other places. And now I believe our people are doing the same. What about the Muslims in these villages?'

'That is what I came to report, sir. Muslims of some villages have started leaving for the refugee camps. Chundunnugger has been partly evacuated. Pakistan army lorries with Baluchi and Pathan soldiers have been picking them up whenever information has been brought. But the Mano Majra Muslims are still there and this morning the lambardar reported the arrival of forty or fifty Sikh refugees who had crossed the river by the ford at dawn. They are putting up at the temple.'

'Why were they allowed to stop?' asked Hukum Chand sharply. 'You know very well the orders are that all incoming refugees must proceed to the camp at Jullundur. This is serious. They may start the killing in Mano Majra.'

'No, sir, the situation is well in hand up till now. These refugees have not lost much in Pakistan and apparently no one molested them on the way. The Muslims of Mano Majra have been bringing them food at the temple. If others turn up who have been through massacres and have lost relations, then it will be a different matter. I had not thought of the river crossings. Usually, after the rains the river is a mile in breadth and there are no fords till November or December. We have hardly had any rain this year.

85

There are several points where people can cross and I have not got enough policemen to patrol the riverside.'

Hukum Chand looked across the rest-house grounds. The rain was falling steadily. Little pools had begun to form in the ditches. The sky was a flat stretch of slate gray.

'Of course, if it keeps raining, the river will rise and there will not be many fords to cross. One will be able to control refugee movements over the bridges.'

A crash of lightning and thunder emphasized the tempo of the rain. The wind blew a thin spray onto the verandah.

'But we must get the Muslims out of this area whether they like it or not. The sooner the better.'

There was a long pause in the conversation. Both men sat staring into the rain. Hukum Chand began to speak again.

'One should bow before the storm till it passes. See the pampas grass! Its leaves bend before the breeze. The stem stands stiff in its plumed pride. When the storm comes it cracks and its white plume is scattered by the winds like fluffs of thistledown.' After a pause he added, 'A wise man swims with the current and still gets across.'

The subinspector heard the platitudes with polite attention. He did not see their significance to his immediate problem. Hukum Chand noticed the blank expression on the police officer's face. He had to make things more plain.

'What have you done about Ram Lal's murder? Have you made any further arrests?'

'Yes, sir, Jugga budmash gave us the names yesterday. They are men who were at one time in his own gang: Malli and four others from village Kapura two miles down the river. But Jugga was not with them. I have sent some constables to arrest them this morning.'

Hukum Chand did not seem to be interested. He had his eyes fixed somewhere far away.

'We were wrong about both Jugga and the other fellow.' The Inspector went on: 'I told you about Jugga's liaison with a Muslim weaver's girl. That kept him busy most nights. Malli threw bangles into Jugga's courtyard after the dacoity.'

Hukum Chand still seemed far away.

'If your honour agrees, we might release Jugga and Iqbal after we have got Malli and his companions.'

'Who are Malli and his companions, Sikh or Muslim?' asked Hukum Chand abruptly.

'All Sikhs.'

The magistrate relapsed into his thoughts once more. After some time he began to talk to himself. 'It would have been more convenient if they had been Mussulman. The knowledge of that and the agitator fellow being a Leaguer would have persuaded Mano Majra Sikhs to let their Muslims go.'

There was another long pause. The plan slowly pieced itself together in the subinspector's mind. He got up without making any comment. Hukum Chand did not want to take any chances.

'Listen,' he said. 'Let Malli and his gang off without making any entry anywhere. But keep an eye on their movements. We will arrest them when we want to . . . And do not release the budmash or the other chap yet. We may need them.'

The subinspector saluted.

'Wait. I haven't finished.' Hukum Chand raised his hand. 'After you have done the needful, send word to the commander of the Muslim refugee camp asking for trucks to evacuate Mano Majra Muslims.'

The subinspector saluted once more. He was conscious of the honour Hukum Chand had conferred by trusting him with the execution of a delicate and complicated plan. He put on his raincoat.

'I should not let you go in this rain, but the matter is so vital that you should not lose any time,' said Hukum Chand, still looking down at the ground.

'I know, sir.' The subinspector saluted again. 'I shall take action at once.' He mounted his bicycle and rode away from the rest house onto the muddy road.

Hukum Chand sat on the verandah staring vacantly at the rain falling in sheets. The right and wrong of his instructions did not weigh too heavily on him. He was a magistrate, not a missionary. It was the day-to-day problems to which he had to find answers. He had no need to equate them to some unknown absolute standard. There were not many 'oughts' in his life. There were just the 'is' s. He took life as it was. He did not want to recast it or rebel against it. There were processes of history to which human beings contributed willy-nilly. He believed that an individual's conscious effort should be directed to immediate ends like saving life when endangered, preserving the social structure and honouring its conventions. His immediate problem was to save Muslim lives. He would do that in any way he could. Two men who had been arrested on the strength of warrants signed by him should have been arrested in any case. One was an agitator, the other a bad character. In troubled times, it would be necessary to detain them. If he could make a minor error into a major investment, it would really be a mistake to call it a mistake. Hukum Chand felt elated. If his plan could be carried out efficiently! If only he could himself direct the details, there would be no slips! His subordinates frequently did not understand his mind and landed him in complicated situations.

From inside the rest house came the sound of the bathroom door shutting and opening. Hukum Chand got up and shouted at the bearer to bring in breakfast.

The girl sat on the edge of the bed with her chin in her hands. She stood up and covered her head with the loose end of the sari. When Hukum Chand sat down in the chair, she sat down on the bed again with her eyes fixed on the floor. There was an awkward silence. After some time Hukum Chand mustered his courage, cleared his throat and said, 'You must be hungry. I have sent for some tea.'

The girl turned her large sad eyes on him. 'I want to go home.'

'Have something to eat and I will tell the driver to take you home. Where do you live?'

'Chundunnugger. Where the Inspector Sahib has his police station.'

There was another long pause. Hukum Chand cleared his throat again. 'What is your name?'

'Haseena. Haseena Begum.'

'Haseena. You are *haseen*. Your mother has chosen your name well. Is that old woman your mother?'

The girl smiled for the first time. No one had paid her a compliment before. Now the Government itself had called her beautiful and was interested in her family.

'No, sir, she is my grandmother. My mother died soon after I was born.'

'How old are you?'

'I don't know. Sixteen or seventeen. Maybe eighteen. I was not born literate. I could not record my date of birth.'

She smiled at her own little joke. The magistrate smiled too. The bearer brought in a tray of tea, toast and eggs.

The girl got up to arrange the teacups and buttered a piece of toast. She put it on a saucer and placed it on the table in front of Hukum Chand.

'I will not eat anything. I have had my tea.'

The girl pretended to be cross.

'If you do not eat, then I won't eat either,' she said coquettishly. She put away the knife with which she was buttering the toast, and sat down on the bed.

The magistrate was pleased. 'Now, do not get angry with me,' he said. He walked up to her and put his arms round her shoulders. 'You must eat. You had nothing last night.'

The girl wriggled in his arms. 'If you eat, I will eat. If you do not, I will not either.'

'All right, if you insist.' Hukum Chand helped the girl up with his arm around her waist and brought her to his side of the table. 'We will both eat. Come and sit with me.'

The girl got over her nervousness and sat in his lap. She put thickly buttered toast in his mouth and laughed when he said 'Enough, enough,' through his stuffed mouth. She wiped the butter off his moustache.

'How long have you been in this profession?'

'What a silly question to ask! Why, ever since I was born. My mother was a singer and her mother was a singer till as long back as we know.'

'I do not mean singing. Other things,' explained Hukum Chand, looking away.

'What do you mean, other things?' asked the girl haughtily. 'We do not go about doing other things for money. I am a singer and I dance. I do not suppose you know what dancing and singing are. You just know about other things. A bottle of whisky and other things. That is all!'

Hukum Chand cleared his throat with a nervous cough. 'Well . . . I did not do anything.'

The girl laughed and pressed her hand on the magistrate's

face. 'Poor Magistrate Sahib. You had evil intentions, but you were tired. You snored like a railway engine.' The girl drew her breath in noisily and imitated his snoring. She laughed more loudly.

Hukum Chand stroked the girl's hair. His daughter would have been sixteen, seventeen, or eighteen, if she had lived. But he had no feeling of guilt, only a vague sense of fulfilment. He did not want to sleep with the girl, or make love to her, or even to kiss her on the lips and feel her body. He simply wanted her to sleep in his lap with her head resting on his chest.

'There you go again with your deep thoughts,' said the girl, scratching his head with her finger. She poured out a cup of tea and then poured it into the saucer. 'Have some tea. It will stop you thinking.' She thrust the saucerful of tea at him.

'No, no. I have had tea. You have it.'

'All right. I will have tea and you have your thoughts.'

The girl began to sip the tea noisily.

'Haseena.' He liked repeating the name. 'Haseena,' he started again.

'Yes. But Haseena is only my name. Why don't you say something?'

Hukum Chand took the empty saucer from her hand and put it on the table. He drew the girl closer and pressed her head against his. He ran his fingers through her hair.

'You are Muslim?'

'Yes, I am Muslim. What else could Haseena Begum be? A bearded Sikh?'

'I thought Muslims from Chundunnugger had been evacuated. How have you managed to stay on?'

'Many have gone away, but the Inspector Sahib said we could stay till he told us to go. Singers are neither Hindu nor Muslim in that way. All communities come to hear me.'

'Are there any other Muslims in Chundunnugger?'

'Well . . . yes,' she faltered. 'You can call them Muslim, Hindu or Sikh or anything, male or female. A party of *hijras* (hermaphrodites) are still there.' She blushed.

Hukum Chand put his hand across her eyes.

'Poor Haseena is embarrassed. I promise I won't laugh. You are not Hindu or Muslim, but not in the same way as a *hijra* is not a Hindu or Muslim.'

'Do not tease me.'

'I won't tease you,' he said removing his hand. She was still blushing. 'Tell me why the *hijras* were spared.'

'I will if you promise not to laugh at me.'

'I promise.'

The girl became animated.

'There was a child born to someone living in the Hindu locality. Without even thinking about communal troubles the *hijras* were there to sing. Hindus and Sikhs—I do not like Sikhs—got hold of them and wanted to kill them because they were Muslim.' She stopped deliberately.

'What happened?' asked Hukum Chand eagerly.

The girl laughed and clapped her hands the way *hijras* do, stretching her fingers wide. 'They started to beat their drums and sing in their raucous male voices. They whirled round so fast that their skirts flew in the air. Then they stopped and asked the leaders of the mob, "Now you have seen us, tell us, are we Hindus or Muslims?" and the whole crowd started laughing—the whole crowd except the Sikhs.'

Hukum Chand also laughed.

'That is not all. The Sikhs came with their kirpans and threatened them saying, "We will let you go this time, but you must get out of Chundennugger or we will kill you." One of the hijras again clapped his hands and ran his fingers in a Sikh's beard and asked, "Why? Will all of you become like us and stop having children?" Even the Sikhs started laughing.'

'That is a good one,' said Hukum Chand. 'But you should be careful while all this disturbance is going on. Stay at home for a few days.'

'I am not frightened. We know so many people so well and then I have a big powerful Magistrate to protect me. As long as he is there no one can harm a single hair of my head.'

Hukum Chand continued to run his hands through the girl's hair without saying anything. The girl looked up at him smiling mischievously. 'You want me to go to Pakistan?'

Hukum Chand pressed her closer. A hot feverish feeling came over him. 'Haseena.' He cleared his throat again. 'Haseena.' Words would not come out of his mouth.

'Haseena, Haseena, Haseena. I am not deaf. Why don't you say something?'

'You will stay here today, won't you? You do not want to go away just yet?'

'Is that all you wanted to say? If you do not give me your car, I cannot go five miles in the rain. But if you make me sing or spend another night here you will have to give me a big bundle of notes.'

Hukum Chand felt relieved.

'What is money?' he said with mock gallantry. 'I am ready to lay down my life for you.'

For a week, Iqbal was left alone in his cell. His only companions were the piles of newspapers and magazines. There was no light in his cell, nor was he provided with a lamp. He had to lie in the stifling heat listening to night noises—snores, occasional gunshots, and then more snoring. When it started to rain, the police station became more dismal than ever. There was nothing to see except rain falling incessantly, or sometimes a constable running across between the reporting rooms and the barracks. There was nothing to hear except the monotonous patter of raindrops, an occasional peal of thunder, and then more rain. He saw little of Jugga in the neighbouring cell. On the first two evenings, some constables had taken Jugga out of his cell. They brought him back after an hour. Iqbal did not know what they had done to him. He didn't ask and Jugga said nothing. But his repartee with the policemen became more vulgar and more familiar than before.

One morning a party of five men were brought to the station in handcuffs. As soon as Jugga saw them he lost his temper and abused them. They protested and refused to leave the reporting room verandah. Iqbal wondered who the new prisoners were. From the snatches of conversation that he had overheard, it seemed that everyone was on a spree, killing and looting. Even in Chundunnugger, a few yards from the police station, there had been killing. Iqbal had seen the pink glow of fire and heard people yelling, but the police had made no arrests. The prisoners must be quite out of the ordinary. While he was trying to figure out who the newcomers were, his cell was unlocked and Jugga came in with a constable. Jugga was in a good humour.

'Sat Sri Akal, Babuji,' he said. 'I am going to be the servant of your feet. I will learn something.'

'Iqbal Sahib,' the constable added, relocking the cell, 'teach this budmash how to go on the straight and narrow path.'

'Get away with you,' Jugga said. 'Babuji thinks it is you and the Government who have made me a budmash. Isn't that so, Babuji?'

Iqbal did not answer. He put his feet in the extra chair and gazed at the pile of papers. Jugga took Iqbal's feet off the chair and began pressing them with his enormous hands.

'Babuji, my kismet has woken up at last. I will serve you if you teach me some English. Just a few sentences so that I can do a little *git mit*.'

'Who is going to occupy the next cell?'

Jugga continued pressing Iqbal's feet and legs.

'I don't know,' he answered hesitantly. 'They tell me they have arrested Ram Lal's murderers.'

'I thought they had arrested you for the murder,' said Iqbal.

'Me, too,' smiled Jugga, baring his row of even white teeth studded with gold points. 'They always arrest me when anything goes wrong in Mano Majra. You see, I am a budmash.'

'Didn't you kill Ram Lal?'

Jugga stopped pressing. He caught his ears with his hands and stuck out his tongue. 'Toba, toba! Kill my own village bania? Babuji, who kills a hen which lays eggs? Besides, Ram Lal gave me money to pay lawyers when my father was in jail. I would not act like a bastard.'

'I suppose they will let you off now.'

·'The police are the kings of the country. They will let me off when they feel like it. If they want to keep me in, they will trump up a case of keeping a spear without a license or going out of the village without permission—or just anything.'

'But you were out of the village that night. Weren't you?'

Jugga sat down on his haunches, took Iqbal's feet in his lap, and started massaging his soles.

'I was out of the village,' he answered with a mischievous twinkle in his eye, 'but I was not murdering anyone. I was being murdered.'

Iqbal knew the expression. He did not want to encourage Jugga to make further disclosure. But once the subject had been suggested, there was no keeping Jugga back. He began to press

Iqbal's feet with greater fervour.

'You have been in Europe many years?' asked Jugga lowering his voice.

'Yes, many,' answered Iqbal, vainly trying to evade the inevitable.

'Then, Babuji,' asked Jugga lowering his voice further, 'you must have slept with many mem-sahibs. Yes?'

Iqbal felt irritated. It was not possible to keep Indians off the subject of sex for long. It obsessed their minds. It came out in their art, literature and religion. One saw it on the hoardings in the cities advertising aphrodisiacs and curatives for ill effects of masturbation. One saw it in the law courts and market places, where hawkers did a thriving trade selling oil made of the skin of sand lizards to put life into tired groins and increase the size of the phallus. One read it in the advertisements of quacks who claimed to possess remedies for barrenness and medicines to induce wombs to yield male children. One heard about it all the time. No people used incestuous abuse quite as casually as did the Indians. Terms like *sala*, wife's brother ('I would like to sleep with your sister'), and *susra*, father-in-law ('I would like to sleep with your daughter') were as often terms of affection for one's friends and relatives as expressions of anger to insult one's enemies. Conversation on any topic—politics, philosophy, sport—soon came down to sex, which everyone enjoyed with a lot of giggling and hand-slapping.

'Yes, I have,' Iqbal said, casually. 'With many.'

'*Wah, wah,*' exclaimed Jugga with enthusiasm and vigorous pressing of Iqbal's feet. '*Wah*, Babuji—great. You must have had lots of fun. The memsahibs are like *houris* from paradise—white and soft, like silk. All we have here are black buffaloes.'

'There is no difference between women. As a matter of fact, white women are not very exciting. Are you married?'

'No, Babuji. Who will give his daughter to a budmash? I have to get my pleasure where I can get it.'

'Do you get much of it?'

'Sometimes . . . When I go to Ferozepur for a hearing and if I save money from lawyers and their clerks, I have a good time. I make a bargain for the whole night. Women think, as with other men, that means two, or at the most three times.' He twirled his moustache. 'But when Juggut Singh leaves them, they cry *"hai, hai"*, touch their ears, say *"toba, toba"* and beg me in the name of God to leave them and take the money back.'

Iqbal knew it was a lie. Most young men talked like that.

'When you get married, you will find your wife a match for you,' Iqbal said. 'You will be holding your ears and saying *"toba, toba"*.'

'There is no fun in marriage, Babuji. Where is the time or place for fun? In summer, everyone sleeps out in the open and all you can do is to slip away for a little while and get over with things before your relations miss you. In winter, men and women sleep separately. You have to pretend to answer the call of nature at the same time at night.'

'You seem to know a lot about it, without being married.'

Jugga laughed. 'I don't keep my eyes shut. Besides, even if I am not married, I do a married man's work.'

'You also answer calls of nature by arrangement?'

Jugga laughed louder. 'Yes, Babuji, I do. That is what has brought me to this lockup. But I say to myself: if I had not been out that night, I would not have had the good fortune of meeting you, Babuji. I would not have the chance to learn English from you. Teach me some *git mit* like "good morning". Will you, Babuji-sahib?'

'What will you do with English?' Iqbal asked. 'The sahibs have left. You should learn your own language.'

Jugga did not seem pleased with the suggestion. For him, education meant knowing English. Clerks and letter writers who wrote Urdu or Gurmukhi were literate, but not educated.

'I can learn that from anyone. Bhai Meet Singh has promised to teach me Gurumukhi, but I never seem to get started. Babuji, how many classes have you read up to? You must have passed the tenth?'

Tenth was the school-leaving examination.

'Yes, I have passed the tenth. Actually I have passed sixteen.'

'Sixteen! *Wah, wah!* I have never met anyone who has done that. In our village only Ram Lal has done four. Now he is dead, the only one who can read anything is Meet Singh. In the neighbouring villages they haven't even got a bhai. Our Inspector Sahib has only read up to seven and the Deputy Sahib to ten.

95

Sixteen! You must have lots of brain.'

Iqbal felt embarrassed at the effusive compliments.

'Can you read or write anything?' he asked.

'I? No. My uncle's son taught me a little verse he learned at school. It is half English and half Hindustani:

Pigeon—kabootur, oodan—*fly*
Look—dekho, usman—*sky*

Do you know this?'

'No. Didn't he teach you the alphabet?'

'The A.B.C.? He did not know it himself. He knew as much as I do:

A. B. C. where have you been?
Edward's dead, I went to mourn.

You must know this one?'

'No, I don't know this either.'

'Well, you tell me something in English.'

Iqbal obliged. He taught Jugga how to say 'good morning' and 'goodnight'. When Jugga wanted to know the English for some of the vital functions of life, Iqbal became impatient. Then the five new prisoners were brought into the neighbouring cell. Jugga's jovial mood vanished as fast as it had come.

By eleven o'clock the rain had dwindled to a drizzle. The day became brighter. The subinspector looked up from his cycling. Some distance ahead of him, the clouds opened up, unfolding a rich blue sky. A shaft of sunlight slanted across the rain. Its saffron beams played about on the sodden fields. The rainbows spanned the sky, framing the town of Chundunnugger in a multicoloured arc.

The subinspector drove faster. He wanted to get to the police station before his head constable made an entry about Malli's arrest. It would be awkward to have to tear off pages from the station diary and then face a whole lot of questions from some impertinent lawyer. The head constable was a man of experience, but after the arrests of Jugga and Iqbal the subinspector's confidence in him had been somewhat shaken. He could not be relied on to handle a situation which was not routine. Would he know where to lock up the prisoners? He was a peasant, full of awe of the educated middle class. He would not have the nerve to disturb Iqbal (in whose cell he had put a charpoy and a chair and table). And if he had put Jugga and Malli together in the other cell, they would by now have discussed the murder and dacoity and decided to help each other.

As the subinspector cycled into the police station, a couple of policemen sitting on a bench on the verandah got up to receive him. One took his cycle; the other helped him with his raincoat, murmuring something about having to go out in the rain.

'Duty,' said the subinspector pompously, 'duty. Rain is nothing. Even if there was an earthquake, duty first! Is the head constable back?'

'Yes, sir. He brought in Malli's gang a few minutes ago and has gone to his quarters to have tea.'

'Has he made any entry in the daily diary?'

'No, sir, he said he would wait for you to do that.'

The subinspector was relieved. He went into the reporting room, hung his turban on a peg and sat down in a chair. The table was stacked with registers of all kinds. One large one with its yellow pages all divided into columns lay open before him. He glanced at the last entry. It was in his own hand, about his leaving Mano Majra rest house earlier that morning.

'Good,' he said aloud, rubbing his hands. He slapped his thighs and ran both his hands across his forehead and through his hair. 'Right,' he said loudly to himself. 'Right.'

A constable brought him a cup of tea, stirring it all the time.

'Your clothes must be wet!' he said, putting the tea on the table and giving it a last violent stir.

The subinspector picked it up without looking at the constable. 'Have you locked Malli's gang in the same cell as Jugga?'

'*Toba! Toba!*' exclaimed the constable, holding his hands up to his shoulder. 'Sir, there would have been a murder in the police station. You should have been here when we brought Malli in. As soon as Jugga saw him he went mad. I have never heard such abuse. Mother, sister, daughter—he did not leave one out. He shook the

97

bars till they rattled. We thought the door would come off its hinges. There was no question of putting Malli in there. And Malli would not have gone in, any more than a lamb would into a lion's cage.'

The subinspector smiled. 'Didn't Malli swear back?'

'No. He really looked frightened and kept saying that he had nothing to do with the Mano Majra dacoity. Jugga yelled back saying that he had seen him with his own eyes and he would settle scores with all of them and their mothers, sisters and daughters, once he was out. Malli said he was not afraid of him any more since all Jugga could do now was to sleep with his weaver girl. You should really have seen Jugga then! He behaved like an animal. His eyes turned red; he put his hand on his mouth and yelled; he beat his chest and shook the iron bars; he swore that he would tear Malli limb from limb. I have never seen anyone in a rage like that. We could not take any chances, so we kept Malli in the reporting room till Jugga's temper was down. Then we moved Jugga into the Babu's cell and put Malli's men in Jugga's.'

'It must have been a good tamasha,' said the subinspector with a grin. 'We will have some more. I am going to release Malli's men.'

The constable looked puzzled. Before he could ask any questions, the subinspector dismissed him with a lordly wave of the hand.

'Policy, you know! You will learn when you have been in the service as long as I have. Go and see if the head constable has had his tea. Say it is important.'

A little later the head constable arrived, belching contentment. He had the smug expression of one ready to protest against any commendation of his efficiency. The subinspector ignored the modest smile the other wore and asked him to shut the door and sit down. The head constable's expression changed from contentment to concern. He shut the door and stood on the other side of the table. 'Yes, sir. What are the orders?'

'Sit down. Sit down,' the subinspector said. His voice was cool. 'There is no hurry.'

The head constable sat down.

The subinspector rotated the sharp end of a pencil in his ear and examined the brown wax which stuck to it. He got a cigarette out of his pocket and tapped its tip on the matchbox several times before lighting it. He sucked it noisily. The smoke poured out of his nostrils, rebounded off the table and spread into the room.

'Head Constable Sahib,' he said at last, removing a tiny bit of tobacco from his tongue. 'Head Constable Sahib, there are lots of things to be done today, and I want you to do them personally.'

'Yes. sir,' answered the head constable gravely.

'First, take Malli and his men to Mano Majra. Release them where the villagers can see them being released. Near the temple, perhaps. Then inquire casually from the villagers if anyone has seen Sultana or any of his gang about. You need not say why. Just make the inquires.'

'But, sir, Sultana and his lot went away to Pakistan. Everyone knows that.'

The Inspector put the end of his pencil in his ear again and rubbed the wax on the table. He took a couple of pulls at the cigarette and this time pouted his lips and sent jets of smoke bounding off the register into the head constable's face.

'I do not know that Sultana has gone to Pakistan. Anyway, he left after the dacoity in Mano Majra. There is no harm in asking the villagers if they know when he left, is there?'

The head constable's face lit up.

'I understand, sir. Are there any other orders?'

'Yes. Also inquire from the villagers if they know anything about the mischief the Muslim Leaguer Iqbal had been up to when he was in Mano Majra.'

The head constable looked puzzled again.

'Sir, the Babu's name is Iqbal Singh. He is a Sikh. He has been living in England and had his long hair cut.'

The subinspector fixed the head constable with a stare and smiled. 'There are many Iqbals. I am talking of a Mohammed Iqbal, you are thinking of Iqbal Singh. Mohammed Iqbal can be a member of the Muslim League.'

'I understand, sir,' repeated the head constable, but he had not really understood. He hoped he would catch up with the scheme in due course. 'Your orders will be carried out.'

'Just one thing more,' added the subinspector, getting up from the table. 'Get a constable to take a letter from me to the commander of the Muslim refugee camp. Also, remind me to send some constables to Mano Majra tomorrow when the Pakistan army chaps come to evacuate Muslim villagers.'

The head constable realized that this was meant to help him understand the plan. He made a mental note of it, saluted a second time and clicked his heels. 'Yes, sir,' he said, and went out.

The subinspector put on his turban. He stood by the door looking into the courtyard of the station. The railway creeper on the wall facing him had been washed by the rain. Its leaves glistened in the sun. Policemen's dormitories on the left side had rows of charpoys with bedding neatly rolled on them. Opposite the dormitories were the station's two cells—in reality just ordinary rooms with iron bars instead of bricks for the front wall. One could see everything inside them from anywhere in the courtyard. In the nearer cell, Iqbal sat in a chair with his feet on the charpoy, reading a magazine. Several newspapers lay scattered on the floor. Juggut Singh was sitting, holding the bars with his hands, idly staring at the policemen's quarters. In the other cell, Malli and his companions lay sprawled on the floor talking to each other. They got up as the head constable and three policemen with rifles entered carrying handcuffs. Juggut Singh took no notice of the policemen going into the adjoining cell. He thought that Malli was probably being taken to court for a hearing.

Malli had been shaken by Juggut Singh's outburst. He was frightened of Juggut Singh and would sooner have made peace on the other's terms than go about in fear of violence—for Jugga was the most violent man in the district. Juggut Singh's abuse had made that impossible. Malli was the leader of his own band and felt that after Jugga's insults he had to say something to regain his prestige in the eyes of his companions. He thought of several nasty things he could have said, if he had known that Juggut Singh was going to return his offer of friendship with abuse. He felt hurt and angry. If he got another chance he would give it back to Jugga, abuse for abuse. Iron bars separated them and in any case there were armed policemen about.

The policemen handcuffed Malli and his companions and linked all the handcuffs to one long chain attached to a constable's belt. The head constable led them away. Two men armed with rifles kept the rear. As they emerged from their cell, Jugga looked up at Malli and then looked away.

'You forget old friends,' said Malli with mock friendliness.

'You don't even look at us and we pine away for you.'

His companions laughed. 'Let him be. Let him be.'

Jugga sat still with his eyes fixed on the ground.

'Why are you so angry, my dear? Why so sad? Is it somebody's love that torments your soul?'

'Come along, keep moving,' said the policemen reluctantly. They were enjoying the scene.

'Why can't we say *Sat Sri Akal* to our old friend? *Sat Sri Akal,* Sardar Juggut Singhji. Is there any message we can convey for you? A love message maybe? To the weaver's daughter?'

Jugga kept staring through the bars as if he had not heard. He turned pale with anger. All the blood drained from his face. His hands tightened around the iron bars.

Malli turned round to his smiling companions. 'Sardar Juggut Singh seems a little upset today. He will not answer our *Sat Sri Akal.* We do not mind. We will say *Sat Sri Akal* to him again.'

Malli joined his manacled hands and bent low near Juggut Singh's iron bar door and started loudly, '*Sat Sri . . .*'

Jugga's hands shot through the bars and gripped Malli by the hair protruding from the back of his turban. Malli's turban fell off. Jugga yelled murderously and with a jerk brought Malli's head crashing against the bars. He shook Malli as a terrier shakes a piece of rag from side to side, forward and backward, smashing his head repeatedly against the bars. Each jerk was accompanied by abuse: 'This to rape your mother. This your sister. This your daughter. This for your mother again. And this . . . and this.'

Iqbal, who had been watching the earlier proceedings from his chair, stood up in a corner and started shouting to the policemen: 'Why don't you do something? Don't you see he will kill the man?'

The policemen began to shout. One of them tried to push the butt end of his rifle in Jugga's face, but Jugga dodged. Malli's head was spattered with blood. His skull and forehead were bruised all over. He began to wail. The subinspector ran up to the cell and hit Jugga violently on the hand with his swagger stick several times. Jugga would not let go. The subinspector drew his revolver and pointed it at Jugga. 'Let go, you swine, or I will shoot.'

Jugga held up Malli's head with both his hands and spat in his face. He pushed him away with more abuse. Malli fell in a heap with his hair all over his face and shoulders. His companions helped him up and wiped the blood and spit off his face with his turban. He cried like a child, swearing all the time, 'May your mother die . . . you son of a pig . . . I will settle this with you.' Malli and his men were led away. Malli could be heard crying till he was a long way from the police station.

Jugga sank back into the stupor he had been in before he lost his temper. He examined the marks the subinspector's swagger stick had left on the back of his hands. Iqbal continued shouting agitatedly. Jugga turned round angrily. 'Shut up, you babu! What have I done to you that you talk so much?'

Jugga had not spoken rudely to him before. That scared Iqbal all the more.

'Inspector Sahib, now that the other cell is vacant, can't you shift me there?' he pleaded.

The subinspector smiled contemptuously. 'Certainly, Mr Iqbal, we will do all we can to make you comfortable. Tables, chairs—an electric fan maybe?'

Mano Majra

When it was discovered that the train had brought a full loud of corpses, a heavy brooding silence descended on the village. People barricaded their doors and many stayed up all night talking in whispers. Everyone felt his neighbour's hand against him, and thought of finding friends and allies. They did not notice the clouds blot out the stars nor smell the cool damp breeze. When they woke up in the morning and saw it was raining, their first thoughts were about the train and the burning corpses. The whole village was on the roofs looking toward the station.

The train had disappeared as mysteriously as it had come. The station was deserted. The soldier's tents were soaked with water and looked depressing. There was no smouldering fire nor smoke. In fact there was no sign of life—or death. Still people watched: perhaps there would be another train with more corpses!

By afternoon the clouds had rolled away to the west. Rain had cleared the atmosphere and one could see for miles around. Villagers ventured forth from their homes to find out if anyone knew more than they. Then they went back to their roofs. Although it had stopped raining, no one could be seen on the station platform or in the passenger shed or the military camp. A row of vultures sat on the parapet of the station building and kites were flying in circles high above it.

The head constable, with his posse of policemen and prisoners, was spotted a long way away from the village. People shouted the information to each other. The lambardar was summoned.

When the head constable arrived with his party, there was

quite a crowd assembled under the peepul tree near the temple.

The head constable unlocked the handcuffs of the prisoners in front of the villagers. They were made to put their thumb impressions on pieces of paper and told to report to the police station twice a week. The villagers looked on sullenly. They knew that Jugga budmash and the stranger had nothing to do with the dacoity. They were equally certain that in arresting Malli's gang the police were on the right track. Perhaps they were not all involved; some of the five might have been arrested mistakenly. It was scarcely possible that none of them had had anything to do with it. Yet there were the police letting them loose—not in their own village, but in Mano Majra where they had committed the murder. The police must be certain of their innocence to take such a risk.

The head constable took the lambardar aside and the two spoke to each other for some time. The lambardar came back and addressed the villagers saying: 'The Sentry Sahib wants to know if anyone here has seen or heard anything about Sultana budmash or any of his gang.'

Several villagers came out with news. He was known to have gone away to Pakistan along with his gang. They were all Muslims, and Muslims of their village had been evacuated.

'Was it before or after the murder of the Lala that he left?' inquired the head constable, coming up beside the lambardar.

'After,' they answered in a chorus. There was a long pause. The villagers looked at each other somewhat puzzled. Was it them? Before they could ask the policemen any questions, the head constable was speaking again.

'Did any of you see or talk to a young Mussulman babu called Mohammed Iqbal who was a member of the Muslim League?'

The lambardar was taken aback. He did not know Iqbal was a Muslim. He vaguely recalled Meet Singh and Imam Baksh calling him Iqbal Singh. He looked in the crowd for Imam Baksh but could not find him. Several villagers started telling the head constable excitedly of having seen Iqbal go to the fields and loiter about the railway track near the bridge.

'Did you notice anything suspicious about him?'

'Suspicious? Well . . .'

'Did you notice anything suspicious about the fellow?'

'Did you?'

No one was sure. One could never be sure about educated people; they were all suspiciously cunning. Surely Meet Singh was the one to answer questions about the babu; some of the babu's things were still with him in the gurudwara.

Meet Singh was pushed up to the front.

The head constable ignored Meet Singh and again addressed the group that had been answering him. 'I will speak to the bhai later,' he said. 'Can any one of you say whether this man came to Mano Majra before or after the dacoity?'

This was another shock. What would an urban babu have to do with dacoity or murder? Maybe it was not for money after all! No one was quite sure. Now they were not sure of anything. The head constable dismissed the meeting with: 'If anyone has any authentic information about the moneylender's murder or about Sultana or about Mohammed Iqbal, report at the police station at once.'

The crowd broke into small groups, talking and gesticulating animatedly. Meet Singh went up to the head constable who was getting his constables ready to march back.

'Sentry Sahib, the young man you arrested the other day is not a Mussulman. He is a Sikh—Iqbal Singh.'

The head constable took no notice of him. He was busy writing something on a piece of yellow paper. Meet Singh waited patiently.

'Sentry Sahib,' he started again as the other was folding the paper. The head constable did not even look at him. He beckoned one of the constables and handed him the paper saying:

'Get a bicycle or a tonga and take this letter to the commandant of the Pakistan military unit. Also tell him yourself that you have come from Mano Majra and the situation is serious. He must send his trucks and soldiers to evacuate the Muslims as early as possible. At once.'

'Yes, sir,' answered the constable clicking his heels.

'Sentry Sahib,' implored Meet Singh.

'Sentry Sahib, Sentry Sahib, Sentry Sahib,' repeated the head constable angrily. 'You have been eating my ears with your "Sentry Sahibs". What do you want?'

'Iqbal Singh is a Sikh.'

'Did you open the fly-buttons of his pants to see whether he was a Sikh or a Mussulman? You are a simple bhai of a temple. Go and pray.'

The head constable took his place in front of the policemen standing in double file.

'Attention! By the left, quick march.'

Meet Singh turned aback to the temple without answering the eager queries of the villagers.

The head constable's visit had divided Mano Majra into two halves as neatly as a knife cuts through a pat of butter.

Muslims sat and moped in their houses. Rumours of atrocities committed by Sikhs on Muslims in Patiala, Ambala and Kapurthala, which they had heard and dismissed, came back to their minds. They had heard of gentlewomen having their veils taken off, being stripped and marched down crowded streets to be raped in the market place. Many had eluded their would-be ravishers by killing themselves. They had heard of mosques being desecrated by the slaughter of pigs on the premises, and of copies of the holy Quran being torn up by infidels. Quite suddenly, every Sikh in Mano Majra became a stranger with an evil intent. His long hair and beard appeared barbarous, his *kirpan* menacingly anti-Muslim. For the first time, the name Pakistan came to mean something to them—a refuge where there were no Sikhs.

The Sikhs were sullen and angry. 'Never trust a Mussulman,' they said. The last Guru had warned them that Muslims had no loyalties. He was right. All through the Muslim period of Indian history, sons had imprisoned or killed their own fathers and brothers had blinded brothers to get the throne. And what had they done to the Sikhs? Executed two of their Gurus, assassinated another and butchered his infant children; hundreds of thousands had been put to the sword for no other offence than refusing to accept Islam; their temples had been desecrated by the slaughter of kine; the holy Granth had been torn to bits. And Muslims were never ones to respect women. Sikh refugees had told of women jumping into wells and burning themselves rather than fall into the hands of Muslims. Those who did not commit suicide were paraded naked in the streets, raped in public, and then murdered. Now a trainload of Sikhs massacred by Muslims had been cremated in Mano Majra. Hindus and Sikhs were fleeing from their homes in Pakistan and having to find shelter in Mano Majra. Then there was the murder of Ram Lal. No one knew who had killed him, but everyone knew Ram Lal was a Hindu; Sultana and his gang were Muslims and had fled to Pakistan. An unknown character—without turban or beard—had been loitering about the village. These were reasons enough to be angry with someone. So they decided to be angry with the Muslims; Muslims were basely ungrateful. Logic was never a strong point with Sikhs; when they were roused, logic did not matter at all.

It was a gloomy night. The breeze that had swept away the clouds blew them back again. At first they came in fleecy strands of white. The moon wiped them off its face. Then they came in large billows, blotted out the moonlight and turned the sky a dull gray. The moon fought its way through, and occasionally, patches of the plain sparkled like silver. Later, clouds came in monstrous black formations and spread across the sky. Then, without any lightning or thunder, it began to rain.

A group of Sikh peasants gathered together in the house of the lambardar. They sat in a circle around a hurricane lantern—some on a charpoy, others on the floor. Meet Singh was amongst them.

For a long time nobody said anything apart from repeating, 'God is punishing us for our sins.'

'Yes, God is punishing us for our sins.'

'There is a lot of *zulum* in Pakistan.'

'That is because He wants to punish us for our sins. Bad acts yield a bitter harvest.'

Then one of the younger men spoke. 'What have we done to deserve this? We have looked upon the Muslims as our brothers and sisters. Why should they send somebody to spy on us?'

'You mean Iqbal?' Meet Singh said. 'I had quite a long conversation with him. He had an iron bangle on his wrist like all of us Sikhs and told me that his mother had wanted him to wear it, so he wore it. He is a shaven Sikh. He does not smoke. And he came the day after the moneylender's murder.'

'Bhai, you get taken in easily,' replied the same youth. 'Does it hurt a Mussulman to wear an iron bangle or not smoke for a day—particularly if he has some important work to do?'

'I may be a simple bhai,' protested Meet Singh warmly, 'but I know as well as you that the babu had nothing to do with the murder; he would not have been in the village afterwards if he had. That any fathead would understand.'

The youth felt a little abashed.

'Besides that,' continued Meet Singh more confidently, 'they had already arrested Malli for the dacoity . . .'

'How do you know what they had arrested Malli for?' interrupted the youth triumphantly.

'Yes, how do you know what the police know? They have released Malli. Have you ever known them to release murderers without a trial and acquittal?' asked some others.

'Bhai, you always talk without reason.'

'Accha, if you are the ones with all the reason, tell me who threw the packet of bangles into Jugga's house.'

'How should we know?' answered a chorus.

'I will tell you. It was Jugga's enemy Malli. You all know they had fallen out. Who else would dare insult Jugga except he?'

No one answered the question. Meet Singh went on aggressively to drive his point home. 'And all this about Sultana, Sultana! What has that to do with the dacoity?'

'Yes, Bhaiji, you may be right,' said another youth. 'But Lal is dead: why bother about him? The police will do that. Let Jugga, Malli and Sultana settle their quarrels. As for the babu, for all we care he can sleep with his mother. Our problem is: what are we to do with all these pigs we have with us? They have been eating our salt for generations and see what they have done! We have treated them like our own brothers. They have behaved like snakes.'

The temperature of the meeting went up suddenly. Meet Singh spoke angrily.

'What have they done to you? Have they ousted you from your lands or occupied your houses? Have they seduced your womenfolk? Tell me, what have they done?'

'Ask the refugees what they have done to them,' answered the truculent youth who had started the argument. 'You mean to tell us that they are lying when they say that gurudwaras have been burned and people massacred?'

'I was only talking of Mano Majra. What have our tenants done?'

'They are Muslims.'

Meet Singh shrugged his shoulders.

The lambardar felt it was up to him to settle the argument.

'What had to happen has happened,' he said wisely. 'We have to decide what we are to do now. These refugees who have turned up at the temple may do something which will bring a bad name on the village.'

The reference to 'something' changed the mood of the meeting. How could outsiders dare to 'something' to their fellow villagers? Here was another stumbling block to logic. Group loyalty was above reason. The youth who had referred to Muslims as pigs spoke haughtily: 'We would like to see somebody raise his little finger against our tenants while we live!'

The lambardar snubbed him. 'You are a hotheaded one. Sometimes you want to kill Muslims. Sometimes you want to kill refugees. We say something and you drag the talk to something else.'

'All right, all right, Lambardara,' retorted the young man, 'if you are all that clever, you say something.'

'Listen, brothers,' said the lambardar lowering his voice. 'This is no time to lose tempers. Nobody here wants to kill anyone. But who knows the intentions of other people? Today we have forty or fifty refugees, who by the grace of the Guru are a peaceful lot and they only talk. Tomorrow we may get others who may have lost their mothers or sisters. Are we going to tell them: "Do not come to this village"? And if they do come, will we let them wreak vengeance on our tenants?'

'You have said something worth a hundred thousand rupees,' said an old man. 'We should think about it.'

The peasants thought about their problem. They could not refuse shelter to refugees: hospitality was not a pastime but a sacred duty when those who sought it were homeless. Could they ask their Muslims to go? Quite emphatically not! Loyalty to a fellow villager was above all other considerations. Despite the words they had used, no one had the nerve to suggest throwing them out, even in a purely Sikh gathering. The mood of the assembly changed from anger to bewilderment.

After some time the lambardar spoke.

'All Muslims of the neighbouring villages have been evacuated and taken to the refugee camp near Chundunnugger.

Some have already gone away to Pakistan. Others have been sent to the bigger camp at Jullundur.'

'Yes,' added another. 'Kapoora and Gujjoo Matta were evacuated last week. Mano Majra is the only place left where there are Muslims. What I would like to know is how these people asked their fellow villagers to leave. We could never say anything like that to our tenants, any more than we could tell our sons to get out of our homes. Is there anyone here who could say to the Muslims, "Brothers, you should go away from Mano Majra"?

Before anyone could answer, another villager came in and stood on the threshold. Everyone turned round to see, but they could not recognize him in the dim lamplight.

'Who is it?' asked the lambardar, shading his eyes from the lamp. 'Come in.'

Imam Baksh came in. Two others followed him. They also were Muslims.

'Salaam, Chacha Imam Baksh. Salaam, Khair Dina. Salaam, salaam.'

'*Sat Sri Akal,* Lambardara. *Sat Sri Akal,*' answered the Muslims.

People made room for them and waited for Imam Baksh to begin.

Imam Baksh combed his beard with his fingers.

'Well, brothers, what is your decision about us?' he asked quietly.

There was an awkward silence. Everyone looked at the lambardar.

'Why ask us?' answered the lambardar. 'This is your village as much as ours.'

'You have heard what is being said! All the neighbouring villages have been evacuated. Only we are left. If you want us to go too, we will go.'

Meet Singh began to sniff. He felt it was not for him to speak. He had said his bit. Besides, he was only a priest who lived on what the villagers gave him. One of the younger men spoke.

'It is like this, Uncle Imam Baksh. As long as we are here nobody will dare to touch you. We die first and then you can look after yourselves.'

'Yes,' added another warmly, 'we first, then you. If anyone

110

raises his eyebrows at you we will rape his mother.'

'Mother, sister and daughter,' added the others.

Imam Baksh wiped a tear from his eyes and blew his nose in the hem of his shirt.

'What have we to do with Pakistan? We were born here. So were our ancestors. We have lived amongst you as brothers.' Imam Baksh broke down. Meet Singh clasped him in his arms and began to sob. Several of the people started crying quietly and blowing their noses.

The lambardar spoke: 'Yes, you are our brothers. As far as we are concerned, you and your children and your grandchildren can live here as long as you like. If anyone speaks rudely to you, your wives or your children, it will be us first and our wives and children before a single hair of your heads is touched. But Chacha, we are so few and the strangers coming from Pakistan are coming in thousands. Who will be responsible for what they do?'

'Yes,' agreed the others, 'as far as we are concerned you are all right, but what about these refugees?'

'I have heard that some villages were surrounded by mobs many thousands strong, all armed with guns and spears. There was no question of resistance.'

'We are not afraid of mobs,' replied another quickly. 'Let them come! We will give them such a beating they will not dare to look at Mano Majra again.'

Nobody took notice of the challenger; the boast sounded too hollow to be taken seriously. Imam Baksh blew his nose again, 'What do you advice us to do then, brothers?' he asked, choking with emotion.

'Uncle,' said the lambardar in a heavy voice, 'it is very hard for me to say, but seeing the sort of time we live in, I would advise you to go to the refugee camp while this trouble is on. You lock your houses with your belongings. We will look after your cattle till you come back.'

The lambardar's voice created a tense stillness. Villagers held their breath for fear of being heard. The lambardar himself felt that he ought to say something quickly to dispel the effect of his words.

'Until yesterday,' he began again loudly, 'in case of trouble we could have helped you to cross the river by the ford. Now it has been raining for two days; the river has risen. The only crossings are by trains and road bridges—you know what is happening there! It is for your own safety that I advise you to take shelter in the camp for a few days, and then you can come back. As far as we are concerned,' he repeated warmly, 'if you decide to stay on, you are most welcome to do so. We will defend you with our lives.'

No one had any doubts about the import of the lambardar's words. They sat with their heads bowed till Imam Baksh stood up.

'All right,' he said solemnly, 'if we have to go, we better pack up our bedding and belongings. It will take us more than one night to clear out of homes it has taken our fathers and grandfathers hundreds of years to make.'

The lambardar felt a strong sense of guilt and was overcome with emotion. He got up and embraced Imam Baksh and started to cry loudly. Sikh and Muslim villagers fell into each other's arms and wept like children. Imam Baksh gently got out of the lambardar's embrace. 'There is no need to cry,' he said between sobs. 'This is the way of the world—

> *Not forever does the bulbul sing*
> *In balmy shades of bowers,*
> *Not forever lasts the spring*
> *Nor ever blossom flowers.*
> *Not forever reigneth joy,*
> *Sets the sun on days of bliss,*
> *Friendships not forever last,*
> *They know not life, who know not this.*

'They know not life, who know not this,' repeated many others with sighs. 'Yes, Uncle Imam Baksh. This is life.'

Imam Baksh and his companions left the meeting in tears.

Before going round to other Muslim homes, Imam Baksh went to his own hut attached to the mosque. Nooran was already in bed. An oil lamp burned in a niche in the wall.

'Nooro, Nooro,' he shouted, shaking her by the shoulder. 'Get up, Nooro.'

The girl opened her eyes. 'What is the matter?'

'Get up and pack. We have to go away tomorrow morning.' he announced dramatically.

'Go away? Where?'

'I don't know . . . Pakistan!'

The girl sat up with a jerk. 'I will not go to Pakistan,' she said defiantly.

Imam Baksh pretended he had not heard. 'Put all the clothes in the trunks and the cooking utensils in a gunny bag. Also take something for the buffalo. We will have to take her too.'

'I will not go to Pakistan,' the girl repeated fiercely.

'You may not want to go, but they will throw you out. All Muslims are leaving for the camp tomorrow.'

'Who will throw us out? This is our village. Are the police and the government dead?'

'Don't be silly, girl. Do as you are told. Hundreds of thousands of people are going to Pakistan and as many coming out. Those who stay behind are killed. Hurry up and pack. I have to go and tell the others that they must get ready.'

Imam Baksh left the girl sitting up in bed. Nooran rubbed her face with her hands and stared at the wall. She did not know what to do. She could spend the night out and come back when all the others had gone. But she could not do it alone; and it was raining. Her only chance was Jugga. Malli had been released, maybe Jugga had also come home. She knew that was not true, but the hope persisted and it gave her something to do.

Nooran went out in the rain. She passed many people in the lanes, going about with gunny bags covering their heads and shoulders. The whole village was awake. In most houses she could see the dim flickers of oil lamps. Some were packing; others were helping them to pack. Most just talked with their friends. The women sat on the floors hugging each other and crying. It was as if in every home there had been a death.

Nooran shook the door of Jugga's house. The chain on the other side rattled but there was no response. In the gray light she noticed the door was bolted from the outside. She undid the iron ring and went in. Jugga's mother was out, probably visiting some Muslim friends. There was no light at all. Nooran sat down on a charpoy. She did not want to face Jugga's mother alone nor did she want to go back home. She hoped something would happen—something which would make Jugga walk in. She sat and waited and hoped.

113

For an hour Nooran watched the gray shadows of clouds chasing each other. It drizzled and poured and poured and drizzled alternately. She heard the sound of footsteps cautiously picking their way through the muddy lane. They stopped outside the door. Someone shook the door.

'Who is it?' asked an old woman's voice.

Nooran lost her nerve; she did not move.

'Who is it?' demanded the voice angrily. 'Why don't you speak?'

Nooran stood up and mumbled indistinctly, *'Beybey.'*

The old woman stepped in and quickly shut the door behind her.

'Jugga! Jugga, is it you?' she whispered. 'Have they let you off?'

'No, *Beybey*, it is I—Nooran. Chacha Imam Baksh's daughter,' answered the girl timidly.

'Nooro? What brings you here at this hour?' the old woman asked angrily.

'Has Jugga come back?'

'What have you to do with Jugga?' his mother snapped. 'You have sent him to jail. You have made him a budmash. Does your father know you go about to strangers' houses at midnight like a tart?'

Nooran began to cry. 'We are going away tomorrow.'

That did not soften the old woman's heart.

'What relation are you to us that you want to come and see us? You can go where you like.'

Nooran played her last card. 'I cannot leave. Jugga has promised to marry me.'

'Get out, you bitch!' the old woman hissed. 'You, a Muslim weaver's daughter, marry a Sikh peasant! Get out, or I will go and tell your father and the whole village. Go to Pakistan! Leave my Jugga alone.'

Nooran felt heavy and lifeless. 'All right, *Beybey*, I will go. Don't be angry with me. When Jugga comes back just tell him I came to say *'Sat Sri Akal'*. The girl went down on her knees, clasped the old woman's legs and began to sob. *'Beybey*, I am going away and will never come back again. Don't be harsh to me just when I am leaving.'

114

Jugga's mother stood stiff, without a trace of emotion on her face. Inside her, she felt a little weak and soft. 'I will tell Jugga.'

Nooran stopped crying. Her sobs came at long intervals. She still held onto Jugga's mother. Her head sank lower and lower till it touched the old woman's feet.

'*Beybey.*'

'What have you to say now?' She had a premonition of what was coming.

'*Beybey.*'

'*Beybey! Beybey!* Why don't you say something?' asked the woman, pushing Nooran away. 'What is it?'

The girl swallowed the spittle in her mouth.

'*Beybey*, I have Jugga's child inside me. If I go to Pakistan they will kill it when they know it has a Sikh father.'

The old woman let Nooran's head drop back on her feet. Nooran clutched them hard and began to cry again.

'How long have you had it?'

'I have just found out. It is the second month.'

Jugga's mother helped Nooran up and the two sat down on the charpoy. Nooran stopped sobbing.

'I cannot keep you here,' said the old woman at last. 'I have enough trouble with the police already. When all this is over and Jugga comes back, he will go and get you from wherever you are. Does your father know?'

'No! If he finds out he will marry me off to someone or murder me.' She started crying again.

'Oh, stop this whining,' commanded the old woman sternly. 'Why didn't you think of it when you were at the mischief? I have already told you Jugga will get you as soon as he is out.'

Nooran stiffed her sobs.

'*Beybey*, don't let him be too long.'

'He will hurry for his own sake. If he does not get you he will have to buy a wife and there is not a pice or trinket left with us. He will get you if he wants a wife. Have no fear.'

A vague hope filled Nooran's being. She felt as if she belonged to the house and the house to her; the charpoy she sat on, the buffalo, Jugga's mother, all were hers. She would come back even if Jugga failed to turn up. She could tell them she was married. The thought of her father came like a dark cloud over her lunar hopes.

She would slip away without telling him. The moon shone again.

'*Beybey*, if I get the chance I will come to say *Sat Sri Akal* in the morning. *Sat Sri Akal*. I must go and pack.' Nooran hugged the old woman passionately. '*Sat Sri Akal*,' she said a little breathlessly again and went out.

Jugga's mother sat on her charpoy staring into the dark for several hours.

Not many people slept in Mano Majra that night. They went from house to house—talking, crying, swearing love and friendship, assuring each other that this would soon be over. Life, they said, would be as it always had been.

Imam Baksh came back from his round of Muslim homes before Nooran had returned. Nothing had been packed. He was too depressed to be angry with her. It was as hard on the young as the old. She must have gone to see some of her friends. He started pottering around looking for gunny bags, tin canisters and trunks. A few minutes later Nooran came in.

'Have you seen all your girl friends? Let us get this done before we sleep,' said Imam Baksh.

'You go to bed. I will put the things in. there is not much to do—and you must be tired,' she answered.

'Yes, I am a little tired,' he said sitting down on his charpoy. 'You pack the clothes now. We can put in the cooking utensils in the morning after you have cooked something for the journey.' Imam Baksh stretched himself on the bed and fell asleep.

There was not much for Nooran to do. A Punjabi peasant's baggage consists of little besides a change of clothes, a quilt and a pillow, a couple of pitchers, cooking utensils, and perhaps a brass plate and a copper tumbler or two. All that can be put on the only piece of furniture they possess—a charpoy. Nooran put her own and her father's clothes in a gray battered steel trunk which had been with them ever since she could remember. She lit a fire in the hearth to bake a few chapatties for the next day. Within half an hour she had done the cooking. She rinsed the utensils and put them in a gunny bag. Flour, salt and the spices that remained went in biscuit and cigarette tins, which in their turn went inside an empty kerosene oil can with a wood top. The packing was over.

All that remained was to roll her quilt round the pillow, put the odds and ends on the charpoy and the charpoy on the buffalo. She could carry the piece of broken mirror in her hand.

It rained intermittently all night. Early in the morning it became a regular downpour. Villagers who had stayed up most of the night fell asleep in the monotonous patter of rain and the opiate of the fresh morning breeze.

The tooting of motor horns and the high note of truck engines in low gear plowing their way through the slush and mud woke the entire village. The convoy went around Mano Majra looking for a lane wide enough to let their trucks in. In front was a jeep fitted with a loud-speaker. There were two officers in it—a Sikh (the one who had come after the ghost train) and a Muslim. Behind the jeep were a dozen trucks. One of the trucks was full of Pathan soldiers and another one full of Sikhs. They were all armed with sten guns.

The convoy came to a halt outside the village. Only the jeep could make its way through. It drove up to the centre and stopped beside the platform under the peepul tree. The two officers stepped out. The Sikh asked one of the villagers to fetch the lambardar. The Muslim was joined by the Pathan soldiers. He sent them out in batches of three to knock at every door and ask the Muslims to come out. For a few minutes Mano Majra echoed to cries of 'All Muslims going to Pakistan come out at once. Come! All Muslims. Out at once.'

Slowly the Muslims began to come out of their homes, driving their cattle and their bullock carts loaded with charpoys, rolls of bedding, tin trunks, kerosene oil tins, earthen pitchers and brass utensils. The rest of Mano Majra came out to see them off.

The two officers and the lambardar were the last to come out of the village. The jeep followed them. They were talking and gesticulating animatedly. Most of the talking was between the Muslim officer and the lambardar.

'I have no arrangement to take all this luggage with bullock carts, beds, pots and pans. This convoy is not going to Pakistan by road. We are taking them to the Chundunnugger refugee camp and from there by train to Lahore. They can only take their clothes, bedding, cash and jewellery. Tell them to leave everything else here. You can look after it.'

The news that the Mano Majra Muslims were going to Pakistan came as a surprise. The lambardar had believed they would only go to the refugee came for a few days and then return.

'No, Sahib, we cannot say anything,' replied the lambardar. 'If it was for a day or two we could look after their belongings. As you are going to Pakistan, it may be many months before they return. Property is a bad thing; it poisons people's minds. No, we will not touch anything. We will only look after their houses.'

The Muslim officer was irritated. 'I have no time to argue. You see yourself that all I have is a dozen trucks. I cannot put buffaloes and bullock carts in them.'

'No, Sahib,' retorted the lambardar stubbornly. 'You can say what you like and you can be angry with us, but we will not touch our brothers' properties. You want us to become enemies?'

'Wah, wah, Lambardar Sahib,' answered the Muslim laughing loudly. '*Shabash*! Yesterday you wanted to kill them, today you call them brothers. You may change your mind again tomorrow.'

'Do not taunt us like this, Captain Sahib. We are brothers and will always remain brothers.'

'All right, all right, Lambardara. You are brothers,' the officer said. 'I grant you that, but I still cannot take all this stuff. You consult the Sardar Officer and your fellow villagers about it. I will deal with the Muslims.'

The Muslim officer got on the jeep and addressed the crowd. He chose his words carefully.

'We have a dozen trucks and all you people who are going to Pakistan must get on them in ten minutes. We have other villages to evacuate later on. The only luggage you can take with you is what you can carry—nothing more. You can leave your cattle, bullock carts, charpoys, pitchers, and so on with your friends in the village. If we get a chance, we will bring these things out for you later. I give you ten minutes to settle your affairs. Then the convoy will move.'

The Muslims left their bullock carts and thronged round the jeep, protesting and talking loudly. The Muslims officer who had stepped off the jeep went back to the microphone.

'Silence! I warn you, the convoy will move in ten minutes;

whether you are on it or not will be no concern of mine.'

Sikh peasants who had stood apart heard the order and went up to the Sikh officer for advice. The officer took no notice of them; he continued staring contemptuously over the upturned collar of his raincoat at the men, cattle, carts and trucks steaming in the slush and rain.

'Why, Sardar Sahib,' asked Meet Singh nervously, 'is not the lambardar right? One should not touch another's property. There is always danger of misunderstanding.'

The officer looked Meet Singh up and down.

'You are quite right, Bhaiji, there is some danger of being misunderstood. One should never touch another's property; one should never look at another's woman. One should just let others take one's goods and sleep with one's sisters. The only way people like you will understand anything is by being sent over to Pakistan: have your sisters and mothers raped in front of you, have your clothes taken off, and be sent back with a kick and spit on your behinds.'

The officer's speech was a slap in the face to all the peasants. But someone sniggered. Everyone turned around to look. It was Malli with his five companions. With them were a few young refugees who were staying at the Sikh temple. None of them belonged to Mano Majra.

'Sir, the people of this village are famous for their charity,' said Malli smiling. 'They cannot look after themselves, how can they look after other people? But do not bother, Sardar Sahib, we will take care of Muslim property. You can tell the other officer to leave it with us. It will be quite safe if you can detail some of your soldiers to prevent looting by these people.'

There was complete confusion. People ran hither and thither shouting at the tops of their voices. Despite the Muslim officer's tone of finality, villagers clamoured around him protesting and full of suggestions. He came up to his Sikh colleague surrounded by his bewildered co-religionists.

'Can you make arrangements for taking over what is left behind?'

Before the Sikh could answer, a babel of protests burst from all sides. The Sikh remained tight-lipped and aloof.

The Muslim officer turned around sharply. 'Shut up!' he yelled.

The murmuring died down. He spoke again, punctuating each word with a stab of his forefinger.

'I give you five minutes to get into the trucks with just as much luggage as you can carry in your hands. Those who are not in will be left behind. And this is the last time I will say it.'

'It is all settled,' said the Sikh officer, speaking softly in Punjabi. 'I have arranged that these people from the next village will look after the cattle, carts, and houses till it is over. I will have a list made and sent over to you.'

His colleague did not reply. He had a sardonic smile on his face. Mano Majra Sikhs and Muslims looked on helplessly.

There was no time to make arrangements. There was no time even to say goodbye. Truck engines were started. Pathan soldiers rounded up the Muslims, drove them back to the carts for a brief minute or two, and then onto the trucks. In the confusion of rain, mud and soldiers herding the peasants about with the muzzles of their sten guns sticking in their backs, the villagers saw little of each other. All they could do was to shout their last farewells from the trucks. The Muslim officer drove his jeep round the convoy to see that all was in order and then came to say goodbye to his Sikh colleague. The two shook hands mechanically, without a smile or a trace of emotion. The jeep took its place in front of the line of trucks. The microphone blared forth once more to announce that they were ready to move. The officer shouted 'Pakistan!' His soldiers answered in a chorus 'Forever!' The convoy slushed its way toward Chundunnugger. The Sikhs watched them till they were out of sight. They wiped the tears off their faces and turned back to their homes with heavy hearts.

Mano Majra's cup of sorrow was not yet full. The Sikh officer summoned the lambardar. All the villagers came with him—no one wanted to be left alone. Sikh soldiers threw a cordon round them. The officer told the villagers that he had decided to appoint Malli custodian of the evacuated Muslims' property. Anyone interfering with him or his men would be shot.

Malli's gang and the refugees then unyoked the bullocks, looted the carts, and drove the cows and buffaloes away.

Karma

All that morning, people sat in their homes and stared despondently through their open doors. They saw Malli's men and the refugees ransack Muslim houses. They saw Sikh soldiers come and go as if on their beats. They heard the piteous lowing of cattle as they were beaten and dragged along. They heard the loud cackle of hens and roosters silenced by the slash of the knife. But they did nothing but sit and sigh.

A shepherd boy, who had been out gathering mushrooms, came back with the news that the river had risen. No one took any notice of him. They only wished that it would rise more and drown the whole of Mano Majra along with them, their women, children, and cattle—provided it also drowned Malli, his gang, the refugees, and the soldiers.

While the men sighed and groaned, the rain fell in a steady downpour and the Sutlej continued to rise. It spread on either side of the central piers which normally contained the winter channels, and joined the pools round the other piers into one broad stream. It stretched right across the bridge, licking the dam which separated it from the fields of Mano Majra. It ran over the many little islands in the river bed till only the tops of the bushes that grew on them could be seen. Colonies of cormorants and terns which were used to roosting there flew over to the banks and then to the bridge—over which no trains had run for several days.

In the afternoon, another villager went around to the houses shouting, 'Oi Banta Singh, the river is rising! Oi Daleep Singha, the river has risen! Oi listen, it is already up to the dam!' The people just looked up with their melancholy eyes signifying, 'We have heard that before.' Then another man came with the same message, 'The river has risen'; then another, and another, till everyone was saying, 'Do you know, the river has risen!'

At last the lambardar went out to see for himself. Yes, the river had risen. Two days of rain could not have caused it; it must have poured in the mountains after the melting of the snows. Sluice gates of canals had probably been closed to prevent the flood from bursting their banks; so there was no outlet except the river. The friendly sluggish stream of gray had become a menacing and tumultuous spread of muddy brown. The piers of the bridge were all that remained solid and contemptuously defiant of the river. Their pointed edges clove through the sheet of water and let it vent its impotent rage in a swirl of eddies and whirlpools. Rain beat upon the surface, pockmarking it all over. The Sutlej was a terrifying sight.

By evening, Mano Majra had forgotten about its Muslims and Malli's misdeeds. The river had become the main topic of conversation. Once more women stood on the rooftops looking to the west. Men started going in turns to the embankment to report on the situation.

Before sunset the lambardar went up again to see the river. It had risen more since his visit in the afternoon. Some of the clusters of pampas which had been above the water level were now partly submerged. Their stalks had gone limp and their sodden snow-white plumes floated on the water. He had never known the Sutlej to rise so high in so short a time. Mano Majra was still a long way off and the mud dam looked solid and safe. Nevertheless he arranged for watch to be kept all through the night. Four parties of three men each were to take turns and be on the embankment from sunset to sunrise and report every hour. The rest were to stay in their houses.

The lambardar's decision was a quilt under which the village slept snug and safe. The lambardar himself had little sleep. Soon after midnight the three men on watch came back talking loudly, in a high state of excitement. They could not tell in the gray muffled moonlight whether the river had risen more, but they had heard human voices calling for help. The cries came from over the water. They may have been from the other side or from the river itself.

122

The lambardar went out with them. He took his chromium-plated flashlight.

The four men stood on the embankment and surveyed the Sutlej, which looked like a sheet of black. The white beam of the lambardar's torch scanned the surface of the river. They could see nothing but the swirling water. They held their breath and listened, but they could hear nothing except the noise of the rain falling on the water. Each time the lambardar asked if they were sure that what they had heard were human voices and not jackals, they felt more and more uncertain and had to ask each other: 'It was clear, wasn't it, Karnaila?'

'Oh yes. It was clear enough. *"Hai, hai"*—like someone in pain.'

The four men sat under a tree, huddled around a hurricane lamp. The gunny sacks they used as raincoats were soaking wet; so were all their clothes. An hour later there was a break in the clouds. The rain slowed down to a drizzle and then stopped. The moon broke through the clouds just above the western horizon. Its reflection on the river made a broad path of shimmering tinfoil running from the opposite bank to the men under the tree. On this shining patch of moonlight even little ripples of water could be seen distinctly.

A black oval object hit the bridge pier and was swept by the stream towards the Mano Majra embankment. It looked like a big drum with sticks on its sides. It moved forward, backward and sideways until the current caught it again and brought it into the silvery path not far from where the men were sitting. It was a dead cow with its belly bloated like a massive barrel and its legs stiffly stretched upward. Then followed some blocks of thatch straw and bundles of clothing.

'It looks as if some village has been swept away by the flood,' said the lambardar.

'Quiet! Listen,' said one of the villagers in a whisper. The faint sound of a moan was wafted across the waters.

'Did you hear?'

'Quiet!'

They held their breath and listened.

No, it could not have been human. There was a rumbling sound. They listened again. Of course, it was a rumble; it was a

123

train. Its puffing became clearer and clearer. Then they saw the outlines of the engine and the train itself. It had no lights. There was not even a headlight on the engine. Sparks flew out of the engine funnel like fireworks. As the train came over the bridge, cormorants flew silently down the river and terns flew up with shrill cries. The train came to a halt at Mano Majra station. It was from Pakistan.

'There are no lights on the train.'

'The engine did not whistle.'

'It is like a ghost.'

'In the name of the Lord do not talk like this,' said the lambardar. 'It may be a goods train. It must have been the siren you heard. These new American engines wail like someone being murdered.'

'No, Lambardara, we heard the sound more than an hour ago; and again the same one before the train come on,' replied one of the villagers.

'You cannot hear it any more. The train is not making any noise now.'

From across the railway line, where some days earlier over a thousand dead bodies had been burned, a jackal sent up a long plaintive howl. A pack joined him. The men shuddered.

'Must have been the jackals. They sound like women crying when somebody dies,' said the lambardar.

'No, no,' protested the other. 'No, it was a human voice as clear as you are talking to me now.'

They sat and listened and watched strange indistinguishable forms floating on the floodwaters. The moon went down. After a brief period of darkness the eastern horizon turned gray. Long lines of bats flew across noiselessly. Crows began to caw in their sleep. The shrill cry of a koel came bursting through a clump of trees and all the world was awake.

The clouds had rolled away to the north. Slowly the sun came up and flooded the rain-soaked plain with a dazzling orange brilliance; everything glistened in the sunlight. The river had risen further. Its turbid water carried carts with the bloated carcasses of bulls still yoked to them. Horses rolled from side to side as if they were scratching their backs. There were also men and women with their clothes clinging to their bodies; little children sleeping on their bellies with their arms clutching the water and their tiny buttocks dipping in and out. The sky was soon full of kites and vultures. They flew down and landed on the floating carcasses. They pecked till the corpses themselves rolled over and shooed them off with hands which rose stiffly into the air and splashed back into the water.

'Some villages must have been flooded at night,' said the lambardar gravely.

'Who yokes bulls to carts at night?' asked one of his companions.

'Yes, that is true. Why should the bullocks be yoked?'

More human forms could be seen coming through the arches of the bridge. They rebounded off the piers, paused, pirouetted at the whirlpools, and then came bouncing down the river. The men moved up toward the bridge to see some corpses which had drifted near the bank.

They stood and stared.

'Lambardara, they were not drowned. They were murdered.'

An old peasant with a gray beard lay flat on the water. His arms were stretched out as if he had been crucified. His mouth was wide open and showed his toothless gums, his eyes were covered with film, his hair floated about his head like a halo. He had a deep wound on his neck which slanted down from the side to the chest. A child's head butted into the old man's armpit. There was a hole in its back. There were many others coming down the river like logs hewn on the mountains and cast into streams to be carried down to the plains. A few passed through the middle of the arches and sped onward faster. Others bumped into the piers and turned over to show their wounds till the current turned them over again. Some were without limbs, some had their bellies torn open, many women's breasts were slashed. They floated down the sunlit river, bobbing up and down. Overhead hung the kites and vultures.

The lambardar and the villagers drew the ends of their turbans across their faces. 'The Guru have mercy on us,' someone whispered. 'There has been a massacre somewhere. We must inform the police.'

'Police?' a small man said bitterly. 'What will they do? Write a first information report?'

Sick and with heavy hearts, the party turned back to Mano

Majra. They did not know what to say to people when they got back. The river had risen further? Some villages had been flooded? There had been a massacre somewhere upstream? There were hundreds of corpses floating on the Sutlej? Or, just keep quiet?

When they came back to the village nobody was about to hear what they had to say. They were all on the rooftops looking at the station. After several days a train had drawn up at Mano Majra in the daytime. Since the engine faced eastward, it must have come from Pakistan. This time too the place was full of soldiers and policemen and the station had been cordoned off. The news of the corpses on the river was shouted from the housetops. People told each other about the mutilation of women and children. Nobody wanted to know who the dead people were nor wanted to go to the river to find out. There was a new interest at the station, with promise of worse horrors than the last one.

There was no doubt in anyone's mind what the train contained. They were sure that the soldiers would come for oil and wood. They had no more oil to spare and the wood they had left was too damp to burn. But the soldiers did not come. Instead, a bulldozer arrived from somewhere. It began dragging its lower jaw into the ground just outside the station on the Mano Majra side. It went along, eating up the earth, chewing it, casting it aside. It did this for several hours, until there was a rectangular trench almost fifty yards long with mounds of earth of either side. Then it paused for a break. The soldiers and policemen who had been idly watching the bulldozer at work were called to order and marched back to the platform. They came back in twos carrying canvas stretchers. They tipped the stretchers into the pit and went back to the train for more. This went on all day till sunset. Then the bulldozer woke up again. It opened its jaws and ate up the earth it had thrown out before and vomited it into the trench till it was level with the ground. The place looked like the scar of a healed-up wound. Two soldiers were left to guard the grave from the depredations of jackals and badgers.

That evening, the entire village turned up for the evening prayers at the gurudwara. This had never happened before, except on Gurus' birthdays or on the New Year's Day in April. The only regular visitors to the temple were old men and women. Others came to have their children named, for baptisms, weddings and funerals. Attendance at prayers had been steadily going up since the murder of the moneylender; people did not want to be alone. Since the Muslims had gone, their deserted houses with doors swinging wide open had acquired an eerie, haunted look. Villagers walked past them quickly without turning their heads. The one place of refuge to which people could go without much explanation was the gurudwara. Men came pretending that they would be needed; women just to be with them, and they brought the children. The main hall where the scripture was kept and the two rooms on the side were jammed with refugees and villagers. Their shoes were neatly arranged in rows on the other side of the threshold.

Meet Singh read the evening prayer by the light of the hurricane lamp. One of the men stood behind him waving a fly whisk. When the prayer was over, the congregation sang a hymn while Meet Singh folded the Granth in gaudy silk scarfs and laid it to rest for the night. The worshippers stood up and folded their hands. Meet Singh took his place in front. He repeated the names of the ten Gurus, the Sikh martyrs and the Sikh shrines and invoked their blessing; the crowd shouted their amens with loud 'Wah Gurus' at the end of each supplication. They went down on their knees, rubbed their foreheads on the ground, and the ceremony was over. Meet Singh came and joined the men.

It was a solemn assembly. Only the children played. They chased each other around the room, laughing and arguing. The adults scolded the children. One by one, the children returned to their mothers' laps and fell asleep. Then the men and women also stretched themselves on the floor in the different parts of the room.

The day's events were not likely to be forgotten in sleep. Many could not sleep at all. Others slept fitfully and woke up with startled cries if a neighbour's leg or arm so much as touched them. Even the ones who snored with apparent abandon, dreamed and relived the scenes of the day. They heard the sound of motor vehicles, the lowing of cattle and people crying. They sobbed in their sleep and their beards were moist with their tears.

When the sound of a motor horn was heard once more, those who were awake but drowsy thought they were dreaming. Those that were dreaming thought they were hearing it in their dreams. In their dreams they even said 'Yes, yes' to the voice which kept asking 'Are you all dead?'

The late night visitor was a jeep like the one in which the army officers had come in the morning. It seemed to know its way about the village. It went from door to door with a voice inquiring, 'Is there anyone there?' Only the dogs barked in reply. Then it came to the temple and the engine was switched off. Two men walked into the courtyard and shouted again: 'Is there anyone here or are you all dead?'

Everyone got up. Some children began to cry. Meet Singh turned up the wick of his hurricane lantern. He and the lambardar went out to meet the visitors.

The men saw the commotion they had created. They ignored the lambardar and Meet Singh and walked up to the threshold of the large room. One looked in at the bewildered crowd and asked: 'Are you all dead?'

'Any one of you alive?' added the other.

The lambardar answered angrily, 'No one is dead in this village. What do you want?'

Before the men could answer two of their companions joined them. All were Sikhs. They wore khaki uniforms and had rifles slung on their shoulders.

'This village looks quite dead,' repeated one of the strangers, loudly addressing his own companions.

'The Guru has been merciful to this village. No one has died here,' answered Meet Singh with quiet dignity.

'Well, if the village is not dead, then it should be. It should be drowned in a palmful of water. It consists of eunuchs,' said the visitor fiercely with a flourish of his hand.

The strangers took off their shoes and came inside the large hall. The lambardar and Meet Singh followed them. Men sat up and tied their turbans. Women put their children in their laps and tried to rock them to sleep again.

One of the group, who appeared to be the leader, motioned the others to sit down. Everyone sat down. The leader had an aggressive bossy manner. He was a boy in his teens with a little beard which was glued to his chin with brilliantine. He was small in size, slight of build and altogether somewhat effeminate; a glossy red ribbon showed under the acute angle of his bright blue turban. His khaki army shirt hung loosely from his round drooping shoulders. He wore a black leather Sam Browne: the strap across his narrow chest charged with bullets and the broad belt clamped about his still narrower waist. On one side it had a holster with the butt of a revolver protruding; on the other side there was a dagger. He looked as if his mother had dressed him up as an American cowboy.

The boy caressed the holster of his revolver and ran his fingers over the silver noses of the bullets. He looked around him with complete confidence.

'Is this a Sikh village?' he asked insolently. It was obvious to the villagers that he was an educated city-dweller. Such men always assumed a superior air when talking to peasants. They had no regard for age or status.

'Yes, sir,' answered the lambardar. 'It has always been a Sikh village. We had Muslim tenants but they have gone.'

'What sort of Sikhs are you?' asked the boy, glowering menacingly. He elaborated his question: 'Potent or impotent?'

No one knew what to say. No one protested that this was not the sort of language one used in a gurudwara with women and children sitting by.

'Do you know how many trainloads of dead Sikhs and Hindus have come over? Do you know of the massacres in Rawalpindi and Multan, Gujranwala and Sheikhupura? What are you doing about it? You just eat and sleep and you call yourselves Sikhs—the brave Sikhs! The martial class!' he added, raising both his arms to emphasize his sarcasm. He surveyed his audience with the bright eyes daring anyone to contradict him. People looked down somewhat ashamed of themselves.

'What can we do, Sardarji?' questioned the lambardar. 'If our government goes to war against Pakistan, we will fight. What can we do sitting in Mano Majra?'

'Government!' sneered the boy contemptuously. 'You expect the government to do anything? A government consisting of cowardly bania moneylenders! Do the Mussalmans in Pakistan apply for permission from their government when they rape your sisters? Do they apply for permission when they stop trains and kill everyone, old, young, women and children? You want the government to do something! That is great! *Shabash*! Brave!' He gave the holster on his side a jaunty smack.

'But, Sardar Sahib,' said the lambardar falteringly, 'Do tell us what we can do.'

'That is better,' answered the lad. 'Now we can talk. Listen and listen very carefully.' He paused, looked around and started again. He spoke slowly, emphasizing each sentence by stabbing the air with his forefinger. 'For each Hindu or Sikh they kill, kill two Mussulmans. For each woman they abduct or rape, abduct two. For each home they loot, loot two. For each trainload of dead they send over, send two across. For each road convoy that is attacked, attack two. That will stop the killing on the other side. It will teach them that we also play this game of killing and looting.'

He stopped to gauge the effect he had created. People listened to him with rapt openmouthed attention. Only Meet Singh did not took up; he cleared his throat but stopped.

'Well, brother, why do you keep quiet?' asked the lad, throwing a challenge.

'I was going to say,' said Meet Singh haltingly, 'I was going to say,' he repeated, 'what have the Muslims here done to us for us to kill them in revenge for what Muslims in Pakistan are doing. Only people who have committed crimes should be punished.'

The lad glared angrily at Meet Singh. 'What had the Sikhs and Hindus in Pakistan done that they were butchered? Weren't they innocent? Had the women committed crimes for which they were ravished? Had the children committed murder for which they were spiked in front of their parents?'

Meet Singh was subdued. The boy wanted to squash him further. 'Why, brother? Now speak and say what you want to.'

'I am an old Bhai; I could not lift my hands against anyone—fight in battle or kill the killer. What bravery is there in killing unarmed innocent people? As for women, you know that the last Guru, Gobind Singh, made it a part of a baptismal oath that no Sikh was to touch the person of a Muslim woman. And God alone knows how he suffered at the hands of the Mussulmans! They killed all his four sons.'

'Teach this sort of Sikhism to someone else,' snapped the boy contemptuously. 'It is your sort of people who have been the curse of this country. You quote the Guru about women; why don't you tell us what he said about the Mussulmans? "Only befriend the Turk when all other communities are dead." Is that correct?'

'Yes,' answered Meet Singh meekly, 'but nobody is asking you to befriend them. Besides, the Guru himself had Muslims in his army . . .'

'And one of them stabbed him while he slept.'

Meet Singh felt uneasy.

'One of them stabbed him while he slept,' repeated the boy.

'Yes . . . but there are bad ones and . . .'

'Show me a good one.'

Meet Singh could not keep up with repartee. He just looked down at his feet. His silence was taken as an admission of defeat.

'Let him be. He is an old bhai. Let him stick to his prayers,' said many in a chorus.

The speaker was appeased. He addressed the assembly again in pompous tones. 'Remember,' he said like an oracle, 'remember and never forget—a Muslim knows no argument but the sword.'

The crowd murmured approval.

'Is there anyone beloved of the Guru here? Anyone who wants to sacrifice his life for the Sikh community? Anyone with courage?' He hurled each sentence like a challenge.

The villagers felt very uncomfortable. The harangue had made them angry and they wanted to prove their manliness. At the same time Meet Singh's presence made them uneasy and they felt they were being disloyal to him.

'What are we supposed to do?' asked the lambardar plaintively.

'I will tell you what we are to do,' answered the boy, pointing to himself. 'If you have the courage to do it.' He continued after a pause. 'Tomorrow a trainload of Muslims is to cross the bridge to Pakistan. If you are men, this train should carry as many people dead to the other side as you have received.'

A cold clammy feeling spread among the audience. People coughed nervously.

'The train will have Mano Majra Muslims on it,' said Meet Singh without looking up.

'Bhai, you seem to know everything, don't you?' yelled the youth furiously. 'Did you give them the tickets or is your son a Railway Babu? I don't know who the Muslims on the train are; I do not care. It is enough for me to know that they are Muslims. They will not cross this river alive. If you people agree with me, we can talk; if you are frightened, then say so and we will say *Sat Sri Akal* to you and look for real men elsewhere.'

Another long period of silence ensued. The lad beat a tattoo on his holster and patiently scanned the faces around him.

'There is a military guard at the bridge.' It was Malli. He had been standing outside in the dark. He would not have dared to come back to Mano Majra alone. Yet there he was, boldly stepping into the gurudwara. Several members of his gang appeared at the door.

'You need not bother about the military or the police. No one will interfere. We will see to that,' answered the lad looking back at him. 'Are there any volunteers?'

'My life is at your disposal,' said Malli heroically. The story of Jugga beating him had gone round the village. His reputation had to be redeemed.

'Bravo,' said the speaker. 'At least one man. The Guru asked for five lives when he made the Sikhs. Those Sikhs were supermen. We need many more than five. Who else is willing to lay down his life?'

Four of Malli's companions stepped over the threshold. They were followed by many others, mostly refugees. Some villagers who had only recently wept at the departure of their Muslim friends also stood up to volunteer. Each time anyone raised his hand the youth said 'Bravo,' and asked him to come and sit apart. More than fifty agreed to join in the escapade.

'That is enough,' said the lad, raising his hand. 'If I need any more volunteers, I will ask for them. Let us pray for the success of our venture.'

Everyone stood up. Women put their children on the floor and joined the menfolk. The assembly faced the little cot on which the Granth lay wrapped, and folded their hands in prayer. The boy turned round to Meet Singh.

'Will you lead the prayer, Bhaiji?' he asked tauntingly.

'It is your mission, Sardar Sahib,' replied Meet Singh humbly. 'You lead the prayer.'

The boy cleared his throat, shut his eyes and began to recite the names of the Gurus. He ended by asking for the Gurus' blessings for the venture. The assembly went down on their knees and rubbed their foreheads on the ground, loudly proclaiming:

In the name of Nanak,
By the hope that faith doth instill,
By the Grace of God,
We bear the world nothing but good will.

The crowd stood up again and began to chant:

The Sikhs will rule
Their enemies will be scattered
Only they that seek refuge will be saved!

The little ceremonial ended with triumphant cries of *Sat Sri Akal.* Everyone sat down except the boy leader. The prayer had given him a veneer of humility. He joined his hands and apologized to the assembly.

'Sisters and brothers, forgive me for disturbing you at this late hour; you too, Bhaiji, and you, Lambardar Sahib, please forgive us for this inconvenience and for any angry words that I may have uttered; but this is in the service of the Guru. Volunteers will now adjourn to the other room; the others may rest. *Sat Sri Akal.*'

'*Sat Sri Akal,*' replied some of the audience.

Meet Singh's room on the side of the courtyard was cleared of women and children. The visitors moved in with the volunteers. More lamps were brought in. The leader spread out a map on one of the beds. He held up a hurricane lantern. The volunteers crowded round him to study the map.

'Can you all see the position of the bridge and the river from where you are?' he asked.

'Yes, yes,' they answered impatiently.

'Have any of you got guns?'

They all looked at each other. No, no one had a gun.

'It does not matter,' continued the leader. 'We still have six or seven rifles, and probably a couple of sten guns as well. Bring your swords and spears. They will be more useful than guns.' He paused.

'The plan is this. Tomorrow after sunset, when it is dark, we will stretch a rope across the first span of the bridge. It will be a foot above the height of the funnel of the engine. When the train passes under it, it will sweep off all the people sitting on the roof of the train. That will account for at least four to five hundred.'

The eyes of the listeners sparkled with admiration. They nodded to each other and looked around. The lambardar and Meet Singh stood at the door listening. The boy turned round angrily:

'Bhaiji, what have you to do with this? Why don't you go and say your prayers?'

Both the lambardar and Meet Singh turned away sheepishly. The lambardar knew he too would be told off if he hung around.

'And you, Lambardar Sahib,' said the boy. 'You should be going to the police station to report.'

Everyone laughed.

The boy silenced his audience by raising his hand. He continued: 'The train is due to leave Chundunnugger after midnight. It will have no lights, not even on the engine. We will post people with flashlights along the track every hundred yards. Each one will give the signal to the next person as the train passes him. In any case, you will be able to hear it. People with swords and spears will be right at the bridge to deal with those that fall off the roof of the train. They will have to be killed and thrown into the river. Men with guns will be a few yards up the track and will shoot at the windows. There will be no danger of fire being returned. There are only a dozen Pakistani soldiers on the train. In the dark, they will not know where to shoot. They will not have time to load their guns. If they stop the train, we will take care of them and kill many more into the bargain.'

It seemed a perfect plan, without the slightest danger of retaliation. Everyone was pleased.

'It is already past midnight,' said the boy, folding up the map. 'You'd all better get some sleep. Tomorrow morning we will go to the bridge and decide where each one is to be posted. The Sikhs are the chosen of God. Victory be to our God.'

'Victory to our God,' answered the others.

The meeting dispersed. Visitors found room in the gurudwara. So did Malli and his gang. Many of the villagers had gone away to their homes lest they get implicated in the crime by being present at the temple when the conspiracy was being hatched. The lambardar took two of the villagers with him and left for the police station at Chundunnugger.

'Well, Inspector Sahib, let them kill,' said Hukum Chand wearily. 'Let everyone kill. Just ask for help from other stations and keep a record of the messages you send. We must be able to prove that we did our best to stop them.'

Hukum Chand looked a tired man. One week had aged him beyond recognition. The white at the roots of his hair had become longer. He had been shaving in a hurry and had cut himself in several places. His cheeks sagged and folds of flesh fell like dewlaps about his chin. He kept rubbing the corners of his eyes for the yellow which was not there.

'What am I to do?' he wailed. 'The whole world has gone mad. Let it go mad! What does it matter if another thousand get killed? We will get a bulldozer and bury them as we did the others. We may not even need the bulldozer if this time it is going to be on the river. Just throw the corpses in the water. What is a few hundred out of four hundred million anyway? An epidemic takes ten times the number and no one even bothers.'

The subinspector knew that this was not the real Hukum Chand. He was only trying to get the melancholia out of his system. The subinspector waited patiently, and then dropped a feeler.

'Yes, sir. I am keeping a record of all that is happening and what we are doing. Last evening, we had to evacuate Chundunnugger. I could not rely on the army nor my own constables. The best I could do was to ward off the attackers by telling them that Pakistan troops were in the town. That frightened them and I got the Muslims out in the nick of time. When the attackers discovered the trick, they looted and burned every Muslim house they could. I believe some of them planned to come to the police station for me, but better counsel prevailed. So you see, sir, all I got was abuse from the Muslims for evicting them from their homes; abuse from the Sikhs for having robbed them of the loot they were expecting. Now I suppose the government will also abuse me for something or the other. All I really have is my big thumb.' The subinspector stuck out his thumb and smiled.

Hukum Chand's mind was not itself that morning. He did not

seem to realize the full import of the subinspector's report.

'Yes, Inspector Sahib, you and I are going to get nothing out of this except a bad name. What can we do? Everyone has gone trigger-happy. People empty their rifle magazines into densely packed trains, motor convoys, columns of marching refugees, as if they were squirting red water at the Holi festival; it is a bloody Holi. What sense is there in going to a place where bullets fly? The bullet does not pause and consider, "This is Hukum Chand, I must not touch him." Nor does a bullet have a name written on it saying "Sent by So-and-so". Even if it did bear a name—once inside, what consolation would it be to us to know who fired it? No, Inspector Sahib, the only thing a sane person can do in a lunatic asylum is to pretend that he is as mad as the others and at the first opportunity scale the walls and get out.'

The subinspector was used to these sermons and knew how little they represented the magistrate's real self. But Hukum Chand's apparent inability to take a hint was surprising. He was known for never saying a thing straight; he considered it stupid. To him the art of diplomacy was to state a simple thing in an involved manner. It never got one into trouble. It could never be quoted as having implied this or that. At the same time, it gave one the reputation of being shrewd and clever. Hukum Chand was as adept at discovering innuendoes as he was at making them. This morning he seemed to be giving his mind a rest.

'You should have been in Chundunnugger yesterday,' said the subinspector, bringing the conversation back to the actual problem which faced him. 'If I had been five minutes later, there would not have been one Muslim left alive. As it is, not one was killed. I was able to take them all out.'

The subinspector emphasized 'not one' and 'all'. He watched Hukum Chand's reaction.

It worked. Hukum Chand stopped rubbing the corners of his eyes and asked casually, as if he were only seeking information, 'You mean to tell me there is not one Muslim family left in Chundunnugger?'

'No, sir, not one.'

'I suppose,' said Hukum Chand, clearing his throat, 'they will came back when all this blows over?'

'Maybe,' the subinspector answered. 'There is not much for

them to come back to. Their homes have been burned or occupied. And if anyone did come back, his or her life would not be worth the tiniest shell in the sea.'

'It will not last forever. You see how things change. Within a week they will be back in Chundunnugger and the Sikhs and Muslims will be drinking water out of the same pitcher.' Hukum Chand detected the note of false hope in his own voice. So did the subinspector.

'You may be right, sir. But it will certainly take more than a week for that to happen. Chundunnugger refugees are being taken to Pakistan by train tonight. God alone knows how many will go across the bridge alive; those that do are not likely to want to come back in a hurry.'

The subinspector had hit the mark. Hukum Chand's face went pale. He could no longer keep up the pretense.

'How do you know that Chundunnugger refugees are going by the night train?' he asked.

'I got it from the camp commander. There was danger of attack on the camp itself, so he decided to get the first train available to take the refugees out. If they do not go, probably no one will be left alive. If they do, some at least may get through, if the train is running at some speed. They are not planning to derail the train; they want it to go on to Pakistan with a cargo of corpses.'

Hukum Chand clutched the arms of his chair convulsively.

'Why don't you warn the camp commander about it? He may decide not to go.'

'Cherisher of the poor,' explained the subinspector patiently, 'I have not told him anything about the proposed attack on the train because if he does not go the whole camp may be destroyed. There are mobs of twenty to thirty thousand armed villagers thirsting for blood. I have fifty policemen with me and not one of them would fire a shot at a Sikh. But if your honour can use influence with these mobs, I can tell the camp commander about the plans to ambush the train and persuade him not to go.'

The subinspector was hitting below the belt.

'No, no,' stuttered the magistrate. 'What can influence do with armed mobs? No. We must think.'

Hukum Chand sank back in his chair. He covered his face with his hands. He beat his forehead gently with his clenched fist. He

137

tugged at his hair as if he could pull ideas out of his brain.

'What has happened to those two men you arrested for the moneylender's murder?' he asked after some time.

The subinspector did not see the relevance of the inquiry.

'They are still in the lockup. You ordered me to keep them till the trouble was over. At this rate it seems I will have to keep them for some months.'

'Are there any Muslim females, or any stray Muslims who have refused to leave Mano Majra?

'No, sir, not one remains. Men, women, children, all have left,' answered the subinspector. He was still unable to catch up with Hukum Chand's train of thought.

'What about Jugga's weaver girl you told me about? What was her name?'

'Nooran.'

'Ah yes, Nooran. Where is she?'

'She has left. Her father was a sort of leader of the Muslims of Mano Majra. The lambardar told me a great deal about him. He had just one child, this girl Nooran; she is the one alleged to be carrying on with the dacoit Jugga.'

'And this other fellow, didn't you say he was a political worker of some sort?'

'Yes, sir. People's Party or something like that. I think he is a Muslim Leaguer masquerading under a false label. I examined . . .'

'Have you got any blank official papers for orders?' cut in Hukum Chand impatiently.

'Yes, sir,' answered the subinspector. He fished out several pieces of yellow printed paper and handed them to the magistrate.

Hukum Chand stretched out his hand and plucked the subinspector's fountain pen from his pocket.

'What are the names of the prisoners?' he asked, spreading out the sheets on the table.

'Jugga budmash and . . .'

'Jugga budmash,' interrupted Hukum Chand, filling in a blank and signing it. 'Jugga budmash, and . . . ?' he asked taking the other paper.

'Iqbal Mohammed or Mohammed Iqbal. I am not sure which.'

'Not Iqbal Mohammed, Inspector Sahib. Nor Mohammed Iqbal. Iqbal Singh,' he said, writing with a flourish. The subinspector looked a little stupefied. How did Hukum Chand know? Had Meet Singh been around calling on the magistrate?

'Sir, you should not believe everyone. I examined . . .'

'Do you really believe an educated Muslim would dare to come to these parts in times like these? Do you think any party would be so foolish as to send a Muslim to preach peace to Sikh peasants thirsting for Muslim blood, Inspector Sahib? Where is your imagination?'

The subinspector was subdued. It did seem unlikely that an educated man would risk his neck for any cause. Besides, he had noticed on Iqbal's right wrist the steel bangle all Sikhs wear.

'Your honour must be right, but what has this to do with the preventing of an attack on the train?'

'My honour *is* right,' said Hukum Chand triumphantly. 'And you will soon know why. Think about it on your way to Chundunnugger. As soon as you get there, release both the men and see that they leave for Mano Majra immediately. If necessary, get them a tonga. They must be in the village by the evening.'

The subinspector took the papers, and saluted. He sped back to the police station on his cycle. Gradually, the clouds of confusion lifted from his mind. Hukum Chand's plan became as crystal clear as a day after heavy rain.

'You will find Mano Majra somewhat changed,' the subinspector remarked, casually addressing the table in front of him. Iqbal and Jugga stood facing him on the other side.

'Why don't you sit down, Babu Sahib?' said the subinspector. This time he spoke directly to Iqbal. 'Please take a chair. Oi, what is your name? Why don't you bring a chair for the Babu Sahib?' he shouted at a constable. 'I know you are angry with me, but it is not my fault,' he continued. 'I have my duty to do. You as an educated man know what would happen if I were to treat people differently.'

The constable brought a chair for Iqbal.

'Do sit down. Shall I get you a cup of tea or something before you go?' The subinspector smiled unctuously.

'It is very kind of you. I would rather keep standing; I have been sitting in the cell all these days. If you do not mind, I would like to leave as soon as you have finished with the formalities,' answered Iqbal without responding to the other's smile.

'You are free to go whenever and wherever you want to go. I have sent for a tonga to take you to Mano Majra. I will send an armed constable to accompany you. It is not safe to be about in Chundunnugger or to travel unescorted.'

The subinspector picked up a yellow paper and read: 'Juggut Singh, son of Alam Singh, age twenty-four, caste Sikh of village Mano Majra, budmash number ten.'

'Yes, sir,' interrupted Jugga, smiling. The treatment he had received from the police had not made any difference to him. His equation with authority was simple: he was on the other side. Personalities did not come into it. Subinspectors and policemen were people in khaki who frequently arrested him, always abused him, and sometimes beat him. Since they abused and beat him without anger or hate, they were not human beings with names. They were only denominations one tried to get the better of. If one failed, it was just bad luck.

'You are being released, but you must appear before Mr Hukum Chand, Deputy Commissioner, on the first of October 1947, at ten a.m. Put your thumb impression on this.'

The subinspector opened a flat tin box with a black gauze padding inside it. He caught Juggut Singh's thumb in his hand, rubbed it on the damp pad and pressed it on the paper.

'Have I permission to go?' asked Jugga.

'You can go with Babu Sahib in the tonga; otherwise you will not get home before dark.' He looked up at Jugga and repeated slowly, 'You will not find Mano Majra the same.'

Neither of the men showed any interest in the subinspector's remark about Mano Majra. The subinspector spread out another piece of paper and read: 'Mr Iqbal Singh, social worker.'

Iqbal looked at the paper cynically.

'Not Mohammed Iqbal, member of the Muslim League? You seem to fabricate facts and documents as it pleases you.'

The subinspector grinned. 'Everyone makes mistakes. To err is human, to forgive divine,' he added in English. 'I admit my mistake.'

'That is very generous of you,' answered Iqbal. 'I had always believed that the Indian Police were infallible.'

'You can make fun of me if you like; you do not realize that if you had been going about lecturing as you intended and had fallen into the hands of a Sikh mob, they would not have listened to your arguments. They would have stripped you to find out whether or not you were circumcised. That is the only test they have these days for a person who has not got long hair and a beard. Then they kill. You should be grateful to me.'

Iqbal was in no mood to talk. Besides, the subject was not one he wanted to discuss with anyone. He resented the way the subinspector took the liberty of mentioning it.

'You will find big changes in Mano Majra!' warned the subinspector for the third time; neither Jugga nor Iqbal showed any response. Iqbal laid down on the table the book he had been holding and turned away without a word of thanks or farewell. Jugga felt the floor with his feet for his shoes.

'All Mussulmans have gone from Mano Majra,' said the subinspector dramatically.

Jugga stopped shuffling his feet. 'Where have they gone?'

'Yesterday they were taken to the refugee camp. Tonight they will go by train to Pakistan.'

'Was there any trouble in the village, Inspector Sahib? Why did they have to go?'

'There would have been if they had not gone. There are lots of outsiders going about with guns killing Muslims; Malli and his men have joined them. If the Muslims had not left Mano Majra, Malli would have finished them off by now. He has taken all their things—cows, buffaloes, oxen, mares, chicken, utensils. Malli has done well.'

Jugga's temper shot up at once. 'That penis of a pig who sleeps with his mother, pimps for his sister and daughter, if he puts his foot in Mano Majra I will stick my bamboo pole up his behind!'

The subinspector pursed his lips in a taunting smile. 'You talk big, Sardara. Just because you caught him unawares by his hair and beat him, you think you are a lion. Malli is not a woman with henna on his palms or bangles on his wrists. He has been in Mano Majra and taken all the things he wanted; he is still there. You will see him when you get back.'

'He will run like a jackal when he hears my name.'

'Men of his gang are with him. So are many others, all armed with guns and pistols. You had better behave sensibly if you hold your life dear.'

Jugga nodded his head. 'Right, Inspector Sahib. We will meet again. Then ask me about Malli.' His temper got the better of him. 'If I do not spit in his bottom, my name is not Juggut Singh.' He rubbed his mouth with the back of his hand. 'If I do not spit in Malli's mouth, my name is not Juggut Singh.' This time Juggut Singh spat on his own hand and rubbed it on his thigh. His temper rose to fever heat. 'If it had not been for your policemen in their uniforms, I would like to meet the father of a son who could dare to bat an eyelid before Juggut Singh,' he added, throwing out his chest.

'All right, all right, Sardar Juggut Singh, we agree you are a big brave man. At least you think so,' smiled the subinspector. 'You had better get home before dark. Take the Babu Sahib with you. Babu Sahib, you need have no fear. You have the district's bravest man to look after you.'

Before Juggut Singh could reply to the subinspector's sarcasm, a constable came in to announce that he had got a tonga.

'*Sat Sri Akal*, Inspector Sahib. When Malli comes crying to lodge a report against me, then you will believe that Juggut Singh is not a man of hollow words.'

The subinspector laughed. '*Sat Sri Akal*, Juggut Singha. *Sat Sri Akal*, Iqbal Singhji.'

Iqbal walked away without turning back.

The tonga left Chundunnugger in the afternoon. It was a long, uneventful journey. This time Jugga sat on the front seat with the policeman and the driver, leaving the rear seat all to Iqbal. No one was in a mood to talk. Bhola, the driver, had been pressed into service by the police at a time when it was not safe to step out of the house. He took it out on his skinny brown horse, whipping and swearing continuously. The others were absorbed in their own thoughts.

The countryside also was still. There were large expanses of water which made it look flatter than usual. There were no men or women in the fields. Not even cattle grazing. The two villages they passed seemed deserted except for the dogs. Once or twice they caught a fleeting glimpse of someone stepping behind a wall or peering round a corner—and that someone carried a gun or a spear.

Iqbal realized that it was the company of Jugga and the constable, who were known Sikhs, that really saved him from being stopped and questioned. He wished he could get out of this place where he had to prove his Sikhism to save his life. He would pick up his things from Mano Majra and catch the first train. Perhaps there were no trains. And if there were, could he risk getting onto one? He cursed his luck for having a name like Iqbal, and then for being a . . . Where on earth except in India would a man's life depend on whether or not his foreskin had been removed? It would be laughable if it were not tragic. He would have to stay in Mano Majra for several days and stay close to Meet Singh for protection—Meet Singh with his unkempt appearance and two trips a day to the fields to defecate. The thought was revolting. If only he could get out to Delhi and to civilization! He would report on his arrest; the party paper would frontpage the news with his photograph: ANGLO-AMERICAN CAPITALIST CONSPIRACY TO CREATE CHAOS (lovely alliteration). COMRADE IQBAL IMPRISONED ON BORDER. It would all go to make him a hero.

Jugga's immediate concern was the fate of Nooran. He did not look at his companions in the tonga or at the village. He had forgotten about Malli. At the back of his mind persisted a feeling that Nooran would be in Mano Majra. No one could have wanted Imam Baksh to go. Even if he had left with the other Muslims Nooran would be hiding somewhere in the fields, or would have come to his mother. He hoped his mother had not turned her out. If she had, he would let her have it. He would walk out and never come back. She would spend the rest of her days regretting having done it.

Jugga was lost in his thoughts, concerned and angry alternately, when the tonga slowed down to pass through the lane to the Sikh temple. He jumped off the moving vehicle and disappeared into the darkness without a word of farewell.

Iqbal stepped off the tonga and stretched his limbs. The driver and the constable had a whispered consultation.

'Can I be of any more service to you, Babu Sahib?' asked the policemen.

'No. No, thank you. I am all right. It is very kind of you.' Iqbal did not like the prospect of going into the gurudwara alone, but he could not bring himself to ask the others to come with him.

'Babuji, we have a long way to go. My horse has been out all day without any food or water; and you know the times.'

'Yes, you can go back. Thank you. *Sat Sri Akal.*'

'*Sat Sri Akal.*'

The courtyard of the gurudwara was spotted with rings of light cast by hurricane lamps and fires on improvised hearths over which women were cooking the evening meal. Inside the main hall was a circle of people around Meet Singh, who was reciting the evening prayer. The room in which Iqbal had left his things was locked.

Iqbal took off his shoes, covered his head with a handkerchief and joined the gathering. Some people shifted to make room for him. Iqbal noticed people looking at him and whispering to each other. Most of them were old men dressed like town folk. It was quite obvious that they were refugees.

When the prayer was over, Meet Singh wrapped the massive volume in velvet and laid it to rest on the cot on which it had been lying open. He spoke to Iqbal before anyone else could start asking questions.

'*Sat Sri Akal*, Iqbal Singhji. I am glad you are back. You must be hungry.'

Iqbal realized that Meet Singh had deliberately mentioned his surname. He could feel the tension relax. Some of the men turned around and said '*Sat Sri Akal.*'

'*Sat Sri Akal*,' answered Iqbal and got up to join Meet Singh.

'Sardar Iqbal Singh,' said Meet Singh, introducing him to the others, 'is a social worker. He has been in England for many years.'

A host of admiring eyes were turned on Iqbal, 'the England returned'. The '*Sat Sri Akals*' were repeated. Iqbal felt embarrassed.

'You are Sikh, Iqbal Singhji?' inquired one of the men.

'Yes.' A fortnight earlier he would have replied emphatically 'No', or 'I have no religion' or 'Religion is irrelevant.' The situation was different now, and in any case it was true that he was born a Sikh.

'Was it in England you cut your hair?' asked the same person.

'No, sir,' answered Iqbal, completely confused. 'I never grew my hair long. I am just a Sikh without long hair and beard.'

'Your parents must have been unorthodox,' said Meet Singh

144

coming to his aid. The statement allayed suspicion but left Iqbal
with an uneasy conscience.

Meet Singh fumbled with the cord of his shorts and pulled up
a bunch of keys dangling at the end. He picked up the hurricane
lantern from the stool beside the scriptures and led the way
through the courtyard to the room.

'I kept your things locked in the room. You can take them. I
will get you some food.'

'No, Bhaiji, do not bother, I have enough with me. Tell me,
what has happened in the village since I left? Who are all these
people?'

The bhai unlocked the door and lit an oil lamp in the niche.
Iqbal opened his kit bag and emptied its contents on a charpoy.
There were several copper-gold tins of fish paste, butter and
cheese; aluminum forks, knives and spoons, and celluloid cups and
saucers.

'Bhaiji, what has been happening?' Iqbal asked again.

'What has been happening? Ask me what has not been
happening. Trainloads of dead people came to Mano Majra. We
burned one lot and buried another. The river was flooded with
corpses. Muslims were evacuated, and in their place, refugees have
come from Pakistan. What more do you want to know?'

Iqbal wiped a celluloid plate and tumbler with his
handkerchief. He fished out his silver hip flask and shook it. It was
full.

'What have you in that silver bottle?'

'Oh this? Medicine,' faltered Iqbal. 'It gives me an appetite for
food,' he added with a smile.

'And then you take pills to digest it?'

Iqbal laughed. 'Yes, and more to make the bowels work. Tell
me, was there any killing in the village?'

'No,' said the bhai casually. He was more interested in
watching Iqbal inflating the air mattress. 'But there will be. Is it nice
sleeping on this? Does everyone in England sleep on these?'

'What do you mean—there will be killing?' asked Iqbal,
plugging the end of the mattress. 'All Muslims have left, haven't
they?'

'Yes, but they are going to attack the train near the bridge
tonight. It is taking Muslims of Chundunnugger and Mano Majra

145

to Pakistan. Your pillow is also full of air.'

'Yes. Who are they? Not the villagers?'

'I do not know all of them. Some people in uniforms came in military cars. They had pistols and guns. The refugees have joined them. So have Malli budmash and his gang—and some villagers. Wouldn't this burst if a heavy person slept on it?' asked Meet Singh, tapping the mattress.

'I see,' said Iqbal, ignoring Meet Singh's question. 'I see the trick now. That is why the police released Malli. Now I suppose Jugga will join them, too. It is all arranged.' He stretched himself on the mattress and tucked the pillow under his armpit. 'Bhaiji, can't you stop it? They all listen to you.'

Meet Singh patted and smoothed the air mattress and sat down on the floor.

'Who listens to an old bhai? These are bad times, Iqbal Singhji, very bad times. There is no faith or religion. All one can do is to crouch in a safe corner till the storm blows over. This would not do for a newly married couple,' he added, slapping the mattress affectionately.

Iqbal was agitated. 'You cannot let this sort of thing happen! Can't you tell them that the people on the train are the very same people they were addressing as uncles, aunts, brothers and sisters?'

Meet Singh sighed. He wiped a tear with the scarf on his shoulder.

'What difference will my telling them make? They know what they are doing. They will kill. If it is a success, they will come to the gurudwara for thanksgiving. They will also make offerings to wash away their sins. Iqbal Singhji, tell me about yourself. Have you been well? Did they treat you properly at the police station?'

'Yes, yes, I was all right,' snapped Iqbal impatiently. 'Why don't you do something? You must!'

'I have done all I could. My duty is to tell people what is right and what is not. If they insist on doing evil, I ask God to forgive them. I can only pray; the rest is for the police and the magistrate. And for you.'

'Me? Why me?' asked Iqbal with a startled innocence. 'What have I to do with it? I do not know these people. Why should they listen to a stranger?'

'When you came you were going to speak to them about

something. Why don't you tell them now?'

Iqbal felt concerned. 'Bhaiji, when people go about with guns and spears you can only talk back with guns and spears. If you cannot do that, then it is best to keep out of their way.'

'That is exactly what I say. I thought you with your European ideas had some other remedy. Let me get you some hot spinach. I have just cooked it,' added Meet Singh getting up.

'No, no, Bhaiji, I have all I want in my tins. If I want something I will ask you for it. I have a little work to do before I eat.'

Meet Singh put the hurricane lantern on a stool by the bed and went back to the hall.

Iqbal put his plates, knife, fork, and tins back into the haversack. He felt a little feverish, the sort of feverishness one feels when one is about to make a declaration of love. It was time for a declaration of something. Only he was not sure what it should be.

Should he go out, face the mob and tell them in clear ringing tones that this was wrong—immoral? Walk right up to them with his eyes fixing the armed crowd in a frame—without flinching, without turning, like the heroes on the screen who become bigger and bigger as they walk right into the camera. Then with dignity fall under a volley of blows, or preferably a volley of rifleshots. A cold thrill went down Iqbal's spine.

There would be no one to see this supreme act of sacrifice. They would kill him just as they would kill the others. He was not neutral in their eyes. They would just strip him and see. Circumcised, therefore Muslim. It would be an utter waste of life! And what would it gain? A few subhuman species were going to slaughter some of their own kind—a mild setback to the annual increase of four million. It was not as if you were going to save good people from bad. If the others had the chance, they would do as much. In fact they were doing so, just a little beyond the river. It was pointless. In a state of chaos self-preservation is the supreme duty.

Iqbal unscrewed the top of his hip flask and poured out a large whisky in a celluloid tumbler. He gulped it down neat.

When bullets fly about, what is the point of sticking out your head and getting shot? The bullet is neutral. It hits the good and the bad, the important and the insignificant, without distinction. If there were people to see the act of self-immolation, as on a cinema screen, the sacrifice might be worth while: a moral lesson might be conveyed. If all that was likely to happen was that next morning your corpse would be found among thousands of others, looking just like them—cropped hair, shaven chin . . . even circumcised—who would know that you were not a Muslim victim of a massacre? Who would know that you were a Sikh who, with full knowledge of the consequences, had walked into the face of a firing squad to prove that it was important that good should triumph over evil? And God—no, not God; He was irrelevant.

Iqbal poured another whisky. It seemed to sharpen his mind.

The point of sacrifice, he thought, is the purpose. For the purpose, it is not enough that a thing is intrinsically good: it must be known to be good. It is not enough only to know within one's self that one is in the right: the satisfaction would be posthumous. This was not the same thing as taking punishment at school to save some friend. In that case you could feel good and live to enjoy the sacrifice; in this one you were going to be killed. It would do no good to society: society would never know. Nor to yourself: you would be dead. That figure on the screen, facing thousands of people who looked tense and concerned! They were ready to receive the lesson. That was the crux of the whole thing. The doer must do only when the receiver is ready to receive. Otherwise, the act is wasted.

He filled the glass again. Everything was becoming clearer.

If you really believe that things are so rotten that your first duty is to destroy—to wipe the slate clean—then you should not turn green at small acts of destruction. Your duty is to connive with those who make the conflagration, not to turn a moral hose-pipe on them—to create such a mighty chaos that all that is rotten like selfishness, intolerance, greed, falsehood, sycophancy, is drowned. In blood, if necessary.

India is constipated with a lot of humbug. Take religion. For the Hindu, it means little besides caste and cow-protection. For the Muslim, circumcision and kosher meat. For the Sikh, long hair and hatred of the Muslim. For the Christian, Hinduism with a sola topee. For the Parsi, fire-worship and feeding vultures. Ethics, which should be the kernel of a religious code, has been carefully removed. Take philosophy, about which there is so much hoo-ha. It is just muddleheadedness masquerading as mysticism. And Yoga, particularly Yoga, that excellent earner of dollars! Stand on your head. Sit cross-legged and tickle your navel with your nose. Have perfect control over the senses. Make women come till they cry 'Enough!' and you can say 'Next, please' without opening your eyes. And all the mumbo-jumbo of reincarnation. Man into ox into ape into beetle into eight million four hundred thousand kinds of animate things. Proof? We do not go in for such pedestrian pastimes as proof! That is Western. We are of the mysterious East. No proof, just faith. No reason; just faith. Thought, which should be the sine qua non of a philosophical code, is dispensed with. We climb to sublime heights on the wings of fancy. We do the rope trick in all spheres of creative life. As long as the world credulously believes in our capacity to make a rope rise skyward and a little boy climb it till he is out of view, so long will our brand of humbug thrive.

Take art and music. Why has contemporary Indian painting, music, architecture and sculpture been such a flop? Because it keeps harking back to B.C. Harking back would be all right if it did not become a pattern—a deadweight. If it does, then we are in a cul-de-sac of art forms. We explain the unattractive by pretending it is esoteric. Or we break out altogether—like modern Indian music of the films. It is all tango and rhumba or samba played on Hawaiian guitars, violins, accordions and clarinets. It is ugly. It must be scrapped like the rest.

He wasn't quite sure what he meant. He poured another whisky.

Consciousness of the bad is an essential prerequisite to the promotion of the good. It is no use trying to build a second storey on a house whose walls are rotten. It is best to demolish it. It is both cowardly and foolhardy to kowtow to social standards when one believes neither in the society nor in its standards. Their courage is your cowardice, their cowardice your courage. It is all a matter of nomenclature. One could say it needs courage to be a coward. A conundrum, but a quotable one. Make a note of it.

And have another whisky. The whisky was like water. It had no taste. Iqbal shook the flask. He heard a faint splashing. It wasn't empty. Thank God, it wasn't empty.

149

If you look at things as they are, he told himself, there does not seem to be a code either of man or of God on which one can pattern one's conduct. Wrong triumphs over right as much as right over wrong. Sometimes its triumphs are greater. What happens ultimately, you do not know. In such circumstances what can you do but cultivate an utter indifference to all values? Nothing matters. Nothing whatever . . .

Iqbal fell asleep, with the celluloid glass in his hand and the lamp burning on the stool beside him.

In the courtyard of the gurudwara, the fires on the hearths had burned to ashes. A gust of wind occasionally fanned a glowing ember. Lamps had been dimmed. Men, women and children lay sprawled about on the floor of the main room. Meet Singh was awake. He was sweeping the floor and tidying up the mess.

Somebody started banging at the door with his fists. Meet Singh stopped sweeping and went across the courtyard muttering, 'Who is it?'

He undid the latch. Jugga stepped inside. In the dark he looked larger than ever. His figure filled the doorway.

'Why, Juggut Singhji, what business have you here at this hour?' asked Meet Singh.

'Bhai,' he whispered, 'I want the Guru's word. Will you read me a verse?'

'I have laid the Granth Sahib to rest for the night,' Meet Singh said. 'What is it that you want to do?'

'It does not matter about that,' said Jugga impatiently. He put a heavy hand on Meet Singh's shoulder. 'Will you just read me a few lines quickly?'

Meet Singh led the way, grumbling. 'You never came to the gurudwara any other time. Now when the scripture is resting and people are asleep, you want me to read the Guru's word. It is not proper. I will read you a piece from the Morning Prayer.'

'It does not matter what you read. Just read it.'

Meet Singh turned up the wick of one of the lanterns. Its sooty chimney became bright. He sat down beside the cot on which the scripture lay. Jugga picked up the fly whisk from beneath the cot and began waving it over Meet Singh's head. Meet Singh got out

150

a small prayer book, put it to his forehead and began to read the verse on the page which he happened to have opened to:

He who made the night and day,
The days of the week and seasons.
He who made the breezes blow, the waters run,
The fires and the lower regions.
Made the earth—the temple of law.
He who made creatures of diverse kinds
With a multitude of names,
Made this the law—
By thought and deed be judged forsooth,
For God is True and dispenseth Truth.
There the elect his court adorn,
And God Himself their actions honours.
There are sorted deeds that were done and bore fruit,
From those that to action could never ripen.
This, O Nanak, shall hereafter happen.

Meet Singh shut the prayer book and again put it to his forehead. He begun to mumble the epilogue to the morning prayer:

Air, water and earth,
Of these are we made,
Air like the Guru's word gives the breath of life
To the babe born of the great mother Earth
Sired by the waters.

His voice tapered off to an inaudible whisper. Juggut Singh put back the fly whisk and rubbed his forehead on the ground in front of the scripture.

'Is that good?' he asked naïvely.

'All the Guru's word is good,' answered Meet Singh solemnly.

'What does it mean?'

'What have you to do with meaning? It is just the Guru's word. If you are going to do something good, the Guru will help you; if you are going to do something bad, the Guru will stand in your way. If you persist in doing it, he will punish you till you repent, and then forgive you.'

'Yes, what will I do with the meaning? All right, Bhaiji. *Sat Sri Akal.*'

'*Sat Sri Akal.*'

Jugga rubbed his forehead on the ground again and got up. He threaded his way through the sleeping assembly and picked up his shoes. There was a light in one of the rooms. Jugga looked in. He recognized the head with tousled hair on the pillow. Iqbal was sleeping with the silver hip flask lying on his chest.

'*Sat Sri Akal,* Babuji.' he said softly. There was no reply. 'Are you asleep?'

'Do not disturb him,' interrupted Meet Singh in a whisper. 'He is not feeling well. He has been taking medicine to sleep.'

'*Achha,* Bhaiji, you say *Sat Sri Akal* to him for me.' Juggut Singh went out of the gurudwara.

'No fool like an old fool.' The sentence kept recurring in Hukum Chand's mind. He tried to dismiss it, but it came back again and again: 'No fool like an old fool.' It was bad enough for a married man in his fifties to go picking up women. To get emotionally involved with a girl young enough to be his daughter and a Muslim prostitute at that! That was *too* ludicrous. He must be losing his grip on things. He was getting senile and stupid

The feeling of elation which his plan had given him in the morning was gone. Instead there was one of anxiety, uncertainty and old age. He had released the budmash and the social worker without knowing much about them. They probably had no more nerve than he. Some of the leftist social workers were known to be a daring lot. This one, however, was an intellectual, the sort people contemptuously describe as the armchair variety. He would probably do nothing except criticize others for failing to do their duty. The budmash was a notorious daredevil. He had been in train robberies, car holdups, dacoities and murders. It was money he was after, or revenge. The only chance of his doing anything was to settle scores with Malli. If Malli had fled when he heard of Jugga's arrival, Jugga would lose interest and might even join the gang in killing and looting the victims of the ambush. His type never risked their necks for women. If Nooran was killed, he would pick up another girl.

152

Hukum Chand was also uneasy about his own role. Was it enough to get others to do the work for him? Magistrates were responsible for maintenance of law and order. But they maintained order with power behind them; not opposing them. Where was the power? What were the people in Delhi doing? Making fine speeches in the assembly! Loudspeakers magnifying their egos; lovely-looking foreign women in the visitors' galleries in breathless admiration. 'He is a great man, this Mr Nehru of yours. I do think he is the greatest man in the world today. And how handsome! Wasn't that a wonderful thing to say? "Long ago we made a tryst with destiny and now the time comes when we shall redeem our pledge, not wholly or in full measure but very substantially."' Yes, Mr Prime Minister, you made your tryst. So did many others.

There was Hukum Chand's colleague Prem Singh who went back to fetch his wife's jewellery from Lahore. He made his tryst at Feletti's Hotel where European sahibs used to flirt with each other's wives. It is next door to the Punjab Assembly building where Pakistani parliamentarians talked democracy and made laws. Prem Singh whiled away time drinking beer and offering it to the Englishmen staying in the hotel. Over the privet hedge a dozen heads with fez caps and Pathan turbans waited for him. He drank more beer and forced it on his English friends and on the orchestra. His dates across the hedge waited patiently. The Englishmen drank a lot of beer and whisky and said Prem Singh was a grand chap. But it was late for dinner so they said, 'Good night Mr . . . Did not catch your name. Yes, of course, Mr Singh. Thank you very much, Mr Singh. See you again.' . . . 'Nice old Wog. Can hold his drink too,' they said in the dining room. Even the orchestra had more beer than ever before. 'What would you like us to play, sir?' asked Mendoza the Goan band leader. 'It is rather late and we must close down now.' Prem Singh did not know the name of any European piece of music. He thought hard. He remembered one of the Englishmen had asked for something which sounded like 'bananas'. 'Bananas,' said Prem Singh. '"We'll Have No Bananas Today." Yes, sir.' Mendoza, McMello, DeSilva, DeSaram and Gomes strummed 'Bananas'. Prem Singh walked across the lawn to the gate. His dates also moved along to the hedge gate. The band saw Prem Singh leave so they switched onto 'God Save the King'.

153

There was Sundari, the daughter of Hukum Chand's orderly. She had made her tryst with destiny on the road to Gujranwala. She had been married four days and both her arms were covered with red lacquer bangles and the henna on her palms was still a deep vermilion. She had not yet slept with Mansa Ram. Their relatives had not left them alone for a minute. She had hardly seen his face through her veil. Now he was taking her to Gujranwala where he worked as a peon and had a little room of his own in the Sessions Court compound. There would be no relatives and he would certainly try it. He did not seem particularly keen, sitting in the bus talking loudly to all the other passengers. Men often pretended indifference. No one would really believe that she wanted him either—what with the veil across her face and not a word! 'Do not take any of the lacquer bangles off. It brings bad luck,' her girl friends had said to her. 'Let him break them when he makes love to you and mauls you.' There were a dozen on each of her arms, covering them from the wrists to the elbows. She felt them with her fingers. They were hard and brittle. He would have to do a lot of hugging and savaging to break them. She stopped daydreaming as the bus pulled up. There were large stones on the road. Then hundreds of people surrounded them. Everyone was ordered off the bus. Sikhs were just hacked to death. The clean-shaven were stripped. Those that were circumcised were forgiven. Those that were not, were circumcised. Not just the foreskin: the whole thing was cut off. She who had not really had a good look at Mansa Ram was shown her husband completely naked. They held him by the arms and legs and one man cut off his penis and gave it to her. The mob made love to her. She did not have to take off any of her bangles. They were all smashed as she lay in the road, being taken by one man and another and another. That should have brought her a lot of good luck!

Sunder Singh's case was different. Hukum Chand had had him recruited for the army. He had done well. He was a big, brave Sikh with a row of medals won in battles in Burma, Eritrea and Italy. The government had given him land in Sindh. He came to his tryst by train, along with his wife and three children. There were over five hundred men and women in a compartment meant to carry '40 sitting, 12 sleeping'. There was just one little lavatory in the corner without any water in the cistern. It was 115° in the shade;

but there was no shade—not a shrub within miles. Only the sun and the sand . . . and no water. At all stations there were people with spears along the railings. Then the train was held up at a station for four days. No one was allowed to get off. Sunder Singh's children cried for water and food. So did everyone else. Sunder Singh gave them his urine to drink. Then that dried up too. So he pulled out his revolver and shot them all. Shangara Singh aged six with his long brown-blonde hair tied up in a topknot, Deepo aged four with curling eyelashes, and Amro, four months old, who tugged at her mother's dry breasts with her gums and puckered up her face till it was full of wrinkles, crying frantically. Sunder Singh also shot his wife. Then he lost his nerve. He put the revolver to his temple but did not fire. There was no point in killing himself. The train had begun to move. He heaved out the corpses of his wife and children and came along to India. He did not redeem the pledge. Only his family did.

Hukum Chand felt wretched. The night had fallen. Frogs called from the river. Fireflies twinkled about the jasmines near the verandah. The bearer had brought whisky and Hukum Chand had sent it away. The bearer had laid out the dinner but he had not touched the food. He had the lamp removed and sat alone in the dark, staring into space.

Why had he let the girl go back to Chundunnugger? Why? he asked himself, hitting his forehead with his fist. If only she were here in the rest house with him, he would not bother if the rest of the world went to hell. But she was not here; she was in the train. He could hear its rumble.

Hukum Chand slid off his chair, covered his face with his arms and started to cry. Then he raised his face to the sky and began to pray.

A little after eleven, the moon came up. It looked tired and dissipated. It flooded the plain with a weary pale light in which everything was a little blurred. Near the bridge there was very little moonlight. The high railway embankment cast a wall of dark shadow.

Sandbags, which had guarded the machine-gun nest near the signal, were littered about on either side of the railway tracks. The signal scaffolding stood like an enormous sentry watching over the scene. Two large oval eyes, one on top of the other, glowed red. The two hands of the signal stood stiffly parallel to each other. The bushes along the bank looked like a jungle. The river did not glisten; it was like a sheet of slate with just a suspicion of a ripple here and there.

A good distance from the embankment, behind a thick cluster of pampas, was a jeep with its engine purring gently. There was no one in it. The men had spread themselves on either side of the railway line a few feet from each other. They sat on their haunches with their rifles and spears between their legs. On the first steel span of the bridge a thick rope was tied horizontally above the railway line. It was about twenty feet above the track.

It was too dark for the men to recognize each other. So they talked loudly. Then somebody called.

'Silence! Listen!'

They listened. It was nothing. Only the wind in the reeds.

'Silence anyhow,' came the command of the leader. 'If you talk like this, you will not hear the train in time.'

They began to talk in whispers.

There was a shimmy-shammy noise of trembling steel wires as one of the signals came down. Its oval eye changed from red to a bright green. The whispering stopped. The men got up and took their positions ten yards away from the track.

There was a steady rumbling sound punctuated by soft puff-puffs. A man ran up to the line and put his ear on the steel rail.

'Come back, you fool,' yelled the leader in a hoarse whisper.

'It is the train,' he announced triumphantly.

'Get back!' repeated the leader fiercely.

All eyes strained toward the gray space where the rumbling of the train came from. Then they shifted to the rope, stiff as a shaft of steel. If the train was fast it might cut many people in two like a knife slicing cucumbers. They shuddered.

A long way beyond the station, there was a dot of light. It went out and another came up nearer. Then another and another, getting nearer and nearer as the train came on. The men looked at the lights and listened to the sound of the train. No one looked at the bridge any more.

A man started climbing on the steel span. He was noticed only when he had got to the top where the rope was tied. They thought he was testing the knot. He was tugging it. It was well tied; even if the engine funnel hit it, the rope might snap but the knot would not give. The man stretched himself on the rope. His feet were near the knot; his hands almost reached the centre of the rope. He was a big man.

The train got closer and closer. The demon form of the engine with sparks flying from its funnel came up along the track. Its puffing was drowned in the roar of the train itself. The whole train could be seen clearly against the wan moonlight. From the coal-tender to the tail end, there was a solid crust of human beings on the roof.

The man was still stretched on the rope.

The leader stood up and shouted hysterically: 'Come off, you ass! You will be killed. Come off at once!'

The man turned round toward the voice. He whipped out a small kirpan from his waist and began to slash at the rope.

'Who is this? What is he . . . ?'

There was no time. They looked from the bridge to the train, from the train to the bridge. The man hacked the rope vigorously.

The leader raised his rifle to his shoulder and fired. He hit his mark and one of the man's legs came off the rope and dangled in the air. The other was still twined round the rope. He slashed away in frantic haste. The engine was only a few yards off, throwing embers high up in the sky with each blast of the whistle. Somebody fired another shot. The man's body slid off the rope, but he clung to it with his hands and chin. He pulled himself up, caught the rope under his left armpit, and again started hacking with his right hand. The rope had been cut in shreds. Only a thin tough strand remained. He went at it with the knife, and then with his teeth. The éngine was almost on him. There was a volley of shots. The man shivered and collapsed. The rope snapped in the centre as he fell. The train went over him, and went on to Pakistan.

I Shall Not Hear The Nightingale

Paracelsus: *I am he that aspired to know: and thou?~*
Aprile: *I would love infinitely and be loved.*

To
Dharma
Who aspires to know.

Please read this note
before reading the novel.

The chief characters in this story are Sikhs.

The Sikh community was founded by Guru Nanak in the 15th century in an attempt to unite the Hindus and the Muslims who had been warring against each other for many centuries. Nanak was succeeded by nine other Gurus (teachers) of whom the last, Govind Singh, turned them into a military brotherhood. The Sikhs became rulers of the Punjab in the 18th century. They were defeated by the British in six fiercely contested battles. Their valour won the admiration of their conquerors and they were recruited in large numbers by the British. They were the best and the most trusted soldiers of the Indian army.

The Sikhs believe that the spirit of Nanak passed from one Guru to the other. The words Guru or the great guru are used to refer to them collectively as well as for God. Their sacred book, the ADI GRANTH, is read and worshipped in temples called Gurudwaras. In well-to-do homes, a room is set apart for the Granth and all members read a hymn or two every day. On the birthdays of the Gurus and on the first of every month the whole family foregathers for a ceremonial when specially chosen passages are read and pershad—a syrupy batter made of flour, sugar and clarified butter—is distributed. There are frequent references to the ceremony of the first of the month in this novel.

Sikhs wear their hair and beards unshorn. They also add the suffix Singh to their names. They have two modes of greeting. One is to say 'Sat Sri Akal', which means 'God is Truth'. In the other mode one person says, 'Wah guru ji ka khalsa'—'the Sikhs are the chosen of God'—and the other replies, 'Wah guru ji ki Fateh'—'and victory be to our God'.

There are some other Indian words which appear in this story. The word Sahib is used when addressing anyone with respect. It is not only used for a white man or a white woman (memsahib) but also for all Sikhs (Sardar Sahib). The suffix ji also serves somewhat the same purpose as in Bibiji (mistress) or Bhraji (brother).

The word *bus* means enough and *achha* all right. Namaste is the Hindu form of greeting.

Characters in the Story

Buta Singh—Senior Magistrate
Sabhrai—Buta Singh's wife
Sher Singh—Buta Singh's son
Champak—Sher Singh's wife
Beena—Buta Singh's daughter
Madan Lal—Wazir Chand's son and famous cricketer
Sita—Wazir Chand's daughter and friend of Beena

❧

Shunno—Maid servant
Mundoo—Thirteen-year-old boy servant
Dyer—Alsatian dog

❧

John Taylor—Deputy Commissioner of the District
Joyce Taylor—Wife of the Deputy Commissioner

❧

Jhimma Singh—Lambardar (village headman) and police
informer

❧

Time : April 1942 to April 1943

Chapter I

'There should be a baptism in blood. We have had enough of target practice.'

The trunk of a tree thirty yards away bore imprints of their marksmanship. Its bark was torn; in its centre was a deep, yellow gash oozing a mixture of gum and sap. From one branch dangled a row of metal heads of electric bulbs; their glass was strewn on the ground and shone like a bed of mica. Littered about the tree were tin cans and tattered pieces of cardboard sieved with holes.

'What about it, leader?' asked the smallest boy in the party slapping the butt of his rifle. 'We should sprinkle blood on our guns and say a short prayer to baptize them. Then they will never miss their mark and we can kill as many Englishmen as we like.'

Sher Singh smiled. He tossed his revolver in the air and caught it by the handle. He took careful aim at an empty sardine can and fired another six shots. The bullets went through into the earth kicking up whiffs of dust. His Alsatian dog, Dyer, began to whine with excitement. He leapt up with a growl and ran down the canal embankment. He sniffed at the tin and pawed it gingerly to make sure that it was dead, then picked it up in his mouth and shook it from side to side. He ran back with it and laid it at his master's feet.

'Why waste good bullets on tin cans and trees? What have they done to us?' asked another member of the party.

'That is why I say we should have a baptism in blood,' repeated the little boy.

'We will have our blood baptism when the time comes,' replied Sher Singh pompously. 'Let us be prepared for action.

When duty calls, we will not be found wanting.'

'Brother, it is an old Hindu custom to baptize weapons before using them. Our ancient warriors used to dip their swords in a tray of goat's blood and lay them before Durga, Kali or Bhavani or whatever name the goddess of destruction was known by. We should keep up the tradition.'

Sher Singh could not make up his mind. He had never killed anything before. Even the sight of a headless chicken spouting blood as it fluttered about had made him turn cold with horror. He had been full of loathing for the cook who had wrenched off the fowl's head, and had given up eating meat of any kind for some months. But this was different. They were training to become terrorists. They had to learn how to take life—to become tough. He more than the others, because he was their leader.

'My gun is thirsty,' went on the little boy. 'If it can't get the blood of an Englishman or a toady it must drink that of some animal or bird.'

There was a general murmur of assent. Only Sher Singh was reluctant. 'You don't want to smear the blood of a jackal or a crow on your guns, do you? What else can you find this time of the year? The shooting season closed two months ago.'

'We will find something or other round about the swamp,' assured Madan. 'There may be deer coming to drink. Perhaps a duck or two which could not migrate.'

That decided him finally. Madan was the strong man of the University. He had won his colours in many games and had played cricket for his province. His performance against a visiting English side—he had carried his bat after scoring a century—had made him a local hero. He had brought the other boys with him and would have been the leader of the band except that he knew little of politics. And it was Sher Singh, and not he, who had arranged the smuggling of rifles and hand grenades from across the frontier. Although Sher Singh had assumed the leadership of the group, Madan was its backbone. He was both Sher Singh's chief supporter and rival: one whose presence was an encouragement and a challenge at the same time.

'OK, brother, OK,' said Sher Singh in English and stood up. We must be quick. It will be dark in an hour.' He collected the empty cases lying on the ground and put them in his pocket. The

boys also stood up and brushed the dust off their clothes. They put
their guns in the jeep. One of them volunteered to stay back.

Sher Singh loaded his rifle and led the party down the canal
bank towards the marsh. Dyer ran ahead barking excitedly.

They crossed the stretch of chalky saltpetre and got to the edge
of the swamp. There were no birds on the water. On the other side
was a peepul tree on which there was a flock of white egrets. Right
on the top was a king vulture with its bald red head hunched
between its black shoulders. Beneath the tree were bitterns wading
in the mud. The birds were over a hundred yards away; well
beyond Sher Singh's range of marksmanship.

The party surveyed the scene and considered the pros and
cons of taking a shot from that distance. The vulture stuck out its
head and the egrets began to show signs of nervousness. Suddenly
there came the loud, raucous cry of a Sarus crane followed by
another from its mate. They were in a cluster of bulrushes not fifty
yards away. The boys sat down on their haunches and stopped
talking. The cranes continued calling alternately for a few minutes
and than resumed their search for frogs. The vulture and the egrets
on the opposite bank went back to sleep.

'Kill one of these. They are as big as any black buck,' whispered
the small boy.

'Who kills cranes?' asked Sher Singh. 'They are no use to
anyone. And I am told if one of a pair is killed, the other dies of
grief.'

'If you are going to funk shooting birds, you will not do much
when it comes to shooting Englishmen,' taunted Madan. 'You will
say, "Why kill this poor chap, his widow and children will weep",
or "His mother will be sad". Sher Singhji, this is what is meant by
baptism in blood; get used to the idea of shedding it. Steel your
heart against sentiments of kindness and pity. They have been the
undoing of our nation. We are too soft.'

That was enough to provoke Sher Singh—particularly as it
came from Madan. 'Oh no! nothing soft about me,' he answered
defiantly. 'If it is a Sarus crane you want, a Sarus crane you will
have. Come along Dyer—and if you bark, I'll shoot you too.'

Sher Singh got down on his knees and crawled up behind the
cover of the pampas grass, his dog following warily behind. He
stopped after a few yards and parted the stalks with the muzzle of

his rifle. One of the birds was busy digging in the mud with his long beak; the other was on guard turning its head in all directions, looking out for signs of danger. Sher Singh decided to be patient. He wanted to get a little closer and also get enough time to take aim. Missing a bird of that size would be bad for his reputation.

After a few minutes, he looked through the stalks again. Both the cranes were now busy rummaging in the reeds. He crept up another ten yards, Dyer behind him. He paused for breath and once again parted the pampas stalks with the muzzle of his rifle. One of the birds was again on the lookout. Sher Singh drew the bead on the other—at the easiest spot to hit: the heavy, feathered middle of its body. The sentry crane spotted Sher Singh. It let out a warning cry and rose heavily into the air. Its mate looked up. Before it could move, Sher Singh fired. The bullet hit its mark. A cloud of feathers flew up and the bird fell in the mud. Dyer ran across to seize it. The boys came up from behind, clapping and shouting.

Sher Singh clicked open the catch; the metal case of the bullet flew out and fell on the ground. He picked it up and put it in his pocket. He blew into the barrel and saw the smoke shoot out of the other end. He was a jumble of conflicting emotions of guilt and pride. He had mortally wounded a harmless, inedible bird. But this was his first attempt to take life and it had succeeded. Then his friends came up, slapped him on the back and shook his hand by turn. The feeling of remorse was temporarily smothered.

The shot had not killed the crane. It flapped its wings and dragged itself out of the pool of blood a few feet farther towards him and pecked away fiercely with its long, powerful beak. The snarling and snapping Alsatian kept a discreet distance. Then the other crane flew back and began to circle overhead, crying loudly. It dived down low over the dog to frighten it away.

'Leader, give the other one its salvation too. Let them be together in heaven or hell.'

'Yes, let's see you take a flying shot,' added Madan.

The argument appealed to Sher Singh. The anguished cry of the flying crane was almost human. If he did not silence it, it would continue to haunt him for a long time. If both of the pair were dead, perhaps they would be together wherever cranes went after death. Sher Singh took out the magazine of his rifle and pressed six bullets in it. He followed the crane's flight with his barrel and fired when the bird was almost above him. The bullet went through one of the wings. The bird wavered badly in its flight and some feathers came floating down. Sher Singh fired the second shot. Then the third and the fourth and emptied the magazine. The crane flew away across the swamp, ducking nervously as the bullets whistled by in quick succession.

Sher Singh blew the smoke out of the barrel once more.

In his excitement he forgot to pick up the empty cases.

'Its time is not up yet,' said Madan to console him. 'Put this one out of its agony.'

Once having embarked on the bloody business, Sher Singh could not stop half way. He walked up to the injured bird and put his right foot on its neck. The crane began to kick violently and gasp for breath. Its beak opened wide showing its thin, long tongue. Sher Singh took out his revolver and fired two shots into its body. The bird's dying gurgle was stifled in its throat. Its legs clawed the air and then slowly came to a stop in an attitude of prayer. Blood started trickling from its beak and a film covered its small black eyes.

'This one is finished. Let us take it to the jeep and baptize our weapons in its blood.'

Two of the boys caught the crane by the wings from either end and dragged it out of the swamp. Dyer sniffed at the dead bird's head dangling between its trailing legs and began to run round in circles yapping deliriously. Sher Singh saw his handiwork and a lump came up in his throat. He did not respond to the backslapping and hilarity of his companions.

Before they got clear of the swamp the other crane flew back and started circling over them. They saw it high above in the deep blue sky catch the light of the setting sun; then heard its cries piercing the stillness of the dusk. Sher Singh ignored requests to have another go at the flying bird; in any case it was too high and the light was failing fast. When they got to the canal bank, it became dark. The crane flew lower and lower till they could see its gray from with its long legs almost above their heads. They shoo'd it off. The bird disappeared in the dark only to come back again and again. Its crying told them it was there all the time, trying to reclaim its dead mate. Sher Singh wanted to get away from the place as fast as his jeep could take him. That was not to be.

When they got to the jeep, they saw a Sikh peasant talking to the boy they had left behind. He was obviously waiting for them. When the man saw what the boys had brought, he spat on the ground: 'Sardarji, why did you have to take the life of this poor creature? Is anyone going to eat it?' He spoke to Sher Singh as Sher Singh was the only one carrying a gun.

'Oi Sardara, what do you know about these things? Be on your way,' answered the boy holding one end of the crane's wings.

The peasant spat again, the spittle fell near the foot of the boy who had spoken rudely. 'The shooting season closed two months ago and you are still going about killing birds. Have you a licence?' he asked.

'Oi, who do you think you are?'

The peasant stood up. He was a big man standing well over six feet. He was also broad and hairy. Long strands of hair trickled out from all sides of his clumsily-tied turban. A thick, black beard covered most of his chest. He carried a bamboo staff shod with iron at either end.

'Keep quiet,' said Sher Singh angrily silencing his companion; then turned calmly to the peasant. 'There is no open or closed season for birds like these; that is only for game.'

'Nevertheless you have to have a gun licence,' continued the other truculently. 'I am the headman of the village beyond the swamp. I heard the firing. It sounded like machine-gun practice. You have to show me all your arms licences.'

'There is only one gun,' said Sher Singh with presence of mind. 'I will show you mine.'

He fished out his father's shot-gun licence from his pocket and wrapped a five rupee note in its folds. He put his arm around the peasant's shoulder and took him aside: 'Come along, Lambardar Sahib, you have become angry for no reason. You can see the licence and anything else you like.'

Madan felt that he was entitled to join them. Before Sher Singh could hand over the licence, Madan spoke to the headman: 'Lambardarji, you know who you are talking to? This is Sher Singh, son of Sardar Buta Singh, Magistrate. You have heard the name of Sardar Buta Singh, I hope.'

The headman turned to Sher Singh. He looked at him for a brief moment and then took Sher Singh's hands in his. The scowl on his face turned to a broad, friendly grin. 'Who doesn't know of Sardar Buta Singh?' he asked. 'But how should I have known! Do forgive me, Sardar Sahib.'

'Not at all,' answered Sher Singh. 'It is you who must forgive us for speaking rudely! You are a lambardar and we should respect you!'

'I am your slave,' said the peasant, touching Sher Singh's knee. 'The slave of your slaves. You must come to my humble home for some water or something.'

'That is very kind of you; we will another day. Do see my licence. And this is for your children.'

'No, no, Sardar Sahib,' protested the headman. 'Do not shame me. I am not short of money. By the Guru's blessing I have plenty to eat and drink. I only need your kindness. If you step into the hut of Jhimma Singh I will ask nothing more. Your slave is named Jhimma Singh.'

They rejoined the party. The headman's mood had changed completely. 'Babuji,' he said, addressing them all, 'If you are fond of shikar, you only have to say the word and I will arrange one for you. I could get the villagers to beat through the fields and you could shoot to your hearts' content. Partridge, hare, deer, wild pig—anything.'

'We will ask you when the shooting season opens,' answered Madan.

'Now you are making fun of me; I was only doing my duty as a headman. Sardar Buta Singh is the king of this district, who dare tell his son when he can or cannot shoot? Isn't that so Bubuji . . . Babuji . . . what is our name?'

Before Madan could reply, Sher Singh answered, 'He is Mr Nasir Ali; he is a captain in the army.'

The boys took up the game eagerly and introduced each other to him with false names. The peasant shook hands with all of them. 'What have I to do with names? You are all friends of Sardar Sher Singh, that is enough for me,' he said with a knowing smile.

'If we have your permission,' said Madan taking the peasant's hand again. 'It is getting very late and I have to report at the cantonment by nine.'

'Of course, of course, Captain Sahib. Please forgive me for detaining you. You promise to let me know when you come next time?'

They all promised and parted the best of friends.

The boys threw the dead crane into the canal without the ceremonial baptism and turned back homewards.

It was evident that Sher Singh was still upset. One of the boys tried to draw him out. 'That was a narrow escape,' he said cheerfully. 'You know what these village headmen are! All informers. They would inform against their own parents to please the police. Leader, you were very clever in not letting him know Madan's name. Wasn't he?'

'Very clever. Great presence of mind,' they agreed.

'He knows mine,' said Sher Singh grimly.

Madan felt he had to explain. 'If I had not mentioned your father's name, he would not have let us go. He will never dare to say a word about you to anyone, you take my word for it. I know his type. He will probably come to you with presents of tins of clarified butter or farm produce. Really, you have no need to worry.'

Sher Singh did not answer. They all fell silent.

When they got to the end of the canal road, they found the way barred by the gate meant to keep off general traffic. The gateman heard the car and came out of his hut with his log book. Sher Singh took it from him and entered a name and a car number and handed it back. The gateman took the log book and examined the entry in front of the headlight. He looked at the number plate on the jeep and came back. He spoke politely but firmly: 'Sardar Sahib, I do not know English but I am not illiterate. You have put in a wrong number for the car. I will have to report it to the canal officer.'

'It is not his car, it is mine,' replied Madan promptly. 'He does not know the number. You enter the correct number and report it to anyone you like. Tell them it was the car of Mr Wazir Chand, Magistrate, driven by his son, Madan Lal. Now open the gate.'

The tone of authority did not fail to impress the gateman. He walked quietly to the gate and unlocked it. He salaamed as the jeep went past.

Everyone was convinced that Madan had atoned for his earlier indiscretion—if any. Even Sher Singh felt he had been a little mean in his resentment. 'If we let ourselves be bothered by informers and canal road gatemen, we won't get far with our plans. To hell with them. Revolutions cannot be stopped by vermin,' he proclaimed loudly.

'Indeed not,' added Madan. 'And what has anyone learnt anyhow? That you have a gun. Of course you have a gun—and a licence for it too. And that your father's jeep used the canal road! What more?'

Sher Singh felt very relieved. His fears were purely imaginary. He pulled up the jeep. 'I've had too much tea,' he announced. 'I will dedicate its remains to the lambardar and the gateman.'

They roared with laughter and leapt out of the jeep. They lined up along the deserted road. 'On the headman,' said one.

'On the headman and all informers.'

'On the headman, all informers, and all Englishmen.'

'No,' said the smallest boy, 'mine is for the Englishmen's memsahibs.' They laughed louder and continued laughing for a long time.

'Quiet!' ordered Sher Singh. 'Listen.'

The laughter died down and they listened. Above the purring of the motor engine they heard the cry of the Sarus crane. They looked up into the black sky studded with stars. A large gray form flew up from the side of the road they had come. It circled over the jeep a couple of times and landed right in front of the glaring head lights. The crane called to its mate.

'It's been following us all the way; thinks we've got the other one in the car,' said the little boy. Even he could not bring himself to repeat the suggestion that Sher Singh should kill the bird. 'Brother Sarus,' he said addressing the crane, 'your dear mate is in heaven. Don't cry. Go and find yourself another wife.'

The crane turned to him without any sign of fear. It spread out its enormous wings and charged. The boy ran round the jeep. Dyer began to growl and bark but even he did not have the courage to attack the angry bird. Other boys came up yelling loudly and the crane retreated. It kept calling all the time.

The boys got back into the jeep and Sher Singh stepped on the accelerator as hard as he could. They heard the crane calling above them for a little distance till they mixed with the traffic going into the city.

❧

After dropping the boys near the main bazaar and Madan at his

house, Sher Singh drove home. He took the jeep into the garage
which was at the back of the house alongside the servants' quarters.
He locked the box containing the rifles and handgrenades and put
it back in the trench in the center of the garage (meant for the
mechanic to examine the car from the bottom) and covered it with
greased rags and motor tools. He took his father's shot-gun, bolted
and locked the garage door and leant back against the wall to spend
a few moments with himself before facing his wife and parents.
Quite involuntarily he looked up into the sky. The figure of the
crane flying in the dark and its crying came back to his mind. Then
the picture of the wounded bird kicking its legs, the deafening
reports of the pistol shots and the end of its struggle in an attitude
of prayer like the effigies of ancient English kings on their
tombstones. Now that Madan and the other boys were not there,
the sense of assurance also left him and he began to be assailed with
doubts. Would the headman report him to the police and the police
to the Deputy Commissioner? Mr Taylor had been particularly
good to his father whom he trusted more than any other officer in
the district; that trust would be lost for ever. His father's career in
service and hopes of recognition for what he was doing for the war
would be dashed. And what would Buta Singh do if he came to
know that his son had been misusing the jeep given by the
government to further war work, to take out terrorists training for
sabotage and to destroy people like him and Taylor?

It was strange, thought Sher Singh, that he had not really
considered these possibilities before committing himself to the
venture. He had somehow believed that he would muddle
through, getting the best of the two worlds: the one of security
provided by his father who was a senior magistrate, and the other
full of applause that would come to him as the heroic leader of a
band of terrorists. Now for the first time he realized how utterly
incompatible the two were and he simply had to make a choice. He
began to feel tired and depressed. There was his home with its high
walls like those of a fortress. They enclosed the courtyard and the
lit up rooms; it looked snug and friendly. From within came
reassuring sounds: the voices of his mother and sister welcoming
the dog who had gone in and his wife shouting to the servant to go
and see why the young master was taking so long in the garage.
And there was the world outside—dark and lonely. The gardener

had flooded the lawn; it looked like a black sheet. Fireflies flitted about the ghostly forms of orange trees.

The courtyard door opened and the boy servant, Mundoo, came out to look for him. Sher Singh handed the shot-gun to the boy and went indoors.

Although he had no appetite, he sat down to dinner to avoid the women nagging him. His wife and sister joined him. His mother, Sabhrai, who never ate before her husband had been served, also sat down with them.

'Did you get anything?' asked Champak.

'No, there is very little game about this time of the year. I thought I might get a pigeon or two, but we didn't come across any.'

'I am glad,' interrupted his mother. 'I don't like this business of killing poor, harmless birds.'

'Where is father?' asked Sher Singh.

'He hasn't come back from the Club,' answered his mother. 'He had to ask a friend to give him a lift since you had taken the car. He was cross.'

'How was I to know he wanted it?'

'Son, it is not our car,' remonstrated Sabhrai gently. 'It has been given to your father for war work. He doesn't mind your using it but you must ask him. Also, he said if you are keen on shikar, you should apply for a licence and have the gun transferred to your own name.' She added, after a pause, 'If you ask for my advice, I would say, "Sell the shot-gun". It is the cause of sin. To take the life of innocent creatures is sin.'

Sher Singh did not contradict her. Sabhrai tried to make up. 'You did not kill anything, so you don't have to bother.' She changed the subject abruptly. 'Why don't you help your sister with her examinations now that you have the time? She has to go out to other people's homes to prepare for them.'

'No, thank you,' interrupted Beena hastily. 'Sita is giving me all the help I need. She is the best in our class.'

The mother and daughter began to argue. It gave Sher Singh the chance to get away. 'This heat has given me a headache,' he complained and stood up. 'I am going to bed.'

'Yes, you must be tired,' agreed his mother. 'Champak, press his head, he will sleep better.'

175

'I will,' replied Champak standing up. She bent her head to receive her mother-in-law's blessing. *'Sat Sri Akal.'*

'Sat Sri Akal,' replied Sabhrai lightly touching Champak's shoulder.

'Sat Sri Akal,' said Sher Singh.

'Live in plenty. Live a long age,' replied Sabhrai taking her son's hand and kissing it. 'Sleep well.'

Sher Singh and Champak retired to their room on the side of the courtyard.

It was one of Sher Singh's grievances that since his marriage he had to give up sleeping in the open because his wife wanted privacy. The rest of the family slept on the roof and the courtyard was visible from it. So they had to be in the room and suffer the hot air churned up by the ceiling fan. They had been married only one year and Champak felt that wasn't asking too much. She forestalled his complaint. 'You have a bath and let the breeze of the fan dry you. That is the advantage of having a room of one's own. I will press your head and legs and you will sleep nicely.'

Sher Singh did as he was told and let his wife press his limbs. The service demanded returns to which he attended with as much enthusiasm as he could muster.

Neither the day's fatigue nor the sex produced the deep sleep they are reputed to produce. For a long time Sher Singh lay awake, staring at the ceiling and the walls. He saw the emblems of strength with which he had surrounded himself. Above the mantel piece was a shield with the Sikh sabers crossed behind it. On his desk, the porcelain bust of the Maratha warrior Sivaji; on the wall facing him a colour print of Govind Singh showing the Guru on horseback—his falcon with its wings outspread on his hand. On the other wall was a panel of photographs pinned on a wooden board. They showed him with the Student Volunteer Corps which he had organized the year before at the University. The one in the centre was of him in uniform taking the salute at a march-past; another, receiving Mahatma Gandhi when he had come to visit his college; and two more shaking hands with V.I.P.s. He saw these things and felt ashamed that the simple killing of a bird should have upset him. He had shrunk in his own estimation. He tried to recover his faith in his own courage and his future. He tried to seek solace from Madan's assurance that all the headman could tell was that Sher Singh had used his father's jeep and shot-gun—nothing more. It was of little avail. He could not sleep. Four figures kept going round and round in his tortured mind. They were those of Madan, the headman, his father, and Mr Taylor. Then he began to dream. He saw himself crossing railway lines. There were four tracks with trains coming towards him from either side. He crossed one track and a train came up from the other direction. He jumped clear of the train on to the third track—only to find yet another train almost on him. He jumped clear of that too but found himself right in front of the engine on the fourth. He woke with a cry of terror and looked round for his wife. His cry had not woken her. She lay like a nude model posing for an artist: one hand between her thighs covering her nakedness and the other stretched away to expose her bust.

Sher Singh wiped the cold sweat from his forehead. He put on his pajamas and looked out of the window; it was dark without a trace of gray anywhere. He looked at the clock on the table; it was just after 3 a.m. He went back to bed and tried to sleep. Once more the four figures came back: Madan, the headman, his father, and Taylor. When sleep overtook him again, he found himself crossing the rail tracks once more. This time he kept reminding himself in his dream that this was only a dream. When one of the trains bore upon him he woke up—but without the cry of terror. The sky had turned gray and the morning star shone brilliantly. His mother and Shunno were already up and at work in the kitchen. He sat down in his armchair and tried to calm himself. A drongo started calling. Crows began to caw softly in their morning sleep and sparrows twittered dreamily—uncertain whether or not it was time to get up. Then all the crows began to caw furiously and all the sparrows began to chirrup. The spell was broken. A kite perched itself on the roof of the kitchen and let out its shrill piercing cry for food: . . . kreel . . . kreel . . . kreel.

Sher Singh got up to face another day.

૪

It was the New Year's Day by the Hindu calendar. Sabhrai was expecting all the family in the temple for the first-of-the-month ceremony. Shunno, the maid-servant, came twice to say the others were waiting. Sher Singh had a quick bath and hurried to the room set apart for worship. His father and sister sat cross-legged on the floor facing the Granth, Buta Singh wore his magisterial dress of gray turban, black coat, and white trousers. A band of muslin ran round his chin and over his turban (it was meant to press his beard in shape). His gray drooping mustache fell on either side of the band. Both his sister, Beena, and his mother, Sabhrai, wore bright pink headpieces above their white Punjabi dresses. The prayer room also wore a festive appearance. The Holy Granth had been specially draped in silks for the occasion, with roses, marigolds, jasmines strewn in front of it. From the four points of the velvet canopy above the holy book hung chains of coloured paper. From either side, sticks of incense sent spirals of scented smoke upwards to the canopy till the breeze of the ceiling fan scattered them about the room.

Sabhrai was reading the Granth quietly. She looked up and spoke to her son: 'We have been waiting for you for the last hour. Your father is in a hurry. He has to go to see the Deputy Commissioner.'

'How was I to know this was New Year's Day?' answered Sher Singh. 'Nobody told me.' Everyone knew that Sabhrai's remarks were really meant for her daughter-in-law. Before Champak could make her excuses, Buta Singh intervened. 'Let us get on with the service instead of arguing.' he said.

Sabhrai picked up the fly whisk lying beneath the cot on which the Granth was placed and began to wave it over her head. She started with the hymn to Spring:

It is spring and all is seemly—
The bumble-bee and the butterfly
And the woodlands in flower.
But there is a sorrow in my soul,
For the Lord my Master is away.

If the husband comes not home, how can a wife
Find peace of mind?
Sorrows of separation waste away her body.

The Koel calls in the mango grove,
its notes are full of joy.

But O Mother of mine, It's like death to me
For there is a sorrow in my soul.

How shall I banish sorrow and find blessed peace?

Spake the Guru: Welcome the Lord in your soul
As a wife welcomes her master when she loves him.

Everyone bowed as the last words trailed off. Buta Singh invoked the Guru loudly. Sabhrai ran the palms of her hands along the broad pages of the holy book and placed them on her eyes.

Shunno came in carrying a steaming tray, placed it on a low stool in front of the Granth, and sat down in a corner.

On the verandah outside, Mundoo bullied little children from the neighbouring houses into keeping quiet and sitting in a row. Behind him, whining impatiently, was Dyer.

Sabhrai closed the massive Granth, holding the ends reverently in her hands and then let it open as if it had a will of its own. She scanned the opening lines of the first verse and, having assured herself that they prophesied no misfortunes to her family, read in a calm clear voice:

When I think of myself
Thou art not there;
Now it is Thee alone
And my ego is swept away.

As billows rise and fall
When a storm sweeps across the water;
As waves rise and relapse into the ocean
I will mingle with Thee.

How can I say what Thou art
When that which I believe is not worthy of belief?

It is as a king asleep on the royal couch
Dreams he is a beggar and grieves;
Or as a rope mistaken for a serpent causeth panic.
Such are delusion and fear.

179

Why should I grieve?
Why be panic stricken?

If God is in every heart
And in every soul
He is in mine.

He has many manifestations
Yet is closer to us than our hands or feet.

These passages were always listened to carefully as prophetic announcements on problems which were uppermost in their minds. To Sher Singh the only lines that had significance were those asking him to discount delusions that caused fear and panic. The Guru himself had given him a personal assurance that he had mistaken a rope for a serpent and had really nothing to worry about. He was not religious or superstitious; nevertheless the words had a strange reassuring effect.

The ceremony ended with a short invocation recited by Buta Singh during which everyone remained standing. It was followed by the distribution of the pershad—a hot syrupy batter made of flour, sugar, and clarified butter. There was an awkward silence which made people conscious of the noise they made eating.

Buta Singh took off the beard-band and wiped his greasy hands on his beard and mustache. He looked at his wrist watch. 'I must be going,' he announced in a tone of finality and stood up. 'A quick cup of tea and I must run.'

Everyone made a last obeisance in front of the Granth and went out into the verandah and put on their shoes. Sabhrai threw Dyer's share of the pershad into the air. The Alsatian leapt up and caught it in his mouth. They all adjourned to the breakfast table.

Buta Singh opened the morning paper. The family sat in silence waiting for him to say something. Sher Singh was particularly nervous. Would his father ask his about taking the government jeep for a private outing? 'The war seems to be going badly for the English,' he said at last, putting down the paper.

'Things are not too good for them,' answered his son, somewhat relieved.

Shunno brought a tray full of fried chapatties and vegetables.

Sabhrai poured out the tea. The meal continued to be described as 'tea' although it was the main meal of the day, combining both breakfast and lunch.

'You take a lot of interest in politics,' continued Buta Singh, sipping his cup of tea. 'What do you think will happen to the British? The Japanese have driven them out of Burma. This chap Rommel has defeated them in Africa. German submarines sink British ships in English ports. They seem to be losing on every front.'

Sher Singh was always somewhat non-committal on political topics when talking to his father. 'I think we should be more concerned with what will happen to us,' he replied. 'We are far too concerned with other people. Our Communist friends are only worried about what will happen to Russia; others think only of what will happen to Britain. Very few of us are bothered with our own future.'

Buta Singh noticed the attempt to snub him. He ate a few pieces of chapatti and curry before replying. The long pause was meant to convey disapproval of his son's tone of talking. 'You can say what you like,' he said at last, 'but I do believe that in this war our interests and that of the English are identical. If they lose, we lose. If we help them to win, they will certainly give us something more than we have now. We should know who are our friends and who are our enemies. The English have ruled us for over a hundred years, and I don't care what you say, I believe they have treated us better than our own kings did in the past; or the Germans, Italians, or Japanese will do if they win and take over India. We should stand by the English in their hour of trouble.'

'Why don't they let us help them? Gandhi is willing. Nehru is willing,' said Sher a little warmly.

'Don't talk like a child,' replied Buta Singh also warming up. 'What does their willingness amount to? Nothing. Are the British short of recruits? Despite your Gandhis and Nehrus more turn up than are wanted. And what are you to do with your Muslims? They don't want a free India until the country is cut up and they get their Pakistan. One should bargain with knowledge of one's weakness.'

It was only in recent years that Buta Singh had begun to think in terms of bargaining with the British. Before that, loyalty to the Raj had been as much an article of faith with him as it had been with his father and grandfather who had served in the army. He, like them, had mentioned the English king or queen in his evening prayer. 'O Guru, bless our Sovereign and bless us their subjects so that we remain contented and happy.' Then things had begun to change. Gandhi had made loyalty to the British appear like disloyalty to one's own country and traditions. Larger and larger numbers of Indians had begun to see Gandhi's point of view. People like Buta Singh who had been proud of being servants of His Britannic Majesty were made to feel apologetic and even ashamed of themselves. Loyalty became synonymous with servility, respect for English officers synonymous with sycophancy. What shook the faith of people like Buta Singh was the attitude of the new brand of Englishmen coming out to India. Buta Singh would have withstood the affection of people like Taylor. Other English officers had kept their distance from Indians and set up the pattern of the rulers and the ruled. Taylor, on the other hand, not only met Indians as equals, made friends with his subordinates, but also openly expressed his sympathies with Gandhi and Nehru. At first Buta Singh had looked upon Taylor's professions with suspicion. When he was convinced of the Englishman's sincerity, he began to look upon him as an oddity—an oddity he respected and liked.

Buta Singh could not comprehend why any Englishman would like to see the end of British rule in India. But many besides Taylor had begun to say so. And most of the Indians were actively agitating for its end. In this state of flux Buta Singh had decided on a muddle-headed and somewhat dishonest compromise. When he was with Englishmen he protested his loyalty to the Raj. 'At my age, I cannot change,' he would say. When he was amongst his own countrymen he would be a little critical of English ways. He let his son cast his lot with the Nationalists and did not object to his organizing the students and making political speeches. He explained his son to Taylor as 'of your way of thinking'. By many people, Buta Singh was described as double-faced; any compromise in a situation like the one in which Buta Singh found himself would appear to unsympathetic people as double-faced.

They ate in silence. Buta Singh finished his meal with a loud belch. 'Oi, water for my hands.'

Mundoo brought a jug of water and basin and handed his

master a cake of soap. Buta Singh washed his hands and rinsed his mouth without getting up from his chair. He belched again and dried his hands and mouth with the towel. A bit of curry stuck to his mustache.

'A bulbul on the bough,' said Sabhrai with a smile. Buta Singh wiped his mustache with the towel again.

'Now!'

'Still on the bough,' said Sabhrai giggling. Buta Singh brushed his mustache a third time.

'Now!'

'It has flown,' they all replied in a chorus and burst out laughing. The atmosphere changed to one of hilarity. Sabhrai noticed her husband glance at his watch. She made another attempt. 'Will any of you have the time to go to the Temple today?' she asked.

'I have to see Deputy Commissioner first,' answered her husband. 'On days like these there is always danger of Hindu-Muslim riots; all magistrates have to be on duty. I will go if I have time.'

'I have to be there,' replied Sher Singh. 'We have organized a meeting outside the temple.'

'You go in the temple before you go to your meeting,' snapped his mother.

'And,' added Buta Singh with indulgent pride, 'don't say anything which may cause trouble. Remember my position. I do not mind your hobnobbing with these Nationalists—as a matter of fact, it is good to keep in with both sides—but one ought to be cautious.'

'O no, no,' answered Sher Singh. 'I know what to say and what not to say.'

It was not customary to consult the girls. Beena was expected to go with her mother unless there were good reasons for not doing so. She knew her only chance of getting away was to bring up the subject while her father was still there. 'There are only a few weeks left for my exams. I had promised to go to Sita's house to work with her. We help each other with the preparation.'

'Why can't she come here?' asked Sabhrai. She had been getting more and more difficult about Beena going to Sita's house. Her sharp tone made Buta Singh react adversely. He came to his daughter's rescue.

'Let her go to Sita. There will be nobody in the house today to give her lunch or tea. I will drop you at Wazir Chand's house.'

That ended the argument. Buta Singh's word was never questioned. The only one left was Champak. Sabhrai was not very much concerned with her plans. If she came to the temple, she would not say anything. If she decided to shut herself in her room with her radio at full blast—as she often did—she would still say nothing. Nevertheless Champak felt that the situation demanded some explanation from her. 'I haven't washed my hair for a long time. If it dries in time, I will go in the afternoon—if I can find anyone to go with. Otherwise I'll stay at home and put away the Granth after evening prayers.'

Buta Singh looked at his wrist watch. 'I must be going,' he announced with a tone of finality and stood up. 'Get your books and things, Beena.'

⁂

'Baisakhi Day! All the world is on holiday but we have to work. Others go to their temples, mosques, or Gurudwaras; this is our temple and mosque.'

Buta Singh made this comment to his colleagues sitting in a circle in the verandah of the Deputy Commissioner's house. They had all been told the evening before to present themselves at 10 a.m. sharp. 'I would like to know what the Sahib would say if this were Christmas Day,' he added.

His colleagues refused to be provoked. 'They are our rulers,' exclaimed one. 'What they order we obey.'

'I agree with Sardar Buta Singh,' said another. 'But who is to bell the cat?'

'Sardar Sahib, you are the seniormost amongst us. Why don't you tell the Deputy Commissioner not to summon us on religious holidays?' asked Wazir Chand with a smile. He had a way of talking to people which made them feel small or stupid; Buta Singh found his tone particularly irritating. He did not mind the attempt to trip him—that was fair according to the rules of the game—but he objected to being taken to be so simple as to fall into so obvious a trap.

'I am quite willing to tell the Sahib; I don't care,' answered Buta Singh. 'Don't you know that I told the last Deputy Commissioner? He kept sending for me on every religious festival saying, "Duty first, duty first". I told him plainly: "Sahib, duty or no duty, I am going to the Gurudwara. If you do not like it, here is my resignation." That made him quiet. Mr Wazir Chand, it is not leadership we lack but unity. I say one thing to the Sahib and another goes behind my back and says something else.'

Wazir Chand knew the last remark was meant for him. 'Sardar Sahib, you are a big man and we are but small radishes from an unknown garden,' he said with mock humility. 'You lead and we follow. Don't you agree?' he asked, turning to the others.

There was a murmur of assent. Buta Singh was angry. Before he could retaliate, the Deputy Commissioner's orderly interrupted them. 'The Sahib sends his salaams,' he said, addressing Buta Singh.

Buta Singh's anger vanished; the Sahib had sent for him first. He rose with deliberate ease to impress the others that he took this sort of thing in his stride. He stopped in front of the hat-rack to adjust his tie and turban. He gave his beard a gentle pat, and went in.

Taylor received him in his dark, air-cooled office. They shook hands and Buta Singh took a chair on the other side of the working table. Taylor helped himself to a cigarette and pushed the box in front of his guest. Buta Singh shook his head.

'Beg your pardon, Buta Singh. I keep forgetting I mustn't offer a cigarette to a Sikh.'

'That is all right, Sahib. Just an old superstition,' explained Buta Singh. His reaction to a similar indiscretion by a fellow Indian would have been a little more emphatic.

Taylor lit his cigarette; a cigarette usually determined the length of the interview.

'Sorry to have sent for you on a holiday; it's something like Christmas for you, isn't it? I hope you don't mind.'

'Mind?' queried Buta Singh in a tone of righteous indignation. 'Mind, Sahib! It is our duty. What impression would the people in Delhi get if they heard that while these Japanese are at our gates, we can't even keep law and order in our towns just because it is Baisakhi Day and the magistrates want a holiday? Sahib must have seen what the American paper, *The New York Times* has said: "India talks—Japan acts!" There is some truth in that. Air raid warnings in Calcutta, bombs dropping on Colombo, and here, our so-called Nationalists and Muslims are quarrelling about little details with the English instead of getting on with the work.'

'I wish other Indians talked like you, Buta Singh! I rely on you to guide them. I do not anticipate any trouble today but one never knows. A small incident may lead to a major riot. There are some politicians looking for trouble. I am told there are many meetings this afternoon.' Taylor paused to drop the ash off his cigarette. As Buta Singh made no comment, he continued, 'The Superintendent of Police informs me that your son has also organized a meeting of students. I told him not to bother about him. "If he is Buta Singh's son," I said, "we can trust him, even if he is a Nationalist or a Communist or anything else."'

'You are most kind, Sahib. He is a young man and you know what youth is! Hot and full of ideas. But he is all right. He is, as you say, Buta Singh's son. And through his hobnobbings with these Gandhi-capped Congress wallahs and Red flag wallahs, Buta Singh knows what is going on in the city and whom to watch.' Buta Singh's accent and vocabulary changed when he spoke to Englishmen. 'Wallah' figured prominently in his speech.

Taylor stubbed his half-smoked cigarette. Buta Singh understood that the interview was over. 'What are the orders for the day, Sahib?' he asked, standing up.

'No orders, Buta Singh,' answered Taylor, coming up. 'Just tell the magistrates to leave information of their movements so that we can get them quickly at short notice; you can organize that. I will be at the fair. Shall I see you there?'

Buta Singh was not going to lose the opportunity of being seen in Taylor's company by milling crowds. Almost the entire Sikh population of the district turned up to see the procession and the fair outside the walls. 'Yes sir. I will be there in the afternoon and then with the procession.'

'Well, see you later, Buta Singh. Your excellent work in the collection of war funds and in recruiting soldiers will not go unrewarded. I will speak to the Commissioner.'

'Thank you, Sahib. Thank you. You are most kind.' Buta Singh knew that this was a reference to the next Honours list. That sort of thing still mattered although other things mattered more. 'Sir, I have a small request to make.'

'Yes.'

'You know, sir, I do not like to ask for personal favours.'

'Yes, yes, Buta Singh. Anything I can do for you, I will. What is it?'

'Sir, my work in collecting funds and furthering the war effort has caused a lot of envy. I receive letters threatening my life. I am not afraid, but if I could get a police guard at my house for a few days, it would stop evil designs. If it is at all inconvenient . . . .'

'No, no. I will speak to the Superintendent of Police; this is a very small matter. Well, goodbye, Buta Singh. And thank you once more.'

'There is nothing to thank me about, sir. I thank you, sir. Goodbye, sir.'

Buta Singh emerged from the meeting wreathed in smiles. '*Chhutti!*' he announced triumphantly clicking his thumb and middle finger in the air. 'Holiday! Go home or wherever you like.'

'Why, what happened?' asked his brother magistrates getting up from their chairs.

'Why do you want to know? I promised you a holiday and I have got you a holiday. Haven't I been true to my word?'

Buta Singh extended his hand. The magistrates smacked it in turn. 'Can I be of any other service?' he asked with exaggerated politeness when Wazir Chand touched him with his limp hand.

'Long live Sardar Buta Singh!' answered Wazir Chand.

&

Wazir Chand's home was very much like Buta Singh's except that it was Hindu instead of Sikh and not so concerned with religion and ritual. As a matter of fact the only evidence of religion in the house was a large colour print of Krishna whirling a quoit on the mantel-piece of the sitting-room. Wazir Chand's wife occasionally put a garland of flowers round it and touched the base of its frame as a mark of respect. She did the same to a portrait of Mahatma Gandhi which was kept discreetly away in the bedroom.

The real 'God' in Wazir Chand's home was the son, Madan Lal. He was a tall, handsome boy in his early twenties. Being the only son, he had been married as soon as he had finished school and had become a father in his second year at college. He had not made much progress in his studies, but had more than compensated for that shortcoming by his achievements in sports. His promotion from one class to another had to be arranged by the college authorities. He was doing his sixth year at the college and had not yet taken the degree which normally took four. But the mantle-piece of every room in the house displayed an assortment of silver trophies which he had won in athletics and other team games. He had been captain of the University cricket eleven for three years and had played for his province against a visiting English side. His performance at this match had made him a legend in the Punjab. There were few days in the year when the sporting columns of the papers did not have some reference to his activities. This was a matter of great pride for his parents. They gave in to every one of his whims; they practically worshipped him.

The only thing in common between the tall and broad Madan and his slim, small sister, Sita, was their good looks. He was bold and easy with strangers; she almost tongue-tied and shy. His obsession for games was matched by her aversion to any form of sport. He avoided books; she spent all her time with them. He had barely scraped through the exams he had passed; she had won the highest scholarship for girls in the University. The combination of the athletic prowess of one and the academic distinction of the other and the looks of both had made them the most sought after couple in the University circles. It was after several months' abject admiration and hanging around that Beena had succeeded in getting to know Sita.

Beena's anxiety to please Sita made her gushing and enthusiastic about everyone and everything in Wazir Chand's home. She addressed Sita's parents in English as 'uncle' and 'auntie'. Madan and his wife she addressed as 'brother' and 'sister' in Punjabi. She spent hours playing with their son and teaching him to call her 'auntie'. Sita was just Sita; but Beena repeated her name as often as she could in every sentence almost as if she feared losing her if she did not.

Madan had just returned from an early morning practice at the nets when Beena came in. His shirt was drenched with sweat and clung to his body displaying a broad hairy chest. Although it was hot, he carried his white flannel blazer on his shoulder. Its outside pocket bore the insignia of the University with rows of letters in old Roman embossed in gold lace beneath. He was playing with his son who was trying to walk in his father's cricket boots. The scene was too overpowering for Beena. She rushed to the child, picked him up and covered him with kisses.

'Ummm, ummm. Little darling wants to wear Papa's shoes. *Namaste Bhraji.*'

'*Sat Sri Akal,*' replied Madan without getting up or removing the cigarette from his lips.

Beena hugged the child and wheeled him round and round; her pigtails flew in the air. The child began to whimper. She thrust him into his father's lap. 'He likes you more than he likes me. Bhraji, where is Sita and Lila sister and Auntie and Uncle?'

'Father has gone to see the Deputy Commissioner. Mother is in the kitchen. Sita is studying. Lila is in her room; she is not feeling too well. And yours sincerely is at your service.' Madan got up and bowed.

Beena ignored his pleasantry. '*Hai!* What's wrong with Lila sister?' she asked with exaggerated concern; she frequently used 'hai' to express it. 'Nothing serious, I hope. I must go and see her.'

'No, no, it's nothing, really nothing. Just a little out of condition,' answered Madan. 'She is in her room.'

Beena picked up the child once more and hurried to Lila's room, Lila explained that she was not really ill; the feeling of nausea came on only in the mornings. When Beena persisted in her inquiries, Lila patted the back of her hand and said she would understand better when she was married. Beena understood and blushed with embarrassment. She sat with Lila till Sita came to take her away. 'Madan says he can take us to a matinee show this afternoon. We can work for two or three hours and go with him. Lilaji, you will be all right by the afternoon, won't you?'

'I'd better not go. The stuffy atmosphere of the cinema will make me sick and your brother will get cross with me. You two go with him.'

Beena had a twinge of conscience. Studies were considered sacred enough to excuse going to the temple. But in her home the cinema was still associated vaguely with sin. The only time the family went to the pictures was to see the life of some saint or other or some story with a religious theme. Regular cinema goers were contemptuously described as tamasha-lovers. If her mother learned that she had spent the afternoon at a cinema instead of the temple, she would use it as an excuse to stop her coming to Sita's house. 'No, I really could not. I haven't asked my mother,' said Beena quickly.

'She would not object if you came with us. I am sure she would not,' assured Sita.

'And yours sincerely is not going to invite you every day,' added Madan in his half-baked stage manner as he came in. 'Besides we won't tell anyone. We will go in when the show has started and you can cover your face during the intermission.' He drew his hand across his face to imitate a woman drawing her veil.

'It's not as bad as that,' answered Beena laughing. 'If I had asked first, it would have been better.' Before she could check herself in her imaginary flight to freedom she heard herself say: 'Of course I'll go with you but we must work first.'

During the time that Beena went over her notes and textbooks in Sita's room she was bothered by what she would say when she got back. If she said nothing and her parents found out it would take many months to re-establish her credit. Perhaps she could mention it casually as something she had been compelled to do. She was seventeen and wasn't going to be bullied by her illiterate mother any more. Pictures could be instructive; maybe this one would have a religious theme and she could persuade her mother to see it too. By the time they left the house, her mind was a muddle of fear and rebellion.

A tonga was sent for the two girls. They took their seats in the rear while Madan rode on his bicycle behind them. He wore a new silk shirt with short sleeves and carried his white flannel blazer on his shoulder; the gold crest and rows of initials glittered in the sun. He kept up a loud conversation with the girls, in between nodding and waving to the many acquaintances he met on the road.

The cinema was crowded. Peasants who had turned up for the Baisakhi festival from neighboring villages were mulling round the cheaper ticket-booths and around the stalls selling soft drinks. The tonga made its way through the crowd and drove up to the porch. Two cinema assistants rushed to take Madan's bicycle. He was a regular visitor and had admirers all over the city. Besides, he was the son of a magistrate; and magistrates, policemen, their friends and families, had privileges which go with power.

The manager of the cinema came out to welcome them and show them to their seats. Madan took out his wallet and pulled out a ten rupee note. The manager caught his hand and pressed the note and wallet back into Madan's pocket. 'No question of money,' he protested. 'It's on the house.' Madan whispered in his ear that the other girl was Buta Singh's daughter. The manager turned to Beena with an obsequious smile. 'How is your revered father?' he asked, rubbing his hands. Beena replied politely that he was well. 'So glad to hear it. We pray to God he should always remain well. Do convey my respects to him. And any time any of your family want to come to the cinema, please ring me up. It will be an honour for us—a great honour.' Beena promised to convey the information to her father.

The party was conducted to a box reserved for V.I.P.s and pressed to take something to eat or drink. The manager withdrew after extracting a promise that his hospitality would be accepted during the intermission.

Madan took his seat between the two girls. He lit a cigarette and the box was soon full of cigarette smoke and the smell of eau de cologne with which he had daubed himself.

The lights were switched off and the cries of hawkers of betel-leaves, sweetmeats, and sherbets, and the roar of hundreds of voices died down. First came a series of coloured slides advertising soaps, hair oils, and films that were to follow. The literate members of the audience read their names loudly in chorus. Then the picture started and the few recalcitrant talkers were silenced by abuses loudly hurled across the hall.

Madan stubbed his cigarette on the floor and lit another one. In the light of the flame he saw his sister completely absorbed in the film. He held his cigarette in his left hand and put his right lightly on the arm of Beena's chair.

Beena's mind was still uneasy about the consequences of the escapade. She tried to drive away unpleasant thoughts by concentrating on the film and enjoying the feeling of being with Sita and her brother. He looked so dashingly handsome in his silk shirt, flannels, and sports blazer; he smoked with such compelling nonchalance and exuded that heavenly, cool, and clean fragrance of good eau de cologne.

Madan's hand slipped down the arm of the chair and came in contact with Beena's elbow. For a moment she held her breath. He seemed to be engrossed in the film and could not have realized how far his hand had travelled. She did not remove her elbow lest the gesture offend him. It was pleasant to have him so close. His hand stayed where it was till the lights came on for the intermission. He casually smoothed his hair and began discussing the film with his sister.

The manager reappeared followed by a relay of bearers carrying trays of soda pop, ice-cream, and fried potatoes. He started talking to Sita. Madan turned to Beena. 'You know, your brother and I have become great friends. For so many years we have been in the same University and it is only now we have got to know each other. He is the most popular man in the students' circles.'

'More popular than you, Bhraji? I don't believe it. We have all seen you play cricket; so has everyone in the world, my God!'

'Cricket is nothing,' said Madan with disdain. 'Our brother, Sher, will go far. He is almost certain to be elected President of the Students' Union. He is the best candidate and I am getting all my friends to vote for him.'

'Your name alone should win him the election. Everyone in the city knows you. We were at the match when you scored your century against the English eleven. I . . . everyone . . . was so proud of you. Sixer after sixer. Oh, it was wonderful.'

'It is nothing. You could be a good cricketer if you tried. You have an athletic figure.'

Beena blushed. That was the fist time anyone had paid her a compliment, and it was Madan, *the* Madan. 'Oh Bhraji, I am no good. I couldn't see the cricket ball coming towards me at that speed.'

'Yes, you could. With those eyes of yours you could hit anything for six,' said Madan, bending close to her to avoid the manager or his sister overhearing.

'*Hai Bhraji*, you are really terrible. Making fun of a girl like me!'

The conversation was interrupted by the bearers coming to collect empty glasses and plates. The manager was still rinsing his hands with invisible soap. He took his leave promising to appear again at the end of the show.

As soon as the lights went out, Madan put his hand on the arm of Beena's chair. This time she knew it was not an accident. She could hardly believe that anyone, let alone Madan, would want to make a pass at a plain and simple girl like her. It was unbelievably flattering. But he was married and it was obviously wrong. Beena had no doubt about Madan's intentions as his fingers closed round her elbow. Would he get angry if she withdrew? What would Sita say if she saw? Madan began to caress her arm. Beena did not move. Then his hand brushed against her breast. She shrank away into the farther corner of her chair. Madan calmly lit another cigarette and took no further notice of her.

When they came out of the cinema, the road as far as one could see was a jostling mass of peasants, tongas, bicycles, and hawkers. Around the ticket booths men were clustered like bees on a hive. Streams of weary, blinking people came out from the many exits; newcomers stood around impatiently for their turn to go in.

A tonga was waiting for them in the porch and a cinema attendant had Madan's bicycle ready. The manager was there bowing, smiling, and still rubbing his hands. He bade them farewell after many reminders that they were to consider the cinema as their own. They went through the crowd with the tonga-driver shouting at the pedestrians loitering on the road. Madan cycled slowly behind. Whenever the tonga stopped, he put his foot on the ground and then cycled on with a slight push. Throughout the journey he did not talk to or even look up at Beena.

Beena was dropped home first. She said a hurried 'Namaste' and disappeared inside the house. Fortunately for her only Champak was in and she seemed too taken up with the radio programme to bother. Beena went to her room and bolted it from the inside. She flung herself on her bed and lay there in the heat. When it got dark she switched on her table lamp and continued lying on her bed staring blankly at the ceiling.

❧

There is no wine in the world as heady as applause; and it has the same effect. It temporarily subdues anxiety and restores confidence.

Even before Sher Singh arrived on the scene, there was a large crowd to receive him. The uniforms and smartness of the Students Corps impressed the peasants more than the volunteers of the Nationalist and Communist Parties in their slovenly shirts and loose pajamas. The S.V.C. also used modern techniques to draw the masses. Although they were largely Sikhs (hence Madan and the Hindu boys of the terrorist gang were not present), it was not Sikh religious songs they played over their microphone. They started off with the most popular songs from the films and large numbers of peasants came over from the other meetings which had nothing better to offer than political tirades or religious sermons. Thereafter they switched on to martial music. The Volunteers paraded up and down the fair grounds keeping step with the military march which blared from the microphone. Then Sher Singh arrived, like a field marshal coming to inspect his troops. There was much shouting of commands and saluting. He unfurled the S.V.C.'s black flag with silver sabers crossing on it. He took the salute at the march-post and went up to the rostrum to address the throng.

The fear of discovery of the activities of the day before, the sinister figure of the village headman, and the wrath of his father, receded into the dim background.

Sher Singh knew that there were police reporters in the audience and whatever he said would be reported to Mr Taylor by the evening. A war was on and the police were armed with powers to arrest and detain at will. He had to be cautious with his words. There was a limited range of subjects to choose from, but an infinite variety of forms of expression. He started in a tone of humility. He paid homage to the Gurus, repeated the well-known facts of the day they were commemorating, and then switched on to political problems. 'Comrades, we meet at a critical time. The enemy is at our gates.' He paused to let his words seep in then he lowered his voice to a confidential whisper. 'Comrades, we not only have the enemy at our doorstep, we have enemies within our own house.' He raised his voice: 'Those who sacrifice the interests of the motherland for foreign countries are our enemy No.1. They have been rightly named as the *Kaum nashts*—destroyers of the race.' He paused for applause. The audience had heard the pun on the word 'Communist' before so there was no response. Sher Singh went on: 'There are also people who want to cut off the limbs of Mother India and make another state of Pakistan. They too are our enemies.' Even this did not arouse any applause. His Volunteers were not doing their duty. Sher Singh worked himself into a fury and let his voice rise to a crescendo. 'But we are Sikhs who do not fear any enemies. We shall destroy all those who stand in our way.' A roar of applause went up. One of the Volunteers ran up to the mike and shouted, 'Sher Singh,' and the Volunteers in the crowd answered, 'Long live.' The crowd joined in. Sher Singh allowed the applause thirty seconds and then raised his hands demanding silence. He started again. 'Comrades . . .' He could not proceed further because of a clamour from the farther end of the marquee. People shouted to say that they could not hear. The mike was dead. Volunteers rushed up to test it. They tapped it, yelled, 'Hullo, Hullo. One, two, three, four. Hullo, hullo, hullo.' But the mike refused to respond. The mechanic fumbled with the battery and it suddenly came to life with a piercing boom. Sher Singh tried again. 'Can you hear me now?' The heads at the far end nodded. 'Comrades,' he started. Once more they waved their hands to say 'No.' The mike was dead again. This time even the mechanic's fumbling with the wires did not bring it back to life. The meeting dispersed.

Sher Singh knew it was no use losing his temper; in nine cases out of ten, meetings ended because of mechanical breakdowns. In any case he had said the two important things he wanted to say and the crowds had seen him and his S.V.C.

Sher Singh spent the morning with his Volunteer friends going round the stalls at the fair and standing them soda pop. In the afternoon he watched the procession pass by. It was over a mile long with brass bands, parties of singers, men demonstrating sword and stick play, more parties of singers on top of motor lorries, in trucks and bullock carts—ending with the flower-bedecked van which carried the Holy Granth guarded by five Sikhs with drawn swords. By then it was late and he was too tired to go to the temple. He decided to look up Madan and tell him about the big turnout at his meeting. He might also get to know Madan's pretty sister whom he had seen but never met.

Sher Singh collected his bicycle from the stand at the fair

ground and cycled down to Wazir Chhand's house. He put the cycle against the pillar of the porch and went into the verandah. The wire-gauze door leading into the courtyard was bolted from the inside and the house seemed empty. Sher Singh rattled the door and shouted, *'Koi Hai?'* He heard Madan's mother shout to the servant to see who was at the door. The servant came up and without opening the door informed Sher Singh that no one was at home.

'I have come for Beena. She came over to study with Sita Bibi.'

'The Bibijis have gone to the cinema,' answered the boy. 'They went with our Babu. Will you come in and wait for them?'

'I will come again.'

'What is your name?'

Sher Singh did not answer. He picked up his bicycle and rode home.

৵

Absence of privacy is a phenomenon that pervades all life in India, urban and rural, of the rich and the poor. It has been so for many centuries and the weight of tradition is heavy against those who live in society and still wish to be alone. Rooms of Indian palaces seldom had any doors and those that did could rarely be bolted from the inside. There was never any need for doors because the most intimate of relationships could apparently be consummated and enjoyed under public gaze. Examine any old painting depicting a love scene. There will be the prince and his paramour in different stages of disarray—one of his hands on her bosom, the other holding the pipe of his hookah. Standing by will be female servants fanning away flies, sprinkling scented water, or serving wine. In the background there will be a party of musicians and singers.

Amongst the poor, shortage of living space has always made privacy an expensive luxury.

Things have not changed very much over the centuries. Amongst the westernized well-to-do class, although separate bedrooms and bathrooms are provided for members of a family, the spirit remains the same: to want to be alone is to be queer. Amongst the middle, lower middle, and the working classes, the joint family system requires large numbers of kinsfolk to live under the same roof. They eat together, sleep together—men in one row, women, in a different part of the house, in another—go and relieve themselves in groups, bathe in rivers or by wells in company and accept the possibility of relations watching sexual intimacies through keyholes.

The cheek-by-jowl existence in an Indian joint family has many consequences. In the first place, an Indian whose soul yearns to know itself has no option but to take the extreme step of renouncing life and seeking solitude as a hermit. It combines an inner craving with outward respectability. This certainly is one, if not the most important, reason why so many in the country take to the ascetic life of the Yogi.

Another consequence of the absence of privacy is that the art of making love, which demands the strictest privacy as well as leisure, is practically unknown. In the land of the *Kama Sutra* (the sacred Hindu thesis on the art of love) and phallus worship, sex is practised in conditions which provide neither the time nor the opportunity for a man to rouse the passions of his woman to that fever heat which makes her yearn for lusty fulfilment. The institution of the honeymoon where a young married couple can make each other's physical acquaintance is unknown except amongst the anglicized upper middle class. For the rest, a newly married girl's first few experiences follow a soulless pattern. After some days her mother-in-law will persuade her to take a tumbler of milk to her husband before he goes to sleep (other members of the household having been told to be away for the time). More likely, the girl will go to a tryst in the fields after dark on the pretext of answering the call of nature. She will be brutally ravished by her impatient husband equally anxious to hurry back home to keep up the appearance of having gone out to ease himself. That is all most Indian women know of sex—an unpleasant subjection to men's desires—necessary in order to have sons, bearable because of its brevity. To the mass of Indian womanhood, the sixty-five ways of kissing and petting, the thirty-seven postures of the sex act so beautifully portrayed in stone on temple walls make as much sense as a Greek translation of the treatise *Kama Sutra* itself. Unfulfilled sexual impulses result in an obsession with sex and in many perversions which result from frustration: sadism, masochism, and

197

most common of all, exhibitionism.

People, when they are left alone, find that they cannot help behaving in an odd way. This is strange because one would expect those who do everything under public gaze to be less inhibited, and therefore have less to get out of their systems than those who enjoy privacy. However, the one desire which those who live in crowds have to suppress is that of self-discovery. This is suddenly aroused in momentary solitude and is expressed in acts which appear quite mad. Thus a man, normally sober and steady, who finds himself alone in a railway compartment, may get the urge to sing loudly, expose himself, or even indulge in adolescent pastimes. He will continue to behave oddly till he gets used to the idea of being alone.

Buta Singh's home had made some concessions to Western notions in the matter of privacy. There were separate bedrooms for everyone with the married couple having a bathroom of their own. Champak spent as much time as she could in her own room with her radio. She was also given to taking a long time at her bath. On religious holidays, because everyone went out, she stayed at home. She could then stroll about the courtyard in her dressing gown with her hair loose about her shoulders, and she could also sing loudly to herself.

On Baisakhi day Sabhrai had ordered Mundoo to stay at home to scrub kitchen utensils and heat the water for Champak's bath. Champak protested there was no need for hot water, but her mother-in-law had her way. 'Hair washes better with hot water,' she had insisted.

Champak sulked in her room. She switched on the radio and lay on her bed reading her favourite film magazine. After some time, she flung the magazine on the floor and looked out into the courtyard. Mundoo sat on his haunches scrubbing a big brass pitcher with ash. Beside him, on a smoking hearth, was a large tin canister.

'Oi Mundoo, is the water hot or not?'

The boy patted the canister with his dirty hands. 'No, Bibiji, not yet. It will be ready in a few minutes.'

He went down on his hands and knees and blew into the hearth. Smoke and ash whirled round the hearth and into his eyes. He stood up and wiped his tears with the hem of his greasy shirt.

All he wore besides the shirt was a red loin cloth which only covered his front. His buttocks were bare except for the string which ran between them.

'Bring it into the bathroom when it is ready.'

Champak got up, opened her wardrobe, fished out a shaving set hidden in the folds of her saris and went into the bathroom. She did not close either the door behind her or the other one which opened into the courtyard. Mundoo was not going to restrict her movements. He was just a servant and a grubby little boy at that. She decided to ignore his presence.

After a few minutes she came back to her bedroom without anything on. She put the shaving set back in its place and stood in front of her full length dressing-table mirror to inspect the results of the operation and admire the contours of her chocolate brown body. She loosened her hair and turned round to see how she looked from behind. Her hair fell to the point at which her buttocks rose like softly rounded water-melons. There were dimples on either side of her rear waist. She turned round once more, inhaled deeply, and lifted her breasts with the palms of her hands and then ran her fingers round her nipples till they became rounded like berries. She clasped her arms above her head and wriggled her hips in the manner of hula-hula dancers. She drew her belly in as much as she could and stroked it with her hand down on either side to her knees. She studied her face and figure in all the postures she had seen in photographs of nude models. She found the reflection in the mirror to her satisfaction.

In the courtyard, Mundoo finished washing the kitchen utensils and was on his hands and knees once more blowing into the hearth. He looked like a frog with the wrong end up.

Champak smiled to herself and went back to the bathroom. She shut the door opening into the courtyard without bolting it and shouted for the bath water. She turned the tap full on into the bucket and began to hum the tune coming over the air.

Mundoo lifted the canister of hot water by the wooden rod which ran through it on the top. It was heavy; he carried it a few paces at a time. When he reached the bathroom door he put it down to regain strength to take it over the threshold. He gripped the handle with both hands, knocked the door open with his forehead, and carried it in. He put the canister beside the bucket and looked up.

'Why don't you knock or call before you come into the bathroom?'

Champak hid her nakedness with her hands between her knees. Her raven black hair fell on either side of her neck. Her breasts looked out from between her arms. Mundoo stared stupidly at her without replying and then started to back out of the door.

'What shall I mix the water in? Both the bucket and the canister are full.'

Mundoo turned off the tap, tilted the bucket a little to let some of the water run out, and began to pour the hot water from the canister with a small copper mug. His eyes never rose above Champak's knees, nor left them. Champak remained as she was, hiding her nakedness with her hands, watching the boy's embarrassment.

'In future, knock before you come in. Sometimes I have no clothes on.'

ॐ

'I must tell you what happened today. My God! I nearly died of shame.' Champak always added 'my God' or 'by God' whenever she wanted to emphasize something. She also had the habit of turning the conversation to herself. It was either some compliment paid to her, a pass made at her in the street, or someone looking at her lecherously. It invariably ended the same way, 'my God,' or, 'by God,' the embarrassment had nearly killed her. Her husband paid little attention to these anecdotes, and that evening he had matters of greater importance on his mind so he barely heard what she had to say.

'You should not have stayed alone in the house all day; you should have come to the fair. What a turnout at my meeting! First we had a march-past of the Student Volunteer Corps. No one had seen such smartness from civilians before. The S.V.C. has come to mean something. Then I addressed the meeting. There was absolute pin-drop silence.' 'Pin-drop silence,' was a favourite among his repertoire of clichés. 'Packed to capacity', 'sacrifice our all', 'eschew all differences' were some of the others which figured frequently.

'*Achha*! Wonderful!' she responded enthusiastically. 'You will become a minister in the Government one day and we will have a flag on the top of our house; we will have an official car and peons in uniform. Then we can dismiss this useless Mundoo of yours. Really you've no idea what he is like?'

'Oh, yes, I have,' interrupted Sher Singh impatiently. 'He is just a poor, underpaid boy. The condition of domestic servants is one of the most pressing problems of urban society. We work them twenty-four hours of the day, underpay, underfeed, and underclothe them. Their living quarters are filthy. They are abused and beaten at will. They are dismissed without notice after a disgraceful search of their belongings. It is scandalous. It must stop. I will stop it.' Sher Singh found it hard to switch from oratory to multitudes to talking to individuals.

'I am sure you will. But this Mundoo . . . really.'

'What's wrong with him? He's no different from other servants. The trouble is we never can see our own faults. Whenever I have difficulty with people, I put myself in their shoes and see their point of view. It is a very good principle.'

Sher Singh and his wife were too full of themselves to listen to each other's tales. They both abandoned the attempt.

It was hot. The ceiling fan only churned the air inside the room. Other members of the family slept on the roof in the cool of the moonlight. Even Dyer, who never left his master's side when he was at home, refused to be in the room at night. Sher Singh had to suffer because of his wife. He looked at his watch. 'It's after eleven. I didn't realize it was so late. I've had such a tiring day.' He put up his arms and yawned.

'Your mother hasn't come back from the temple. The procession could not have ended.'

'I don't know about her but I could hear father's snores from the courtyard. And there is a light in Beena's room. She must be studying.'

Sher Singh gave himself a long look in the mirror before taking off his turban and uniform. He went into the bathroom, poured a few mugs of water on his body, and came back dripping to dry himself under the fan. He saw himself in the mirror. His paunch showed no sign of reducing. He pulled it in and thought how much nicer it would be if it always stayed there. He bent down and touched his toes three times and re-examined the effect on his middle. He put on his thin muslin shirt and pajama. Before switching off the light he looked round the room to see if everything was in place. Champak had taken off her kimono and lay stark naked on her belly. She had the pillow between her arms, her legs were stretched apart. Sher Singh knew what this meant. 'My God I feel fagged out,' he said wearily and switched off the light.

Champak stretched out her hand and caught her husband's. 'Now it's dark, I can tell you about this Mundoo of yours. He's not all that innocent, you know!'

'Oh? What did he do?' asked Sher Singh yawning at the same time.

'Come over and I'll tell you,' she mumbled, tugging at his hand.

Sher Singh rolled over on to her bed and let her put her hand on his arm. 'When I bathe, he keeps peeping through the crevices of the door.'

'How do you know?'

'I know. And today he burst into the bathroom on the pretence of bringing in the hot water. I didn't have a stitch on me. Not one thing! My God, I nearly died of shame.'

'Why don't you bolt the bathroom door?'

'Never occurred to me; I thought everyone was out. In any case he should have knocked before coming in.'

'I suppose so. He's only a little fellow,' he said. 'Let's go to sleep.' A minute later he began to breathe heavily.

Champak's body twitched. She moaned as if in a nightmare and snuggled closer to her husband. She caught his hand and took it lower down her body. Sher Singh knew there was no way out.

'What have you done?'

'Just to give you a little variety.'

❧

When the procession came back to the temple from its round of the city, it was well past midnight. Only a handful of men and women were there to welcome it back. Sabhrai and Shunno were amongst them. They had walked behind the decorated motor-van which carried the Holy Book for the first mile or so till the heat and jostling from the crowd had become too much for them. They came back to the temple to await its return. Shunno went to the open-air kitchen to help other volunteers wash and clear up the mess, over 10,000 people having been fed there that morning. Sabhrai sat beside the platform, on which there was another copy of the Granth, listening to the recitation.

By sunset the mammoth mile-long procession of the afternoon had been reduced by half; an hour later only a few hundred people remained. When it came to the temple there were just the men carrying gas lamps, some volunteers, and the five men who had marched with drawn swords all the way. A last quick prayer was said and the Granth was laid to rest.

Sabhrai and Shunno came out into a deserted street. There were no tongas or taxis at the stand, so they had to walk home; the mistress in front and the maid-servant a few paces behind her. One side of the narrow street was whitewashed by the moonlight; a dark shadow slanted down from the other. People slept on platforms in front of their shops. The road was occupied by stray cows placidly chewing the cud and Brahmany bulls who roamed about bellowing into the stillness.

Part of their way lay through the prostitutes' quarter, where there was some life. Several tea shops, pan leaf and soda pop stalls were still open. Long-haired pimps sat in groups gossiping. From some balconies came the whining of harmoniums and the tipety-tipety tum-tum of the tabla; from some others the shrill notes of singing and the jingle of bells. Farther down the street were women who did not pretend to combine dancing or singing with their real profession. They sat on their doorsteps under the lights of hurricane lamps to display their heavily made-up faces and artificial jewellery.

Sabhrai and her maid-servant aroused no comment; only the pimps stopped talking and turned round to see them. (Vice responds only to vice; it seldom dares to accost virtue.) Shunno drew her veil across her nose, came alongside her mistress, and whispered an angry comment on the profession of street women. Sabhrai ignored her remark and started mumbling her prayers. Shunno dropped back. She cast surreptitious glances at the women and tried to overhear the negotiations between them and their patrons. They came out of the bazaar and its warm smell of stone and sewage to the grassy cool of the municipal garden. It was bathed in silvery moonlight; the fragrance of the lady of the night pervaded the lawns. The women quickened their pace. Save for the croaking of frogs and the challenging cries of watchmen from the roofs of neighboring houses, it was still.

When they got home, everyone was asleep. Mundoo lay on the kitchen floor. Shunno kicked him with her bare feet till he woke up and sent him to the servants' quarters. She went up to the roof with her mistress.

Sabhrai said another short prayer sitting cross-legged on her bed. When she lay down, Shunno began massaging her feet and legs.

'Go to sleep. You must be tired.'

'It doesn't matter. You will sleep better if I press you a little.'

Sabhrai knew that the maid-servant wanted to say something. She did not openly encourage Shunno to gossip; neither did she discourage her more than to occasionally call her a gossip-monger.

'Everyone is asleep,' said Shunno to reassure her mistress.

'I thought Beena was stirring,' whispered Sabhrai to indicate that she knew what was on Shunno's mind.

'Beena Bibi, are you asleep?'

There was no answer.

'No, she must be asleep. It is long after midnight,' assured Shunno. After a few minutes, she spoke again.

'Bibiji.'

Sabhrai mumbled inaudibly.

'Bibiji, are you feeling sleepy?'

'No.'

'Bibiji,' continued Shunno in low tones 'One shouldn't say such things, but . . . '

'But what?'

'If you don't take it ill, this house our Bibi Beena has started going to, the one with those hairless Hindus, is not a very good one.'

'Bus, bus, enough! You know nothing about them.'

'I am just telling you what I have heard, it is my duty. If something happens don't blame me for not telling you what people say.'

'What do they say?'

'The son is said to have bad habits. One hears he spends his time playing cricket and going to cinemas. He has other habits too . . . . One hears his wife is very unhappy.'

'Bus, bus! You are always slandering people . . . . Who told you?'

'Who told me? All the world knows.'

'Accha, accha! Go to sleep and don't gossip.'

'Whatever I say is gossip,' grumbled Shunno. 'As you wish! *Sat Sri Akal.*'

'*Sat Sri Akal.*'

Shunno heaved herself up and went down the stairs praising the Guru.

Sabhrai sat up in the bed once more and repeated the prayer for the night to wipe out the effect of Shunno's words. She, too, had heard stories of Wazir Chand's son. But Sher had made friends with him and Beena almost worshipped his sister, Sita. And Wazir Chand was a colleague of Buta Singh. Sabhrai did not know what she could do without upsetting the rest of her family. She had infinite faith in the Guru and was sure of His special interest in her husband and children. He had helped her husband to rise to the position of senior magistrate. He would no doubt get her Sher to settle down to a steady occupation and find Beena a nice husband, not necessarily rich, just well off, but a good Sikh with his hair and beard unshorn. That was not too much to ask or hope for. Sabhrai shut her eyes and invoked His blessings for her family with all the fervour she could command.

ง

'These English are funny.'

It was not usual for Buta Singh to be in good temper at breakfast. 'Bhai, yesterday was great fun,' said he, making a second attempt to interest his family. When no one asked him why, he continued of his own accord. 'These English, they don't know anything about our customs. Yesterday the Deputy Commissioner offered me a cigarette. I said, "Sahib, today you have done this and I do not mind because we are old friends, but don't do it again." Then he started apologizing.'

The family took Buta Singh's stories of his candour with English officials with a pinch of salt. 'Did you tell him that Baisakhi is a big day for us and he should not ask people to be on duty?' asked his wife fanning flies away with a hand towel.

'He apologized himself. He said since I was the only one who really knew the people in the city, he had to rely on me. He also tried to bribe me with promise of a title. I said, "Sahib, you keep your titles. I don't care for such things."'

'Sardarji,' said Shunno chiming in, 'there is a policeman with a bayonet at our gate since the morning.'

'Oh yes, I had almost forgotten that part of Mr Taylor's orders,' said Buta Singh in a lordly way. 'The seniormost official in the district is to have a sort of decorative guard outside his house just like the one outside the Deputy Commissioner's. I don't think the other magistrates will like that.'

'It will hurt their eyes,' commented Sher Singh expanding with filial pride.

Buta Singh suddenly realized that his daughter had spent the whole of the day before at Wazir Chand's. 'How are you getting on with the preparations for your exams?'

'I worked yesterday at Sita's house,' answered Beena. She made one attempt to clear her conscience. 'We worked all morning and got so tired that nothing would stay in our heads. So we decided . . . .'

'No, no, it is foolish to force the mind to things it cannot retain,' interrupted her father, trying to make up. 'When I was at college, I never worked more than two hours at a stretch. When I got tired, I used to take a walk in the fresh air; fresh air is best. Some of the boys used to go off to the cinema after working all day. When the eyes are tired, the stuffy atmosphere in a cinema can do them no good.'

Beena did not have the nerve to mention the pictures after that. Sher Singh realized that and decided to keep the knowledge of his sister's escapade to himself and question her when the occasion arose. Buta Singh had not finished talking about himself. 'The Guru was merciful; yesterday went off peacefully. Our Sahib was scared: "There will be a Hindu-Muslim riot . . . The Communists will be up to mischief." I said, "Sahib, don't worry, all will be well." He also wanted to know about your meeting.'

'The place was packed to capacity.'

'I hope you didn't say anything indiscreet.'

'O, no! There's no such danger.'

'You have to be careful. Many people would like to create mischief for the family. It is wise to be cautious.'

Buta Singh rose form the table, 'I better inquire from Mr Taylor whether he slept well or had nightmares of riots.' The family obliged with a laugh.

Buta Singh left. Sabhrai turned to her brood with maternal aggressiveness. 'Did you go to the Gurudwara or just carry on your *buk buk* nonsense?' she asked her son.

Sher laughed. 'There are so many to say prayers for me. You must have said one, Champak another.'

It gave Champak an opportunity to enter into the family discourse. 'I had a very quiet day all alone. I washed my hair and listened to the hymns relayed from the temple by the radio. Then I said my evening prayers and put the Granth to rest. It was very peaceful.'

Chapter II

The last thing Shunno did every night before retiring was to fill a brass jug with water, put a *keekar* * twig in it, and leave it on a stool outside the kitchen. Every morning while it was still dark she came in, lit the fire, and put the tea kettle on the hearth. She put the keekar twig in her mouth, picked up the jug, and went out into the garden or the vacant plot across the road. She performed her morning functions behind a bush and washed her privates with the water she carried. She scooped up a little mud and used it as soap to rinse her hands. She chewed the twig till one end was reduced to a soggy, fibrous pulp and brushed her teeth with it. She tore off a strip of the bark and scraped her tongue with such vigour that it made her retch and spit. She returned to her quarters and bathed under the tap in the garden and went back to the house to get tea ready. All this she did before the earliest risers, the drongos, had started calling or even a suspicion of gray had appeared on the eastern horizon.

Shunno was a peasant woman and had not changed her way of living in the city. Her regular habits had helped to keep her in rude, rustic health. Although she was fat and nearly fifty, she could work fourteen hours a day without any sign of fatigue. She had never been known to be ill, she had not even known a cold or a headache. Her eyes were clear, with the white and black whiter and blacker than other people's. She had an even row of teeth not one

* Acacia arabica

of which had ever given her trouble. She could crack almonds and walnuts as if her mouth had been fitted with a nut-cracker. Shunno was the despair of men servants employed as additional help. Since she could run the house single-handed, she soon reduced them from being fellow-servants to her own personal slaves. She bossed them till they couldn't stand it any more. They were dismissed for the same reason: making improper advances to her. The compromise had been found in hiring the thirteen-year-old Mundoo whom she could not easily accuse of impropriety and who would submit to her bullying. On the night of the New Year's Day she had kicked him several times.

Shunno loved to talk, like most women of her age and frustrations. (She had become a widow before she was twenty.) Her sexual instincts had been sublimated in hard work, religion, and gossip. She spared no one, not even members of the family for which she had worked for nearly thirty years. The only reason why she had failed to create misunderstandings between them was because they knew her well.

Despite her tongue, Shunno was a God-fearing woman. She said her prayers, went to the Gurudwara and, on religious festivals, helped menfolk in the community kitchen. She was not narrow in her faith. She also went to Hindu temples, bathed in the river every Tuesday morning, respected Brahmins and cows. Even Islam was not beyond her religious pale. She visited tombs of Muslim fakirs, left offerings with their guardians, and consulted them on her imaginary ailments. She never let a beggar, be he a Hindu, Sikh, or a Muslim, return empty-handed from Buta Singh's door.

Shunno's one grievance with life was that no one took her seriously. Although her master and mistress disapproved of her forays into other faiths, they said nothing to her. But the younger members of the family made fun of her. They often insinuated that her visits to the river had motives other than spiritual. And since she was never known to have been ill, it did not take much to twist her accounts of visits to Muslim medicine men.

Shunno did not tell anyone about her new ailment for the first few days. Many times during the previous month she had returned form her early morning performances with a slimy feeling between the thighs; her left hand which she used to wash her bottom felt as if it had been dipped in glue. She had to wash again with fresh water before she felt clean.

On the morning of the first of Jeth (early May), Shunno got up earlier than usual; she had to get the morning tea and the pershad ready. She had also to sweep the Gurudwara room and prepare it for the first-of-the-month ceremony. She went to the corner of the garden and after she had finished, washed her person with water she carried in her brass jug. She got the same clammy feeling which she had had before. She decided to get some of the kitchen work out of the way before going to the tap for a second wash. Half an hour later, in the light of the gray dawn, she noticed some red stains on her Punjabi trousers. She examined her left hand; it was also smudged with crimson. She filled a pail with fresh water and hurried to her quarter. She took off her trousers and splashed water between her thighs. It trickled down her legs tinged with red. She felt weak and slumped down on her charpoy. After a few minutes she woke up Mundoo and told him to tell the mistress that she was unwell. That was the first time in the many years of service in Buta Singh's home that Shunno had not turned up at the Gurudwara for the first-of-the-month ceremony.

ર૪

It was Mundoo who brought the steaming tray of pershad. He had changed his shirt and covered his head with a kitchen duster for the occasion. He also felt entitled to stay on in the room instead of being outside with the dog and the urchins of the locality.

As soon as the final prayer had been said and the pershad distributed, Buta Singh asked the question which was in everyone's mind: 'Where is Shunno?'

'She says she is not feeling well,' piped up Mundoo, beaming. 'She looks all right.'

'She came in the morning to light the fire; she put the pershad on the hearth and then went back. I will go and see what is wrong with her. She has never been ill before,' said Sabhrai, very concerned.

'It must be the heat,' added Buta singh. 'Yesterday the temperature touched 115 in the shade! The courtroom was like an oven.' He made a grimace and went on: 'I was hearing a murder case; the place was packed with Sikh villagers. They obviously do not bathe every day. The smell of sweat and clarified butter was terrible.'

210

Sabhrai did not like derogatory references to Sikhs and changed the subject abruptly. 'A lot of things are going to happen this month,' she said. 'Beena is going to take her examination; Sher, you've got something on too, haven't you?'

'Yes, the election of the University Union.'

'We ought to have a complete reading of the Granth Sahib. All of you must help.'

'You better get a professional reader. Most of us will be busy and will not be able to do much reading,' pleaded Buta Singh.

'I don't like hiring outsiders to do our prayers; it hasn't the same effect. If none of you can spare the time, I will do it all on my own,' said Sabhrai with determination. They knew they would have to come to her rescue. This was one of the ways she imposed religion on them and although they said nothing, they did not like it. Before they could pursue the matter further, Mundoo came and announced that some people were waiting to see Buta Singh. They had an appointment.

&

'What are the orders for me?'

This was Buta Singh's way of getting down to business straightaway; it also had the note of humility which, coming from a man of his status, created a favourable impression.

The deputation of Hindu merchants had been sitting cross-legged on the chairs in the verandah talking to the policeman on duty. As Buta Singh came out the policeman sprang to attention, brought his rifle to his shoulder, and slapped the butt in salute. The visitors got up quickly, slipped their feet into their shoes, and greeted him: 'We touch your feet. *Sat Sri Akal* . . . Orders? You order and we obey. You are the emperor, we are your subjects.'

It was a proud moment for Buta Singh. His politeness became more exaggerated. He joined his hands to greet them and escorted them to the sitting room. They took off their shoes and sat down. After a while Buta Singh asked them whether they would like something to drink and, without waiting for a reply, asked again: 'What are the orders for me?'

The visitors again protested that they were the ones to receive orders not give them. After some shuffling of feet, clearing of throats, and nodding to each other, the eldest in the group spoke: 'Sardarji, our request is for a licence to take out a religious procession next week.'

'You know the Deputy Commissioner has promulgated an order banning all meetings and processions,' replied Buta Singh without looking up.

'We know that, Sardar Sahib. We will be honest with you. The Sikhs have had their procession and the Muslims have had theirs; then there was no order to ban them. When it comes to our turn, our kismet is bad.'

'If it is for a Hindu procession, why do you come to me? Go and ask a Hindu official to speak to Mr Taylor. Ask Mr Wazir Chand.'

'Sardar Sahib, for us you are a Hindu. What is the difference between a Hindu and a Sikh? You tell us.

'Yes, Sardarji,' joined the others in a chorus. 'We are like brothers. No difference at all.'

'I never said there was any difference; I think we are the same community. You started by saying something about Hindus and Muslims and Sikhs.'

'Please forgive us,' said the eldest with his hands joined. 'It was only a manner of speaking. Most of our homes have Sikh forms of worship. We give our sisters and daughters in marriage to Sikhs. We are kinsmen. Why, brothers, isn't that the truth?'

'Truth?' protested one. 'Why, there is no greater truth.'

The others nodded approval. The eldest started again. 'Why should we hide anything from you! We did approach Mr Wazir Chand first but he refused to help. He said, "If you want to get anything from Taylor Sahib, ask Sardar Buta Singh." We would not have put you to this trouble if we hadn't been told by everyone in the world that the only man who can do it is Sardar Buta Singh.'

'This is only your kindness. I will do the best I can,' said Buta Singh getting up.

The visitors also got up and slipped their feet back into their shoes. 'When shall we present ourselves?'

'Come and see me some time tomorrow—at the law courts.'

'Sardar Sahib,' spoke another, 'we have pinned all our hope on you. You do this for us and we will sing your praises the rest of our lives.'

'We will remain ever grateful,' exclaimed the others.

'Acchaji Namaste . . . . Some water or something?' asked Buta Singh mechanically and without waiting for a reply dismissed them: 'Namaste.'

'This is like our own home. We would ask for anything we want. *Sat Sri Akal.'*

ॐ

John Taylor was an Englishman and a member of the Indian Civil Service. He was only twenty-eight but these two qualifications had led to his being made the Deputy Commissioner and the virtual ruler of an area larger than two English counties, with a population of nearly a million natives.

Taylor did not belong to the class which had produced the builders of the Empire. He was the son of a school master. His wife, Joyce, had been a nurse—a very pretty nurse. He had met her at the hospital where he had been sent for a medical check-up before joining the service. From the very start, they found themselves isolated from the English community. They found the snobbery of the senior English officials a little irksome. They did not share their views about the role of Englishmen in India. Although Taylor, as the English Deputy Commissioner, was elected President of the exclusively European Club, he never went to it. His wife avoided the company of other memsahibs and restricted the duties, which her status imposed on her, to purely Indian circles. But their attempts to make friends with Indians were not very successful. The Indians refused to be treated as equals; they refused to be frank and outspoken; and at some stage or other they tried to exploit their association. So the Taylors gave up trying to find friends in India. They spent their after-office hours together—going out riding, taking long walks, or just being at home. They disliked people invading the privacy of their home and Taylor had issued strict instructions that no one was to call at the house except on the day set apart for visitors. He had a repertoire of little tricks by which he put subordinates, who tried to be familiar, in their places. He kept them waiting. He took a long time to answer simple questions; he lit a cigarette or casually knocked tobacco out of his pipe on the heels of his shoe while the other was on pins and needles waiting for a reply. At times he was just abrupt; sometimes even rude.

Buta Singh believed that Taylor had a personal regard for him and would always treat him with special consideration. As minutes accumulated to make half-an-hour and then three-quarters, doubts began to assail his mind. 'Did you give Sahib my card?' he asked the orderly.

'Immediately, sir. Sahib looked at it but said nothing.'

Buta Singh had always tipped the Deputy Commissioner's staff and had no fears about his card having been deliberately withheld. He could not understand why the Sahib had not come out to greet him or ask the *chaprasi* to show him in. 'Didn't he say whether or not I was to wait; or does he want me to see him in his office at the law courts?' he asked.

'He was having his tiffin with the memsahib. We have orders never to come in when he is at tiffin. But your case is different. I put the card on a plate and took it in. He looked at it but didn't say a word.'

Buta Singh began to feel thoroughly uncomfortable. If it had not been for the fact that Wazir Chand had admitted his inability to get permission for the Hindu procession, Buta Singh would never have taken on the task. He had reasoned that if he failed, it would not do him much damage; if he succeeded, his prestige amongst the Hindus of the city would greatly increase and that of Wazir Chand suffer. He was beginning to doubt the wisdom of his venture. He knew that Taylor did not like people coming to his house unless sent for and he was a stickler for appointments. He had fondly believed that those rules did not apply to him. Now he was not so sure of himself. It could, of course, have an innocent explanation and Taylor might apologize for keeping him waiting; in that case he would forgive him graciously.

'What is it, Buta Singh?'

That is all Taylor said as he came out. He was still in his riding breeches and was smoking his after-breakfast cigarette. His shirt was drenched with perspiration and stuck to his chest.

Buta Singh stood up. 'Good-morning, sir . . . I . . . I do not like disturbing Sahib at his residence unless it is something urgent.'

'Well, what is it?'

'Sahib's order banning meetings and processions is being misconstrued by mischief makers as being directed only against the Hindus because it was promulgated after the Sikh and Muslim celebrations,' said Buta Singh without a pause.

'That is absolute nonsense. I am fed up of hearing about this Hindu, Sikh, Muslim business. Can't you people get these notions out of your heads? The order has nothing to do with favouring one community or the other; and I don't give a damn about what some silly people say. Is that all?' Taylor's cigarette shook in his hand as he took it to his mouth.

'Sir, I felt it my duty to report. A deputation of the city's leading Hindus called on Mr Wazir Chand when they heard that the order was to be passed. They wanted him to request you to postpone its promulgation by a few days. Mr Wazir Chand might have spoken to you about it.' Buta Singh had not intended to take this line; but neither had he expected this kind of reception. Slight inaccuracies did not vitiate a substantial truth.

'Wazir Chand said absolutely nothing. Changing the date of the order would have been a simple matter, but I do not like to take back my orders.'

'Perhaps Mr Wazir Chand got frightened of Sahib's temper,' said Buta Singh a little nervously. Taylor threw the cigarette on the floor and squashed it under his foot. The growl on his face disappeared. 'Why should anyone be frightened of me? It's this heat and the work which make me ratty. I am sorry, Buta Singh, I never asked you to sit down. Do take a chair.'

'No, thank you, sir. You have not had your bath. Your shirt is wet and you might catch a cold if you don't change quickly.' Buta Singh decided to cash in on the changed mood. 'I won't keep you one minute more, sir. And I apologize again for bothering you at home. I know you don't like it, but I felt it was my duty to inform you.'

'Buta Singh, you mustn't misunderstand my temper. I am sorry if I sounded impolite. I did not mean to.'

Buta Singh's face lit up with a broad smile. 'Sir, I have to work with you every day. If I started misunderstanding your anger—which I must say is very rare—our work would stop. I have always said, and will say again, that it is a subordinate's duty to understand his officer's moods as well as his method of work. When you tick me off, I consider it a privilege because then I know

215

I have made a mistake and have been given an opportunity to correct myself.'

This was too much for Taylor. 'Well, I don't know if I agree with you, Buta Singh. Now this business of the procession. Don't you think it is wrong to withdraw an order? It can be construed as a sign of weakness.'

'You are absolutely right, sir. I suggest that you let it stay; only give the Hindus special permission to take out a procession along a well-defined route and during hours when there is no chance of a disturbance.'

'That's much the same thing as withdrawing the order.'

'No, sir, not at all. This will be a special dispensation for a few hours. After all you are not banning people going in procession with a wedding or a funeral!'

'That's true. OK. You make out an order and put it up for my signature in the office.'

'Perhaps Sahib should send for the Hindu delegation and convey the order personally. It will be better than letting someone else do it. That will also avoid wrong interpretations by mischief makers.'

Taylor thought for a moment. 'I think you are right. Tell them to come and see me at the law courts.'

'Right, sir. I will bring them in personally. Good morning, sir. Change your shirt before you catch a chill.'

&

Beena had reason to be in a bad temper. Without any reason her mother had started an argument about going to Sita's house. 'Why don't you work at home instead of going to Sita's every day?' she had asked. 'Because Sita is very good at her studies and can help me.' 'Why don't you ask her to come here?' 'Because it is much quieter there. Here there are you and Champak. There, there is no one.' 'What's happened to Madan's wife and child?' 'I don't know; she has gone to her parents.' Then her mother came out with a suggestion which made Beena positively angry. 'Your sister-in-law is left alone in the house when I go away. Today even Shunno is not in. You take her with you.'

'What will she do there?' asked Beena in an exasperated tone.

'We go away to study in Sita's room, what will she do, kill flies?'

'She can knit or read; she is lonely. Anyhow, I do not like you being alone in the houses of strangers. People talk.'

'Talk about what? What do I do there?'

'I do not care; you have to obey your mother. You take Champak with you today and see how it goes. If she does not like it, she can come away.'

Beena walked out of the room in a huff. 'After today, I am never going to Sita's. I don't care if I pass or fail.'

Champak did not protest as much as was expected. Although she was being deprived of a chance of being alone in the house, her curiosity about Wazir Chand's household, which had become the chief topic of conversation over the last month, had been thoroughly roused. Buta Singh often spoke of Wazir Chand, sometimes critically, as people do about their colleagues. Beena was full of the family, particularly Sita. And her husband had begun to see a lot of Madan. She had never met him but had seen him play against the English eleven. 'I am not at all lonely here,' she said in the dutiful tone she adopted in speaking to her mother-in-law. 'But if you want me to go with Beena, I will.'

There wasn't much conversation in the tonga. Sabhrai made some feeble attempts to make up but Beena continued to reply in gruff monosyllables. When they got to Wazir Chand's, the roles between mother and daughter were reversed. Sitting in the verandah was Madan, smoking and reading a newspaper. It wasn't such a quiet place to study after all; Sabhrai felt she had done well to bring her daughter-in-law along. Beena knew her mother would not believe her if she told her that Madan was not usually at home in the mornings. 'Bhraji, you haven't gone to college today?' she asked begging for an explanation.

'I am taking the day off. *Sat Sri Akal, auntyji.* This is the first time you have put your foot in our home; it will rain today.' He threw down his half-smoked cigarette and crushed it under his foot. 'Do come in.'

'I will another day, son. I am late for the Gurudwara. Look after your sisters and see them home when Beena has finished studying.'

'Do you have to say that? Of course, I will see them home. Have absolutely no worry.'

217

The tonga drove away with Sabhrai.

Beena did not bother to introduce Champak. She did not seem to need an introduction or to be put at ease. 'You go and work and don't bother about me,' she said making herself comfortable on the drawing room sofa. 'I will stay here and do my knitting. I have promised to knit your brother a sweater before the winter.'

Beena went off to Sita's room and Champak took her knitting out of her bag. Madan came in from the verandah. 'Would you like something to drink? Shall I send for some cold butter-milk?'

'No, thank you, I am not thirsty. I will ask for anything I want. After all this is like my own home.'

'Absolutely!' he emphasized warmly. 'You must consider this your own home. Don't wait on formalities.'

Madan seemed uncertain of the next step. He went over to the radio set, took off the embroidered velvet covering, and began to fiddle with the knobs. He could not find a station on the air and switched it off. Champak went on with her knitting without taking any notice of him. But as he moved towards the door she asked, 'Bhraji, when is sister coming back?'

'She has gone to her parents for the summer. It is very hot here and it wasn't good for her and the little boy's health.'

Madan looked out on to the verandah and slowly opened the door.

'There is nothing wrong with sister's health, I hope?' she asked, putting down the knitting in her lap.

'No, just the heat,' he replied turning back. He realized that his presence was not unwelcome. It was up to him to make the next move. 'Your husband and I have become great friends.'

'Nowadays he talks of nothing but you. He is a great admirer of yours.'

'And I am a great admirer of his. He is a wonderful orator. Today he is only the leader of the students; tomorrow he will become a leader of the country. I am sure he will be a minister or something really big one day.'

Champak laughed. She took up her knitting again and without looking up said, 'I suppose you have thousands of admirers all over the city since you scored that century against the English eleven. You saved your country's honour that day.'

Madan smiled and sat down in the armchair facing the sofa.

'Have I your permission?' he asked, taking out a cigarette from the case. He lit it without waiting for a reply. He sent a jet of smoke straight at Champak; then tried to fan it away with his hands.

'Where does cricket get you? In five years I will be forgotten. Sher will be the Chief Minister of the Province and you his great lady. When I come to your door you will ask your servant: 'Madan? Who is Madan? I don't know any Madan. Send him away.'

'You are making fun of me. How can anyone forget the great cricketer, Madan! You know, Bhraji, one of the sixers you hit, the ball came flying towards me. I thought it would hit me right here in the middle.' She dug her finger in the center of her low cut shirt to indicate the spot. She flung away her thin muslin head-covering, put her arms behind her head and smiled.

Madan looked from the spot between her breasts to her face. Their eyes met and were fixed on each other for a few seconds.

'My husband,' said Champak looking away, 'takes no exercise and has started to get a paunch. You should teach him cricket.'

'I will teach him anything you command; I will be always at your service,' replied Madan putting his hand across his chest and bowing slightly.

'If you make fun of me, I will not talk to you.' Champak took off her shoes and tucked her feet under her on the sofa. She put aside her knitting and said with a deep sigh, 'This will never get done and you know whose fault it will be!'

'I am a great sinner,' answered Madan bowing again. They both laughed. They sat and talked of many things: Sher Singh's election, the growing friendship between the families, the hot weather, films and film-stars. Then the clock on the mantelpiece struck twelve and Champak got up; one of her knitting needles fell on the floor. Madan picked it up and came near her to hand it back. 'You are wearing khas? On a hot day it reminds one of rain. I think it is the best perfume in the world; better than anything made in France.'

'Is that all you know of perfumes, Mr Madan?' she answered coyly. 'For your information this is French and is called "*chasse garde*", which means "hunting forbidden". So there!' She tapped him on his chest. One of the buttons of his shirt was open; she buttoned it, then picked a piece of thread off his sleeve and slowly released it in the air.

'Hunting forbidden! What does it mean?'

'Find out for yourself.'

'It's a silly name for a perfume.'

'Isn't it? I am sure the girls have done enough work for the morning. We must get home now. Namaste.'

'Namaste. And don't forget humble folk like us when you are the wife of the Chief Minister,' said Madan joining his hands as if in prayer.

Champak caught his hands in hers and pressed them. 'Don't make fun of me. I don't like it.'

≈

Sher Singh always had a good look at himself in the mirror before taking off his uniform. He examined his profile from both sides and then gave himself a steady stare to study the effect it could have on other people. At these moments he was reminded of newsreels showing busty Russian women soldiers marching fifty abreast through Moscow's Red square on May Day parades. The crash of bands, the deep-throated chorus, and, above all, the command to salute, gave him a tingling sensation along his spine. If no one was looking, he would stretch his hand sideways and like Hitler clutch his belt with his left hand. Thereafter he looked at himself again in the mirror as each garment came off.

Champak was already in bed waiting for him, so he could not go through the saluting ceremony. However, the Russian troops in the Red Square started a sequence of thought. 'You know what these bastard Communists want to do now?'

'What?'

'They want our peasants to fight the Japanese army. They say we must help Russia to win the war.'

The statement did not register on Champak whose notions of politics and geography were somewhat hazy. She gave a non-committal answer: 'Funny, isn't it?'

'It's not funny at all; it's serious. For the Communists, one day it is an imperialist war, the next day it becomes the People's War. One day they call the Muslim League a tool of British imperialism, the next they describe it as the only true representative of the Muslims. One day they decry the demand for Pakistan, the next day they support it. They say what Moscow tells them to say. It is always Russia this and Russia that. They never think of India. I will teach them a lesson one day. My S.V.C. will knock the hell out of them.'

'Incidentally, you have a great admirer.'

Admirers always interested Sher Singh. 'Oh! and who would admire me?'

'Your dear sister's friend, Madan.'

Sher Singh felt a little uneasy. He recalled Beena's going to the pictures with Madan and his sister on New Year's Day and her keeping quiet about it. He was not sure if it meant anything, but it made him uneasy. 'What did he say?'

'He said you were sure to become the Chief Minister one day.'

Sher Singh laughed. The cinema episode could not have meant anything since Sita had also gone with them and Madan was married. But why had she kept it a secret?

'And he said he was going to get his friends to vote for you in the Union election. He said you were sure to win.'

'Madan is a first-rate chap. We have got to know each other recently but I know he is one of those to whom loyalty to friends comes above everything else. Don't you think so?'

'I have only met him once. You should ask your dear sister. I think she will agree with you. The way she goes on, "*Bhraji* this and *Bhraji* that", I think she is a little gone on him.'

'He is a bit of a rascal,' admitted Sher Singh.

'You are telling me! He's a big rascal. The way he looked at me! My God, it made me feel as if I had no clothes on. He had his eyes fixed on my breasts all the time. I couldn't look up.'

Sher Singh knew what the turn of conversation to sexual matters before bedtime meant. 'I don't bother about his morals. I like men who have courage and daring, and he has both.'

'He certainly has daring; I can tell you that after one meeting. I think your mother is quite right in sending someone to keep an eye on Beena—particularly when it is obvious to everyone how she feels about him.'

'Oh, I am hot,' said Sher Singh trying to change the conversation. 'Why can't we sleep out in the courtyard now that the rest of the family sleeps on the roof? It would be much cooler. Even Dyer refuses to stay with me at night.'

'What privacy is there in the courtyard? They can see everything from the roof. There is also that not-so-little Mundoo of yours who sleeps in the courtyard these days. I don't think he likes being on the roof of the servants' quarters next to Shunno.' There seemed no way of stopping Champak from giving a slant to the conversation.

'This heat is terrible,' he grumbled, taking off his vest. 'I feel so sleepy.' he yawned to prove what he said.

'Just take your clothes off; they make you hot. I am going to strip myself. Have you bolted the door?'

Sher Singh bolted the door. He went into the bathroom to pour tumblers of cool water on his hot, sweaty body and went to bed. Fifteen minutes later he went back to the bathroom to wash himself.

❧

A late moon rose over the line of trees and the day's heat was slowly wafted away by a cool breeze. Buta Singh, Sabhrai, and Beena had their charpoys on the roof. The father and daughter were asleep; Sabhrai sat cross-legged on her bed saying her bed-time prayer. The sound of footsteps coming up distracted her attention. Dyer began to growl but as the steps came closer he recognized them and began to wag his tail. Shunno heaved herself up the stairs invoking the assistance of the Guru at each step. She sat down on her haunches beside Sabhrai's bed and began to press her mistress's legs. Sabhrai finished her prayer, made her obeisance, and spoke to the maid-servant in an undertone, 'Where have you been all day? I went to look for you in the servants' quarters in the morning and afternoon.'

'Don't ask me anything,' moaned Shunno. 'It was written in my kismet.' She slapped her forehead and sighed. 'Stretch your legs, I can press them better.'

'What is the matter with you?' asked Sabhrai lying down and stretching her legs.

'*Hai, Hai, Hai. Ho, Ho, Ho,*' wailed Shunno. 'It would be better if you didn't ask. I have died of shame.'

'What is the matter?' asked Sabhrai impatiently.

'Bibiji, I am so ashamed, I can't even talk.' Shunno explained her ailment at length.

222

'How old are you?'

'I don't know; between forty-five and fifty-five.'

'It may be more serious than you think! Bleeding at this age can be dangerous. Did you go to a doctor?'

'It is all right. If it is written that I have to die, I will die.'

'Have you been to a doctor?'

'What do doctors know? Only God knows. I went to the Peer Sahib. He has some miraculous prescriptions which his ancestors have left him. Many women, who had remained barren for years and whose husbands threatened to take other wives, have been cured by Peer Sahib. He is a magician—a divine magician. Sometimes he writes verses from the Quran Sharif and makes people swallow the paper; sometimes he just blows magic formulas in their ears. There is a big crowd there every day—Muslims, Hindus, Sikhs—everyone. I had to wait till I got a chance to speak to him alone. You can't mention such things before others, can you, Bibiji?'

'Did he give you a magic potion?' asked Sabhrai, sarcastically.

'No, Bibiji, he said he couldn't find out the trouble by feeling my pulse. He has asked me to come another day when there is no one and he can examine me carefully.'

'Won't you be ashamed showing yourself to a Muslim rascal?' hissed Sabhrai.

'Na, na,' protested Shunno. 'Don't use such words for him; he is a man of God. He doesn't charge any fee.'

'Go to sleep. I don't want any pressing.'

Shunno took no notice of her mistress's temper and went on pressing. After a while she started again. 'We have heard other things today.'

'Bus, bus, it seems you can't digest your food without slandering people.'

'As you wish. Don't be angry with me later on for not having warned you in time.'

The mistress relented. After waiting some time for Shunno to continue, she lost patience and asked meekly, 'What is it?

'Don't blame me! We have heard that Wazir Chand's son's wife has gone away to her mother's.'

'She is going to have a baby. What is so important about her going to her mother's to have it?'

'We have heard that she has been turned out; she was old-fashioned.'

Sabhrai made no rejoinder. She had also heard from someone else that Madan had been describing his wife as illiterate.

'Our Beena is growing up fast,' continued the maid-servant after a significant pause.

'What's that to you?' snapped Sabhrai; she knew what it was leading up to.

'It is not good to keep a young girl at home. It is time we thought of her marriage. If you find a nice Sikh boy . . . .'

'*You* find one and then talk.'

Shunno realized that any talk about Beena would only lead to a snub, so she changed the subject. 'Our queen, our daughter-in-law, is idle all day.'

'What shall I do? Beat her?'

'It is not good to be idle all day. She reads stories and listens to film songs over the radio.' As her mistress did not reply, Shunno went on. 'How long has she been married? Isn't this the second year? There are no signs of a child appearing!'

'*You* ask her to have one.'

'I? She doesn't even talk to me; as if I was an enemy. She won't let me press her when she is tired. She is always asking Mundoo.'

Again Sabhrai made no comment.

'This Mundoo is getting very cheeky.'

'Is there anyone in the world you do not malign? Whether you are well or ill, you never curb your tongue form gossip and slander.'

'*Hai, Hai,*' protested Shunno. 'Whatever I say is gossip.'

She pressed her mistress in silence for a few more minutes, then heaved herself up and went down moaning about her age and illness and invoking the Great Guru.

೨

'We Indians have no character.'

When Buta Singh made such statements he excepted himself. But when he added: 'We have still a lot to learn from the English,' the implication was that he had done all the learning there was to be done; it was for other Indians to follow his example. In the past these remarks had been directed to the shortcomings of Wazir Chand's character. Of late Buta Singh had to make his references less pointed because his son and daughter had begun to see a lot of Madan and Sita.

'Some people have boot-licking ingrained in their makeup.' Buta Singh recalled that he had passed that judgment on Wazir Chand more than once and quickly tried to generalize it. 'All these magistrates are great lions in their own homes. When it comes to facing the Sahib, you should see them: each anxious to push the other in front. When Taylor is there, they can't utter a squeak.'

'This has come because of centuries of slavery. Our country has never been free and we have developed a servile mentality. We are frightened of power. Rarely do we get someone who can stand up to it: someone like Sivaji, or Rana Pratap, or our own Guru, Govind Singh.' Sher Singh's heroes were the tough men of Indian history who had fought the Muslims.

Buta Singh acknowledged his son's compliment. 'Those were great men called upon by destiny to save their country. I am talking of common people like us. Take this business of getting permission for the procession. Not one of these Hindus, who give battle with their tongues, would face Taylor and get him to revise his decision. They had to come to me.'

'Did he grant them permission?' asked Sabhrai.

'Of course! Didn't take a minute. It would have been a little awkward if he had asked me why a Sikh had to speak on behalf of the Hindus.'

'Sikhs have always had to help the Hindus,' answered his wife proudly. 'That is nothing new.'

Buta Singh felt the mantle of 'Defender of the Hindus' descend on him. His tone became generous and patronizing. 'There are other things about these English which one must admire. When Taylor realized his order was a mistake—I pointed that out to him—he did not hesitate one moment to alter it. No personal pride or anything.'

'It isn't by accident that they are sitting on half the world as rulers,' joined Sher Singh. 'Look at the way their delegates come to negotiate with Indians who have been put in jail by their own King's Viceroy. No personal pride or anything.' He concluded with his father's words.

'We Indians have a lot to learn from them.

Sher Singh sensed that the remark was directed to him. 'They too have something to learn form us,' he said, taking up the challenge.

'What?'

He did not answer or look up.

'What,' repeated Buta Singh, 'can Indians teach Englishmen?

'O, many things, like . . . like . . . . '

'Like what?'

'Like hospitality . . . tolerance . . . '

'Rubbish! Ask the eighty million untouchables what they think of the tolerance of the caste Hindus. Ask the Hindus and Sikhs about the tolerance of the Muslims.'

'You can find examples like that everywhere. Most white people are anti-semitic. It's not only Hitler who has been putting Jews in gas chambers, the Russians have killed many. Everywhere in Europe and America there is prejudice against them and only because they have better brains and talent than the others. We do not have any racial discrimination.'

'No? What is untouchability if not racial?

'We do not kill our untouchables.'

'Because they have never had the courage to revolt. What religion of the world other than the Hindu—and I include the Sikhs in the Hindus—has degraded humanity in the same way?'

The friendly family discussion turned into an acrimonious debate. Sabhrai did not like it. 'Why must you start arguing at home? Don't you get enough from the lawyers in the courts?' she asked angrily.

'One must not get things wrong,' answered Buta Singh lamely and got up. 'One should be able to see one's faults and learn from other people. Being contented with one's lot is not good enough.'

Sher Singh did not reply. He knew anything he said would irritate his father more and occasion another long sermon. But as soon as Buta Singh left, Sabhrai provoked him into another argument. 'Why do you have to contradict your father in everything he says?' she asked him aggressively. 'It is not nice to argue with one's elders; you should listen to what they have to say.'

'I wasn't arguing. I was . . . '

'Sherji never argues,' interrupted Beena. 'Other people argue with him.'

They started laughing.

'And why are you so much against the English? What have they done to you?' asked Sabhrai coming back to the subject.

'I am not against them; I am for my own country. If they stayed in England, I would have nothing against them.'

'Is that what you say at your meetings? Do you tell the British Government to go back to England?'

'That, and other things.'

'Well, don't say them in this house. We eat their salt, and as long as we eat it, we will remain loyal.'

Sher Singh's temper shot up. 'Who eats whose salt? They suck our blood.'

'This is no way to talk, son,' remonstrated Sabhrai gently. 'You are welcome to your views, but do not say things which you know may embarrass your father. At least we eat *his* salt.'

Sher Singh got up. Sabhrai felt she had upset her son. 'Tell me, son,' she asked, putting her hand on his shoulder, 'what will you get if the English leave this country?'

'I? Nothing. But we will be free.'

'Then what will happen? What sweetmeats will we get?'

Sher Singh could not answer simple questions like these; at least not in words his illiterate mother could understand.

He became lyrical—'Spring will come to our barren land once more . . . once more the nightingales will sing.'

227

Chapter III

In June the sun scorches
The skies are hot
And the earth burns like an oven.
The waters give up their vapours,
Yet it burns and scorches relentlessly.

When the sun's chariot passes the mountain tops,
Long shadows stretch across the land.
The cicadas call from the glades,
And the beloved seeks the cool of the evening.

If the comfort she seeks be in falsehood,
There will be sorrow in store for her.
If it be in truth,
Hers will be a life of joy.

Spake the Guru: My life and life's ending are at the will of the
Lord
To Him have I surrendered my soul.

۞

The Guru had left out reference to the dust in his description of
the month of Asadh (May/June). First there were the devils
spiralling their way across the parched land.

They were followed by storms which came with blinding fury, flinging dark brown earth in fistfuls in people's faces. Some summers, as in the summer of 1942, there were no dust-devils or dust storms but only dust. The sky turned form a colourless gray to copper red and a fine hot powder started to fall. It fell gently day after day and covered everything under a thick layer of khaki. It got into the eyes till they hurt; it got into the month and one felt the grit between the teeth; if one turned the end of a handkerchief on one's finger-tip inside the ears or nostrils, it came out muddy. Trees stood in petrified stillness with the weight of dust heavy on their leaves. There was neither sunshine not shadow. The sun had become a large orange disc suspended in an amber sky; its light was dissipated in the atmosphere. It was intensely hot without even a suspicion of breeze anywhere.

Sabhrai wiped her forehead with a towel and pressed it on the Holy Book. She spread the cover on it and looked up at her family. They were all there including the dog and they were all well and happy. That was enough for her.

Her husband ran his hand gingerly behind his neck and remarked: 'I've never had prickly heat like this before. It feels like a thousand thorns stuck into the back.'

Sabhrai took no notice of the complaint. They had spent several disturbed nights and everyone's nerves were a little frayed. 'Will you say the supplicatory prayer?' she asked, heaving herself up. 'Don't forget to thank Him for Sher's success at the election. Also mention Beena's examination: if the Guru wills she will pass even if her papers have not been good.'

The family stood up. Buta Singh stepped in front. He shut his eyes and raised his face to the ceiling. With his hands joined across his navel he recited the names of the Ten Gurus, the important shrines, and the martyrs. He thanked the Guru for his son being elected President of the Students Union and invoked special assistance for his daughter and blessings for the rest of the family. They all went down on their knees, rubbed their foreheads in front of the Holy Book once more, and sat down in their places. Shunno stirred the pershad with a dagger.

'Last night it was like an oven,' commented Sher Singh. 'I could not sleep at all. I must have drunk at least twelve tumblers of water but the thirst would not go.'

'It can't last very long. The monsoon has broken in Bombay and it should be reaching the Punjab in another fortnight. As a matter of fact, Mr Taylor, who is a keen bird watcher, told me that he had heard the monsoon bird calling. He said this bird comes all the way from Africa with the monsoon winds and wherever it goes the rain is sure to follow. Now the college is closed, why don't you go to the hills for a few days? Sher, you should take Champak and Beena to Simla. You can rent a house for a couple of months; your mother and I will come over later.' Buta Singh cupped his hands to receive pershad from Shunno.

'I have just taken over the Union and even though the colleges are closed, there is a lot of work to do. Madan said his father has rented a large house in Simla and only he and his sister are going for the present. He suggested our sharing it with them. It may not be a bad idea if Beena and Champak went with them now; I will take off a few days in September before the colleges re-open.' Sher Singh took his share of the pershad in his cupped hands.

Before Sabhrai could say anything, Buta Singh agreed that it was a good idea. 'Of course, I will have to stay in a hotel—Cecil or Clarke's. In Simla one meets many senior officials of the Punjab Government and the Government of India, and a good address is most important. You come to some arrangement with Wazir Chand's family: take half the house and pay half the rent. I will see Taylor and discuss summer plans with him.'

The attitude of Buta Singh and his family to the Wazir Chands had undergone a change. Buta Singh had so completely triumphed over his colleague both in the eyes of the bureaucracy and in the estimation of the local populace that he could afford to adopt a patronizing attitude towards him. Sher Singh and Madan were constantly seeing each other during the elections and there was no doubt in anyone's mind that Sher Singh's easy success was in large measure due to Wazir Chand's son. The opposition that had come from Sabhrai was silenced by Beena's persistent refusal to go to Sita for help in her studies, and a not too subtle insinuation that her poor performance at the exams was a result of her mother's attitude.

The Buta Singhs decided to call on the Wazir Chands to settle the business of going to Simla.

The arrival of Buta Singh and his family created quite a commotion in Wazir Chand's house. They had turned up without warning. To emphasize the degree of familiarity that had developed between them, they trooped in without waiting to be announced.

'Anyone there?' shouted Buta Singh leading the way; Sabhrai, Sher Singh, and Beena followed behind him. They went through the sitting room into the courtyard. Wazir Chand was lying on his belly on a fiber mattress with only a loin-cloth on his person. A servant was vigorously massaging his buttocks and legs with oil. Beside him seated on a chair was his son Madan shaving himself in front of a mirror placed on a stool; one side of his face was still covered with lather. His mother had just emerged from the lavatory at the far end of the courtyard and was scrubbing her water-jug with ashes. Sita, the only one who was dressed and ready, fled to her room utterly embarrassed.

'Oho,' said Buta Singh jovially. 'You are having yourself massaged.

Wazir Chand shook off the servant and got up hurriedly. He unwound the dirty dhoti on which he had been resting his chin and wrapped it round his legs; he spread a newspaper across his greasy, hairy chest. Madan wiped off the lather with a towel and stood up; his face looked like a lawn, only half of which had been mown.

'Don't disturb yourselves,' protested Buta Singh. 'This is like our own home. We are always this way.'

Sher Singh and Beena looked at each other and smiled.

'Sardarji, come into the sitting-room. Oi, ask Sita to come out,' ordered Wazir Chand.

'I will get her,' volunteered Beena and rushed away to Sita's room. Wazir Chand put on a soiled shirt and conducted his guests to the sitting-room. Servants brought in trays of dried fruit and soda. Despite Buta Singh's protests that they had just had breakfast, that this was like their own home, that they would ask for anything they wanted, they were talked into sampling the nuts and drinks placed before them.

The conversation started with the terrible heat and plans to escape to the hills. Then the women made a group of their own and got into a huddle on one side. Buta Singh and Wazir Chand dropped their voices to a conspiratorial whisper to discuss office gossip and politics. 'They are getting a hell of a beating these English, aren't they? Four of their aircraft carriers have been sunk, the Germans have swallowed most of Europe and Russia, the Japanese have them on the run in the East. How long do you think they can hold out?'

'One can never tell,' answered Wazir Chand cautiously. 'So far they seem to be getting the worst of it. But their broadcasts always talk of victories.'

'Don't believe a word! You think they would be willing to talk of a settlement with us if all were going well?'

'You maintain that the English always win in the end,' said Wazir Chand with a mischievous smile. 'Have you begun to change your views?'

Buta Singh felt cornered. 'You will agree that so far they have always won the decisive battles. One never knows how things will turn out, they may still turn defeat into victory.' Buta Singh realized that Wazir Chand had made him contradict himself. He tried to retrieve the situation. 'What is more important than the fate of the English or the Germans or the Japanese is the future of this country. How can our leaders persuade the English to give us freedom if the Muslims do not side with us?'

Buta Singh's zeal in collecting war funds was a popular subject of discussion in magisterial circles. Words like 'freedom', 'our leaders', were new in his vocabulary. Wazir Chand decided to keep Buta Singh on the defensive. 'What does Taylor have to say about it? You see more of him than anyone else.'

'Sends for me morning and evening,' complained Buta Singh. 'You can see he is worried. He is always asking me about British proposals and my views on the Muslim demand for Pakistan. I tell him quite frankly what I think.'

'Your position is different,' conceded Wazir Chand. 'You are the only one he really confides in.'

'You are making fun of me,' said Buta Singh, thoroughly flattered. 'Believe me, he listens to what I say because he gets things straight from me; I don't butter my chapatties for him. He has sent for me again this morning.' Buta singh glanced at his watch: 'Actually we came to discuss this matter of sharing the house in Simla; I believe you have rented a large one.'

'Sardar Sahib, it is your house; you are most welcome. What could give us greater pleasure?

'That is very kind of you, but we must share the rent.'

'No, no,' protested Wazir chand, taking Buta Singh's hands in his. The two magistrates squeezed each other's hands with great affection. Buta Singh looked at his watch again. The conversation died down.

Wazir Chand's wife spoke in a timid, low voice: 'Sherji, you don't ever come to see us.'

'What a thing to say!' said Madan before Sher Singh could answer. 'He is busy being a leader; he has no time for social calls.' He turned to Buta Singh's wife and added: 'Auntie, we are going to ask you for sweets the day Sherji becomes a Minister; he is bound to become one one day. I've got sister Champak to promise us that already.'

'If brothers like you wish him well, then he will achieve everything,' answered Sabhrai. She turned the conversation to what was uppermost in her mind: Madan's relationship with his wife. 'How is our daughter-in-law keeping? You get good news of her?'

'She is with her mother and you know how daughters are in their mothers' homes!' answered Wazir Chand's wife.

Sabhrai was not satisfied. 'I hope she will be going to Simla. It should be good for her health.'

Wazir Chand came to his wife's rescue: 'Of course! The plans are that Madan will first take up his sisters. After he has made all the arrangements for their comfort, he will go and fetch his wife. By then, I hope I will be there or Sherji or Sardar Sahib. There ought to be some man there all the time. Don't you think so?'

'Of course, of course,' agreed Buta Singh. 'I wish Sher could go now, but he insists on staying here for some time.'

'My own arrangements are a little uncertain. If I go at all, it will only be for a day or two to leave my wife and then to bring her back.'

They got down to discussing the plans again. Buta Singh and Wazir Chand went out together and after much protesting on either side agreed to share the rent of the house.

છ

The *chaprasi* returned the visiting card and held up the heavy chick for him to pass under. 'Go in, Sardarji, the Sahib is waiting for you.'

Buta Singh put the card back in his wallet, adjusted his tie and coat, and went in. It was dark; all the doors and fanlights were blocked with thick khas fibre thatching. A cool spray came through each time the coolies outside splashed water on them. A pleasant damp smell of fresh earth pervaded the court room.

A table lamp cast a circle of light on a sheaf of yellow files which Taylor was reading. He wore a white open collar shirt, khaki shorts, and sandals on his feet. A silver tankard of iced beer lay in front of him; froth trickled down its sides and mixed with the beads of frost on the metal. Several feet away on a lower level there was another circle of yellow light under which Taylor's reader sat quietly turning over case files.

'Come in, come in, Buta Singh. Come right in,' said Taylor pushing a chair beside him.

'Good-morning, sir. How cool you have made it here. You have brought Simla down to this hot place. No need to go to the hills.'

Taylor felt slightly uneasy. He knew the conditions in which his Indian colleagues worked. Small cubicles packed with litigants and lawyers squabbling and shouting each other down; smell of sweat and stale clarified butter churned about vigorously by the ceiling fan. No curtains to keep out the glare; no khas to lessen the heat and bring in the aroma of the damp earth. Just bare white walls with red betel spit splattered on the corners and a calendar bearing a photograph of the Governor of the Punjab looking down upon the scene through his monocled eye.

'I would break down under the heat if I didn't have all this,' explained Taylor. 'It is a matter of getting used to it. You Indians can take it because you eat the right food, wear the right clothes . . . not you Buta Singh,' he added laughing as he noticed the other's stiff-collared shirt, necktie, silk suit, and thick crepe-soled shoes. 'I mean the man in the street.'

'Even so, Sahib, it doesn't stop us getting prickly heat, sore eyes, and bleeding through the nose. Last two nights I had a servant rub the soles of my feet with the skin of an unripe melon; and still they burn as if on fire. I am sending my family to the hills to escape this heat.'

That gave Taylor the chance to introduce the subject he had

wanted to discuss with Buta Singh for some days. 'Very good idea! The youngsters must have finished with their colleges. A long three-month break every year is a very good idea.' After a pause he added, 'I was glad to see your son was elected President of the University Union. He can go off to the hills feeling pleased with himself.'

Buta Singh was flattered at Taylor's knowledge and interest in his family. 'Yes sir, God has been good to us. We have much to be grateful for.'

Taylor became more explicit. 'What are his immediate plans?'

'Sir, we were planning to go to Simla. I really wanted to know what your programme was for the summer before deciding.'

'I don't think I will take any vacation this summer. Neither should you just yet. Send the family with Sher Sigh and join them later.'

'Sher is not free yet. You see, sir, as President of the Union he has a lot of work to do. He is a very serious-minded young man.'

'You tell him from me that it is not wise to work during the summer months. Ask him to see me. I'll talk to him.'

'Yes, sir, thank you, sir. I will tell him. All work and no play makes Jack a dull boy.'

Buta Singh purred with gratitude at Taylor's concern for Sher Singh. He was quietly tapping his knees with his hand when Taylor got up and extended his hand. 'Well, goodbye, Buta Singh. And don't forget to give my message to your son. Tell him to drop in whenever he has the time.'

Buta Singh went out into the glare of the noon day sun; it was some time before he could see properly. It took him yet longer to get over the fact that Taylor had sent for him only to ask about his family. Then an uneasy suspicion crossed his mind; perhaps there was more in Taylor's tender inquiries about Sher Singh than he knew.

જ

For the first time in two months, Champak had the house almost to herself. Although Mundoo was there he scarcely mattered.

As soon as the family had dispersed, Champak bolted the doors of the house from the inside and retired to her room. She changed back from her Punjabi dress to her kimono. She switched on her radio and stretched herself on her bed under the ceiling fan.

Mundoo finished the little work Shunno had left for him and dozed against the wall. He heard the music coming from the young mistress's room and sat up. Champak watched his reaction through the chick curtain and turned down the volume. After straining his ears for a few minutes, Mundoo got up, came to Champak's door, and sat down on the floor beside the threshold. Champak got up and went into the bathroom and shut the door behind her. Mundoo heard his mistress leave the bedroom. He lifted the chick curtain over his head to shade him from the sun. He put his head against the door and shut his eyes in musical rapture.

Champak bathed and washed her hair. She was in a carefree mood and kept company with her radio music, singing at the top of her voice. Mundoo heard her singing and splashing water; he felt assured that his listening would not be interrupted for some time. As soon as Champak stopped, he sat up. One of his favourite songs was coming over. The mistress would surely take a couple of minutes with the towel. Mundoo thought he could risk it a little longer.

Champak decided that it would be cooler under the breeze of the ceiling fan. She stepped into her bedroom with her long hair and naked body dripping with water. Mundoo edged back thoroughly frightened.

'Why don't you ask before you come into the room?'

Mundoo murmured something incoherently.

'Fool! Hand me the towel.'

The towel lay on a chair facing her dressing table. Mundoo went across the room and gave it to her.

'You can sit inside and listen,' said Champak and went back to the bathroom. Mundoo came in and sat down beside the table on which the radio was placed.

Champak came back wearing her thin cotton kimono. She had a towel about her shoulders to take the drip form her wet hair. She went to her dressing table with its three full-length mirrors and sat down on a chair facing them. From the corner of her eye she noticed Mundoo looking at her reflection. She casually undid the belt of her kimono and put her feet on the dressing table drawer. The kimono fell on either side of her legs, baring her to the waist. She dabbed talcum powder from the neck downwards to her breasts, belly, and thighs. Then threw her head back and let her wet hair fall behind the chair. She shut her eyes to enjoy the cool breeze and the music.

Mundoo sat and stared at the reflection in the mirrors. He felt hot and the palms of his hands became wet with perspiration. His little virginal mind was swamped with lustful longing. All he could do was to stare, squeeze his hands between his thighs, and drool at the mouth. The torment ceased after a few minutes; he felt tired and ill. He got up to go back to the kitchen.

'Press my legs. I am very tired.'

Champak got up from her chair, flapped the sides of her kimono, and tied the belt. She lay down on her belly clutching a pillow between her arms.

Mundoo began pressing his mistress's feet and ankles with his damp hands.

'Here,' ordered Champak, slapping her calf muscles. 'It hurts here.' She drew up her kimono to her thighs and spread out her legs. The boy pressed without daring to look up. After a few minutes he looked up to press the other leg. His mistress was bare up to her buttocks. She seemed fast asleep. The boy was overcome with a maddening desire. He clutched his mistress by the waist, then sank back exhausted.

'What is the matter with you?' asked Champak waking up.

'Nothing, Bibiji,' answered the boy trembling.

'Go back to the kitchen. You don't know how to press.' Champak let out the boy and bolted her bedroom door. She switched off the radio and fell asleep.

When she woke, the shadow of the wall had spread across the courtyard. Sparrows were gathered by the hundreds for their evening twitters before going to roost. All the family were in except her husband.

Champak's mood changed when her husband came back. She had slept all day, and was wide awake and full of herself. After a perfunctory inquiry about what he had been doing, she came back to her favourite subject—herself. 'I had a very quiet day. All your family was away so I washed my hair and read and read and read. Did you know John Barrymore was dead? He died yesterday. I was very sad. He was my favourite film star. I wish we had someone like him in the Indian films. Our films are just singing and dancing. Nothing else. That reminds me, you must do something about this Mundoo, you really must.'

'What has he been up to?'

'Without knocking or warning he came into the room. I had nothing on, not a stitch. My God!'

Sher Singh knew that this sort of conversation always ended in the same thing and he wasn't in the mood.

'The fellow said nothing. Just gaped at me stupidly with his mouth wide open as if I were something to eat. I ran into the bathroom and put on my dressing gown.'

'Why didn't you tick him off?'

'I did. I told him if he came into my room again without knocking I would have him whipped. He simply said he had come in to listen to the radio. He has got film music in his blood. It's these films that give him ideas. How old do you think he is?'

'I don't know, thirteen, fourteen, or fifteen.'

'I used to be so innocent at that age. We were brought up so strictly and Mummy did not tell us one single thing about life. This fellow, I am sure, knows all about sex already. Don't you think so?'

Sher Singh did not like after-dinner conversation turning to sex, so he changed the subject abruptly. 'It must be the heat or something. I have never felt as tired out as I do today,' He said, speaking through a yawn.

'I'll press your legs and you will sleep much better. Take off your clothes; it is so hot.'

ॐ

Sher Singh was late for breakfast. Shunno knocked at the door twice to say that the others were waiting. He quickly wound his turban (his father objected to people coming to the sitting-room or dining-room bareheaded), brushed his little beard and tied a muslin band round his chin to press it. He hurried to join the family at the breakfast table. He interrupted his father's monologue with a loud '*Sat Sri Akal*' meant for everyone.

'*Sat Sri Akal*,' replied his mother. 'Now that he has no college to go to, Sherji finds it hard to open his eyes before midday.'

'I came back rather late last night. Our meeting did not end till then.'

Buta Singh resumed his discourse. 'As I was saying, these Englishmen take a lot of interest in other people, and it is not just curiosity, it is a genuine concern with their problems. Now Taylor knows all of you by name, what you are doing, how you have fared in your examinations—everything. He has an excellent memory.'

'They have learnt from Americans,' answered Sher Singh. 'They have reduced human relationships to a set of rules. They say you must know the name of the person you are talking to and use it as often as possible. You must know his or her interests and talk about them and never of your own. They write down whatever they have discussed with anyone in their diaries and refresh their memories before the next meeting. It does not mean much because their real desire is to create a good impression about themselves. They are not one bit concerned with the affairs of the person they happen to be talking to.'

Buta Singh did not like the way his son twisted everything he said in favour of Taylor. 'I don't know what you mean. Mr Taylor asked me about your election and where you planned to go for the summer. He also asked you to come and see him. He does not take that sort of interest in everyone or invite people to see him. Many rub their noses on his threshold and are not allowed to enter.'

'He must have politely mentioned my name.'

Buta Singh flared up. 'I don't understand this attitude. Even if he mentioned your name out of politeness, you can at least pay him a courtesy call.'

'What will I say to him?'

Buta Singh was too angry to be coherent. 'I don't know what is happening to young men today. I wonder when you will learn about the world.'

Once more an academic discussion had turned into an unpleasant personal argument between father and son. Sabhrai stepped in. 'Why don't you go to see the Deputy Commissioner if he wants to meet you?'

'I did not say I will not see Mr Taylor,' protested Sher Singh. 'I simply asked what use it will be and you all start getting angry.'

'Don't worry, I will send him,' said Champak smiling. 'I will make him ring up for an appointment today.'

'Good,' pronounced Buta Singh. 'When a man is friendly and also happens to be an important officer, one should take advantage of it. Ring up his P.A., tell him who you are—mention my name—and say the Sahib wanted to see you. He will give you an appointment.'

୨ଈ

When Sher Singh rang up the Deputy Commissioner's office, Taylor himself answered the telephone. Sher Singh's English crumbled to a breathless stutter punctuated with many 'sirs.' Taylor brusquely ordered him to come on Tuesday which was the visitors' day.

Visitors' day came a week later. Sher Singh had expected to be received alone. When he got there, the Deputy Commissioner's regular hangers-on were already waiting their turn to be called. There were village officials in their starched turbans and baggy trousers, with their pistols strapped on their sides and cartridge belts running across their chests. There were fat businessmen from the city in their thin shirts and dhotis. There were officials in silk suits and ties. They sat in a row of chairs in the verandah. Sher Singh had great contempt for such people; but here he was sitting alongside them waiting his turn to be summoned. His father had terrified him into submission. He had visiting cards specially printed so that one could be sent in to the Deputy Commissioner. He had his own silk suit altered and made Sher Singh wear it instead of the militant looking open collared bush shirt made of coarse hand-spun cloth. The process of humiliation was carried a step further by the reception Sher Singh got at Taylor's bungalow. One of the regular callers, a colleague of Buta Singh, recognized him and proceeded to introduce him to all the others. 'Wah bhai, wah,' he went on after the introductions were over. 'We used to ask how long will it be before this disciple of Gandhi will become his father's real son! Today in your European outfit you look like the heir of Sardar Buta Singh.'

'Yes, Sardarji,' drawled another who looked like a common informer: stiffly starched turban with its plumes waving in the air and a shifty, cunning look in his lecherous, antimonied eyes. 'What is there in Gandhi's followers? When an Englishman says, "Git awt you biladee," they will run like jackals. Sardar Sher Singh, your father is a wise man. You should follow in his footsteps.'

Sher Singh did not say a word. He was angry with his father for having sent him and angry with himself for having come. He felt angrier with his wife—he always felt angry with her when he could not find reasons for his temper—for not having stopped him from coming. And of course he felt angry with Taylor for having suggested his calling on a Tuesday and belittling him by keeping him waiting with the crowd of sycophants. 'Never again,' he kept saying to himself. This time he would go through the ordeal even if it meant sitting out till the last snivelling, fawning caller had had his say, but never again.

Sher Singh was still immersed in his angry thoughts when the orderly came to say that the Sahib would receive him. Him, Sher Singh, before any of the crowd of corrupt businessmen wanting to be made honorary magistrates; before the boot-licking peasant informers begging for the privilege of being seated beside the Deputy Commissioner at formal functions! It could be because he was Buta Singh's son; it could be because he was the leader of the students. In either case it was something which raised him above the sort of people who called on Taylor. Sher Singh's temper cooled a little.

The orderly conducted him through the verandah, lifted the chick, and peered in. Taylor was dictating to his stenographer. The orderly asked him to wait till the Sahib had finished.

Taylor finished dictating. The stenographer read out what he had taken down and left. Taylor picked up the first visiting card on his table, turned it about, and put it down. He lit his pipe, and after looking vacantly into space for some time, tapped the bell on his table. The orderly raised the chick and hustled Sher Singh into the room.

'Good morning, sir!' said Sher Singh a little nervously. Taylor picked up the visiting card again and scrutinized it carefully. He did not hear the greeting.

'Good morning, sir,' repeated Sher Singh a little louder.

'Hm?'

'Good morning, sir,' said Sher Singh a third time.

Taylor looked up and smiled. 'Oh, good morning, Sher Singh, good morning. Didn't notice you come in. Do sit down,' he said, pointing to a chair.

'Good morning, sir,' stammered Sher Singh for the fourth time. 'Thank you, sir.'

'Well, how are you? And how is your good father? I haven't seen him for some days.'

'Very good, sir. Very good, sir. Thank you.'

'I am glad. And how are your politics? You are a leader of the students, aren't you? Your father told me you had become President of the Students' Union. He is very proud of you.'

A kind word from anyone one fears or hates has quicker and greater impact than it has from another—and Sher Singh had worked up both fear and hatred for Taylor. The Deputy Commissioner's friendly tone and praise won him over completely. He did not know what to say. 'It is nothing, sir, nothing,' he replied with gratitude. He could hardly believe his own ears when he heard himself say, 'It is all the kindness of people like you. The students were being led astray by these Communists and other political groups. At a time like this, when the enemy is at our gates, we should be united and strong. The way the English are standing up to their adversities should be a lesson to us.'

'Things are not going too well for us, are they?' queried Taylor. He picked up a shiny metal tube from his table and tossed it in the air several times. Sher Singh was not sure what it was but he was fascinated by the object. Taylor went on: 'It could put ideas in the minds of people who do not like us. Of course, we can rely on our friends. The Sikhs have a long tradition of loyalty to the British. We trust them more than any other community in India. And you know, your father is my closest colleague. He is a very good man.'

'Yes, sir. Thank you, sir.'

Taylor smiled looking straight at Sher Singh. He put one of the tubes to his lower lip, blew into it and made it whistle. It was an empty cartridge. Sher Singh went pale.

Taylor continued in his friendly manner: 'Well, I mustn't keep you from your work,' he said. 'It's nice of you to have come. Drop in any time you want to see me about anything—not on a visitor's morning like today—any other day. And if I can do anything for you, don't hesitate to ask me.'

Sher Singh stood up and saw two other cartridges lying on the table beneath the table lamp.

'Nice of you to have called.'

'Goodbye, sir. Thank you very much, sir.'

'Goodbye. Remember me to your father. What do you Sikhs say—*Sat Sri Akal*. That's right, isn't it? I am told it means 'God is truth.'

'Yes, sir.'

'*Sat Sri Akal.*'

Sher Singh walked out of the room and left the bungalow without saying goodbye to the other visitors. He brushed off the orderlies who ran after him to collect their tip. As soon as he was out of the gate, he pulled off his tie and thrust it into his coat pocket; then took off the silk coat and hung it on his shoulder. He walked aimlessly down the road till he found a quiet spot. He sat down on the grassy curb with his head between his knees. He was angry, humiliated, and frightened. He wanted to cry but no tears would come into his eyes. He sat like that for a long time till the anger and humiliation receded to the background and only fear remained. Fear of what Taylor might do to him, fear of what the whole family would have to say for the way he had disgraced his father.

For the first time in many years, Sher Singh went to the big temple in the city to pray.

Chapter IV

To know India and her people, one has to know the monsoon. It is not enough to read about it in books, or see it on the cinema screen, or hear someone talk about it. It has to be a personal experience because nothing short of living through it can fully convey all it means to a people for whom it is not only the source of life, but also their most exciting impact with nature. What the four seasons of the year mean to the European, the one season of the monsoon means to the Indian. It is preceded by desolation; it brings with it the hopes of spring; it has the fullness of summer and the fulfilment of autumn all in one.

Those who mean to experience it should come to India some time in March or April. The flowers are on their way out and the trees begin to lose their foliage. The afternoon breeze has occasional whiffs of hot air to warn one of the days to come. For the next three months the sky becomes a flat and colourless gray without a wisp of a cloud anywhere. People suffer great agony. Sweat comes out of every pore and the clothes stick to the body. Prickly heat erupts behind the neck and spreads over the body till it bristles like a porcupine and one is afraid to touch oneself. The thirst is unquenchable, no matter how much one drinks. The nights are spent shadow-boxing in the dark trying to catch mosquitoes and slapping oneself in an attempt to squash those hummings near one's ears. One scratches and curses when bitten; knowing that the mosquitoes are stroking their bloated bellies safely perched in the farthest corners of the nets, that they have gorged themselves on one's blood. When the cool breeze of the morning starts blowing, one dozes off and dreams of paradise with ice cool streams running through lush green valleys. Just then the sun comes up strong and hot and smacks one in the face. Another day begins with its heat and its glare and its dust.

After living through all this for ninety days or more, one's mind becomes barren and bereft of hope. It is then that the monsoon makes its spectacular entry. Dense masses of dark clouds sweep across the heavens like a celestial army with black banners. The deep roll of thunder sounds like the beating of a billion drums. Crooked shafts of silver zigzag in lightning flashes against the black sky. Then comes the rain itself. First it falls in fat drops; the earth rises to meet them. She laps them up thirstily and is filled with fragrance. Then it comes in torrents which she receives with the supine gratitude of a woman being ravished by her lover. It impregnates her with life which bursts forth in abundance within a few hours. Where there was nothing, there is everything: green grass, snakes, centipedes, worms, and millions of insects.

It is not surprising that much of India's art, music, and literature is concerned with the monsoon. Innumerable paintings depict people on roof tops looking eagerly at the dark clouds billowing out from over the horizon with flocks of herons flying in front. Of the many melodies of Indian music, Raga Malhar is the most popular because it brings to the mind distant echoes of the sound of thunder and the pitter-patter of raindrops. It brings the odour of the earth and of green vegetation to the nostrils; the cry of the peacock and the call of the koel to the ear. There is also the Raga Desha which invokes scenes of merry-making, of swings in mango groves, and the singing and laughter of girls. Most Indian palaces had specially designed balconies from where noblemen could view the monsoon downpour. Here they sat listening to court musicians improvising their own versions of monsoon melodies, sipping wine and making love to the ladies of their harem. The commonest theme in Indian songs is the longing of lovers for each other when the rains are in full swing. There is no joy fuller than union during monsoon time; there is no sorrow deeper than separation during the season of the rains.

An Indian's attitude to clouds and rain remains fundamentally different from that of the European. To the one, clouds are symbols of hope; to the other, those of despair. The

245

Indian scans the heavens and if cumulus clouds blot out the sun his heart fills with joy. The European looks up and if there is no silver lining edging the clouds his depression deepens. The Indian talks of someone he respects and looks up to as a great shadow; like the one cast by the clouds when they cover the sun. The European, on the other hand, looks on a shadow as something evil and refers to people of dubious character as people under a shadow. For him, his beloved is like the sunshine and her smile a sunny smile. He escapes clouds and rain whenever he can and seeks sunnier climes. An Indian, when the rains come, runs out into the streets shouting with joy and lets himself be soaked to the skin.

The fact that the monsoons come at about the same time every year gives expectation a sort of permanent place in the Indian's mental calendar. This does not happen with other people, for example the Arabs, who also thirst for water and bless its descent. (If the Arabs had the monsoon turning up with the same regularity, their calendar would have taken note of changes of seasons instead of being linked with the vagaries of the moon.) All the different calendars current in India are a dexterous combination of the lunar and the solar systems. As a result, the correspondence between the month and the season is much closer. On the official day heralding Spring, the chill winds of winter mysteriously vanish and a warm breeze begins to blow. Similarly, while the coming of the monsoon may be any day in June or July by the Roman calendar, more often than not the first of Sawan will see it in full force all along the Western ghats and well inland up to the plains of the Punjab.

Sawan is the month for lovers. Just as Spring turns a young man's fancy to thoughts of love, in Sawan an Indian girl longs to be in her lover's arms. If her lover is not there, she languishes away singing songs of sadness. That spirit is expressed by the Guru in his composition on the monsoon, in which, following the literary tradition of the time, he describes God as the Great Lover and the devotee as His mistress yearning for union with Him.

> *The season of rains is here*
> *My heart is full of joy*
> *My body and soul yearn for my Master.*
> *The Master is away and if He return not,*
> *I shall die pining for Him.*

The lightning strikes terror in my heart.
I stand alone in my courtyard
In solitude and in sorrow.
O Mother of Mine, I stand on the brink of death.
Without the Lord I have no hunger
Nor no sleep;
I cannot bear the clothes on my body.

Spake the Guru: She alone is a wife true
Who loseth herself in the Lord.

❧

The monsoon had burst some time after midnight. The thunder and
lightning was enough to wake the dead but people had just lain in
bed pretending that they were asleep. It came as usual: first a few
heavy drops and everyone announced to everyone else, 'It is going
to rain,' then suddenly it began to pour. There was shouting on all
the roof tops and much bustle and activity as servants ran from
their quarters to help bring the charpoys and bedding down into
the verandahs. It took some time to get back to sleep again—but
not too long. Nerves which had been frayed by the heat were
soothed. And the sound of water spouting down from the roof, the
gurgle of the gutters and of the rain falling in torrents was like a
lullaby.

❧

'Today we have Simla here,' said Buta Singh. He made the remark
in the hope that his son would start some conversation. When Sher
Singh said nothing. Buta Singh made another attempt. 'What
wonderful weather we are having,' he repeated looking out of the
door of the temple room. The chicks had been rolled up. The rain
pock-marked the puddles as it fell.

'Yes,' answered Sher Singh without looking up; he held his
father chiefly responsible for what he had suffered at Taylor's
hands, and had avoided meeting him for some days. Buta Singh
had sensed that the meeting had not been a success and wanted to

know what had happened. 'How did your interview go?'

'It was on the morning meant for visitors; there were many others there.' The tone of resentment was unmistakable.

'Did you have to wait long?'

'No! He sent for me before any of the others.' Now father and son were on the same ground. Sher Singh mellowed at the thought that Taylor had sent for him first.

'He is specially kind to me,' added Buta Singh glowing with pride. 'One should take full advantage of his friendship. You should not bother about what people say. After all you are the President of the Students Union and may be seeing him in connection with the students' demands.'

Sher Singh recalled Taylor playing with the empty cartridge and the two lying on his table.

Sabhrai interrupted their conversation. 'You have plenty of time to talk about these things later on; why start on them in the Gurudwara?' she said crossly. She opened the Granth and, without scanning it silently before reading as she was wont to do, began to recite:

> *O, Black Buck, why lovest thou*
> *The pasture of fenced-in fields?*
> *Forbidden fruit is sweet but for a few days*
> *It entices and ensnares*
> *Then leaves one sorrowing . . . .*

Sabhrai had brought a pen and paper to take down the passage to send to her daughter and daughter-in-law who were away in Simla. The verse made her a little uneasy but it was the Guru's word and she copied it down as it had come. Shunno distributed the pershad to her husband and son and the children outside.

It was obvious that Sher Singh was not in a mood to talk; Buta Singh made no further attempt to make him do so. Sabhrai broke the silence at the breakfast table. 'I wonder what the girls are doing today?' she asked.

'The monsoon couldn't have got to the hills yet,' answered her husband. 'They must be having a good time strolling about on the Mall looking at the shop windows or meeting friends.'

'I wasn't thinking of that. I was wondering if they'd know it was the first of the month and go to a temple or at least say their prayers.'

૨ન

There were no rickshaws available to take them out to the picnic. Madan had looked for them at the stands and on the roads and drawn a blank: all had been reserved by the English folk the day before. 'They give bigger tips than we do,' he explained.

'We can't walk all the way to Mashobra and back,' complained his sister. 'It is more than seven miles from here. And now we have the lunch things ready.'

'The best I could do was to reserve bicycles in the Carpenters' Bazaar,' said Madan. 'He had only three left. One of us could take the other on the back.'

After all the preparations, the girls were in no mood to spend the day at home. They set out with their lunch packed in a basket and their raincoats slung across their shoulders. In Simla, most people carried raincoats as a matter of style; news of the advancing monsoon had provided the habit an additional excuse. They came to the shop owned by the Sikh who combined making furniture, toys, and walking sticks, with hiring out cycles. Of the three bicycles, two were ladies': these were taken over by Sita and Beena. Madan took the man's.

For the first mile the road climbed steeply, so there was no question of anyone cycling. When they came to the flat stretch they noticed that there were no carriers on any of the cycles. The only possible way Champak, who could not cycle, could get a lift was by riding on the handlebar of Madan's. Nothing was said on the subject. But, instead of mounting their cycles, they went on walking. Madan was in great form. He made funny remarks about the people they passed—in Punjabi about the English and in English about the Punjabis.

Mashobra bazaar and hotel was crowded with holiday makers so they went a little farther to an old rest house in the midst of pine trees. Madan found an isolated spot above the roads. They hauled their cycles up the hillside and flung themselves on the bed of the pine needles.

They ate their lunch and again spread themselves on the

ground for an afternoon. It was pleasant lying in the sun, breathing the warm, resiny odour of the pines and listening to the breeze soughing through the trees. There were a few white clouds. Lammergeyers circled lazily, high above in the deep blue of the sky. In the valley below a barbet started calling in its agitated, breathless way. Then a woman started to sing in a plaintive voice which seemed to fill the valley to the brim. Beena sat up to listen. She looked at her companions; they seemed to be fast asleep. She got up and quietly walked away in the direction from where the song was coming.

The hill woman stopped singing as soon as she saw Beena and began to call to her goats. 'Hurrieyeh . . . urrieyey. Aoh, aoh, aoh.' The goats paused in their grazing and looked up.

'Why have you stopped singing? I came to hear you.'

'What singing, Bibi? This is only to while away the time. We poor people can't go to the cinemas and learn new songs . . . aoh, aoh.' The goats looked up again, saw their mistress busy, and resumed their nibbling. The woman sat down on her haunches. She was old and full of wrinkles but her smile had the gay abandon of youth. She had a flat gold coin of the size of a rupee on one side of her nose and her arms were full of cheap glass bungles. 'What can we sing, Bibi,' she repeated. 'Aoh, urreieyh.'

'Your song was better than the songs in the films. Why don't you go on?' asked Beena sitting down at little distance from her. The old woman just looked down at her feet.

'Have you a family?' asked Beena to encourage the other to talk.

'Family? Don't ask me anything. Five daughters!' she replied, slapping her forehead. 'It was written on my forehead; I cannot grumble.' She smiled baring a set of pearl white teeth.

'What's wrong with having five daughters?'

The peasant woman spat on the ground between her legs. 'One has got to get them married; that costs money. We can't pay our debts and now we have to borrow more because the eldest is thirteen. We are marrying her off next month. You can't keep a young girl in the house, can you?' *You* must be married.'

'No, I am single.'

'You rich people have no worries. It's us poor folk who can't get enough to fill our bellies. Five daughters and nothing to give to any one of them.' She smacked her forehead again. 'It is all written there'—and she smiled again. Her worries did not last long.

Beena took off one of her gold bangles. 'Give this to your eldest for her dowry. And now sing me a song.' Beena flung the bangle on the ground.

The hillwoman picked it up and placed it on her open palms. 'Bibi! You are unmarried and will need it yourself. Take this back.'

'No! I don't take back anything I have given. Now sing.'

The woman came up to Beena, touched her feet, and began a loud sing-song of blessing. 'Bibi, may all your wishes be fulfilled! May you get a handsome bridegroom; may you be the mother of seven sons; may you . . . .'

'Stop! Stop!' laughed Beena. 'You have seven sons yourself; one will be enough for me. Now sing.'

'I will sing you a song of a young girl waiting for her lover.'

She began to hum. When she had the notes correct she put the palm of her hand across her left ear and started to sing. Once more her soft, plaintive voice rose above the roar of the stream and the crying of barbets and flooded the valley like the sunshine. Beena shut her eyes and listened to the invocation to the gods to grant a young girl's wishes: to bring her lover back home in time to hear to koel calling in the mango groves and see the rain falling in torrents; to make him take her till every part of her body was full of pleasure and full of pain.

The singing stopped suddenly. Beena opened her eyes. The old woman had drawn her veil. Beena looked up. There was Madan standing beside her. 'What sin have I committed that I should not be allowed to hear the singing?' he asked with a smile.

'*Hai Bhraji*, I didn't hear you. I thought you were asleep.'

'How can sleep come to me when you are away!'

Beena's face coloured up. The hillwoman got up, wrapped her grass in a bundle, and called to her goats. 'Aoh, aoh. Urrieyeh. Bibi, a thousand blessings on you. We will always pray for you.' She hurried down the hillside driving the flock of goats in front of her.

'Are you angry with me? You haven't spoken to me all day.'

Beena stood up. Madan took her hands in his and pressed them against his heart. 'You don't love me,' said Madan with a leer.

'How can you say a thing like that? I like you more than anyone else . . . I also like your wife and your sister. I am very fond of you all,' she replied. She could not bring herself to utter the word 'love.'

Madan let go her hands and assumed a very hurt expression. 'Let's go back.'

'Please don't be angry with me,' pleaded Beena. She came up to his side and took his hand. He did not reply; he withdrew his hand from hers and started to walk back. 'Please don't be angry with me, *Bhraji*, please!' she pleaded tearfully. 'I'll do anything you want me to do, but don't be cross with me. I will do anything . . . .

Madan stopped and turned to her. He held her firmly by her arms. 'You swear you will do anything I ask?'

'I swear.'

'Come to my room tonight when everyone is asleep.'

&

Later in the afternoon more clouds appeared in the sky and a black wall came up on the southern horizon. There were flashes of lightning which could be seen across the bright sunlight.

'I think the monsoon is here at last. We should get back home before it starts,' said Sita.

They sat up and saw the black clouds towards the south looking like a range of mountains. The cicadas had begun to call. Then the bells of St Crispin's Church in Mashobra began to toll for evensong.

'We must have tea at the Gables Hotel,' said Madan. 'They have excellent sandwiches and cakes. They charge you just the same whether or not you eat them.'

'In which case we better eat all they give us,' said Champak laughing. 'We have no dinner ready and it will be too late to cook anything.'

They got their things together and began to walk homewards. The road was too rough to cycle and was crowded with people going to the Gables Hotel for tea. By the time Madan found a table and got a bearer to serve them, the wall of black clouds from the southern horizon had spread over the sky and a strong breeze sprung up. People started to leave. Rickshaw coolies and syces of horses were agitating to get their clients to move before the downpour started. They were amongst the last to be served. Madan

was in a bad temper. He did not mince his words with the bearer.
'You serve Indians after the English people have finished! Is their
money better than ours?'

The bearer grinned sheepishly. 'No, sir, for us all are the same.
They were in a hurry; it might start raining any moment.'

'Don't Indians get wet?'

The bearer shuffled his feet uncomfortably.

'Jao—go' roared Madan, 'get me the bill.'

Madan's outburst gave him a sort of right to command. He
proceeded to order everyone. 'I think you girls should be on your
way,' he told his sister and Beena. 'I shall be slower as I have to
bring Champak. We may catch you up at the Carpenters' Bazaar.
But don't wait for us. Go home and get something hot ready; tea
or something.'

The two girls got up. 'Don't go too fast,' warned Madan. 'The
road will be crowded with horses, rickshaws, and mule caravans.'

'We can look after ourselves,' replied Sita. 'Don't be too long.'
They waved a farewell and left on their cycles.

Madan scrutinized the bill carefully before paying. When the
bearer brought him his change, he left a large tip on the plate and
asked for a packet of cigarettes. The bearer brought him the
cigarettes. Madan lit one, stretched his legs on another chair, and
relaxed. After everyone had left, he stubbed his cigarette, looked
up at the sky. 'We'd better be moving,' he said at last and got up.

They walked up the road to the Mashobra bazaar and stopped
to survey the scene. The twilight was rapidly sinking into the night.
Across a range of hills, the lights of Simla sparkled in stellar
profusion all over Jacko Hill. Shopkeepers were putting up the
shutters of their shops; smoke oozed through the crevices of the
wooden planks smelling of wood and spices and tobacco. There
were muffled sounds of the hubble-bubble of the hookah, of
coughing and spitting and subdued conversation. The chirping of
millions of cicadas was like the deafening roar of a waterfall.

Madan folded his raincoat over the bar of his cycle and
smoothed it with his hand. Champak came on the other side. He
put his arm around her waist and gently raised her on to the
raincoat. He put his right leg across to the other side and got on the
saddle. Once more he put his arm round Champak's waist and
brought her closer to him till her head touched his chin and her

thighs were between his knees. He let the cycle roll down the hill.

They had hardly gone a hundred yards when it began to rain.
'We will get wet,' said Champak turning her face backwards.

'We'll stop under the cliff which is sheltered from rain.'

When they came to the cliff, they saw many people with bicycles, taking shelter. Madan slowed down but did not stop. 'I know a house farther down the road which has an arched entrance thickly covered with wild roses; that will be better.'

The house was another half-mile. By the time they got to it their clothes were completely wet. Madan put the bicycle against the wall and opened the gate. They went in and stopped under the arch made by the creeper. There were no roses, but honeysuckle, which grew with it, was in full bloom. Its acid-sweet smell was heavy in the dark, leafy tunnel.

'I am absolutely drenched,' said Champak holding out her shirt in the middle. 'How foolish of us to sit on the raincoat instead of wearing it. You put it on before you catch a chill.'

'We can share it,' answered Madan. He spread the raincoat over his shoulders and put his arms around her waist. She leaned back and let her head rest on his chest.

'Your shirt is soaked,' she said turning back. She opened the slit below the first button and drew her finger across his chest. 'You will catch a cold,' she murmured turning away from him and pressing her head back on to his chest.

'You are also wet,' replied Madan in a whisper. He undid the top button of her shirt and let his hands slip on to her warm, rounded breasts. She turned her face up to him; their mouths met with hungry passion. Madan gently pushed her against the wall on the side and kissed her on her eyes and glued his lips on hers. The breath in his nostrils became heavy.

Champak wriggled out of his grasp: 'What will the girls say if we are late?'

'What will they say? They must have been held up by the rain! What else?' He waited for her reaction. She flung her arms about his neck and bit him fiercely on the nose. Madan kissed her on her nose, chin, and neck; then buried his face between her breasts. She pushed him back. 'Not here,' she whispered. 'Somebody will see us.'

Madan became impatient. As he moved towards her his

shoulder brushed against a pole supporting the arch on which the roses and honeysuckle grew. A heavy shower of raindrops came down from the leaves. 'You see,' said Champak laughing, 'the gods also say not here. Come along.'

Madan caught her by the arm. Before he could pull her towards him, a tinkle of bells came round the corner and a line of mules carrying wooden crates filed past. The muleteers coming behind paused by the gate and then moved on. They had hardly gone out of view when half-a-dozen rickshaws came round the bend. There was more tinkling of bells. 'Hosh . . . bacho,' shouted the coolies as they ran past on their bare feet.

'Even the coolies say, "Careful . . . keep off," said Champak teasing. 'If you behave like a good boy, I will come to your room after the others have gone to bed.'

≈

Sita and Beena did not wait at the Carpenters' Bazaar and went on home to get out of their wet clothes. They changed into their nightdresses and made themselves some tea. Madan and Champak came in an hour later.

'We stopped under the cliff hoping the rain would stop. It was jammed with people. So we came on,' said Champak holding up the hem of her shirt to show how wet it was.

They went to their rooms to change. Madan came back wearing his full-sleeve sports sweater and white flannel trousers. Champak joined them a few minutes later. She wore a bright red kimono. She had put on a fresh paint of lipstick and loosened her long black hair about her shoulders. 'Absolutely wet,' she explained, running her fingers through it and tossed it back. She settled down on the sofa and crossed her legs lotus fashion like a female Buddha.

They had their tea and discussed the monsoon. Beena didn't say a word. Madan lit a cigarette. He did not know how to put her off. Should he take her aside and apologize to her for having made the unbrotherly proposal in a rash moment? Before he could make up his mind Champak yawned and got up. 'I don't know about you people, but I am very sleepy. It is this fresh air and the rain. *Sat Sri Akal.*' Sita and Beena who shared a room also left. Madan got up with a sigh. Beena, he decided, was not the sort who came into men's bedrooms. He switched off the lights in the house and retired to his room.

Beena turned on the table lamp and saw a letter from her mother lying beside it; the servant had left it there. She got into bed and tore open the envelope. As usual, most of it invoked the Guru's blessings for someone or other. In the end she mentioned how the monsoon had burst the night before the first of Sawan and how cool it had become. Then followed the passage from the Granth:

> O, Black Buck, why lovest thou
> The pasture of fenced-in fields?
> Forbidden fruit is sweet but for a few days
> It entices and ensnares
> Then leaves one sorrowing . . .

There was a postscript asking her to read it to Champak and also to write back soon and give a detailed account of how they were getting on in Simla and whether or not Madan's wife had joined them.

Beena put the letter under her pillow and switched off the table lamp. The confusion that already existed in her mind became worse confounded. The desire to go into Madan's room brought a feverish longing in her body. It was followed by visions of Madan's wife and child; and the hot perspiration turned cold and froze on her. Then came the figure of Madan in his cream-coloured, hand-knitted sports sweater and flannel trousers—tall, handsome, and overpowering—stripping her and taking her as a man should take a woman; and the fever wracked her system. Once more the implications of what would follow—her mother's cold censorious eyes, the words in the letter burning through the thickness of the pillow . . . 'Forbidden fruit is sweet but for a few days. It entices and ensnares, then leaves one sorrowing.' The images followed each other in quick succession, alternately rousing hot passion and immersing her in cold water. After an hour of sleepless tossing in bed, her mind became possessed by one figure, a mammoth one, of Madan smoking, smiling, and beckoning her. Others receded to a dim background and the fever took complete possession of her.

She heard Sita's steady breathing. She whispered her name

several times to make sure. She got out of her bed, picked up the letter from under the pillow, and tiptoed out of the room. She decided to see if Champak were also asleep. She could say she had just seen her mother's letter and brought it to give to her.

The rain fell on the corrugated tin roof with a deafening roar and drowned all sounds of creaking wood and opening and shutting of doors. Beena called softly to Champak and then tiptoed to her bed. It was empty; even the bedcover had not been removed. She went to the adjoining bathroom and slowly pushed open the door; it too, was empty. She tiptoed through the sitting-room to Madan's room. The door was shut. She put her palms gently on it and pressed. It was bolted from the inside. She put her ear against it and heard sounds of human voices. She stood rooted to the ground like a statue. All longing turned to cold, sickening hate. She went back to Champak's bedroom and left her mother's letter on the pillow. She opened her bedroom door and went out on to the balcony. She stood in the pouring rain staring steadily at Madan's window. An hour later a light came on in his room and was extinguished a few minutes later. Another light came on in Champak's room which also went off after a couple of minutes. And all was dark and silent save the thunder of rain on the roof.

❧

The meeting with Taylor did not help to settle the issue for Sher Singh; it only introduced an element of fear to the confusion that already existed. At the two extremes were the Deputy Commissioner and the terrorists: one stood for the status quo with the power to maintain it; the others, for change and the insecurity that is the price of change. In the case of terrorism, the price could be one's life. Presiding over the two extremes was his father with his conveniently dual morality: 'Keep up with both sides.' For him loyalties were not as important as the ability to get away with the impression of having them. To be found out was stupid, even criminal. There was also his temper, of which Sher Singh was as scared as he was of the police. He had his tacit approval of his association with the Nationalists, but he knew that if Buta Singh learned that he had got mixed up with the terrorists, his father would disown him and throw him out of the house. In addition to

257

these factors, there was his own temperament. Despite his love for his country, he knew he was not the sort who ever burnt his bridges himself.

On the point of principle, Sher Singh felt that his mind was quite clear: he was a Nationalist and although he had worn a silk suit and tie when he called on the Deputy Commissioner, that was to save Taylor's feelings. Or was it the fear of his father? He could have told Taylor that he did not believe in the hocus-pocus of traditional Sikh loyalty to the British. In proportion to their numbers, more Sikhs had gone to jail and to the gallows in the freedom movements than those of any other community in India—Hindu, Muslim, or Christian. In any case, talk of loyalty might have made some sense in the 19th century, it was beside the point in 1942.

Britain had to get out of India herself, or be kicked out, and Sher Singh would say that to Taylor's face. Could he? What about his father's views, his career in the service, and his hope of finding his name in the next Honours list? And the unique honour he was getting in the way of an armed police guard outside his house—the sentry who sprang to attention and smacked the butt of his rifle even when Sher Singh passed by with his college friends? Couldn't it somehow happen that these opposing factors would be combined into one harmonious whole? He visualized scenes where his Nationalist and terrorist colleagues honoured him as their beloved leader, where Taylor read an address of welcome, and his father proudly looked on. Such were the dreams with which Sher Singh tried to dope himself. They were based on the non-discovery of one party by the other.

Sher Singh tried to dismiss the cartridges on the Deputy Commissioner's table from his mind. Taylor was known to shoot; they could be from his own rifle. And many people liked playing with empty shells. He tried to reassure himself that a village headman wouldn't dare to report against the son of as powerful an officer as Buta Singh. Deep inside him he also knew that there were flaws in his reasoning. There was evidence to prove that he was being watched. A new sentry had replaced the old one.

The new sentry was politer than the last one and even saluted visitors who came to the house. He asked their names and business before letting them enter. He also became friendly with Shunno and Mundoo, and both the servants got into the habit of gossiping with him when they were free from work. Then one of the terrorists let him down. He used to come to see Sher Singh off and on and was known to Mundoo. One day he turned up with a false beard and moustache and wearing dark glasses. He announced himself to the sentry by a Muslim name. Even the thirteen-year-old Mundoo recognized him. Before Sher Singh could make up his mind whether or not to tell Mundoo not to talk about it to the sentry, the boy had done so. This was the last straw.

Sher Singh decided to get rid of the arms till suspicion had been allayed. But his troubles had only begun. He tried to arrange a meeting. None of the boys would agree to have it in his own home. One had a sister getting married; another had just lost his aunt and there were mourners in the house. One's father was already suspicious; another was sure his house was watched by the police. Sher Singh asked them to meet on the canal bank outside the town and come on their own cycles. They grumbled about the heat and the distance and only agreed when Sher Singh lost his temper and gave them a sermon on the greater battles to come. But neither the sermon nor the bad temper would persuade them to take over the illicit arms and keep them in their homes. 'They are safer in your house than ours. No one will dream that Sardar Buta Singh's son can be a terrorist, no one will dare to search a magistrate's home.' Sher Singh repeated with exasperation that he was wanting to remove the arms precisely because he was already under suspicion. They offered him much advice but refused to budge from their position: 'They have to be with either you or Madan; and Madan is away.'

Sher Singh left them, raging and cursing wildly. He realized later that by his behaviour he had turned fellow conspirators into potential informers. If there were trouble he would be the only one involved. The headman, and perhaps Taylor, knew only of him; the arms were also in his possession. He simply had to get rid of them.

He decided to throw everything into the well in the garden, then changed his mind because it was too obvious a place and the first thing anyone looking for the arms would do would be to send a man down into the well. He planned to put them in the jeep and dump them into the canal. Before he could do anything about it, the jeep was taken away. The driver said that it was wanted for emergency service elsewhere. He could not risk taking the stuff in a taxi or a tonga and once more he reverted to the plan of throwing them into the well. One evening he went out to reconnoiter. He discovered that the sentry who stood by the gate all day, slept by the parapet of the well at night. So the rifles, pistols, and hand grenades remained where they were. Sher Singh just tried to forget their existence.

Then the village headman came to call on him.

ॐ

Buta Singh had strong views about people coming to see him in his house—particularly if they were unimportant. His principle was that the only place for business was the office: the home was for rest and the family. 'Otherwise,' he used to say, 'fellows not worth the price of a broken shell could destroy the peace of the home.' He had issued instructions to his servants to tell callers to see him at the law courts. Naturally he was angry when Mundoo casually announced at breakfast, 'Sardarji, there is a peasant waiting to see you. He has been waiting since the morning. He says he has come all the way from his village.'

'Haven't I told you a hundred times not to allow peasants in the house! Tell him to see me at the courts.'

'Not you, Sardarji. He wants to see the small Sardarji,' answered Mundoo turning to Sher Singh.

'Me? What peasant wants to see me?' Sher Singh got up from the table and went out to the verandah. He saw the village headman sitting by the gate talking to the sentry. After a few moments of reflection he went back to join his parents at the breakfast table. Before they could ask him any questions, he ordered Mundoo to take a tumbler of buttermilk and some chapattis for the visitor.

'Who is the man?' asked Buta Singh.

'Just a villager we met when we were out on the canal bank one day. He was very good to us and gave us tea and food.'

'We? Who's we?'

'Madan and I.'

'Of course! One should always return hospitality,' said

Sabhrai, backing her son.

'That is all right,' said Buta Singh, 'but one should not encourage these people too much. They always try to take advantage.'

Buta Singh went off to the law courts and Sabhrai to the kitchen. Sher Singh stayed on to plan his line of approach. He felt cross with Madan for having got him into this mess and having gone away to Simla. But there it was and he had to face the situation alone. At least he could find out whether or not this fellow had told the police or Taylor about the shooting of the crane and given the Deputy Commissioner the fired bullets. He would have to be tactful. Perhaps the best approach would be to give him hope of getting something or other from Buta Singh and keep him hoping till things were easier.

Sher Singh opened the offensive with an enthusiastic greeting. '*Wah, wah,*' he exploded warmly, 'you are sitting outside and this your own home! Come inside.'

The headman had just finished the tumbler of buttermilk that Mundoo had brought him. He belched loudly and brushed his moustache with the back of his hand. He got up and made a quick move to touch Sher Singh's feet. Sher Singh stopped him half-way, put his arm round the other's shoulders, and conducted him to the sitting room. The headman left his shoes by the threshold and went in. He smoothed the sofa with his hands and slowly sank into it. Sher Singh sat down beside him. The headman took his host's hand in his. 'What wonderful palaces you live in,' he exclaimed, looking from the carpet, to the pictures on the walls, the radio set covered in embroidered velvet, up to the whirring ceiling fan.

'What palace? This is our poor home that you have blessed by putting your feet in it. Tell me what service I can do for you. More buttermilk or tea? Our buttermilk is not as good as yours. You get the best milk, butter, and yogurt.'

'Sardarji, there is no *ours* and *yours*; it is all given by the Great Guru, the True Emperor. You order me and I will bring you an excellent milch buffalo—twenty seers of milk a day and thick with cream. Next time I come I'll get you a tin of pure clarified butter. Your heart will rejoice.' He squeezed Sher Singh's hands with great affection.

They talked of the joys of village life, of crops and cattle. Sher

Singh got no closer to the real subject. His patience began to run out; he glanced at his watch.

'You working people!' exclaimed the headman giving Sher Singh another sympathetic squeeze. 'You have to go somewhere. I only came to have a sight of you. Now I have been blessed with that, I can return happily.'

Sher Singh sniggered; then came to the point—first with the bait. 'If you want my father to do anything for you, tell me. I can speak to him. If you want to be on the panel of assessors in Sessions trials, or entitled to a seat at the Commissioner's durbars, or anything like a gun licence . . . just anything.'

'Sardarji, all I want is your kindness. The Great Guru, the True Emperor, has given me all I want. I am a headman and an assessor; I am entitled to sit on a chair at formal occasions; I also have a gun and a pistol. I have cows and buffaloes; plenty to eat and drink and no debts to pay. If I want anything who else can I go to except you! All I want is your kindness.' He smacked Sher Singh on the thigh and added, 'All right, you go to your important business.'

'It isn't all that important,' answered Sher Singh. He knew he was losing the game; he had grossly underestimated the peasant's cunning. He made a headlong plunge. 'Friend,' he whispered, 'You didn't by any means tell Taylor Sahib about our shooting party of the other day?'

'I tell Taylor Sahib about you? Sardarji, how can you say such a thing?' The headman looked utterly scandalized.

'I know you couldn't have told against your brother. Taylor had empty bullets lying on his table and I thought they might have been mine.'

'Here, Sardarji, are the bullet cases,' said the headman untying the knot of a dirty handkerchief. There were three: on Taylor's table there were also three. Sher Singh had emptied his magazine which took six bullets. He stretched out his hand to take the cases. The headman withdrew the handkerchief and retied the knot. 'No, Sardarji, they are my property. They remind me of the lucky day when I met you.'

Sher Singh felt cornered and helpless. And that in an encounter with a slovenly Sikh peasant with a shaggy, unkempt beard; a rustic whose clothes were full of grease, whose skin had layers of dirt on it and whose head was undoubtedly full of lice.

'Sardarji, who were those Hindu boys with you that day?' asked the peasant again taking Sher Singh's hands in his.

'Friends,' answered Sher Singh. He wasn't going to give the fellow any more information even if they had let him down. 'They were not all Hindus,' he added quickly. He recalled introducing them with Muslim names.

The headman didn't seem perturbed. 'One of them was a gentleman; the tall chap in trousers . . . You know the boy who introduced us!'

'Yes, he is an important officer—a lieutenant in the army.'

'Wonderful!' exclaimed the headman. 'Big people like you should only have big friends.' After a short pause he remarked, 'He looked like a college boy.'

'Yes, he looks younger than he is.'

They sat in silence for some time. Sher Singh felt like ordering the fellow out of the house or having the servants beat him up. He decided to keep calm and make one more attempt to get round his adversary. He got up abruptly and went to his room. He came back with five ten-rupee notes stuffed in his trouser pockets. 'All right, Lambardarji, *Sat Sri Akal* . . . and here is a little present for your children from me.' He thrust the money in the headman's hands.

'Sardarji, what is this? I am your slave. I have no children and if I had any they would also be your slaves. You don't have to give me anything.'

'You have come to my house for the first time; you must have something, otherwise it will be an ill omen. Buy some sweets for your wife and relations.'

Fifty rupees proved too much for the Lambardar. He accepted them with lavish expressions of praise. 'You are an emperor . . . I shall always sing your praise.'

Sher Singh paid the money but the headman didn't give him a chance to ask for the return of the spent bullets. He kept up a flow of flattery till he left the house.

Sher Singh's illusions about Taylor not knowing of his activities were shattered. He also realized that he had paid the first instalment of blackmail money and many more would undoubtedly follow.

Chapter V

Sabhrai was possessed of that sixth sense which often goes with people of deep religious convictions. It had been proved so often that her family believed that she had some sort of intuition which told her of events to come. Once she had returned from her village many days before she was expected, just as her husband was being taken to the hospital for an emergency operation to have his appendix taken out; she had left long before the telegram summoning her had been delivered. Once again she had come to her son's bedside, who, in her absence, had been suddenly taken ill with typhoid fever. On her arrival she had not shown any surprise but behaved like a doctor who had been sent for and was expected to get down to his job straightaway. She had got down to hers at once: with softly murmured prayers and gentle ministrations of her hands which had the healing touch. There were many other instances. Perhaps they were mere coincidences to which men of science would attach little importance. Her family had learnt to know better. Therefore, when she suddenly declared her intention to go to her daughter in Simla, neither her husband nor her son asked her for the reason.

The monsoon had settled down to a routine of rain. People no longer risked sleeping in the open or on their rooftops; too often had a clear starlit sky suddenly become overcast and without warning it had begun to pour. Buta Singh, Sabhrai, and Sher had taken to sleeping in the verandah under a ceiling fan. Dyer slept on the floor beside his young master on a trough of sand on which water was sprinkled from time to time. The servants slept in the humid heat of their quarters.

Sabhrai always felt uneasy when all the members of her family were not with her. She talked about those who were away, wrote them long letters full of quotations from the scriptures and sermons to be good. She thought of them in her prayers—particularly with the last one she said before going to sleep. She was doing this the night before she announced her intention to go to Simla. She sat cross-legged in her bed telling the beads of her rosary. After the prayer she shut her eyes and thought of her family by turn. For many days her main concern had been her daughter, Beena. That evening she could think of nothing else and even at prayer her mind had strayed from her God and her Gurus to her daughter. When she went to bed the argument went on in her mind. Although Beena was not alone, she was unprotected. She could be the victim of Madan's wiles. Madan's wife had probably not turned up in Simla. Even if she had, she was not likely to be able to keep her husband straight. For some reason men were inclined to be more promiscuous when their wives were pregnant. Sabhrai tried to drown these ugly thoughts with more fervent praying. But they persisted and when she finally went to sleep somewhat exhausted, they turned into a nightmare. She dreamt that her daughter was being pursued by a band of hooligans wanting to ravish her and was frantically calling for help. As the pursuers gained ground, Sabhrai's agitation changed from dream to reality. When they bore upon her child, she yelled at them and opened her arms to protect her daughter. One of them tried to kiss Sabhrai by force. She began to moan. Dyer got up and came to her bedside and sniffed enquiringly in her ear, then licked her on the nose. Sabhrai woke up with a start and smacked the dog on the face. Her husband and son also woke up.

'What is the matter?' asked Sher Singh turning to his mother.

'This Dyer of yours. He puts his cold nose against my face. Don't know what's come over him.'

Dyer was told off by all three and slunk back to his place. Father and son resumed their snoring. Sabhrai returned to her prayers.

At the breakfast table next morning she was quieter than usual. When her husband and son had finished discussing the morning's news, she said, 'We haven't heard from Beena for some days.'

'She must be having a good time. After examinations no one wants to be worried with reading or writing—not even letters,' answered her son.

The concern on Sabhrai's faced indicated that she had other things on her mind.

'You must be imagining she is ill. No one falls ill in the hills,' assured Buta Singh.

'Has Madan's wife joined them in Simla?' she asked.

'I don't know, but I can find out,' answered Sher Singh.

'I would like to know.'

Neither father nor son followed the trend of her thoughts. That evening when Sher Singh told her that he had found out from Wazir Chand's house that Madan's wife was still with her parents, Sabhrai stated firmly, 'I should go to Simla.'

'I asked Wazir Chand myself,' replied Sher Singh somewhat nonplussed. 'He said Madan's wife would rejoin her husband after having her baby which is expected in a month or two.'

After a pause, Sabhrai repeated: 'I ought to go to Simla. Beena wants me.'

'Why do you get so bothered and impatient?' protested her son. 'Champak is there; so are Sita and Madan. And if there were anything wrong, they would send us a telegram.'

'No, I will go tonight.'

To such determination there was no answer. It only aroused apprehension: anything that could bother Sabhrai so much was not to be trifled with. Buta Singh waited for his son to volunteer to accompany his mother. Sher Singh did not look up from his plate. 'All right,' said Buta Singh at last, 'I will send one of my orderlies with you.'

ॐ

Sabhrai reached the house in Simla as the siren boomed across the hills and valleys to announce the middle of the day. She found the doors and windows wide open with no one about. She left the orderly to haggle with the rickshaw coolies and went in. The sitting room had not been swept; the dinner table was littered with the remains of the morning's breakfast; one tea cup had cigarette stubs floating in a mixture of tea and ash. The next room was obviously her daughter-in-law's: on the table beside the bed was a photograph of her son. The door of the room beyond that was shut. Sabhrai opened it gently. One bed was empty; her daughter was fast asleep in the other. She had a woollen scarf round her neck and was breathing heavily through her mouth. Her nose was raw and there were marks of dried tears on her cheeks. She had a heavy cold.

Beena opened her eyes as Sabhrai's soft hand touched her forehead. Sabhrai sat down beside the pillow and took her daughter's head in her lap. Beena clutched her mother by the waist and burst into tears. Sabhrai began to chant:

'The True, The True
The Great Guru.'

The mother pressed her daughter's head as she chanted. The girl cried, sobbed, sighed, and then fell silent.

'You have no fever?'

Beena shook her head.

'When did you catch the cold?'

'Night before last. We were all drenched.'

'The True, The True
The Great Guru.'

Sabhrai was still with her daughter when Madan and the two girls returned. She heard the servant tell them of her arrival and Madan's loud guffaw, '*Wah ji wah*! It is our good kismet that has brought auntie to our home. Where is she?'

'I will get news of my Sardarji,' added Champak jovially. 'He is such a bad correspondent.'

The three came into the bedroom, led by Madan. They bowed to her to receive her blessings

'Auntie, you did not write about your coming: I would have come to receive you at the taxi stand.'

'No, son, it was only yesterday that I decided to leave; there was no time to write a letter. And I do not like sending telegrams.'

They sat down on Beena's bed. 'First tell me the news of my Sardarji. Why didn't you bring him with you? I don't like it here without him. Now you have come, I can go back,' said Champak.

'Everyone is well. Sherji is very busy with whatever he is doing. He leaves early morning and seldom turns up for dinner.'

'He's got into the rut of leadership,' explained Madan. 'It is very demanding, but it will take him far, very far.'

Sabhrai changed the subject abruptly. 'Madanji, have you good news of your wife?'

'It is quite some time since she wrote,' he replied without any hesitation, 'but you know what girls are when they are with their mothers! All must be well otherwise I would have certainly heard.' He did not let Sabhrai pursue the subject further. 'Auntie, we must celebrate your arrival. I will take you all to Davicos for tea. They have a European band and all the world turns up. It will do Beena good; fresh air is good for a cold.'

Beena waved her hand to say no.

'I think I will stay with Beena,' said Sabhrai.

'Bibiji, you go, I will stay with her,' insisted Champak.

'No, no, no,' protested Beena angrily, 'I don't want anyone to stay with me. I have no fever. I will sit out in the garden in the sun. I don't want to meet people; I can hardly talk. My nose is clogged.'

'That's settled then,' said Madan triumphantly. 'I will book a table. We will steal some of the sandwiches and small cakes and bring them home for Beena.' He laughed at his own joke.

After lunch they left Beena at home and went out for tea. The sun had come out after two days and people came out of their homes as ants emerge out of their holes after rain. The Mall, on which the big stores and restaurants were, was crowded. The Viceroy sped past in his Rolls Royce. The Muslim Chief Minister of the Punjab strode down the slope like an elephant at a ceremonial prade; he wore a white turban whose stiffly starched plumes waved in the air. He was surrounded by a horde of bowing and scraping ministers and civil servants. Behind him followed a train of liveried coolies, bearing his crest on their blue turbans, pulling brightly polished rickshaws. Fashionable women, both English and Indian, strolled about showing off their clothes and exuding expensive French perfumes. Batches of college students went up and down the three hundred yard stretch of road displaying their college badges and eyeing girls. It was like a fashion parade where everyone was both the mannequin and the audience. Madan had his admirers all along the route. He stopped every few yards to greet them and exchange the three stock questions which people ask each other at holiday resorts: 'When did you come up? Where are you staying? How long will you stay?' And then rejoined Sabhrai and the girls.

Davicos Restaurant was jammed. The air was thick with cigar smoke, perfume, and the smell of whiskey. Sabhrai drew one end of her shawl across her face.

The steward conducted them to their table at the farther end of the hall close to the orchestra. Madan surveyed the room, waved to the people he knew, and sat down. 'Auntie, you would hardly believe there is a war on and these English chaps are getting the beating of their lives,' he said to Sabhrai.

Champak answered, 'When they work, they work hard. When they have a good time, they have a really good time. So my Sardarji says.'

'You don't know what the Germans and the Japanese are doing to them! And so far they have had the Indians to go to the front to receive the enemies' bullets. That won't last for long. When it starts here, they will forget about having a good time; then they will think of their maternal grandmothers.'

Sabhrai looked up sharply. Before she could speak, the bearer came with the tray of teacups and started laying them out on the table. A soon as he left, Madan started again, 'Auntie, you think we Indians can do nothing! Wait and see what happens; you just wait and see. We will give them a shoe-beating such as they have never had before.'

Sabhrai did not want to be rude to Madan; nor let him get away with saying things she did not like. She remonstrated gently, 'Son, your father and uncle would not like to hear you talk like this.'

'Auntie, you have old-fashioned ideas.'

'I am an old woman.'

They had their tea without further conversation. Madan turned his chair away to look at the crowd and resumed waving and smiling to his friends.

The setting sun broke through the clouds and came streaming through the large bay windows of the restaurant. It was a magnificent view. Immediately below them was the unshapely mass of gray and red of the tin roofs of Simla's bazaar. Kites dive-bombed into the narrow streets and reappeared with food in their talons. They fought in the air and went whirling down in pairs. Beyond the bazaar yawned an enormous valley with its terraced fields and tiny farm houses; in the centre of the valley was a silver stream with its banks flecked with white where the washermen had spread their clothes to dry. Beyond all these were the vast plains of Hindustan with the river Sutlej winding its way through the golden haze like a gilded serpent. The sun went down behind a range of low hills. The twilight spread over the city and the mountains like the hand of benediction. Some English people came across with their whiskey glasses to admire the scene; many Indians followed their example.

Sabhrai got up. She did not like to be surrounded by people smoking and drinking. The evening star was up in the deep blue sky and it was time for prayer once more.

The bill had to be paid so Madan suggested their going ahead. Champak volunteered to stay and come with him; it was her only chance to agree to explanations if any were called for. Sita went home with Sabhrai.

Madan and Champak came out in the brightly lit and crowded street. They went across to the ridge which was less crowded. There were many benches on the sides but they were all occupied.

'Can't we find any place where we can be alone for a few minutes?' asked Champak, taking Madan's hand.

'Let us go to the tennis club,' he replied. 'After dark there is no one there.' He marvelled at the woman's daring.

They went down a steep road and came to the Club. The courts were absolutely dark and deserted. They found a bench and sat down. Madan pulled Champak onto his lap. He pressed his lips on hers and his hands sought the cord of her trousers. Champak pushed him back rudely and stood up. 'I did not come for this,' she hissed angrily. 'I am not a bazaar woman who sleeps with men in the open.'

'I am sorry,' replied Madan tamely. 'I thought you wanted to say something to me alone.'

'Say, not do,' she replied. She sat down beside him and took his hand in hers. She put her head against his shoulder. 'I am so worried and you don't care at all.'

'What are you worried about?'

'Why do you think the old woman has turned up suddenly?'

'I don't know. But why should that worry you?'

'You don't know her. She gets to know things that no one else knows. Besides, I think Beena suspects and she may tell. I am going mad, I will kill myself?' Tears rolled down her cheeks. 'Why did I do it? Why, why, why!' she sobbed.

'Why does Beena suspect?'

She told him of the letter left on her pillow the night she had come to him.

Madan put his arm round her shoulders and kissed her on the ear. 'Beena will never tell. You take it from me, never.'

'How are you so certain?' she asked, looking up with her tear-stained eyes.

Madan kissed her tears away. 'Because she wanted to come to me herself. I did not agree. She can never say a word against you.'

Champak's concern changed to anger. 'The slut! How can she raise her eyebrows at me? Or her old, pious mother point an accusing finger at me?'

'I told you no one can say anything.' Madan raised her on his lap and once more his hands went exploring. They did not meet any resistance—nor any response.

'Nevertheless I have been bad. It was absolute madness.' She kissed him on his lips and got up. 'No more of this. Never again.'

271

Chapter VI

In the absence of Sabhrai, Shunno automatically became the mistress of the household. She played her role well. She pandered to Buta Singh's whims and mothered Sher Singh. She also resumed bullying Mundoo. She nagged him all the time and occasionally smacked him. With no one left to complain to, Mundoo decided to repeat the trick which had earlier on put Shunno out of action for twenty-four hours. At the end of a day when he had enough of Shunno's tongue—she had even pulled his ears till he had screamed—he took all the gum and red ink from Beena's table and emptied it into Shunno's jug of water.

Shunno took her responsibilities seriously. Despite the recurrence of the mysterious disease, she attended to her master's breakfast, prepared the dinner, and told Mundoo to warm it before serving it. She asked for permission to be absent for the day. Buta Singh was too well-bred to ask a woman questions about her illness. He offered to get a doctor from the municipal hospital. But Shunno did not believe in Western-trained doctors and their bitter medicines. She had faith in vaids and hakims brought up on ancient Indian and Arabic systems. She had more faith in the prescriptions of holy men who combined spiritual ministrations with medicine. Peer Sahib was such a man.

&

Peer Sahib was a young man under thirty years of age. He had inherited the guardianship of the tomb of an illustrious ancestor—respectfully referred to as Hazrat Sahib—who had made many converts to Islam in days gone by. Hazrat Sahib had lived in the open under a jujube tree. When he died he was buried under the shade of the same tree and his tomb became an object of worship. People came from distant towns and villages and it started drawing a handsome income in offerings. The mud and brick of the tomb was replaced by marble slabs and a red headstone with a niche for an oil lamp. Then a large brick courtyard was built to enclose it. And, finally, rooms were put up for the guardian of the shrine who was always chosen from amongst the descendants of the Hazrat Sahib's brothers. The incumbent had to devote himself to the study of the Koran, the Traditions, Islamic law, and medicine. He also had to remain celibate, and succession went from uncle to nephew.

Like his predecessors, Peer Sahib spent most of the day praying and giving spiritual guidance to the men and women who flocked to the tomb. He did not know much about medicine, but since most of the people who came to consult him were more sick in mind than in body, he was able to minister to their needs His following, though largely Muslim, had also a sprinkling of Hindus and Sikhs.

Shunno had chosen a good day to call on the Peer Sahib. The three-day celebrations of the anniversary of the illustrious ancestor's death had ended and the crowds had departed. There were only a few people sitting under the shade of the jujube tree which was alive with the twittering of sparrows. The tomb was draped in a green cloth on which were strewn rose petals and copper coins. The courtyard was littered with paper and crumpled plates made of leaves sewn together. Seventy-two hours of non-stop singing, dervish dancing, prayer, and sermon, had left everyone and everything exhausted. Shunno joined the group by the grave.

'Peer Sahib is asleep. He won't be up for a long time,' said one of the women. 'The anniversary of the Hazrat Sahib's ascent to heaven ended yesterday, and Peer Sahib is very tired.'

'I will wait. I have come a long distance from the city.'

An hour later, Peer Sahib emerged from his room in the corner of the courtyard. He was a tall, wiry man with closely cropped hair. Unlike most Muslim divines, he did not grow a beard; only a scissor-trimmed stubble spread from one ear to the other. He had a thin moustache which fell below his chin on either side in the fashion of the Mongol, Genghis Khan. He wore large earrings and a necklace of amber beads the size of pigeon eggs over his black silk shirt. He was handsome in an austere sort of way—high cheek bones and sunken eyes. He had no loose flesh over his big, bony frame. Women found him compelling since he carried an air of spiritual disdain towards their sex.

He filled his brass jug from a pitcher which stood on a stool beside his door and washed his face. He gargled noisily and spat the water on the wall; then splashed more water on his head, face, and hands and held up his hands in the air to dry (the Prophet had never used a towel). He came to his congregation praising Allah in his rich, bass voice.

'Salaam, Peer Sahib; may Allah bring plenty to you,' exclaimed the Muslims and put offerings of a few pice each on the tomb. Shunno touched the holy man's feet and placed something wrapped in a towel in front of him. Peer Sahib looked away. Shunno removed the towel and uncovered a silver plate with slices of coconut and five shining rupees.

Five rupees was many times more than the measly copper pice the faithful had offered. Peer Sahib saw them from a corner of his eye; but he was not one to express interest in money—particularly when it came from an infidel woman. He looked up to the sky and said: 'May Allah be merciful to you, my daughter, and fulfil your wishes. The offerings are not for us; we have nothing to do with money. If you want to give something in the name of the Almighty, place it on the tomb of our revered ancestor, now sitting in the lap of Allah.'

Shunno did as she was told. It gave her a peculiar pleasure to have a man, young enough to be her son, call her daughter.

'It is time for our evening prayer. Ask what you have to ask; then we must devote ourselves to the praise of our Maker.'

The women asked what they wanted, got the Peer Sahib's blessings, and departed with their children and menfolk. Shunno waited until the last one had left; her troubles could not be mentioned in public.

'Daughter, what is it you desire?'

'You are a Man of God who can remove all affliction.'

'Allah is the remover of ills; we are only his slaves. What ails you, my child?'

Shunno only shifted her weight from one leg to another.

'We haven't much time. The sun is setting and we must pray. If it is a child you want, we will give you an amulet to wear when you are being intimate with your man. If Allah is pleased, your womb will fill again and again.'

Shunno blushed. She nearly fifty and children! How far this young man of God was from worldly things! Perhaps he did not know the first thing about sex. Such were the pure in heart!

'Peer Sahib, my man was summoned by the Great Guru thirty years ago,' she explained. 'I do not want to child. My troubles are of a different sort.' She drew her veil across her face and hurriedly whispered her ailment to the holy man. 'You are the only one who can cure me. I have no faith in English-trained doctors, nor in hakims or vaids. If you make me well, I will give you all you want. I will give marble for the headstone of the tomb of your great one.'

Peer Sahib pondered in silence.

'Daughter, this will need careful examination. Would you not rather see a lady doctor?'

'You are the knower of all secrets; what is it that I can hide from you? I have no fear.'

'Then wait till we have finished our evening prayer.'

The Peer Sahib bolted the door of the courtyard. He washed himself once more and faced west towards Mecca. He put his hands to his ears, turned his face to the heavens, and in his rich mellifluent voice beckoned the faithful to prayer. His voice floated across space with no one to hear it, for habitation was a long way off. Peer Sahib himself hearkened to his call and proceeded to whisper his prayer and go through the series of genuflections. He sat on his shins with his palms open as if he were reading them like an open book. He turned his face to the right and blessed those on his right side. He turned his face to the left and blessed the rest. He rubbed his face with his palms and stood up still praising Allah. The short twilight gave way to the night. The sparrows on the jujube tree were silent. Only the dogs barked in the distance.

Peer Sahib brought an earthenware lamp from his room, lit it, and placed it in the niche in the headstone of the tomb. He whispered yet another prayer for the peace of the departed soul, again holding his hands in front of him like an open book. He went back and brought another oil lamp. 'Daughter, let us see your trouble,' he said holding the lamp up to his shoulder.

'Here? In the open?'

'The door of the courtyard is shut. No one comes here after sunset.'

'If you look away, I can take my clothes off.'

The Peer Sahib turned his face to the wall. Shunno undid the cord of her trousers and underwear and slipped them below her knees. She laid herself on the floor beside the tomb and covered her face with her hands.

'See.'

The holy man turned and saw a fat middle-aged woman lying bare from the navel to her ankles. He held the oil lamp in his left hand and sat down beside her. The aroma of jasmine and sweat filled his holy nostrils; the infidel woman had perfumed her privates. '*Aaoozo Billabé Minash Shaitanur* . . . I seek the protection of Allah from Satan,' said he getting down to his job, 'there is no power except that of God . . . *Allah Billah*.' With his large calloused, peasant's hands he stroked the soft flesh of the woman's under belly and the sides of her thighs. There was no visible evidence of any disease.

'Turn over.'

Shunno turned over baring her enormous wrinkled behind. The Peer Sahib's healing hands went gently over the sagging buttocks down to the back of her thighs and up again. He explored the depths with his fingers and saw what there was to be seen by the help of the oil lamp. He could not find a clue to Shunno's mysterious ailment.

'Turn over.'

Shunno complied once more. Peer Sahib came over and examined more carefully. His scrutiny was no longer confined to clinical ends. With the vows of celibacy to which he was committed, sex got little chance of natural expression. He had had to be satisfied with his own devices or occasionally take liberties with little boys sent by their mothers to learn the scripture. These were not the normally accepted expressions of sex and therefore did not violate the rules of celibacy as he interpreted them. Neither did intercourse with an infidel woman who might in this way be brought on the right path. And it was obvious she had come with something of the sort in mind. So the Peer Sahib put the other lamp also in his ancestor's grave and obliged.

Shunno made a nominal protest at the start: 'Na, na, someone will see,' and then accepted the inevitable. She had almost forgotten what sex was. Her instincts had been buried under a thick pack of conventional morality prescribed for a Hindu widow—religion, charity, gossip about sex, but no sex. Here was a man twenty years younger, strong and virile with an untamed lust savagely tearing off the padding of respectability with which she had covered herself. He stirred up the fires of a volcano which had all but become extinct. It was all wrong, but it was deliciously irresistible. It was like an itch which begs to be scratched till it draws blood.

The two lay on the hard brick floor of the starlit courtyard till the early hours of the morning with only the slumbering sparrows and the winking oil lamps on the Hazrat Sahib's tomb to witness the goings on. Not a word of affection or explanation passed between them.

Shunno repeated the visit several times with several shining sliver rupees. Her temper improved: she stopped nagging or beating Mundoo. Instead she brought him sweets from the bazaar. There was no reason for Mundoo to take recourse to bottles of gum and red ink.

The cure was a complete success.

ॐ

Neither her intuition nor her shrewd insight into human character gave Sabhrai a clue as to what had passed between Beena and Madan—or between Madan and Champak. For one, Beena's cold led her off the scent; she believed that it was her daughter's illness which had been mysteriously conveyed to her. And she was pleased to have yet another confirmation of the prowess of knowing whenever any member of her family needed her. For another, Madan completely won her heart with his attentions. At the breakfast table he read out the news and translated it for her in Punjabi. Her own family had hardly even taken any notice of her in their political discussions which were carried on exclusively in

English. When they went out, he preferred walking with her rather than with the girls. He introduced her, an old-fashioned Punjabi woman, to his college friends always adding: 'You know the mother of our future Chief Minister, Sardar Sher Singh.' It did not sound as if he were pulling her leg. Her suspicions were completely allayed. She settled down to enjoying the blue skies and the pine-scented air of Simla. She hoped that her husband and son would join her. But neither said anything about his plans. When the exam results were announced, there was an exchange of telegrams. Both the children had passed: Sita, as expected, in the first division and Beena in the third. From then on there was little communication between the family. But the days went by pleasantly.

A month later, events took place which not only shook the country but almost destroyed Sabhrai's family. Neither her sixth sense nor the Guru speaking through the Holy Book gave her any warning. She learnt of them from the headlines of the daily newspaper read out by Madan.

The fresh cold air of Simla had been getting the better of Sabhrai and she had been getting up later and later every day. One morning she had only finished her bath when the servant came in to say that breakfast was on the table. She did not want to keep her hosts waiting and decided to postpone her prayers.

Madan never smoked in front of Sabhrai. That morning he did not throw away the cigarette he was smoking nor get up from his chair. 'Listen to the rumblings before the earthquake, auntie,' said he, and proceeded to tell her of the breakdown in the negotiations between the British and Indian leaders. He told her that the Nationalists had called a meeting at Mahatma Gandhi's hermitage to decide on the next step. Meanwhile the police had begun arresting demonstrators; in Dacca alone over 700 had been arrested in one day. There had been riots in many towns.

He stubbed out his cigarette and lit another. 'These bloody English won't learn till they get a real shoe-beating,' he said angrily.

'Is there any trouble in the Punjab,' asked Sabhrai.

'There have been a few arrests including some in Simla yesterday. But no rioting or violence—not so far.'

'Not by the people perhaps, but by the police,' added Sita. 'Last evening I saw a boy volunteer—he couldn't have been more than fourteen or fifteen—come up the steps of the lower bazaar to picket an English store on the Mall. A European sergeant hit him full in the face. He fell and must have rolled down at least a dozen of those horribly steep steps when one of the crowd came to his help. The sergeant went down and arrested the picket as well as the man who had helped him. I saw them taken to the police station. The boy must have had some of his teeth knocked out; he was bleeding profusely. There was an uproar on the Mall and many shops closed in protest.' Sita seldom spoke this way. Her cheeks were flushed.

'Bastards,' muttered Madan in great anger.

After a pause Champak said: 'I suppose this will go on and on.'

'This sort of thing never stops,' replied Madan.

'Then I must get back to my husband. He mixes with such queer types and gets excited very quickly. Bibiji, don't you think I should go back? I will do exactly as you tell me.'

Sabhrai did not say anything. Champak sensed that her mother-in-law would not object. 'If you give me permission, I will leave tomorrow.'

'You have never travelled alone,' interrupted Sita. 'These are dangerous times; Madan Bhraji can go with you. We can look after ourselves for a few days.'

'No, no!' protested Champak. 'He can put me in a taxi. I am bound to meet somebody at the Kalka railway station who can see me home.'

'That is out of the question,' started Madan in a tone of authority. 'Of course, I will go with you. You are not the only one who wants to see Sherji; I also want to see my brother. He is doing all the work amongst the students and I am having a good time in Simla. I will send him up for a few days' rest.'

It was agreed that the two would leave the next day.

Madan went to the bazaar to book places in the taxi which was to take them down to the plains. Most of the Indian bazaar was shut. All European and some Muslim-owned shops on the Mall were open. Nationalist volunteers in Gandhi caps came up the long flights of stairs to picket them. Knots of people collected at a safe distance to watch.

Madan saw the scene narrated by his sister enacted before his eyes. Encouraged by the audience, one of the volunteers shouted defiantly, 'Victory to Mahatma Gandhi,' and waved his tricolour flag. A white sergeant walked up to him. The volunteer cowered down and covered his face with his arms. The sergeant hit him from below on the chin and sent him flying backwards down the steps. Two constables ran after him and brought him back handcuffed. His nose was bleeding and he cried like a child. Madan's blood boiled within his veins; his hands itched to get round the sergeant's throat.

All that afternoon and evening and the next day, till it was time to take the taxi, they talked nothing but politics. A national crisis had overtaken them and completely swamped their personal problems. Beena did not dare to sulk or even hint that Champak and Madan travelling together might cause people to talk. It seemed treasonable to mention such trifles—particularly when Madan seemed so concerned with the fate of his country and Champak so worried about her husband.

ॐ

Rumours of road blocks and attacks on trains had caused a lot of cancellations; Champak and Madan had the taxi all to themselves. The momentous events taking place in the country and their own secret desires seemed to create a conflict in their minds which made talking of either one or the other somewhat difficult. They sat in silence at the two ends of the rear seat looking at the mountainous scenery—the lush green hillsides and endless stretches of valley lost in the haze of tropical sunshine. Champak, who normally took this journey badly, was able to do the sixty miles of tortuously winding road without feeling sick. They came down from the cool breezes of fir and pine of the high Himalayas to the hot, dusty plains of the Punjab.

The railway station at Kalka was crowded with English soldiers and coolies. From the hill cantonments of Taradevi, Kasauli, Degshai, and Sanawar, British soldiers and officers had come down in lorry loads to go to distant towns to quell the disturbances which had broken out. The European refreshment room was packed with officers drinking iced beer under the mad whirl of ceiling fans. Madan, who had always preferred going there rather than to any of the Indian varieties (Hindu vegetarian, Hindu non-vegetarian, or the Muslims), went straight to the Hindu non-vegetarian. He asked Champak to order the dinner and went out to buy the railway tickets.

At the ticket booth he was informed that all the first and second class accommodations had been reserved for the officers and soldiers. In the inter and the third class there were no reservations—nor any privacy. Madan bought two seconds despite the clerk's warning that he would find no berths on the train. He went to the platform on which his train was standing. A group of Indian ticket collectors were busy checking reservations. Madan took the youngest by the hand, put his arm round his shoulders, and drew him away to a quiet spot.

'Brother, I have to have a second class coupé at any cost and you have to find it for me.' He slipped a ten-rupee note into the collector's hand.

The collector gave the note a quick glance and thrust it into his pocket. A ten rupee tip for a man whose monthly salary was 50 rupees was nothing to scoff at. Madan also looked familiar and important; he spoke with the tone of confidence which goes with authority. 'It is going to be extremely difficult,' replied the collector. 'The whole train is packed with British tommies; their reservations were made two days ago. But I'll try.' After a pause he asked. 'Are you by any chance Mr Madan, the famous cricketer?'

'The same, your humble servant,' replied Madan with a bow. They shook hands.

The collector took out the ten rupee note and put it back in Madan's hand. 'Keep this. Put your luggage in this second class coupé and I will put a reservation slip in your name.'

Madan forced the note back into the collector's pocket. 'What I give once I never take back. After all, getting British soldiers out of a train in these times is not easy. It needs a man of courage to do that.'

The flattery worked. 'Mr Madan, if you can hit them for sixers, I can write them down on my penis. You will say one day that you met Mussadi Lal, the ticket collector of Kalka. My name is Mussadi Lal.' He slapped his chest in a gesture of of defiance. They shook hands once more.

Mussadi Lal took out a key from his pocket and unlocked the glass frame alongside the door of the compartment. He took out the card marked 'Reserved for B.O.R.s No. 171/172,' tore it up and flung the bits in the air with contempt. He wrote out another one in the name of Mr and Mrs Madan and put it in its place.

'Here!' he said slapping his chest again. 'What will you say!' They shook hands a third time.

'Mr Mussadi Lalji, I'll sing your praises. If there were a few more brave people like you, India would have been free many years ago.'

The collector accepted the compliment; they shook hands for the fourth time and said goodbye.

Madan joined Champak for dinner. He ordered two bottles of beer and drank them in the Hindu refreshment room which had no licence to sell liquor nor a permit to allow consumption of alcoholic beverage. Madan was above these pretty rules and regulations; and now he was celebrating his victory over the British army.

He ate his dinner with relish and relaxed with a cigarette. When it was finished, he got up, took Champak by the elbow: 'Let's go.' On the way to the compartment he bought some betel leaves charged with lime paste, cardamoms, and scented betel nuts. He ordered a couple of iced bottles of lemonade to be left in the coupé and told the coolie to spread the bedding rolls on the berths. He left Champak to change while he took a stroll on the platform.

The train was due to leave at midnight but most of the upper class passengers had retired and put up the shutters of their compartments. The inter and third classes were also quiet with people dozing on each other's shoulders. The hawkers had packed up and left. The platform was deserted except for the railway staff.

Many soldiers were still in the refreshment rooms drinking beer when the guard's whistle summoned them to the train. They trudged out in the sweltering heat with their heavy packs on their backs and their Sten guns slung on their shoulders. Most of them found their berths indicated on the counterfoils they carried. Only two remained. They went up and down the platform peering at reservation slips to find one that matched their own. The engine driver blew the warning whistle. The soldiers began to shout for the guard. Instead of the guard, they found Mussadi Lal walking quickly away towards the end of the platform.

'Hey, you, Babu. Where's our berths?'

'Sir?'

'Them places to sleep on you know! *Charpoy bashin!*' One of them shut his eyes and put his cheek against his hand. 'Unnerstan?' The other showed him the counterfoil. Mussadi Lal examined it carefully and consulted the reservations in his book.

'Sir, I have no record of this reservation. There is no place on the train. You can go by the morning express.'

'Mawhnin? Wot you talkin Babu? Court martial if we don't get there tomorrer. Court martial you know?' The soldier unslung his Sten gun, stuck the nozzle in Mussadi Lal's belly and explained 'Tatatatatatattat—bang.' He fell back a step to indicate the effect of the firing. 'Unnerstan? Give us them berths or we'll stick the gun up your tail. Hurry-Juldi.'

The guard blew his whistle and waved his green lantern. The engine gave another blast and jerked the train into movement.

'Sir,' stuttered Mussadi Lal, 'there is no time now. I will ask the guard to let you sit in his compartment. He may find you a place at the next station.'

The tommies began to shout. 'We are fighting for the King and country. Our f . . . King and your f . . . country and you can't find a charpoy on this 'ere trayn?'

Many shutters were let down and genteel ears heard the inebriated tommies blaspheme and curse on the deserted platform. The shutters were quickly put up. The train began to gather speed.

'Where's the f . . . guard's van?'

Mussadi Lal and the two soldiers ran to the tail end of the train. The guard stood in the open door of his van. Mussadi Lal breathlessly explained to him in Hindustani, 'Let these whites who sleep with their sisters get in till they can find a place. They are drunk and may let off their guns. One never knows with these people!'

The soldiers leapt into the guard's van hurling insults to the King and country. Mussadi Lal waved them a goodbye and then shook his arm from the elbows to make an obscene gesture. 'Ride on my pony if there is no room on the train,' he roared.

The occupants of the soldiers' berths did not hear the abuse. The musical hum of the fan and the tipity, tipity, tap of the wheels beating time drowned all unpleasant noise. A cool breeze came through the shutters smelling of the green rain-washed forest.

Champak went into the bathroom and took a shower. She came back wearing her transparent kimono. She went to the window and let down the shutter. A gust of wind blew the kimono on either side, baring her from her feet to her waist. Her hair flew wildly like the snakes on Medusa's head. Madan got up, switched off the lights, and came towards her.

'Can't you bear to see me as I am? Why do you want it dark?'

Madan pressed the switch. Champak took off her kimono, tossed it on the rack and lay down on the berth.

'Now you can switch off the lights if you want to.'

Madan stared at the girl stretched out on the white bedsheet. He had never seen a woman like that—not even his own wife.

'Don't look at me like that; it makes me ashamed of my nakedness,' said Champak turning her back and hiding her face. 'You look as if you had never seen a woman.'

Madan switched off the light and came to her. 'No, I have never seen one with absolutely nothing on—never,' he said hoarsely.

'I still have my wrist watch.'

Chapter VII

Sher Singh saw the morning paper before his father. He read the news of the arrests of the Indian leaders and of the strikes and demonstrations taking place all over the country—except in the Pu.ıjab. At the breakfast table he read out the headlines to his father. They were discussing the consequences of the action taken by the Government when an orderly came with a message asking Buta Singh to come to Taylor's bungalow at once.

Sher Singh took the paper to the sitting room and scanned the details. As he went from page to page he realized that everywhere in India the people were protesting; only the Punjab was peaceful. He thought of his own inactivity. He too was doing nothing except lie on the sofa and get worked up. Just then Mundoo brought the post and handed him a letter. It was a cyclostyled circular in English with the caption, 'A Manifesto of the Hindustan Socialist Republican Army.' It drew attention to the arrests of the leaders and asked the youth of India to arise and rid themselves of foreign rule. It did not mince its words. 'Shoot English officials and the Indian toadies who serve them. Destroy roads and bridges; cut telegraph and telephone wires; create chaos and paralyze the administration. This is your sacred duty. Long live the revolution.' Sher Singh examined the postmark. The letter had been posted the evening before from the city. He had heard of the terrorist organization which went under the name of the Hindustan Socialist Republican Army but had never met anyone who belonged to it. Could someone have told them that Sher Singh was a secret sympathizer?

Sher Singh stayed at home and brooded. He listened to the news over the radio each time it came on. Each time it was the same story—demonstrations, violence, arrests everywhere—except in the Punjab. Wasn't it time for him to throw caution to the winds and strike a blow? He was like the rest of his countrymen, frittering away his energies in quarrelling with his colleagues. How could he get them to collaborate in any plan of action which required courage and daring for its execution? He spent that day and night in these thoughts and decided that the hour of trial had come. At some time or the other in their lives, men had to gamble with fortune. Those that won, became great; those that lost, lost; those that refused to take the chance, made up the mass of mediocrity.

Next morning one of the boys of his group turned up at the house. He walked straight into his room. 'Sher Singhji,' he said without a word of greeting or explanation, 'the time for quarrels is over, we have to do something.'

'Do what?' asked Sher Singh sitting up.

'Something or other. You are our leader, we will follow you.'

Sher Singh ran his fingers through his thin beard, pulled out some hairs and examined them thoughtfully. After a minute he answered, 'O.K. I will be in your house in half-an-hour. Ask the others to come too. Tell them to come at different times with books on their carriers; there are bound to be a lot of policemen about.'

A few minutes later, Sher Singh cycled out of the house with his hockey kit on the carrier behind him. In the bag were also six hand grenades which had been lying with him for many months.

All the boys who had taken part in the shooting practice were there; only Madan was missing. Since he was in Simla, and there was no time to waste, they got down to business. The first thing they did was to take on oath of secrecy. They spread out the Indian tricolour flag on the table and put their hands on it. Someone produced a picture of Mahatma Gandhi and set it in the centre.

'No, not Gandhi,' said Sher Singh. 'What has he to do with bombs and pistols? We are not launching a campaign of passive resistance. We will take the oath in the name of our martyrs. Have you a picture of Bhagat Singh?'

The host fetched a card with the photograph of the handsome, clean-shaven Sikh terrorist who had been hanged twelve years earlier and laid it on the flag. They took the oath to liberate their country from foreign rule. Then Sher Singh got down to explaining the line of action. 'The call is to destroy means of communication,' he said. 'A few bridges blown up, a few roads barricaded, and the British Army will be stuck where it is.'

'How is a bridge blown up?'

'They are heavily guarded. We'll have to kill many soldiers before we can tamper with a bridge.'

'I have never blown up a bridge,' replied Sher Singh, 'but we can learn. We will try our hand on something small and unguarded. I have six hand grenades. I am sure they will knock down one of the canal bridges. Later on we can have a go at a bigger one—perhaps a railway bridge.' Sher Singh opened his bag and showed them the grenades.

'What do you do with them?'

Sher Singh unfolded a piece of paper on which he had written down the instructions and read them out.

'Let us blow up the little bridge near where you shot the crane.'

'That's what I had in mind too,' agreed Sher Singh. 'It is in a deserted spot. We can test the power of these grenades without anyone bothering us.'

They agreed to go back to their homes and meet in the afternoon outside the city. Sher Singh decided to stay where he was rather than go back home and be seen again by the sentry at the gate of the house.

The group reassembled a few hours later and made for the canal. They wore coloured sports shirts and carried their hockey sticks. They passed many policemen on the way but no one took any notice of them. When they reached the bridge, there was still daylight. Some of the boys took off their clothes and jumped into the canal; others went with Sher Singh to examine the bridge. It was barely ten feet wide, made of red bricks. The thick layer of dried dung showed that it was mainly used by cattle. They came back and joined the bathers.

The sun set and the short twilight quickly darkened into night. There was no moon. It was silent except for the croaking of frogs. Sher Singh took out his flashlight and produced one of the grenades. 'I suppose the first honour goes to me,' he said gravely.

'Sure, leader. But tell us how it is done,' they said, closing round him.

They went down the canal embankment to take cover. Sher Singh stood up. He pulled out the pin of the grenade with his teeth, counted five, hurled it on the bridge, and sat down. The grenade bounced off the parapet and fell into the water with a loud splash and exploded. It sent a jet of water flying into the air. The next one, thrown by one of the other boys, exploded on the bridge and sent up the debris all round. So did the remaining four. The boys ran up through the dust and the smoke to see the damage they had caused. Sher Singh flashed his torch. There were big dents in the center of the bridge and the parapet had been knocked off at several places; but it was still serviceable. They mounted their bicycles and sped back as fast as they could.

Sher Singh went to the bazaar near the railway station where there was a row of eating places. He sat down on a steel chair on the pavement and ordered himself a plate of meat and raw onions; he ate onions to his heart's content when his wife was away. The cook slapped a few chapatties and baked them in the oven. Sher Singh had his dinner on the pavement along with a motley crowd of peasants and labourers, and listened to the music coming over the radio. He heard the nine o'clock news. He heard about the Allied victories in the face of Fascist advances and the calm in the country despite thousands of arrests. It did not irritate him any more. He knew they were lying.

Sher Singh got home after 10 p.m., his mouth still on fire from the chillies and raw onions he had eaten. Finding his wife at home was not a pleasant surprise. She made it unpleasanter. 'Hullo, hullo, when did you turn up? You did not send any word!'

Champak was too angry to talk. She just looked out of the window. Sher Singh came to her and put his arms round her shoulders. 'Don't be cross. How could I have known you were coming?'

'This is what you do when I am away.'

Champak covered her nose with her handkerchief; the reek of raw onions was overpowering. Sher Singh kissed her on the back of her neck and then on the cheeks. She shook herself free. 'Now I suppose it is my turn. I am just the wife you can have whenever you want . . . after you've had your own good time,' she said bitterly. The suspicion of infidelity amused Sher Singh. He became more amorous. 'I am not like one of those chaps . . . like your

Madan,' he said laughing. 'That type go about sleeping with anyone they can. For me it is only you. I was at a meeting, that is why I am late. If I had known you were coming I would have left it and come straight home.'

The reference to Madan changed Champak's attitude. 'I've been waiting for you all day. I nearly died of worry,' she complained. 'You must not be out late these days. These are dangerous times.'

Sher Singh promised not to be late again. They forgave each other in their usual way. Only Champak kept thinking how different this was from the evening before. That man's breath was perfumed with cardamoms and scented betel nuts; and this man's! She could not avoid smelling the onions even when she breathed through her mouth.

&

The orderly took Buta Singh's cycle from him and stood it against the wall. Buta Singh unfastened the metal bands he wore round his shins to save his trousers being soiled and put them in his pocket. 'Have the others come?' he asked.

'Yes, sir, but not all; the Sahib is waiting for them. He has ordered me to inform him as soon as everyone is here. Please sit down.' He held up the heavy khas fibre chick. Buta Singh ducked under it and joined his fellow magistrates. They stood up to shake hands with him.

'Buta Singh, give us some news. You are in the know. What itches the Sahib today?'

It was a Muslim colleague and with Muslims it was not wise to be honest about politics. They pretended to be against the idea of Pakistan when they were with non-Muslims but gave it their support in every way they could.

'It must be the arrests of the Nationalist leaders. I suppose he expects trouble in the city,' answered Buta Singh.

'The police brought papers of some of these Gandhi disciples to my house yesterday,' continued the Muslim a little maliciously. 'I sentenced them to six months' detention under the Defence of India Rules.'

Buta Singh knew that if the papers had concerned a Muslim

289

supporter of Pakistan, the same magistrate would have argued with the police. In that case the police would undoubtedly have arranged to bring the papers to somebody like Wazir Chand or himself and they would have taken pleasure in locking up the Muslim for six months. That was the accepted method of dispensing justice from the lowest tribunal to the highest.

Four magistrates, including Wazir Chand, arrived together. The newcomers greeted the others very cordially and took their seats—the Muslims with the Muslims, Hindus and Sikhs with the Hindus and Sikhs. That sort of division took place automatically.

Wazir Chand embraced Buta Singh and the two sat down next to each other. Their families had brought them closer than they believed possible.

'Did daughter Champak reach home safe and sound?' asked Wazir Chand.

'Champak! Is she back? I left home very early.'

'Yes, Madan escorted her from Simla; that is why I am late. She wanted to come back to Sher. Youth, you know! How long can a young wife keep away from her husband?' Wazir Chand smiled mischievously.

'It is good she is back. Sher has been very lonely and working too hard with his student organizations. Everything else O.K.?'

Wazir Chand wagged his head contentedly and then asked in a whisper, 'What is all this about?'

'I suppose he wants us to do special duty. He's expecting trouble after the arrests of the leaders.'

The *chaprasi* came out and asked the magistrates to come into the sitting room. He held the chick up for them and they filed in. Taylor got up and shook hands with them. He was smoking his pipe and looked completely unruffled: he was keeping up the tradition of the British Civil Service of appearing calm in times of crisis. He pretended that it was the sort of meeting he called on the eve of religious festivals.

He did not ask them to sit down but dismissed them with a short speech: 'Gentlemen, I am sorry to have sent for you at short notice. You have no doubt read the news of the arrest of some political leaders. We are not concerned with the rights or wrongs of the decision; we have to carry out the orders of the Government. Our hands are strengthened by the fact that the Government of the

Punjab thoroughly disapproves of the position taken by the leaders of the Nationalist party and fortunately the Nationalists have very little following here. We are not expecting any trouble from our own people but mischief makers may come in from other provinces. We have to be vigilant. We have powers to detain people on suspicion. These powers are not to be abused; but we must not hesitate to make use of them whenever necessary. We have to co-operate with the police in maintaining law and order. If you have any information of importance or need my advice, come to me without hesitation. That is all for the moment. Thank you.'

Taylor turned away without shaking hands again. He paused at the door. 'Buta Singh, do you mind waiting! I want to have a word with you.'

A minute later Taylor came back to the sitting-room and asked Buta Singh to sit down beside him on the sofa. He knocked his pipe against his heel and blew in it. He filled it with tobacoo, lit it, pressed the tobacoo with the matchbox, and took a few puffs with noisy 'Um ums.' Buta Singh was quite used to the trick; it no longer played on his nerves. He waited patiently for the Englishman to begin.

'Buta Singh, I am a little worried and want your advice.'

'Whatever little service I can perform! I am at your disposal.' Buta Singh rubbed his hands with obsequious eagerness.

Taylor produced a copy of a cyclostyled leaflet. Buta Singh read the exhortation by the Hindustan Socialist Republican Army to rise against the British. 'The Police Commissioner has given me this thing,' continued Taylor. 'The envelope bears a city postmark. He says we can presume it was also printed here. That is the most he can say. It may be the doing of some one individual who may do nothing more. It is also possible that there is some sort of organization in the city which has violent aims and is planning to put them in effect. If that is so it must be tracked down and its plans nipped in the bud.'

'Before it can do any mischief,' added Buta Singh.

'Precisely.'

They both became silent. Buta Singh expected Taylor to tell him what he wanted him to do. Taylor believed the hint was good enough. Then, seeing that Buta Singh had not taken the cue, added, 'Can you help in tracking down these people?'

'If Sahib assigns me this duty, I will carry it out. I should have thought this sort of job is more for a policeman than for a magistrate.'

Taylor relit his pipe; it did not need relighting. Could he make the suggestion directly or would Buta Singh take offence? 'Buta Singh, I wasn't thinking of official action. These chaps are obviously some young hotheads who have got a little worked up. If we knew who they were, we could keep an eye on them and save them from their own acts. Even talk to them in a friendly way.'

Buta Singh realized what Taylor was driving at; he kept his eyes fixed on his feet.

'Don't misunderstand me, Buta Singh,' said Taylor quickly. 'I am not suggesting anything dishonourable. Your son could do a good service to his friends and his country. You know we are anxious to get out of India and hand over the reins of power to you people as soon as the war is won. But we will not leave the country to the Japanese or the Germans. And these acts are calculated to do just that—hand over India on a silver platter to the Fascist powers.'

Buta Singh did not look up.

'I seem to have upset you, Buta Singh; I am sorry. Let's forget about it. I'll let the Police Commissioner handle it in his own way.'

'I will speak to my son, sir,' answered Buta Singh at last.

'No, no, don't. Just forget about the whole affair.' Taylor got up abruptly and shook hands. Just as Buta Singh was going out of the room, he called him back. 'Oh, I almost forgot. Last time your son came to see me, he asked for a licence for a rifle. I have made one out for him. Give this to him with my compliments. Goodbye. And don't bother about what I said.'

Chapter VIII

Taylor did not have to do any more than ignore Buta Singh and the strain became too much for the old man. He came unbidden a week later and assured the Deputy Commissioner that he would get the required information. Another week passed. Buta Singh's resolve to speak to his son remained unfulfilled for the simple reason he never saw him. When he left for the law courts the boy was still in bed; when he came back, he was away. He had dinner with his daughter-in-law. Every time he asked her, 'Where is Sher?' she replied, 'I do not know'—and nothing more. Night after night he whiled away the hours doing his files waiting for his son to return. Night after night, he nodded, dozed off to sleep, woke up again, switched off the light, and went to bed resolved to broach the subject next day. There were many questions he wanted to ask. When had Sher Singh decided to buy a rifle? Why didn't he mentioned it to him? Why hadn't he told him that he had asked Taylor for a licence? It did cross Buta Singh's mind that the boy might be up to no good in wanting the weapon; it did not occur to him that he might already be owning one illegally. Buta Singh planned to utilize the situation to get round his son to try and get the required information. No, that was a horrid expression. To cooperate in keeping peace and order and save India from a Fascist invasion. Sher Singh might not see it that way unless it was put tactfully. It was worth waiting for. If Sher Singh did what he was asked, the New Year's Honours list would certainly have something for his father.

Then came the first of the month. Buta Singh resolved that was to be the day. Three days before the date he told the servants and Champak that everyone was to be present at the Gurudwara in time. On the morning itself, he was up before anyone else and went to the servants' quarters to get Shunno and Mundoo to sweep the room and put things ready. He knocked on his son's bedroom door and told him not to be late. He had decided to bring up the subject casually at breakfast as a sort of follow up of the discussion on the morning's news.

Things seemed to go as planned. Everyone turned up at the Gurudwara as told. Sher Singh looked fresh and cheerful. So did Champak. She wore a close fitting Punjabi dress which accentuated the largeness of her bosom and narrowness of her waist. It was odd, thought Buta Singh, how the girl he saw every day without taking much notice of her looked more fetching one morning than on another! There were several children outside, with Mundoo as usual bossing them and the dog. Shunno brought in the tray of pershad and placed it in front of the Granth. Buta Singh picked up the fly-whisk and began to wave it over his head with one hand; with the other, he looked for the right page to read. He was not used to conducting the prayer and it made him slightly nervous. He found the chapter and put the fly-whisk down. He removed his beard-band and brushed his mustache off his lips. He placed his forehead reverently against the Book and shut his eyes to say a private prayer for the fulfilment of his own wishes. His eyes were still shut when he became conscious of someone entering the Gurudwara. The man had prostrated himself before the Granth. He stood up and announced his arrival by greeting everyone at the top of his voice, *'Wah guru ji ka Khalsa, Wah guru ji ki Fateh.'* ('The Sikhs are the Chosen of God, Victory be to our God.') It was the village headman.

Buta Singh's face flushed with anger but he kept it under control. This was a temple where anyone could come and worship and there was nothing he could do about it. He read the passage for the month quietly to himself, made his obeisance, and left. Champak followed him.

At the breakfast table Buta Singh kept the newspaper in front of him to cover the scowl on his face. He did not want to be irritable with Champak, but he could not help saying with suppressed wrath: 'I don't understand the sort of people your husband mixes with! Low, third class types! He should use his intelligence a little more.'

Champak did not look up from her plate.

Buta Singh could not bring up the subject that morning. He swore to himself to do it in the evening even if it meant sitting up later than before.

That night Buta Singh waited a long time for his son to return home. Once again the vigil was in vain.

৯৬

Sher Singh took the headman to the sitting room and ordered breakfast for him.

'Sardarji, why do you put yourself to all this trouble?' asked the headman, munching a thickly buttered toast. He wiped the butter off his mustache with the hem of his shirt and gave it a twirl. 'You should not have bothered. This is like my own home.'

'You've come from such a long distance,' answered Sher Singh in the same tone, 'this is nothing.'

'Why nothing, Sardarji? This is everything! All I want is your kindness.' He picked up the tumbler of buttermilk, cleared his lips of his billowing mustache, and drank it up it one long gulp. He emitted a loud belch which tapered off into praise of the Great Guru, the True Emperor. He combed his beard with his fingers and placed a heavy hand on Sher Singh's knee. 'Tell me some news.'

'What news? Life just goes on.'

The headman belched again and stroked his beard patiently. 'Oh, congratulations!' he said as if he had just recalled something.

'Congratulations for what?'

'Congratulations for what! This is no way to talk to friends. You know very well; the gun licence. Taylor Sahib's clerk told me he had issued one for you and given it to your revered father.'

'Oh, when?'

'Again you hide things from friends! When we first met you said you had a licence and now I discover you have been given one only fifteen days ago. You ask the big Sardar, your father.'

Sher Singh wondered why Buta Singh had not questioned him about the rifle. Nor had he handed him the licence given by Taylor. Did he know that the rifle was already in the house? In any case

Sher Singh was relieved that the headman would not be able to blackmail him any more.

'Here, friend, what do you say! You were worried about these things.' The headman thrust the three empty rifle bullets in his hand. Sher Singh wanted to fling them in the peasant's face, call him a dirty pig, spit at him, and kick him out of the house. But he quietly took the shells and put them on the table. This was the last time he was going to see this fellow, why not let the meeting end peacefully?

The headman gave no indication of wanting to leave. He combed his beard, twirled his mustache, and slapped Sher Singh's knee. 'Tell me some news.'

'What news? Life just goes on.'

'*Wah ji wah!* Great men do great deeds.' The peasant smiled mischievously and pinched Sher Singh's thigh. What was he up to now? 'Great deeds, great men,' he said with a sigh. He continued after a significant pause: 'Tell me, you know how to make bombs?'

'Bombs?'

'Bombs?'

'How should I know anything about making bombs. Why, do you need some?' asked Sher Singh, laughing nervously.

'Is this friendship or a chaff of chick-peas? Our little canal bridge is full of holes. Had the poor thing done any harm to anyone? My best bullock broke its leg in one of the holes. It had cost me three hundred rupees. I said, it doesn't matter if my three hundred are drowned; this is my friend's hobby! But these canal chaps have been trying to find out. They came to ask me You see, the bridge is within the area of my village. I said nothing to them.'

Sher Singh felt cornered once more. It was humiliating for a well-to-do, educated, rising politician like him to be put on the spot by an illiterate, uncouth, peasant informer. 'Sardar Sahib, I will say nothing about you. Once one makes friends, come what may, one must prove true to that friendship. Don't you agree?'

Sher Singh agreed.

'I could never say anything about you,' the headman repeated. 'But who are these Babus with you? Something should be done about them.'

Sher Singh wanted to yell like a madman. Instead he maintained a sullen silence. The headman continued: 'I ask nothing of you, but these Babus must pay for my bullock. I will say nothing to the canal people; they can go and have their mothers raped, but these Babus . . . .'

'I will get you the money.'

The headman clasped him by both the knees. 'No, brother, not you. If I take anything from you, may I be cursed as if I had eaten the flesh of the sacred cow. But these Babus, are they relations of ours? If you tell me who they are, I could get the money from them myself.'

'No, I will get it for you. This evening at seven o'clock at the bridge.'

ੴ

There wasn't another place within cycling distance of the city which was as desolate as the spot near the little bridge over the canal. For several miles on all sides the land was flat as a pancake. It also looked like a pancake: a stretch of yellow with a layer of fine powdery saltpetre. Nothing grew on it except bushes of calotropis and thorny saguaro cactus. There was also the marsh. Most of it was a muddy swamp with reeds growing in some places. The only evidence of human life was a footpath along the canal bank which no one ever seemed to use, and the little bridge, which if used at all, was probably used by stray cattle. The flat waste of saltpetre, scrub, and swamp had an eerie loneliness about it.

The boys came in their sports kit carrying their hockey sticks as they had done a few days earlier. Near the bridge, they divided themselves in three groups. Two groups, of four each, took their positions fifty yards on either side of the bridge behind calotropis bushes. The remaining four, including Sher Singh and Madan, sat in the open on the bridge. The bridge had no holes in it as alleged by the village headman. Nor did Sher Singh have the three hundred rupees to pay him for the bullock which had broken its leg.

Sher Singh looked at his watch. It was 7:15 p.m. The sun had set. In another ten minutes the twilight would darken into night.

'Perhaps you should have come alone. He might have taken fright seeing four of us here,' said one of his companions a little wearily.

'Of course I could have come alone. I've told you several times

297

he was most keen to meet you. He certainly isn't the sort who would be frightened of people like us. You know what Sikh peasants think of city dwellers! And this chap, you might remember, is a few inches taller than Madan and fat and full of hair; he looks like a gorilla. I wouldn't like to meet him alone in the dark.' Sher Singh laughed a little nervously. 'If he doesn't turn up in another ten minutes, we will go back. He can have his mother raped.'

They all hoped the ten minutes would pass quickly and they could go to their homes.

Suddenly, the Lambardar appeared from behind them. The boys jumped when he greeted them with a loud *'Wah guru ji ka Khalsa, Wah guru ji ki Fateh.'* A leather belt charged with cartridge ran down from his shoulder to the waist. At the lower end was a holster with the black butt of a revolver sticking out. 'The entire congregation is here,' he said cheerfully and sat down beside them.

'You said you wanted to meet them; that is why they are here. I said to myself, 'If my brother asks a favour, I should do it for him.' Sher Singh introduced the boys—this time with their correct names.

The headman shook hands with the three boys. 'What have I to do with names? All I want to know is that they are my brother's friends and that is enough for me,' he said with a broad smile.

The twilight was fading rapidly and, as usual, it was the peasant who was more at ease. 'Tell me some news,' he said quite unconcerned and slapped Sher Singh on the thigh.

'What news? Life just goes on.'

Madan changed the tone of polite humbug.

'Lambardara, you said your bullock had broken its leg in a hole in the bridge. There are no holes in the bridge.'

The headman was quick to react to the rude tone; 'What do you know about bullocks, Babuji? You stick to your shopkeeping and account books.'

'You want us to pay you three hundred rupees for a damaged bullock. We have brought the money but we must have proof before we pay. Show us the hole in the bridge and your lame bull.'

For a moment the headman believed the money was in his grasp. Then his shrewd rustic sense told him they were bluffing. 'I don't give any proofs. This is not a court of law.'

The tone cleared the atmosphere. They all stood up.

'In one breath you call Sher Singh "brother", said Madan sharply, 'in the other you want to make money off him. What sort of bastardy is this?'

'Keep your tongue in check. You know who you are speaking to?'

'Yes. A police informer. The son of a pig . . . A raper of his mother.'

The Lambardar's hand went to his holster. Before he could draw his weapon two of the boys fell on him. He shook them off like a wounded wild boar shakes off pye-dogs at the end of a chase. Madan and Sher Singh covered him with their pistols.

'Put your hands up or I'll shoot you like the filthy dog you are.'

The headman extended his arms towards Sher Singh as if to embrace him. 'Brother, you also have become angry!' he said appealingly.

Sher Singh stepped back and fired. The headman bent over with a loud 'Hai.' His hand moved to his gun. The boys behind him saw and gave warning. Madan fired a second shot. The headman let out another loud 'Hai,' sagged down on his knees and slowly stretched himself on the path. Blood poured out of his wounds. His last words were not addressed to God or the Great Guru but to his killers. 'I'll sleep with your mothers . . . I'll sleep with your sisters . . . I'll . . . .' It made it easier for them to finish him off. Each one of the boys fired a shot in the headman's body so that the crime was shared. They unstrapped the holster and the cartridge belt and dragged the corpse down the slope towards the swamp. It was warm and twitching. An occasional gurgle came out of the dead man's throat. They dumped it into a ditch and covered it with earth and stones. They dug up and relevelled the path where he had fallen and bled. They washed their hands in the canal and made for the city as fast as they could.

There was a brief farewell at parting. The boys were to leave the city immediately for different destinations. Madan was to return to Simla.

Sher Singh was left alone to face his amorous wife, his ill-tempered father—and himself.

299

Chapter IX

In a country of 400 million people living in congested rusticity, events like births and deaths are reduced to their proper insignificance. That does not mean that the birth of a son does not occasion joy or the death of a kinsman no grief. They do. Only the rejoicing at the arrival of another infant in a family which has to live on the produce of ten acres of impoverished land becomes progressively more a matter of form than of reality. After the first child or two, births are simply looked upon as something which follows nocturnal pastimes as day follows night. Since there are no other diversions in the village and it is not easy to restrict sexual intercourse to a few messy days in the month, one child comes after another as the new year comes after the old. Its arrival is accepted with resignation as a blessing of the Almighty, Omniscient God who knows what is best. But little importance is attached to it. In the case of death, the reactions are somewhat confused. There is sorrow at the loss of a loved one; there is also relief that there is one mouth less to feed. In any case God seems to manifest His power more at death than at birth. (Human beings have a not too unimportant role in creating new life: it is only rarely that they become instruments of destruction. Killing is largely God's monopoly. When the Lord giveth, He lets mankind have some share in the giving. But when the Lord taketh away, He does it at His own sweet will.) So deaths are accepted with even more resignation than births—and as little fuss.

Jhimma Singh was one of many brothers. Being the eldest, he inherited the official function of headman of the village from his father. Thereafter he acquired possession of most of his father's property. He loved his brothers and arranged marriages and employment for them as farm labourers in newly colonized lands a few hundred miles away to the north-west. Malicious tongues spread poison and turned the brothers against him. They took him to court to get possession of their share of the land. But providence, assisted by clever lawyers, triumphed over their evil designs. Then they tried violence. That too went against them. They were imprisoned on charges of attempted murder and Jhimma Singh was given a revolver to defend himself. He gained the confidence of the local police officials by his hospitality; they let him look after the affairs of the village and Jhimma Singh became virtually its ruler. Anyone who has had to live the hard way, literally fighting for survival at every step, doesn't set much store by values like truth, honesty, loyalty, or patriotism. Neither did Jhimma Singh. Each little success meant more envy and more danger from the envious. He had to seek the help of the police to protect him. In turn they expected him to keep an eye on miscreants. He became a paid informer.

Jhimma Singh's only failure in life was the inability of any one of his three wives of produce a child. After the first had remained barren for five years, he married her niece. Following a few years of fruitless matrimony with the niece, he cast his protective mantle on a young widow whose provocative figure and dark eyes had given Jhimma Singh visions of many sons. She also let him down. Now the land he farmed, the land he leased out to tenants, his own brick-built house, his wives' jewellery, and his account in the savings bank, which was said to have grown from some hundreds to fabulous thousands, was his to give away or squander. This prosperity hurt his fellow villagers, particularly his relations. Although everyone feared him and some even sided with him in his lawsuits, not one of them loved him.

It wasn't very surprising then that for a week no one should have bothered about his disappearance. He was known to go away to the city for two or three days without telling his wives. As in the past, they assumed he had been called away on urgent business. After a week they became anxious and started going round to other homes asking the women to find out from their menfolk if they had seen Jhimma Singh. When no one came forth with any news of him for another week, the anxiety changed to alarm and a report was lodged at the police station by one of the tenants at the urging of Jhimma Singh's first wife. It mentioned the enmity of his brothers and their previous attempts to murder him. Once again the brothers were arrested, interrogated, and beaten up. Nothing came of it. No corpse, no case. They were set at liberty. The Police Commissioner was notified that the most trusted informer in the district had disappeared—probably murdered by one of his many relations and no trace could be found of either the victim or the murderer. The Commissioner sent the file to the Deputy Commissioner to have the case closed as 'untraced'. He was a little surprised to find that instead of the usual words 'Seen. File,' with the illegible initials, there was an order asking him to come over to discuss the case. What followed startled the Police Commissioner.

The Deputy Commissioner handed the Police Commissioner a warrant to search the house of Sardar Buta Singh, the seniormost Indian magistrate of the district. He gave him another one, to arrest Sher Singh. Taylor refused to disclose his source of information. All he said was: 'Be gentle to the old man. I suggest you send him over to see me and then search the house. You may find something. In any case, take his son to the police station and give him the works. Get some of your tough Anglo-Indian sergeants to handle him. It will not be hard to make him talk.'

Buta Singh had firmly decided to speak to his son after the headman had left. That evening Sher Singh came home early but straightway retired to bed complaining of a severe headache. Next morning, he did not turn up for breakfast and Buta Singh went to see him in his room. The boy looked pale and jaundiced and would not speak at all. A doctor was sent for but he could not diagnose anything. Nevertheless it was plain to any one that he was very sick; one could scarcely bring up a delicate subject with him in that state of health. After many days in bed, his health improved and he started moving about the house. He still wore a sallow, furtive look and avoided meeting people. Buta Singh waited patiently. At

last came the first of the month. The father came to the conclusion
that matters had been allowed to drift for too long and the time had
come to settle the business once and for all. He would talk to his
son after the morning ceremony.

Autumn had set in and there was a nip in the morning air.
Inside the Gurudwara it was cozy because of the thick carpet and
the incense. Sher Singh, Champak, and Shunno were inside.
Mundoo, as usual, was lording it over the children and the dog
outside. Buta Singh uncovered the Holy Book to start reading. He
saw the figure of a policeman through the chick. He kept his temper
under control and proceeded to look for the appropriate passage.
He pressed his forehead reverently on the Book and looked up once
more. There was yet another policeman outside talking excitedly
to Mundoo. He took off his shoes and came into the Gurudwara.
This was too much for Buta Singh. He hollered angrily at the top
of his voice: 'What is your business?' The constable saluted and
said: *'Huzoor,* the Police Commissioner is waiting for you outside
in his car. The Deputy Commissioner has sent him to fetch you. It
is most urgent. I crave forgiveness for disturbing you in the
Gurudwara; I was ordered to do so.'

The reference to the Police Commissioner and Mr Taylor
changed Buta Singh's tone. He did not proceed with the reading.
He left at once and asked Champak to carry on. Shunno followed
her master; she wasn't going to be left out of things.

'You do the reading instead of your father,' said Champak
with a smile.

Sher Singh did not smile back. 'I can't. I am not feeling too
well.'

'What is the matter?' asked Champak.

'I don't know, I don't feel well.'

Champak put her hand on his forehead. 'You have no fever
but you have cold-sweat. I'll get Mundoo to make your bed. You
come and lie down. Mundoo, Oi Mundoo,' she cried. 'The
policemen seem to have frightened away the servants.'

She went out and shouted for the boy again. Mundoo came
wailing. 'A policeman beat me. They have come inside the house.
When I asked them what they were doing, one fellow slapped me.'

Sher Singh went deathly pale. Had they found out? Had one
of the boys told on him? His wife looked at him for some

explanation. 'I will see what is happening,' he said weakly. 'You go to your room.'

There were policemen all over the place: in the courtyard and the sitting room; in the garden and at the gate. Sher Singh came out into the verandah followed by Dyer. Two white sergeants were sitting in the armchairs with their legs on the table, smoking. A head constable stood by them with handcuffs dangling from his belt. A policewoman in a khaki sari was leaning on a Black Maria in the porch. 'You want to see my father?' asked Sher Singh timidly.

'You Buta Singh's son?' asked one of them knocking the ash off his cigarette.

'Yes . . . sir.'

'Head constable, search this fellow. And send someone inside to search his woman.'

The two resumed their smoking. The policewoman went inside. The head constable took Sher Singh by the hand. Sher Singh felt he ought to protest. He mustered up all the courage he had and spoke: 'What is this about? How dare you put your hands on me! What authority . . . .'

One of the sergeants got up slowly from his chair and came up to him. 'You want to know what authority we have to search you?'

'Yes,' answered Sher Singh through the spittle that clogged his throat.

'Man, this bugger wants to know why we want to search him,' said the sergeant turning to his companion. 'We better tell him.'

Without warning the sergeant struck his knee sharply into Sher Singh's privates. As he doubled over with pain, the sergeant hit him on the face with the back of his hand. Sher Singh's turban came off and fell on the ground; his long hair scattered about his face and shoulders.

'Cheeky nigger. That'll teach . . . .'

The sergeant could not complete the sentence. Dyer leapt at him with savage fury and knocked him down. He tore the collar off the white man's coat and went for his throat. The constable lashed out with his iron handcuffs; the other sergeant laid out with his swagger stick and kicked the dog with his hobnailed boots. Policemen came running with their iron shod bamboo poles to beat him. At last the Alsatian gave up. Blood flowed from his face and back, the bone of one of his legs had been fractured.

'I'll shoot the bloody pariah,' raged the sergeant getting up and drawing his pistol. His coat was torn, his face scratched and bitten.

The other sergeant put his hand on the pistol. 'No, mun. Old Deecee will kick up a hell of a row if you shoot the bloody cur. You know how mad these f . . . Englishmen are about dogs!'

The sergeant put back his pistol in the holster and wiped the blood off his face: 'Suppose I'll have to have anti-rabies shots. A Sikh's dog is bound to be mad.'

It took two constables with their long bamboo poles to keep the battered Alsatian at bay.

Sher Singh slumped on the floor of the verandah with his arms covering his face and began to cry. He hated himself for crying but he could not stop. The two people he feared and loathed most, Anglo-Indians and Muslim policemen from northern Punjab, had insulted and beaten him in his own home and all he could do was to cry like a child. Even his dog had shown more fight.

'Take this bloody patriot to the station and put some red hot chillies up his arse,' ordered the sergeant to the head constable. 'If he has any illusions of being a magistrate's son, knock them out of him.'

The head constable put the handcuffs on Sher Singh's hands and said gently: 'Come along, Sardar Sahib.' Sher Singh rolled up his hair into a chignon and picked up his turban. His eyes were inflamed with hate and humiliation. When he tried to stand there was a stab of pain in his testicles. He held them with his manacled hands and slumped down again. The head constable took the turban from him and put his arm round his waist and helped him up on to his feet. He whispered in his ears: 'Be a man. Don't degrade yourself before these white bastards.' Sher Singh limped into the van.

The search lasted an hour. They ransacked every room in the house. A man was sent down the well. They found nothing—not even the rifle for which Taylor had made out a licence in Sher Singh's name. The illicit arms remained unnoticed in the pit in the center of the empty garage.

The policewoman came out to report that she had searched Champak and her belongings but had recovered nothing. The sergeants rode off on their motorcycles. The two policemen who had been keeping the Alsatian at a safe distance took their seats in the van. Sher Singh heard the defiant barking and snapping of the dog following the Black Maria till it gathered speed on its way to the police station.

≈

The Police Commissioner dropped Buta Singh at Taylor's house. There were no other magistrates present nor were there any chairs laid out for them. Taylor's bearer came out and held open the wire-gauze door. 'The Sahib is at *chota hazri* and wants you to join him.'

Buta Singh had been inside Taylor's drawing room but no farther. Mrs Taylor came in to greet him. 'Come in, Sardar Sahib, and join us for breakfast.' She led him to the dining room.

'Very kind of you, madam. I had my tea before coming,' answered Buta Singh lying. 'Very kind of you. Good morning, sir.'

'Good morning, Buta Singh,' answered Taylor putting down the morning paper. 'Come and join us. You have met my wife before, haven't you? Joyce, you know Mr Buta Singh.'

'Of course! One more cup of tea won't do you any harm.'

'No harm,' sniggered Buta Singh. 'No harm. Thank you. Very kind of you, madam.' Buta Singh sat down and allowed himself to be talked into having eggs and bacon, toast and marmalade, and three cups of tea. He could now bring up Taylor's breakfast menu casually with his colleagues and his family. It would be fun talking about bacon in front of the Muslim magistrates. Had Taylor some special favour to ask for this reception? Probably to pursue the subject of getting information from Sher Singh.

When breakfast was over, Taylor conducted Buta Singh to his study. He didn't light a cigarette to time the interview but took out his pipe and tin of tobacco.

'Sahib seems to have something special on his mind this morning. What service can I tender?'

Taylor lit his pipe. 'I wanted to have a general talk with you about things; one seldom gets the time to do that. I also have to ask you about a particular subject which we will come to later on. I hope you don't mind my being personal. How long . . . .'

'Nothing personal, sir,' interrupted Buta Singh. 'I have no secrets to keep from you. Ask me anything you like.'

'I was going to ask how long had your family been connected with the British Government?'

'Sir,' warmed Buta Singh, 'sir, we can almost go back to the days of Sikh rule. On the annexation of the Punjab and the disbanding of the Sikh forces my great grandfather, who was a subedar and had fought against the British in the Anglo-Sikh wars, joined the British army. He served under John Lawrence. He also fought under Nicholson in the Mutiny of 1857 and was awarded a medal for the capture of Delhi; we still have it in the family. My grandfather was also in the British army. He rose from the ranks and retired as a Jemadar—in those days to be a Jemadar was a big thing for an Indian. My father did not join the army, but he recruited many soldiers in the 1914–18 war and our family was given lands in the Canal Colonies. I have kept up the tradition of loyalty to the British Crown and will do so till the day I die.' He became breathless with the excitement he had generated in himself. It did not seem to affect Taylor who coolly lit his pipe once more.

'What about your son?'

'What about my son? He may hobnob with the Nationalists but he will have to be loyal to the British as long as Buta Singh lives,' he replied, smacking his chest. 'Otherwise I will disown him. After I am dead, he can do what he likes.'

Taylor still seemed unimpressed. 'I appreciate your sentiments of loyalty, Buta Singh, but I do not agree with you about the future of India; and I am British. I feel we should pull out of this country as soon after the war as we can and let you Indians manage your own affairs. I, for one, have no intention of continuing in the Indian Civil Service a day after the cease-fire. In fact I am not on the side of Mr Churchill but on that of Mr Gandhi and Mr Nehru—except, and this is important, I do think the war has to be won first. Otherwise the Nazis and the Fascists will put the clock back for you and for us. I may be wrong, but that is my belief.'

Englishmen like Taylor confused Buta Singh. It wasn't entirely his fault. He had only known Englishmen who believed in the British Empire as they did in the Church of England; who stood to attention even if a bar of their national anthem came over the air while somebody was fiddling with the knob of a radio set; who believed that 'natives' were only of two kinds—the Gunga Dins, whom they loved like their pet dogs because of their dogged devotion to the Sahibs, and the Bolshies, whom they hated.

'Mr Taylor, you may be right. I am an old man and I cannot change. I am for the British Raj. If it goes, there will be chaos in this country as there was chaos before the British came.' Buta Singh felt mean. There were limits beyond which flattery should not go; his frequently did. Only if the Englishman accepted it, he would feel better.

'What does your son have to say on the subject?'

That gave Buta Singh the opportunity to redeem himself. 'Of course he disagrees with me and is more of your point of view. He is young and you know what youth is!'

'Yes,' answered Taylor absent-mindedly. 'But what do you do when there is a conflict of loyalties? What would you do if you discovered that he had been mixed up not only with the Nationalists but also with terrorists?'

Insinuations about duplicity made Buta Singh angry. 'I would disown him. I would throw him out of the house,' he replied emphatically.

'You are a harsh judge, Buta Singh. Children are meant to be understood, not thrown out when there is a difference of opinion.'

'We teach our children to respect and obey their parents,' said Buta Singh. 'I am sure European parents do the same, sir.'

'It may be a hard thing to say, but, despite the close living in joint families and the formal respect paid to the elders, there is less contact, understanding, or friendship between parents and their children in India than in Europe.'

Buta Singh didn't understand the trend of the conversation. Taylor seemed to be beating about the bush. Then out of the blue he came out with a wholly irrelevant question. 'Did you know Jhimma Singh, headman?'

'Jhimma Singh? No, who is he?'

'I hope he is; he certainly was. A big, burly, black chap. Apparently he knew your son and was on visiting terms with him.'

'Oh yes, sir, I know,' answered Buta Singh. 'I think he came to my house some time ago when I was at prayer in the Gurudwara. I remember him. I didn't know his name was Jhimma Singh. What about him, sir?'

Taylor went through the process of emptying, refilling, and relighting his pipe. Sometimes these tactics worked.

'What about Jhimma Singh, sir?'

'I have reason to believe that the day he came to your house was the last day he was seen alive. Further, I have reason to believe that your son, Sher Singh, was perhaps the last man to see him alive.'

Buta Singh's face fell. 'What is this you say, Sahib?'

'Jhimma Singh was a headman and a police informer. He had been informing me about your son's activities with a group of boys who practised rifle shooting near his village. You recall I gave you a licence for one! I hoped that it would bring the whole business out in the open and you would have put a stop to it. Well, it didn't work out that way. These lads then tried to blow up a bridge on the canal. Jhimma Singh told me about that too. The only one of the gang he knew was your son. Then suddenly he disappeared. I am pretty certain he has been murdered. I may, of course, be wrong.'

Buta Singh sank back in his chair and covered his face with his hands. Large tears rolled down his cheeks and disappeared in his beard. 'My nose has been cut. I can no longer show my face to the world,' he sobbed.

Taylor took the Sikh magistrate's hairy hand in his own. 'Buta Singh, this is extremely unpleasant for me but I have to do my duty. Let me tell you all. Your house is being searched in your absence now. I have also ordered Sher Singh to be taken into custody. We have nothing to go on except what Jhimma Singh has told me and that, you as a magistrate know, is not enough. If Sher Singh had anything to do with the headman's disappearance it is for him to tell. It is on him we have to rely for information about his accomplices as well. If he gives it, I may consider granting him a King's pardon. Of course, if he had nothing to do with the affair, or refuses to talk, the case will not be reopened.'

'How shall I face the world?' moaned Buta Singh and again covered his face with his hands. Taylor got up and asked the bearer to get a cold drink. Mrs Taylor came in carrying a tray with three glasses of orange juice. She put it on the table and sat down on a chair beside the magistrate. She put her hand gently on his knee. 'Buta Singh, pull yourself together and have a drink. I was told the Sikhs were brave people! This is not being very brave, is it?'

Buta Singh blew his nose and wiped his tears with his handkerchief. Mrs Taylor held the glass of orange juice for him. 'Come along, drink it. And don't fret. What's happened has happened.'

The magistrate's hand shook as he gulped down his glass of orange juice. He brought up a deep sigh. 'How can I thank . . .' He broke down again and started to sob in his handkerchief. The Taylors sat quietly and let him cry his heart out. Then Taylor spoke in a firm voice: 'Buta Singh, I have given you fifteen days' leave. Your house will continue to be guarded as before. If you want to be spared the embarrassment of visitors you can tell the policeman to keep them out. You can see your son as often as you want to. You can give him whatever advice you deem fit; it is for you to decide. I repeat, if he is willing to give us the names of his accomplices, he will be made a Crown witness and be granted the King's pardon. If not, he must face the consequences of his act.'

Buta Singh sank back in his chair and covered his face with his hands. Large tears rolled down his cheeks and disappeared in his beard. 'My nose has been cut. I can no longer show my face to the world.' He sobbed.

In the Himalayas it is not the advent but the end of the monsoon which is spectacular. There are not months of intense heat which turn the plainsman's longing for rain into a prayer for deliverance from a hot purgatory. People of the hills look upon the monsoon as they do on other seasons. One brings snow, one the blossoms, one the fruit; also one brings the rain. For another, in the mountains the monsoon is heavier and for days the hills and valleys are blotted out by sheets of rain. It is misty, damp and cold, and people pray for the sunshine. Their prayers are answered some time in September or October. The monsoon is given a grand farewell with fireworks. Thunder explodes like firecrackers and lightning illumines the landscape as if flares were being dropped from the heavens. The sky is no longer a mass of shapeless gray; it is an expanse of aquamarine full of bulbous white clouds which change their shapes and colours as they tumble away. The mists lift as if waved away by a magic wand, unfolding rain-washed scenery of snow-capped mountains on one side and an infinity of brown plains intersecting a thousand golden streams on the other. The air is cleaner. It has the crispy cold of the regions of perpetual snows; it also has the insinuating warmth of the regions of perpetual sunshine.

Some days of autumn have more of 'God's in His Heaven' than others. This was one of them. When they came out into the garden, the sun had just come up over the hills and touched the snow range across the valley with a glow of pink. The forests of deodar stood on the mountainside patiently waiting for a long day of mellow sunshine. There wasn't a cloud in the deep blue sky: only lammergeyers drifting lazily with the noiseless ease and grace of gliders. It was too good to be true; and like all times that are too good to be true, there was mixed with the sense of elation, an apprehension that it would not last long, and perhaps, not end as well as it had begun.

They had their breakfast in the garden where the dew lay like whitewash on the lawn. The borders were thick with chrysanthemums, sunflowers, and hollyhocks. After breakfast they went for a stroll on the Mall. The crowds had considerably thinned as most of the government offices had shifted back to the plains and some of the larger stores had closed down for the month. They walked up and down the road a couple of times and then went into Davicos for coffee. After the coffee, Madan took the girls with him to watch the finals of a football tournament played on the race-course in the valley at Annandale. Sabhrai went down to the temple in the lower bazaar to spend the rest of the day.

When Sabhrai returned home late in the afternoon, the servant handed her a telegram; it had been delivered some hours earlier. She tore it open and looked at the hieroglyphics. 'What does it say?' she asked anxiously.

'I can't read English,' replied the boy, a little surprised that she should ask him.

'Go and ask somebody to read it and come back quickly.'

The boy went to the neighbours' homes and came back half-an-hour later to say that the masters were out and none of the servants could read. Sabhrai took the telegram from him. She paced up and down the verandah; she walked up to the gate and came back; she went down the road a little distance, came back home, and paced up and down the verandah again. She looked at the telegram over the over again. The only letters she could piece

together were those that spelled her husband's name; the rest made
no sense to her. At long last Madan and the girls came home.
Sabhrai met them at the gate with the telegram. Madan read it out
aloud first in English and then translated it for her in Punjabi. She
was right, it was from here husband.

'Return immediately. Buta Singh.'

Chapter X

Sabhrai's sixth sense told her nothing about the drama that had taken place. She realized that nothing could be wrong with her husband because he had sent the telegram. Whatever had happened had happened to her son. If he were sick or had met with an accident, his wife was there to look after him. Why should Buta Singh send for her in this manner unless Sher Singh was dying or was already dead? The more she thought of it, the more certain she became that the telegram had something to do with her son; and that he was either in mortal danger or had succumbed to it. She sat up in her bed and prayed all through the night. Next day on her way down to the plains and again all night in the train, her thoughts and prayers were for her Shera.

It was still dark when she woke up Beena and asked her to wash, change, and roll up the beddings. She asked her to come and sit beside her. 'Pray for your brother,' she said to indicate that she had an inkling of what had happened. They sat cross-legged on the berth wrapped in their shawls and recited the morning prayer. The black nothingness outside the window pane became a dimly-lit landscape beyond continuous waves of telegraph wires which rose and fell from pole to pole. The sun came up over the flat land and lit up the yellow squares of mustard, the solid greens of sugarcane, and blocks of mud villages. They came to the suburbs of the city. Mud huts gave way to brick buildings, and open fields to evil smelling ditches where men sat on their haunches, shamelessly baring their bottoms and relieving themselves.

The train drew in on a noisy crowded platform full of coolies in red uniforms. Sabhrai and Beena looked for a familiar face, but could not recognize anyone. The orderly came from the servants' compartment and took charge of the luggage. They were counting their pieces when an Englishwoman approached them. She touched Beena on the arm and asked, 'Are you Sardar Buta Singh's daughter?'

'Yes.'

'I am Mrs Taylor. Good-morning. And this I presume is your mother. *Sat Sri Akal*, Sardarini Sahiba. We have met before.'

Sabhrai joined her hands and answered the Englishwoman's greeting. It took the mother and daughter some time to realize that the Deputy Commissioner's wife had come to receive them. Sabhrai lost her composure and whispered agitatedly into her daughter's ear. Joyce Taylor saw the consternation on their faces. 'Don't be alarmed Sardarini Sahiba, all is well,' she said putting her hand on Sabhrai's shoulder. 'Your husband and son are in the best of health; you will see them soon. I had nothing to do this morning so I thought I'd come along to fetch you and spare you a long tonga ride.'

Beena translated this to her mother and they smiled gratefully at Mrs Taylor. Things must have changed for an English Deputy Commissioner's wife to take the trouble to receive the family of an Indian subordinate. They were too bewildered to think that there might be other reasons. Beena gave the coolies more than twice their due to prevent them nagging and making a scene in front of the Englishwoman.

There was nothing at home to indicate a crisis. There were two policemen on duty, instead of one. They came to attention and saluted as the car went in. Nobody came out to receive them while they were unloading their luggage. That didn't surprise them. Buta Singh was likely to be at the Courts; Sher Singh would be out somewhere and Champak in her room. But where was Dyer? He was always the first to greet members of the family returning home and had to be restrained from putting his paws on their shoulders and licking their faces. As soon as Mrs Taylor had said goodbye and left, Beena shouted for the dog. He came round the house, hopping on the three legs; the fourth was in plaster. There was a gash on his nose on which flies were clustered. He whined as he came to his mistress and let out a long piteous howl. 'Hai, Dyer, what's happened to you?' Who's hurt my little son?' Sabhrai fanned the flies off with her headpiece and put her arms round the dog. 'Didn't Sher take you to the doctor?'

Champak came out of the wire gauze door. Her hair was scattered untidily on her face. Her eyes were red and swollen. She wore a plain white cotton sari without any make-up or jewellery—like a widow in mourning. Sabhrai's heart sank. Was her son dead? Hadn't the Englishwoman said he was in good health!

'What has . . . ?'

Champak clasped her mother-in-law round the waist and burst out crying. Sabhrai, who had never particularly cared for Champak, stroked her head. 'The True, The True, The Great Guru,' she chanted.

Beena could not stand it any more. 'What has happened? Why don't you tell?' she shrieked.

Buta Singh came out in the verandah. He, too, was shabbily dressed in a white shirt and pajamas. His beard had not been pressed and he wore no turban. 'What is all this crying for?' he asked at the top of his voice. 'You behave as if he were dead. Perhaps that might have been better.'

'The True, The True, The Great Guru. What words are these? Where is my son, my Moon, my little Ruby. Where is he?' Tears streamed down Sabhrai's face. 'Why don't you tell me?'

Even her tears did not appease Buta Singh's temper. 'My nose has been cut; I can no longer show my face to anyone.'

'What has he done? Why don't you tell me where he is.'

'He's in jail. Where else can he be?'

'The Great Guru. The Great Guru. Who has been born to put my child in jail! What did he do?'

'Murder, what else! I can no longer show my face to anyone. All my life's work has been thrown into a well.'

'The True, The True, The Great Guru.'

They went into the sitting room. After a few minutes, Sabhrai regained her composure and asked her husband to explain what had happened. Buta Singh did so in a bitter voice, mincing no words. He ended on a note of self-pity. 'All my years of loyal service thrown into the well . . . . Just when I am due to retire and expect to be rewarded, my son cuts my nose. I wouldn't be surprised if the little land we have in reward for services were confiscated and I were given no pension. I do not understand this complete lack of regard for one's parents. And Champak must have known about his goings on with these bad characters. I wouldn't be surprised if that rascal Madan were one of them. To whom can I show my face now?'

Champak began to sob once more. Sabhrai spoke sharply. 'You are only concerned with yourself. Don't you want to save your child's life?'

The snub had a salutary effect on Buta Singh's temper. He relapsed into a sullen silence.

'What are we to do?' asked Beena at last.

'I don't know. I've gone mad,' replied her father.

'We shall have a non-stop reading of the Granth for two days and nights. The Guru will be our guide,' said Sabhrai quietly.

'Yes, yes,' commented Beena impatiently, 'we will do that, but we must do something about getting Sherji out of jail. Have you been to see him?' she asked her father.

'No. I don't want to see him.'

Champak's sobs became louder. Sabhrai put her arms round her. Buta Singh felt guilty. 'If the Deputy Commissioner had not been so kind to me, the police would have beaten him straight. Even now, he has promised that if Sher tells them all about the crime, he will grant him the King's pardon.'

'Will he have to give the names of his accomplices?' asked Sabhrai.

'The police already know about them; they know everything. These other chaps were probably the ones to implicate Sher. It is only by the Deputy Commissioner's kindness that Sher can avail himself of the King's pardon. The others would give anything to have the other offer made to them.'

'Will he have to become an informer?' asked Beena.

Buta Singh got angry again. 'These are stupid words. I am telling you that the police don't need an informer; they know everything. They are only willing to give Sher an excuse to save his life because the Deputy Commissioner is keen to help him.'

'Why haven't you told Sher of this offer?' asked Sabhrai.

Buta Singh felt cornered. 'I've been out of my senses. If it hadn't been for the Taylors, I don't know what would have happened to me! What more can a man do than offer your son's life back to you?'

'You must see Sherji,' said Beena, 'and tell him about Mr Taylor's offer.'

'We will first do the non-stop reading of the Granth,' said Sabhrai firmly. 'The Guru will guide us. We will do what He commands.'

ᐧ᭟

Being the only son, Sher Singh had been pampered in his childhood and allowed to have his own way in his adolescence. Despite this, the two things he hankered after were affection and esteem. The one he sought through popularity amongst friends; the other through leadership. The applause that came from his family and his colleagues was offset by his early marriage. Champak, despite her expressions of admiration, gave him an uneasy feeling of being a failure. To impress her became an obsession. The form it took was to hold out visions of a successful political career by which he would take her to dizzy heights of eminence along with him. The more his physical inadequacy gnawed his insides, the more daring he became in his political activity. From fiery speeches, he went on to uniforms and discipline; from those to belief in force: the worship of tough men and love for symbols of strength, like swords crossed over a shield. These, with the possession of guns, pistols, cartridges, and the handsomely masculine Alsatian as a companion, completed his martial padding. Living with these symbols of strength and among people who vaguely expected him to succeed, Sher Singh came to believe in his own future and his power. He did not realize that strength was not a natural development of his own personality but nurtured behind the protection provided by his father's position as a senior magistrate and a respected citizen. He was like a hot house plant blossoming in a greenhouse. The abuse, beating, and arrest were like putting that plant out in a violent hailstorm. His bluster and self-confidence withered in the icy cold atmosphere of the police station.

Sher Singh had never been beaten before in his life. Being kicked in the groin and hit in the face had been a shattering experience. He touched the depths of humiliation and anger. He

317

had always feared and hated Anglo-Indians. They did the Englishman's dirty work, spoke his language in their own ugly Hobson-jobson, full of vulgar abuse, but had none of his cricketing spirit. They were the Hydes of the English Dr Jekyll. He had also envied and hated Punjabi Mussulmans. They were physically stronger and more virile than his type of Sikh. And on that fatal morning an Anglo-Indian sergeant had hit him in the face with the back of his hand and a Mussulman constable had told him to face his ordeal like a man. He had wept from fear; he had wept in anger; he had wept in hate. At the end of two days of weeping, his system was drained of anger and hate; only fear remained: the fear of another thrashing and the greater one of death by hanging.

After a few days, life in the police station became such a routine that it seemed to Sher Singh as if he had been there all his life. Every hour a brass gong was struck, it told the time and regulated the life of the station. At the stroke of six, the reveille was sounded and everyone had to get up. There was much sucking of keekar twigs, spitting, and gargling around the taps where policemen and prisoners took turns to bathe. An hour later they were given highly brewed tea and stale bread. Thereafter the courtyard rang with exercise and drill orders. Anglo-Indian sergeants drove in on their noisy motorcycles and took charge. Policemen went out in batches for traffic duty or investigation or to make arrests. Black Marias were brought in; prisoners were handcuffed, fettered, and taken to the law courts. They were brought back in the evening, locked up and fed. Anglo-Indians drove out more noisily than when they came. After the evening roll-call, there was another call of the bugle and the lights were switched off everywhere except in the reporting room. Then it was silent save for an occasional shriek of cry for mercy from the cells behind the courtyard where prisoners were interrogated. Through all this the brass gong marked the hours.

What Sher Singh dreaded most was a visit from his father. He had ruined the latter's career and he would now have no chance of getting an extension of service or a title in the next Honours list. The Government might even deprive him of his pension. Buta Singh was sure to denounce him and refuse to let him come back home—if ever he got away alive. Without Buta Singh there was no chance of reconciliation with the rest of the family. Sabhrai was the type of Indian woman who believed that her husband was a God and would do little more than plead for her son after the initial outburst was over. Champak would probably be sent away to her parents and not be heard of till he came out of jail—if that ever happened. It was an amazing thought that he had hardly missed her. His sister, Beena, did not really matter. The only one he really missed was his dog. Dyer's defense of his master had made a deep impression on his mind. He had often visualized his picture in uniform on large posters with his handsome Alsatian beside him. Now he visualized the same picture of himself as a sad disillusioned man with a distant philosophic look, loved by no one except his dog, who fixed his doting eyes on his master. He wished they would let Dyer share his cell.

Then there was the interrogation. Sher Singh knew his turn would come soon. The sergeant who had hit him said so every morning when he went round the cells: 'Well, Sardar, how are your plans for turning the British out of the country getting on? We must discuss them soon; perhaps I can help you, hm?'

How much did the police know?

Sher Singh tried to work that out hour after hour, day after day. It was obvious that he was the only one of the group they had arrested so far. Madan, who had got him in this mess, was back in Simla having a good time; the others were scattered in different places. Could one of them have been a spy? No, because then his arrest would have followed immediately after the murder. Unless one of the gang had also been arrested and had talked, the police could not possibly know anything about it.

How much should he tell to get away without a beating?

೭ಎ

One afternoon a constable came to the cell, put two cane chairs against the wall, and said casually: 'The Sahibs want to talk to you.' The 'Sahibs' came slapping their putteed legs with their swagger sticks. They were the same two who had arrested him. Sher Singh got up from his chair—more out of fear than out of politeness. He did not greet them because he knew the greeting would not be answered. The sergeants sat down. One of them pulled Sher Singh's chair nearer him with his toes and put his feet on it. Sher

Singh's only option was to squat on the floor or to keep standing. He kept standing. He was conscious of his arms hanging at his sides as if he were at attention.

'Well, Sardar, are you still plotting to get the British out?' He turned to his companion. 'Great leader this chap, mun. You wouldn't know looking at him, would you?'

The other nodded his head slowly, scrutinizing Sher Singh from head to foot. 'One never knows with these niggers.'

'One doesn't, does one!'

'Not unless one sticks a greased pole up their bums.'

They had their eyes fixed on him; they scratched their chins as if contemplating the course of violence. Sher Singh could do nothing except look down at his hands or at their feet.

'Is this chap also involved in the killing of that fat Sikh lambardar?'

'No mun! He's after bigger game. He wants to shoot the Guv or the Viceroy. Don't you? Speak, you big leader of the revolution! Don't you?'

Sher Singh felt the blood drain out of his system. Were they going to beat him? Why didn't they ask him a specific question and give him a chance to answer?

'Oi,' shouted one of them to the constable outside, 'ask the sub-inspector to *juldi karo*. We can't waste the whole afternoon with this fellow.'

The constable ran across the courtyard. The sub-inspector came with a sheaf of yellow files tucked under his arm. They got into a huddle. Sher Singh watched them carefully as they whispered into each other's ear. The older of the two sergeants pushed aside the file with disdain: 'Wot you wasting your time for on this chap if the other fellows have already given us all the names?'

'I don't know, Sahib,' answered the sub-inspector feigning surprise. 'Mr Taylor, Deputy Commissioner, say he Sardar Buta Singh's son, give him chance to be informer and save his life.'

'So that's it! You hear, mister? The DeeCee wants to give you a chance to save your bloody neck from hanging because of your old Bap. We have all the information we want from your pals. It's a water-tight case. You confirm what they have said and we might consider granting you pardon. Otherwise you hang with the rest of the buggers.'

Sher Singh found his voice with great difficulty: 'What did they say?'

'The bugger wants to know what the others have said? Clever fellow isn't he? Don't try tricks with us, old chap. We've known too many like you.'

The Indian sub-inspector was more polite—obviously wanting to curry favour with Buta Singh. 'Sardar Sahib,' he said in Punjabi, 'as the Sahibs have told you, we have all the information we need from your associates. This is a very serious case; you can be sentenced to death for conspiracy to wage war against the King Emperor. Mr Taylor wants to reward the loyal services of your respected father and has ordered us to give you the chance to be a Crown witness. If your statement confirms what the other conspirators have said and is truthful about the crimes you have committed, the Government may decide to grant you pardon. Do you understand?'

'Yes.'

Three pairs of eyes were fixed on him.

'Could I consult a lawyer?'

'Rape your sister,' exploded one of the sergeants. 'We want to give you a chance to save your neck and you want to bring lawyers here! Give him the rod properly greased.'

The Indian sub-inspector again took charge of the situation with a mixture of servility and firmness. 'Sardar Sher Singh, you have not appreciated our point. We know everything already and really have no need for your statement. It is only for your own good. If Taylor Sahib insists on sparing your life because of Sardar Buta Singh, we can make you talk; you know that, don't you?'

Sher Singh made no answer to the threat.

Three pairs of eyes continued to transfix him. He did not know what to say. But he knew that if they used any violence he would tell all he knew without considering the rights or wrongs of making the confession. He made one last attempt to postpone the decision. 'Could I at least see my father?'

'Now he wants to see his Bap. What's wrong with this fellow?'

'Perhaps he will want to see his Ma too,' added the other.

'You don't believe what we say?' asked the Indian subinspector angrily. 'It is because your father has been rubbing his nose at Mr Taylor's threshold every day that you are being given his opportunity!'

'It is very kind of you but I would like to speak to my father before making any statement.' For the first time Sher Singh spoke firmly, and that because an Indian subordinate had dared to talk disparagingly of his father.

The three officers went back into a huddle and then rose up together. The one with his feet on the chair kicked it towards Sher Singh. 'O.K. You see your bloody Bap. We'll talk to you later.'

'And if you want our advice on how to kick the British out of India, don't hesitate to ask.'

They roared with laughter and left.

❧

The non-stop reading of the Granth did not bring any peace in Buta Singh's home. What was worse, the Guru did not indicate the line of action as Sabhrai had promised. And soon after the ceremonial reading was over, Buta Singh resumed his sulking and self-pity. He refused to see Sher Singh in the lock-up, and would not let anyone else see him. He began to insinuate that Champak must have known of her husband's activities and had done nothing to stop him. When Champak's parents heard of it, they came over and took her back home. At last Sabhrai's patience came to an end. One morning she boldly announced her intention to see her son. Buta Singh was adamant. The crisis was averted by the arrival of the officer in charge of the police station. He told them that Sher Singh had expressed the desire to see his father before making a statement and that Mr Taylor had specially requested Buta Singh to comply with his son's wishes.

Buta Singh refused to comply. He thought that, in the circumstances, the refusal to obey Taylor would more than ever prove his loyalty to the Government and disapproval of his disloyal son. The responsibility fell automatically on Sabhrai. She accepted it readily, not because she had any advice to give her son on the statement he was to make, but because her heart ached to see her son and to clasp him to her bosom. She asked her husband to tell her what she was to say to Sher Singh about the confession.

Buta Singh explained the legal situation to her again. She

asked: 'If the police already know the names of his associates why do they want them all over again from Sher?' He explained, as he said, for the twentieth time, because they wanted to give him a chance to get away. Why, she went on, were they so keen on letting him get away? For the hundredth time, answered her husband, because Mr Taylor was so kind and friendly to a family which had a long record of loyalty. Why, persisted Sabhrai, if the police really knew the names of Sher's associates hadn't they arrested any of them? Oh really, Buta Singh couldn't be bothered to go over things again and again. Sabhrai had developed a stubborn indifference to rudeness and irritation and asked her husband point blank: 'What will happen if he refuses to make a confession?'

'What will happen? As far as I am concerned, my service, pension, and the land granted by the Government all go. But that is a small matter; in addition, the boy will be hanged.'

Sabhrai shut her eyes: 'The True, the True. The Great Guru, the Great Guru.'

She turned to her daughter. 'Have you any advice for your brother?'

'I only want him back,' she replied full of emotion. 'I don't care what he says or does, but he must come home now.'

Buta Singh felt that he should not let the matter be postponed indefinitely. 'Will you go tomorrow morning? I have to tell the sub-inspector.'

'What is the hurry? We have waited so many days. We should think about it a little more.' answered Sabhrai.

Buta Singh launched into another tirade. When he finished telling her how little she appreciated the gravity of the situation, how stubborn and stupid she had become of late, Sabhrai got up. 'I will talk to the inspector myself,' she said.

The sub-inspector stood up and saluted Sabhrai.

'Have you come from the police station where my son is kept?'

'Yes, Mataji, your son is in our care.'

'Tell your senior officer I will come to the police station four days from now. I will come, not my husband. I would also like to bring my son's dog with me. He has missed his master very much.'

'Very good, Mataji. I will tell the Inspector Sahib. Is there anything you want to send to your son or any message you want me to give him.'

Sabhrai thought for a while. 'If you wait for a moment, I will give you something for him.' She went into the house and came back with a small prayer book wrapped in velvet. 'Give this to my little Ruby and tell him to say his prayers regularly. Tell him that the Guru is with him in body and in spirit. *Sat Sri Akal.'*

The sub-inspector was a Muslim. Nevertheless he put the Sikh prayer book reverently to his forehead and then kissed it. 'Mataji, I will give it to him myself. Allah will protect your son from harm.'

For the next three days Sabhrai shut herself away from the world. Her sanctuary was not the Gurudwara but her own bedroom. She sat in her armchair with her legs tucked beneath her and murmured her prayers. Her only companion was Dyer. She had never taken much notice of the dog but since her son's arrest she had tried to give him the affection Sher Singh had given. Dyer sat in front of his mistress with his chin stretched on the floor and his eyes dolefully fixed on her. After each prayer she would speak to him: 'Dyer, son, will you come with me to see Sher?' Dyer would prick up his ears at his master's name and cock his head inquiringly from side to side. 'Nobody takes you out for walks these days?' Like all dogs, Dyer knew the word 'walk.' He would get up with a whine and come to his mistress wagging his big tail. 'That's all right, son. Mama will take you out when you are well. And when my Moon comes home, we will all go for walks together, won't we?' And Dyer would again be full of questions cocking his head from left to right, right to left. Sometimes he would get too excited, put his paws in his mistress' lap, and lick her face. She would push him away gently, for this she did not like. She would wipe her face with her headpiece, wash her hands in the bathroom, and start praying again. An hour later the whole thing would be repeated: 'Dyer, son, will you come with me to see my Shera?'

The evening before the interview, she had her dinner with her husband and daughter and told them she was going to spend the night at the temple in the city. They did not ask her any questions. She wrapped herself in her Kashmir shawl, for it had become bitterly cold, and went away on a tonga.

When Sabhrai took off her slippers outside the main gate, the man in charge of shoes was already packing up. 'Brother, keep my shoes for the might; I will take them in the morning.' He gave her a ticket, put out his hurricane lantern, and locked the shoe-shed.

Not many people stay in the temple after the evening service is over. Visitors from other towns retire to the quarters provided for them; beggars are driven away by armed guards who patrol the sacred premises. Only those stricken with sorrow spend the midnight hours in different corners crying and praying for peace. These no one disturbs.

Sabhrai washed her hands and feet in the cistern at the entrance and went down the marble stairs gripping the silver railing on the side. The waters of the sacred pool and the milk-white of the marble walls glistened in the moonlight. The gilded dome of the shrine had a ghostly pallor. Sabhrai bowed towards the shrine. She walked along the side-walk and up the narrow passage, which ran level with the water, to the central place of worship. The room was dimly-lit by a blue electric bulb; the diamonds and rubies in the ceiling twinkled like stars on a dark night. In the centre of the floor the sacred Granth lay wrapped on a low cot. In the corners of the room were huddled figures of men and women, some asleep, some in prayer. Sabhrai made her obeisance and went out. She found a spot from where she could see the dome of the temple and the reflection of the moon and the stars in the dark waters of the sacred pool. She sat down on the hard and cold marble floor. An icy wind blew over the water, through the trellised fence, into her bones. But it was absolutely still and peaceful. The city was asleep; only the gentle clop clop of ripples on marble and the boom of the tower clock striking the hours disturbed the heavy silence.

Sabhrai did not know what prayer one recited during the night; so she went through all she knew by heart. When she had finished, the clock struck two. But the tumult in her mind was not stilled. They were going to hang her son if he did not mention the names of the other conspirators. Hang her little Shera whom she had borne and fed by her own breasts. She began to sob. She stifled her sobs and tried to meditate. How could she meditate with Shera crying for help: 'Mother, they will hang me and I am only twenty-one.' Tears coursed down her cheeks, hot and unceasing. She wiped them with the hem of her shirt and blew her nose. She felt her son's presence between her arms, and more tears flooded down. Why did she feel alone in this awful predicament? Her husband had no doubts; he wanted Shera to confess. So, obviously, did her daughter and daughter-in-law. Sher mattered as much to them as he did to her. Did they really believe that the police knew everything or were they doping their consciences with the thought? And what did Shera himself want to do? Surely it was really for him to decide rather than for her? And if she were the only one with doubts, couldn't she be mistaken?

So the tumult continued and the tears continued to course down her cheeks. Her gray head was full of dew and her limbs stiff with cold and damp. Why did the Guru not guide her in her hour of need? Had she lost faith? She recalled the time when she had come to this very temple to take part in the cleaning of the sacred pool. The water had been pumped out and the enormous carp that ate out of people's hands had been put away in another tank. Millions of Sikhs had volunteered to carry on their heads the slime which had accumulated for over a hundred years. People said that the hawk of the last Guru would come to see the cleaning. Non-believers had laughed their vulgar laughter, shrugged their shoulders, and said: 'What can you do to people like that?' But the hawk had come. With her own eyes she had seen it swoop down from the heavens, scattering the thousands of pigeons that nested in the temple precincts. It had perched on the pinnacle of the golden dome, preened its lustrous white plumage, and looked down on the throng waist deep in slime and mire. The people had wept and prayed. Over and over again men had hurled the Guru's challenging cry: 'Ye who seek salvation, shout,' and the crowd had roared back: 'God is Truth.' People with faith had seen; those without faith neither saw nor believed that others had seen. Sabhrai also recalled the terrible days when the Sikhs wanted to take over their shrines from the clutches of corrupt priests and the police had decided to help the priests against the people. They had killed and tortured passive resisters. But for each one who was killed, beaten, or imprisoned, another fifty had come. Word had gone round that whenever a band of passive resisters prayed with faith, the Guru himself would appear in their midst and all the lathi blows the police showered on them would fall on him and not on them. That was exactly how it had happened. Frail men and women, who had not known the lash of a harsh tongue, had volunteered and taken merciless beatings without wincing. The police had tired and the priests had panicked. The faith of the Sikhs had triumphed. Was her faith shaking? She tried to dismiss all other thoughts and bring the picture of the last warrior Guru to her mind. He came as he was in the colour print on her mantelpiece: a handsome bearded cavalier in a turban, riding his roan stallion across a stream. On his right hand was perched his white falcon with its wings outspread. *There* was a man. He had lost all his four sons and refused to give in to injustice. She was to lose only one. How had the Guru faced the loss of his children? She began to recite his stirring lines:

> 'Eternal God, who art our shield
> The dagger, knife, the sword we wield
> To us protector there is given
> The timeless, deathless Lord of Heaven.

It went on, its short staccato lines infusing warm blood into her chilled veins and making her forehead hot with anger. She was a Sikh; so was her son. Why did she ever have any doubts?

By the time the prayer ended, the gray light of dawn had dimmed the lesser stars—only the morning star shone a pure, silvery white. At last there was peace in her soul. She got up and went to the women's enclosure to bathe. The water was bitter cold and she shuddered as she went down the steps. She bobbed up and down naming members of her family with each dip with five extra ones for her Shera. She had brought no towel and dried herself in the breeze. She got back into her clothes, wrapped the warm shawl about her shoulders, and went to the inner shrine where the morning prayer was about to begin.

The priest unwrapped the Granth and read the passage for the day.

> 'Lord, thou art my refuge
> I have found Thee and my doubts are dispelled.
>
> I spoke not, but Ye knew my sorrow
> And made me to meditate on Thy holy name.
> Now I have no sorrow; I am at one with Thee

327

You took me by my arm
And led me out of Maya's winding maze
You set me free of the trap of attachment.

Spake the Guru: Thy fetters are fallen
Thou who wert estranged
Are united to Thy Lord.'

Sabhrai made her obeisance to the Granth and went out. At the entrance to the temple she scraped a palmful of dust that had come off the feet of pilgrims and tied it up in a knot in her headpiece. She took her slippers from the shoe stand and went home.

આ

The silence at the breakfast table was broken by the sound of a car drawing up in the porch. Mundoo came in to say that the Deputy Commissioner had sent his car to take Sabhrai to the police station. Buta Singh was very moved: 'What fine people these Taylors are! They have taken the trouble to find out and sent their car. Almost as if Sher were their own son.'

'The Guru will reward them for their kindness,' said Sabhrai. 'Those who are with you in your sorrow are your real friends. God bless them.'

The entire household, including the servants and orderlies, came to see Sabhrai off on her mission. Dyer, who had missed a car ride ever since the jeep had been taken away, cocked his unbelieving ears when his mistress asked him to come along. He gave a bark of joy and hopped onto the seat beside her. They drove off to the police station.

The Deputy Commissioner's car with its Union Jack and chauffeur in police uniform was well known to the staff of the police station. The sentries saluted as it went through the gates and the Anglo-Indian sergeants sprang to attention. Taylor's personal bodyguard stepped out of the front seat and opened the door. Dyer hopped out, followed by Sardarini Buta Singh.

The sergeants recognized the dog. They also realized that the native woman was Buta Singh's wife. The chauffeur enlightened them. They slunk away to the reporting room and let the Indian staff take over. The Muslim sub-inspector conducted Sabhrai to her son's cell.

Dyer was the first to greet his young master. He rushed at him, barking deliriously. He went round in circles, whining, pawing, and licking, and would not let Sabhrai get near her son. Sher Singh patted the dog on the head and pushed him aside gently. Mother and son clasped each other in a tight embrace. Sher Singh's pent up emotions burst their bounds and he began to cry loudly in his mother's arms. Sabhrai hid her unmanly tears by holding him to her bosom. She kissed his forehead again and again. They rocked in close embrace with the dog leaping about the cell, yapping and barking joyously.

'Could you leave us alone, sub-inspector Sahib?' asked Sabhrai addressing the officer.

'Certainly Mataji,' he replied, drying his eyes. 'Stay here as long as you like. Can I bring you some tea or something to eat?'

'No, son, just leave me here for a few minutes. I won't be long.

The sub-inspector went out and ordered the inquisitive group of constables back to their barracks.

Mother and son sat down on the charpoy. Dyer put his head in his master's lap.

'How pale you are! Do they give you enough to eat?'

'They give me all I want; I don't feel hungry. I could not even eat the food you sent me.'

'I did not send you anything.'

'Oh? The Deputy Commissioner's orderly brought it every day. I thought it was from home; it was Indian.'

'God bless him and his wife. Son, your father would not let me send you anything.'

'Is he very angry with me?'

'He had to be angry. You have poured water over all his ambitions.'

'What does he want me to do? The police tell me he wants me to make a statement naming the boys who were with me.'

'Yes. He thinks that is the only thing that will save you.'

'Have you all thought the matter over?'

'We have talked of nothing else. Everyone says that if the police already know about the others, there is no harm in making

329

a statement. And Taylor Sahib is showing you a special favour in letting you be the only one to get away.'

After a long pause Sher Singh asked: 'Has Champak said anything?'

'What can she say except to want you back! Her eyes are inflamed with too much weeping. She would accept any course which would bring you back home as soon as possible. What is your own opinion?'

'I . . . ,' said Sher Singh hesitantly, 'I have no opinion. I will do exactly what you people tell me to do. If it is true they know all about the affair, there seems no point in hiding anything any more.'

Sabhrai shut her eyes and rocked to and fro. After a while she asked, 'Son! Have they been beating you?'

Sher Singh looked down at his feet. The memory of the first thrashing came back to him. 'No, but they beat everyone who comes here. I can hear their cries every night.'

Sabhrai shut her eyes again and chanted as she rocked: 'The Great Guru! The True . . . Are you afraid?'

'Who is not afraid of a beating? Only those who get it know. It is easy to be brave at the expense of other people.' He stroked Dyer's head and tickled him between his front legs. 'Then are you all agreed that I should make a statement? What do you advise me?'

'I am an illiterate native woman, what advice can I give in these matters, son? I only ask the Guru to guide you. What He says is my advice.'

Sher Singh gave her time to tell him what the Guru had to say on the subject. Sabhrai simply closed her eyes and resumed rocking herself and chanting. 'The True, the True, The Great Guru.' Tears began running down her cheeks. Sher Singh put his hand on her knees: 'Mother, what do you want me to do?'

She dried her tears and blew her nose. 'Son, I spent last night at the Golden Temple asking the Guru for guidance. I do not know whether I got it right. In any case His orders were for me; not for you.'

'What did He say, Mother? Why don't you tell me?'

'He said that my son had done wrong. But if he named the people who were with him he would be doing a greater wrong. He was no longer to be regarded as a Sikh and I was not to see his face again.'

She undid the knot in her headpiece in which she had tied the dust collected at the temple and pasted it on her son's forehead with her palm. 'May the Guru be with you in body and in spirit.'

Chapter XI

Chapter XI

'Dear Taylor Memsahib. I am an uneducated Punjabi woman who cannot write nice words of thanks in English. Ask one of your clerks to read this to you. God bless you for what you have done. You wanted to share the grief of a mother whose child has been stricken. There is no greater act of kindness in the world. May the Guru's blessings be on you, your Sahib, and on your children. May you have many sons. May God ever keep your household full of plenty and keep sorrow and suffering away from your door.'

Sabhrai folded the paper with her shaking hands. Her head shook and she had difficulty in licking and sealing the envelope. She asked Shunno to give it to the Deputy Commissioner's chauffeur, who had driven her back from the police station, and then light a fire in her bedroom. By the time Shunno came back with old newspapers and firewood, Sabhrai was in bed with her quilt wrapped about her. Despite her will power, her teeth began to rattle and she began to shiver violently.

'Bibiji, you have fever,' said Shunno in alarm. 'You must have caught a chill.'

Sabhrai wanted to tell her to get on with her work, but no words would come out of her mouth. She shivered and shook; her forehead was hot, her body cold. Shunno quickly lit a fire. She came to her mistress and began to press her. The fit of shivering was soon over, Sabhrai relaxed in her warm bed and fell fast asleep in the heated room.

Neither her husband nor her daughter got a chance to ask her about her interview with Sher Singh. She had gone straight from the car to her room. An hour later, Shunno came to tell them she was asleep. They knew that she had been away all night and needed rest. If she had had anything really important to tell them, she would have done so before retiring. Obviously, thought Buta Singh, everything had gone according to plan and his son's release would now be a matter of time, an unpleasant time, with other arrests, and a public trial where Sher Singh, being the Crown witness, would be branded as a traitor. It would finish Sher's political career—but only for a time, for public memory was notoriously short. In any case it would save the boy's life. It would also save Buta Singh's face vis-à-vis Taylor who had trusted and relied on him and had been so good to his family in the worst crisis in his life. Buta Singh felt that at long last the nightmare of the past month was coming to an end. He was full of gratitude to Taylor and to God; even to Sabhrai—his illiterate, superstitious, half-companion of the past thirty years.

Sabhrai did not stir all afternoon. Beena tiptoed in and out of the darkened, stuffy room several times to see her. By evening she grew somewhat nervous and came to her mother's bedside. Sabhrai seemed to be in deep slumber. Beena watched her quilt for some time before she noticed the reassuring heave of her breath. She looked at her watch. Eight hours of continuous sleep was long enough. If Sabhrai stayed in bed longer, she would not be able to sleep at night; and she had not eaten all day. Beena called her softly. There was no sign of waking. She put her hand on her mother's forehead. It burnt with fever. Beena ran out to her father and told him. Buta Singh hurried in. They whispered to her, then called out loudly. She did not answer. They felt her pulse beat rapidly. Buta Singh sent his orderly to fetch a doctor.

જી

The doctor took her temperature and examined her chest and back with his stethoscope. He asked a few question and then told the family that Sabhrai had pneumonia. Her temperature was over 104° and she was in a state of delirium. But pneumonia was no longer something to be scared of, he assured them. The new American drug had got the better of it. He prescribed a medicine and gave detailed instructions about the nursing. He would call again in the morning.

Buta Singh and Beena took turns at watching over Sabhrai, and Shunno pressed her mistress's feet intermittently all through the night.

Next morning Buta Singh scanned the paper more carefully than he had done for a long time. There were no arrests of terrorists reported. Perhaps it was too early for the police to act or the boys had absconded. He felt as if he had been given one more day of respectability with the citizens. Would he be able to explain away his son's action? If his name appeared in the next Honours list (which would be published in another ten days), no one would ever accept his explanations. They would say that he had forced his son to betray his colleagues so that he could get his O.B.E or C.I.E., or one of the other titles that the British had invented for the Indians. What would it matter in the end! He would retire to his village with his pension and property intact. His family would be safe. He would be able to get his son a good job; Taylor would surely continue to help him.

In the crisis, the Englishman seemed to have become Buta Singh's only hope. It would be Christmas in three days. Perhaps he should make the Taylors some gesture of gratitude for what they had done. He knew they were very particular about accepting gifts from subordinates. His case was different; he was a friend as well. Besides, the circumstances warranted a symbolic expression of thanks. Christmas was a good opportunity to do so. In any case he would send it from his wife to Mrs Taylor.

After the doctor had come and gone, Buta Singh asked his orderly to go to the bazaar and buy three dozen of the best Malta oranges with blood-red centers. He busied himself in composing a letter to go with the gift.

Respected Mrs Taylor,

Pray accept this humble gift of oranges for Christmas Day. They are the first pick of the year from our garden. I hope you will like them. To you and your noble husband, our most respected Deputy Commissioner, my husband and children owe their all. Madam will do us an honour by receiving this very little gift on the auspicious occasion of the birthday of the World Savior, Lord Jesus Christ.

Your humble servant,
Sabhrai
(Sardarini Buta Singh)
wife of
Sardar Buta Singh, B.A. (Hons),
Magistrate First Class.

Buta Singh read the letter over several times. Did it sound too servile? No, he decided, nothing sounds too obsequious to the recipient. The only important thing was that the gift should not be returned because a snub in these circumstances would be hard to take. Also, other people should not get to know about it and make fun of him.

The basket of oranges and the letter were sent off three days before Christmas. To Buta Singh's great relief, it was not returned. Mrs Taylor accepted the gift and, in accordance with Indian custom, left two oranges and a five rupee note as tip for the orderly. She held the orderly to inform his mistress that she would come over personally to thank the Sardarini.

Mrs Taylor came to call next morning. Buta Singh had already told his daughter about the oranges. 'I said they came from our garden because it sounds better,' he explained blandly. 'I sent them from your mother. Mrs Taylor has been specially good to her.'

'How extremely kind of you to send us the first pick from your garden,' said Mrs Taylor as she stepped out of the car and held out her hand.

'Oh nothing, Mrs Taylor. A very humble gift. It was most kind of you to accept.'

'And this is your daughter? We met at the station. How are you? Where is the Sardarini Sahiba? I must thank her for the wonderful oranges. I'll try my Hindustani.'

'She is very ill,' answered Beena. 'She has been in a state of delirium for the last two days.' Buta Singh realized that his daughter was contradicting his story of the oranges being sent by Sabhrai. He broke in quickly, 'No, nothing, it is just a little cold and fever. The doctor said it would be controlled by the new American drug. It costs me thirty-five rupees each day. But I say, "Money

335

does not matter." Of course you can see her.' He opened the door to usher her in.

'I was a nurse before I married John,' explained Mrs Taylor. 'Perhaps I can be of some help.'

Buta Singh went on, 'You have done enough of helping. We will not forget it all our lives.'

Sabhrai's room was warm and dark. A fire smouldered in the chimney. The windows were shut and there was an oppressive odour of mint and eucalyptus. Under the table-lamp beside her bed were an assortment of bottles of medicine, a thermometer, and a tumbler of water. There was also a picture of the first Guru in a silver frame, and a rosary. Beside the bed on the floor was a basin of margosa leaves for her to be sick in. Shunno drew her veil across her face as her master came in and went on rubbing the soles of her mistress's feet.

Joyce Taylor was surprised that in an educated Indian home there should be so much disregard of the elementary rules of hygiene. Her nursing past got the better of her recently acquired status as the wife of the Deputy Commissioner. 'Why have you got the room so hot and stuffy?'

'You see, madam, she has caught a cold and draughts are not good for her,' explained Buta Singh.

'Rubbish! Open the doors and windows at once. She needs fresh air. Have you kept a temperature chart?'

Joyce Taylor opened the windows herself and took the temperature chart which lay under the tumbler of water. She examined it carefully. Then she put her hand under the quilt and felt Sabhrai's pulse.

Mrs Taylor put her cold hand on Sabhrai's hot forehead and gently pushed back her eyelids. Sabhrai kept her eyes open but there was no look of recognition in them.

'How are you, Sardarini?'

Sabhrai's lips quivered; she was trying to say something.

'Taylor's Memsahib has come to call on you. Don't you recognize her?' asked Buta Singh loudly in Punjabi.

There was another quiver of her lips. Then tears welled in her eyes and rolled off into her ears. Joyce Taylor wiped Sabhrai's tears with her handkerchief and gently pressed her hand on her eyes. 'Go to sleep like a good girl. You'll soon be well.' She asked Buta

Singh about the doctor and scrutinized the prescription he had made out.

'Very expensive medicine this new thing,' said Buta Singh.

'Next time you send for the doctor, let me know. I would like to have a word with him,' she ordered. She gave a friendly pat on Sabhrai's cheek and got up. 'You mustn't allow any visitors for some days. There must be no excitement at all. She is very ill.'

࿏

Among happily married people there grows up a private language of accent, emphasis, and gesture which makes privacy between them almost impossible. If they have shared a common past, they get to know each other's reactions to particular situations and have an instinctive knowledge of each other's attitude to any set of new circumstances. Sometimes, long forgotten tunes come up in their minds and without any reason at all they find themselves humming the same notes at the same time. Then there are ways of behaviour which indicate to no one but themselves what the other has in mind. Even at the dinner table the way the wife will pass the bread, or, later, the way she will walk up to her room will tell the husband that she wants to be slept with that night. It is not so simple when she wants favours others than sexual. Nevertheless the husband will become aware of something brewing in her mind long before it is put in words.

There was nothing subtle about Joyce Taylor's fidgets the evening after she had returned from the Buta Singh home. It continued throughout dinner and she remained close to her husband afterwards. This was contrary to the normal practice of giving him an hour with his files before rejoining him for coffee.

'Something on your mind, dear?' Taylor asked at last.

'Yes and no. I mean there is something but I don't know exactly what it is.'

'That doesn't get us very far. What have you been doing with yourself all day?'

'The same as any other day—apart from calling on old Buta Singh and his family. Curious lot, aren't they?'

'How did it go?'

'Not too bad. I don't understand the Old Walrus with his

obsequious "respected Memsahib" and "our noble Deputy Commissioner".'

'Don't be too hard on the old stick; he's been brought up like that. The English are his Mai-Bap, Father-Mother when they are about; when they are not, he is more himself. But he is all right. Does his job honestly and has certainly done more for the war effort than any other officer in the district.'

'What I cannot understand is if he really feels that way about the British Raj, that he should have a son mixed up with terrorists.'

'Well! In a way you have the history of Indo-British relationships represented by Buta Singh's family tree. His grandfather fought against us in the Sikh wars; his father served us loyally. He has continued to do so with certain reservations. His son is impatient to get rid of us. Poor Buta Singh is split between the past and the future; that is why he appears so muddled in the present. He is not as much of a humbug as he appears to be.'

'One knows where one stands with the younger generation of Indians. They certainly do not want to have anything to do with us.'

'I am not so certain of that either,' answered Taylor. 'The boy in the police lock-up is in as much of a muddle as his father.'

'What do you mean? He wants India for the Indians, he is willing to kill the English if he can't get rid of them in any other way.'

'It isn't as clear as that. You heard about the Alsatian dog he has—the one which attacked one of the police officers who arrested him and which Sardarini took to the police station! Well, he named him Dyer, quite obviously because it was the most hated name he could think of : General Dyer fired on a crowd in this very city and killed several hundred men and women. In giving a dog that name, he expressed his loathing for the General. Now apparently he loves the dog more than his own relations.'

'I don't know if that indicates much,' laughed Joyce.

'No, except that it is all a bit muddled.'

Taylor began to show signs of impatience. 'Let's have coffee. I can do my work later on; there isn't very much to do.'

She ordered the coffee and the two came into the study. He lit his pipe. 'How is the family taking the boy's arrest?'

'I couldn't find out. The Walrus did all the talking; I couldn't get a clue from him. John, how does the case against the boy stand?'

'So far there is no evidence at all. The police haven't made up their minds what to do with him. They have means of making people talk when they want to. They never fail.'

'You mean torture.'

'You can call it that. It may be nothing more than a threat or an inconvenience. With educated city dwellers like Sher Singh they should have no difficulty.'

The bearer brought in the coffee. They drank it in silence. Joyce still showed no signs of leaving. When she noticed her husband impatiently emptying his pipe, she asked him in a nervous, high-pitched voice: 'John, you can't keep that boy in prison indefinitely till he confesses to a crime he may never have committed. That's the sort of thing we are fighting against in this war.'

Taylor filled his pipe and lit it before answering. 'A man is missing; it can be presumed that he is dead. If someone had told me about his disappearance a little earlier, I would have put the police on the right track. He had been seeing me regularly.'

'What makes you think Buta Singh's son killed him?'

'It is only a guess. He had seen some boys including Sher Singh at target practice; he brought me the fired bullets. They also tried to blow up a little bridge on the canal. He told me about that too.'

'Yes, yes,' she cried impatiently, 'but how did they know he was telling you these things?'

'Buta Singh's son was certainly aware of it; I had it conveyed to him that I knew. I hoped it would stop his goings on.'

'It is possible one of the others killed him without Sher Singh having anything to do with it.'

'It is possible but highly improbable.'

Joyce Taylor had no more arguments but was still reluctant to give up. 'How long do you deprive a man of his liberty because of probability of guilt?'

Taylor looked a little surprised at her vehemence. 'Not for long; if there isn't any further evidence. You seem very wrought up today. What is the matter?' He ran his fingers through her hair. She let her head drop on his shoulder.

'John, will you promise me something?'

'What is it, dear?'

'You won't be cross with me for interfering in your business?'

'I promise not to be cross, but I am likely to say no.'

After a long pause she continued: 'The Walrus's wife—the Sardarini—is ill, very ill.'

'Oh!' exclaimed Taylor, a little surprised. 'This is the first I have heard about her illness. What is the matter with her?'

'The doctor has diagnosed it as double pneumonia. Apparently before interviewing her son she spent the night praying at the Golden Temple. She must have got the chill there.'

Taylor was not a religious man, but this sort of devotion moved him. 'I am very sorry to hear that. She has the dignity of an ancient people behind her. Without knowing her I have respect for her. If you like, I can ask the English Army doctor to see her.'

'I do not think she has the will to live. Unless she gets back that will, no doctor will able to help her.'

Taylor continued stroking her hair.

'John, why can't we give her a Christmas present which will mean something to her? Really mean something.'

Taylor got up, carrying his wife in his arms as if she were a child. He kissed her and put her on her feet. 'They don't believe in Christmas; they are not Christians. Come along now. Time for bed.'

❧

The Muslim sub-inspector entered the cell with a conspiratorial smile on his face. 'Congratulations, Sardar Sher Singh. A hundred, hundred congratulations.'

'What about?' asked Sher Singh feigning ignorance. He knew in prison there could only be one reason to congratulate anyone.

'If you give us some sweets, I will tell you.'

'Even so?'

The sub-inspector dramatically held out a piece of yellow paper. 'An order for your release. Tomorrow morning you will be discharged. Mr Taylor's orders are that your respected parents should not be told but that you should be taken home as a surprise for the Big Day. Tomorrow is Christmas, you know!'

'Christmas for the Christians,' said Sher Singh disdainfully. 'Tell me, what happened about the case? Am I being released on bail?'

'No, no, Sardar Sahib. Discharged! Finished! Holiday! There was no evidence against you.'

'I thought you had all the evidence for some case or other from the boys who had confessed.'

'Oh, you are still yesterday's child, Sardar Sher Singh! You will get to know the ways of the Punjab police when you grow up. No one has been arrested so there are no confessions. You have nothing to worry about. Go home and have a good time. Some day when you are a big man, a minister or something, think of poor sub-inspector Wali Dad who gave you the good news.'

'That is very kind of you.'

Sher Singh pondered. Next day was Christmas. There would be no newspapers. 'I don't suppose it would be possible for you to delay my release by a day.'

The sub-inspector looked puzzled. 'Don't you want to go home? It is the Deputy Commissioner's order. If it is disobeyed, I'll have my plug taken out. It is not only because it is the Big Day tomorrow but also because your respected mother is in indifferent health.'

'Oh! no one told me about that.' Sher Singh really didn't believe it. Probably Taylor was trying to be a boy scout and an Oriental monarch in one—releasing a prisoner on Christmas Day to save the life of a dying mother. 'Would you do me a favour? Could you take a message to a friend of mine. He is Mr Wazir Chand's son, Madan. He is my best friend.'

'Mr Madan, the famous cricketer? With great pleasure. I will deliver it personally. I know his respected father, Mr Wazir Chand, Magistrate.'

Sher Singh took up a piece of buff coloured paper from a large pad and wrote:

Dear Madan,

You will be glad to hear that I am being released tomorrow. Please convey this information to all my friends in the University (but not to my parents for whom I want it to be a pleasant surprise).

The police did their worst to get information from me but

341

they failed. I am proud to have been able to serve my God and my country. We should exploit this little service I have done to our best advantage. Greetings to all the comrades in arms.

Long live the Revolution.

Your brother,
Sher.

He put the letter in an envelope and sealed it. 'This is private, sub-inspector Sahib. I shall be grateful if the inspector does not read it before it is forwarded.'

'What will you say when you are a great man? Wali Dad did me a little service,' said the sub-inspector. He shook Sher Singh with both hands and put the letter in his pocket.

Sher Singh was flushed with excitement. At long last it had come. An imprisonment and a heroic stand against torture by the police. What more could anyone ask for? He would be the hero of the city for the next few days. If he kept up the citizens' interest and faith in him, a political career was his for the asking. What about his father? The Government could not penalize him for something it had been unable to prove against his son! He would make it up to him by his success. And his father had almost certainly more than made it up with Taylor. All was well. Sher Singh knew his star was in the ascendant once more. He hardly thought of his mother's illness. In fact, he did not believe there was any truth in it. It must be another canard let loose by his father to get round Taylor.

Madan did not fail his friend. He spent the whole of Christmas Eve going round to all the college hostels and telling the boys to turn up at the police station at the crack of dawn. He informed the Nationalist Party office and persuaded them to hire a brass band and get an open car to take Sher Singh in procession. He got hold of press photographers and newspaper correspondents, all of whom had been obliged to him for exclusive interviews and pictures of sporting events. In publicizing Sher Singh they were on a safe wicket. Father, a senior magistrate—son, a student leader on the road to fame and power.

From the early hours of the morning crowds of students

carrying garlands of marigolds and roses began to collect outside the police station. By eight o'clock, the crowd had swelled to three or four thousand. An open car decorated with buntings and flowers drew up and took its place behind the brass band made up of retired Sikh soldiers. When the gate of the police station was opened there were thunderous cries of 'Long live the revolution' and 'Long live Sher Singh'. There were no white sergeants on duty on Christmas Day, and the Indian police officers were not unduly perturbed at an unlawful assembly at their doorstep. All said and done, it was to honour the son of a magistrate.

Sher Singh was escorted out by a couple of sub-inspectors. Camera bulbs flashed. The band leader ordered his men to attention. The drum beat a loud tattoo and then opened with the slow bars of 'God Save the King.' There was an uproar. The band leader had his baton snatched out of his hand. The anthem whimpered to a standstill amid roars of laughter. The crestfallen band leader started again. This time with 'It's a long, long way to Tipperary.'

Sher Singh shook hands with his police escort and was immediately submerged in embraces and garlands. Madan led him to the car through a crowd cheering and yelling wildly. He stood beside Sher Singh in the open car, waved his hand and shouted, 'Sher Singh.' The crowd roared back, 'Long live.' Sher Singh raised both hands asking for silence. Everyone shushed everyone else. The band stopped—still a long, long way from Tipperary.

'Comrades,' said Sher Singh in a voice charged with emotion, 'I will cherish the honour you have done me today for the rest of my life. I am proud that I was called upon to do a small duty to my country and I did it.' The crowd interrupted him with loud cheers. He raised his hands, demanding attention. 'I have been a guest of the King Emperor.' The crowd roared with laughter. 'You all know how well the King Emperor—may peace be upon him—looks after his guests. . . .' The crowd roared again. Sher Singh worked himself into a fury. He thumped his garland laden chest. 'But they could not break the spirit of this son of India and God willing they never will.' Madan hurled his voice across the sea of human heads, 'Sher Singh'—the sea thundered back 'Long live.' Sher Singh joined his hands and bowed his head in humble acknowledgment. He was deeply moved by the affection of the crowd and by his own words.

There were tears in his eyes.

The band struck up a slow march and the procession began to move. Sher Singh sat on the rear acknowledging the cheers and bowing to people who kept loading him with garlands and hurling rose petals at him.

&

On Christmas morning, Buta Singh and his daughter were having breakfast in Sabhrai's bedroom. Mrs Taylor's warning that she was to be left strictly alone had been ignored. It was an old custom to be by the bedside of a sick, person, and so they were—all the twenty-four hours—eating, sleeping, and gossiping. Sabhrai had remained in a state of delirium with the fever never falling below 104°. She opened her eyes sometimes and tried to speak, but only an inaudible whisper escaped her lips.

Buta Singh looked up from his plate and wiped the egg off his mustache with his napkin. 'Sounds like a wedding procession. They have started early.' Beena sat still. She heard the shouting of slogans. 'Couldn't be a wedding party; sounds more like a political procession.' The music and the shouting came nearer and nearer till it was inside the house. They got up and hurried out of the room. The band was playing in their porch. The garden, the driveway, and road were jammed with boys chanting 'Long live the Revolution.' As Buta Singh appeared on the scene the chanting changed to 'Long Live Buta Singh. Long live Sher Singh.' A dozen young men rushed forward to congratulate the magistrate. It was then he noticed his son loaded with garlands. The father and son fell into each other's arms. All differences of opinion, all rancour which had poisoned their relationship over the past months were submerged in the applause of triumph.

&

It was Sabhrai's ninth day in bed. On the ninth day the fever usually subsides and the patient is on the mend—unless, of course, there is a relapse. In which case, the process starts all over again. Nobody could say that the family had not done their best in looking after her. They never left her bedside for a moment. Her husband and daughter took turns to watch over her all through the night. During the day, there were other relations or servants always present. Shunno showed great endurance in keeping the house going and also being with the mistress at all hours; pressing her tired limbs, talking to her when she mumbled in her delirium, comforting her with words in baby language and with prayer. The doctor's instructions about the medicine and diet were also strictly carried out. As books of medicine prescribed, Sabhrai sweated profusely all night and in the morning her temperature was down by four degrees. She was obviously turning the corner.

She was awakened from her half delirious sleep by Beena embracing her and shouting in her ears that Sher Singh was back home. She heard the band and the slogans and the people talking excitedly. She saw many strange faces in her room till it was full of bright eyes and glistening teeth. She vaguely guessed what could have happened. Or was it another dream which would end in the nightmare of awakening?

Then her son appeared. His sister had reloaded him with garlands. He came and fell on her and smothered her with tears, kisses, and crushed flowers. His sister gently pushed him away; Mrs Taylor had said 'No excitement.' The physical touch of her son convinced Sabhrai that her son was free. She could not reason out why he was free. She had herself urged him on the way to death but merciful God had sent him back to her. Her lips quivered but no words came: only a long drawn moan and then a flood of tears.

When the doctor came an hour later, Sabhrai was in a state of complete collapse. In the excitement that prevailed in the house no one realized that this was the crucial ninth day. The doctor examined the chart and discovered that she had a relapse. But even he could not bring himself to being angry with as important a man as Buta Singh and on a day when there was so much rejoicing. Hadn't his only son been delivered from the jaws of death? He told the family that the son's coming had been too much for the patient and the fever would continue for another period. He assured them that Sher Singh's release would act like a tonic and she would pull through.

Five days later, Sabhrai got another dose of the sort of tonic the doctor had spoken of. On New Year's Eve, the correspondent of *The Tribune* turned up with garlands. This time they were for Buta Singh. He had been given the C.I.E. in the New Year's Honours list. Buta Singh refused to believe it. 'Not until I see in print!' he insisted. An hour later it was in print in the special supplement published for the Honours list. By then Buta Singh's colleagues had also learned of it. All the district's officers, clerks right down to the orderlies, and peons, turned up with garlands of flowers and gold thread. Those who knew the family invaded the house right into Sabhrai's bedroom to congratulate and garland her. It went on till late into New Year's Eve. Next morning it was the turn of the citizens who read of the honour conferred in the paper. So for more than twenty-four hours, the house was full of laughter, gaiety, and flowers. Even Sabhrai in her dazed state knew that God was back in His heaven because all was well with her family.

Sabhrai had not known many illnesses in her carefully regulated life and had considerable powers of resistance. Nevertheless more than a fortnight of high fever, which had touched 105°, come down and shot up again, had wasted her body and begun to tell on her heart. This was not noticed by the doctor. When the second period of fever came to an end, the family was more careful. In any case the period of excitement was over.

For two days Sabhrai had no fever; she was exhausted and looked deathly pale. She lay all day long staring at the ceiling above her and slowly telling the beads of her rosary. If she wanted anything she would slowly raise her hand for Shunno and whisper instructions in her ears. On the third day she seemed well on the way to recovery and was allowed to sit up in bed propped up with pillows.

The fourth day started well. She was in better form than ever. The family were having their breakfast in her bedroom. Her husband was airing his views on politics. 'This man Hitler must be an amazing character. He has raised the German people from defeat to such greatness. If India could produce a man like him, all would be well.'

Sher Singh took that sort of remark personally. 'The crisis produces the man,' he said pompously. 'India can only be ruled by strong men. This democratic business of votes for everyone, elections, assemblies, committees, is nonsense. I don't believe in it.'

After Sher Singh's short detention his pronouncements on politics had acquired sanctity.

Buta Singh swallowed a mouthful of curry. A stringy bit of vegetable stuck to his walrus moustache and began to dance up and down as he poured out platitudes with great earnestness. 'Absolutely right! What does a vote mean to illiterate semi-savage people! It may be all right in England, but not in India. What is the point of creating a jungle of committees and rules so that no one can see the way out? In our own administration they do the same. It doesn't take me in. I don't take any notice of committees. No red tape for me,' he said sitting back. The stringy piece of curry also sat back on his moustache. It looked funny but Buta Singh was talking so seriously that no one could draw his attention to it. 'If I had allowed myself to be fooled by files and rules of procedure I wouldn't have got where I have. It takes a shrewd man to see through them.'

A faint smile came on Sabhrai's pale face. She raised her hand with her rosary dangling between her fingers. Shunno got up and put her ear close to her mistress's mouth; then put her hands on her mouth and went into an irrepressible giggle. The family looked round. After two months of sighing, sorrowing, and sickness, Sabhrai had cracked a joke.

'What is it?' asked Beena.

Shunno could not speak; she was convulsed with laughter. The smile still played on Sabhrai's pallid face. Beena came close to her and she whispered the same words into her daughter's ear. Beena also burst out laughing.

'Tell us the joke too,' said Buta Singh, smiling eagerly. Beena held her laughter. 'Mama says there is a bulbul on the bough.'

Everyone including Buta Singh began to laugh. He brushed his moustache with his napkin and asked: 'Has it flown?'

Sabhrai nodded her head slowly still smiling.

'Thank god you are smiling today,' said Beena. She put her arms round her mother and kissed her on her cheeks and forehead.

Serious political discussion was over and everyone was happy. The joke was repeated to the doctor and other visitors who came. They dispersed to go to their work——to the law courts and the college.

❧

347

More people die between nine and eleven in the morning than at any other time of the day or night. Body temperature falls to its lowest degree in the early hours and after a short struggle the heart gives in.

But death was far from Sabhrai's mind on the morning she died. She lay propped up on her pillow looking out of the window. The ixora creeper grew outside and was in full bloom with clusters of scarlet flowers peeping in beside the frame. A pair of magpie robins were apparently contemplating matrimony. She could not see the hen, but the cock flew up to the window sill to serenade his sweetheart. Like a ballet dancer he ran across the sill in quick, short steps and came to a sudden halt. He jerked his wings behind him as a man tucks his thumbs in his waistcoat pocket. His tail went up, his chest swelled. He raised his head to the flowers and a full-throated song burst out of his tiny beak in sheer ecstasy. He pirouetted, ran back, and repeated the performance as if to an encore from his audience. Sabhrai knew that God certainly was in His heaven and all was right with the world.

There were a few things which bothered her mind. She had not understood why Sher Singh had been released. Had he ignored her advice and confessed? She did not feel strong enough to question him; she would do so when she was better. The first thing to do was to send him to fetch Champak from her parents. And now this calamity was over and Beena had taken her degree, it was time they got down to finding her a husband.

Sabhrai was immersed in these thoughts when the ormolu clock wound itself and after a preliminary *Kirr* struck the half hour. She looked round. There it was on the mantelpiece with its ivory face with faded gold spots. She had brought it with her in her dowry and it had kept the hours ever since. Only the clear metallic tinkle had gone. Sabhrai put her pillows flat and lay down. She felt very tired. Half an hour later, the ormolu clock again wound itself and after a long *Kirr* struck ten as if its nose were clogged with a heavy cold—*thig, thig, thig . . . .*

Sabhrai felt her feet go icy cold. She called out to Shunno as loud as she could. The maidservant hurried from the kitchen to her mistress's beside. 'Send for my family,' whispered Sabhrai. 'My time has come.'

'The True, The True. Don't say such things, *Beybey*! Let the time come to our enemies.'

'Don't talk. Send for my family. My time is drawing near.'

Shunno rushed out of the house to the sentry and asked him to get the Sardar and other members of the family together. Neither she nor the sentry thought of the doctor. What use are doctors when one's time is up?

Shunno came back to the room. Even she could see that Sabhrai was not wrong. She began to press her mistress's feet chanting in loud sing-song: 'The True, The True. The Great Guru.'

Sabhrai shook her head. 'Read me the passage for the month. I was ill and nobody read it out to me.'

Shunno fumbled with the pages of the prayer book, found the month of Magh, and began to read loudly:

> The Lord hath entered my being;
> I make pilgrimage within myself and am purified.
> I met Him
> He found me good
> And let me lose myself in Him.

> Beloved! If Thou findest me fair
> My pilgrimage is made,
> My ablution done.
> More than the sacred waters of the Ganga
> Of the Yamuna and Tribeni mingled
> at the Sangam;
> More than the seven seas.
> More than all these, charity, almsgiving, and prayer,
> Is the knowledge of eternity that is the Lord.

> Spake the Guru:
> He that hath worshipped the great giver of life
> Hath done more than bathe in the sixty and eight
> places of pilgrimage.

'Shall I read anything else?' asked Shunno coming closer to her mistress.

Sabhrai shook her head again. 'When is the first of Phaggan?'

'I don't know. Many days yet.'

349

'Don't forget to clean the Gurudwara and make the pershad. Wake up everyone in time and ask my Sardarji to read the prayer.'

Shunno began to sob. 'Beybey, why do you talk like this? You will read it yourself. We will sit and listen.'

Sabhrai ignored her sobs. She put her hand on her servant's shoulder. 'Now read the morning prayer to me.'

Shunno drew a chair beside her mistress's pillow. She never sat on a chair in the house but that was the only way she could get close to her. She picked up the prayer book and began to recite. Sabhrai lay back on her pillow and shut her eyes. She folded her hands across her navel and began telling the beads of her rosary.

Buta Singh was the first to arrive. 'Have you sent for the doctor?' he asked Shunno in an agitated tone. Sabhrai opened her eyes and spoke to her husband. 'I don't need a doctor, she whispered. 'Let me go to my Guru with your blessings.'

Buta Singh began to sniff. A few minutes later Beena turned up. She saw the pallor on her mother's face and heard her father sobbing in his handkerchief. Sabhrai opened her eyes again and put her hands on her daughter's head.

'May the Guru keep you from evil.'

'Mummy, don't talk like this. In the name of the Guru, don't,' she sobbed.

The tears gave way to a gloomy silence. Buta Singh and Beena sat on Sabhrai's bed and pressed her arms and feet. Sabhrai fell asleep utterly exhausted. Sher Singh was the last to arrive. Sabhrai woke up as soon as he came in—just as if she had been waiting for him all the time. She smiled and beckoned him to come close to her. She whispered in his ear: 'I shall not hear the nightingales, my son. May the Guru give you long life.'

Sher Singh was more emotional than the others and began to cry loudly. His father and sister broke down again.

'What is all this noise?' asked Sabhrai audibly. 'You want me to go with the noise of crying in my ears! Say the morning prayer—all together. And do not stop till it is over.' They suppressed their crying and began to chant together.

There is one God.
He is the supreme Truth.
He, the Creator,
Is without fear and without hate.

He, the omnipresent,
Pervades the universe.
He is not born.
Nor does He die to be reborn again.
By His grace shalt thou worship Him . . .

Sabhrai joined her family in the recitation. She seemed to be at complete peace with the world. An unearthly radiance glowed in her pale face. A few verses before the epilogue her voice became faint and then her lips stopped moving.

Chapter XII

In India an old person's death is a matter of rejoicing; a young person's one of sorrow. In the case of the former, they decorate the bier with paper flags and buntings and often hire a band to lead the funeral procession. Married women put vermilion in the parting of their hair and wear their bridal jewellery. Mothers ask their children to walk beneath the stretcher on which the corpse is carried so that they may have as long a life as that of the deceased. During the seven or ten days prescribed for mourning, there is much ceremonial but little sorrow. On the death of a young man, woman, or child, grief refuses to be confined by custom and expresses itself with savage abandon. Relations and friends of the bereaved indulge in orgies of crying, wailing, and beating of breasts till sorrow in drained of all tears.

Sabhrai was neither too old nor too young. By conventional methods of calculation, she had died before her time because she had left a daughter unmarried. So her going had to be condoled with the necessary concern expressed for Beena's future. Except for that, it was like the death of any other person who had had a fair innings though not a full one.

Four hours after her death she was carried to the cremation ground with practically half the city following in procession behind her flower-bedecked bier. The Taylors and many other officials had sent wreaths. There amongst a dozen other pyres in different stages of burning—some fiercely ablaze, others barely glowing under a mound of ashes—they put together a pile of logs and placed her body on them. They uncovered her face for a few minutes for all to see. She slept with a smile still hovering on her face. They put more logs on her, sprinkled them with clarified butter and rose water. A last prayer was said to consign her body to the Great Guru who had earlier in the day claimed her soul. Sher Singh took round a burning faggot and set the pyre aflame.

Three days later, he and his father went back to the cremation ground, sprinkled water on the ashes, and picked up whatever had escaped the all-consuming fire: knuckles, knee-caps, ankles, and other unrecognizable little bits of bone. They put them in a sack and took them home. The sack was placed under the cot on which the Granth lay. It had to stay there till Sher Singh could take time off to go to the Beas and scatter its contents in the river.

For the first two days no fire was lit in Buta Singh's house. The Wazir Chands brought food from their house and persuaded the family to eat. Everyone slept on the floor and most of the day was spent listening to the recitation of the Granth. Then relations turned up by the dozens and Champak and Sita had to organize their feeding and comfort; Beena was too distracted to be of any help. It was almost like a wedding—crowds of children shouting and playing about in the courtyard and a lot of coming and going of friends and relations. Men came wearing sad expressions on their faces: 'Very sorry to hear the news. How did it happen?' each one would ask. 'It was God's will. When the time is up, who can stop its coming?' would be Buta Singh's weary answer. They sat down on the carpet and were soon busy discussing business affairs till the next visitor arrived with the same sad face and the same question. 'Very sorry to hear the news. How did it happen?' 'It was God's will. When the time is up . . . .' Then as was customary, Buta Singh himself asked them to leave and go back to their work.

The women were more expressive. They drew veils as they came in, sat down on the ground, clasped each other by the shoulder, and rocked to and fro in silent embrace for a minute or two. Then they broke into a whine which changed to loud lamentation or beating of breasts till someone stopped them. They blew their noses in the hems of their shirts, wiped their tears with the backs of their hands, sighed, and turned to subjects closer to their hearts: a minute account of Sabhrai's last hour (followed by more crying). And then, 'Did Auntie Sabhrai fix her daughter up anywhere? How old is the girl now?' This lasted ten days. Then the relatives and the visitors departed and the family was left to itself.

Came the first of Phaggan.

In accordance with Sabhrai's wishes, Shunno swept the Gurudwara, opened the Granth, and got the family together. None of them was looking forward to it because this was an occasion closely associated with Sabhrai and for the first time in the living memory of any one of them, she was missing—and yet mysteriously present. She seemed to pervade the Gurudwara like the incense which rose spirally from the stick and then scattered lazily all over the room.

Buta Singh took Sabhrai's place in reading the Granth. He had resolved to keep his emotions under control. He read the verse on the month of Phaggan without faltering.

> *She whose heart is full of love*
> *Is ever in full bloom.*
> *She is in bliss because she hath no love of self.*
> *Only those that love Thee*
> *Conquer self-love.*
> *Come Thou and abide in me.*

> *Many a lovely garment did I wear*
> *But the Master willed not, and*
> *His palace doors were barred to me.*
> *When He beckoned, I went*
> *With garlands and strings of jewels and raiments of*
> *finery.*

> *Spake the Guru:*
> *A bride welcomed in the Master's mansion*
> *Hath found her true Lord and love.*

Buta Singh decided to say a few words to his family. 'Sabhrai has really found her true Lord and love, we . . . .' He put his head on the Granth and began to sob. The whole family broke down and wept quietly. He gave up the attempt. After a while he proceeded to read the passage for the day:

> *My eyes are wet as if nectar had dropped with the dew*
> *and washed them.*

My soul is athrill and full of gratitude.
For the Guru rubbed the touchstone with my heart
And found it was burnished gold.

Buta Singh was now in control of his emotions and decided to make another attempt. 'I only wanted to say this. I hope and pray that all of us will live up to the ideals of truth Sabhrai stood for. She was like the gold the Guru speaks of. She has left us and the light is gone out of our home. We must try to find our way in life in the same way as she did: through the Guru's words.'

355

Chapter XIII

Buta Singh had learnt not to rely too much on his memory. He did not make notes on the subjects he had to discuss, but usually numbered them and had symbols which fixed them in his mind. If it was only one thing he had to bring up, it didn't need much memorizing—and of course he thought of God, because there was only one God. Two didn't offer much difficulty either; it was 'just two things I had to ask you,' as one said even if there were more things to ask. There was no symbol for two. For three, there was the Trinity of Brahma the Creator, Vishnu the Preserver, and Siva the Destroyer. Four was always causing trouble, but the mere fact that it caused trouble was good enough to remind him that he must have had four points to discuss. For five there were the 'Five Beloved Ones'—the first batch of converts to the Sikh faith made by the last Guru. And beyond five it was too much to expect symbols to remind him of what they were, they had to be put down in his notebook.

Buta Singh went over the 'Five Beloved Ones' one by one. First in importance was to thank Taylor for the honour done him in the New Year's Honours list; he had given up hope of it altogether after his son's arrest. Two, was to thank Mrs Taylor—if he saw her—or tell Mr Taylor to convey to his wife his thanks for all the kindnesses shown to the family over the terrible months they had gone through. Third, was the business of his son, which he had not understood clearly. If his son had revealed the truth—as he must have for Buta Singh to get his title—why had there been no other arrests? And why had he been released in such a dramatic manner?

He had not asked his son because that was not the sort of thing one talked about—particularly when the son was being made so much of for his heroic stand against police torture. Taylor might drop a hint as to what had really happened. Fourth in order of importance was Sher Singh's future. Couldn't Taylor help him to get a job in the Government of India and save the boy from the vagaries of a political life? He was bound to know people in Delhi and an Englishman's recommendation was so much more effective than any Indian's. Indian V.I.P.s were always recommending people for jobs in the strongest terms and therefore no one took them seriously. A mildly worded letter from a junior English official could do miracles. That was four. Five! What was the fifth? Oh yes, the memorial to Sabhrai. He couldn't afford very much, but he would donate 4,000 to 5,000 rupees and perhaps Mr Taylor could suggest a charity and later on open or inaugurate it. Sabhrai had been such a good wife. Illiterate, but with some sort of charm that attracted sophisticated Europeans like Mrs Taylor. The thought brought tears to Buta Singh's eyes. He adjusted his black tie—he had bought one especially for his first call on the Deputy Commissioner after Sabhrai's death—and left the house going rapidly over 'The Five Beloved Ones.'

Taylor was friendlier than ever before. He came out into the verandah to receive Buta Singh and took him inside. There was his wife, too, with the appropriate expression on her face. 'I was so sorry to hear about the Sardarini; I really was. I couldn't have felt the loss of any relation of my own more keenly. She had that something about her which makes people think of their own mothers. She reminded me of mine.'

'Thank you; very kind of you, madam. What God wills happens.' This was the fifth subject on the list; she was upsetting the order. How could one switch from that to being honoured in the New Year's list! 'Madam and madam's husband have been most kind to me and my family. I cannot find words to express my heartfelt gratitude.'

Joyce Taylor made a one word comment: 'Rubbish.' Her husband softened it. 'Not at all, Buta Singh. The last few months must have been somewhat trying for you all.'

Trying! These British with their understatements! It was like going through hell. Buta Singh answered in the same tone, 'Yes, sir, very trying.' Joyce Taylor went out to order tea. Buta Singh got the chance to tick off the first of the 'Five Beloved.'

'Sir, I must thank you again for my title. It is a great honour.

'I am glad it came through, Buta Singh. You have done so much for the war effort. I was not sure if the people at the top would appreciate it. I was afraid somebody might distort this business of your son's and hold it against you. People are apt to be like that.'

'For that I have to thank my late wife, sir. She was the one to give good counsel to my son. I was too angry and disappointed at his disloyal behavior. He had washed out the loyal services of four generations. I was relieved that in the end he redeemed it.'

Taylor looked a little puzzled. The expression on the Indian's face convinced Taylor that Buta Singh did not know what had passed between his wife and son in the lock-up. Taylor decided not to tell him. 'Your wife must have been a great influence on the family,' he remarked.

'She was old-fashioned and would not learn English, answered Buta Singh. 'You know, sir, I got her many teachers, but she absolutely failed to learn the language. She was a very religious woman—she prayed all the time. This was again number five. His son came before her. 'She was very keen that Sher Singh should give up politics and take up a steady job. If he could be fixed up somewhere in the government of India, I would be very happy.'

Taylor knew what the other was driving at. 'Sure, Buta Singh, I shall be only too pleased to help. Not that I count for much in the government of India.

'How can you say that, sir? One word from you and everything will be done.' Buta Singh was happy. He would bring up the subject again when he had found out what to apply for and to whom.

Mrs Taylor came in carrying the tea-tray. She poured out the tea and handed Buta Singh his cup. Buta Singh took a noisy sip and put away the tea. Now for the fifth. He pulled a long face to preface the subject. 'Mrs Taylor, I want to seek your very kind advice on an important matter. I wish to erect a memorial for my late wife—a small library or a ward in a hospital or some such thing. I would be most grateful if you could advise me.'

'How thoughtful of you, Sardar Sahib! I will be delighted to help. Since she was so religious perhaps she would have liked to have given something to a religious institution—like a temple. I believe having wells dug is also a very popular form of charity in this part of the world. You must have known her mind?'

'You are right; she was very religious.' Buta Singh pondered. He couldn't possibly get Mr or Mrs Taylor to do anything with the building of a new Gurudwara or having a well dug in some village. The object of the charity would be lost. 'You see she was illiterate,' he repeated 'If I had asked her, she would have said, "Anything you like." That is why I ask you.'

'If you like I can find out what is needed in the city; we are short of practically everything. I will certainly let you know.'

Buta Singh was very pleased. He had succeeded in drawing Mrs Taylor into his plans. Now he needed no appointments to come here nor would he have to sit with other magistrates in the verandah waiting his turn to see Taylor. The 'Five Beloved Ones' had been satisfactorily dealt with. He finished his tea and put aside the cup. 'I must not waste your precious time,' he said, getting up. 'I will come and pay my respects again to you, Mrs Taylor. Goodbye, sir.'

'Goodbye, Sardar Sahib. It is so nice to see you cheerful after such a long time.'

'Thank you, madam. As a famous English poet has said, "All's well that ends well."'

Delhi

I asked my soul: What is Delhi?
She replied: The world is the body and Delhi its life.
Mirza Asadullah Khan Ghalib

This novel which took me over 20 years to write I dedicate to my son
Rahul Singh and his friend Niloufer Billimoria

Contents

A Note from the Author   364

Delhi   365

Lady J.H.T.   377

Bhagmati   392

Musaddi Lal   413

Bhagmati   447

The Timurid   455

Bhagmati   462

The Untouchables   481

Bhagmati   494

Aurangzeb Alamgir: Emperor of Hindustan   501

Bhagmati   520

Nadir Shah   524

Bhagmati   547

Meer Taqi Meer   549

Bhagmati   586

1857   590

Bhagmati   663

The Builders   665

Bhagmati   694

The Dispossessed   696

Bhagmati   720

A Note from the Author

In this novel I have tried to tell the story of Delhi from its earliest beginnings to the present times. I constructed it from records chronicled by eye-witnesses. Hence most of it is told in the first person. History provided me with the skeleton. I covered it with flesh and injected blood and a lot of seminal fluid into it. It took me twenty-five years to do so. I am not sure whether I have succeeded in my venture.

Some chapters in an earlier draft were published in *Evergreen Review* of New York and *The Illustrated Weekly of India*.

New Delhi   *Khushwant Singh*
15 September 1989

Delhi

I return to Delhi as I return to my mistress Bhagmati when I have
had my fill of whoring in foreign lands. Delhi and Bhagmati have
a lot in common. Having been long misused by rough people they
have learnt to conceal their seductive charms under a mask of
repulsive ugliness. It is only to their lovers, among whom I count
myself, that they reveal their true selves.

To the stranger Delhi may appear like a gangrenous accretion
of noisy bazaars and mean-looking hovels growing round a few
tumble-down forts and mosques along a dead river. If he ventures
into its narrow, winding lanes, the stench of raw sewage may bring
vomit to his throat. The citizens of Delhi do little to endear
themselves to anyone. They spit phlegm and bloody betel-juice
everywhere; they urinate and defecate whenever and wherever the
urge overtakes them; they are loud-mouthed, express familiarity
with incestuous abuse and scratch their privates while they talk.

It is the same with Bhagmati. Those who do not know her find
her unattractive. She is dark and has pock-marks on her face. She
is short and squat; her teeth are uneven and yellowed as a result of
chewing tobacco and smoking beedis. Her clothes are loud, her
voice louder; her speech bawdy and her manners worse.

This is, as I say, only on the surface— like the evil-smelling oil
people smear on their skins to repel mosquitoes, midges and other
blood-sucking vermin. What you have to do for things to appear
different is to cultivate a sense of belonging to Delhi and an
attachment to someone like Bhagmati. Then the skies over Delhi's
marbled palaces turn an aquamarine blue; its domed mosques and

pencil-like minarets are spanned by rainbows, the earth exudes the earthy aroma of khas, of jasmine and of maulsari. Then the dusky Bhagmati glides towards you swaying her ample hips like a temple dancer; her mouth smells of fresh cloves and she speaks like her imperial Majesty the Empress of Hindustan. Only when making love does she behave, as every woman should, like a lusty harlot. It is a simple formula: use your heart not your head, your emotion not your reason. I make Delhi and Bhagmati sound very mysterious. The truth is that I am somewhat confused in my thoughts. What I am trying to say is that although I detest living in Delhi and am ashamed of my liaison with Bhagmati, I cannot keep away from either for too long. In these pages I will explain the strange paradox of my lifelong, love-hate affair with the city and the woman. It may read like a *Fucking Man's Guide to Delhi: Past and Present* but that is not what I mean it to be.

৯

The plane touches down at Palam at 2100 hours, one hour behind schedule. 'Air-India planes used to arrive on the dot till the government took it over,' says someone. A voice over the speaker system orders us to remain seated. 'Why?' I demand of an air hostess gliding past me. She confides in my ear: 'Health!' India, mother of most diseases known to mankind, does not want to add any more to her list. We sit encapsuled in light, talking in whispers and preventing our newspapers form rustling.

Someone slaps the plane with a heavy hand: thump, thump. The steward yanks open the door. Two men in medical white waft in with a gust of hot air. They go down the aisle distributing printed forms. We busy ourselves filling in the answers: Where did you spend the last ten days? Nine days? Yesterday? One man takes a canister out of his pocket and strides up the aisle spraying us with hospital smell. We can disembark.

We file out. Near the base of the ramp attached to the first class exit stands an enormous grey Rolls-Royce bearing the President's three-faced lion insignia on its numberplate. Beside the car, stand the President's ADC and an orderly with an armful of flowers. Behind them are half-a-dozen photographers with cameras raised to their noses. A white woman carrying a fur coat on one arm and a hat-box in the other comes down the steps. Flash bulbs explode. The ADC clicks his heels and salutes. He takes the white woman's fur coat and hat-box and hands them to the orderly. He garlands the woman, presents her with the bouquets and salutes her again. She flashes her teeth at him. They get into the Rolls-Royce. The Rolls-Royce purrs away into the dark.

Who is she?

We are herded together and directed to follow an Air-India official. We shade our eyes against the glare of airport lights and showers of moths. We skirt past long-snouted bandicoots skating on their bellies and enter a door marked 'International.' A large poster with a picture of Pandit Nehru bids us *Welcome to India*.

A police sergeant scrutinizes our health forms and stacks them in the 'out' basket on his table. A sub-inspector inspects our passports, stamps them and hands them back to us. A customs officer gives us sheafs of forms to fill in triplicate. Three each for what we have bought abroad; three each for what we have in foreign currency. We spend half-an-hour filling them. Customs men eye us to see if our expressions betray undeclared items. We look bored; our expressions betray nothing.

Forty minutes later trollies rattle into the customs shed. Coolies offload cases on the floor. I locate my valise and grab a customs inspector. I have bought nothing and have no foreign currency. He does not believe me. He examines my declaration forms and my passport. He opens my valise and fires a stream of questions as he digs into my clothes.

'Any whisky-shisky?'

'No.'

'No tape recorder?'

'No.'

'Transistor-shranzistor?'

'No.'

'Camera-shamera?'

'No.'

'Watch-shotch?'

'No.'

He grabs my hand and examines the shiny new Vulcan alarm watch on my wrist. I bought it at Beirut's duty-free shop in the airport store for thirty-five pounds.

'How much?'

I produce a receipt for the watch I bought for my cook which is tucked in my hip-pocket. 'Seven pounds.'

He is a bad loser. He chalks my valise as if he were writing 'Fuck off.' One takes a lot from these customs bastards.

A porter grabs my valise. We pierce through a wall of clamorous taxi-drivers and find a cab. The porter dumps my valise on the rear seat and exclaims: 'Okay sir, salaam!' Airport rules say don't tip porters. He takes five rupees off me.

The Sikh cab-driver has a Sikh friend in the front seat. Twenty minutes later we arrive at my destination. The cab-driver lights a match and reads the meter, 'Eighteen fifty plus two for the luggage. Twenty fifty.'

'Eighteen fifty?' I pack as much disbelief as I can into my voice. It is more than double what I paid on my way out to Palam airport a few weeks ago.

'Eighteen fifty,' repeats the cabbie. His friend lights another match and reads: 'Eighteen fifty. See meter.'

One Sikh may argue with one Sikh. One Sikh must never argue with two Sikhs—certainly not after dark. I pay twenty rupees fifty paise plus another two rupees as tip.

The night-watchman of our block of apartments is also a Sikh. When I go out of Delhi, I leave the key of my flat with him. He is an honest fellow but a little soft under his turban. He was discharged from the army for his eccentricities. Although he was only a truck-driver he never forgets he once wore a soldier's uniform. He jumps up from his charpoy and orders himself: 'Salute!' And salutes me as if I were the colonel of his regiment. 'How was his Majesty the King of England?' he asks me in English.

'England now has a Queen.'

He thinks that a matter of small detail. 'Very well, sir. Did you ask His—beg pardon—Her Majesty, why he/she did not answer my letters?'

'Budh Singh, how long have you been like this?' I enquire very gently. Budh (knowledge) Singh gets this way three times in the year; then he becomes a Budhoo (simpleton) Singh. One has to be very gentle with Budhoo Singh.

His eyes burn. 'You think I mad?' he screams. 'You want dismiss me?' I do not answer. He unlocks the door, switches on the light and lets me in. He carries my valise to the unlit bedroom mumbling to himself. He comes back and presents me the key of the apartment with both his hands like a vanquished general surrendering his sword. 'Sir, here is your key and here is your job!'

'Budh Singh, I only asked you how long you have been like this,' I say taking the key.

'Yes, but I know truth,' says he peering into my eyes. 'Public say Budh is Budhoo again. Sahib sack him when he back from foreign. I say *Hunooz Dilli Door Ast*: you know what that mean? It is a long way to Delhi.'

'But I am back in Delhi,' I remind him. He looks at me more intensely. 'Okay! Forgive and forget.'

He assures me the apartment has been swept, furniture dusted. 'All okay. Cold machine okay, air-condition okay. Come and look,' he commands. I follow him to the bedroom and press the switch. *Click*. No result. *Click, clock, click, clock*. No result. 'Excuse me, bulb fooze,' explains Budh Singh. He presses another switch. The burst of light gives him a shock. He leaps in the air and pirouettes like a dancing dervish.

He puts a finger to his turban and explains. 'Springtime something happen here. Don't mind, salute!'

'It will pass,' I reassure him. He comes close to me till his beard almost touches mine. He says in a conspiratorial whisper, 'Excuse me! Your *hijda* come many time to enquire if you back.'

Budh Singh does not like my mistress Bhagmati because she called him Pagal (mad) Singh. Budh Singh has never forgiven her. He calls her a him or a *hijda* (hermaphrodite). Bhagmati has a small bosom and a heavy voice. 'Excuse me,' he confides to my beard, 'everyone is talking about it. They say, take woman, take boy—okay! But a *hijda*! That's not nice. Don't mind my saying so!'

I say nothing. Budh Singh takes it as a reprimand. He stands stiffly to attention, salutes for the umpteenth time and orders himself: 'Right turn!' He turns right. 'By the left, quick march.' And marches out with measured steps.

Hah!

I peel off my clothes and go into the bathroom. I turn on the tap. A muddy ooze trickles down into the bucket. It is followed by a little muddy water. Then a fart. No water. I give up.

I go to my study, pick up the phone and dial the number of

the caretaker on night duty. Two girls are on the line yakking away about their Daddyji and Uncleji. I put down the receiver, slap a mosquito against my paunch and try again. They are still at it; this time about their Mummyji and Auntyji. I put down the receiver, extract fluff out of my navel, inhale its shitty smell and try a third time. They are exulting over the piquancy of the chaat in Bengali market: 'Yum! Yum!' I lose my temper and tell them that it is almost midnight and they should be doing what their Mummyjis are doing to their Daddyjis. 'Some dirty fellow on our line,' says one. 'Will buzz you later. Ta-ta.'

I dial my number. Engaged. Three minutes later I dial again. Engaged. I dial Complaints. The man at the other end tells me to dial Assistance. I dial Assistance. This operator tells me: 'Number out of order please, dial Complaints.' I give up.

I go to my bedroom to let the air-conditioner cool my naked flesh and raw temper. It welcomes me with a distinct lowering of tone, but soon its drone lulls me to slumber. In a short while, however, it resents my indifference and goes off in a sulk. The bedroom becomes like the Black Hole of Calcutta.

Power cut. No light, no fan. I come out into my patch of garden and flop into a canechair. It's hot, humid, dark and still. There are a few stars, but they are very very far away. And there are too many mosquitoes. I think angry thoughts. I will write letters to the papers about delays at the airport, the manners of customs inspectors, cheating by cab-drivers, the inefficiency of the electricity company, Delhi telephones, Delhi water supply . . . Then I think of Bhagmati. I wonder how much whoring she has done while I have been away. She likes to tell me of her exploits because she knows it rouses my desire for her. I sit in the dark many hours. I am angry, I am wanton. Then less angry, more wanton. A pale, old moon wanders into the sky. A light goes up in the temple behind my apartment. The electricity is back when it is not needed. I get up and drag my feet into the sitting-room.

I switch on the table-lamp. 5.15 a.m. I throw open the window. The curtains flutter. A cool breeze fragrant with the madhumalati which covers the outside wall drives away the dank fuzz of yesterday's dead air. I sink into my armchair and gaze out of the window. Streetlights go off with a silent bang. Through the foliage of the mulberry tree appears the grey dawn.

Flying foxes wing their soundless way back to perch on massive arjun trees. The old lady who lives in the apartment above mine slish-sloshes along the road. She stops by my hibiscus hedge, looks around to see if anyone is looking, quickly plucks some flowers, thrusts them in her dupatta and slish-sloshes on towards the temple. Her old man follows her. He also stops by my hedge, looks around to see if anyone is listening, presses his paunch, and lets out a long, painful fart. He walks on with a lighter step and a 'who did that?' look on his face. A light goes on in the opposite block. A woman draws the curtains, ties her untidy hair into a bun and stretches her arms towards me. More lights are switched on and off. The morning star is barely visible in the pink sky. Crows begin cawing to each other. Sparrows start quarrelling in the mulberry tree. The muezzin's voice rises to the heavens. Temple bells peal to awaken the gods from their slumbers. The milkman cycles round the block with a noisy clanging of milkcans. Another cyclist follows tinkling his bell and shouting *'Paperwalla! Ishtaitman. Taim of India, Hindustan Taim, Express, Herald, paperwalla!'* I hear the shush of papers being pushed under my door. I stay in my armchair. The morning breeze wafts the light of dawn into the room. It is cool, fragrant, pregnant with sadness and longing; it is the *bad-i-saba*—the morning breeze—sacred to lovers. And I am back in my beloved city.

❦

I settle down to the *Hindustan Times*. The front page has a picture of the white woman who came off the plane last night. 'Lady Hoity-Toity says it's great to be back home in Delhi.' So that's who she is! She has come to collect material for a book on archaeology. She is staying with the President at Rashtrapati Bhavan.

I glance over the headlines and look at the pictures.

My cook-bearer enters with a welcoming grin. I give him the Japanese watch I bought for him. His grin changes into a smile. He gives me a mug of black coffee and asks me if I will be in for lunch. No. Dinner? Yes, but I may be late, so leave it on the table. What would I like? I know he's thinking of Bhagmati because she eats only Indian food and I eat Anglo-Indian *ishtoo* or *sawset* with *kashtar* for a *putteen*. I do not know how, when or where I will find

Bhagmati. But I am not going to tell him, so I reply, 'Anything.' He goes away constipated with curiosity.

It is time to catch up with Delhi. A quick shower and I am off in my Hindustan Ambassador. More roads and round-abouts have had their names changed. The Windsors, Yorks, Cannings and Hardinges have been replaced by the Tilaks, Patels, Azads and Nehrus. There are red flags outside a petrol station with three men chanting, 'Death to petrol-stationwalla.' Red flags outside Dr Sen's nursing home. Six men yelling, 'Death to Doctors.' Red flags outside Food and Agriculture Ministry building. Four men in garlands sit cross-legged on the lawn. A placard in front of them says *Third Day of Relay Hunger Strike*. A procession with saffron flags goes along Parliament Street chanting, 'Our religion and our country are one. The cow is our mother. Death to cow-eaters.' On the lawns of Connaught Circus there is a political meeting. The speaker yells into the mike: 'All together cry—*Jai Hind*.' The crowd obeys: '*Jai Hind*.' The man at the mike is not happy. 'That's not good enough. We cannot fight those Chinese pigs with such feeble voices, can we? Let your voices be heard as far as Peking. All together—*Jai Hind*.'

'JAI HIND.'

Pekingese pigs piss in your pants. With enemies like Indians you've nothing to lose except your piddle.

I park my car beside the stalls of the Tibetan 'antique' dealers on Janpath (once Queensway). The same brand of American tourists bargain for the same kind of brass and stone bric-à-brac. The same set of Sikh fortune-tellers mumble the same kind of romances and travel to foreigners. One fellow spots my Marks-and-Sparks T-shirt. 'You come from *phoren*, you go *phoren* again,' he assures me. 'One minute you give me and I tell you love-affairs. Rich, white lady passioning for you. I tell you name. I tell you how to make her and her much fortune your own.' I speak to him in Punjabi. 'Tell these things to the *Amreekans*, I have no money.' He knows his victim. 'Money?' he sneers indignantly, 'Money is dirt on back of hand. You great future. Much riches. Much love-affairs with *phoren* ladies. One evil star stopping you. Close palm.' Without thinking I clench my fist. 'Now open.' I unclench my hand. There is a black spot in the middle of my palm.

'See!' he says triumphantly, 'Black star! You give rupee one only. From *Amreekans* I take rupees ten. I tell you how conquer black star.' I give him a rupee and am instructed in the art of seducing foreign women. 'Sardarji, your lady love name begin with J.H.T. Yes?' I know no woman with the initials J.H.T. He goes on: 'When you get white lady with J.H.T. in name you remember Natha Singh, world-famous palmist-astrologer.'

I arrive at the All India Cooperative Coffee House. More red flags. One banner says *Give us our demands.* A man hands me a leaflet listing the demands. I roll it up and return it to him with an obscene gesture. He returns the compliment. Nasty man!

I cast my eyes over the noisy throng. Can't see anyone I'd care to be with. I buy a copy of *Delhi Underworld* from the news-stand, grab a table just as it is vacated and tilt three chairs against it. I plunge into my weekly ration of Delhi scandals. A Minister of Cabinet (name to be disclosed next week) has impregnated his daughter-in-law. There's nepotism for you! Free service to the son! 'Confessions of a Connaught Circus Girl.' Poor thing complains of misuse by the Indian staff on an African embassy. She says Africans are better endowed than Indians. They also pay more money. A college lad writes a letter complaining that his step-mother raped him while his father was out on tour. Editor appends angry footnote in italics: *'How can you put your instrument in the same place as your father's which gave you birth? . . . . Your stepmother is disgrace to Indian womanhood.'* He promises to give advice on how to deal with such women in the next issue. I drool over drawings of 'sex cats' with bosoms like the protrusions on the fenders of American cars. The next issue also promises a full disclosure of goings-on in Tihar Jail (women's section). Bhagmati has told me quite a lot about that. She's been to Tihar many times.

I see two of our gang come in. One is a photographer, the other a journalist. Both claim to be Delhi's champion womanizers. They see me and advance with their arms wide open. 'Hullo, hullo. How's the little one?' asks the photographer, tapping my middle. 'Did it do its duty to the memsahibs?' I tap his fly: 'And how's Delhi's champion stud bull?' He shrugs his shoulders. 'Fifteen days no action. I stick to my motto: when you find a woman, fornicate, when you do not, be celibate. No self-abuse, no boys, no *hijdas*.' That's hitting me below the belt.

'And you great pen-pusher, what's your Qutub Minar been up to?' I ask the journalist. He's a big fellow with pubic-sized growth on his face. He also replies in verse. 'When I get a woman I copulate. When I don't, I masturbate. No complaints. The great Guru is in His Heaven and the *mashooka* in my bed!' He plucks a hair out of his beard and examines it with philosophic detachment. A third friend joins us. He is an Upper Division Clerk in the Ministry of Defence. He is utilizing his unutilized sick leave. He disapproves of this kind of talk! 'Five million Indians are dying of hunger in Bihar and all you fellows can think of is women.' He shakes his foot, then jerks his legs like the arms of a nutcracker. He puts his feet on the chair and continues to amuse himself. A fart escapes his fat arse: *poonh* He is embarrassed. He puts his feet down and apologizes: 'Sorry, it was a slip of the tongue.'

Another of our cronies comes along. He is a politician of sorts and our political expert. He made a name during the last famine by organizing a 'miss-a-chappati-a-week' movement. Now he is contemplating a similar campaign for family planning based on the slogan 'If you want good luck: In one week only one . . . .' The slogan hasn't got off the bed yet. We return to sex and corruption and inefficiency and five million starving in Bihar. We drink many cups of coffee and nibble many plates of cashewnuts. So passes the morning.

A heavy depression overtakes me. I take leave of my coffee-house friends and drive along the Ring Road which skirts the old city. I pass along the Mughal city wall and Zeenat Mahal's mosque. I slow down at the electric crematorium. No customers, no smoke. I move on through the arches of three bridges to Nigambodh Ghat cremation ground on the Jamna. I park my car and go in.

What's happened to the Delhiwallas? They are not even dying as they used to! Only one pyre burning and three heaps of smouldering ashes. No mourners. I walk up to the edge of the bank to see if there is any life there. Quite a scene!

Down the steps running into the river is a corpse draped in a red shroud. A dozen men and women are screaming and beating their breasts. A Brahmin priest pushes them aside, chants Sanskrit mumbo-jumbo and sprinkles water on the body A middle-aged man uncovers its face. It's a young girl—very waxen and in deep slumber. The man stares at her face, moans and shakes his head in disbelief. A woman on the other side of the corpse smacks her forehead many times and clasps the dead girl in her arms. Other people gently remove the wailing couple and cover up the face of the corpse. The priest puts out his palm. Somebody gives him a rupee. He looks at the silver coin with disdain, then clip-clops up the stairs in his wooden sandals. The mourners lift the bier and follow him. They put the corpse on the ground and begin to make a platform of logs. The middle-aged couple resume their mourning. The woman throws dust in her hair and smacks her head with both her hands, screaming, '*Hai! Hai! Hai!*' The man again uncovers the dead girl's face, gazes intently for a minute and then groans, '*Hai Rabba!*' He cannot take his eyes off the dead child. He presses her arms and legs, massages the soles of her feet. The pyre is ready. The corpse is lifted and placed on it. More wood and pampas stalks are placed over the body and a brass *lota* full of clarified butter emptied on it. A man lights a stick with a bundle of rags soaked in kerosene and takes the torch round the pyre. It bursts into flames. Another man takes a sharp-pointed bamboo pole, prods the flaring, crackling pyre to locate the dead girl's head and then lunges into her skull.

The parents bury their faces in the dust, slap the ground and wail. The Toofan Mail from Calcutta rumbles over Jamna's iron bridge towards Delhi railway station.

I leave Nigambodh Ghat with the heat of the flames on my face and the helpless cry of the stricken parents ringing in my ears. There is real grief! It stabs through the heart like a needle. There, but for the grace of God, it could have been I pouring dust onto my head to mourn the death of my child! Here, by the grace of God, I am driving my Ambassador back to my apartment! What are my irritations, envies and frustrations compared to the sorrow of the people I have left behind! They will go home and miss their daughter. I'll get home and drink my Scotch.

Budh Singh awaits me. He presents arms with his stave. I refuse to be embarrassed. He comes closer and confides. 'Excuse me, sir, your *hijda* came to see you. I told her you have not come back from *phoren*. I hope you not angry with me Take a woman, take a boy, but a *hijda* . . . .'

I could slap Budhoo Singh across his bearded face. Instead I gently shut the door behind me and fix myself a drink.

That's Delhi. When life gets too much for you all you need to do is to spend an hour at Nigambodh Ghat, watch the dead being put to the flames and hear their kin wail for them. Then come home and down a couple of pegs of whisky. In Delhi, death and drink make life worth living.

Lady J.H.T.

I am nibbling my second sandwich with my second Scotch. The phone rings. 'Is that 420420?' It is. 'Sir, please speak to the Secretary, Ministry of Education.'

'How are you, old cock?' (The Secretary and I are on Delhi's old cock network). He does not wait for an answer and proceeds. 'This is about Lady Hoity-Toity. You must have read about her in the morning papers! Famous archaeologist, cousin of the Queen, Guest of the President, V.V.I.P. etc., etc. Good contact; maybe a good lay. She wants to examine some old sites to see if she can dig up something. Everything laid on. Limousine, caviar, champagne. Everything that our poor country can afford. Can you take her around?'

'Sure!'

'Fine! The car will pick you up at five in the morning. Don't keep her Ladyship waiting. Have a nice fuck.'

Before I can explode 'Five!' he puts down the receiver. I reason with myself. One early morning compensated by a lifetime of name-dropping. How does it go? 'Sound, sound the clarion, fill the fife, throughout the sensual world proclaim, one crowded hour of lusty loving, is worth an age without a name.' I'd have a whole day with a world celebrity, with a bit of luck, seduce her and go down in the pages of history as one of her lovers.

I could take her to Moti Mahal on Qawwali Nite. People would ogle, whisper, envy. And to my friends: 'Jane said to me...' 'Who is this Jane *yaar*...?' 'You don't know Lady Jane Hoity-Toity...? Cousin of the Queen... renowned archaeologist! Well, we were digging for this grey earthenware pottery . . . we became close friends . . . ' I turn in early. I get little sleep. The scene at the cremation ground haunts me. I switch on the light often to see the time. The alarm clock bursts my eardrum at 4.30 a.m. Quick shit, quick shower and half-an-hour later I am standing outside my apartment.

It is March. Fragrant dawn. The morning star shines brighter than the dying moon. The block of apartments is lit by the headlights of a car. A truck thunders by. Again the silence and the morning star and the fresh morning breeze. The eastern horizon gets lighter. Big bats wing their way home. Another car. And another. My watch says 5.40. My temper begins to rise. I could have had another half-an-hour in bed. The glare of headlights blind me. A Rolls-Royce rolls up and a flunky in red and white uniform steps out and asks whether I am I. Yes. He opens the front door. I find myself wedged between the chauffeur and the flunky. I take a quick look back; a vast seat occupied by a diminutive figure wrapped in fur. She nods her colourless white face and asks, 'Are you the guide?'

'Yes Madam,' I reply gruffly. When she discovers who I am she will feel very silly. The thought soothes my temper.

'Purana Qila,' I order the chauffeur.

'No,' she squawks from the rear. 'Tilpat. He's been told where to go.' So she knows Delhi! What am I supposed to do? Act the court jester to Her Royal Bitchiness of Kennelpore!

We go along the Mathura-Agra Road, cross the ancient Barapulla bridge. The Rolls-Royce switches off its headlights. The morning light reveals scores of defecating bottoms. We go over the railway bridge, past Friends Colony and through the stench exuded by the sewage disposal farm. We bump past the Road Research Institute. We go through the village Badarpur, turn off the main highway and ride into the rising sun. The fields are littered with defecators; some face us with their penises dangling between their haunches; others display their buttocks—barely an inch above pyramids of shit. The Indian peasant is the world's champion shitter. Stacks of *chappaties* and mounds of mustard leaf-mash down the hatch twice a day; stacks of shit a.m. and p.m. We cross the western Jamna canal. Tilpat hoves into view rising on a hillock above a sea of young wheat. The chauffeur announces,

'Tilpat, Madam.'

'We're there, are we!' she exclaims. Her voice is hoarse, asthmatic. 'Pull up somewhere. I'd like some breakfast.'

I tell the chauffeur to drive on to the end of the road. I switch on my Oxbridge. 'There's a palm grove beyond the village. Your Ladyship can have breakfast in peace without half of Tilpat gaping at you.'

She winces at my *haw haw*.

'Sounds lovely! I am dying for a cup of hot coffee. Bet you are too!'

I ignore her invitation. I'll punish her till she says sorry. We skirt round Tilpat. The road ends abruptly beside a temple in a grove of date-palms. The flunky hurls himself out to open the rear door. I follow him.

Lady Hoity-Toity emerges out of her ermine cocoon. I get a full view. Fifty-fivish, small (a little over five feet), bosomless, bottomless, scraggy, sexless. Muddy blonde hair, muddy blonde down all over her leathery pink skin. Cuts on the sides of the jaw indicate a surgical face-lift. She is, as the Bard put it, 'beated and chopp'd with tann'd antiquity'. Dress: grey cardigan, powder-blue denims, khaki canvas boots. Nothing feminine about her except her little size, blue eyes and a bracelet strung with gold coins.

The Presidential hamper is opened on a Presidential collapsible table. Egg sandwiches, steaming hot coffee.

'You speak uncommonly good English,' says she, offering me a cigarette. 'Bet you were schooled in England.'

I shake my head at the cigarette. 'Haileybury.' Haileybury sounds safe and very Blighty.

'Old East India school!' she says very patronizingly.

'And surely that's a King's tie!'

'It is.' I hold up the tie I have no right to wear.

'My husband is also a King's man. When were you up?'

'Seven years ago.' Her husband must be at least thirty years older than I. No danger of being caught out.

'What did you read?'

'History.'

She beams. 'So did my husband! Who was your tutor?'

I will get into trouble if I let her go on questioning me. 'I spent more time on the sports ground than in tutorials.'

She smiles. She makes up to me. 'I am awfully sorry. I took you to be a professional guide. They should have told me. Do forgive my discourtesy.'

'Don't give it a thought! Your Ladyship has Delhi's worst unpaid guide at her service.'

'You are a joker! We'll get on. My name is Jane. What's yours?' She extends her hand. Bony, strong, cold. 'Singh. A very distinguished name shared by fifty million Sikhs, Rajputs, Banias, Thakurs, Gurkhas, Biharis and many others.' She chortles happily. We are old friends. I tell her I was on the same plane. I flatter her. 'Those camera bulbs flashing! I thought you were a film star. You could be one.'

'Liar! I like compliments not flattery.' She wheezes a mixture of cough and laughter.

We sip coffee, munch egg sandwiches and engender rapport.

'What do you know about Tilpat?' she asks.

'Not much. Legend has it that it was one of the Pandava's five villages. You know about the Pandavas?'

She nods. 'Tell me again.'

'The Pandavas demanded of their kinsmen, the Kurus, their share of the inheritance consisting of five villages: Panipat, Sonipat, Indrapat, Baghpat and Tilpat. When the Kurus refused, they went to war. The battle was fought at Kurukshetra, seventy miles north-west of here. The Pandavas, helped by Krishna, won. You know the *Gita*?'

She nods again. 'Part of the *Mahabharata*, isn't it? Krishna's sermon on the righteous war .... Wasn't there a woman with many husbands somewhere in the story?'

'Draupadi! She was wife to all the five Pandava brothers. Arjun, the third brother, won her at an archery contest. When he brought her home and said, "Mama, see what I've got!", his Mama without looking back replied: "Be a good boy and share it with your brothers." So like an obedient Indian son he did as he was told.

'After the Pandavas had settled the hash of the Kurus, they retired to the Himalayas: all good Indians go to the Himalayas to die when they grow old. It is possible that the people living on that mound are descendants of the Pandavas who stayed at home.'

'Last time I was here they'd dug up grey earthenware pottery

at Tilpat. I examined the specimens: certainly 1000 BC or earlier.'
She speaks in a tone of authority and emphasizes it by pouring the
dregs of her coffee on the ground. The flunky runs up to take her
cup. We gaze at Tilpat which is lit by the sun. It is a huddle of
mud-huts around a few brick-houses and a temple.

A herd of cows and buffaloes come from Tilpat towards us.
Boys run around to prevent them straying into cultivated fields.
Girls follow picking up blobs of steaming dung and putting them
in their baskets. Cows eye the Rolls-Royce and shy away. Buffaloes
snort at its fenders and meander along. Boys let the cattle scatter
in the palm grove. They put their staves between their legs and sit
down on their haunches a few feet away from us. The girls line up
behind them.

'What do they want?' demands Lady Hoity-Toity.

'What do you want?' I translate.

'Nothing,' replies one of the boys, 'just looking.' I repeat the
reply in English. A villager alights from his bicycle and asks what
is going on. 'Nothing,' reply the boys. The cyclist joins them. More
villagers come along. Within a few minutes we have quite an
audience.

'*Bhai*! Is this a *tamasha*? Is it a zoo?' I ask them with kindly
sarcasm.

They snigger, they shuffle. But continue to sit and stare. A lad
asks me, 'Is this a mem or a sahib?'

The girls look at each other and giggle. Men grin. The lad gets
cheeky. '*Arre*, it wears a pantaloon like a sahib! It has nothing in
front or behind. How can anyone tell!' More giggles and smirks.
Hoity-Toity senses he has said something about her. She takes my
arm in a firm grip and demands to be told. I tell her. She drags me
towards the lad. 'Ask him to come round the bush and I'll show
him.' I tell the lad. He is overcome with embarrassment.
Hoity-Toity grabs the fellow by his ears and hauls him up to his
feet. 'Come and see for yourself.'

The lad wrenches his ears free and runs away. The boys and
girls scamper away after him. The cyclist cycles off. The other men
melt away. There's the master race for you! There's a woman who,
although she has no breasts to speak of, could give suck to a
regiment of Grenadier Guards!

'That's that!' she says triumphantly slapping imaginary dust off her hands. 'Now I'd like to see a bit of the countryside. The river couldn't be very far from here.'

'A brisk hour's walk.'

'Let's go.'

We set our course eastwards. We go through the palm grove and out into open country. We skirt a swamp. We wade through water courses. The ground becomes sandy. Stunted thuja and casuarina. A herd of deer come bouncing into view and bounce away towards Tilpat. A black buck, its antlers spiralling into the air, comes to a stop a few yards ahead of us. Hoity-Toity raises her arms, takes aim and says 'Bang.' The buck turns its back on us. It has been hit; blood trickles down its rump. It ambles away slowly and sinks exhausted behind a cluster of dark casuarinas. A jeepload of Sikhs armed with rifles and shotguns comes zig-zagging through the bushes. 'Sardarji, did you see a herd of deer go by?' one asks me in Punjabi. He sees the white woman and adds in English, 'And a big black buck. I am sure I hit it.'

I point towards the river: 'Just this moment. It cannot have gone very far.'

'Thanks, thanks.' The jeep races on towards the river.

'I'd put those bloody shikaris against the wall . . . . '

Hoity-Toity smiles. Her blue eyes sparkle. 'No bang, bang. She gives me a patronizing pat on my beard.

'When I was a boy there were herds of blue bull and wild pig within a mile of the city walls. Tigers were seen on the Ridge behind Rashtrapati Bhavan where Your Ladyship is staying. There were hares, partridges, and peacocks in our parks. As for deer, I remember seeing herds fifty strong not twenty miles from here. Today you can't see anything within a hundred miles of Delhi. These foreign bastards with diplomatic privileges have shot all our game. If I had my way, I would shoot the bloody lot.'

'Those chaps in the jeep looked more like your own kind than foreign bastards,' she says.

'I'd shoot them too.'

We trudge along. Scrub gives way to cultivated fields; wheat turning from green to light yellow. A skylark pouring down song on us plummets down into the wheat. Another rises skyward, flutters at one spot and trills away. Then another. And another. The cultivated land ends. Our feet sink in sand. We come to a small pond. A flock of whistling teal rise and whistle past over our heads. I raise my arms, take aim and say, 'Bang, bang .... Good shot Lady Hoity-Toity. Six birds down!' She laughs, 'You are making fun of me.'

We skirt the pond. Our feet are now ankle deep in powdery soil. Suddenly the river bursts into view.

We are on a high bank. Below us stretches the Jamna coiled like a three-mile-long grey python. She seems lifeless but for a red shroud entangled in marigolds that floats lazily downstream. Three turtles scamper down and slosh into the water. On the sandbank on the other side thousands of waterfowl bask in the sun. Terns slice the air. A white-headed fishing eagle flies over the stream scanning its surface.

Lady Hoity-Toity spreads out her arms in wonder. 'It's like a pre-historic reptile! All those bends and curves!' She takes my elbow and lowers herself on to the sand. I sit down beside her. Our feet dangle over the ledge perforated with the nest holes of bank mynahs. She lights a cigarette.

'That's because of Krishna's brother Balaram. Jamna would not yield to his lust so he got drunk and dragged her by the hair zig-zag across the plains of Hindustan.'

A fish takes a somersault on the surface of the stream.

From far away come the thuds of the shikaris' guns. Waterfowl on the opposite bank rise skyward. They pass in a great whoosh, honking and squawking as they go: geese, mallard, brahminy ducks, pintails, pochards .... They fly along the river and back again to land on the stream a hundred yards from us. Peace returns to the Jamna. Once again terns slice the air and the white-headed eagle looks for fish in its heavy, purposeful way.

After a while, Hoity-Toity puts her hand on my knee and asks: 'Is this one of your sacred rivers?'

'Only a fraction less holy than the Ganga! She is Sarjuga, daughter of the Sun; she is also Triyama, sister of Yama the ruler of the dead. And since she was born on Mount Kalinda, she has yet another name, Kalinda-Nandini, daughter of the black mountain. The *Vedas* were washed up by its flood; Krishna bathed in her waters. Madam, the Jamna is so holy that one dip in it washes away the sins of a lifetime. As a matter of fact if I were to push you down the bank, I would be doing Your Ladyship a great favour.' I put my hand on hers.

She extricates her hand. The gold coins on her bracelet jingle. She throws away the stub of her cigarette and digs out a packet of Caporals from her hip-pocket. She hands me the lighter and puts a cigarette in her lips.

I cup my palms to shelter the flame and take the lighter to her lips. I look up. She looks up. Our eyes meet. Hers are as blue as the Bay of Bengal under an aquamarine sky. She knows how to use them. I feel their rapier-like stab through my eyes down to my gullet. I lower my gaze. She blows a mouthful of roasted tobacco smoke into my face. 'Thanks,' she says taking back her lighter. Her hand again comes to rest on my knee.

I play with the coins on her bracelet. They bear masculine names: Jim, Freddy, Dennis, Jacques. 'Boy-friends,' she explains. She bares her yellowing teeth, cough-laughs and spits phlegm on the other side.

'Rich and of all nationalities,' I remark, holding the gold coin inscribed 'Ali'. She laughs again. 'Not all rich; I had some made at my own expense. And not of all nations. India is missing. Perhaps I'll add an Indian this time,' she says, giving me a meaningful leer. She buries her half-smoked Caporal in the sand. 'I really must have a quick *dekho* at the Tilpat excavations and then this other place Suraj . . . Suraj . . . and some four letter obscenity.'

'Kund.'

The obscenity dawns on me. I blush.

'I am an awful tease!' she says patting me on my beard. She stands up and brushes the sand off her little bottom. 'Come along,' she commands, hauling me up by the shoulder.

She is rejuvenated. She strides on ahead. I trudge behind her. I can't make anything of her. I cannot affix any labels to this diminutive yet strong, sexless yet bawdy woman.

We see a small cloud of mobile dust over the bushes. It is the jeep with the shikaris. No black buck in the jeep. They see us. Lady Hoity-Toity bares her teeth and turns a victorious smile on me. They understand. One fellow clenches his fist, shakes his right arm from its elbow and yells abuse.

'What's he saying?' asks Hoity-Toity.

'He's telling me to go and bugger myself.'

'An Oriental accomplishment, no doubt! One of the yogic postures designed to make the ends meet,' she says.

384

The masterful female leads the way through the palm grove back to the Rolls-Royce beside the temple. A crowd of inquisitive rustics has again collected round the car. They disperse as soon as we arrive. We have coffee. And drive into Tilpat.

Word has gone around about how the memsahib dealt with the village lad. The state emblem on the car and the liveried flunkies do the rest. The village headman and his cronies welcome us with a mixture of namaskars, *Jai Hinds* and salaams to the memsahibji. Hoity-Toity nods at them. A charpoy is laid out. A woman with her face veiled brings a trayful of chai in glass tumblers. Hoity-Toity peers into the woman's veil and makes everyone laugh. She refuses to drink the chai but grabs the pipe of a hookah from the hand of a peasant and takes a couple of puffs. They clap their hands and laugh like children. Through me they inform her that the excavated sites have been covered over. 'Have any of you found any strange objects while ploughing or digging foundations for new houses?' They waggle their heads. 'No.'

We take leave of Tilpat. At Badarpur we turn left, go over a railway level crossing and turn left again along a narrow road. We descend through a defile. A peacock scuttles across and takes wing raucously crying *paon, paon.*

'A real live peacock!' exclaims Hoity-Toity.

'The place is infested with them.'

'And humans! India seems to be infested with human beings.' She waves towards the buses, scooters, cars and bicycles in the parking lot at Suraj Kund. Picnickers are scattered everywhere. Transistors, tape recorders and gramophones compete with the snake charmers' pipes.

Our arrival causes a stir. By the time we pull up alongside the verandah of the rest-house, transistors have been toned down; three snake charmers blow lustily through their gourd pipes; an old man with a king cobra twined round his neck approaches us. 'Christmas!' exclaims Lady Hoity-Toity. 'I don't like snakes and I don't like picnickers.' She surveys the scene for a moment, shudders a long *ooh* of disgust. 'How long do we have to stay here?' she asks.

'There's this amphitheatre. Then there is an old dam about two miles from here, village Anangpur another mile beyond the dam. There are the remains of the wall which protected Anangpur. It'll take us most of the afternoon and evening.'

She's a lady of quick decisions. She orders the flunky to unload the hamper. She goes in, examines the room and the bathroom, sniffs at the towels, turns up her nose at the bundle of clipped newspapers in a box beside the toilet. She dictates the order of the day to the chauffeur, 'Take the car back. Come back around 9 p.m.' She does not ask me if I am free till 9 p.m.

The flunky puts the hamper and her suitcase on the floor. The chauffeur and the flunky salute and take their leave. She flops into an armchair, glances at her wrist-watch and says, 'I am dying for a drink. Be a darling and mix me a gin and tonic. And help yourself to anything you like—Scotch, champagne, beer, gin—all on your old President.'

I act the butler. I mix Her Ladyship a gin and tonic. While I am still making up my mind what to take, I have to mix her another and light her cigarette. I make myself a dry martini and sit down on the edge of the bed. I raise my glass. She ignores the gesture. 'Tell me about this place Suraj . . . Suraj . . .'

'*Kund* to rhyme with the German *Bund*. Simply means pond.' I tell her about the Tomar Rajputs who ruled Delhi in the seventh and eighth centuries and their chieftain Surajpal after whom the amphitheatre is named.

She holds out her glass, 'Be a honey!'

I be a honey and give her another gin-tonic. 'And this dam and the village?' She puts her legs on either arm of her armchair just as she would do to let a man enter her. How can I talk of the Tomar Rajputs with her opening her thighs in this wanton manner? I try to keep my mind off her middle. 'The dam was built by another Tomar, Anangpal. He also built the fortified town Anangpur; we can go there in the afternoon. Then he shifted his capital westward and built a citadel of red sandstone which came to be known as Lal Kot.'

She's lost interest in my lecture. Her eyes are drooping. 'Go on,' she orders.

'No, I won't,' I reply rudely. 'You are half-asleep.'

She laughs, coughs, spits. She throws her cigarette on the floor and squashes it under her foot. 'Forgive me! I'll have a wash and get out of this,' she says holding her blue denims. 'Won't be a jiffy.' She pulls out a skirt from her case and goes into the bathroom. The bathroom has a curtain which only covers the middle part of the doorway. It also has a door; she does not shut the door. She unzips her denims and hangs them on a peg. She wears white lace panties to cover her little bottom. She bends over the basin to wash her face. I know she is doing it to rouse my curiosity. My curiosity rises. She buries her face in a towel. She turns round, bends over and slips on her shirt.

'*Chalo,*' she says. '*Juldi* (quick). Is that right?'

We step out. It is quieter. The snake charmers are bundled under trees and the picnickers are huddled round their transistors; the women are frying pooris. Boys in bum-tight trousers, girls in bosom-and-bum-tight long shirts stroll about the amphitheatre.

Hoity-Toity examines a bush of thorny caparis in flower. She looks across the ridge and is entranced. On one side is the vast Romanesque amphitheatre with large steps going down to the pool. A man is washing himself on a slab of stone. A safe distance from him a couple of moorhens are bobbing up and down. Swallows skim over the water in unending circles. On the other side is a densely wooded valley of flame trees and wild date-palm. She clasps her hands beneath her chin in adolescent wonder: 'So that's the flame of the forest! How perfectly beautiful! Where is the Sun temple?' she asks.

I point to the flights of steps on the other side of the amphitheatre. I lead her down the large steps to the pool. Then up the same steps to the ruins of the Sun temple. I show her some of the surrounding countryside: massive boulders with flame and acacia sprouting from the sides.

'I have had enough for the morning. I am hot and hungry,' I plead. 'Aren't you?'

She glances at her wrist-watch. 'Okay! My watch says time for another gin-tonic and a bite.'

We return to the rest-house. I mix more gins and tonics and lay a plateful of tandoori chicken and Russian salad on the table. I help myself to a bottle of chilled lager and some kababs. She gobbles up her lunch and brusquely orders me out of the room. 'I must have my siesta. Wake me up at 4.30. We can do your dam and fortified village in the evening.' She does not care to find out whether there is another room or even a chair for me, just puts me out on the verandah and shuts the door. 'Shake me up; I sleep heavily.'

I scrounge a chair from the kitchen, put my feet up against a column and make myself comfortable. I watch the picnickers dozing under the trees. My head is heavy with sleep. I close my eyes. I am roused by the snake charmers' pipes. The picnickers are packing up while the snakewallas make a last attempt to extract something from them. I doze. I hear charabancs, cars, scooters leave. The snake charmers' pipes fade away in the distance. Only pye-dogs snap and snarl over garbage left by the picnickers. I daydream. Hoity-Toity is trying to seduce me. I am not very difficult to seduce. I have no conscience about Bhagmati. Bhagmati is a whore; why should I feel guilty about her? I am taking Hoity-Toity when Bhagmati turns up and asks, 'Couldn't you find anyone better than this old memsahib?' It would be nicer if Hoity-Toity was younger and her mouth did not smell of gin-tonics, roasted tobacco and old age!

It is 4.30 p.m. I press open the door of Hoity-Toity's room and shut it behind me. She sleeps with the bedsheet drawn over her head like a corpse in a shroud. I shake her by what appears to be her shoulder. She flings the sheet off her face. 'What time is it?

I tell her.

She yawns and stretches her arms. Yellow, fungoid growth in her armpits. She props herself against her pillow and holds the bedsheet under her chin. 'Be a darling and hand me a cigarette.' I give her a cigarette and light it for her. She sends jets of smoke through her nostrils, *ahs* and *oohs* with pleasure. 'Hand me my dressing-gown,' she says pointing to the garment hanging on the latch of the bathroom door.

I get her the dressing-gown. She leaps out of bed. Stark naked: small, wrinkled breasts; nipples looking downwards and dejected; wrinkled belly with a slight paunch beneath the navel; scraggy-brown pubic hair. I put the gown round her shoulders and close my hands over her breasts. She turns to stone. 'What do you think you are trying to do?' she demands.

'Well I . . .'

'Well, you what? Don't get silly notions in your head.' She picks up her shirt and denims lying at the foot of the bed and walks into the bathroom. She does not bother to shut the door. I do not bother to look.

She comes back, puts her hands on my shoulder. 'Don't be

cross. I'm a bit of a cock-teaser.' She gives me a smelly kiss on the nose to seal her forgiveness. My feelings are hurt, I want to hurt her. Her halitosis encourages me to be rude to her. I snigger. 'What's the joke?' she asks.

'You! You remind me of my city Delhi. We have a saying: "Ruins proclaim the past splendour of an ancient monument."'

She shrivels. 'That's not a nice thing to say.'

We step out of the bungalow as strangers. We walk alongside with a wall of silence between us. It is hot. Sandstone boulders burn under the sun. In the shade of trees sit peacocks panting for breath with their beaks open. We walk a mile or more without exchanging a word or looking at each other.

We come to the end of the Ridge. In front stretch cultivated fields growing wheat and mustard. Out of the flat sea of green and pale yellow rise rocky islands covered with the flame. Beyond the islands is the village Anangpur. It is the kind of scene that cannot be appreciated by people with a wall of misunderstanding between them. I take Hoity-Toity's hand and ask, 'Isn't it beautiful?' She replies, 'Isn't it! Let's sit down somewhere.'

I lead her by the hand. We descend on Anangpal's dam. We turn our backs to the fields and sit down facing a valley of date-palms. Fifty feet beneath us is a pool of water, crystal clear. It sparkles as minnows' bellies catch the sun. From a date-palm darts a halcyon kingfisher aglitter with peacock-green and molten-gold. It hovers helicopter-like above the pool, drops like a stone into the water and is off with a wiggling minnow in its beak. The pool returns to its placid self; once more fish move in shoals of grey dots. Suddenly they leap into the air like a shower of sparks, plop back and dart to the sides of the pool. A snake wriggles upwards, raises its head above the surface and wriggles back nosing its way through the shadows of submerged rocks. Hoity-Toity smokes yet another Caporal and throws the butt into the pool. Minnows come back for the cigarette. The stub bobs up and down like an angler's float, then goes down into the water.

We spend the rest of the afternoon walking through the fields of Anangpur. We watch a camel-driven Persian wheel. We watch Gujar women patting buffalo dung on their walls. We skirt round Anangpur and see the ruins of its battlement. As the sun goes over the Ridge we retrace our steps to the dam. We return through the valley of palm trees, wading through swamps overgrown with bulrushes. As the sun sets, we are back in the rest-house.

Not a human being in sight. The chowkidar puts chairs and a table out for us and retires to his quarters. I bring out the President's Scotch. We sit with our legs on the table and sip our whisky. After a long walk, it is like elixir in the entrails. I stretch out my hand to her. She gives me hers to hold. We watch the sky turn a luminescent grey. Flocks of parakeets streak across squawking as they flash by. It is peacock time. They cry lustily from the valley of the date-palms. Two perched on the roof of the rest-house return their calls. Then the twilight hush. Hoity-Toity stands up and stretches her limbs. I stand up as well. She nestles her head against my chest. 'Thank you! It's been a lovely day.' She kisses me on my mouth. I enfold her in my arms, lift her off her feet and kiss her all over her leathery face. 'Would you like to make love to me?' she asks very humbly.

'Yes, let's go inside.'

We get as far as the verandah. The President's Rolls-Royce catches us with its headlights. I swear: 'Fuck!'

Very frustrating! Also somewhat of a relief. I do not have to waste my *bindu* on a battered, malodorous woman. I can preserve it for Bhagmati who despite the bashing she gets from men goes for sex with the zest of a newly-wed nymphet. And her mouth smells like a bush of cardamom in springtime.

Hoity-Toity becomes the Lady once more—cold and aloof. She sits at the other end of the seat. When we pull up outside my apartment, she says very dryly: 'Thanks for everything. Do look me up when you are in London.'

'It was a pleasure.' I do not invite her to come in. There is the omnipresent Budh Singh armed with his stave. As soon as I step out of the Rolls-Royce he springs to attention and yells: 'Parade, present arms! *Thak, thak, thak.*' As Hoity-Toity leans out to wave to me, he intones a Punjabi version of 'God Save our Gracious Queen.'

I wave to Hoity-Toity. I acknowledge Budh Singh's salute and ask: 'How's everything?'

'Parade, slope arms! *Thak, Thak.* Everything okay. Your *hijda* is waiting for you. I let it in because you were so *gussa* with me yesterday. Excuse my saying so, take a woman, take a boy, but a *hijda* . . .'

390

I complete his sentence for him. 'That's not nice.' And hurry indoors.

Bhagmati

She sits cross-legged in my armchair turning over the pages of a book. Her left hand is clenched into a fist with a cigarette sticking out of her fingers. She sucks noisily at the cigarette and flicks the ash on my carpet. Her hair is heavily oiled and arranged in serried waves fixed by celluloid clips shaped like butterflies. She wears a pink sari of glossy, artificial silk with a dark blue blouse of the same material. A pair of white slippers with ribbon bow-ties on their toes lie in front of the chair. Bhagmati is the worst-dressed whore in Delhi.

The light of the table-lamp reveals a layer of powder and rouge on her face. It does not lighten the colour of her black skin or hide the spots left by small-pox. The kohl in her eyes has run down and smudged her cheek-bones. Her lips are painted crimson. Her teeth are stained with betel-leaf. Bhagmati is the plainest-looking whore in Delhi.

'Ajee! You are back from *vilayat!*' she exclaims as I enter. And without giving me the chance to say yes, continues, 'What kind of books do you keep? They have no pictures.' She waggles her head with every sentence and gesticulates with her hands in the manner of *hijdas*. 'No pictures, only black letters like dead flies.' She changes the subject. 'Did you ever think of your poor Bhagmati when you were riding those white mares in London?' Bhagmati is the coarsest whore in Delhi.

Bhagmati is not a woman like other women. She's told me something of her past life; I've discovered the rest myself.

Bhagmati was born in the Victoria Zenana Hospital near Jamia

Masjid. When her father asked the doctor, 'Is it a boy or a girl?', the doctor replied, 'I am not sure.' Her parents already had three boys. So they gave their fourth child a girl's name, Bhagmati. When a troupe of *hijdas* came to their home to sing and dance and said, 'Show us your child. We want to see if it is a boy or a girl, or one of us,' her father abused them and drove them away without giving them any money. The *hijdas* gave her parents no peace. Whenever they came to the locality to sing or dance at births or weddings they would turn up at their doorstep and say, 'Show us your last born. If it is one of us, let us take it away.'

Bhagmati's mother had two more chldren—both girls. Both times her father had taken Bhagmati with him to the hospital and asked the doctor to examine her and say whether she was a boy or a girl. Both times the doctor had looked at her genitals and said, 'I am not sure; it is a bit of both.' Bhagmati was then four years old. When the troupe of *hijdas* visited them after the birth of their last child, her father gave them twenty-one rupees and said, 'Now I have three sons and two daughters, you can take this one. It is one of you.'

The troupe of *hijdas* adopted Bhagmati. They taught her to sing, clap her hands and dance in the manner of *hijdas*. When she was thirteen her voice broke and became like a man's. She began to grow hair on her upper lip, round her chin and on her chest. Her bosom and hips which were bigger than a boy's did not grow as big as those of girls of her age. But she began to menstruate. And although her clitoris became large, the rest of her genitals developed like those of a woman. This time she went to see the doctor herself. He said, 'You can do everything a woman can but you will have no children.'

There are as many kinds of *hijdas* as there are kinds of men and women. Some are almost entirely male, some almost entirely female. Others have the male and female mixed up in different proportions—it is difficult to tell which sex they have more of in their makeup. The reason why they prefer to wear women's clothes is because it being a man's world every deviation from accepted standards of masculinity is regarded as unmanly. Women are more generous.

Bhagmati is a feminine *hijda*. When she was fifteen, the leader of the troupe took her as his wife. He already had two *hijda* wives;

but such things do not matter to them. Instead of shunning her as a rival, the wives stitched Bhagmati's wedding-dress and prepared her for the nuptial bed. They shaved the superfluous hair on her face and body and bathed her in rose-water. They escorted her to their husband's room. They had their eyes and ears glued to the crevices in the door. Later they often made love to her. Bhagmati had small-pox when she was seventeen. 'They gave me up for dead,' she said. 'They threw me in a hospital where people were dying like flies. Seetla Mai (goddess-mother of small-pox) spared me but left her fingerprints all over my face.'

When men came to expend their lust on hijdas—it is surprising how many prefer them to women—Bhagmati got more patrons than anyone else in her troupe. She could give herself as a woman; she could give herself as a boy. She also discovered that some men preferred to be treated as women. Though limited in her resources, she learnt how to give them pleasure too. There were no variations of sex that Bhagmati found unnatural or did not enjoy. Despite being the plainest of hijdas, she came to be sought by the old and young, the potent and the impotent, by homosexuals, sadists and masochists.

Bhagmati regards a bed in the same way as an all-in wrestler regards the arena when engaged in a bout where no holds are barred. Bhagmati is the all-purpose man-woman sex maniac.

Although Bhagmati is a freelance, she continues to live with her husband and co-wives in Lal Kuan. She puts whatever she earns in the community kitty. In return she has a roof over her head, and a meal whenever she wants it. When she is ill, they look after her. When she is arrested for soliciting they furnish bail; when she is sentenced by the magistrate, they pay the fine.

How did I get mixed up with Bhagmati? That's a long story which I will tell you later. How did she come to mean so much to me? I am not sure. As I have said before I have two passions in my life; my city Delhi and Bhagmati. They have two things in common: they are lots of fun. And they are sterile.

'Where have you been blackening your face?' I ask her flopping down on the sofa.

'*Ajee!*' she exclaims saucily digging her finger into her chin. 'I go blackening my face but you go riding big cars and old, white women! What kind of justice is this?'

'You've been gossiping with Budh Singh.'

'That *pagal!*' she dismisses him with a wave of her hand. 'He lied to me. He said you would not be back for fifteen days. But something in my heart told me you were back.' She stubs the half-smoked cigarette on my table and sticks it behind her ear. With the thumb and finger of the hand she makes a circle. She inserts the index finger of the other hand in and out of the circle and asks: 'How was it?'

I told you she is the coarsest whore in Delhi.

'Must you be so vulgar?'

'*Uffo!*' she exclaims, 'Today you call us vulgar; God knows what you will be saying tomorrow!' She comes and sits on the floor, takes off my shoes and socks and begins to massage my feet. It is very pleasant. She massages my ankles, my calf muscles and the insides of my thigh. Every now and then her hands wander up for a spot-check. Very casually she undoes my fly-buttons, plants a soft kiss on my middle and comes over me. I don't have to do a thing except lie back and enjoy myself. I told you Bhagmati knows exactly what anyone wants at any time.

How did Bhagmati come into my life? That's in the past tense—three years ago.

At the time I was engaged in writing the biography of an industrialist. I was provided with a staff of research assistants to sift through his correspondence. We were allotted a few rooms in one of the newer suburbs called Patel Nagar across the Ridge which had at one time marked the western extremity of the two cities of Delhi, the Old and the New.

It took me some time to discover that the shortest way to my office was along a road which ran atop the Ridge. It was also the most picturesque; from many places you could get a view of the two cities. On either side of the road were bushes of sesbania, vasicka and camel thorn; huge boulders of red sandstone were strewn about everywhere. There were flowering trees, flame, coral and the flamboyant gulmohar. Ridge Road as it was known had earned a bad name.

A car or two had been held up, there had been a case of assault or robbery. The newspapers did the rest. Pedestrians and cyclists avoided it now and cars sped by without stopping. It was usually deserted. It was on this road that I first met Bhagmati.

It is curious how the first encounter remains so indelibly printed on the mind while the affair that follows is soon blurred.

I can recall every detail of our first meeting.

It was some time in April. It was very hot. I had put in a couple of hours of work in my air-cooled office which I had heavily curtained against the glare of daylight. (I read and wrote under the orb-light of an anglepoise lamp). Suddenly the electric current was cut off: those days as now this was a frequent occurrence in Delhi. For a while I waited in the stifling dark, then decided to call it a day. It was noon with a dust-laden grey sky and a scorching hot wind blowing more dust. I drove onto the Ridge Road. Through clusters of waving sesbania I could see a dense pack of houses on either side. But no signs of life, not even a kite wheeling in the sky. A hundred yards or so ahead of me I saw two cyclists struggling against the wind. And beyond them what appeared to be a body stretched halfway across the shimmering tarmac. I saw the cyclists stare at the body, hesitate a little, and then push on. I pulled up on the side. The cyclists turned back.

It was a woman lying with her arms and legs stretched out as if crucified. Her eyes were half-open; a little froth and blood trickled down her mouth. There was a damp patch beside her sari. I looked at her bosom to see if she was breathing: the flapping of the sari made it difficult to be sure. 'Is she dead?' I asked the cyclists who had joined me.

They peered into the woman's face. '*Mirgee* (epileptic fit)!' exclaimed one of them. He found a twig and thrust it between the woman's teeth. 'That will stop her from biting her tongue.' He took off one of his shoes and placed it on the woman's face. 'This is the best thing for *mirgee* . . . the smell of old leather.'

I noticed the woman's bosom heave. It was a very small, almost non-existent bosom, encased in a cheap, printed, artificial silk blouse. What else did I notice? Feet, very black. Toe-nails painted bright crimson. Inside of the palms stained with henna.

Very short and somewhat plump. About twenty and altogether too dark to be considered attractive by Indian standards. The little I could see of her face was pitted with pock-marks.

'What is she doing on the Ridge by herself?' I asked.

'Only the Guru knows!' exclaimed one of the cyclists.

'These are bad times,' said the other. He removed his shoe from the woman's face and slipped it on his foot. 'She'll be all right in a few minutes.' Then without giving me a chance to say anything the two rode off.

The woman began to moan and shake her head. She raised her hand and drew a circle with her finger.

'Are you all right?' I asked her.

She nodded her head. I wiped the bloody forth on her mouth with her own sari and helped her to her feet. She smelt of sweat and urine.

'*Chukkur,*' she explained, again drawing a circle with her finger. 'Be kind and take me to a bus-stand.' It was a hoarse, masculine voice.

I hesitated. Was it a trap? I had heard of people being blackmailed in this way. But I had little choice. And my conscience was clear. I helped her into the rear seat of my car. She slumped down and closed her eyes. I passed the cyclists. In the rear-view mirror I saw them dismount and one of them write something in his pocket-book. It was obvious he was taking down the number of my car. What had I landed myself into?

'Where would you like to be dropped?'

No answer. I looked back. She was fast asleep—or perhaps having another fit. What was I to do? Take her to a hospital? They'd ask questions and send for the police. Take her to a police station? Oh no! Not the Delhi police! Not in a thousand years!

I drove past Lohia Hospital towards the Parliament and headed down Parliament Street towards Connaught Circus. Then it struck me that I was being very foolish! At any traffic light someone might have noticed the woman lying in a state of collapse and started a riot. I turned back towards the Parliament and took the broad road to Palam airport. At a deserted spot I pulled up to see how she was. I felt her forehead. No fever. I shook her gently by the shoulder. She opened her eyes and mumbled, 'Let me be! I am very tired.' And went back to sleep.

I drove about for an hour before I turned back to my apartment. I parked the car where I usually did alongside my window. The Guru was merciful. None of my neighbours or their servants were about. I opened the rear door and boldly dragged the woman out by her shoulders. 'Come along!'

She allowed herself to be helped out. 'You can sleep here till you feel better,' I said as soon as we were safely indoors. 'Your slave has had enough sleep,' she replied. 'If *huzoor* can show me where to wash, your maidservant will be most grateful.'

I was startled by her florid Hindustani. I showed her the bathroom and explained how the hot and cold water taps operated. I gave her a clean towel, my Princeton T-shirt and a pair of trousers. 'I have no woman's clothes, but you can wear these till your sari is dry.'

She spent a long time in the bathroom bathing and washing her soiled clothes. She waddled into the sitting-room with the Princeton T-shirt hanging loose on her shoulders and holding up the trousers with her hands. My clothes were many sizes too big for her.

I smiled. A blush spread on her pock-marked dark face. 'Too big for me,' she said looking down at the trousers. I poured her a Coke and asked her to help herself to the plateful of mangoes on the dining-table.

'I am very hungry,' she said taking a mango. 'I have not had anything to eat since yesterday.'

'What were you doing on the Ridge at noon?'

'I was on my way home from Tihar.'

'Tihar?'

'You know! The jail! They let me out last evening. I did not have a paisa with me. I spent the night outside a labourer's hovel. They would not let me in. Then I started to walk home. Tihar is a long way away from the city.'

'What took you to Tihar?' I asked her.

She fixed her eyes on me and waggled her head saucily in the manner of a dancer. 'Vagrancy, what else? I am a prostitute.'

'What is your name?'

'What will you do with my name? Your slave is known as Bhagmati.' I had a vague suspicion that there was something besides her flat chest and masculine voice which made her different from other women. 'Where is your home?' I asked her.

'Wherever the dusk overtakes me, I spread my carpet and call it my home. My roof is studded with the stars of heaven.' She had retained all her tartish tartness. 'Your slave's abode of poverty is in Lal Kuan.' My suspicion got stronger. In Lal Kuan was the hermaphrodites' quarters. My curiosity was roused. I'd never known a *hijda*, only seen them go about in groups of fours and fives, sing in their unmelodious male voices, make ungainly movements they called dancing and clap their hands with the fingers stretched backwards. I had heard strange stories of their sex-life and the shapes of their genitals. Despite my curiosity to find out more about her, I asked her if she would like to be dropped home.

'Your honour is very anxious to get rid of me.'

'Not at all! But won't your people be worried?'

'Nobody worries about me!' she replied. 'I come and go as I please. All my husband asks me is how much have you brought?'

'You have a husband?'

'What sin have I committed that I should not have a husband? When I am old and of no use to men, he will look after me.'

She sensed I was one of the types who liked to hear about sex. 'Has *huzoor* never honoured our habitations with his blessed feet?'

'Never.'

'*Inshallah*! Your maidservant may have the honour of turning your steps in that direction.'

I was not used to being propositioned by women—much less a *hijda*. 'Your clothes must be dry,' I blurted. 'Let's go.' She came across the room, sank down on the coir mattress and put her head on my feet.

'In the name of Rama! Do not throw me out! I am too sick to go back to work. If you let me spend this one night here, I swear by Allah I will cause you no further embarrassment. For the sake of your Guru, please!' (How she mouthed the names of Gods—Hindu, Muslim, Sikh!). She looked up at me with tears in her eyes.

Women had spent nights in my apartment. But they had been Europeans or westernized Indian memsahibs aping English mannerisms; never a low-born, Hindustani-speaking *hijda* whore, who obviously catered to perverts of the working-classes:

domestic-servants, soldiers, policemen—at a couple of rupees a shot. I thought to myself that I would not know what to say to her. And she was not very appetizing. 'All right,' I said without much enthusiasm. 'But we must leave the house before my servant comes back. And while you can stay here after he has left for the night you must leave early in the morning. Go and get dressed, your clothes must be dry by now.'

She bent down and kissed my feet. She brushed her tears with the hem of my shirt. She got up and turned her back towards me. The trousers slid down baring her from her waist to her ankles. Whatever other ravages her body might have suffered at the calloused hands of the working-classes, her behind was like that of a schoolboy athlete: taut, dimpled. She looked back over her shoulder and smiled an embarrassed smile. Then bent down, pulled the trousers up to her waist and shuffled back to the bathroom.

While she was changing I made plans for the night. I put two candles on the dining-table. This was my way of communicating with my unlettered cook-bearer. One candle for 'out-for-dinner'; two candles for 'also do not come in with the bed-tea in the morning.'

We left the apartment unnoticed. 'If you would be so kind as to take me for a drive! I would like to eat some fresh air,' she said as she got into the car. 'There are not many car rides written in your slave's kismet.' She tapped her forehead.

'Where would you like to go?'

'Wherever *huzoor's* heart desires to take his maidservant.'

This was a different Bhagmati—relaxed and self-assured. She began to hum and tap a tabla drumbeat on the dashboard when we set off. As we drove past the Ashoka Hotel into the Diplomatic Enclave she began to chant the names of the embassies we passed: '*Amreekee ambassee* . . . .and the *Roosi, Pakistani, Japanee, Germanee.*'

'How do you know all these embassies?'

'Your slave has had the privilege of serving many foreign gentlemen.' she looked sideways at me to watch my reaction.

'They must give you a lot of money.'

'They probably do. But after the pimps and the embassy chauffeurs have taken their share, a couple of rupees is all that falls into your maidservant's apron. Then there is my husband. Allah be thanked! I have enough for a cupful of lentil soup and a chappati to fill this belly.' She slapped her paunch.

'How do you talk to them?'

'*Ajee wah!*' she exclaimed animatedly waggling her head. 'What kind of question is that? They don't need to talk to me. They drink their whisky; they carry on their *git mit* in their own language till they need my services.' She paused, looked sideways at me and added, 'These foreigners have some very curious habits.'

'What do they do?'

'Not all in one session,' she admonished. 'A little today, a little tomorrow. But it will astonish you. They take their pleasure in strange ways. It makes me sick to think of it.' She spat out of the window.

'Will *huzoor* kill me with hunger? Take me to a nice hotel and give me some saffron *pilaf*, some oven-baked chicken and kulfi (ice-cream) and I may tell you more.'

'And be seen with you in public? You want me to cut off my own nose?'

She was squashed. I felt mean. But I was determined not to give in. I turned towards the old city. We went through Delhi Gate and entered Faiz Bazaar. I pulled up outside Moti Mahal. I left her in the car and went to order a packed meal for two. I brought it back to the car: 'All you desire: saffron *pilaf* and nan, chicken and baked fish and *rabdee* of thick clotted cream.' She turned her face away from me.

We drove out of the city along the old wall. Her silence began to irritate me. 'If you are going to sulk, I will put you out of the car right here.' I turned to look at her. She turned away and blew her nose into the hem of her shirt.

'*Accha*, if you are going to behave like this, I will drop you at Lal Kuan.'

At Kashmiri Gate I turned into the city. We drove along Chandni Chowk to where it ended at Fatehpuri Mosque. I turned left towards Lal Kuan. I could sense her nervousness. 'You gave me your word . . .'

'I take it back. You go home,'

'*Hai Ram!*' she exclaimed as we approached the hermaphrodites' quarters. She slid down the seat and grabbed my left foot resting on the clutch. 'I'll do anything you want, but in the name of Rama, don't throw me out here.'

'You promise to behave?'

'I'll be your slave for life.'

I slowed down. Pimps darted across form the pavement. 'Nice new goods, just unpacked . . . college girl . . . virgin of thirteen . . . you no jiggee-jig?' Bhagmati remained hidden where she was, calling upon Hindu and Muslim gods. *'Hai Ramji. . . .Ya Allah.'*

We came out of Lal Kuan to Qazi-ka-Hauz and out of the city wall. 'We are out of Ajmeri Gate,' I announced.

She peered over the rim of the window to make sure before she sat up. *'Huzoor* has a strange sense of humour!' she complained. 'If they had found your maidservant in your car, her throat would have been slit.'

'If you sulk again, I'll take you back.'

At Connaught Circus I pulled up at a drug-store. When I came back she remarked: 'May our enemies be stricken with disease! I trust your honour is in good health?'

'Just the compulsions of age!' I answered. 'A pill to whip up the appetite; another to digest what has been eaten. A third for sound sleep, a fourth to be more wide awake and a fifth to tone up the system.' From the look on her face I could tell she had not bought my story.

Budh Singh, the night-watchman, had got used to seeing me bring women to my apartment. I gave him a tip every month. Although he was crazy, he never created trouble for me. In the dark, he could not tell what I was bringing home. Although it was a common bazaar *hijda* prostitute I felt as awkward as a young groom bringing home his bride. Bhagmati walked with a self-conscious gait.

Few words passed between us while we ate.

'It would be too much to ask a Sikh gentleman for a cigarette,' she exclaimed as she belched. I brought her the cigarette-box. She took two and stuck one behind her ear and waited for me to light the other. As I lit the cigarette she looked me boldly in the eye and blew a jet of smoke in my face; then fanned it away with her hand.

I switched on the fan in the sitting-room and asked her to make herself comfortable on the sofa. 'If you need anything just knock on the door.' I retired to my bedroom.

The hum of the air-conditioner cut out the other sounds in the apartment. I wondered what she was doing. Had I insulted her? Surely living in a brothel she must have got used to being turned down in favour of other inmates! In any case I did not know what one did to a *hijda*. And she had had an epileptic fit that afternoon. What would she sleep in? I had not given her a change of clothes. Naked? She wasn't very beautiful. But what did a *hijda* look like with nothing on?

I felt a desire for sex. I tried to put it out of my mind. A sick, scruffy *hijda*—how could I? I picked up a journal. Her naked figure kept coming over the print. What kind of breasts did a *hijda* have? What shape were her genitals? Did she shave her pubis? I put away the journal and switched off the lamp.

It did not help. I could not put out the notion that I had a strange creature in my apartment; I might never again have the opportunity to add to my knowledge. I switched on the bed-lamp and once again began to turn over the pages of the journal.

The bedroom door was pushed open. The light of the table-lamp sliced Bhagmati's figure in two. She had nothing on. As I had suspected—not real breasts, just protrusions. And she had her hands between her thighs. 'Have I permission to enter?' she asked as she entered. 'This poor wretch has nothing else to offer in return for your kindness.'

I made room for her beside me. She sat down with her face turned away. For a while I stroked her navel and her underbelly. I was roused. I pulled her beside me, fished out a contraceptive from under my pillow and mounted her. She directed me inside her. It was no different from a woman's. She smelt of sweat; I avoided her mouth. She pretended to breathe heavily as if she were getting worked up. Then sensing my coming to a climax she crossed her legs behind my back and began to moan. I dismounted. I felt unclean.

I went to the bathroom and brushed my teeth a second time. I was under the shower when she came in. Without asking for permission she squeezed paste out of my tube and began to massage her gums with her forefinger. As I turned off the shower to dry myself, she turned it on to wash herself. I could not bring myself to see what she really looked like in the middle.

I left her in the bathroom and returned to my bed. I did not want any more of her. To make my intentions clear I switched off my bed-lamp. I heard the shower turned off and after a while the click of the bathroom switch. Once again she came and sat on the edge of my bed. She had daubed herself with my cologne. I felt mean and made room for her.

For a while she lay still with her head tucked beneath my armpit. She began to play with my nipples—first with her fingers, then with her tongue. She placed her head on my chest and began to stroke my paunch—first with her fingers, then with her tongue. She went on till my reluctance was overcome. I rolled over and felt under my pillow. She held my hand and murmured, 'No need of that; I am clean.' Once again she directed me inside her and held me in a vice between her legs. Her tongue darted into my ears; a shiver of a thrill ran down my spine. Then she glued her mouth on mine. This time there was no faking. With a series of violent heaves she sucked my seed into her in a frenzy of abandon.

I lay on top of her—exhausted.

We had another shower together. She was the plainest creature I'd ever made love to. Her pock-marks showed darker than before. Her teeth were stained red with betel-leaf and tobacco. 'What are you staring at?' she demanded looking up through the shower and coyly hiding her nakedness.

'You, who else?' And though I had not the slightest desire for sex left in me I escorted her back to my bed and let her sleep beside me.

I slept as if I had been drugged. It must have been some time in the early hours that I began to dream. It was a mixture of fact and fantasy. Bhagmati lying on the road in a puddle of urine beckoning to me. Bhagmati grabbing me by the neck and pinning me down as a wrestler puts down his adversary. I realized that it was not all a dream and that Bhagmati was in fact lying on top of me. She nibbled my earlobes and gently led me out of my dreamland into her dusky, lusty world. She was taking me as a man takes a woman: clawing my scalp, biting my neck, heaving into my middle with a violence I had not known. I submitted to her lust with supine abandon. I felt the room go in a whirl, all my life-force from the top of the crown to the soles of my feet was sucked into my middle and erupted like lava out of a volcano. The three acts of sex were like the *scala menti* of a mystic's ascent to union with the Divine. The first rung in the ladder was the purgatory; the second, the seeking; the third, the final act of destruction of the individual self (*fana*) and the merging of two lights into one. In simpler terms—that of my relationship with Bhagmati—the process was masturbation, fucking and the body's rapture. But I still did not know how a hijda like Bhagmati was different from a breastless woman.

It was 5 a.m.

While Bhagmati was getting into her sari I opened the safe hidden behind my bookshelf and took out a wad of ten rupee notes.

'What is this?' she asked with feigned surprise when I pressed the money into her hands. She counted the money. 'One hundred! You do not have to give me money,' she said. Then she quickly changed her mind. 'I can't refuse to take what my husband gives me, can I?'

'One hundred thousand husbands!'

She put her arms about my neck. 'As Allah is my witness, hereafter you will be the only one. You have been kind to me. I will be forever indebted to you.'

'Let's go,' I said unlocking her arms.

'You don't believe me?' she demanded. She re-counted the notes and handed them back to me. 'All right, I'll take ten to give to my husband,' she said plucking out one of the notes from my hand. 'Keep the rest for me. I will come for them another day.'

I looked out to see if it was clear. Budh Singh was fast asleep on his charpoy. We tiptoed past him and slipped into my car. Even the starter didn't rouse the watchman from his slumber. It was a clean getaway. We went through a deserted Connaught Circus under Minto Bridge and then onto Ajmeri Gate. 'Drop me here,' said Bhagmati putting her hand on the steering wheel. I pulled up and opened the door. She pressed my hand. 'Your maidservant thanks you a hundred thousand times. Don't forget her.' Then she walked away, barefooted, in the middle of the deserted road.

Bhagmati had not bothered to ask me my name. She had not enquired about the number or even the location of the block of the apartments in which I lived. How would she find her way back to get her money? I certainly had no intention of going into the hijda locality in Lal Kuan to look for her.

Days went by and weeks. With the passage of time I began to think that perhaps Bhagmati was not as much of a whore as I had earlier presumed. And the memory of that one night she had spent with me came back to me with pain. I lost hope of ever seeing her again.

The way Bhagmati re-entered my life made me believe that the gods had decided to have fun at my expense.

I resumed my usual routine of life; a few hours of work in the morning, a round of golf in the afternoon, a cocktail party in the evening followed by a late dinner. In Delhi one could manage to drink and dine off other people all 365 days of the year. The Diplomatic Corps was my cornucopia. I got all the canned food and liquor I needed from diplomats. Scotch which cost a hundred-and-fifty rupees per bottle in Connaught Circus was made available to me by the crate at thirty rupees each or for free. The Corps also catered to my basic needs. Delhi had over a hundred embassies, High Commissions and Legations. Diplomats in Delhi did not have much work to do. Most of their energies were directed to wining and dining officials of the External Affairs and other ministries of the Government of India, cultivating non-official locals, and celebrating their independence days. It was not difficult to find a bored wife or a spinster eager to know Indians and thus ensure a regular supply of imported victual and exotic sex.

At the time I found Bhagmati on the road I had been courting a stenographer working in the West German Embassy. I had met her at a consular reception, discovered that she was a new arrival and like many newly arrived foreigners anxious to get to know Indians. She was not particularly attractive—thirtyish, grey-eyed, thin-lipped, tall and bony. She tied her hair in a bun which made her look severe.

૪

Fraulein Irma Weskermann was an easy conquest. One Sunday I took her round the monuments of Delhi and had Bavarian beer in her apartment. The following weekend I took her to the *son-et-lumiere* at the Red Fort and gave her dinner at Moti Mahal. Since restaurants were not permitted to serve alcohol I carried a hip-flask and when the waiter was not looking poured a slug of Indian whisky in her Coke. I explained that this was all an Indian citizen could afford as the cost of Scotch was prohibitive. She took the hint. (This gambit always worked with the diplomats). Thereafter whenever I invited her home or took her out she brought a bottle of Scotch or wine with her.

Fraulein Weskermann did not seem very interested in sex. Being somewhat sexless in appearance she had cultivated a kind of brashness as a defence mechanism. When I first put my arm round her waist she said, 'Must you?' I answered in the affirmative and added, 'Because I like you.' Thereafter, she began to put her face forward to receive a kiss on her bony cheeks. One evening I said to her, 'Irma, I am beginning to like you more than I should.' 'Zat's nice,' she replied and responded with a kiss. On another occasion I told her, 'Irma, it's terrible but I think I am beginning to fall in love with you.' No woman can resist that. 'How many women have you said zat to before?' she asked. And let me kiss her on her lips. The relationship progressed in the conventional way with a little more intimacy each time. Soon I was fondling her breasts. How long can any woman have her breasts fondled and resist giving herself completely? My hands began to explore further. If they got too close to her middle she would open her grey eyes and firmly say, 'No.' But it was only a matter of time. One evening as I was feeling her between her thighs I said, 'You are ready for it.' A shudder passed through her frame. 'It must neffer, neffer happen,' she said pushing my hand out of her knickers. I apologized and pretended to be hurt. 'It's also my fault, yah?' she replied and made up with a kiss that made my ears burn. I had little doubt that the decks had been finally cleared and at the next encounter the Indo-Germanic affair would be consummated.

I had not reckoned with Bhagmati.

It must have been almost two months after the meeting with Bhagmati that Fraulein Weskermann was dining with me in my apartment. A certain strangeness, loud conversation and forced laughter indicated that she had made up her mind to say 'Yah.' Half-way through the meal we had emptied her bottle of Moselle. She agreed to try a 'tear-drop' of cognac with her coffee. As soon as my cook-bearer left we went to the sofa and proceeded to fondle each other. I whispered into her ear, 'Shall we?' She murmured, 'If you wish. Let me prepare myself.' She picked up her handbag and hurried into the bathroom. I repaired to the bedroom and switched on the air-conditioner. Irma Weskermann emerged draped in my dressing-gown. She looked coy. 'Don't look at me,' she pleaded. 'Switch off the light, please!' I laughed and put my arms round her waist—'We have a saying in Hindustani, "If you are pregnant you have to show your belly to the midwife." If you are going to make love you have to bare your body,'—disrobed her and led her to my bed.

Fraulein Weskermann lay on her back and parted her thighs. I entered her without much emotion. She was not a virgin; she was damp but not very excited. All she did was to let out a moan—aah—and shut her eyes. We lay interlocked without a word or movement. Neither of us seemed to be getting very much out of it. But neither seemed to have the courage to call it off. How different it had been with Bhagmati!

Through the hum of the air-conditioner I heard the doorbell. I looked up. It rang again. 'Somebody at the door?' asked the Fraulein a little alarmed. 'Sounds like it,' I replied. To reassure her I added, 'Who cares!'

She pushed me off. 'Might be a telegram or something important like zat.'

I got up, slipped on my dressing-gown and tiptoed to the door. I peeped through the Judas hole. It was Bhagmati.

The ringing became more insistent. I tiptoed back. Fraulein Weskermann was sitting up in bed. 'Who is it?' she demanded.

'A woman,' I replied foolishly. 'I owe her some money.'

'What a time to visit a man!' she said very acidly.

'It is nothing like that,' I protested. 'She is a sick woman I picked up on the road one morning . . . .'

The bell continued ringing.

'I haf been a big fool,' she said standing up. She picked up her clothes and went into the bathroom. She came out fully dressed. 'Nice to have known you, Mr Singh. Good-bye and haf a naice time.' She opened the door and looked the dazed Bhagmati up and down. 'Excuse me, Madam!' she exclaimed and marched out to her Volkswagen.

I slumped on my sofa and covered my face with my hands. I heard the door close and then Bhagmati's voice pleading, 'If your slave has been guilty of indiscretion she begs a thousand pardons.'

I refused to look at her. 'You could have chosen a better hour.'

'*Huzoor*, your maidservant had an engagement at the *Misri*

408

embassy. I thought I would leave some money with your honour and also offer my humble services. I see I have angered your honour. I must extract a pardon before I rid myself of your sight.'

She sat down at my feet and began to press my legs. 'Your slave had only to turn her face the other side and you were unfaithful to her!' Her hands stroked the insides of my thighs. 'What was the giraffe like?' she asked saucily.

'I'll show you,' I replied and roughly hauled her up into my lap.

'*Arre!*' she exclaimed wagging her head, 'All males of the species are the same. One minute one woman, next minute another.'

৵

Today is the 15th of June. Delhi had its first pre-monsoon shower. It has cleansed the atmosphere of the dust that had been hanging in the air for the past three days. A fresh breeze drives snow-white clouds across the blue sky. The earth is fragrant. The air smells of more rain. How can anyone stay indoors on a day like this?

The choice is between Mehrauli and Okhla. Mehrauli has the Qutub Minar with its gardens, monuments and acres of mango orchards. Okhla has no monuments but it has lots of water. The Jamna has a weir from which a canal branches off. At monsoon time the river is an awesome sight. She is then Triyama, the sister of the ruler of Hades. Delhiwallas who have a death-wish come to Okhla during the monsoons to hurl themselves into the Jamna's muddy arms. Those who have a zest for living come with baskets full of sucking mangoes. They suck them and see how far into the river they can throw their stones. Whether it is Mehrauli or Okhla you have to have a *mashooka* to share the experience: a *mashooka* in whose ears you can whisper: 'I want to take you in the rain till your bottom is full of mud and mine full of the monsoon.'

I hear a tonga pull up outside, I hear argument between the tongawalla and the passenger. The tongawalla shouts, 'There is more money in buggery than in plying a tonga.' The passenger replies in a louder voice, '*Abey ja!* Who would want to bugger you! Nobody will spit on your dirty arse.'

Who could it be except Bhagmati!

Before she can ring the bell I open the door. She comes in swaying her hips and abusing the tongawalla, '*Sala, bahinchod*! I give the sister-fucker one rupee from Lal Kuan to this place and he wants to bugger me for more. There is no justice in the world.' She turns on me. 'Is this a day to sit indoors like a woman in a burqa? I thought you'd like to take me out in your motor car to eat some fresh air and mangoes.'

I'm waiting for an excuse to get out. There is no one I'd like to be with more than Bhagmati. But not with her dressed in that red and blue sari and her head looking like a nest of butterflies. I've bought her a pair of stretch-pants and an open collared shirt which she keeps in my apartment. 'I'll change into my *vilayati* clothes,' she says as she strides on into my bedroom.

She washes off the powder, rouge and lipstick. She plucks out the butterfly-clips from her hair, combs out the waves and ties it up in a bun at the back of her head. Now it is a different Bhagmati: a sprightly little gamine in a canvas kepi, half-sleeved sports shirt and bum-tight stretch-pants. Very chic! No one can tell whether she is a *hijda* or a boy who looks like a girl.

We start with an argument. Bhagmati says, 'It's a day for Okhla. When it rains the entire world goes to suck mangoes by the weir.'

'Not Okhla,' I reply. 'I don't like crowds: least of all Punjabis. There will be a crowd there screaming, shouting, eating, making litter everywhere.'

'If you are ashamed of being seen with me, I'll stay in the motor car,' retorts Bhagmati. It's true. But I am not going to spoil her day. 'I swear by the Guru that is not true! Okhla has too many people, too many monkeys, too many snakes. Once I killed five snuggling behind the water-gauge. Five! One after the other.'

Snakes settle the argument in favour of Mehrauli.

The road to Mehrauli has an endless procession of cycles, tongas, scooters, cars and people on foot. Everyone is shouting ho, ho or singing film songs.

A two-wheeled open cart jammed with women in veils and children comes tearing through the crowd and passes us. The driver puts the handle of his whip on the spokes of the wheel to make them rattle. He yells to everyone to get out of his way. He almost knocks down a Sikh with his wife and four children piled on one bicycle. The Sikh is very shaken. He lets out the foulest abuse he can for a family of Mussalmans. 'Progeny of pigs! You want to kill us?' Out of the huddle of burqas rises a six-year-old David. He loosens his red jock strap, sticks out his pelvis and flourishes his tiny circumcised penis. He hurls back abuse like pellets from a sling. '*Abey Sikhrey*! *Harami* (bastard), you want to sit on my Qutub Minar?'

Daood *Mian*'s Qutub is a mighty two-and-a-half inches long. The other Qutub only 283 feet!

Bhagmati breaks into a helpless giggle. 'What a lovely little penis he has! So much nicer than the tapering things of the Hindus. Is your fellow circumcised?'

'You should know.'

'They all look the same when they are up. Next time I will look when it is asleep.'

We get to the Qutub. The car park is full of cars, the gardens are full of people. While we are trying to make up our minds where to go there is a heavy shower and everyone scurries for shelter. 'Not here,' I say and drive on. We go past the ruins of Metcalfe's mansion, Jamali-Kamali's mosque and enter Mehrauli town. I pull up in the car park alongside Auliya Masjid. The shower turns into a downpour. The Shamsi Talab becomes a part of the cascade pouring into it. We sit in the car playing with each other. Bhagmati slithers down the seat and parts my legs. I am nervous. Any moment someone may peep in the window and want to know what she is up to. 'Not here,' I tell her, pushing away her head. We'll try Jahaz Mahal.'

I take the car a few feet further up the road and park it alongside Jahaz Mahal. We make a dash for the building. There is a crowd of rustics—obviously caught by the rain on their way home. They make way for us. I take Bhagmati down the stairs to the floor which is almost level with the water of the pool. Not a soul. I take Bhagmati in my arms and crush her till she can't breathe. 'You want to break my bones? You want to murder me?' she protests.

'It you die here you would go straight to paradise. The waters of the Shamsi Talab have been blessed by many saints.'

'*Acchaji*! Now you want to finish me! I'll go and tell them I was murdered by my lover. Allah will forgive my sins. In my next birth

I will be born as Indira Gandhi and become a famous daughter of India.'

We resume our flirting. But when you have only one ear, one eye and half-a-mind to spare for sex and have to keep the other ear, eye and half-of-the-mind to confront anyone who suddenly bursts upon you, it is not much fun. Twice we try to have a quickie but both times we are interrupted by voices coming down the steps. In that light no one can tell whether Bhagmati is a boy or a girl—or both. Indians are very understanding about boys amusing each other. Only when it comes to straightforward fucking do they get censorious. We pretend we are deeply interested in archaeology, history, architecture. I light matches, examine the tiles and try to decipher inscriptions on stones.

The downpour continues. Not a break anywhere in the leaden sky. We continue strolling in the cellars examining dark corners by matchlight. I find a stone lying on the ground with some writing on it. I pick it up and bring it to the light. It has a swastika on top, lotus flowers on either side with 'Allah' inscribed on it in Arabic. Beneath it is a legend in Persian:

'Musaddi Lal Kayasth, son of Chagan Lal Kayasth, disciple and slave of Peer Hazrat Khwaja Nizamuddin, Beloved of God by whose blessing he received the gift of a son, Kamal Kayasth. In the reign of Sultan Ghiasuddin Balban, King of Kings, Shah-in-Shah of Hindustan.'

Musaddi Lal

I, Musaddi Lal, son of Lala Chagan Lal, Hindu Kayastha of Mehrauli in the city of Delhi, having lost the light in one eye due to the formation of a pearl and fearing the same fate befalling the other, herewith record some events of my days upon this earth. May Ishwar who is also Allah, and Rama who is also Rahim, bear witness that what I have written is true, that nothing has been concealed or omitted.

I was born in 633 Hijri corresponding to the year 1265 of the Christian calendar. It was the beginning of the reign of Sultan Ghiasuddin Balban. My ancestors had been scribes in the service of the rulers of Delhi. They had served Raja Anangpal, the Tomar Rajput, who built Lal Kot and planted the sacred iron pillar of Vishnu Bhagwan in the middle of the city. They had also served Raja Prithvi Raj Chauhan who renamed the city Qila Rai Pithora. When Mohammed Ghori defeated and slew Raja Prithvi Raj and became ruler of Delhi my ancestors acquired knowledge of Turki, Arabic and Persian and continued in the service of the new ruler. My great-grandfather served under Sultan Qutubuddin Aibak and with his own eyes saw the destruction of Hindu and Jain temples, the building of the Jamia Masjid later called Quwwat-ul-Islam on their ruins and the beginnings of the tower of victory, the Qutub Minar. My grandfather served under Qutubuddin's son-in-law and successor Sultan Altamash. Like a common labourer he dug the earth for the Shamsi Talab at the site where the Sultan had seen the footprints of the Holy Prophet's horse, Buraq, and carried stones on his head to build the mausoleum of the Saint Qutubuddin

Bakhtiyar Kaki. He saw the Qutub Minar completed in AD 1220. It was my grandfather who built the house along the Shamsi Talab where I was born and spent most of my life. He also served under Sultan Altamash's daughter Razia Sultana who ruled over Hindustan for three-and-a-half years. My father, Lala Chagan Lal was a clerk in the Kotwali (police station) of Mehrauli under the mighty Sultan Ghiasuddin Balban and served from AD 1265 to AD 1287. (My father died in the year AD 1280).

Like my Kayastha forefathers, I was trained to be a scribe. A pandit taught me Sanskrit and Hindi. Through my father's influence I was admitted to a madrasa to learn Arabic, Turki and Persian. At first I was treated roughly by the Turkish boys and the sons of Hindu converts to Islam. But when I learnt to speak Turki and dress like a Turk, they stopped bullying me. To save me being harassed, the Maulvi Sahib gave me a Muslim name, Abdul. The boys called me Abdullah.

I was the only child of my parents. I had been betrothed to a girl, one of a family of seven who lived in Mathura. We were married when I was nine and my wife, Ram Dulari, only seven. Four years later, when I was old enough to cohabit, my parents sent the barber who had arranged my marriage to fetch my wife from Mathura. For reasons I will explain later, her parents refused to comply with our wishes. Then tragedy struck our home. My father died and a few days later my mother joined him. At thirteen I was left alone in the world.

The Kotwal Sahib was very kind to me. When he came to offer his condolence, he also offered my father's post to me. It was at that time that my Muslim friends suggested that if I accepted conversion to Islam my prospects would be brighter; I could even aspire to become Kotwal of Mehrauli. And I would have no trouble in finding a wife from amongst the new converts. If I was lucky I might even get a widow or a divorcee of pure Turkish, Persian or Afghan stock. 'If you are Muslim,' said one fellow who was full of witticisms, 'you can have any woman you like. If you are up to it, you can have four at a time.'

A Turk for toughness, for hands that never tire;
An Indian for her rounded bosom bursting with milk;
A Persian for her tight crotch and her coquetry;

An Uzbeg to thrash as a lesson for the three.

There was something, I do not know what, which held me back form being converted to Islam. I suspected that the reason why my wife's parents had refused to send her to me was the rumour that my parents had adopted the ways of the Mussalmans. If I became a Muslim, they would say, 'Didn't we tell you? How could we give our daughter to an unclean *maleech*?'

On the last day of the obsequial ceremony for my mother, my wife's uncle came from Mathura to condole with me. His real object was to find out what I was like and whether I observed Hindu customs. With his own eyes he saw that I had my head shaved, wore the sacred thread and fed Brahmins. I asked the barber to speak to him about sending my wife to me. The uncle did not say anything and returned to Mathura.

After waiting for some days I approached the Kotwal Sahib. At that time people felt that fate had dealt harshly with me and were inclined to be sympathetic. The Kotwal Sahib made me write out a complaint against my wife's parents for interfering with my conjugal rights. He forwarded it to the Kotwal of Mathura with a recommendation for immediate execution. If the family raised any objection, they were to be arrested and sent to Mehrauli.

A week later my wife escorted by her younger sister and uncle arrived at my doorstep. After a few days her uncle and sister returned to Mathura.

Ram Dulari behaved in a manner becoming a Hindu wife. She touched my feet every morning and wore vermilion powder in the parting of her hair. But she cried all the time. And if I as much as put my arm on her shoulder to comfort her she shrank away from me. One night when I went to her bed she started to scream. Our neighbour woke up and shouted across the roof to ask if all was well. I felt very foolish.

Even after one month I did not know what she looked like because she kept her face veiled with the end of her dupatta. If was only from her neck and hands that I made out that she was fair. I also noticed that her bosom was full and her buttocks nicely rounded.

It took me several weeks to realize that my wife did not intend to cohabit with me. She cooked her food on a separate hearth and ate out of utensils she had brought with her. For her I was an unclean, Muslim *maleech*. I tried to take her by force. I beat her. It was no use. I asked her whether she would like to return to her parents. She said that she would only go if I threw her out or when she was taken away on her bier. What was I to do? Could I go to the Kotwal Sahib and ask him to order my wife to spread her legs for me! Gradually, I reconciled myself to my fate. We slept under the same roof but never on the same charpoy.

One morning I took Ram Dulari to see the Qutub Minar. We climbed up to the first storey and I pointed out the mausoleum of the Saint Qutubuddin Bakhtiyar Kaki, the Auliya Masjid alongside the Shamsi Talab, our own little home on the other side. And right below us the tomb of Sultan Altamash. I showed her the slab on which a Hindu stone-mason had inscribed *Sri Visvakarme Prasade Rachita* and stuck it into this Muslim tower of victory. We came down and I took her towards the Quwwat-ul-Islam mosque. I explained to her how the Turks had demolished twenty-seven Hindu and Jain temples and buried the idols of Vishnu and Lakshmi beneath the entrance gate so that Muslims going in to pray could trample on them. She refused to enter the mosque. As we were retracing our steps, she noticed that the figures of Hindu gods and goddesses on the pillars of what had once been a Hindu temple had been mutilated: noses sliced off, arms broken, breasts chopped off. She put her head against a pillar and began to cry. A small crowd collected. I pretended she was not feeling well and pushed her along. If it hadn't been for the fact that I was dressed like a Mussalman and my wife wore a burqa (all Hindu women of rank wore burqas) it could have been very awkward. When we got home I reprimanded her very severely.

The Hindus' hatred of the Mussalmans did not make sense to me. The Muslims had conquered Hindustan. Why hadn't our gods saved us from them? There was that Sultan Mahmud of Ghazni who had invaded Hindustan seventeen times—not once or twice but seventeen times. He had destroyed the temple of Chakraswamy at Thanesar and nothing happened to him. Then Somnath. They said that even the sea prostrated itself twice every twenty-four hours to touch the feet of Somnath. But even the sea did not rise to save Somnathji from Mahmud. They said that Mahmud used to chop off the fingers of the Hindu rajas he defeated in battle; his treasury was full of Hindu fingers. He styled himself as Yaminuddaulah—the right hand of God and Zill-e-llahi, the Shadow of God on earth.

The Muslims had become masters of Hindustan. They were quite willing to let us Hindus live our lives as we wanted to provided we recognized them as our rulers. But the Hindus were full of foolish pride. 'This is our country!' they said. 'We will drive out these cow-killers and destroyers of our temples.' They were especially contemptuous towards Hindus who had embraced Islam and treated them worse than untouchables.

The Hindus lived on the stale diet of past glory. At every gathering they talked of the great days of the Tomars and the Chauhans.

'*Arre bhai*! Who can deny our ancients were great!' I told my Hindu friends a hundred times. 'But let us think of today. We cannot fight the Mussalmans; they are too big, too strong and too warlike for us. Let us be sensible and learn to live in peace with them.' But reason never entered the skull of the Hindu. Everyone in the world knows that if you put the four Vedas on one side of the scale and commonsense on the other, commonsense will be heavier. But not so with the Hindus. They would look contemptuously at me and call me a pimp of the Mussalmans. Their great hero was Prithvi Raj Chauhan who had defeated Ghori once at Tarain in AD 1191. But the very next year, on the same battlefield, he had been defeated and slain by the same Ghori. They had an answer to that too. 'Prithvi Raj's only mistake was to spare the life of the *maleech* when he had first defeated him,' they would reply. Nobody really knows the truth about this Prithvi Raj. A poet fellow named Chand Bardai had made a big song-and-dance about him. This great hero Prithvi Raj married lots of women and even abducted the daughter of a neighbouring raja. But you could not say a word against him to the Hindus. Next to Sri Ramchandraji, it was Samrat Prithvi Raj Chauhan whom they worshipped.

I realized that I belonged neither to the Hindus nor to the Mussalmans. How could I explain to my wife that while the Brahmins lived on offerings made to their gods, the Rajputs and the Jats had their lands, Aheers and the Gujars their cattle, the Banias their shops, all that the poor Kayasthas had were their brains and their reed pens! And the only people who could pay for

417

their brains and their pens were the rulers who were Muslims!

I was disowned by the Hindus and shunned by my own wife. I was exploited by the Muslims who disdained my company. Indeed I was like a *hijda* who was neither one thing nor another but could be misused by everyone.

Then I heard of Nizamuddin. 'Go to the dervish of Ghiaspur on the bank of the river Jamna and all your troubles will be over,' people said. They called him auliya (prophet) and also Khwaja Sahib. But there were many learned Mussalmans who called him an imposter who would soon meet the fate he deserved. As becomes a good Kayastha I did not express any opinion and waited to see which way the wind was blowing.

In due course this Nizamuddin was summoned by the sultan to answer charges of heresy levelled against him. On the day of the trial I took leave from my job and went to the palace.

The very name of Ghiasuddin Balban made people urinate with fear. He had a terrible temper and was known to execute anyone who as much as raised his eyes to look at him. He kept two huge Negroes beside him to hack off the heads of people he sentenced to death.

What a sight it was! The great sultan on his couch flanked by his Abyssinian bodyguards: black djinns with drawn swords! Hundreds of bearded Turkish generals! On one side of the throne-couch stood five ulema dressed in fine silks. Facing them on the other side was a young man not much older than I. He wore a long shirt of coarse black wool and had a green scarf tied round his head. With him were three of his followers dressed as poorly as he. This was Nizamuddin, the Sufi dervish of Ghiaspur.

The sultan first addressed Nizamuddin. 'Dervish, the ulema have complained that you make no distinction between Mussalmans and infidels; that you pose as an intermediary between God and man; that you use words which obliterate the difference between man and his Maker; that your followers indulge in music and dancing in the precincts of the mosque and thus contravene the holy law of the shariat. What do you have to say in your defence?'

Nizamuddin smiled and replied: 'O mighty Sultan, it is true that I do not make any distinction between Mussalmans and Hindus as I consider both to be the children of God. The ulema exhort Your Majesty in the name of the Holy Messenger (upon Whom be peace) to destroy temples and slay infidels to gain merit in the eyes of Allah. I interpret the sacred law differently. I believe that the best way to serve God is through love of his creatures. As for the charge of posing as an intermediary between man and his Maker, I plead guilty. God's Messenger (on Whom be peace) said: "Whoever dies without an Imam dies the death of a pagan." We Sufis follow this precept and believe that he who has no Shaikh is without religion. The ulema know not that Allah cannot be understood through knowledge of books or through logic. His Messenger (Peace upon Him) when asked whether even he did not know God replied "No, not even I. God is an experience."'

The sultan nodded towards the ulema. Their leader went down on his knees and kissed the ground in front of the throne. *'Jahan Panah* (Refuge of the World),' he said addressing the sultan, 'you who are the wisest and the most just of all monarchs do not need such insects as we are to expound the holy law. Your Majesty must know that this man, Nizamuddin, talks of love only to throw dust in the eyes of innocent people.' He unwrapped a copy of the Quran, touched it to his forehead and read out a passage. The crowd broke into a chorus of applause—*Wah! Wah! Subhan Allah!* Few of them understood Arabic. Even fewer understood what the words meant when translated into Turki.

The sultan turned to the dervish and asked him about his claiming unity with God. Nizamuddin replied in very poetic language, 'O Sultan! And O you ulema, learned of the law! And all of you people assembled here! Do you know what it is to love and be loved? Perhaps all you have known and enjoyed is the love of women. We Sufis love God and no one else. When we are possessed by the divine spirit we utter words which to the common man may sound like the assumption of godhood. But these should not be taken seriously. You may have heard of the story of the dove that would not submit to her mate. In his passion the male bird said, "If you do not give in to me, I shall turn the throne of Solomon upside down." The breeze carried his words to Solomon. He summoned the dove and asked it to explain itself. The dove replied, "O Prophet of Allah! The words of lovers should not be bandied about." The answer pleased Solomon. We hope our answer will please the Sultan Balban.'

A murmur of *Wah! Wah!* went round.

The sultan asked the ulema for authority on the subject of music. The ulema opened another book (they had brought many bundles of books with them). Their leader again read out something in Arabic and then translated it into Turki. He looked back at the crowd and a section applauded *Wah! Wah!*

The sultan again turned to Nizamuddin. The dervish had not brought any books. From memory he quoted a tradition of the Prophet about music and dancing. 'When Allah's grace enters one's person it manifests itself by making that person sing and dance with joy. If this be a manifestation of being possessed by Allah, I say *Ameen.*'

The sultan pondered over the matter for a while. He brushed his beard and examined the hair that came off in his hand. The silence was terrible. At last he cleared his throat and spoke in a clear, loud voice! 'We dismiss the ulema's charges against Nizamuddin, dervish of Ghiaspur.'

The crowd broke into loud applause praising the sultan's sense of Justice. Many rushed to the dervish and kissed the hem of his coarse, woollen shirt.

The next morning I asked the Kotwal Sahib about Nizamuddin. 'He's got up there,' he replied pointing up to the sky. 'He has shown many infidels the true path. Go to him any Thursday or on the eve of the new moon and you'll see what miracles he can perform!'

The following Thursday I hired An *ekka* to go to Ghiaspur which was more than a *kos* from Mehrauli. When I got to the hospice and asked an attendant whether I could see the man who was at the palace some days earlier, he replied, 'Khwaja Sahib is meditating in his cell. He only receives visitors in the evening. You can go and eat at the *langar* (free kitchen).'

I went to the *langar*. It was crowded with Muslims and Hindus, rich and the poor, clamouring for a leaf-cup of lentils and a morsel of coarse bread. I had to fight my way through the crowd to grab a chappati. I came out and sat in the courtyard where a party of *qawwals* were singing in Hindi. I was told that the song had been written and composed by one Abdul Hassan, who was very close to the holy man.

Late in the afternoon word went round that the dervish had

emerged from his cell. People buzzed round him like bees round a crystal of sugar. I pushed my way through the throng and when I got to him I kissed the hem of his shirt. Suddenly tears came gushing into my eyes. The dervish put his hand on my head. I felt a tingling sensation run down my spine and the fragrance of musk enveloping my frame. He tilted my tear-stained face upwards and said, 'Just as Allah has let my tunic drink your tears, so may He make your sorrows mine!' As he spoke those words I felt as light as a piece of thistledown floating in the air.

'Abdullah, my son,' he continued, 'you live near the mausoleum of Hazrat Qutubuddin Bakhtiyar Kaki. Go there every morning and recite the ninety-nine names of Allah. Your wishes will be granted. Come whenever your heart is heavy. The doors of our hut of poverty are never bolted against anyone.'

It was on my way back to Mehrauli that I asked myself, 'How does he know that I live near the mausoleum of Bakhtiyar Kaki? How does he know that my Muslim friends call me Abdullah? And if somebody has told him who I am and where I live, how is it that he does not know that I am a Hindu and may not know the ninety-nine names of Allah?'

I could not contain myself. Since there was no one else I could unburden myself to I told my wife all that had passed. For the first time since we had been married, Ram Dulari showed some interest in me. When I ran out of words she asked very timidly, 'Why don't you take me along one day?' In my enthusiasm I took her hand. It went limp in my grasp.

On the first day of the new month of the muslim lunar calendar I took Ram Dulari to Ghiaspur. Our *ekka* was one in a long line on the dusty road. We passed bullock carts loaded with women and children, the men striding along barefoot with their shoes hung on their staves.

There was an immense crowd. A whole bazaar of bangle-sellers, sweet-meat vendors, cloth-dealers and medicine-sellers had gone up. I feared Ram Dulari would not get a chance to have darshan of the holy man. I did not take her to the *langar* as she would not touch anything cooked by Muslims. We wandered round the stalls, watched jugglers and acrobats, dancing bears and monkeys. We sat down under a tree. I began to despair. In an hour the sun would set and the *ekka*-driver would insist that we return to Mehrauli before it became dark. I was lost in my thoughts when a dervish came to me and said: 'Abdul! Isn't your name Abdul or Abdullah? The khwaja Sahib has been enquiring after you.' He led us through a door at the back of the mosque into a courtyard where the holy man was receiving visitors. The dervish forced his way through the crowd with us following close on his heels.

I kissed the hem of the holy man's shirt. Ram Dulari prostrated herself on the ground before him. Khwaja Sahib stretched his hand and blessed her. 'Child, Allah will fulfil your heart's desire. If He wills your womb will bear fruit. Go in peace.' That was all. The crowd pushed us away.

Her womb bear fruit? This man of God who was said to read people's minds like a book had not read Ram Dulari's. From the way she turned away her face I could tell she was embarrassed. On the way back to Mehrauli she avoided touching me. We got off opposite the Auliya Masjid. We walked home as if we had nothing to do with each other. I in front, looking at the shuttered doors of shops as if I had never seen them before; she behind me, enveloped in her burqa.

As soon as we stepped into our courtyard she lit the hearth to warm up food she had cooked in the morning. I lit an oil-lamp in the niche and wrote down the events of the day. She gave me my meal and went back to the kitchen to eat hers. After I had finished I gave her my empty brass plate and went to the bazaar to get a pan-leaf.

By the time I came back Ram Dulari had rinsed the utensils and was lying on her charpoy with her face towards the wall. I blew out the oil-lamp and stretched myself on my charpoy. I could not sleep. I kept thinking about the holy man's promise that we would have children. How could Ram Dulari have them unless I gave them to her? I wondered if she was thinking the same thing. After an hour of turning from side to side I called softly to her, 'Ram Dulari!'

'Hun!'

'Are you asleep?'

'No.'

The gong of the Kotwali struck the hour of midnight. Once again I asked Ram Dulari if she was asleep; she said 'No.'

Something said she might not be averse to my touching her. I got up and went over to her charpoy. 'Can I lie with you?' I asked, 'I feel cold.' She made room for me and replied, 'If you wish.'

I lay beside her. The passion that I had stored up over the months welled in my body. Just as a torrent carries away everything that comes in its way my lust swept aside my fears. I fell on her like a hungry lion. I tore away her sari and tried to enter her. She spread out her thighs to receive me. But no sooner did I reach between them than my seed was spent. I felt ashamed of myself.

Ram Dulari got up to clean herself. She poured water from the pitcher into her brass lota. She put aside her sari and began to splash water between her thighs. Under the light of the stars I saw her pale body, the outlines of her rounded breasts and her broad hips. She dried herself with the same sari and wrapped it round her body. She hesitated, not sure which charpoy to go to. I stretched out my hand to her. She took it and let me pull her beside me. My passion was roused again. She let me remove her damp sari and warm her naked flesh in my embrace. This time I was able to hold myself longer. And she more eager to receive me. A cry of pain escaped her lips. I knew that I had at long last made Ram Dulari mine.

I re-lit the oil-lamp and helped her wash the stains of blood on the bedsheet. By the time we had finished our bodies were again hungry for each other. So passed the whole night.

I was woken by the sun on my face and flies buzzing in my ears.

Ram Dulari had bathed and cooked the morning meal. She was wearing the red sari she had worn when she had come to Mehrauli as a bride. She did not cover her face against me and blushed as she saw me get up from her bed. She ran indoors. I followed her and bolted the door from the inside.

Thereafter I could not have enough of Ram Dulari. I could not take my eyes off her. Every movement she made fired me with desire to take her. Every moment I was away from her was a torment and I hurried back home to be in her embrace. And she became coquetish. '*Ajee*, I am not a whore you can have anytime you like—not unless you pay me for it.' I bought her a nose-pin with a red ruby; I bought her glass bangles of all the colours I could find in the bazaar. For some months our world was narrowed to a small charpoy on which we sported night and day.

Ram Dulari and I became members of a community which worshipped both in Hindu temples and in Sufi hospices. We celebrated Hindu festivals as well as the Muslim. At Dassehra we went to see Ram Lila, on Diwali we lit-lamps on the parapet of our house, at Holi we squirted coloured water on our Hindu friends. On Id we exchanged gifts with Muslims we knew; on the death anniversaries of Muslim saints we went to the mausoleum of Qutubuddin Bakhtiyar Kaki. And at least once a month we went to Ghiaspur and watched the sky at dusk to see if the new moon had risen.

Ram Dulari continued to dress as other Hindu women did. She wore crimson in the parting of her hair, a red dot on her forehead, and a mangalsutra (a necklace of black and gold beads). I continued to dress like a Turk with a skull cap and turban. Like the Turks I sported a neatly trimmed beard and moustache. And I spoke the way they did. If they said *As-Salaam-Valai-Kum* (peace be with you) I replied *Valai-Kum-As Salaam* (and with you too be peace). If they asked me how I was, I replied *Al-hamdu-lillah* (well, by the grace of God). But if they asked me, 'Abdullah when will you become a true Muslim?' I would reply, 'Soon, if that be the will of God—*Inshallah*.' If anyone asked me whether we were Hindus or Mussalmans, we would reply we were both. Nizamuddin was our umbrella against the burning sun of Muslim bigotry and the downpour of Hindu contempt.

So passed the days, weeks and months. By the end of the year Ram Dulari was pregnant and had to go to her parents in Mathura for her confinement. When news of the birth of a son was brought to me I sent plates full of sweets to the Kotwal Sahib and to all our Muslim and Hindu friends. After a few weeks I went to Mathura to bring back my wife and son. Ram Dulari's sisters made a lot of fuss over me They teased me, 'Are you going to have the boy circumcised? Are you going to name him Mohammed or Ali or something like that?' I let them say what they liked. I had great fun with them.

I did not have my son circumcised. I had his head shaved and got a Brahmin to recite mantras. I chose the name Kamal for him—it could be either Hindu or Muslim. In Hindi it meant the lotus

25

flower. In Arabic, pronounced with a longer accent on the second *a*, it meant excellence. We took the child to Jogmaya temple and had the priest daub sandalpaste on his forehead. Then we took him to Ghiaspur and had the Khwaja Sahib bless him. I recorded my gratitude to my *peer* by having his name inscribed on stone as my benefactor and embedding the stone in the outer wall of our home.

People who do not have a guru or a *peer* can never understand what they mean to their disciples. They are more than either father or mother to them. A disciple gives more respect and obedience to his guru than to his father. He is more devoted to his guru than to his mother; he suckles the milk of love from the guru's bosom and snuggles in his lap as would a baby in its mother's. Indeed the guru is more loved by his disciple than the bridegroom is by his bride because the disciple gives to his guru his *tan* (body), *man* (mind) and *dhan* (worldly wealth). The guru is the embodiment of God on earth. What happens when the true guru is away or you choose a wrong guru was abundantly proved to us. When Khwaja Sahib went away to the Punjab all the little towns which comprised Delhi became like a woman whose husband has gone abroad. Dust-storms of chaos began to blow. One calamity followed another.

Sultan Ghiasuddin Balban's eldest son, Prince Mohammed, was killed fighting the Mongols. The mighty sultan who had ruled Hindustan for twenty-two years with an iron hand wept like a woman. He would not eat or sleep or attend to the affairs of the state. He fell ill but would not allow the royal physician to feel his pulse. In a few days he was reduced to a skeleton—and died.

There were many claimants to the throne. They slew each other; I cannot even recall their names. Then Jalaluddin Firoze of the tribe of Khiljis, an old man with one foot in the grave, took his seat on the throne of Delhi. His sons could not wait for him to die. Many of them came under the influence of a false guru called Siddi Maula.

Siddi Maula had a hospice of his own where he ran a *langar* in which confections, the like of which were only cooked in the royal kitchen, were served to the rich and the powerful. The Siddi also had an army of followers to sing his praises. They reeled off the names of the *omarah* and princes of royal blood who paid homage to Siddi. They said Siddi Maula did not care a cowrie shell for worldly wealth or power and had even turned down the post of chief qazi. They said that the daughters of noble houses were eager to marry him but he would not have any of them. *'Ya Allah!* What kind of dervish is this?' I asked myself. 'One foot in God's boat and the other in the courts of kings! Maybe he is one of those who wears the cloak of humility to cover designs of power!'

I saw Siddi Maula and at once knew he was not fit to kiss the dust of the feet of my *peer*, Nizamuddin. He was a rascally-looking fellow with a glossy black beard and moustaches that curled up like scorpion tails. He assumed the airs of an aristocrat and was forever sniffing at a perfumed swab of cotton. Although he was a young man, he had developed a paunch. Even a blind man could see that this Siddi did not believe in fasting or overcoming his *nafs* (desires). He was so busy giving counsel to the rich that he had little time left for the poor. He was a proud man. Of the proud, Mustatraf has said:

> *Tell this fool whose arrogance makes his neck veins swell!*
> *Pride corrupts religion, weakens the mind, destroys*
> *reputations. So take heed!*

It is truly said that a country cannot have two kings any more than a scabbard hold two swords. In Delhi we had the Khilji, Jalaluddin Firoze. And we had Siddi Maula who was known to be conspiring with one of the sultan's sons to overthrow the sultan. It had to be one or the other.

How the old sultan outwitted the dervish is quite a story. He got some people to lodge a report that the dervish had promised to help a faction inimical to the sultan and had in turn been promised the hand of a young, beautiful princess. No sooner did this charge reach the sultan than he ordered the arrest of Siddi Maula. I was in the kotwali when Siddi Maula and a score of his followers were brought in handcuffs. Their feet were in irons. I knew blood would flow and Siddi Maula would curse anyone who sided with his enemies. Why risk the anger of a dervish, even a false one! I wrote a petition to the Kotwal Sahib begging leave for three days as my bowels had suddenly become loose and the hakeem had advised rest.

I learnt of what passed with Siddi Maula from the clerks who came to enquire about my health. Kotwal Sahib had tried to extort a confession from Siddi Maula. He had him beaten, his testicles squeezed, red hot chillies pushed up his anus, his mouth filled with shit and urine. But Siddi Maula had refused to speak. The sultan was very angry. 'Make him and his followers walk through fire. If they come out alive, I will believe they are innocent and let them go,' he said. The next day a huge funeral pyre was prepared near village Baharpur not far from Mehrauli. I could not miss this sight as Siddi Maula was reputed to be able to perform miracles.

The sultan came to watch the spectacle. The pyre was set on fire. Just as the Siddi and his followers were being pushed towards it, the sultan lost his nerve. He sent for the ulema and asked them if an ordeal by fire had the sanction of the holy law. The ulema shook their heads. 'It is the nature of fire to burn,' they said. The sultan cancelled the order and returned to his palace. Siddi Maula and his men were flogged back to the kotwali. The sultan turned his wrath on the Kotwal Sahib. 'If you can't make him talk, send him to us. We will make him open his vile mouth.'

Despite Ram Dulari's remonstrations that I should stay at home I joined a party of clerks going to Shahr-i-Nau—the new city going up in the vicinity of the Qasr-i-hazaar Sutoon, the palace of a thousand pillars.

Siddi Maula and his gang were already present in the Hall of Public Audience when the sultan took his seat. The sultan was in a very bad mood. The way he talked showed clearly that his mind was as infirm as his body, 'Confess your crimes,' he roared, 'or we will have your tongue torn out of your mouth.' And if he confessed he was to have his head cut off.

'Bring the impostor near us,' he commanded. Siddi Maula was brought forward. The old sultan stepped down from his throne. 'Son of Satan! You call yourself a saint and meddle in the affairs of kings!' he shouted as he slapped the dervish across the face. Siddi did not flinch. Although his face was black with bruises and his eyes were almost closed because of the swelling round them, the ends of his moustache were still curled up and his mien was as defiant as ever. The sultan hit him again and screamed, 'Speak, you fruit of fornication!' Siddi spoke in a clear and powerful voice everyone could hear. 'Jalaluddin, listen to the words of Siddi Maula, the dervish of Allah!' he said as if he was speaking to a slave.

'Allah will punish you for laying hands on His servant. At the hands of your own kinsmen will you die. Your carcass will burn in the fires of hell.' Suddenly Siddi Maula spat out a blob of phlegm and blood which covered the sultan's face and snow-white beard.

The old sultan began to rave like a maniac: *'Moozi* (blackguard), bastard, son of a pig!' He turned to his courtiers and abused them, 'Cowards! You allow your ruler to be insulted by this dog!' In the hall there was a party of dervishes of an order known to hate Siddi Maula. They pounced on Siddi and belaboured him till he was reduced to a bloody mess. They dragged him out into the open where he lay like a sack—alive or dead, I do not know. Then an elephant was brought to crush Siddi Maula's head under its foot. His skull burst like a coconut, spilling blood and butter-like fat. My knees buckled under me; I could not stop my body from shaking. I sat down where I was and began to pray. It took me an hour to recover. My friends helped me get home.

What a terrible day it was! When Siddi Maula was taken to Shahr-i-Nau, it was a bright, sunny morning. No sooner was he dead than the sky turned as black as charcoal. A vast cloud of locusts descended on the city. Every tree and every bush became a beehive of crawling, hopping, flying insects. Within a matter of moments the trees were leafless, bushes turned to brambles.

Then followed the worst sand-storm I have ever known. It came like the charge of a phalanx of black elephants smashing walls, uprooting trees, blinding man and beast alike. It was so dark that one could not tell when the sun set and the night came on. 'It is the curse of Siddi Maula,' said Ram Dulari to me as we lay huddled together with Kamal between us.

What Siddi Maula had prophesied came to pass. Sultan Jalaluddin Firoze was murdered by his own nephew, Alauddin Khilji, who was also his son-in-law. I do not know whether the deceased sultan roasted in the fires of hell but we certainly had a foretaste of *gehennum*. The summer's heat turned Delhi into an oven. The sun's rays were so fierce that every day twenty or thirty people died of stroke. There was no rain. Wells dried up. Cattle began to die of thirst. Crops withered. There was no flour or rice or lentils in the bazaars. We had to get provisions at an exorbitant price from distant villages. The city was full of starving beggars dying in the streets. Hindus prayed to their gods. Muslims prayed to Allah. We prayed for the return of our Khwaja Sahib.

Our prayers were answered. One morning a dervish returning from the Punjab informed us that the Khwaja Sahib was only two days march from Mehrauli. That afternoon there was a meeting of the citizens at the mausoleum of Qutubuddin Bakhtiyar Kaki to arrange a suitable reception for him.

When the great day came, citizens in their hundreds poured out of the city gates to welcome the saint.

The Khwaja Sahib looked pale and tired. That was not surprising as he had walked barefoot over hundreds of *kos* of hot, dusty roads. But he had a smile and a blessing for everyone who got close enough to kiss the hem of his cloak or touch his feet. The dervishes had to make a cordon to protect him from the surging crowd. The bazaars were decorated with arches with banners saying *Khush Amdeed* (welcome). Women crowded on the roof-tops showered rose-petals on him. Men smothered him in garlands. A huge procession led by parties of *qawwals* wound its way through the main bazaar of Mehrauli to the mausoleum of Qutubuddin Bakhtiyar Kaki. The Khwaja Sahib begged to be left alone. He went down into one of the cells in the basement of Auliya Masjid and bolted the door from the inside.

At night we heard the rumble of clouds. Mehrauli which had not had a drop of rain during the monsoon season had a heavy shower in autumn. May the mouths of unbelievers be stuffed with dung!

The following Thursday, I took Kamal and Ram Dulari to have *darshan* of the Khwaja Sahib. Such a crowd I had never witnessed at Ghiaspur! It was very hot and my throat was parched. The Khwaja Sahib's words were like nectar cooled in mountain streams of paradise.

'There is only one God though we call Him by different names. There are innumerable ways of approaching Him. Let everyone follow the way he thinks best for him. His path may lead to the mosque or the tabernacle, to a temple full of idols or to a solitary cave in the wilderness. What path you take is not important; what is important is the manner in which you tread it. If you have no love in your heart then the best path will lead you into the maze of deception.' He told us of an incident from the life of the Prophet Musa. Musa heard a poor shepherd praying: 'Where art Thou that

I may serve Thee? I will mend Thy boots, comb Thy hair, give Thee milk from my goats.' Musa reprimanded the shepherd for so speaking to God. God in His turn reprimanded Musa. 'Thou hast driven away one of my true servants.'

It was again to the Prophet Musa that Allah conveyed the essence of true religion. The Almighty said, 'I was sick, and you did not come to see me. I was hungry, and you did not give me food.' Musa asked, 'My God, can you also be sick and hungry?' God replied, 'My servant so-and-so was sick, and my servant so-and-so- was hungry. If you had visited one and fed the other, you would have found me with them.'

The Khwaja Sahib made us memorize some Sufi catechisms:

> *Who is the wisest of wise men?*
> *One who rejects the world.*
> *Who is the saintliest of all saints?*
> *One who refuses to change with changing circumstances.*
> *Who is the richest of rich men?*
> *One who is content.*
> *Who is the neediest of the needy?*
> *One who has no contentment.*

How to be content? I asked myself. The Khwaja Sahib heard the question I had asked only in my heart. 'Reduce your wants to the barest minimum, conquer your *nafs.*'

By the time we came out, the sun had gone behind the walls of the hospice. Kamal had fallen asleep in my lap. *Ekkawallas* were clamouring to get back to Mehrauli.

These were dangerous times. We had to pass through villages inhabited by Jats and Gujars who were notorious robbers. We formed a party of ten or twelve *ekkas;* two dozen men armed with swords and spears rode on either side. We reached Mehrauli without any untoward incident.

It had been a long day. I put Kamal to bed. Ram Dulari brought me a tumbler of milk which I was in the habit of drinking before retiring. I drew her on my lap. She protested: 'All day you hear sermons on controlling your passions, but as soon as it gets dark you want to do this.'

'*Aree!* How stupid can you be! All day you hear sermons about love; but by the evening you forget everything you heard.'

'The Khwaja Sahib did not mean this kind of love,' she replied. 'Hasn't he often said, "If you want to approach God, you must first conquer your desires"? Is this how you overcome your *nafs*?' she asked pressing her bottom on my middle. 'You will never achieve union with God this way,' she giggled.

'Let us first achieve union between ourselves; we can bother about union with the Almighty later,' I replied.

୨ଈ

The days went by. Our Kotwal Sahib became too old to work. He was permitted to retire and go to Mecca. His son-in-law was appointed in his place.

The new Kotwal was a bigot. He spoke very disparagingly of the Hindus. He became a great favourite of Sultan Alauddin Khilji who, as I said before, was the late sultan's nephew, son-in-law and assassin.

Sultan Alauddin Khilji set about despoiling the Hindu kingdoms of the south. His General, Malik Kafur, extended his dominions right up to the seas. He brought thousands of slaves, hundreds of elephants, camels and bullocks carts loaded with gold, silver and precious stones to Delhi. Hindu women were given away to Muslims as rewards for service. Many Hindu temples were destroyed. The sultan paid no heed to the Khwaja Sahib's advice that conquests of the sword were shortlived.

The atmosphere changed so much that even Hindus like me, who had adopted Muslim ways, found life irksome. I did my job, drew my wage and kept my mouth shut. If some Mussalman needled me too much, I sought shelter at Ghiaspur. Not even the mighty sultan who assumed the title *Sikandar-i-Sani* (Alexander the Second) and proclaimed Delhi as *Dar-ul-Khilafa* (Seat of the Caliphate), who had defeated and massacred Mongol invaders by the thousands, who had raised a new city Siri and an enormous madrasa beside the Hauz-i-Alai and who planned to raise another Qutub Minar twice as high as the first, dared to raise his eyebrows in front of our Khwaja Sahib. Once when he expressed a wish to visit Ghiaspur, the Khwaja Sahib replied, 'We will have nothing to do with kings. If the sultan enters our hospice by one door, we will leave by another.'

One day I was at the kotwali singing praise of our Khwaja Sahib. A clerk whose tongue was coated with odious criticisms said loud enough for all to hear, '*Ajee*, what can one say about a gentleman like you! The more one says the less adequate it is! At one place you are Musaddi Lal Kayastha, at another Shaikh Abdullah, some you greet with a Ram Ram, others with a salaam: with Muslims you bow towards the Kaaba; with the Hindus you kiss the penis of Shiva; a courtier in the kotwali, a dervish in the hospice; one foot in a monastery, the other on your woman's charpoy. You get the best of both worlds. Yes sir, the more one praises you, the less adequate it seems.'

I did not return to the kotwali after my midday meal. I lay on my charpoy in the courtyard, gazing at the grey sky and thinking about what that clerk had said. If I'd had the power I would have had the fellow taken to the market-place, his trousers pulled down and ordered every citizen to spit on his bottom.

Ram Dulari sat down beside me and asked, 'What's the matter?'

'Nothing.'

'Can't be nothing. It's written on your face. Why don't you tell me?'

I told her. She listened quietly. When I had finished, she gaped at the wall; I gaped at the sky. 'There are many like us,' I told her. 'There is that poet Abdul Hassan who also calls himself Sultani and Ameer Khusrau. His father was Muslim, his mother Hindu. For Hindus he writes in Hindi, for Muslims in Persian. For Indians he praises everything about India; for Muslims he praises everything in the lands of the Muslims. He flatters the sultan and he flatters the Khwaja Sahib. And he is the favourite of both. He writes poems praising the *omarah* and extracts many *tankas* from them; at the same time he pretends to be a dervish. No one dares to say anything to him because he is Muslim. It is only poor Hindus like us who wish to befriend Hindus as well as Muslims who get spat on by both; we are neither one nor the other. They treat us as if we were *hijdas*.'

'Let our enemies be *hijdas*!' exclaimed Ram Dulari angrily. 'You talk to this man Abdul Hassan or Khusrau or whatever his name is. Ask him for advice.'

'I don't like him. He never says anything without a sting in it.

He is too clever for the likes of me.'

'If you speak nicely to him, he may become your friend.'

'*Aree*! You are very innocent; you don't know the ways of the world. The rich only make friends with the rich. The clever only like admirers and flatterers. Khusrau is both rich and clever. I am not important enough to matter to him. And I will not waste my time pandering to his vanity.'

However, the next day when I went to Ghiaspur I ran straight into this chap Abdul Hassan Ameer Khusrau. As usual he was surrounded by a ring of admirers. Also as usual the only voice you could hear was his. As soon as he saw me he aimed a barbed shaft at me: 'Lala Musaddi Lal alias Abdullah brings his august presence amongst us.' I exchanged greetings with the others without looking at the fellow. His friend, another poet named Amir Hassan Dehlvi, was more amiable. 'Say brother Abdullah, how goes it with you?' he asked. '*Al hamdu-Lillah*,' I replied as I sat down.

Khusrau realized I had taken offence and tried to make up. 'Brother Abdullah I have composed a new riddle for you in Hindi. Let us see if you can get it:

> Twenty I sliced, I cut off their heads
> No life was lost, no blood was shed.'

He had obviously put it to the others before I came. They said in a chorus, 'This is really a clever one!' I could make nothing of it. Khusrau reverted to his ill-mannered self. 'Fool!' he cried, 'The answer is in the riddle itself. It is *nakhoon*. Don't you see *nakhoon* means both nails and no blood? You have to have brains to work out Khusrau's riddles.'

'Allah gave you wisdom, Ishwar gave me the gift of good manners,' I replied in as sharp a tone as I could manage. It hit the mark. Khusrau changed his tone. He was like that, blowing hot one minute blowing cold the next. 'Don't take it ill, brother,' he said. 'We are *dharam bhais* (brothers in faith). Try this one:

> All night he stayed with me
> Came the dawn and out he went;
> At his going my heart bursts
> O friend, was it my lover?

No friend, it was the . . . '

'It was the . . .? It was the . . .?' demanded Khusrau clicking his thumb and finger in my face. Fortunately someone gave an answer. 'No friend, it was the lamp.' Khusrau went on from riddle to riddle. '*Bhai*, the prophecy that you will be greater than Khaqani of Persia has certainly been fulfilled,' remarked one of his cronies. Khusrau did not deny it. 'I am but the dust under the feet of the Khwaja Sahib! If the great Nizamuddin honours me with the title of Toot-i-Hind (The Nightingale of India) and calls me Shaikh Saadi of Hindustan, what power on earth can prevent me from becoming the greatest poet and singer of all time? It's not I, it is the divine spark that the Khwaja Sahib has lit in my bosom that shines in my wretched frame.'

What could anyone say to such mock humility and such bare-faced bragging? It is true that as soon as someone achieves success, people vie with each other to discover newer facets of his genius. So it was about Khusrau. If one man said Khusrau was a great poet, another said he was a greater musician. If a third one said Khusrau was a great statesman, a fourth one would insist he was an even greater swordsman. Khusrau knew the art of spreading stories about himself. Since it was fashionable among Muslims to trace their ancestry to some foreign land, Khusrau who was darker than I and had more Indian blood than Turkish in his veins talked of Turkey as his 'home'. The poetic pseudonyms he had chosen for himself were designed to convey nobility of birth, power and wealth. At first he was Sultani (drop the i at the end and it becomes Sultan). When he became Khusrau he added Ameer (rich) to it. God had given him brains and talent but had forgotten to temper His gifts with modesty. This braggart who compared himself to Shaikh Saadi had not read what had been written about people who chant their own praises:

> *It does not behove a man of wisdom*
> *By his own tongue to praise himself;*
> *What pleasure does a woman beget*
> *If with her own hand she rubs her breast?*

What a change came over Khusrau when the Khwaja Sahib

made his appearance! He was like an actor who takes off a mask which has moustaches painted insolently upwards and puts on another which has them hanging down in humility. The arrogant boaster suddenly turned into an ardent hem-kisser and tear-shedder. And he alone of all the thousands present was always honoured by a pat on the head and a solicitous enquiry, 'Is all well with you, Abdul Hassan?'

On my way back to Mehrauli, I was full of angry thoughts about Khusrau. How was it that other people could not see what a double-faced man he was? He had served innumerable masters. If anyone knew when to turn his back to the setting sun and worship the new one rising, it was Khusrau! He had first been with Sultan Balban's nephew, Malik Chajjoo. How he had extolled Chajjoo! Then he had joined the sultan's younger son and denounced Chajjoo. Next he'd served the heir-apparent; thereafter the ruler of Avadh. When the ruling dynasty was half-Hindu he boasted of the Hindu blood in his veins and extolled the greatness of Hindustan. He praised its betel leaves and its bananas, its chess players and musicians. When the ruler was a Muslim bigot, the same Khusrau proclaimed: 'Do not count Hindus among men for they venerate the cow, regard the crow superior to the parrot and read omens in the braying of an ass!' According to Khusrau what made India the greatest nation of the world was the fact that he, Khusrau, was Indian! I said to myself: This Khusrau is a cunning sycophant. Why should I waste so much of my time and temper on him! By the time the *ekka* pulled up at the stand outside the Auliya Masjid I had made my peace with Khusrau; for me he was just a successful joker, a *khusra* (a castrated male).

Ram Dulari heard my footsteps and undid the latch to let me in. Kamal was already asleep. She warmed milk for me and sat down beside me. I told her of what happened at Ghiaspur. I asked her the riddle about paring nails. She had heard of it and gave me the answer. I asked her about the other one about 'spending all night and going out at dawn.' She nudged me in the belly: 'Do you have anything else on your mind except this?' I took her hand and put it on my member. 'It's not this, you silly woman! It is the lamp.'

She rose and blew out the lamp.

❧

The years drifted by. Despite the thousands of conjugations in which our hips met to pump ecstasy into each other and the Jamna-flood of semen which I poured into her—none of these efforts bore more fruit in Ram Dulari's womb. The hair on my head thinned till there was none left. My right eye began to turn grey; antimonies prescribed by hakeems did not arrest the cataract which soon deprived me of the sight in my left eye. Ram Dulari's hair also turned grey. No sooner did she stop menstruating than she started getting fleshy about her middle. Every time she had to get up from her charpoy, she had to rest her hands on her knees and invoke the assistance of Ramji. At times we lay on the same charpoy. But more often it was with our bottoms that we kissed each other than with our lips. We decided that Ishwar had given us enough and we should devote the days that remained to us in prayer.

Kamal had become a man. He had acquired knowledge of Turki and Persian at the madrasa at Hauz-i-Alai near Siri. I pleaded with the Kotwal Sahib, gave him a handsome *nazrana* of eleven gold tankas and got Kamal appointed in my place as a clerk in the kotwali. Ram Dulari found him a wife from among the daughters of one of the Kayastha families who frequented both the temple of Jogmaya and the hospice at Ghiaspur. From the way Kamal and his wife behaved, we were assured that our branch of the Kayasthas would not end with us.

We began to spend more time at the Khwaja Sahib's hospice in Ghiaspur than in our home in Mehrauli. Then we rented rooms in Ghiaspur and began to live there. We went to Mehrauli to visit our son and daughter-in-law once every month. Kamal brought his wife to see us every Thursday.

We saw the Khwaja Sahib every day. Khusrau was also there more often than he used to be. The years had deprived him of his teeth and cleansed his tongue of its coating of sarcasm. He became quite friendly and began to address Ram Dulari as *bhabi* (sister-in-law). I responded to his friendship and we were often in each other's homes.

What more could one ask for in old age? Peace, prayer, security, friends—all under the shade of a massive banyan tree—and our Khwaja Sahib, Beloved of God (*Mahboob-i-Ilahi*) and Beloved of Man! We lived in the world without being a part of it.

We were like people who stroll through a bazaar without wanting to buy anything.

Rarely did the world intrude into our sanctum. One occasion that I recall was on the death of Sultan Alauddin Khilji. At first we heard that he had died in his sleep and that Malik Kafur, the slave he had raised to the rank of Commander, had taken over the administration till such time as a successor could be named by the *omarah*. Then we heard that Kafur had taken his master's senior widow to his couch, put out the eyes of two princes and murdered many others. The Khwaja Sahib, who seldom bothered about the comings and goings of sultans, put his hands on his ears and exclaimed, 'Tauba!' Even Ameer Khusrau who had, as he said himself, 'woven a false story in every reign' wrote a satire on Malik Kafur which he recited to a gathering in Ghiaspur. We knew that if our Khwaja Sahib said something against someone, he was sure to be punished. So it came to pass. The servants of the palace rose against Malik Kafur and slaked the thirst of their daggers with his vile blood.

Qutubuddin Mubarak Shah, who became the next sultan, did not like our Khwaja Sahib. It did not take flatterers much time to fan the ashes of hate that smouldered in the sultan's breast into a vindictive flame. They said, 'Nizamuddin tells people that he does not give a cowrie shell for anyone; he defies royal commands to lower Your Majesty in the eyes of Your Majesty's subjects. (This was in reference to the Khwaja Sahib not attending Friday prayers in the Quwwat-ul-Islam mosque). He spreads all manner of gossip about Your Majesty and Khusro Khan.'

Who was this Khusro Khan? He was a Hindu Pawar boy captured during an expedition to Gujarat. The men of Gujarat are handsome but effeminate. And, of the Gujaratis, Pawars are known to be the most handsome and at the same time the most womanlike. I never saw this fellow, but he was said to be fair, gazelle-eyed with eyebrows curving like scimitars and buttocks as large as a woman's. By some quirk of fate the sultan who was known for his prodigious appetite for women turned his back upon his well-stocked harem of the beauties of Hindustan, Iran and Turkistan and fell in love with this boy from Gujarat. He had the fellow colour his lips and put kohl in his already dark eyes. They drank out of the same goblet. The royal hakeem was asked to prepare perfumed oil to smear on the boy's bottom. Then yet another change came over the sultan. He started colouring his own lips, smearing his own bottom with scented oil and making the Pawar do to him what he had been doing to the Pawar. As details of the affair travelled from lip to ear more pepper and spice were added to it.

The Muslims were more upset by these goings-on than the Hindus. They said it was a disgrace that a manly Turk should allow an infidel to mount him as a horse mounts a mare. The sultan thought the Muslims were unhappy because his beloved was a Hindu. He ordered the boy to be converted to Islam and re-named Khusro Khan. The two celebrated the occasion by getting drunk and carousing with each other in the open. Bawdy jokes about the Gujarati stallion and the Turkish mare could be heard in the bazaars. They reached the sultan's ears. The ulema who had reason to hate our Khwaja Sahib told the sultan that the source of all the filthy stories about him and Khusro Khan was the hospice at Ghiaspur.

The sultan believed this calumny. He forbade the supply of provisions to the hospice; a police post was established at Ghiaspur to check the coming and going of people.

Strange are the ways of God! Our Khwaja Sahib who was the Sultan of all Sultans, simply wrote the name of Allah on a piece of paper and stuck it on the entrance of the hospice. He announced that the quantity of food cooked in the *langar* kitchen would be doubled. Allah saw to it that we were never short of flour, lentils, salt or ghee. Although the *omarah* discreetly stayed away, the number of poor pilgrims to the hospice increased.

This was like a cup full of chillies in the already hot curry of the sultan's temper. He ordered that the hospice be closed down. But the ways of God are mysterious! He heard of the plight of His Beloved Friend and decided to teach the sultan a lesson. The sinful cohabitation of the sultan and his lover-boy bore its monstrous fruit. Boils erupted on the royal penis and blocked the passage of urine. Physicians applied all kinds of unguents but the boils would not heal nor a drop of urine trickle out. What can medicines do against affliction visited by God! And how long can man live without urinating? Within a few hours the sultan was tossing in agony and crying to Allah for mercy. His mother came to Ghiaspur tearing her hair and pouring dust on her head. She clung to the Khwaja Sahib's feet and would not let him go till he forgave her son. 'Let your son abdicate and give his kingdom to us,' said the Khwaja Sahib. We knew the Beloved of God had some other miracle in mind.

The Queen Mother rushed back to the palace. The sultan was in terrible pain and agreed that as soon as he was able to urinate he would give up his kingdom. 'No,' said our Khwaja Sahib to the emissary, 'first abdicate, then urinate. Write the deed of renunciation in your own hand and put the royal seal on it.'

The sultan was almost on the verge of death when he signed the deed of abdication. As he pressed his seal on the wax, his bladder, which was on the point of exploding, emptied itself of its poisonous contents. The Queen Mother carried the jar containing her son's urine on her head and walked barefoot all the way from the palace to Ghiaspur. Women of the royal harem, eunuchs and guards followed her. She prostrated herself before the Khwaja Sahib and placed the scroll of parchment at his feet. The Khwaja Sahib broke open the seal and read aloud the deed of transfer of the kingdom of Hindustan made by Sultan Qutubuddin Mubarak Shah in favour of Hazrat Khwaja Nizamuddin, dervish of Ghiaspur. He then crumpled up the parchment and dropped it in the jar of urine. 'This is all we dervishes care for earthly kingdoms,' he said and retired to his cell to pray.

When a man's instincts are evil, repentance has a short lease and brief is his gratitude towards those who have done him good. No sooner had the sultan's penis healed than he began to misuse it as he had done before. And since the story of what our Khwaja Sahib had done with the deed transferring sovereignty of Hindustan to him had become common knowledge, the sultan's chagrin got the better of his gratitude. He issued an order reminding Mussalmans they were expected to be at the Quwwat-ul-Islam mosque on the eve of the new moon to pay him homage. He knew that our Khwaja Sahib dedicated this day of the month to the sacred memory of his departed mother. The Khwaja Sahib heard of the order and went to his mother's tomb to pray for guidance. After his prayer he lay down where he was and fell asleep. When he woke he told us that he dreamt of an enormous bull charging towards him. He had caught hold of the beast by its horns and pulled it down into the dust. We did not have to consult a soothsayer to know what the dream foretold.

Came the fateful day and there was the usual congregation to join the Khwaja Sahib at the afternoon prayer. As the shadow of the western wall spread across the courtyard of the mosque, the Khwaja Sahib took some of us with him to the roof to see the new moon. Just as the lower rim of the sun sank below the battlements of Shahr-i-Nau, we saw the pale, silver crescent of the moon. The Khwaja Sahib said a short prayer, ran the palms of his hands over his eyes and beard and recited a Persian verse which went somewhat as follows:

Oh fox! Why did you not stay in your lair?
Why did you join issue with a lion and bring about your doom?

We continued to stroll on the roof enjoying the fresh evening breeze. Both the sun and the moon disappeared. The short dusk turned into a dark night. Suddenly the western horizon was aflame. We heard the sounds of horses' hoofs. It seemed as if an army bearing torches was galloping towards us. Was it the Royal Constabulary sent to arrest the Khwaja Sahib? The Kotwal came in person. He had come not to arrest the Beloved of God but to break the news that the sultan had been murdered and that the city was in turmoil.

The next morning we learnt the details of what had transpired. It appeared that the sultan and his Pawar friend had come to a settled arrangement whereby each played the male and female role on alternate days. To heighten their enjoyment they would go through the elaborate charade of a marriage ceremony. One evening the sultan would arrive as a Turkish groom, sign a contract of marriage with the Pawar and then escort him to the royal couch. This was followed by the feast of deflowering (*dawat-i-valima*) for their cronies. The next evening the roles would be reversed. Apparently on the fateful evening it was the sultan's turn to play the woman and the Pawar's to bestride him. The sultan decked himself out like a Turkish bride, wearing a spider-net veil over loose-fitting garments of silk. The Pawar rode to the palace as a Rajput bridegroom would, accompanied by a band of musicians. They were married by Hindu rites, going round a sacrificial fire to the chanting of mantras. The Pawar then led his Turkish 'bride' to his couch and with much banter proceeded to disrobe 'her'. When the Pawar mounted the Turk, the latter made modest protestations as would a virgin on her first initiation. When the Pawar was fully ensconced he began to play with the sultan's now perfectly healed penis. People who know about such matters say that this is customary in the unnatural cohabitation of male with male. As the Pawar approached the climax of his passion he withdrew his member and rammed it back into the sultan's bottom with great violence. The sultan screamed. The Pawar was overcome with an insane frenzy and crushed the sultan's testicles in his hands. As he was drained of his mad lust, the vapours that had clouded his vision lifted. He acted boldly. He cut off the sultan's head and had his body thrown down from the ramparts. He proclaimed that he had executed the sultan because the people did not want to be ruled by a degenerate transvestite. Thus ended the rule of the sodomite-catamite Sultan Qutubuddin Mubarak Shah. The year was AD 1320.

Delhi had a new king! One sodomite-catamite succeeded another. The Hindu Pawar Rajput from Gujarat re-named Khusro Khan had himself proclaimed emperor of Hindustan under the title Sultan Nasiruddin Mohammed.

We wondered whether the Divine Maker of Destinies would permit the new sultan to go unpunished after He had reduced his partner-in-sin to dust.

Nasiruddin squandered largesse on the *omarah* hoping thereby to buy their loyalty. He sent robes of honour to the governors of the distant provinces. Most accepted them and sent gifts in return. But one, Ghiasuddin Tughlak, who guarded the western frontiers against the Mongols, kicked the trays bearing the robes. No Turk he said would recognize a double-faced *hijda* as his monarch.

The Mussalmans of India rose against Nasiruddin. He had to turn to the Rajputs and the Jats for help. He invited them to take over the defence of Shari-i-Nau. The battle was fought on the outskirts of the city. It appeared that just as the Turks were giving ground, the Muslims of the city rose against the Jats and the Rajputs and turned the tide of battle in favour of their co-religionists. Ghiasuddin Tughlak had Nasiruddin torn limb from limb and his torso thrown over the ramparts. Thousands of citizens were put to the sword. Ram Dulari and I spent the rest of the night praying for the safety of our son and his *bahoo*. (But as becomes wise Kayasthas they had locked themselves inside a room, painted the numeral 786 on the door to indicate that it was the house of a Muslim and so escaped the blood-thirsty Turks).

A wise man has said that a subject should not look at the warts on the face of his ruler but only at the nobility of his features. The new sultan, Ghiasuddin Tughlak, was of noble birth. He had taken a Hindu princess as wife and also had his son, Prince Juna, marry into a noble Hindu family. With a Hindu as his chief consort and a Hindu daughter-in-law we expected the sultan to be lenient towards his non-Muslim subjects. Our hopes were belied. Ghiasuddin Tughlak turned out to be a headstrong tyrant. Flatterers created mischief between him and the Khwaja Sahib. 'Is it right that this old dervish (Khwaja Sahib was over four score years and ten) should receive the homage due only to Your Majesty as God's viceregent on earth?' they asked.

Half-way between Mehrauli and Ghiaspur, Ghiasuddin Tughlak built a new city of gold-coloured bricks with high battlements around it. It came to be known after his tribe as Tughlakabad. He expected everyone to come and pay him homage and praise his handiwork. Everyone did, except our Khwaja Sahib. When Ghiasuddin demanded an explanation our Khwaja Sahib prophesied that the new city would soon be a wilderness inhabited by Gujar robbers.

When this was reported to the sultan, he swore he would teach the Khwaja Sahib a lesson. The foolish man did not know that God spoke through His Beloved Saint, Nizamuddin. God in the role of the Divine Mahout struck the sultan with a goad and made him act like a rogue elephant. He granted him a victorious campaign in his eastern domains and filled him with delusions of invincibility. His courtiers did the rest. 'O mighty Sultan! You who slice off the heads of thousands of your enemies like a reaper gathering wheat, can you not destroy this insignificant dervish?' they asked. Ghiasuddin Tughlak who was only a few marches from Delhi sent orders that before he entered the capital the hospice at Ghiaspur should be razed to the ground.

The Kotwal came with tears in his eyes and placed the royal

command at the Khwaja Sahib's feet. The Khwaja Sahib comforted him: 'Son, I have seen the coming and going of many sultans. When I first came to Delhi, it was Ghiasuddin Balban. Thereafter there was Kaikobad and Jalaluddin Firoze; then there were Alauddin and Qutubuddin of the Khilji tribe followed by Nasiruddin. And now Ghiasuddin Tughlak. That makes seven. Kings come and kings go. The will of Allah is eternal.'

The Kotwal did not understand the meaning hidden in the Khwaja Sahib's words. 'Beloved of God! You are more to me than my father and mother. The sultan is only three marches from Delhi. What am I to do?' he wailed.

'Go home in peace. *Hunooz Dilli Door Ast*! (It is a long way to Delhi),' remarked the Khwaja Sahib.

As soon as the Kotwal returned to Shahr-i-Nau he received the news that the sultan had met with an accident. The next day runners brought the news of his death which had occurred when an archway he was passing under fell on him. This was in AD 1325. Allah is indeed the greatest of plotters and the strength of the feeble! And as the Khwaja Sahib had prophesied, the great citadel that Ghiasuddin had raised was soon deserted; the river Jamna receded from its walls and all its wells dried up. It became the abode of jackals, owls, bats and Gujars. Its once golden walls began to crumble—all that remained intact was the tomb in which Ghiasuddin Tughlak was buried—it was as if Allah wanted him to see what had happened to his dreams of glory.

God is the author of the Book of Destiny in which are written the past, the present and the future. God allowed our Khwaja Sahib to read the chapter on events to come. One day in his sermon the Khwaja Sahib said no one should ever fear death because it was a lover's tryst with his Beloved. 'For ninety years I have been separated from Allah,' he said, 'but every hour of every day of those ninety years I have longed to be reunited with Him.'

His words cast a gloom over Ghiaspur. I sought audience with the Khwaja Sahib. When I came before him I broke down and wept. 'If it is for me you cry,' he said, 'be assured you will follow us soon. And your wife will not linger in this caravanserai very long after you.'

I cried, 'O Beloved of God! Take us with you so that we may continue to serve you in paradise.'

I became very low in spirits. Much as I told myself that life was no longer worth living because I could hardly see or walk unaided and that death would be a release from the sufferings of old age, I was afraid of dying. I would prefer being ill and in pain than going into the dreaded kingdom of Yama. I did not desire union with the Beloved; my toothless Ram Dulari was good enough for me.

One day in the month of *Rabi-us-Sani* of the year 725 of the Hijri of the Prophet (peace be upon Him) corresponding to AD 1324 of the Roman calendar, the Khwaja Sahib told us that he could hear the angels singing songs of welcome. But before he left the world he would purge his body of earthly dross by fasting for forty days. We pleaded with him. 'O Beloved of God! Hakeems say that your body needs nourishment and even a week's fast may be too much for it.' He rebuked us. 'Is this all you have learnt from me? Know you not that fasting and prayer are food for a better life than we lead on earth?'

A pall of melancholy spread over Ghiaspur. The Khwaja Sahib sensed our concern. 'I will be with you till Thursday; on Friday I will depart,' he told us. 'Bury my remains in this courtyard. Do not let Khusrau (he was then in Lakhnauti) come near my grave lest I am tempted to defy the laws of nature and rise to embrace him. The message of Allah and His Holy Prophet (may peace be upon Him) will continue to be delivered to you by my chief disciple Makhdoom Nasiruddin. He will be your guide in this dark world, for he is Roshan Chiragh Dilli, light of the Divine Lamp in Delhi.'

It happened exactly as the Khwaja Sahib had foretold. It was on the morning of Friday, the 18th of Rabi-us-Sani 725 A.H. (3 April 1324) that the Khwaja Sahib's soul winged its way to paradise. What cries of lamentation rent the skies! Hundreds of thousands of people from the neighbouring towns came to Ghiaspur. Women beat their breasts chanting *Ya Allah! Ya Allah!* Hazrat Roshan Chiragh, whom the Khwaja Sahib had named his successor, came out and pleaded in a tearful voice that such demonstrations of grief were forbidden by the holy law; he divided the mourners into different groups and gave them passages from the Quran to chant in unison.

The Khwaja Sahib's body was bathed. The bier was placed in the courtyard of the mosque for the last prayer. Then it was taken out in procession round Ghiaspur. *Qawwals* sang as they went along. The party closest to the bier sang one which began with the following words:

People crave to see thy face
Why hast thou turned thy back on the world?
Whither art thou bound, O Fair One
Beloved of God! Whom hast thou gone to meet?

Someone shouted that the Khwaja Sahib had put his hand out of the shroud. The bier was placed on the ground and the mob surged towards it. It took a while to restore order. The pall-bearers insisted that they had heard the Khwaja Sahib's voice replying to the questions in the song. Hazrat Roshan Chiragh cupped his mouth and spoke loudly into the ears of the Khwaja Sahib. 'Beloved of God! Does thy dervish have to remind thee that speaking after death is against the ordinance of Allah? Go in peace to thy tryst.' He put the Khwaja Sahib's hand back into the shroud and the procession proceeded on its way.

The Khwaja Sahib's sainted dust was interred in the centre of the mosque courtyard. Some people placed oil-lamps on the grave; others lit joss-sticks in the fresh earth. People put their ears to the grave to catch sounds that might come out of it.

&

Khusrau has returned from Lakhnauti. A huge mob has collected to see how he will conduct himself and whether the Khwaja Sahib will rise from his grave to embrace him. Khusrau has come to the hospice wailing and beating his breast like a woman who has lost her husband. Hazrat Roshan Chiragh holds him in a tight embrace. After he has wept his heart out the dervish tells him that the Khwaja Sahib had forbidden him from going to the graveside. Khusrau stops by a kewra bush a few yards away from the grave and fixes his eyes on the spot where his departed friend sleeps. Tears run down his eyes into his beard; he sobs like a child crying for its mother. In a wailing voice he recites:

On her couch sleeps my fair one
Her black hair is scattered over her face.

O Khusrau! 'tis time thou too the homeward path did tread,
The shades of twilight over the earth are spread.

Khusrau shaved his head just as Hindus do on the death of their parents. He gave away his property. He began to wear a coarse cloak of black wool prescribed for the Sufis. As he had prophesied for himself, a few weeks later he took the homeward path. We buried him beside the kewra bush.

ॐ

I come to the last chapter of the book of my life. I hasten to write these lines before my right eye, which has also developed cataract, loses its light and I am no longer able to put pen to paper.

After many weeks of absence Kamal has brought his wife and two children to be left in our care. He says Sultan Mohammed Tughlak has gone mad. For many years we have been hearing of his eccentric habits. In fits of generosity he gives away lakhs of tankas, in fits of madness he cuts off lakhs of heads. He issues copper coins to represent silver rupees and gold tankas. Cunning people forge copper coins and take their value in silver and gold till there is nothing left in the treasury. Kamal says that the sultan has been talking of conquering China and then the rest of Asia. And now he has issued a proclamation transferring his capital from Delhi to Daulatabad 700 miles down towards *gehennum*. He has ordered every man, woman and child to evacuate Tughlakabad and travel southwards with him. This is indeed madness! Delhi by whatever name it is known—Lal Kot, Mehrauli, Shahr-i-Nau or Tughlakabad—has always been the seat of the emperors of Hindustan. Delhiwallas would rather die than live in any other city in the world. Poor Kamal as a government servant must comply with the order; but no sultan's writ has ever extended to the sacred precincts of the mausoleum of Hazrat Khwaja Nizamuddin.

446

Bhagmati

May. The lid is off the fires of *gehennum*. Searing heat, spiralling dust devils, eye-scorching glare, tarmac on the road shimmering like quicksilver. Not a breath of life. No mad dogs, no nothing. Only the noonday sun.

The car seat burns. *'Hai Ram!'* groans Bhagmati and raises her bottom to let the seat get cooler. 'Ouch!' I cry in my wog style. 'Just touch the steering wheel.' I grab her hand and put it on the steering wheel. She withdraws it with a jerk. 'Has some doctor ordered us to go out and get sunstroke?'

We take the Qutub road. Past the mausoleum of Safdar Jang, through the rash of bungalows that have smothered Yusuf Sarai and all the Khilji, Tughlak and Mughal monuments that once dominated the landscape. At Qutub Minar we turn sharp left and go through village Lado Sarai. There is a lot of activity at the well. Jat women vigorously hauling up buckets of water and pouring them into pitchers lined on the parapet. Two young ones bathing. Not a stitch on them. They see our car. They put their hands between their thighs and turn their large buttocks towards us. I slow down to have a good look. A woman picks up a clod of mud and hurls it at us. I laugh. They laugh. These Jat women are tall, full-bosomed, slender-waisted, well-stacked. They carry their pitchers on their heads and stride along flouncing their skirts like the queens of Amazonia. I ask Bhagmati, 'Don't you think these Jat females are the most beddable women in Hindustan?'

'Other men's wives and sisters are always more fuckable than one's own. A home-bred chicken tastes no better than lentils.'

Bhagmati believes in the wisdom of clichés.

We are out of Lado Sarai. And again the hot, shimmering tarmac and an expanse of dun-coloured plains. The shadow of the car speeds ahead of us. A tumulus on our left gradually becomes a stone wall, the stone wall becomes a massive battlement of grey and red rock towering sixty feet or more above the ground. We go along an avenue of ancient banyans. I pull up under the shade. On my left is an arched gateway leading into the citadel of Tughlakabad; on my right a viaduct leads to the tomb of the builder Ghiasuddin Tughlak. Its sloping red walls and white marble dome rise above its fortress-like enclosure.

What's happened to all the urchins who hang around to look after visitors' cars? Midweek, midsummer. No visitors, no urchins. Calls for a celebration. We celebrate.

'What's that?' shouts Bhagmati pointing to a furry hand with black, tapering fingers clutching the rim of the windscreen. Up comes the face of a rhesus monkey with a request for food—*kho-kho-kho-kho*. Bhagmati screams and clings to me. The monkey takes fright, scampers away across the road displaying its bright red posterior.

Bhagmati nestles in my arms, I push her away. There is another somebody at the door. 'Sahib, I'll look after your car.'

Before I can say 'Okay,' another boy turns up. 'Sahib, it is my turn. He looked after the last car; didn't you?'

They begin to quarrel, 'Sahib, didn't I ask you first? Sahib, it's not his turn—you decide.' More urchins come along and clamour for the right to guard my car. I step out, take one by the scruff of his neck. 'This fellow will look after my car. He's the only one I will give money to.'

That settles it. Or does it? Four boys follow us up the path leading to the gate of Tughlakabad fort.

'Sahib, we will show you round the ruins of Tughlakabad.'

'I know them quite well,' I reply. 'We don't need a guide.'

'Sahib this is the main gate of the fort.'

'I know. You don't have to tell me, *jao*.'

'This hollow on the left was a tank; it used to supply drinking water to Tughlakabad.'

'I've told you once, I do not need a guide. Go away.'

'Sahib, these are the remains of the Meena Bazaar, the

women's market.'

I turn on them. 'Bugger off!'

They run away a little distance and shout back at me: 'Bugger off.' Bhagmati and I proceed up the paved pathway through the ruins: gun emplacements, mosques, markets and up to the highest point. We survey the landscape: the Qutub Minar to the west, Ghiasuddin Tughlak's tomb to the south, the ruins of the Qasr-i-hazaar-Sutoon palace and Shahr-i-Nau to the east. We retrace our steps and turn off on a path, thread our way through the debris and goats nibbling at vasicka bushes. We are at the edge of the battlement. A hundred feet below us is a pool full of water buffaloes. This is all that remains of what was once a moat encircling the citadel of Tughlakabad. And what goes by the name of Tughlakabad today is a huddle of flat-roofed brick-houses and mud-huts. The rest of the landscape is a rocky, treeless plain dotted with ruins among which new buildings are erupting like red fungus.

Bhagmati takes my hand.

'*Arre* ! She's taken the Sardar's hand.' The bastards are still there. Bhagmati takes over. 'Will you get away from here or do you want a rod up your arses?' she asks striding towards them. They run away as fast as they can with the goats scampering after them. Bhagmati comes back triumphantly. We sit down on the rampart. She nestles her head on my chest. 'Tell me why are some monkeys' balls and behinds red?'

'I don't know. I am told they become red when they are randy.'

'Do your balls become red when *chotey mian* (the little gentleman) becomes *badey mian* (big gentleman)?'

It takes me a while to catch on. 'I have never looked; besides I am not a monkey.'

'Our fathers' fathers were,' she pronounces very scholar-like. 'I must look next time. I'll bring a flashlight with me.'

We sit and talk and look at the world below us. Bhagmati nibbles my ear and feels my middle to make sure that *chotey mian* is still there.

The sun's rays lose their sting. The sun becomes a large, orange balloon. Lines of crows flap their wings towards the city. Flocks of parakeets streak across the grey sky. From Tughlakabad village a million sparrows rise, wheel over the tops of keekar trees and then settle down on them in a bedlam of twitters.

The orange sun goes down in a haze of dust. Village lads urge their buffaloes to get out of the pond. Their shouts mingle with the chirruping of the sparrows and the forlorn barking of dogs. Then an eerie silence descends on the ancient ruins. Even Bhagmati has run out of words. I tell her of the varieties of silence in a language she does not understand.

> *There is silence where hath been no sound,*
> *There is silence where no sound may be,*
> *In the cold wave—under the deep, deep sea,*
> *Or in wide desert where no life is found,*
> *Which hath been mute, and still must sleep profound;*
> *No voice is hushed—no life treads silently,*
> *But clouds and cloudy shadows wander free,*
> *That never spoke, over the idle ground:*
> *But in green ruins, in the desolate walls,*
> *Of antique palaces, where Man hath been,*
> *Though the dun fox or wild hyaena calls,*
> *And owls, that flit continually between,*
> *Shriek to the echo, and the low winds moan—*
> *These true silence is, self-conscious and alone.*

The evening stars shine in the grey sky. A soft breeze begins to blow. After the hot wind it feels cool, soporific. My eyes are heavy with sleep. I ruffle Bhagmati's hair. She has fallen asleep. I shut my eyes and am lost to the world.

I waken with a feeling of someone looking at me. It is the full moon shining in my face. A papeeha comes out of the grey sky and settles on a crag a few feet away. It raises its head to the moon and fills the haunted landscape with its plaintive cries, *pee ooh, pee ooh.*

'Listen Eugenia!' Her name is not Eugenia but Bhagmati. The bird is not the nightingale but a Hawk Cuckoo.

Nevertheless its full-throated bursts come crowding through the moonlight.

Eternal passion!

Eternal Pain!

❧

Sometime after this I have my encounter with the bees.

Delhi has a rich variety of bees of which one species, the apis historicus Delhiana, is noted for its attachment to the past. Habitat: high vaulted arches with special preference for the pre-Mughal, Mughal, post-Mughal, Lutyens and Baker. Size of hive: the most massive known in the beeworld. Natural enemies: the urchins of Delhi who torment it with stone, brick, dung smoke and flaming rags. Natural victims: unsuspecting, absent-minded old men who visit historical monuments to daydream.

One afternoon I find myself at Hauz Khas. Although it is late April and very hot, this old *madrasa* is so designed that hot winds passing through the maze of its ancient walls turn cool. I am seated on the floor of a colonnaded verandah, reclining against a grey, sandstone column. On my left is a freshly mown lawn with a sprinkler spreading rainbows; the bullock and the lawn-mower both rest in the shade of a neem tree. Facing me is the tomb of Sultan Firoze Shah Tughlak with its lofty plaster-dome black with age. And about fifty feet below me on my right is a muddy pond black with buffaloes. This is all that remains of the huge tank, the Hauz-i-Alai, dug by Sultan Alauddin Khilji to provide water for his new city, Siri. Of the city the only surviving evidence is a litter of disjointed walls and a gate.

The warm breeze-turned-cool drones in my ears. Above my head martins chitter in their mud-feathered nests. From the floor below come the strains of a Hindi film song and the voices of men playing cards. In the lengthening shadow cast by the ancient school of learning, village boys play tipcat. Bhagmati is not with me and the calm and peace of the surroundings are conducive to daydream.

What did they teach at this *madrasa*? Astronomy, astrology, mathematics, chemistry and the Quran? Boys sitting in rows chanting their tables? Whatever happened to Siri and the great tank which supplied its drinking water? Was it still there when Taimur, the club-footed Mongol, sacked Delhi and slew 50,000 of my citizen-ancestors? How long did it take to repopulate the city?

I see the scenes of horror which must have taken place around Hauz-i-Alai during the massacre. Men sitting on their haunches with their hands tied behind them and necks bent low; the flash of scimitars and heads rolling away from bodies; spurts of blood, the tops of spines sticking out. Shrieking, wailing mothers, wives and sisters. Children benumbed with terror. The Mongolian shadow of God on earth enjoying the scene from somewhere near where I am sitting. If only I had been there, armed with a modern sharpshooter's rifle fitted with a telescopic sight, I would have climbed a tree beyond bowshot and shot the lame bastard dead. I would have picked out his generals and one after another sent them to hell. I would have created panic in the ranks of the Mongols, Turks, Tartars and all the other Central Asian savages. The Delhiwallas would then have risen against them, slaughtered thousands like goats and sent the rest screaming back to Samarkand.

A stone narrowly misses my head and crashes down on the floor. I see a pack of urchins scuttling away into Firoze Shah's tomb. 'Oi, oi, oi,' I yell. 'You *harami* . . .' Before I can tell them what I will do to their mothers and sisters, a swarm of apis historicus Delhiana descends on me. I flail my arms. I run like one pursued by the devil. They follow me attacking my face, neck, arms. I unwrap my turban, wrap my face and arms in its folds, and crouch on the ground. I can hear the card-players shouting for help as they run to safety and the grass-mower's bullock bellowing on its way to the village. The assault continues for five hellishly long minutes before it is called off. I pluck dead bees off my body. I pick two caught in the meshes of my beard and get stung on the tips of my fingers. My flesh begins to swell, my fingers become too fat to be useful, my body tingles all over. I run back my car and drive as fast as I can to Ram Manohar Lohia Hospital.

By the time I enter the emergency ward my eyes are almost closed and parts of my body are numb. I muscle my way through the crowd into the clinic. It looks like the third-class passengers' waiting-room of Delhi railway station. Men, women and children are sprawled all over the floor. A bearded patriarch lies on a stretcher tracing patterns on the wall with his legs. There is a cluster round the doctor's table. I push my way through: I am more 'emergency' than most of them. Bee-stings on the neck and the ears can be fatal unless attended to at once. The doctor is talking on the phone. In his left hand he holds the instrument; in his right, a syringe. He talks away as he presses air bubbles out of the needle. Facing him is a fourteen-year-old girl with her chemise raised over

452

her shoulders. My half-shut eyes focus on her young bosom-buds. Her mother glowers at me and turns angrily to the doctor: 'You want to expose my child to the world?' The doctor says, 'One minute,' puts the receiver on the table, stabs the needle into the girl's belly and tells her to come again tomorrow. He picks up the phone. 'Doctor, I've been stung by bees, please...' He says 'Excuse me,' into the phone in English and snaps at me in Punjabi. 'You are not dying! Take your turn.' He apologizes to the phone and lists his favourite restaurants: Moti Mahal, Gaylord, Laguna. He warns the fellow or lady at the other end of the line about crows being served instead of chicken and blobs of blotting-paper mixed in kulfi. Ha ha. I slap my numbed hands on the table and scream. The fellow says, 'Sorry, too many patients. I'll ring later. Ta-ta.' Then he turns to me in a raging temper. 'You beestingwalla, don't you see I am busy?' he says in Punjabi. I reply in my haw haw Oxbridge: 'Busy, my fucking foot! Discussing restaurants and food with some broad while people here are in agony. I'll report you to the Health Minister; I'll write letters to every paper. Who the bloody hell do you thing you are?' English works like magic in independent India. The bugger examines my stings, gives me a massive shot of something and tells me that I am lucky to be alive. Then adds humbly, 'Please forgive me for the delay. I am only an intern.'

The shot does not improve my vision. I go out of the door closest to me. I find myself in a room with a corpse lying on a marble slab and a policeman counting the number of bruises on 'the aforesaid deceased so-and-so'. He asks, 'Are you a relative or something?'

'No, I am the corpse. Count the stings on my dead body.' Before he can retort, I retrace my steps and hurry back to the car.

Budh Singh is alarmed at my appearance. He asks me how and where it all happened. I tell him as best as I can. He raises an admonishing finger and ticks me off. 'I have warned you many times not to go near graveyards. They are full of ghosts. Places where hundreds of thousands have been murdered have hundreds of thousands of ghosts. You were not attacked by bees but by evil spirits of those slaughtered by that Taimur *lang* (the lame one).' He spits into his own hand.

I cannot argue with Budh Singh. I tell him to keep his charpoy near the door so he can hear me if I shout for help. I take my temperature: 103 degrees—high enough to make a man of my age delirious.

I sleep a little, groan a lot. I feel sorry for myself. How close had I come to dying? Scenes from the past come vividly before my eyes. I wonder what kind of savage was this Taimur who revelled in the massacre of innocents! I have his Memoirs. To his own words, I add some gloss.

The Timurid

One night in the spring of the Year of the Ox when we were sixty-two years old we had a strange dream. We saw ourselves in an orchard with trees loaded with fruit. The trees also had many nests and birds were pecking away at the fruit. The gardeners were making a lot of noise to frighten away the birds. We arrived in the orchard armed with a sling and a bag full of pebbles. With our slingshot we drove away the birds and destroyed their nests. The gardeners then prostrated themselves before us and gave thanks to Allah for being thus delivered of the pests.

Whenever the tablet of our mind was heavily over-writ with our designs we were wont to dream about them. We asked the saintly Shaikh Zainuddin Abu Bahr Tatyabady to tell us what this dream signified. The Shaikh, who was the pole star of religion, confirmed that we were about to undertake an expedition to a distant land which was being despoiled because it had too many rulers; that we would drive away these rules, as we had driven away the birds in our dream, take possession of their kingdoms and their subjects would kiss our feet. At the time we were in two minds. We were not sure whether we should conquer China—or proceed towards Hindustan. We consulted Syed Mohammed Gesudaraz, the saint with long hair, whom we had also adopted as our guide in matters of religion. The Syed was more specific. He interpreted the dream as follows: 'The Holy Prophet (on Whom and on Whose progeny be peace) has taken you under His care and protection in order that you propagate Islam in the extensive regions of India.'

By then we had already subjugated most of the kingdoms of Asia. Now Hindustan through its disorders had opened its gates to us.

Nothing happens in this world save as Allah wills it. When we were born in the spring of the Year of the Mouse sparks had flown out of our royal mother's womb and our hands were found to be full of blood. Men of wisdom foretold that the flash of our scimitars would be like sparks of an ironsmith's anvil and we would wade through rivers of blood. We were taken by our parents to be blessed by Shaikh Shamsuddin. He was reading the sixty-seventh chapter of the Holy Book and intoned, 'Are you sure that He who dwelleth in heaven, will not cause the earth to swallow you up . . . and behold it shake (*Taimura*)?' And so we came to be given the name Taimur. Our horoscope had promised that we would be superior to all monarchs of the age, we would protect religion, destroy idols and be the father of our people. At twenty-seven an injury caused a deformity in our foot compelling us thereafter to be more in the saddle than on foot. We knew that behind our backs, common people called us Taimurlang (Taimur the lame) but in our persence they addressed us as the Uncompared Lord of Seven Climes and the Lord of Fortunate Conjunction.

We summoned the *kuriltay* of the nobles who had attached their destinies to our aporn. We told them of our dream and the interpretations made by wise and saintly men. We told them that our object in undertaking the invasion of Hindustan was to bring infidels to the path of true religion and to purify the country from the filth of polytheism and idolatry. We exhorted them to place helmets of courage on their heads, don the armour of determination, gird on the swords of resolution and like alligators dive into the river of blood: if victorious they would gain renown as warriors who had carried the flag of Islam to the farthest horizons of the earth; if subdued they would gain admittance to paradise as martyrs. We told them of the enormous wealth of Hindustan; of the city the Tughlaks had built of gilded bricks that glistened in the sun and of the cistern in this citadel which was said to be filled with molten gold. We warned them of the rising power of infidels and said that if we did not destroy them by stuffing their mouths with lead they would swallow up everything that the line of sultans starting with Mahmud of Ghazna followed by the

Ghors—Mohammed, Qutubuddin Aibak, Altamash and his daughter Sultana Razia—followed by the mighty Ghiasuddin Balban and the house of Khiljis—Jalaluddin, Alauddin—down to the dynasty of the Tughlaks—Ghiasuddin, Mohammed, Firoze and Nasiruddin—had amassed over two centuries.

The minds of Turks are as narrow as their eyes. In order to gain their support and to tie up their tongues, it is necessary not only to excite their zeal for Islam but also their greed for gold. We reminded them that as in the past whatever had fallen into our lap after a victorious campaign we had divided amongst them without keeping anything for ourselves, so would we divide the gold, silver, cattle and slaves that fell into our hands during the expedition to Delhi.

The *kuriltay* was moved by our words. Every man present drew his sword to follow us to victory or paradise.

We decided to send a probing force ahead of us under the command of our grandson, Prince Peer Mohammed Jahangir. The Prince was a youth of only twenty-three summers but he had accompanied us on many campaigns and we had gauged that the star of his destiny was in the ascendant. We summoned him to our tent to apprise him of his duties. 'He who wishes to embrace the bride of royalty must kiss her across the edge of the sword,' we told him. 'We give you the throne of Ghazna. From there you will proceed to Hindustan and capture the city of Multan.' We then told him of the state of affairs in Delhi. Sultan Firoze Tughlak had spent more of his time raising mosques, caravanserais, *madrasas* and laying canals than in keeping his subjects in fear. Rightly had the Holy Porphet (on Whom be peace) said that a just king is the shadow of God on earth and from the dread of that shadow people render him obedience. But Sultan Firoze had allowed infidels to raise their heads. He had also given sancturaty to many traitors who had fled our wrath and thus behaved in an unbrotherly manner towards us. Firoze had been dead ten years but the seeds of disrespect towards the supreme ruler that he had sown had grown into a thicket of nettles and this displeased us.

His sons and grandsons followed each other in quick succession and now Mahmud sat on the throne of the Tughlaks. However, it was not Mahmud Tughlak who ruled Hindustan but two upstarts: Sarang Khan who had Multan under him and his

457

brother, Mallu Khan Iqbal, who crowed over the ramparts of Tughlakabad and the Qasr-i-hazaar Sutoon. The smoke of vanity had clouded their brains.

Soon Prince Mohammed Jahangir marched from Ghazna, crossed the river Indus and besieged Sarang Khan in Multan.

Now it was the Year of the Tiger. We sent messengers throughout our kingdom to announce that we were ready to march on Delhi. The men who flocked to our standard were as numerous as drops of rain—of these the largest number were our own kin, Chughtai Turks of the Barlas clan, who had shared the perils and profits of many campaigns with us. By the time the almond trees ushered in the spring we had upwards of 90,000 cavaliers and cross-bowmen under our command. We led a small task force into the mountains of Kafiristan and carried out great slaughter amongst the tribes of infidels who had defied even the mighty Alexander of Macedon.

By rapid marches we overtook birds in flight and reached the river Indus. We crossed the mighty river and entered the domains of the Tughlaks. Meanwhile our grandson had occupied Multan. We overcame attempts to impede our progress and crossed the rives of the Punjab. We stopped at Pak Pattan to pray at the tomb of Fariduddin Ganj-i-shakar and promised to convey the blessings of the saint to his successor Shaikh Nizamuddin buried in Delhi.

Our expedition had been carefully timed in consultation with astrologers and men of learning who knew the movements of the sun. When we traversed the Punjab, its plains were still muddy from the recent heavy rains of the summer. By the time we arrived on the banks of the river Jamna it was cool; the skies were as blue as the tiles of our palace roof and the breezes as balmy as those during spring in Samarkand.

We rode along the Jamna then in flood and drew rein in full view of the city which Sultan Firoze Tughlak had built and which was known after him as Firozabad or Kotla Firoze Shah. On the top of his palace Firoze had planted a slender pillar fabricated at the time of the infidel Ashoka who had ruled this country over 1500 years ago. It was said to bear inscriptions of Ashoka's prophet named Gautama the Wise. The citizens of Firozabad did not put up any resistance; indeed many Mussalmans came to offer us their services.

Our nobles warned us that the thousands of infidels we had taken as slaves in the Punjab might use the opportunity to rise against us when we were engaged in battle against the Tughlaks. Some advised us to slaughter them before we engaged the enemy. We refused to spill so much blood as there was upwards of 1,00,000 slaves in our custody. Instead we picked a few who had tried to escape and had them brought before us. We ordered them to be beheaded in front of the others as a warning of the fate that awaited those who dreamt of breaking the bondage we had imposed on them. Thus we crushed the thorn of rebellion under our foot before it could prick us.

On the 19th of December 1398 Mahmud Tughlak, misguided by his minister Mallu Khan Iqbal, came out of the city with a great clamour of drums and fifes and a vast army to meet us. His generals confronted us with a line of elephants covered with armour and loaded with archers. They were like slow-moving fortresses. We were prepared for them. We had sharp stakes dug in the ground behind the front line of our cavalry. Like the Cossacks we relied on suddenness of assault and retreat. Our horsemen galloped up to their elephants, discharged their arrows and galloped back. This repeated many times took a fearful toll of the Tughlak's army and drove its commanders to desperation. As their elephants advanced, we retreated. Beasts in the front row got their feet entangled in the stakes; those behind them refused to move forward. We ordered camels (animals which elephants are known to dread) to advance from the sides. We had loads of hay put on their backs and set alight. The remaining elephants turned back in terror exposing the Tughlak's cavalry and footmen to us. We gave the *Tekbir*. Our Turkish warriors replied with full-throated cries of *Allah-o-Akbar* and sprang like lions on their quarry. The Tughlak army broke ranks and fled. Allah, who presides over battlefields, blessed our swords with victory.

Two days later, on Thursday the 21st of December, we encamped in the ancient *madrasa* along the spacious tank called Hauz-i-Alai. We recited the *fateha* at the tomb of Sultan Firoze Tughlak and after the *zohar* prayer commanded the citizens of Siri, Jahanpanah and Mehrauli to make their submission. They came in their thousands, presented *nazranas*, laid their turbans and caps at our feet and craved our fogiveness. A party of ulema presented us with copies of the Holy Quran and appealed to us as a fellow Mussalman not to shed more Muslim blood. They brought us the keys of their townships and pleaded with us to let them arrange a befitting welcome for us. We acceded to their request and asked them to discuss with our generals details of the indemnity to be paid to us.

The next day being Friday the *khutba* was read in our persence at the Quwwat-ul-Islam mosque. We recited *fatehas* at the tombs of Sultan Altamash and Sultan Alauddin Khilji before inspecting the Qutub Minar and the entrance to the Royal Mosque. We marvelled at their craftsmanship: how these Hindvis began their work as giants and finished it like goldsmiths! We decided to take their master craftsmen with us to work on the mosque at Samarkand. We then proceeded to Mehrauli to pay our homage to Saint Qutubuddin Bakhtiyar Kaki and visited the Auliya Masjid where he had performed many austerities. The citizens made a great display of welcome and arranged swimming contests at the Shamsi Talab beside the mosque. We saw signs of prosperity everywhere.

The ladies of our harem were anxious to see Qasr-i-hazaar Sutoon. We allowed them to be escorted thither while we proceeded to Ghiaspur to fulfil our vow to pray beside the tomb of Hazrat Nizamuddin Auliya.

It does not take long for the men of Hindustan to switch their minds from fawning flattery to deadly hate. They began to make excuses for their failure to pay the indemnity we had imposed on them. Under the cover of darkness many stole out of Siri, Mehrauli and Jahanpanah with their possessions. Guards we had posted at the city gates were slain. We ordered out troops to enter these towns and extend the hand of rapine, to slay every able-bodied man and take his women and children as slaves. For the next ten days our men drenched their swords in blood. There was no count of the numbers killed: some said 50,000 others 5,00,000. Nor was there any measure of the quantites of precious stones, gold and silver taken by our valiant soldiers. Even the humblest of our footmen took over tow dozen slaves. The wealth they acquired in Delhi would last our men many generations. We recalled that once the Holy Prophet (on Whom be peace) had appeared in a dream and told us that the Almighty had declared that seventy-two of our line would sit on the throne of sovereignty. That prophecy seemed to be fulfilling itself. We decided to tarry no more.

We loaded innumerable elephants and camels with the wealth of Delhi and with thousands upon thousands of slaves in our train began our slow march homewards. We crossed the river Jamna, ransacked Meerut and proceeded along the foothills. We destroyed, as we had undertaken to do, many temples of idolatry. At one place the brahmins warned us not to touch the image of their god, Krishna, who was said to be so powerful that he could in one night impregnate 1600 women. His image which was made of gold stood as high as ourselves. Under the eyes of the pleading, wailing priests we smashed the idol with our own hands and ordered the priests to be beheaded.

A month later we and our victorious armies were back in Samarkand.

We received sad tidings from Delhi. We were informed that after our departure there was no one to bury the dead. The rotting corpses had spread pestilence and the few who had survived had succumbed to disease. For many months the towns of Delhi were deserted save for crows, kites and vultures by day and owls, jackals and hyaenas by night . . .

But we had fulfilled our life's mission. We had realized early in our youth that just as there is one God in heaven, so the earth can support only one king. In the years granted to us by Allah we strove to bring the nations of the world under our rule. In order to preserve our sovereignty, we took justice in one hand and equity in the other and by the light of these two lamps kept our royal palace illuminated. Many people blamed us for the blood we had spilt. At one time the ill-informed Khwaja Obeyd forbade Muslims to recite the *khutba* in our name because we had also shed the blood of Mussalmans. That night the Holy Prophet (peace be upon Him) had visited Khwaja Obeyd in his dream, refused to acknowledge his salutations and reprimanded him in the following words: 'Although Taimur has shed much blood of my followers, as he has been a friend, the supporter and respecter of my posterity and descendants, why dost thou forbid the people to pray and bless him?'

May Allah forgive us for any sins we may have committed.

Bhagmati

It has rained in the night and the damp fragrance of the earth steals into my bedroom as I wake. It is cold. The hot-water-bottle at my feet has lost its warmth and I shiver under my quilt. Sounds of muffled voices pass along my apartment like the babble of a stream. I switch on the table-lamp. It is 4.30 a.m. I switch off the light, tuck my hands between my thighs and try to go back to sleep. The stream of voices continues. What on earth are these people up to on this cold winter morning?

I am woken with finality by my cook-bearer with a steaming mug of tea. He switches on the electric radiator; the bedroom has a glow of pink warmth. 'It's very cold,' I tell him.

'Yes,' he agrees. 'It rained during the night. Can I serve your *chotta hazri* soon? I'd like to get away early.'

'What for?'

'To see the parade; it is Republic Day. People have been leaving their homes since the early hours to find a place in front to get a good view. Budh Singh also wants leave for the day.'

What could be better than having both out of the way. If only that stupid Bhagmati would know it is a holiday and get to this side of the city before the police put up barricades on the roads (to mark off the route of the parade) we could celebrate *gantantra divas* on the carpet by the fireside. But she never reads newspapers nor listens to anything on the transistor I gave her except film music on Vividh Bharati. However, there is hope. I haven't had sex for many weeks and it's accumulated to explosion point. I ask the cook-bearer to put the breakfast on the table and light a fire in the sitting-room before he and Budh Singh take off.

By the time I come into the sitting-room there is a blazing log fire in the grate. The sky is clear and the sun is streaming through the windows. A regular procession of men, women and children wrapped in shawls, and mufflers goes by on its way to Rajpath and Connaught Circus. I feel very superior in my singular isolation. I can read about it in the papers, hear the commentary on my radio, and, if that Bhagmati has any sense, sing the national anthem and hoist the tri-colour flag atop her quivering torso. There is reason to hope because she seldom misses a holiday.

The stream of humanity ceases to flow. The block of apartments becomes strangely deserted. Everyone has gone to see the caparisoned elephants, camels of the desert patrol, tanks and troupes of folk-dancers. The President, Prime Minister and everyone else who is anybody in Delhi will be there. My window-panes rattle. I switch on the radio and hear the deafening roar of cannon. Twenty-one salvos in honour of the Rashtrapati! He will take the salute of the units of the Army, Navy, Air Force and then proceed to tell the world of Gandhi, his message of non-violence and peace. And there will be Nehru kissing children, being *chacha* (uncle) to all the snivelling little bastards.

The twenty-first cannon explodes. My doorbell rings. Bhagmati has not let me down. 'How wonderful! I thought you'd forgotten. How did you manage to cross over the traffic barriers?' I ask her with unconcealed pleasure.

'The mortal who can stop your faithful servant going where she wants is yet to be born,' she replies, spreading her hands in front of the fire. 'The ice has got into my bones. What kind of *chootias* are these Dilliwallas. Year after year they go out in the cold to see the same parade!'

I make her a cup of coffee and put a slug of rum in it. She is so involved in talking she doesn't notice the smell or the difference in the taste. By the time she has drained the mug she is as warm inside as she is toasted on the outside. And I am possessed by the urge to celebrate *gantantra divas*. I get to the job with an adolescent eagerness. A minute later I lunge into an exultant cry of '*Jai Hind*'. A million Delhiwallas echo '*Jai Hind*' over my radio. It's all over in sixty seconds.

I would like Bhagmati to return to Lal Kuan. But Bhagmati has no intention of obliging me. She is disappointed with me and she is not the sort of person to spare my feelings. 'So many lessons I have taught you but you have forgotten even the first one: patience. How can I get to the second lesson; consideration for the *mashooka*? Lesson three is also very important: when you light a fire, you must see that you put it out before going *phut*. While your *mashooka* is like Sri Lanka burning on Dassehra you are like a fire brigade hose with no water in it, *hain*?'

Horrible bitch! She will give me no peace till I dowse the fire I've lit in her body. She must cool off and I must re-warm myself. I mumble an apology and suggest that we go out before the millions start moving back to their homes. She is in a sulk. She throws up her hands and sighs.

The breeze is cold but the sun is warm. The world looks washed, clean and green. Delhi is at its best and saying it with flowers: roses, poinsettias and bougainvilleas. I drive to the zoo to show her the family of white tigers. Other people have had the same idea and the entrance is crowded. So we opt for the Purana Qila towering over the northern end of the zoo. It is deserted. I take her down the steps of the *baoli* (well) and touch the icy cold water. Then back into the sunlight to Sher Shah's mosque. She covers her head with a scarf. Even after the years I have known her I am not sure whether she is a Muslim or Hindu. She says she is both—and more, because now she is also Sikh. We stroll about in the sunshine. I tell her about this being the site of Indraprastha, the first city of Delhi built by the Pandavas. That invites trouble because she knows all about Draupadi and her five hasbands. She remarks acidly, 'Seeing what the men of today are like, every woman should have five husbands.'

Indian Air Force jets scream across the blue sky leaving streaks of white ribbons behind them. Then follow a clutch of helicopters showering rose and marigold-petals. The Republic Day parade is over. We go up the Sher Mandal tower to get a better view. I tell her that it was a library built by Sher Shah Suri. 'But it has no books,' she remarks waving to the empty octagonal-shaped room on the top. I tell her that the library existed more than 450 years ago. She understands.

We watch the lines of buses, cars and scooters honking, hooting and spluttering down Mathura Road. It is cold and breezy at the western end so we go to the sunny eastern side. 'I know that one,' she says pointing to the marble dome, half-a-mile away from us, 'that is the mausoleum of Humayun Badshah. His begum built it over his tomb. Will you build a tomb like that for me when I die?'

Her irritation is over. She takes my hand in her's. We descend the narrow dark steps together. I miss a step and fall heavily on my bottom. '*Ya Allah!* Be more careful of these murderous steps. If you had fallen on your face, you would have broken your head.'

'That's right,' I tell her cheerfully. 'That's exactly what Emperor Humayun did on these very steps exactly 430 years ago to this day—on 26 January 1530.'

Bhagmati is now impressed with my learning. But she cannot resist a back-hander. 'He must have been running down to meet his begum. I tell you an impatient lover always comes to grief.'

'No he wasn't impatient to bed his begum. He heard the call to prayer and was impatient to meet Allah, so Allah sent for him.'

Bhagmati raises both her hands in front of her face and mumbles something for the soul of the departed emperor. We return home to fan the dead embers of lust and make them glow.

It is a bad day. It had an inauspicious start and much as Bhagmati ministers to me, I cannot rise to the occasion. I tell her I am getting old and nothing will rouse me any more. She tells me, again very acidly, that I am not getting old but indifferent and need a memsahib to re-activate me.

Bhagmati has a sixth sense about other women in my life. I try to ward off her pointed enquiries and avoid meeting her eyes. We pass the afternoon bickering over little things. I pretend to make up by offering to drive her around in the evening to see the Republic Day lighting. Once again she shrugs her shoulders and sighs. She takes very little interest in the grand display of the Secretariats and Rashtrapati Bhavan. The crowds make the going very slow. By the time I get through Parliament Street and Connaught Circus to Ajmeri Gate, it is after 9 p.m. I press two ten rupee notes into her hand as I open the door for her. She looks at them disdainfully, throws them on the seat and disappears into the crowd.

Something has happened to Bhagmati. She is becoming jealous and possessive. 'I know you will ask who I am to object to anything or anyone,' she says on one occasion. She brushes the back of her hand to wipe tears that are not there and continues, 'I am like the Purana Qila you have conquered; now you want the Red Fort and its white marble palaces.'

Sarcasm does not suit Bhagmati's style of speech. She has begun to irritate me. But the more I dodge her, the more she pursues me. Every night after she is through with her chores, she comes to my apartment to see if I am in. If I am not, she questions Budh Singh. And Budh Singh has become something of a mischiefmaker. 'He's gone out with that *Amreekan* Missy Baba,' he tells her.

The American Missy Baba is sixteen-year-old Georgine. Why Bhagmati should worry over a gawky, snub-nosed, freckled, red-headed teenager is beyond me. She never bothered about any of the other women. In any case, what right has a common whore to object to what one of her many patrons does when she is not with him? However Georgine has become an obsession with Bhagmati. I admit that Georgine has also become an obsession with me. I am always talking about her. It was I who first told Bhagmati about her.

It had been a bad year for me. I didn't have many writing assignments and the articles I sold to Indian papers did not get me enough to keep me in the style I was accustomed to. So I registered myself as a guide with the Tourist Department of the Government of India and left my card at foreign embassies and international organizations. During the tourist season between October and March I made quite a bit in tips in foreign currency which I exchanged for rupees at rates higher than the official. I earned commissions from hotels, curio dealers and astrologers for the custom I brought them. Men left me the remains of their bottles of Scotch. Sometimes middle-aged women invited me to their rooms and gave me presents for the services I rendered them.

It was not very hard work. After I had memorized the names of a few dynasties and emperors and the years when they ruled, all I had to do was to pick up a few anecdotes to spice my stories. At the Qutub Minar I told them of the number of suicides that had taken place and how no one could jump clear of the tower and come down in one piece. I told them of Humayun's father, Babar, going round his son's sickbed four times praying to Allah to transfer his son's illness to him and how Humayun had been restored to health and Babar died a few days later. About the Red Fort and its palaces I had picked up a lot of interesting details from the time Shah Jahan had built it—the kings who had sat on the peacock throne and were later blinded or murdered; the British who had taken it after the Mutiny of 1857; the trials of INA officers, down to 15 August 1947 when Lord Mountbatten had lowered the Union Jack and Nehru hoisted the Indian tri-colour on the ramparts. Having once done my homework, there was little more to do than impress the tourists with my learning.

After a while I began to enjoy my work. Although I did not find anyone who would give me a free round-the-world ticket, I could boast that the world came to me. Once a cousin who had found a job as a worker in England told me of the number of white girls he had 'killed'. They were English girls working in the same factory. I told him that I had 'killed' many more Europeans, Americans, Japanese, Arabs and Africans, sitting where I was in Delhi, without having to pay a counterfeit four-anna coin to anyone. The fellow began to drool at the mouth and scratch his testicles with envy.

The only thing that troubled me was that I never got a chance to make friends with anyone. All the Marys, Janes, Francoises and Mikis darlinged and honeyed me for a day or two then vanished for ever. After a few weeks I could not recall their names or faces. All I could recollect was the way they had behaved when I bestrode them. Some had been as lifeless as the bed on which we lay; some had squirmed and screamed as they climaxed. A few had mouthed obscenities, slapped me on the face and told me to fuck off.

It was different with the American Missy Baba, Georgine.

My contact with the US Embassy was a man named Carlyle. I do not know what he did in the embassy except that he looked after what he called 'visiting firemen'. He had tried out other guides. Once he was assured that 'I did no hanky panky' with visitors, he put a lot of custom my way. Americans were my best customers. Despite their brash manners they were more friendly and generous than other foreigners. I was particularly careful with Carlyle's 'visiting firemen'. I was respectful, polite and kept my distance. I opened car doors for them, did not angle for tips or look eagerly at their tape recorders, cameras and ball-point pens. (I knew they would leave some memento for me). I did not take them to emporia to earn commissions but helped them with their shopping at the best and cheapest stores. I never made passes at Carlyle's introductions and only obliged those who insisted on my obliging them.

My Oxbridge accent impressed Americans more than it did the other nationalities; to them I was a gentleman guide, a well-to-do fellow fallen on evil days, which was true.

Carlyle introduced me to Georgine. Georgine was Mrs Carlyle's niece and had come to Delhi to spend her Christmas vacations. 'This is Georgine,' Carlyle said without mentioning her second name, 'and this is your guide,' without mentioning mine. I bowed. She said, 'Hi.'

As I said before, she was very young, gawky, freckled, pimpled, snub-nosed—but also large-bosomed and even larger-arsed. She wore a tight-fitting sweater with 'Arizona' printed across her boobs and bum-tight jeans frayed at their ends. I asked her what interested her more, people or monuments. She shrugged her shoulders, stuck out her tongue and replied in a voice full of complaint: 'How should I know? A bit of both, I guess.' She proceeded to take snapshots of the Carlyles, the house, the car—then handed me her mini-camera so she could be in the pictures as well. She spoke very fast and dropped the g's at the end of most words: goin', comin', gettin', seein'. She was very animated and spoke with her grey eyes and hands; she interspersed her speech with noises like unh, shucks, crikey — and was constantly sticking out her red tongue.

'What are we waitin' for?' she demanded turning to me the first day after she had finished the photo session.

I opened the rear door of the car for her. She ignored me and bounced into the front seat beside the chauffeur. I took my place in the rear seat. 'Miss. . . .'

'The name is Georgine.'

'Miss Georgine, have you. . . .'

'Not Miss Georgine; just plain and simple Georgine, if you don't mind.'

'I was going to ask you, if you had read any Indian history. We are going to see. . . .'

'That's a stoopid question to ask an American high school girl. Why in the name of Christ should I have read Indian history?' I decided to keep cool. We passed through Delhi Gate into Faiz Bazaar. 'What are all these jillions doin'?' she demanded.

'They are no jillions, they are vegetable-sellers. They. . .'

She turned round as if to make sure I was human. 'You don't know a jillion? It is the highest number—more than millions of millions. Even the dumbest American kid knows that.'

'Oh, I see,' I replied tamely. 'The population of Delhi has more than trebled in these last twenty years. It is over four million now.'

'I don't want to know that!' she snapped.

We went out of Faiz Bazaar—on our left the Royal Mosque, Jamia Masjid, on our right the massive red walls of the Fort. She ordered the chauffeur to stop and took more snapshots. We drove up to the entrance of the Red Fort. While I queued up to buy a ticket for her, she took photographs: Chandni Chowk, the tongas, hawkers, beggars, everything. She stopped outside the entrance to take pictures of the guards, looked up at the towering walls and exclaimed, 'Yee!'

No sooner had we entered the arcade with its rows of shops aglitter with brass, gold-and-silver thread embroidery, miniature Taj Mahals and other bric-a-brac, than she stretched her arms wide and exclaimed, 'I want everythin' in this crummy bazaar. How much?' She went from shop to shop picking up things and putting them down with a grunt. But she was canny. She parried every attempt to sell her anything. A marble-seller would say, 'Yes memsahib, some *marbil-varbil*?' and she would shake her head and reply firmly, 'No thanks.'

We came to the Naqqar Khana gate. I cleared me throat. She pulled out her Murray's Guide and said: 'Don't tell me. This is where drums were beaten, right? And that red buildin' in front is the Dear one somethin'-or-the-other where the kingee received common folk, right?'

'Right on the mark. It is the Diwan-i-Am, the Hall of General Audience. You don't need a guide, you know everything.'

'No. I don't,' she snapped. Armed with Murray's Guide she instructed me about Emperor Shah Jahan, when he had lived, when he had built the palaces, pointed out the figure of Orpheus behind the throne, the Rang Mahal, the 'Dreamin' Chamber', the octagonal

Jasmine tower and the 'Dearonee . . . '

'Diwan-i-Khas.'

'Where kingee sat on the peacock throne to receive noblemen. Right?'

'Right.'

'Goodee! That pearly mosque built by the kingee's son who locked up Dad and became King Orangeade.'

'Aurangzeb.'

'Aren't I clever?'

'Very! You could make a handsome living as a professional guide.'

'I could at that! I am thirsty. Can I get a carton of milk or a Coke some place?'

'Coke, yes. Milk, no.'

We returned to the arcade. She drank two bottles of Coke, pressed her belly and belched. 'Sorree! I feel good.'

It usually took me over an hour-and-a-half to take visitors round the Red Fort. Georgine did it in twenty minutes. I picked up a marble Taj Mahal encased in glass and nodded to the shopkeeper. He wagged his head to indicate I could have if for free. 'Miss . . . . I mean Georgine, this is for you. With my compliments.'

'Me? What for?' she demanded blushing. She grabbed it from my hands and clasped it to her big bosom. 'It's lovely. Thank you.' She gave me a peck on my nose, 'And that's for you bein' so nice to a horrid girl.'

This time she took the rear seat beside me. When I asked the chauffeur to take us to the Royal Mosque, she protested: 'Nope. One mornin' one buildin'. Okay?'

'That would take us a whole month to do Delhi.'

'Goodie! You can spend every mornin' with me. Won't you like that?'

We drove through Chandni Chowk, Khari Bawli and Sadar Bazaar. Georgine kept taking snapshots and making unintelligible sounds. She suddenly turned round, stared at me and giggled. 'Gawd! You are a funny lookin' man!' she exclaimed. 'If somebody had told me last week that I'd be ridin' around with a darkie with a bandage round his head and a beard round his chin, I would have died.' I made no comment. She sensed my resentment. 'Don't mind me,' she added, 'I am always sayin' such dumb, stoopid things.

Anyway what have you got under that bandage?' I made no reply. She grunted 'unh' and said no more till we were back in Carlyle's home. As she got out of the car she asked, 'Can I pull your beard?' Before I could raise my hand to protect myself she grabbed it in her hand and gave it a violent tug. She threw three ten rupee notes on the seat, jumped out with the miniature Taj in her arms, and with a jerk of her big bottom ran to the door. 'Bye! See you tomorrow.'

The bloody bitch! I muttered to myself. What she needs is to be put across the knee, her jeans ripped off and a few hard smacks on her large, melon-sized bottom. Followed by buggery.

At the Coffee House I found myself telling my cronies about Georgine. I didn't like my Sikh journalist friend referring to her as 'another quail I had trapped.' Nor the politician warning me against carnal knowledge of a girl of sixteen. When I came out of the Coffee House, it was late in the afternoon. The jamun trees were alive with the screeching of parakeets. I wanted to fill my chest and yell her name so loudly that it would be heard all over Connaught Circus; 'Georgine' —and the traffic would come to a halt, 'Georgin' —and the parakeets would stop screaming. And the only sound to be heard would be 'Georgine, Georgine, Georgine,' echoing round and round the Circus.

That evening I told Bhagmati about Georgine. As usual she did not like my being so enthusiastic about anyone except her. I tried to laugh it off by reminding her that Georgine was forty years younger than me. That did not reassure her. And when I took her with greater gusto than usual, she asked, 'What is the matter with you today?' Meaning: You are not taking me but that fat-bottomed sixteen-year-old white girl.' She was right.

I was less exuberant in the morning. However, I spent twenty minutes in my cold, damp bathroom dyeing my beard. By the time I turned up at Carlyle's house I was apprehensive of the kind of reception I would get.

Georgine was outside soaking in the sun. She looked more grown up. 'How do you like my new hair-do?' she asked turning her head sideways. The hair was bunched on top of her head and tied in a chignon. It made her neck look longer and bared her small pink ears.

'Very nice! Makes you look like a lady.'

'I *am* that. Shucks!'

In the car she asked me if I slept with my turban on my head.

I replied: 'If you were a little older, I would have said, "Come and find out for yourself!"'

Her face flushed. 'You are an ole lech! You makin' a pass at me or somethin'?'

It was my turn to be embarrassed. 'I said if you were older and I meant a lot older. I must be older than your father.'

'I don't buy that kind of crap!'

I laid on some flattery. White people are not used to flattery and succumb very easily. She gave me an opening by taking my hand and apologizing: 'Don't be mad with me. I don't mean to be nasty.'

'You are not nasty,' I replied taking a grip on her hand, 'you are the nicest Missy Baba I've met.'

'Messy what?' she asked, raising her voice.

'Not messy, Missy. No flattery, it is not often I have anyone as pretty to take around.'

'Unh' she growled. 'I am not pretty or good lookin' or anythin' like that.'

But it was clear my compliment had hit the mark. Her face had gone pink with happiness and after a pause she said, 'You're a nice ole man. Can I call you pop? I don't know your name anyhow.'

Girls are more easy to seduce when they are sixteen than when they are a year or two older. At sixteen they are unsure of themselves and grateful for any reassurance you can give them about their looks or brains—either will do. Georgine, despite her brashness, proved very vulnerable. I took her to the Coffee House to, as I said, 'show you off to my friends.' She blushed again and repeated, 'You are an ole lech, you know? But I like you.'

At the Coffee House we sat in the section marked 'Families Only'. I ordered a Coke for her and went to greet my friends. They were not very complimentary about Georgine. Said my Sikh journalist friend: 'From the way you described her, I thought you had picked up a Marilyn Monroe. Nice fat boobs and bum though!'

'She's no Noor Jahan,' opined the political expert. 'Like any American schoolgirl. Must have a nice pussy. But you must be madder than I thought; you try any tricks with that one, you will be in for seven years rigorous imprisonment.'

Ugly, vulgar words. I rejoined Georgine. 'What did they have to say about your girl-friend?' she asked.

'Girl-friend? Oh, you mean you?' I replied pretending to have been taken by surprise. 'They said you were very beautiful.'

'Liar! I bet you a hundred dollars, they said, "What are you doin' with a lil girl like that? Foolin' around with anyone under seventeen can land you in a jail." How 'bout that for a guess?'

'Wrong, wrong, wrong,' I protested vehemently. I could see she was happy.

This time she put my fee in an envelope and gave it to me with 'Thanks a whole lot.'

That evening I was by turns exhilarated and conscience-stricken. In my confusion I rang her up without having anything to say to her. Her uncle picked up the phone. 'You must not let Georgine make a nuisance of herself,' he said, 'and let me have your bill for the time she's been with you.' He put down the receiver without asking me why I had rung. But I was excited to know that Georgine had paid me without telling her uncle.

I decided to use the information at an appropriate moment. Meanwhile I became bolder in my compliments. Since she changed her hair-style every day I got many opportunities to say something that would please her. One day she dressed herself in a bright red sari. It did not suit her, nor did she know how a woman in a sari should walk—like most Caucasians she had a masculine stride. I said, 'How charming,' and she replied: 'Oh, thank you, I thought you'd sort of like to see me in your native costume.' I explained that the sari was not native to Punjab and that a salwar-kameez would look even nicer on her. 'O great!' she exclaimed. 'I must have these thingees at once.' I took her to a tailor and while she was choosing the material I told him in Punjabi to send the finished products with the bill to me. Georgine could not make up her mind. What she liked best she said was too expensive for her. So she settled for the second best. I spoke to the tailor (again in Punjabi) to use the material of her first choice.

'You think it will look nice on me?' she asked me when we were in the car.

'I am sure it will. We have a word in our language *jamazebi* which means the ability to fit into any clothes. I think you will look nice in anything you wear.' (Far from being *jamazeb*, because of her large bosom and broad hips she had difficulty fitting into

473

readymade clothes). 'You are nuts,' she said dismissing the compliment. 'I know none of the nice things you say are true, but I like you sayin' them. So don't stop, O—Kay?'

Getting her into my apartment was easy. Two days after she had been measured, I offered to drive her around in my own car. When I went to pick her up, I said, as casually as I could, 'Your things have been delivered to my apartment. Would you like to pick them up before we go sightseenig?'

'O—Kay.'

She looked around admiringly at my books and pictures. 'Nice, comfy pad,' she remarked.

'Thank you. Do sit down.'

She took off her shoes, bounced onto the settee and crossed her legs. '*Nunc!* What you starin' at?'

I quoted Ghalib, first in Urdu and then translated it for her: 'She has come to my house. Sometimes I look at her, sometimes I look at my house.'

'That means you're pleased to have me here. Where are my thingees?'

I brought the bundle and untied it. 'I didn't order that one; it was too expensive, you remember? That old tailor is tryin' to rob me. All you Indians try to touch us Americans. You think we're a bunch of suckers, don't you?'

'He's not charging you any more for this material. He knew you liked it better, so he's just made it for you.'

She was nonplussed. 'I am sorry. That's very nice of him. And this?' she asked, opening out a sequined dupatta, 'It is very pretty, but I didn't ask for this.'

'That goes with the other things. Nothing extra.'

She draped it over her head and looked around for a mirror. 'Where can I try them on?' she asked, taking the bundle under her arm. I showed her to my bedroom. I was left alone for some time. I poured out a whisky and gulped it down neat. I moved from the chair to the sofa.

Georgine came out in Punjabi clothes. The dupatta was like a small white cloud studded with stars haloing her red hair, face and shoulders. The clothes fitted her: it seemed as if she were formed to wear Punjabi clothes. 'How's that?' she asked pirouetting on her toes.

'Very becoming! Much nicer than anything you've worn.'

'Thank you, I sort of like it too.'

She came and sat beside me on the sofa. She opened her handbag, 'How much does he want for this?'

My voice stuck in my throat, I forced it out. 'Nothing. Allow me the privilege of making this a present. Please!'

'Thank you and all that. But I know you can't afford it.'

'Yes I can; and it'll make me very happy.'

'Okay, if it'll make you happy.' She turned round and gave me a quick kiss on my beard, 'Thank you, pop.'

The kiss paralysed my tongue. After a while I was able to say: 'And I owe you money. You paid me for the outings out of your own money, didn't you?'

'How do you know?'

'I rang up your uncle.'

She turned scarlet. 'That was a dumb thing to do! What did he say?'

I took her hand in mine. 'Don't worry. I did not tell him you had paid me. Now I can earn a double fee.'

'You cunning ole Oriental!' she laughed. 'I'm relieved to know my ole uncle doesn't know.'

'Why didn't you tell him?'

'I dunno.'

The initiative was now mine. 'Maybe you wanted to be with me without his knowing.'

'Maybe,' she replied tossing back her hair.

Any experienced lecher knows that one should not waste words with a teenager because when it comes to real business she gets tongue-tied or can only say 'No.' It is best to talk to her body with your hands. That excites her to a state of speechless acceptance. I ran my fingers up and down her lower arm. She watched them till goose pimples came up. Thereafter all I had to do was to put my arm around her waist, draw her towards me and smother her lips, eyes, nose, ears and neck with kisses. She moaned helplessly. I slipped my hand under her kamiz and played with her taut nipples. Then I undid her pyjama cord and slipped my fingers between her damp thighs. A little gentle ministration with the hand made her convulse and she climaxed groaning 'O God! O God!' She lay still like a human-sized rubber doll. I put my hand on her bosom. She slapped it and pushed it away. She picked up her clothes and went to the bedroom. She came back in her jeans, tossed the bundle of salwar-kameez and sequined dupatta on the settee and strode out of the apartment.

That was the last I saw of Georgine.

She was the last customer Carlyle put my way. I do not know whether what I had done amounted to having carnal knowledge of a girl below the age of consent. But for many long days and nights I pondered over the words in the Mahabharata: 'As two pieces of wood floating on the ocean come together at one time and are again separated, even such is the union of living creatures in this world.'

*

After many years I have come to Delhi by train. The railway station has changed. But not beyond recognition. The platforms bear the same numbers they did fifty years ago. The same line of coolies in dark-red shirts and dirty white dhotis, bearing metal brassards with identification numbers on their arms, line up on their haunches along the platform. There are the mynahs chittering and quarrelling with cows. The same hawkers; the same melodious cries: lemon-soda-*barraf* (ice); chai, *garam* (hot) chai. And the same all pervading stench of shit, urine and phenyl.

It is an early morning in October. Pleasantly cool and somewhat misty, presaging the advent of winter. I skirt past people sleeping on the platform, go up the stairs, across the footbridge over rail tracks with mounds of shit on the sides, and down the stairs alongside the retiring-rooms. No one asks me for my ticket. I come out of the station and face the Company Gardens with is Hardinge library. Clean, frest air. Motor scooters and taxis are lined up on the road as far as the eye can see. The drivers are sprawled on the seats, snoring lustily. I hail a passing tonga. The tongawalla is wrapped up in a dirty shawl. He eyes me suspiciously. He is Muslim. I am Sikh. 'Where to?' he demands. 'Raisina! How much for Raisina?' He hasn't heard anyone use Raisina for New Delhi for many years and rightly concludes I am an old Delhiwalla. Raisina is also a good four miles away and will therefore have more money to it. 'Give me whatever you wish; a taxi would cost you over ten rupees. You are my first customer so this will be my *boni*.' I clamber up on the rear seat and place my valise beside him in the front.

He decides to go through the city; it is shorter, not crowded at this hour and safer than the deserted Ring Road. So we set off through the Company Bagh to the Fountain which has not spouted water in half-a-century. On the balcony of Roshan-ud-Daulah's mosque men are lined up for prayer. Alongside is Sees Ganj Gurdwara festooned with coloured bulbs. There is much coming and going of worshippers. Swarthy, long-bearded men in blue and yellow armed with spears guard the entrance.

The tonga turns left. I see the ramparts of the Red Fort. The tonga turns right into Dariba. Herds of Hindu women in white carrying brass plates full of flowers and coconuts are shuffling along towards the Jamna. We emerge from Dariba with the Jamia Masjid towering above us. The sun has just caught the eastern minaret in its noose. Hundreds of figures wrapped in sheets sleep on the broad steps. A weary oil-lamp flickers on the headstone of Sarmad's grave. It has been given a fresh coat of green; withered jasmine and marigold are strewn over it. We go through a very smelly Urdu Bazaar, past the lane leading to Razia Sultana's grave, the high-plinthed Kali Masjid and out of the old walled city through Turkman Gate. The air is fresher. Hundreds of RSS boys drill with staves under the podium in the wide acres of the Ram Leela ground. Middle-aged Punjabis take their walking-sticks for brisk walks. We pass the massive equestrian statue of Shivaji brandishing his sword towards New Delhi. 'When did they put this up?' I ask the tongawalla. 'Two years ago,' he mumbles as he gives the statue a baleful look. We go down below the Minto rail bridge and up again into Connaught Circus. 'Drop me at the Coffee House on the other side,' I tell him. We drive round the colonnaded shopping centres and pull up outside the Coffee House. 'How much?' I ask him as he hands me my valise. 'Whatever pleases you, you are doing the *boni*; and I have yet to feed my son,' he says patting the flanks of his horse. The horse has apparently had plenty to drink; it sends a powerful jet of wine-coloured fluid splashing on to the asphalt road. I hand him a tenner. He fumbles for change in his pocket. 'Keep it; give your son a good feed.' He invokes Allah's blessings on me, my kith and kin and drives off.

I buy the six English daily papers published in the city. It is a waste of fifty paise six times over. But old habits die hard. I flip through pages to read the announcements of citizens who have 'left for their heavenly abode'. Quite a few have. I don't know any of them. Nor any whose loss is mourned in verse and syrupy prose in the Memoriam columns. *Delhi Diary* states it is a sectional holiday for the Sikhs on account of the anniversary of the martyrdom of Guru Tegh Bahadur. And the column alongside mentions the promulgation of Section 144 of the C P C forbidding the assembly of more than five persons in certain areas. The Inspector General of Police states that 'goondas, miscreants and anti-social elements have been rounded up.' You don't have to read between lines to know that trouble is anticipated.

By the time I have disposed of my idli-sambar and the papers, the regulars who have little to do besides being regulars at the Coffee House are at their respective tables holding forth on political developments. My regulars have dwindled. The bald, beady-eyed photographer left for his heavenly abode last year; the farting clerk in the Ministry of Defence who resented our calling him a farter has dropped us. That leaves the Sikh journalist and the political expert. They are not getting along too well. The Sikh journalist arrives first, plucks a hair from his sparse beard and says, 'You are back! When?' and orders coffee. The politician follows: 'I thought all goondas had been rounded up,' he says in lieu of greeting. The journalist, usually quick-witted, is stuck for a proper retort. I ask, 'What's all this fuss about today? We've had hundreds of the Guru's martyrdom anniversaries without Section 144 and the police *bandobast*.' The politician—he is Hindu—fires another barbed shaft at us: 'You can never trust the Sikhs. They couldn't do much when their Guru was executed, so better three hundred years later than never. Isn't that so?' The Sikh journalist explodes, 'We settled our scores with the Msulims long ago. It is you Hindus, whose mothers and sisters they raped, who provoked us against them. You can't bear to see Sikhs and Muslims becoming friendly.' I try to defuse the tension. 'How different would have been the story of India if instead of Aurangzeb, Dara Shikoh had become Emperor of India!'

The politician proffers his version: 'He would not have executed your Guru and the Guru's son would not have had any excuse to make you grow all this fungus around your chins. Also

India would have become a real Hindustan—the land of the Hindus; and . . . .'

'And,' interrupts the Sikh journalist, 'if there had been no bearded Khalsa the only thing your Hindu ancestors could have offered in the way of defence against invaders like Nadir Shah and Abdali would have been their bare buttocks to be buggered.'

'Don't *buk buk*,' snaps the politician warming up.

'You are doing all the *bakwas* not I.'

So does the past cast its baleful shadow on the present. But nowhere do the shadows of history assume such bizarre patterns as they do in Delhi's Coffee House. I pick up my valise and leave the two to dispute the past.

🐾

Bhagmati bursts in like a hurricane, flailing her arms and spouting torrents of words. 'The Sikhs are up in arms. They are all over the city carrying long swords and are marching towards their gurdwara in Chandni Chowk. Do you know what they are saying? Three hundred years ago someone murdered their Guru in Dilli so they are going to murder every Dilliwalla today. Does that make any sense?'

'Why don't you ask your friend Budh Singh?'

'*Hai Ram*! You should have seen the way he looked at me! He asked me, "On whose side are you, Badshah Aurangzeb's or our Guru's?"'

'On whose side are you?'

'He is mad. I told him as politely as I could, "I am on no side—neither Emperor Aurangzeb's nor your Guru's." You know what he says to me? "So you are neutral, *hain*? If you were a man or a woman you would have been on one side or the other." But I shut him up for all time to come; he will never bandy words with me again. I said, "*Arre*, son of Budhoo Singh! The great Bhagwan who lives up in the heavens can perform many miracles. He can make a Bhangi (sweeper) into a Brahmin. He can turn a timid Bania (shopkeeper) into a Kshatriya (warrior). He can make a poor *hijda* into a man or a woman. But even Bhagwan cannot put sense into the skull of a *budhoo* like you."'

479

Bhagmati flops into the sofa with a triumphant *'hoon'*. She takes out a cigarette and flings the matchbox across the room to me. I go over and light her cigarette. 'You think there will be trouble in the city? There are policemen everywhere. Truckloads of them in Chandni Chowk and Nai Sarak and Qazi-ka-Hauz and Ajmeri Gate and Connaught Place—everywhere!'

'Maybe!' I reply. I have been a little off colour for some days and have not much appetite for Bhagmati. She has shown me a way out of my difficulties. 'That's the route the Sikh's procession is to take this afternoon. And they will be in all the gurdwaras including the one right behind this apartment. You will be safest with your husband in Lal Kuan. I can drop you there.'

Bhagmati looks at me very suspiciously. I don a sanctimonious look. I tell her that I had forgotten about the anniversary of the martyrdom of the ninth Guru, Tegh Bahadur. I tell her that it is a day for prayer not fornication. Bhagmati is very superstitious about having sex on sacred days. She often says, 'We have three sixty-four days to do this; one day of abstinence won't kill us.'

She finishes her cigarette. I give her twenty rupees. 'What's this for?' she asks as she tucks the notes in her bra. I drive her back to Lal Kuan.

The Untouchables

It was a few days before Diwali that news of the Badshah Jahangir's death was heard in Dilli. No one was allowed to light a lamp or kindle a fire in their hearth for some days. Our elders said that anyone seen smiling or heard laughing during the next forty days would have his head cut off. My mother would not let me go out to play with the other boys lest I forgot not to shout or laugh. That is why although I was only a small boy I can never forget that badshah's death.

When I asked my Bapu the name of the badshah who had died, he said, 'What will you do with the badshah's name?' None of the sweepers or cobblers in Rikabganj knew his name. Only the Mussalmans who lived in the sarai alongside the mosque and the contractor, Lakhi Rai, who lived in a big stone house with his wives, eight sons and their wives knew the badshah's name. These Mussalmans and Lakhi Rai's family went about with long faces as if their own mother's mother had died. Some people feel very big if they can cry over the deaths of big people.

'What have we poor untouchables to do with kings!' I remember my Bapu saying. 'They are all the same to us. One goes, another comes, *zulum* goes on.'

I did not know who *zulum* was. When I was a little older my Bapu told me that *zulum* was not a man but what the rich did to the poor. We untouchables were the poorest of the poor. No one did anything to us except run away if we came near them. That, said my Bapu, was also a kind of *zulum*. It was in our karma. We had done bad things in our previous births. That was why we were born black and had to do all the dirty work.

My Bapu called every badshah a *zalim*. This one who had just died, said my Bapu, was a very bad man because he drank more wine than Uncle Reloo who was drunk most of the time. Uncle Reloo told me that the badshah could drink twenty cups of arrack and eat tolas of opium every day and yet poke his queen and the other women of his harem every night. He told me that his queen had been married before. But when she saw the badshah who was only a prince at the time she knew at once that he would become a badshah. So she put some magic powder in his cup of wine and made him fall madly in love with her. The prince had the busband murdered and when he became badshah he made her his queen. Uncle Reloo said that it was not the badshah but this queen who had ruled over Hindustan.

It was not so much the badshah's drinking or womanizing that had made my father angry with him as what he dad done to our Guru. 'What is it to us how much he drinks and whose mother he fucks,' he used to say, 'but perish the man who raises his hand against our Guru.' Most of us untouchables of Rikabganj had attached ourselves to the lotus feet of the Guru and begun to call ourselves the Sikhs of Nanak. No one had seen Nanak or the Gurus who came after him to save us. The badshah who had just died had killed our fifth Guru Arjun and put his son Hargobind in jail. So there was no reason for us to beat our breasts on this badshah's death.

If there was a death in our family we did not light lamps at Diwali or squirt coloured water at Holi for at least one year. But the Mussalmans have strange csutoms. Three full moons after the death of the Badshah a fellow came from the city kotwali and began to beat his drum in front of the mosque. When everyone had collected he shouted: 'All you people listen to the order of the new badshah.' Then he gave his name which was as long as the road from Rikabganj to Paharganj—His Majesty Abul Muzaffar Shahabuddin Mohammed Sahib-i-Qiran Sani, Shadow of God on Earth, King of Kings, Monarch of the Universe, Emperor of Hindustan. He told us that we were to light our homes and pray for his long life.

We untouchables had no oil to light our homes and we had no temples to go and say our prayers in. So we decided to see how others lit their homes and prayed for the new badshah's long life.

My mother gave me a clean shirt to wear. Everyone wore their best clothes. The sweepers and cobblers of Rikabganj formed a party. The men in front danced to the beat of the drum; women followed, singing as they went along. I took hold of Uncle Reloo's hand. He was more fun to be with than Bapu. Aunt Bimbo was happy. 'You stick to your *chacha* and don't let him drink or get into mischief,' she said.

We drank lots of sherbet which was served free outside nawabs' mansions and we ate lots of sweetmeats which were also given free by rich tradesmen. My Bapu did not give me any money but I got a handful of coins in the scramble when a nawab showered them from his elephant.

The new badshah who called himself Shah Jahan or King of the World was not as *zalim* as his father had been. Although he had killed his brothers' families when he came on the throne, he did not hurt any one else. But Uncle Reloo who knew everything told me that like his father, grandfather and great-grandfather and others before them, this badshah also liked women. His favourite was a queen whom he kept pregnant from the day he married her. In the fourteen years they were married she had fourteen sons and daughters. She couldn't take any more and died giving birth to her fourteenth child. The badshah was so sad that he decided to make the biggest and most beautiful grave over her body. This was very good news for the stonemasons of Paharganj. They moved to Agra. It took over twenty years to make. People who came from Agra said it was higher than our Qutub Minar and much more beautiful than the tomb of Badshah Humayun at Arab-ki-Sarai. One day Aunt Bimbo asked Uncle Reloo: 'When I die, will you make a Taj Mahal for me?' He replied: 'You die first, we'll talk about a Taj Mahal for you aferwards.'

Some years after he became king, this badshah, Shah Jahan, came to Dilli. He liked our city very much and said: 'I am going to live here.' He sent for his chief builder, Mukarram Khan, and told him: 'Make a big fort along the river Jamna, and inside that fort make palaces for myself and my queens. I also want the biggest mosque in the word.' Mukarram Khan bowed three times before the badshah and replied: 'Badshah, peace be upon you! If Allah wills I will build you as big a fort as at Agra with as many canals and gardens and fountains. You will also have the world's biggest and most beautiful mosque. I will build it on Bhojla Hill so it can be seen from Palam and Qutub.' Then Mukarram Khan asked Ustad Ahmed and Ustad Hira to make maps. When that was done he asked the badshah to come to Dilli. 'Badshah, peace be upon you! Now put down the foundation stone, so we can get on with work.'

What years they were! Everyone got work. We gave up skinning dead cows and buffaloes and carrying other people's shit. Lakhi Rai got a contract to supply labour. As I was now old enough, he gave me a job to carry mud and stones.

Dilli began to change. Every day a new building! Every day the city wall rising higher! Every day new minarets and domes rising into the sky! And so it went for many years. When the work was finished we had nine days of tamasha. Princes showered silver coins on the crowds. The badshah rode through the city on his biggest elephant and scattered gold coins by the palmful. His courtiers said, 'We won't call Dilli Dilli any more. We will rename it Shahjahanabad.' But Dilli is Dilli and no king or nobleman can give it another name.

When a person is busy making money he forgets his God. As soon as he has made ninety-nine rupees he wants to make a hundred. For the years I was working in the city I hardly ever thought of my Guru. When my Bapu died and I became the head of the family, the Guru's agent sent for me. I went along with the messenger to the agent's camp. He reclined against a big pillow set on a big charpoy. I thought he was the Guru himself and so I went down on my knees and rubbed my forehead on the ground in front of him.

'Who are you?' he asked me.

'I am Jaita Rangreta of Rikabganj,' I replied.

'Are you a Sikh of Guru Nanak?' he asked.

I told him I was what my Bapu had been.

'You paid nothing for your father's soul nor on the accession of the new Guru,' he said.

I replied that I had no money left as I had to feast all the Rangretas in Rikabganj on my Bapu's death. His servant smacked me on the back of my neck and exclaimed angrily. 'You argue with the Guru's agent!' I had to borrow money from Lakhi Rai to pay him. I said to myself, 'At least I am something—a Sikh of Guru Nanak. I do not know what it means but it is better than being nothing but a Rangreta untouchable.' Thereafter every year I had to give this agent of the Guru something when he came to Dilli. Although he never allowed me to go near him or even touched my money with his own hands (his servants did that) I felt different. I was told that the new Guru did not like people to cut their hair or their beards. So I let the hair on my head grow long and wrapped a turban over it. I had quite a growth of beard on my face. The Mussalmans did not allow Hindus to wear beards but they did not bother us untouchables. We bearded Rangretas began to look different from other untouchables. And although after the building of Dilli was over I had to become a sweeper again, if anyone asked me who I was I would reply: 'I am a Sikh of Guru Nanak.'

For some years after the building of Shahjahanabad, the badshah liked Dilli more than Agra. Then he began to like Agra more than Dilli. His visits to our city became less and less frequent. Tradesmen and artisans began to move back to Agra. People began to say that very soon Shahjahanabad would become like the other old cities of Dilli: Mehrauli, Siri, Chiragh, Tughlakabad, Kotla Firozeshah and Kilokheri—the abode of Gujars, jackals, hyaenas and the owls.

I did not earn very much sweeping drains and cleaning latrines and had to borrow money from the Bania and Lakhi Rai. I had to pay interest on their money and when I was unable to do that they refused to lend me any more. Because of this I was forced to take employment in the executioner's yard attached to the kotwali in Chandni Chowk. This was really dirty work: first I had to get used to seeing a man's head being hacked off; then see his arms and legs cut off. After this had happened it was my job to put the pieces together and lay them out for the people to see. As I worked I could hear the onlookers avoiding me as if I were a murderer. Every evening there were at least three to four unclaimed corpses to be carted off and dumped in the river or on the garbage mound. What will man not do to fill his belly!

As I said before, I did not like this work. I did not like to shout *dom, dom* whenever I went out with the cartload of corpses. I did not like people covering their children's eyes against me and blocking there nostrils against the smelly load I carried. Even the sentries at the city gates would draw aside to let me pass. I used to console myself by recalling my Bapu's words: 'Son, only two people can pass through the gates of Shahjahnabad without being questioned: the King and the untouchable!'

It was on one of his visits to Dilli that Badshah Shah Jahan was taken ill. They tried to keep it secret but within a few hours everyone knew about the sultan's ailment mainly through the badshah's doctor who was a gossip. This is how it happened. The badshah had got up at night and complained of pain in his belly. The queen had sent for the hakeem who lived in Ballimaran. The hakeem told many people of having had no sleep because he had to stay up all night with a patient whose name he could not disclose—which is how news of the badshah's ailment spread.

When I came to work one of the *doms* shouted '*Chhuttee* (holiday)! Orders from the palace, no executions today.' Executions were only stopped on religious holidays or if the king or one of his queens or their princes was ill and desired to earn merit and good health. By the time the sun had risen over the walls of Red Fort people were gathering in groups and speaking in whispers. Butchers were forbidden to slaughter animals; mullahs were ordered to pray to Allah to restore the king to good health; priests were ordered to clang their temple bells. Shops closed. People hurried to their homes and barricaded their doors. At night they dug holes under their hearths to bury their gold and silver.

The king it turned out was constipated. The hakeem gave him a purgative made of laburnum pods. For two days and nights the king emptied his bowels till there was nothing left in them and he started shitting blood. But big people's illnesses are always made to sound big. The simple shutting and opening of the royal arse-hole was made to sound as if the world was coming to an end. At first he was said to be dying of constipation; then he was said to be dying of dysentery.

My Bapu used to say that when a father hiccups his sons go for his purse. That was certainly true about the badshah's four sons. No sooner had they heard of their old man's illness than their hands were on the hilts of their swords. But they wanted to make sure he was really dying before they drew them. So they sent messengers to Dilli with gifts for their father. The old fellow knew these tricks as he had tried them in his own time. He seated himself at the window of his palace so that the crowd could see him. He had prayers of thanksgiving said in the mosques. However, his sons were not fooled and started raising armies to march to Agra and Dilli. The badshah decided to get to Agra and sit on his throne before one of his boys got to it. Despite this, one after another his sons proclaimed themselves kings of Hindustan. First, Shuja who was in Bangladesh from where the sun rises put a crown on his head and said: 'I am King of Hindustan.' A few days later Murad, who was somewhere in the south, sat himself on a throne and said: 'I am King of Hindustan.' Aurangzeb was more clever. He went to Murad and told him: 'Let me help you defeat our brothers. Then we will lock up our old man who is now too feeble to rule and you can become King of Hindustan. I will then go off to Mecca and pray for you.' Dara who was the badshah's eldest and the favourite son was incensed at the behaviour of his brothers. He said, 'My father is King of Hindustan. After him, I will be King of Hindustan because I am his eldest son. Shuja, Murad and Aurangzeb are bastards. I will kill them.'

We were not sure which of the sons would make the best king. The contractor Lakhi Rai was in favour of Dara. 'He is the eldest and the eldest son always succeeds his father. Besides he is god-fearing and treats Hindus and Muslims alike,' he said. The Muslims did not like Dara. They said he was a *kafir* because he made the stone gods of the Hindus equal to Allah and his Prophet. Their favourite was the third son Aurangzeb.

At this time there was a Yahoodi fakeer, Sarmad, who went about naked like a Naga sadhu. Sarmad told everyone in the bazaars that Dara would win. The people of Dilli were frightened of Sarmad because he was a friend of God and could ask Him for any favour he wanted. One day I casually told one of the Muslims at the sarai what fakeer Sarmad was saying. The Mussalman spat on the ground and exclaimed: '*La haul valla quwwat!* That shameless fellow who dangles his penis before women! If I ever catch him alone I will cut it off and throw it to the dogs.'

Fakeer Sarmad was wrong. The king's sons fought each other as hungry dogs fight over a bone. Dara's son, Sulaiman Shikoh, defeated Shuja. Meanwhile Murad and Aurangzeb defeated Dara, captured Agra and made their old father prisoner. Then this fellow Aurangzeb tricked his brother Murad: he got him drunk, tied him up and threw him into a dungeon. He then finished off Shuja, Dara and Dara's sons. This was how we had a new badshah—Aurangzeb—while the old badshah Shah Jahan was still alive. The Mussalmans in the sarai were happy. They said that the new badshah was a good man. He did not drink wine; he did not have concubines or courtesans; he did not allow dancing and singing in the palace; he ate little, slept little and prayed a lot. He spent on himself only what he earned by making copies of their holy book and selling them. They said if all kings had been like him, Hindustan would have long ago been rid of *kafirs*. Alamgir was the name they used for him—'Alamgir, *Zinda Peer*, is a living saint,' they said.

Lakhi Rai was not happy. The new badshah did not give him any contracts. One day many years later when I was eating his leftovers in his courtyard I told him that the Mussalmans said Aurangzeb was a man of God because he did not drink wine or womanize. He lost his temper and said, 'What about that slut Hira Bai?' Then he got frightened and made me swear that I would never tell anyone of what he had said. But I could not get Hira Bai's name out of my mind. I asked the Bania, who also sometimes gave me his leftovers, about her. He made a ring with the thumb and index finger of his left hand and pierced it with a finger of his right hand. 'But that Hira Bai is dead,' he said. The Bania did not like Aurangzeb because he had imposed jazia tax on the Hindus. 'Don't tell anyone I told you,' he said in a low voice, 'but a tribe called the Marathas are going to finish him. Their leader Shivaji has stuck a big bamboo pole up the bottoms of these Mughals. Haven't you heard how this Shivaji tore out the bowels of one of the badshah's generals with his hands? In the name of Rama, don't breathe a word about this to anyone or they will slit my throat.'

I couldn't keep secrets. One day I asked the Mussalman cook at the sarai if he had ever heard of Shivaji. He almost spat in my face. 'Where did you pick up the name of that dirty *kafir*?' he asked angrily. 'He murdered the brave General Afzal Khan who was embracing him as a friend. That is the kind of *moozi* he is. The badshah has sent an army against him. If Allah wills, the rat will be flushed out of his hole and destroyed. *Inshallah!*'

Some months later the Mussalman cook gave me an extra large portion of leftovers. He looked very happy. 'Have you heard of that Shivaji of yours? He has been captured and brought in chains to Agra. He will be sent to hell.' When I told this to the Bania, he said it was a lie and that Shivaji had come of his own free will to talk to the king. For many days everyone in Dilli was talking of this man Shivaji. The Mussalmans said he was a great villain and that the king would cut off his head. The Hindus said he was a great hero. Then we heard that he had escaped and returned to his mountain kingdom in the Deccan. 'Dindn't I tell you so?' said the Bania to me. 'They can never catch him. Ramji is his protector.'

The king was very angry. He ordered Hindu temples at Varanasi and Mathura to be destroyed. The Bania who was so frightened of the Mussalmans called the badshah a *zalim*. 'Whenever there is too much *zulum*,' he said, 'God sends an avatar to destroy *zalims*. It is written in the Gita.' Even Lakhi Rai who kept up with the Mussalmans wagged his head and said, 'This is Kaliyuga (the dark age), God will send an avatar to save us.'

The *zulum* went on but no avatar came to stop it. When the Jats and Brahmins of village Tilpat, which is a few kos in the direction of the rising sun, claimed land which belonged to their temple, the badshah sent his army against them and blew up their village. Their leader, Gokula Jat and all his supporters were brought to Dilli and executed. No avatar came to save them.

Three years later there was a worse *zulum* at Narnaul. A sect of sadhus called Satnamis were slain by the thousand. No avatar came to save them or punish the *zalim* badshah.

I asked Lakhi Rai about the coming of the avatar. He just shook his head. I asked him whether our Guru could be the avatar. 'Which Guru?' he asked. 'There are so many. And all they do is to send their agents to collect money.' That was strange talk from Lakhi Rai!

I began to lose faith in the Guru. The Mussalmans in the sarai made fun of him. 'Who is this robber you worship?' one fellow asked me. The mullah of the mosque (may his mouth be filled with dung!) said: 'The badshah will soon bring this Guru of yours to the path of obedience and teach him that the only way of approaching Allah is through His only Messenger, Mohammed—upon whom be peace.' Although I knew nothing about this Guru I did not like Mussalmans talking like that about him. When the Guru was captured at Agra and brought to Dilli in chains, the Mussalmans mocked: 'We told you this Guru of yours is a robber! The entire gang will be hanged.

I saw the Guru and three Sikhs who had been arrested with him. I said to myself: 'If he is an avatar he will save himself and destroy the *zalims*.' I prayed that he would fly out of his cell or perform some other miracle so that I could show my face to the Mussalmans of Rikabganj.

But who cares for the prayers of poor untouchables? There was this judge Qazi Abdul Wahab. His Allah had made him so deaf that everyone called him *behra qazi*. He sentenced the Guru and his three followers to death. He ordered their bodies to be displayed in front of the kotwali for everyone to see. For the first time even the timid Lakhi Rai became brave. 'This must not happen,' he said to me. 'The Guru has refused to save his life, but we must not allow them to dishonour his body.' The rich contractor addressed me as Jaitaji. Before this he had always called me 'Jaitoo' or worse 'O, *choorha* (sweeper).' How was I to know Lakhi Rai was not a spy? I kept quiet. Silence is the best friend of the poor.

Strange things happened in Dilli that autumn. Dassehra passed without any Ram Lila or the burning of the effigies of Ravana and his brothers. The Hindus said the badshah had forbidden the celebration of Hindu festivals. The Muslims said that this was a lie and said they knew why Hundus were not celebrating their most important festival. A few days later came Diwali. Not a light in anyone's house! Not a sound of a cracker! No fireworks! No one sending sweets to anyone! The whole world was like a dark, moonless night. You know how much darker the night looks when you expect millions of oil-lamps twinkling and there are none! So no Diwali for the Hindus. And the Mussalmans feeling as if ants were crawling up their bottoms! The mullahji of the sarai mosque asked Lakhi Rai very discreetly why he had not lit any lamps on Diwali night. 'The death of a very near and dear one,' he replied. All the Hindus seem to have lost someone near and dear to them,' exclaimed the mullahji very sarcastically.' I hope it is not because someone very near and very dear is going to die, yes?'

Lakhi Rai did not answer. The mullahji turned his temper on me. 'And you, Jaitoo! Have you lost your mother's mother that you did not light lamps at Diwali?' I replied: 'Mullahji, in poor men's houses there is a death every day. We never have enough oil to light a lamp. If you gave me money, I would have lit up every home in Rikabganj.' He mumbled in his beard, 'You have learnt to talk big, haven't you?'

Everyone in Dilli was talking about the miracle the Guru would perform. They said anyone who raised his hand against him or his companions would go blind. The Kotwal could not find anyone in Dilli to carry out the sentence of death and had to send for one Jalaluddin all the way from Samana in the Punjab. This Jalaluddin hated the Sikhs and their Gurus.

A few days after the Diwali-without-lights, Jalaluddin cut off the heads of the Sikhs captured with the Guru. Jalaluddin did not go blind; nothing happened to him. Now it was the turn of the Guru. The *behra qazi* said, 'Jalaluddin, we'll cut off the Guru's head on Thursday. His body will be exposed to public gaze after prayer on Friday. Everyone in Dilli will see which is mightier, the sword of Islam or the neck of an infidel!' Everyone in the world knows that whenever the blood of a good man is spilled in Dilli, the Great God who lives in the sky makes His anger known. On Thursday the sun came up like a ball of fire. Everyone said: 'Something terrible is going to happen today.' Even the Mussalmans were anxious and hoped the badshah who was away beyond the Punjab would get to know and would cancel the order of the *behra qazi*. The Kotwal told me that he had prayed all night. 'It will be very bad for the Mussalmans if this Guru is martyred,' he said shaking his head.

The Guru performed no miracle. With the name of God on his lips he permitted the monster Jalaluddin of Samana to sever his head from his body. The town-crier went round beating his drum and yelling that 'justice' had been done and that the Guru's body would be exposed in front of the kotwali for two days and nights for all to see and learn a lesson.

I brought the news to Rikabganj. In the afternoon all the Sikhs and Hindus of Rikabganj gathered under a tree. No one said anything. The men sighed and the women wept. The Mussalmans of the sarai watched us from a distance. Even they seemed to be touched by our grief.

As I sat in that crowd listening to the sighing and whimpering a strange feeling came over me. We had done nothing to save the life of our Guru—and now they were going to expose his naked body to the gaze of crowds and for animals to tear and birds to peck! What kind of devotees were we? My blood boiled within me; I felt very hot and angry with myself. Most of the Guru's disciples were high-born Kshatriyas and Jat peasants who boasted loudly of their bravery. They had done nothing to save their Guru. I, an untouchable, could teach these high-caste fellows how a Guru's Sikh should act. It might cost me my life, but I would win the respect of the world for my untouchable brethren.

I slipped away. Lakhi Rai saw me get up and followed me. 'I have some work for you Jaitaji,' he said, putting his hand on my shoulder, adding meaningfully, 'if you are man enough to do it.' This was the first time he had touched me. I was not sure of this rich contractor—one can never be sure of rich people. I replied, 'I have to be on duty at the kotwali.' Lakhi Rai said: 'I will come with you. I also have business at the kotwali.' What was his game? I really did not care to find out. However, I felt not Lakhi Rai's but my Guru's hand on my shoulder. I was not afraid of anyone in the world—not of the badshah or the *behra qazi* or that Jalaluddin; not even of the Mughal soldiers or the Kotwal and his constabulary.

Lakhi Rai had several bullock carts lined up on the road. They were loaded with bales of cotton. His eight sons were with him. As he was a government contractor, he and his family were allowed to carry weapons. All the men were armed with swords and spears. Lakhi Rai always guarded his caravans in this way and everyone knew him. We left Rikabganj in the afternoon.

When we reached Paharganj, the sun suddenly disappeared. The wind dropped. Hundreds of kites began circling above us. We could see a dark brown wall come sweeping in from the west. As we came to the city wall, the circle of kites moved overhead towards the Royal Mosque. Then the storm overtook us with a fury I would not have thought possible.

The guards at Ajmeri Gate had muffled their faces with the ends of their turbans and waved us on. The storm swept us through Qazi-ka-Hauz, through Lal Kuan and past Begum Fatehpuri's mosque into Chandni Chowk. We arrived at the kotwali.

Who knows the inscrutable designs of the Guru? The dust-storm had turned the day into night. Every door and window had been shut against the dust. The guards had bolted themselves in their barracks. And the only sound was the howling of the wind.

I had no difficulty in finding the Guru's body. I touched his feet and then slung his body over my shoulders. I took his head in my hands and walked through the blinding dust-storm. Lakhi Rai and his sons also touched the Guru's feet. We laid his body and head on one of the bullock carts, piled bales of cotton over it and turned our carts around. The same storm that had driven us into Chandni Chowk drove us backwards through the same bazaar, out of Ajmeri Gate to Paharganj. When we arrived at Rikabganj, the wind suddenly dropped and the dust disappeared. The night had come on.

Lakhi Rai's wife and daughters-in-law had made a pyre of sandalwood in the centre of their courtyard. We placed the Guru's body on it. All the family touched his feet. Lakhi Rai said a short prayer and lit the pyre. His wife brought out a shawl and wrapped the Guru's head in it. 'Take this to the Guru's son in Anandpur,' she said, handing me the bundle. 'The Guru will take you there in safety.'

៛

As I went up the ridge, I looked back to make sure no one was following me. In the distance the flames of the funeral pyre in the courtyard of Lakhi Rai's house flickered. The storm had gone as suddenly as it had come and the sky was clear and full of stars. It was a few days after the full moon. I quickened my steps. By the time the moon came up, I was many kos from Dilli on the way to Anandpur.

At last the Guru had performed the great miracle. He had given a carrier of shit and stinking carcasses the privilege of carrying his sacred head in his arms. Hereafter anyone who called me unclean would have his mouth stuffed with dung. I was now Jaita Rangreta, the true son of the Guru.

Bhagmati

I haven't seen Bhagmati in weeks and, worse, haven't even thought of her—so engrossed have I been in a series I've been doing for Doordarshan TV, entitled 'The Delhi you do not know'. I began with monuments in the suburbs of Mehrauli—the tombs of Altamash, Sultan Ghari, Balban and Jamali-Kamali. I threw in a few dilapidated mosques and some *baolis*. The appearance on Doordarshan has brought me an unexpected bonus—a letter from a lady saying she had watched the programme and would like to meet me. She has signed herself by her first name, Kamala. Neither Miss nor Mrs nor anything else about who she is—what age or what she does for a living. The address is the room number of an army mess. Usually women who write letters to men they do not know turn out to be serious-minded bores. However, something impels me to write back to say that I would be happy to meet her. And this is when I think with some guilt of Bhagmati.

I spend an hour or two in the library of the India International Centre where I have asked Kamala to meet me. Since she knows what I look like she should find it easy to locate me.

Though I usually love flipping through the magazines and papers at the Centre, this morning I find I cannot keep my mind on what I'm reading but keep looking up at every woman who comes in. Will she be fifteen or fifty? Fat or slim? Fair or dark? And what the hell does she want to get to know me for? To bore me or to get laid?

At last she comes in and walks straight towards me, holds out her hand and says with a smile, 'I am Kamala.'

I get up, take her hand and reply, 'Pleased to meet you. Let's have some coffee in the garden.'

She is small, dark and looks in her thirties. We find a table, I order coffee for two. I open the dialogue: 'What is your full name, Kamala what?'

'You are very curious. Okay, I am Kamala Gupta, wife of Brigadier Gupta. We have three school-going children—one girl, two boys.'

I express surprise. 'Mother of three! You look young enough to be in college.'

She beams with pleasure. 'Not as young as you think. I am over forty. Been married more than twenty years. People mistake my daughter to be my younger sister.'

'Are you a Delhi girl?'

'No. I am Tamil. My husband is from Delhi itself.'

The 'itself' is her first Indianism. It could as well have been 'Delhi only'.

'Convent of Jesus and Mary, Miranda House and arranged marriage,' I guess.

'Wrong on all three. Modern School and St Stephen's College where I met my husband and eloped with him. Later forgiven by parents on either side for intercaste, interstate marriage. He is a Bania, I am a Mudaliar. He speaks Hindi; I speak Tamil. We speak English. Our children speak all three.'

'Sounds wonderful! Where is the rest of the family?'

'My husband is posted at a non-family station. The children are in boarding schools in Mussoorie. I've been allowed to stay on in the army mess. We get together during vacations.'

There is a lull in the dialogue. I try to size her up. She is lost in the depths of her coffee-cup. 'A paisa for your thoughts,' she says breaking the silence. 'I can tell you what you are thinking—why did this woman want to meet me?'

'You tell me.'

'Well, I have nothing much to do. Can't stand army wives. So I thought I'd write a book or something. Your programme on TV gave me an idea. Why not something on Delhi and its monuments? What do you think?'

'There are hundreds of them in the market.'

'Maybe. But they are all the same. None of them have those

495

things you were showing on your programme. I know many old
havelis lost in tiny lanes nobody knows about. My husband was
born and brought up in Parathe Vali Gali. Ever heard of it?'

'Heard yes, seen never.'

'There you see, even you don't know! Ever heard of Gali
Namak Haraman? I bet you haven't. You show me what I have not
seen. I'll show you what you have not seen. And we do a book
together. What do you say?' She puts out her hand as her part of
the deal. I take it as my part of the deal. 'Done.' And give it a gentle
squeeze. It is firm but leathery.

We chat for an hour. It seems as if we have known each other
for years. I have little doubt that I can extract more out of the deal.

I drop her outside the army mess, an old building raised
during the war to house American G.I.s. She agrees to meet me at
the Centre the following Sunday to be driven round the sites I had
shown on TV. 'Better the Centre than the mess. Too many prying
eyes and bitchy wives,' she says as she waves good-bye.

୨ବ

She is there waiting for me at the gate with a small basket
containing two thermos flasks and a box of sandwiches. 'Much
better to carry your own stuff than go to those crowded cafeterias
or *dhabas*,' she explains.

I give her a miniature jade Ganapati that I had lying with me.
'It is my good luck totem. I always carry one in my wallet. This one
is to see nothing goes wrong with our friendship.'

She cradles the figurine in both he palms and kisses it. 'Thank
you. I am sure it will bring me luck.'

As we pass the Qutub Minar, she remarks: 'I believe that the
latest research has proved that this is a Hindu monument.'

'So is the Taj Mahal and the Red Fort,' I add sarcastically.
'Where did you pick up this bullshit. All these buildings have the
names of the builders and the dates of completion inscribed on
them in Arabic. You've been reading Hindu fascist propaganda?'

We spend the morning in Mehrauli. I park the car alongside
Auliya Masjid. We walk along the Shamsi Talab, past Jahaz Mahal
into the crowded streets. I take her to the mausoleum of
Qutubuddin Bakhtiyar Kaki and show her the tombs to Mughal

kings in the neighbouring graveyard. At Emperor Bahadur Shah's tomb I tell her about the execution of Banda Bairagi and 700 of his Sikh followers. 'He was ordered to kill his own child before they hacked him to pieces, limb by limb.'

'When?'

'Sunday, 19 June 1716.'

'You must hate Muslims,' she mutters. 'You remember the day and date as if it was your birthday.'

'No, I don't hate Muslims,' I protest. 'Banda had slaughtered them by the thousands before they caught him and his bands. Those were savage times.'

I take her to Jamali-Kamali's mosque. She pours out the coffee, gives me a sandwich. She takes out a notebook and a ball-point pen. 'Tell me of the places we've seen this morning. If I don't write it down I'll forget everything.'

I go over the itinerary while she makes notes and sips her coffee. When I come to Banda, she repeats, 'I don't believe you like Muslims.'

Once again I lodge a protest: 'Most of my friends are Muslims, not Hindus or Sikhs.'

'You couldn't possibly like someone like Aurangzeb—a man who killed his brother and nephews and put his father in prison. He destroyed Hindu temples and had one of your Gurus executed. How can you like a character like that? If you ask me, all our Hindu-Muslim troubles of today can be traced back to Aurangzeb.'

'My dear young lady, you've been properly brainwashed! You've never been told that this Aurangazeb also gave grants to build Hindu and Sikh temples.'

'That's news to me. You've just made that up.'

She asks to be dropped at the corner of the road near the army mess.

Our next tour is to be in the city where she will act as my guide and mentor. This time I give her another miniature Ganapati made of crystal! 'This is to double your luck.' This time she gives me a kiss on my beard. We drive up to the Red Fort where I park the car. She takes me into Chandni Chowk. 'I can't take you through Dariba or the Parathe Vali Gali; I have many in-laws living there who may want to know what I am doing with a Sardarji.'

'And I don't want to be shown round Lal Kuan. I have friends living there.' I reply.

'Friends in Lal Kuan? What kind of friends?' she asks suspiciously.

'Very respectable, very likeable. I'll tell you about them in course of time.'

We branch off onto Nai Sarak, into a narrow lane. She points out several old havelis and shrines beneath peepal trees. At places the stench from open sewers is overpowering. Stray cows, hawkers, and scooters and passers-by make the going difficult. It gives me the excuse to occasionally hold her hand. She presses mine whenever I do so. There is no want of response.

After an hour-and-a-half of wandering through winding lanes we find ourselves behind the Jamia Masjid. We cross the maidan to get to the parking lot outside the Red Fort.

'Drop me at Connaught Circus,' she says. 'I have some shopping to do.'

I know it is an excuse to avoid being seen with me by the other residents of the mess. I am somewhat puzzled by her attitude. When I suggest she come to my apartment, she says no firmly, though in our conversations she makes no secret of her being unhappy with the life she is leading. 'What kind of life does an army wife lead? The husband is away for weeks and months. When he gets back for a few days he can think of nothing besides sex. He gets as much of it as he wants whether his wife likes it or not. And then he is off again, while the wife is left twiddling her thumbs.'

If it isn't going to be my apartment and she is not going to let me come to her room, where in Delhi can we find a place where we can do what we are heading for? The initiative has passed out of my hands to hers. But I am determined to bring matters to a head. If she says no, I will drop her.

Our third rendezvous at the Centre is on a warm October afternoon. I give her yet another Ganapati—this one made of ivory. 'How many Ganapatis are you going to give me?' she asks as she kisses me on the lips. We drive away towards Purana Qila.

'You know what I'd really like to give you?' I ask her in the car.

'No, tell me.'

'What I'd really like to give you is a baby.'

She does not bat an eyelid but keeps looking straight ahead of her. After a while she replies, 'That may take some doing as I had my tubes sewn up when I had the third child. But there is no harm in trying, is there?'

How does one cope with a woman like this one? I flush with embarrassment. I grab her hand and kiss it. We do not bring up the subject all afternoon as we trudge round the monuments. On the way back she asks me to take her to the INA market to buy fruit and provisions. 'You stay in the car,' she orders. 'I won't take very long.'

I know she doesn't want to be seen with me in the market which is frequented by government officials and armed forces personnel. She comes back after a few minutes followed by a coolie carrying apples, tins, biscuits and cheese in a basket. He dumps the basket on the rear seat. This time she asks me to drive to the mess. 'I can't carry all that stuff up to my room,' she explains. 'You can have a quick drink with me.'

I carry the basket and follow her up the stairs and down a verandah. She has the last room. She unlocks the door and switches on the light. I can see she is relieved that no one has seen us come in. 'I don't mix with my neighbours,' she says. 'They are a nosey lot.'

I dump the basket in her kitchenette. She puts some of her purchases in a tiny fridge and others on the shelf. 'I am afraid all I can offer you is army rum. Can't afford anything else. With soda or water?'

'I've never had it. Give it to me on the rocks.'

It is a sparsely furnished bed-sitter. She sits on her bed; I on the sofa. I take a sip of the sweet, smelly rum. It is raw, rough and heady. I cannot think of what to say. I break the silence with the first thing that comes to mind. 'The other day you said something about Aurangzeb being a bigot. That's not how Muslim historians see him. Even the ordinary Muslims of today think he has been unfairly maligned.'

She laughs. 'Can't you think of anything more interesting to talk about with a woman than a dead emperor?'

'I could say how lucky I am being in the company of an attractive woman. But where will that get me?'

'You know very little about me. Not even how attractive I can be. You've not even tried to find out,' she says. She removes her sari *pallu*, undoes the clasp of her blouse and exposes her breasts. 'Have you seen anything like these before? And on a woman who has suckled three children?'

I certainly had not. Ebony black, perfectly shaped and taut as that of a virgin of sixteen. Blacker nipples pointing directly at me. 'You have the most perfectly shaped bosom I've ever seen, the pictures of nudes included,' I say. I have a strong urge to get up and sit beside her. She notices my hesitation. 'Feel them. Nothing flabby about me.'

I go and sit beside her. I run my palms over her bosom; they are firmer than any I have ever encountered. I lay her head on her pillow and run my tongue round her nipples. 'This is coming in your way,' she says removing my turban from my head. My long hair spreads over her face. She pulls me down by it and presses my head closer to her bosom . . . . I stop for a breather and take a look at her face. She has closed her eyes and is breathing heavily. As I press my lips on hers she opens her mouth to entangle her tongue in mine. My hand goes reconnoitring over her buttocks and then between her thighs. 'Come inside and give me the baby you promised,' she murmurs.

I do her bidding. She is a quick comer. It is all over in a matter of seconds. I go back to my rum on the rocks. She gets up, plucks a cigarette from her bedside table and lights it. 'Now that we've got this off our minds, you can tell me about Aurangzeb,' she says.

Aurangzeb Alamgir: Emperor of Hindustan

In the name of Allah, the Beneficent, the Merciful and in the name of His Messenger, the Refuge of the World, I, Abdul Muzaffar Mohiuddin Mohammed, on whom Allah in His Divine wisdom bestowed the sovereignty of the Empire of Hindustan, pen this brief account of the ninety years of his life and forty-eight years of his reign. I do this so that Allah who is just will punish those who have transgressed against truth in writing about me. And may He forgive His humble servitor for presenting his side of the story in his own words.

This sinner, full of iniquities, was born in Dohad, a small town in the province of Gujarat. A poet composed for us the title *Aftab-e-Alamtab* meaning 'The Sun whose Radiance would take the World in its embrace'. Another bard composed the chronogram: *Gauhar-e-Taj-Muluk-Aurangzeb* meaning 'Aurangzeb a Pearl in the Emperor's crown'. The letters of both these titles when added up gave the year of our birth, 1027 Hijri corresponding to 1618 of the Christian calendar. We were born on the 15th day of Zi'qad (3 November) under the dual signs of Libra and Scorpio. Astrologers predicted that our character would partake of the qualities of both: justice and mercy from the scales; and from the scorpion which carries venom in its tail, tenacity of purpose and the power to destroy those who dared to trample on our rights.

At the time of our birth our Sire, then known as Prince Khurram, was Viceroy of the Deccan and his Sire, Jahangir,

Emperor of Hindustan. Our royal mother who reposes in the peace of the marble mausoleum in Agra named after her as the Taj Mahal, bore fourteen children in fourteen years of happy conjugation. Seven of these children were summoned to paradise by Allah. Of the seven who were permitted to sojourn in the world, the eldest, Jahanara, was followed by Dara Shikoh, Shuja and Roshanara Begum. This creature of dust was the fifth surviving child and the third son of our parents. After us came Murad. Gauhar Ara made her entrance into the world the same day as our revered mother took leave of it on 7 June 1631.

Since the memory of mortals begins to accumulate only after the sixth or the seventh year, we remember little of our childhood. We were told later that our grandfather, Emperor Jahangir, being for some reason displeased with our father, had our elder brother Dara Shikoh and ourselves taken as hostages to reside with him at Lahore. We were then eight years old.

The Emperor appointed men of wisdom and piety to be our teachers. Mir Mohammed Hashim Gilani and Aitmad Khan taught us the sacred word of Allah, the traditions of our holy Prophet (on Whom be peace). We were also taught Persian, Turki, Hindi and the art of calligraphy. We were content to learn whatever was considered worthy of learning. Indeed what more is there to learn than the word of God and the precedents of His chosen Messenger! However, Dara Shikoh preferred reading the books of infidels and holding discourses with heretics. He gave up saying his prayers and fasting during Ramadan. On one of his fingers he wore a ring with the word *prabhu* inscribed in Devnagri characters. He also bestowed patronage on men who created the likeliness of living things on paper and stone, singers, lute-players, dancers and such others. The gift of intellect that God had given him he magnified into something of his own making. He became haughty in his manner, pompous in his speech and arrogant towards the *omarah*. Of such it has been truly said: 'If the blanket of man's fate has been woven black, even the waters of Zam Zam and Kausar cannot wash it white.'

As often happens in families, some members were closer to each other than to others. Our father's favourite children were the two eldest, Jahanara Begum and Dara Shikoh, and the two were perforce drawn closer to each other than to any of their other brothers or sisters. Although we maintained equal affection towards all our kin, Roshanara sought our company more than that of her other brothers. Likewise the youngest, Gauhar Ara, attached herself to Murad.

Our father, Shah Jahan, when he became Emperor of Hindustan in October 1627, once spoke of his four sons in the following words: 'Dara Shikoh has made himself an enemy of good men; Murad has set his heart on drinking; Shuja has no good trait except contentment. The resolution and intelligence of Aurangzeb prove that he alone can shoulder the burden of ruling India. But he is physically weak.'

We had seen only fifteen summers when we proved to the world that just as our heart did not lack resolution our arms did not lack strength. In the early hours of one morning, when the sun had only made its presence known to the minarets of the Royal Mosque, a vast concourse assembled along the sandbanks of the river to watch a fight between two elephants—Sudhakar armed with spearlike tusks and Surat Sundar which, despite its tusks being removed, was as big as its adversary. The beasts had been fed on hashish. After entangling with each other for some time, Sudhakar, goaded by its mahout and angered by the yelling of the people, suddenly wrenched itself free, turned upon the crowd and crushed many people under its mighty feet. Everyone except us fled in panic and terror. Seeing us alone, Sudhakar charged towards us. We held our horse in check. As the maddened elephant bore down upon us we struck its forehead with our spear with such force that it was stunned to a halt. However, with a swipe of its trunk it knocked down our horse beneath us. We rose to our feet, drew our sword and slashed its trunk. By then others, including Shuja and Raja Jai Singh, galloped up and attacked the beast. The other elephant, Surat Sundar, came back into the fray as well and chased Sudhakar off the ground. His Majesty chided us for our rashness. We replied: 'Death drops the curtain even on emperors; that is no dishonour. The shame lay in what our brother did.' Since Shuja had done whatever he could, it was apparent to everyone that our words were aimed at Dara Shikoh for he had behaved like a coward. His Majesty pretended as if he had not heard us. He had us weighed against gold coins which he presented to us and bestowed on us the title of *Bahadur* (the brave). A few months later he appointed us governor of the Deccan. Dara Shikoh's heart became heavy with envy.

At the age of seventeen we were married to Dilras Bano Begum, daughter of Shah Nawaz Safawi. The following year Murad, then only fourteen, married Dilras Bano's younger sister and so, besides being our brother, he also became our brother-in-law. Though we were in the prime of youth, and youth has its compulsions, we wasted little time on the nuptial couch. Living in camp amongst our comrades-in-arms became us more than dallying with the ladies of the harem. Gilani Sahib, our teacher, had impressed upon us that a ruler should always be on the move; being in one place gives the impression of repose and repose brings a thousand calamities. We realized early that it is bad for kings as it is for water to remain in the same place; stagnant water goes putrid and a stagnant king's power slips out of his hands. Unlike other monarchs of Hindustan and the nobility of the times, no more than five women enjoyed our intimacy; they produced ten children from our seed. Only one of these women we really and truly loved but her sojourn was brief and bore no fruit.

&

We were thirty-five years old. The searing heat of summer had given way to the season of dark clouds, cool breezes and rain. We had gone to call on our aunt at Burhanpur and were strolling in her deer park along the banks of the river Tapti. We heard the laughter of young girls at a swing and stopped where we were in order to save them embarrassment as they were unveiled. The girls began to sing in chorus. We caught some words of their song which was about a young bride pining for her groom. They were singing in raga megh malhar which was appropriate for the time and the season. One voice rose above the others; dulcet, clear it seemed to spread over the verdant greenery like drops of dew glittering under a morning sun. Our feet were drawn towards the voice. The girls fled from our presence but the voice stayed. Till then only our ears had been bewitched. What we saw bewitched our eyes as well: a young girl clad in diaphanous white, her jet black hair hanging down to her waist, her hands clasping the bough of a tree loaded with mangoes—exposing her chemise bursting outward. She continued to sing as she swayed and regarded us with her large gazelle-like eyes. We stood rooted to the earth a few footsteps from this apparition of matchless beauty. The girl leapt up, plucked a mango from the branch and tossed it towards us. It hit us on our heart and we felt we had been struck by lightning. Then the girl turned and ran away into the palace. 'Allah be praised!' we exclaimed. 'Is that a mortal or a *houri* from paradise!' One of our companions who had joined us replied. 'Sire! Allah forgive me if I am wrong but that could be no other than your aunt's slave, Hira Bai. Her fame as the comeliest of women and a nightingale amongst singers is the talk of the Deccan.' We tarried for a while to recover our composure. But when we paid our respects to our *mausi* (mother's sister) Saliha Bano, she could read our misfortune in our countenance and in the confusion of words in which we addressed her. We implored her assistance to give us our heart's desire. 'Take all the women of my harem and in return give me Hira Bai,' we beseeched her. Saliha Bano said she would do anything, even sacrifice her life for us but was afraid of what her husband Saif Khan, governor of Burhanpur (who was notorious for his ungovernable temper), might say. Our friend and companion, Murshid Quli Khan, undertook to murder Saif Khan. But we restrained him from acting against the shariat law. Instead Murshid simply went to Saif Khan and put our proposal as bluntly as he could. Saif Khan pondered the matter and then informed our aunt that he would exchange Hira Bai for one of our slaves, Chattar Bai.

It was thus that Hira Bai was brought in a palanquin to our harem. For many months we thought of nothing but her and sought no company save hers. From her hand we even took a cup of wine which had hitherto been an abomination to us—and would have as gladly sipped it even if it had been deadly poison. She herself forbade us to do so. Stories of our infatuation were carried by tale-bearers to Dara who further poisoned our father's ears against us. He was reported to have told the Emperor: 'See the piety and abstinence of that hypocritical knave! He has gone to the dogs for the sake of a wench of his aunt's household.'

Allah in His infinite wisdom decided that we were straying from the path of duty and took Hira Bai from us. We buried her in Aurangabad beside a tank full of our tears.

Our father was given to lending his ear to gossip and the prattle of soothsayers. It was narrated to us that once an impostor who passed for a holy man gave His Majesty two apples and said that as long as the smell of the fruits remained on his hands no illness that afflicted him would take a fatal course. When asked which of his sons would destroy his dynasty the knave is said to have replied, 'Aurangeb.' We who had kissed our father's hands many times never detected the smell of apples on them. And far from destroying the kingdom, we extended its domains beyond the furthest limits known to our forefathers. Nevertheless our father's mind was poisoned against us; it was reported to us that to mock our fair complexion and our character he had described us as 'a white snake'.

An incident confirmed our suspicions. One evening Jahanara Begum, while carrying a candle to her bedchamber, stumbled and let the flame touch her muslin garments. She suffered grievous burns; two maidservants who took her in their embrace to smother the fire were burned to death. Dara Shikoh delayed sending the news to us. Consequently, it was only after a month that we were able to reach Agra. His Majesty was out of countenance with us and relieved us of the governorship. All our explanations were ignored. Ultimately we wrote in anguish: *If His Majesty wishes that of all his servants I alone should pass my life in dishonour and at last perish in an unbecoming manner, I have no recourse but to obey . . . . Ten years ago I realized this fact; I knew my life was a target.*

Later the same year Dara Shikoh invited us to his palace by the river Jamna. Having been slighted by him many times we preferred to keep our distance from him by staying near the entrance, whereupon he incited the emperor to rebuke us about the necessity of keeping our rank. We were forbidden from attending court for seven months.

This was only one among many such incidents. The emperor put us away as if we were not of his seed. To our brothers and their sons he sent presents of gold and jewellery on their birthdays; never to us or our children. Recommendations we made for promoting loyal servants were turned down. We were accused of misappropriating the wealth of Golconda which had fallen into our hands and even of eating Deccani mangoes meant for the emperor's table. It was reported to us that, while on a visit to Delhi, the emperor had recognized Dara as the future King of Hindustan. He appeared in the darbar wearing a robe of honour conferred by the emperor and sat on a gold chair placed beside the peacock throne. If Dara is speaking the truth, which is seldom, His Majesty apparently said to him: 'My child, I have made up my mind not to do any important business or decide on any great undertaking henceforth without your knowledge and without consulting you first . . . . I cannot sufficiently thank Allah for blessing me with a son like you.'

As we have said before, and will say a hundred times, we had no desire for power or kingship. But, as our teachers had often reminded us, since Allah in His wisdom had given us birth in a dynasty of kings, it was our duty to serve humanity and to spread Islam by making mankind bear witness to the true faith. Gilani Sahib used to say that Hindustan was like a piece of bread given by the Bestower of Gifts to our ancestors Taimur, Babar, Humayun, Akbar, Jahangir and Shah Jahan. He used to impress upon us that though Allah was bountiful, it was the duty of those who received his bounty to extend the domain of Islam. 'Make the best of life,' he said, 'but remember it is transitory: only the name of Allah is immortal.'

> *When in the garden enjoy every moment,*
> *Every moment of every day.*
> *Spring passes into summer, summer into autumn,*
> *And the flowers of henna*
> *Shall wither away.*

While Dara Shikoh clung to his father's apron at Delhi and Agra, we administered the Deccan, restored order in Balkh, Badakshan, Kandahar and Multan. We measured swords against the misguided Persians. We were continuously on the move from one field of battle to another. The only part of our life which never changed was the routine of our devotions. It mattered not to us where we were or how critical the battle, as soon as it was time for prayer we put aside our weapons and turned our face towards Mecca to pay homage to our Maker.

Misguided historians have written many falsehoods about the way we came to acquire sovereignty over Hindustan while our father Emperor Shah Jahan was still alive. They have maligned our name as a scheming self-seeker and a plotter. They forget that the holy book says: 'God is the best of plotters.' We were but the instrument of His design.

The stars and saints had foretold the shape of things to come. Our agent in the court of our father had informed us that once the emperor had asked a saint, who could read the book of future events, which of his four sons would sit on the peacock throne. The saint asked him the names of his sons.

'Dara Shikoh is the eldest,' replied the emperor.

'His fate will be the same as of his namesake Darius who fell to Alexander.'

'Shuja is the second.'

'Though his name means 'fearless', he is not without fear.'

'Murad is our youngest.' (His majesty, as was his wont, often overlooked our existence).

'Though his name means ambition, he will not achieve it.'

'Then there is Aurangzeb.'

'He has been justly named for he alone is fit for the throne. Wisdom and fortune are closely connected to each other. He who lacks wisdom will have no fortune either.'

We were in Burhanpur when we received the news that His Majesty had been taken ill on 6 September 1657. Our agent in Shahjahanabad sent us a message in code saying that His Majesty had been unable to pass motions or urine for several days and the physicians attending on him despaired of his ruling Hindustan for much longer.

We instructed or agent to keep us posted on His Majesty's state of health and at the same time ordered our agents in the courts of our brothers to keep us informed of every move they made. In our letter praying for his speedy recovery, we sought His Majesty's permission to attend on him at Delhi.

His Majesty sent us a very curt note to say that rumour-mongers had exaggerated a minor stomach upset; that he was in perfect health and proceeding to Agra. At the same time our agent in Delhi informed us that the royal hakeem, on being given a handful of gold mohurs, had expressed the opinion that unless Allah performed a miracle His Majesty's sojourn in this troublesome world might soon be over. Our dear sister Roshanara

Begum, who was in attendance on His Majesty, also sent us a cryptic message hinting at the machinations of our brothers and wishing us success.

We advised our brothers Shuja and Murad to behave in a manner becoming of the descendants of Taimur and Babar. They did not heed our counsel. First Shuja, who was in Bengal, proclaimed himself Emperor with the title Abul Fauz Nasiruddin Mohammed Taimur III, Alexander II, Shah Shuja Bandar Ghazi. A few weeks later Murad, who was in Gujarat, proclaimed himself monarch of Hindustan with the title Maruwwajuddin and asked us to join him in the march to Agra. Being unable to govern his hot temper he soiled his hands by murdering his minister, Ali Naqvi, on suspicion of conspiring with Dara Shikoh. Our agent in Agra sent us news that Dara Shikoh had already made himself master of the Red Fort where His Majesty was convalescing and had opened negotiations with the infidel Rajputs to help him become the Emperor of Hindustan.

We pondered the matter for many days. We could not believe our brothers would behave in this unseemly manner. Dara Shikoh's pretensions disturbed us most. If he became king, the empire of Hindustan would cease to be Dar-ul-Islam and the work of our Mughal forefathers, and the Afghan and Turki monarchs before them, would come to nought.

There was another matter which caused much disturbance in our mind: the viciousness of sibling rivalry. We knew that kingship knows no kinship. No bridge of affection spans the abyss that separates a monarch from his sons; no bonds of affection exist between the sons of kings. Sired though they may have been by the same loins, lain in succession in the same womb and suckled the same breasts, no sooner are they old enough to know the world than they understand that they must destroy their siblings or be destroyed themselves.

Since the Mughals had ruled over a domain larger than that ruled by any other dynasty in the world, it was the Mughals who had spilt more royal blood than any other succession of monarchs. Our great ancestor Zahiruddin Babar had laid the foundation stone of the empire in Hindustan in 1526. His two sons, Humayun and Kamran, had then drawn their swords against each other. Allah had granted the throne to Humayun and so he took the light out of the eyes of his brother and sent him off to Mecca to die. When Akbar succeeded Humayun he disposed of Kamran's only son. Likewise Emperor Akbar's reign was disturbed by the revolt of his beloved son Salim Jahangir—who in his turn had to keep his own impatient son Khusrau in confinement. The same fate had befallen our father who had also to suffer his sons Dara Shikoh and ourselves being taken hostage. When Allah bestowed the empire of Hindustan on our father, he was compelled to remove his own brothers Dawar Baksh and Shahryar along with their male progeny. Truly does the prophet Jeremiah say: 'Fathers have eaten sour grapes and the children's teeth are on edge.'

Only one of us four brothers could sit on the peacock throne; for the other three it had to be the scaffold. The Hindvis summed it up in an aphorism: *taj ya takhta* (the crown or the gibbet). A kingdom is like a scabbard which can hold only one sword at a time

The ambition to be Emperor of Hindustan possessed Dara Shikoh like a fever; his ambition had been fed by assurances given to him by a mad charlatan, Sarmad, who went about the streets of Delhi without as much as a loin-cloth to clothe his nakedness. This Sarmad had proclaimed that Dara would be King of India.

Allah who knows the innermost secrets of our hearts knew that we had no thought of royalty when we responded to Murad's request to join him on the march to Agra. Our only aim was to save the empire from falling into the hands of an enemy of Islam like Dara Shikoh.

Soon our worst fears were confirmed. The infidel Rajputs aligned themselves on the side of Dara Shikoh. His son Sulaiman Shikoh and the Rajput Jai Singh defeated Shuja near Benares. He sent another Rajput, Jaswant Singh of Jodhpur, against us and Murad. We routed his army and proceeded apace towards our goal. Dara Shikoh met us at Samugarh, ten miles from Agra. Once more our swords were crowned with success. While we gave our thanks to the Granter of Victories, Murad, as was his wont, took the daughter of the grape to bed and remained drunk for many days.

Even in the flush of victory we penned respectful words to our father, the Emperor: 'Obedience was my passion as long as power was vested in your venerable hands, and I never went beyond my limit, for which the all-knowing Allah is my witness. But owing to your Majesty's illness Prince Dara Shikoh, usurping all authority and bent upon propagating the religion of the Hindus and idolaters and suppressing the faith of the prophet, had brought chaos and anarchy throughout the empire. Consequently I started from Burhanpur lest I should be held responsible in the next world for not providing a remedy for disorders.'

Our victorious armies arrived at Agra. Dara fled. Then Jahanara Begum sent us a note of remonstrance saying: 'Your armed advance is an act of war against your father. Even if it is directed against Dara is it no less sinful, since the eldest brother both by common law and common usage stands in the position of the father.' We felt it was time to kill the serpent of falsehood with the staff of truth. 'Dara is doing everything to ruin his younger brothers. Witness how he has crushed Shuja already,' we wrote in reply. 'He has poisoned the Emperor's ears against us.'

His Majesty, though old and sick, continued to weave the net of intrigue against us. He sent us gifts including the famous sword *Alamgir* and invited us to visit him in the fort. He flattered us for our piety and addressed us as 'His Holiness'. Our spies warned that preparations were afoot to have the women of the harem assassinate us as soon as we set foot in the palace. We refused to walk into the trap laid for us and cut off the water channel that ran from the river into the fort. In his next communication, His Majesty pleaded for our sympathy: 'Why should I complain of the unkindness of fortune, seeing that not a leaf is shed by a tree without the will of Allah? Only yesterday I was master of nine lakh troops, and today I am in need of a pitcher of water! Praise be to the Hindus who offer water to their dead, while my devout Muslim son refuses water to the living!'

We ordered water to be sent to His Majesty but declined to call upon him till we were assured of our safety. When on 8 June 1658 the gates of the Red Fort were thrown open to us, we beseeched the emperor and Jahanara Begum to move into the palace with their retinue and ordered our trusted eunuch Etabar Khan (aptly named by its parents) to allow no one save our beloved sister Roshanara Begum to come and go whenever it pleased her.

Then we decided to go in pursuit of Dara Shikoh who had fled to Delhi. But we first had to deal with Murad. After the victories that Allah had granted us, he had lost his balance of mind. In his camp there was nothing but music, dancing, win-bibbing and revelry. It became clear as daylight that if the reins of the empire were left in Murad's hands, the empire's chariot would soon be wrecked. We decided to let Murad retire to a place where he could drink and carouse to his heart's desire without any harm to the empire of the Mughals.

We also heard reports that while in his cups Murad not only foolishly boasted of having won the victories that Allah had bestowed upon us but had also confided to his drinking companions that after finishing with Dara and Shuja he would turn his attention to us. We did not allow such impious thoughts which poisoned our ears to poison our heart but resolved thereafter not to be misled by Murad's professions of affection and kept a watch on his actions.

We awaited Murad at Mathura, a city regarded as holy by the Hindus. When he arrived we invited him to our tent, and with our own hands offered him a cup of wine which we, as a pious Muslim, heartily abominated. Murad drank many cups. Slave girls in our employ massaged his besotted limbs and divested him of his weapons. On a sign made by us, the girls put gold handcuffs on his hands and feet. We ordered that he be given generous libations of opium and wine for as long as he lived. Then we proceeded on our march. We arrived in Delhi and took the management of the city's affairs in our hands.

Dara fled before our victorious army leaving the entire country at our feet. With our father too old and too ill to bear the burden of the empire and our brothers having proved inept we were compelled to overrule our hearts desire to retire to a hermitage and instead forced to take upon us the crown of thorns which adorns the heads of kings. This we did (after consulting astrologers) on 21 July 1658. We received felicitations from monarchs of distant lands: Iran, Bokhara, Mecca and Ethiopia.

It took us another year to remove the thorn of Dara from our side. Our troops pursued him through the Punjab, Rajasthan, Gujarat and in a skirmish at Seorai scattered his following as the breeze of autumn scatters dead leaves. Dara was finally captured trying to flee to Afghanistan. A few weeks after the celebrations of our first anniversary as King of Hindustan had ended, our loyal servant Malik Jeewan brought him, his sons and entourage in chains to Delhi.

We consulted the ulema. With one voice they replied that by the holy law the punishment for heresy was death. Our dear sister, Roshanara, equally related to Dara as she was to us, expressed the same opinion. Dara Shikoh begged us to pardon him.

'My brother and my king,' he wrote to us,' my execution is an unnecessary preoccupation for your lofty mind. Grant me a house to live in, and a maid from my former retinue to attend to my needs, and I will devote my life in retreat to praying for your good.'

We did not wish to enter into controversy with Dara Shikoh. At the bottom of his petition for pardon we appended one line in Arabic: 'You usurped authority and you were seditious.'

The fate of Dara Shikoh excited the passions of the misguided citizens of Delhi. They wept in sympathy with him and pelted the loyal Malik Jeewan who had brought him to justice with pots full of urine and excreta. Though our heart was heavy with sorrow we again reminded ourselves that kingship knows no kinship and signed the warrant of death. He was separated from his son Siphir Shikoh and executed on the evening of 30 August 1659. His severed head was brought to us in the Red Fort for inspection. The next morning his headless body was paraded through the streets of Delhi before being interred in a vault of the tomb of our great, great-grandsire, Emperor Humayun.

Dara's son, Sulaiman Shikoh, who had fled into the mountains was likewise apprehended and brought in irons to Delhi. On the morning of 5 January 1661, he was led to our presence in the Diwan-i-Khas. We had not seen him for many years and were struck by his handsome and manly bearing. We had to remind ourselves that though the skin of the serpent may be beautiful, within it there is deadly poison. We explained to him the enormity of the crimes committed by his father and himself and ordered him to be sent to prison in Gwalior fort where he was executed.

We had yet to deal with the charlatan Sarmad who had falsely prophesied the crown to Dara Shikoh. Apart from going about naked in front of men and women alike his attachment to a Hindu boy had become scandalous. Although professing Islam, he was reported to have used expressions lowering the dignity of the Prophet. We summoned him to our presence and questioned him about his prophecy. The villain had the audacity to reply: 'God hath given him (Dara) eternal sovereignty!' We further asked him if it was true that he only recited half the *kalima*—'There is no God but Allah'—leaving out 'and Mohammed is His Prophet'. He replied:

> *The Mullahs say, Mohammed rose to the skies*
> *But I say, 'God came to him'—the rest is lies!*

Sarmad juggled with words: 'I am absorbed in the negative and hence have not yet arrived at the positive.' Questioned about his nakedness, he replied that the Prophet Isaiah also went about naked. We ordered him to be executed in front of the steps of the Royal Mosque in full view of the populace. It was later reported to us that his severed head acknowledged the truth by reciting the entire *kalima*.

While our father lived we decided to stay away from Agra. We had a small mosque built besides the Diwan-i-Khas so that we did not have to disturb the prayers of other Mussalmans by the screen that was provided for kings. It took us five years to complete it and we gave it the name Moti Masjid—because it did indeed look like a pearl without blemish. We spent many hours in this mosque praying and telling the beads of our rosary.

It was not written in the tablet of our fate to see our father. For many months he kept sending us letters accusing us of conduct unbecoming of a son and wickedness towards our brothers. We thought it was time to state the bitter truth. Our father, despite his predicament and his grey beard, was reported to be indulging himself in wine and carousal. 'Kingship means protection of the realm and guardianship of the people, not the enjoyment of bodily repose or lusts of the flesh,' we wrote. We also reminded him that after the way he had disposed of his collaterals when he ascended the throne, it did not befit him to point an accusing finger at us or threaten us with the wrath of Allah. To put an end to this pointless dialogue we wrote: 'If God had not approved of my enterprise, how could I have gained victories which are only the gift of God?'

In January 1666, our father was taken ill and at his desire his bed was placed in the octagonal Jasmine Tower from which he could gaze on the Taj Mahal. On the evening of the 22 January 1666, with the name of Allah on his lips, he passed out of this world into paradise.

Urgent affairs of state kept us in Delhi for two weeks. Then, as soon as we were able, we repaired to Agra and with our tears washed the sacred earth in which our parents were laid.

It was not till two years after our father had been summoned to paradise that we first took our seat on the peacock throne. We then felt we should fulfil the mission that we had been charged with by Allah. We ordered our commanders Mir Jumla, Shaista Khan and others to extend the domains of Islam to the furthermost corners of Hindustan. Our victorious armies marched eastwards to Chatgaon, northwards over the mountains to Tibet, westwards beyond Kabul and southwards beyond Karnatak. In turn we crushed the Jats, the Rajputs, mischievous sects of the Satnamis and Nanak Prasthas who had raised their heads against us. We ravaged the lands of the wily Marathas and forced their leader, Shiva, to pay homage to us. We levelled temples of idolatry to dust and raised mosques on their ruins. We imposed the jazia tax on non-believers to induce them to tread the righteous path. In everything we did, our only guide was the holy law of the shariat. We forbade the distillation of liquor and severely punished those we suspected to be under its influence. It was a common saying that when we ascended the throne there were only two men in all Hindustan, ourselves and the chief qazi, who did not drink. Within a few years we made drink a rarity. Since drinking was often indulged in to the accompaniment of dancing and singing, we forbade them too. We forced prostitutes and dancing girls to marry or leave our empire. Once when musicians and singers carried fake biers of corpses of music and dance, and accosted us as we were going for our Friday prayers, we told them to bury the corpses so deep that they would never rise again. Our Mussalman subjects were happy with our ordinances and acclaimed us as *Zinda Peer* (a Living Saint.)

We waged a ceaseless war against the infidel. wherever he raised his serpentine hood we crushed it under foot. Most of our later years were spent in the Deccan contending with the mountain rats that Shiva had bred. We caught his son Sambha and sent him to eternal damnation. However, we realized that the land would not be purged of idolatry in our lifetime and exhorted our sons to keep up the crusade.

Other kings would have treated the state treasury as their

personal property and wasted it in extravagant living, women, wine, jewels and monuments. We looked upon ourselves as God's chosen custodian to use it for the good of the people. On ourselves we spent no more than the poorest of our subjects. We sewed prayer caps and made copies of the holy Quran: whatever we got for them in the market we spent on our food and personal raiment. How many monarchs who ruled empires as large as ours could claim to have lived like dervishes as we had done?

We had only three sisters left in our world. Roshanara, who had been closest to us, had of late shown indifference to our wishes and had been indiscreet in her behaviour towards strangers. Before we could fully remonstrate with her, Allah summoned her to His court. She had in her lifetime designed her own resting place. She used to spend many evenings in this garden and had a variety of exotic, fragrance-emitting shrubs planted alongside water channels and tanks. She had desired that her tomb should have the sky as its vault so that the dew and the rain that Allah sent down could refresh her remains. Her wishes were carried out.

We turned to Jahanara Begum and pleaded that now that people who had come between us had gone, she should show us the affection due from an elder sister to her brother. On the anniversary of our coronation we presented her with 1,00,000 gold pieces, fixed a pension of 1,700,000 rupees and invested her with the title of *Padshah* Begum. She agreed to share our loneliness and guide us with her counsel. When she was summoned by Allah we commanded that in all historical documents she should be referred to as *Sahibat-uz-Zamani*, because she was indeed the mistress of the age. In accordance with her wishes, she was buried near the tomb of Hazrat Nizamuddin Auliya. On the tombstone we had inscribed a Persian couplet she had composed:

> Let green only conceal my grave:
> Grass is the best covering for the tomb of the meek.

In the spring of the year AD 1706 when the last of our brothers and sisters, Gauhar Ara Begum, was summoned by Allah to His presence we knew it was our turn to fold up our prayer mat. We were in Ahmednagar when our health began to deteriorate. We realized that Ahmednagar was to be the end of our travels. Our beloved daughter Zeenat-un-Nissa, to whom Allah had given the gift of prayer (which she had translated into a large mosque in Delhi) and our ageing wife Udaipuri Begum ministered to our needs. A hundred hakeems felt our pulse every day; but what can mortals and medicaments do against Allah's decrees? We divided our time between re-reading the tablet of our deeds in our mortal's existence of ninety lunar years, and of what rewards and penalties awaited us on the day of judgement.

What now sorrowed us most was the treacherous path taken by the progeny of our own loins. Mohammad Sultan had earlier blackened his face by joining his uncle Shuja against us, and now Akbar went over to the infidels. Azam, to whom we had given Dara's daughter as wife, turned out to be a worthless braggart. We had to put him in prison for a year to keep him away from wine and to teach him to govern his temper. Our youngest, Kam Baksh, had neither ambition nor competence, but of all the slights that our children had aimed at us, none hurt us more than the conduct of our gifted daughter Zebu-un-Nissa to whom Allah had given the gift of poetry (she composed verse under the pseudonym 'Makfhi'). She encouraged her brother Akbar to carry on treasonable conduct against us and with a heavy heart we were constrained to order her to be detained in Salimgarh fort. She aimed her last barbed shaft at us:

> *I have experienced such cruelty and harshness in this land of*
> > *Hind,*
> *I shall go and make myself a home in some other country.*

Saying which she went to the land of the dead.

We had reposed faith in our eldest-born, Muazzam. Even he betrayed our trust during our victorious campaigns against Bijapur and Golconda by treating with the enemy. We did not let our affection stand in the way of justice and had him put in prison and forbade him to either cut his hair or pare his nails or drink anything except water. We kept him in confinement for seven full years.

Came the summer of 1705. As we camped in village Devpur, on the banks of the river Krishna, a severe fever seized us. In our delirium we recited a quatrain of Shaikh Ganja:

> *When you have counted eighty years and more,*
> *Time and Fate will batter at your door;*
> *But if you should survive to be a hundred,*
> *Your life will be death to the very core.*

A nobleman attending our sickbed added the last lines:

> *In such a state lift up your heart: remember*
> *The thought of God lights up a dying ember.*

We had little will to tarry longer in the world and the succession of fevers that ravaged us confirmed our hope that before long Allah would summon us. In one of these feverish bouts we composed another couplet:

> *A moment, a minute, a breath can deform,*
> *And the shape of the world assumes a new form.*

We thought it proper to address words of counsel to our errant sons. To Azam we wrote: 'I came alone and I go as a stranger. I do not know who I am, nor what I have been doing. The instant which has passed in power has left only sorrow behind it. I have not been the guardian and protector of the empire. Life, so valuable, has been squandered in vain. God was in my heart, but I could not see Him. Life is transient, the past is gone and there is no hope for the future . . . .I fear for my salvation, I fear my punishment. I believe in God's bounty and mercy, but I am afraid because of what I have done . . . .'

And to Kam Baksh: 'Soul of my soul . . . .I am going alone. I grieve for your helplessness; but what is the use? Every torment I have inflicted, every sin I have committed, every wrong I have done, I carry its consequences with me. Strange that I came into the world with nothing, and now I am going away with this stupendous caravan of sin! Wherever I look, I see only God . . . . I have sinned terribly and I do not know what punishment awaits me . . . .'

These were not words written by an old man who feared death

when he knew his end to be near but who feared that he was taking leave of life without fulfilling his mission. We saw the infidel Marathas, Rajputs, Jats and Sikhs rising in arms all over Hindustan. And we saw how feeble of mind and purpose were the progeny we were leaving behind. We knew that after we were gone the empire of the Mughals founded by Babar would begin to totter to its fall and only tumult remain: *Azma hama fasad baki.*

We had already chosen our place of rest, a simple, unadorned grave in the courtyard of the tomb of the saintly Shaikh Zainuddin at the foot of Daulatabad fort.

We knew our end was near. Our companions also understood that the time for farewell was nigh. They asked us if we would give away our elephants and diamonds in charity to ward off the final hour. Our tongue had lost its speech but we scribbled on a piece of paper that such practices were not becoming to Muslims. 'Give all you want out of the treasury to the poor. And build no mausoleums over my body,' we wrote. 'And carry this creature of dust quickly to the first burial place and consign him to the earth without any useless coffin.'

Bhagmati

All my life I have been tormented by ghosts. Since Delhi has more ghosts than any other city in the world, life in Delhi can be one long nightmare. I have never seen a ghost nor do I believe they exist. Nevertheless for me they are real. I have tried to overcome this 'ghostophobia' by exposing myself to the dying and the dead, visiting cremation grounds and graveyards. It has not helped very much. I come back feeling at peace with myself and imagine that I have exorcised the fear. But no sooner does the day begin to die, than spirits of the dead come alive. Doors open by themselves, curtains rustle without any breeze and I feel the invisible presence of dead people around me. The only one to whom I have confessed these fears is Bhagmati because she believes in ghosts. She is not sympathetic. She laughs and calls me *baccha* (child) and adds, 'When I die, I will come to lie with you. Then you will be free of this childish fear. But if I catch you making love to someone else, I will never let you have one night of sleep.' (She has not yet forgiven me for fucking Kamala, the Brigadier's wife. But Kamala is gone now with her husband to a family posting so Bhagmati is no longer as angry with me!).

Of the many encounters I have had with ghosts, there is one I can never forget. This was some years ago. I was rung up and told that my uncle was very sick and I should see him before he died. This uncle had been dying for many years. Asthma had reduced him to a bearded skeleton with large, fiery eyes. He had been a kind of living ghost for a long time and something told me I should keep away from his bedside. But my morbid fascination with death, and wailing over the dead, made me ignore my inner promptings and so presently I found myself in a room full of solicitous relatives seated round the sick man's bed. Some were praying, others whispering to each other. He was reclining against a bolster with his head tucked between his knees. His wife sat beside him holding a spittoon full of phlegm. He began to cough—a long never-ending cough—then raised his head. His wife held the spittoon under his chin and yellow, pus-like phlegm drooled down his black beard into the receptacle. The wife wiped his beard with a towel and told him I had come to see him. He fixed his large eyes on me without a trace of recognition. Then he lowered his head between his knees. A minute later he fell sideways with his eyes and mouth wide open. He was dead.

My aunt slapped her forehead with both her hands and screamed, '*Hai*! I am dead! People, I have become a widow!' She smashed her glass bangles against the bedpost. Others came crowding round to comfort her. Someone closed the dead man's eyes and mouth, tied a band round his chin and stuffed wads of cotton in his nostrils. The wailing continued for some time followed by the loud chanting of prayer: 'There is One God. He is the Supreme truth,' etc. etc.

It was monsoon time and the sky was clouded. But I dared not sleep alone in my apartment. I had no means of locating Bhagmati and persuading her to spend the night with me. I asked Budh Singh to put my bed out on the lawn behind my apartment as the air-conditioner was out of order. The lawn was overlooked by other apartments and the comforting sound of human voices and lights from the servants' quarters drifted down to it. I fixed a mosquito net and lay down in the gauzy security it provided.

Despite all these measures I could not shut my eyes. Whichever way I tried I could see the dead uncle's eyes staring at me. The lights went out one by one. The human voices faded into an eerie silence. A grey moonlight spread over the sky. Owls screeched in the mulberry tree. I saw one flit across, dart down on to the road and carry off a mouse Of their own volition my eyes had closed and I was re-living the scene of the death in the morning. The dead man came alive. With measured steps he walked across the lawn towards me, parted the flaps of my mosquito net and brought his face close to mine. I was petrified with terror. I lost my voice. Then a gurgle rose in my throat and burst out into a loud moan. The dead man shook me by the shoulder and exclaimed, '*Wah Guru! Wah Guru!* It's only I, Budh Singh. It has begun to rain. Let me take your bed inside.'

I was bathed in a cold sweat. I saw the lights go up in the neighbouring apartment. A voice asked: 'What's the matter?' Budh Singh answered for me: 'Nothing! He was having a nightmare.'

I went indoors, switched on the lights in all the rooms and told Budh Singh to go. I sank down in my armchair and began a silent argument with myself. I felt very foolish. I had made an ass of myself. Now Budh Singh would tell everyone how his sixty-year-old master had behaved like a frightened child.

I resolved to get the better of this stupid, irrational phobia. It was 3.30 a.m. I got into my trousers and walked out into the drizzle, determined to take the dead in my stride. I strolled down the deserted road to Lodhi Park. It had many tombs. I would sit on them I decided and say 'hullo' to the chaps lying buried underneath.

First I called on Mohammad Shah, the third ruler of the Sayyid dynasty who died in 1444. Big, octagonal-shaped mausoleum on a high plinth. I told him he had no business to be there because the park belonged to the Lodhis. He didn't say anything but the bats in the dome replied: 'He came here first; the Lodhis came later. And that fellow Sikandar Lodhi has even less right to be here because he spent more time in Agra than in Delhi.'

I went out into the drizzle again towards the Bara Gumbad mosque built by Sikandar Lodhi. Beautiful dome! Exactly like the bosom of Kamala, the woman from the south, the land of coconuts: firmly rounded, with its taut nipple poking the sky. I walked round the mosque, sat on a dilapidated grave and examined the Sheesh Gumbad which was a few metres away. Its dome was a little less wanton. The surrounding frills of coloured tiles which looked like lace brassieres in the daytime were not visible in the grey moonlight. From the mosque to Sikandar Lodhi's tomb. My nerve began to fail me. The fellow was buried inside a square garden with high walls. I could not trust myself in the enclosure at night. What if some ghost blocked my exit?

I went up the steps and down again. I tried twice but both times I failed to go further than the entrance. 'Taken as visited,' I assured myself. In any case the fellow didn't like Delhi and I didn't have to bother with him. Besides it was his son Ibrahim Lodhi who let himself be defeated and killed by the Mughal, Babar, at Panipat. So no more honour was due to the Lodhis.

By now the eastern horizon had turned bright and the drongos were announcing the dawn. Early morning walkers were striding over the Athpula bridge. An open-air yoga class had assembled on the grass opposite Bara Gumbad. The living world was awake; the world of the dead had retired for the day.

Nadir Shah

Many years ago, when we shepherded our father's flocks of goats, ate the bread of humility and slept on a couch of sand, we had a dream. We dreamt that from a shepherd we had turned into a fisherman and in our net we had trapped a fish with four horns. A fish, we knew, was the emblem of royalty. We also knew that it was in the nature of an empty stomach to produce illusions of grandeur. Nature provides that a man who slaves all day should spend the hours of the night in a palace full of *houris* whereas a king who wields the sceptre by day should have his sleep disturbed by nightmares of rebellion and assassination. Thus does Allah dispense justice; to one man He gives pleasure by day, misery by night; to another He gives travail from sunrise to sunset, the joys of paradise from sunset to sunrise.

However, the dream remained embedded in our memory. When we became ruler of Isphahan we consulted a seer who had mastered the science of interpreting dreams. A fish, he confirmed, was indeed the emblem of royalty, and its four horns symbolized four kingdoms. In short, Allah had destined us to rule over four domains. We were ruler of Isphahan and had become *Padishah* (Emperor) of Iran. Afghanistan would soon yield to us. What could the fourth kingdom be save Hindustan?

We were besieging the city of Kandahar when we had a second dream. We dreamt that Hazrat Ali Murtaza came to us and with his own blessed hands girdled our waist with the all-conquering sword, Zulfiqar. We pondered this dream. We recalled that when someone had asked him: 'How far is it from the east to the west?'

The Blessed One had replied: 'A day's journey by the sun.'

'Tahmas Quli Khan,' we said to ourselves, 'the road to Delhi beckons you!' And so it came to pass. A few days later we received an invitation to come to Delhi. It was not from Nasiruddin Mohammed Shah, who was then seated on the throne of the Mughals, but from two noblemen of his court—Asaf Jah Nizam-ul-Mulk, who was governor of the Deccan, and Saadath Khan, who was governor of an equally important province eastward of Delhi known as Avadh. The secret manner in which the invitation was delivered to us, and the way it was worded, convinced us that its authors knew the art of impregnating sentences with more than one meaning.We said to ourselves: 'Nadir Shah, you have ruled over men long enough to know the art of striking the heads of serpents with the hand of your foe!'

We use the word 'foe' for the Mughal because he had shown grave discourtesy towards us. He neglected to maintain commerce between his court and ours, was negligent in answering our letters and had even detained our envoys in Delhi. And what could better describe men like Nizam-ul-Mulk and Saadath Khan who, while eating their master's salt, were plotting for his downfall than the vile serpent which crawls on the ground but is ever ready to bite the man who stands above it?

On important matters we deemed it wise not to dilute our judgment by watering it with the advice of lesser men. We dipped the pen of diplomacy in the ink-well of our own interests and had the reply written on the parchment of stratagem. We neither accepted nor rejected the invitation; we only enumerated the difficulties we would encounter on the way to Delhi. The deep defiles of the Sulaiman and Hindu Kush mountains through which we would have to traverse, the warlike tribes of the Afghans and Pathans that we would have to contend with, the ill-will that the subedars of Kabul and Lahore had against us. We ended our epistle with a reference to the powerful army that the Mughal Emperor was said to have under his command. The reply to our letter would tell us whether those who had invited us were conspiring to wield us as a sword in their hands or whether their fount of loyalty had been so poisoned by their sovereign's ill-use that they would become pliable weapons in ours.

We did not have to wait very long for their reply. They not

only pledged assistance to us but also sent us copies of letters they had addressed to other *omarah* advising them to look upon us as their redeemer. They informed us that their monarch, 'His Imperial Majesty Nasiruddin Mohammed Shah employs his time in wine and women . . . . The great heritage of the Mughals is being squandered and may soon pass into the hands of the infidel Marathas.'

Reports of Mohammed Shah's profligacy had come to our ears from other quarters. It had been reported to us that he was seldom without a mistress in one arm and a glass of wine in the hand of the other. He was known as 'Rangeela', the colourful monarch. Although he was said to be well-versed in Persian he had not heeded the admonition of Shaikh Saadi: 'Account as an enemy the passion which is between thy two loins.'

> *He whose wishes you fulfil will obey your orders*
> *But passion when obeyed will forever command.*

We took Kandahar and Ghazni and then the city of Kabul. The whole of Afghanistan, which was nominally a part of the Mughal's domains, yielded to us. We thought it best to address Mohammed Shah in the following words: 'Be it clear to the enlightened mind of Your High Majesty that our coming to Kabul, and possessing it ourselves thereof, was purely out of zeal for Islam and friendship for you. We never could have imagined that the wretches of Deccan (the infidel Marathas) should impose a tribute on the dominions of the King of Mussalmans. Our stay on this side of Attock is with a view, that, when these pagans move towards Delhi, we may send an army of our victorious Qazilbash to drive them to the abyss of hell . . . . History is full of the friendship that has subsisted between the Kings of Iran and Your Majesty's predecessors. By Hazrat Ali Murtaza we swear that excepting friendship and concern for religion we neither had, nor have, any other interest. If you suspect the contrary you may. We always were, and will be, a friend of your illustrious house.'

Mohammed Shah did not reply to our letter. 'Ameen,' we said to ourselves, 'but we will not allow an Islamic kingdom to be despoiled by heathens just because it has the misfortune to be ruled over by a man who thinks that paradise is a garden where fountains spout grape-juice and common harlots are as bewitching as *houris.'*

We sent another letter to Mohammed Shah. In the letter we stated our terms clearly enough to pierce his besotted skull. We told him that we would soon be taking the road to Delhi to put the House of the Mughals in order and to restore the Kingdom of Hindustan to Islam. Our price for so doing would be four crore rupees in silver and the ceding of four northern provinces of the Mughal empire to Iran. Our experience of Mohammed Shah's earlier conduct persuaded us to append a warning. 'We expect a reply within forty days,' we wrote.

Forty days went by. Then the whole year. Not only did we get no answer, but our envoy was not allowed to leave Delhi.

We ordered a general muster. Men were drawn to our ever-victorious standard as moths are drawn to a lamp and they were as willing to sacrifice their lives for us as winged insects are for the love of the flame. There were Quzilbashes and Turks and Georgians, Uzbegs, Afghans, Pathans and Biloches. We enlisted engineers and gunners from Inglistan, France and Italia. Very soon we had 1,25,000 men under our command.

On 6 November 1738, kettle drums were biaten and we started our long march to Delhi. It had already turned cold. In the valleys through which we passed the nights were bitter with frost. The tribes which inhabited the region between Kabul and plains of the Punjab, being robbers by nature, often looted our baggage. We would have liked to have taught them a lesson but the affairs of Hindustan demanded that we quicken our steps.

We arrived at the western mouth of the Khyber. We had been told that this pass was like a trap and that large bands of robbers had assembled on the mountaintops to prey on us. We made a brief halt and joined our men for the *maghreb* prayer. As the sun was about to set we gave orders to strike camp and proceed forward. While the robbers slept in the warmth of their quilts we rode through the fifty miles of the treacherous defile with no light to guide us save that of the stars that twinkled in the clear, cold sky. By the time the robbers were rubbing their eyes to the rising sun we were on the outskirts of the city of Peshawar. We captured Peshawar without any difficulty.

We pressed on. We crossed the broad stream of the Indus after which this country is named and entered the vast champaign of the

Punjab so named after the five (*punj*) rivers (*ab*) that flow through it. The land was flatter than any we had visited, but at that time of the year, not unpleasing to the eye. For many marches the snowcapped hills were visible towards the north and the west. How much more beautiful snows appear at a distance than when one has to wade through them!

The skies were as blue as lapis lazuli; the sun as warm as amethyst. The khaki plains were dotted with oases of green wheat, mustard and sugarcane. There was an abundance of game: partridges, peacocks and herds of deer. Many varieties of waterfowl swarmed over the ponds and rives. We were told that tigers, panthers and leopards were also to be found in plenty. In the middle of these islands of prosperity were villages walled like fortresses. Most of the inhabitants—being Muslim—knew that we had come to save the country from the infidel Marathas and were friendly towards us. For provisions that we took from them we paid in silver and gold. If our men were found taking anything by force we had their heads chopped off; if they molested Indian women we had them castrated and gave their month's wage and their testicles to their victims.

Zakarya Khan, governor of Lahore, made a show of resistance before he came to us with the shawl of submission over his head. He pleaded that he had misunderstood our motives for coming to Hindustan. We knew he was lying. We recalled the saying of Hazrat Ali Murtaza: 'Accept his excuse who seeks your forgiveness,' and allowed him to kiss our feet and offer twenty lakh rupees towards the expenses of our troops.

We spent sixteen days in the pleasant surroundings of Shalimar Gardens, a few miles south of the city. The days began to get longer, the sun began to get warmer. At Shalimar the silk cotton trees burst into large red blossoms. Gardeners said that from the colour of the simbal (that was what the natives called it) one could foretell the heat of the summer to come; the brighter its fiery red the fiercer the sun's rays would be.

Our agents in Delhi informed us that Mohammed Shah had raised a huge army to impede our progress towards Delhi. We ordered our troops to resume march as we realized that if we tarried much longer in Lahore the spring would turn to summer and the heat would become too oppressive for our warriors.

We followed our advance guard till we arrived at the village Tilauri where our tents had been pitched. A few musket shots away the Mughal army was entrenched between the town of Karnal and the canal named after one Ali Mardan Khan.

The next morning we rode out to see the disposition of the enemy's forces. He had indeed come in great strength—upwards of 3,00,000 men. Yet it was apparent that the Mughal was still a baby in the art of war. Despite being twice as numerous as us, and possessed of over 2000 war elephants, thousands of camels mounted with swivels, parks of artillery and innumerable cavalry, he had thrown high breastworks about his forces, and thus deprived himself of the power to strike at us. Allah had verily deprived him of sense and delivered him into our hands!

We ordered our mobile columns to cut off the Mughal's food supplies. Verily has the learned Saadi said: 'When a warrior is full, he will be brave in fight; but if his belly is empty, he will be brave in flight'. We let our enemy go hungry for a few days. When his stomach was empty we struck him at various points to create confusion in his mind. He fired his artillery in all directions without ever hitting us.

On the afternoon of 14 February 1739, driven by hunger, the vast army that the Mughal had collected emerged from its earthworks to give us battle. First a wall of elephants was sent against us. We sent camels loaded with burning naphtha on their backs to meet them. The elephants took fright, turned tail and trampled over their own host. Before the Mughal could restore order in his ranks we sent our cavalry to charge him. Our lion-hunting warriors broke the lines of the enemy. In a two-hour engagement, 20,000 of the enemy were killed and many more taken captive. Among those mortally wounded was Samasmudaulah, regarded as one of the pillars of the Mughal court. This nobleman was also reputed to be a patron of poets. We were truly sorry to hear of his death.

We allowed the dust of defeat to settle on Mohammed Shah's face before agreeing to receive him. And who did he send to plead for him but Asaf Jah Nizam-ul-Mulk, who had invited us to Hindustan! This man had been untrue to his master's salt; but as he had also become the instrument of our designs we bestowed on him a robe of honour and agreed to let Mohammed Shah lay the sword of submission at our victorious feet.

The following day Nasiruddin Mohammed Shah, Emperor of Hindustan, came to our presence. He feared that we might take his life and stopping outside our tent sent a eunuch in with a copy of the Quran as a pledge of our forgiveness. We kissed the Holy Book and asked our dear son, Prince Nasrulla Khan, to bring in the Mughal. Mohammed Shah entered our tent, bowed and placed his sword at our feet. We rose and embraced him. We told him to banish fear from his mind. 'Our policy towards our enemies is open war, not treacherous assassination,' we said.

He did not believe us. When food was laid before him, we saw the veil of suspicion drop over his frightened visage. We took his plate and placed ours before him. We did the same with the goblets of wine. To reassure him further, with our own hands we poured a cup of *kahwa* and handed it to him. Since kindness failed to kindle the flame of friendship in his breast we thought it best to give him some plain words of advice.

'It is strange that you should be so unconcerned and regardless of your affairs that notwithstanding the fact that we wrote you several letters, sent you an ambassador to testify to our friendship, you did not think it proper to send us a satisfactory answer!' We paused for a reply but Mohammed Shah maintained a mute silence. We continued: 'You show no concern for your affairs; when we entered your empire you did not send an envoy to ask who we were, or what our design was! None of your people came with a message or salutation, nay, not even with an answer to our salutation to you!'

We pointed to him the errors he had committed in the conduct of the battle. 'You foolishly cooped yourselves up in your trenches, not considering that you could not remain within barricades without either water or grain. You have seen what has happened!'

The Mughal's head remained lowered in shame. We did not want to leave him with any misgivings of our motives for coming to Hindustan. 'Only your indolence and pride has obliged us to march so far,' we told him. 'We shall not take the empire from you. But we have been put to extraordinary expense; our men, on account of the long marches, are much fatigued, and in want of necessities. We must proceed to Delhi, and remain there for some days until our army is refreshed and the compensation that Asaf

Jah Nizam-ul-Mulk has agreed to is made to us. After that we shall leave you to look after your own affairs.'

Mohammed Shah listened to us without as much as raising his eyes from our feet. We gave him permission to leave. We had it conveyed to him that his Empress, Malika-ul-Zamani, and his son Sultan Ahmed be sent as hostages to our camp.

We proceeded onwards to Delhi with the Mughal King following in our train. When we arrived outside the capital of the Mughals, we detached a posse of Qazilbash cavalry to escort the Mughal king to his palace and prepare the city to receive us.

Our camp was pitched in a suburb called Shalimar where the *omarah* had their pleasure houses amidst the greenery of massive banyan trees whose branches hung down to the earth. Here also were orchards of a fruit called the mango, much relished by the natives. At the time, they were in flower—barely visible clusters of pale green which attracted a pestilence of flies, bees and spiders. The mango tree was also the favourite abode of a black bird of the size of a crow called the koel which screamed incessantly all through the day. Besides mangoes, the orchards had a large number of guavas which were again not in season. How different spring was in our gardens in Khorasan and Meshed! There, when the new leaf burst through the brown of grapevine, the days and nights were filled with the melodious songs of nightingales. We said to ourselves, 'Allah! One day in Iran is worth a hundred in Hindustan.'

The next day we entered the city of the Mughals through the northern gate which opened into Lahori Bazaar. We left most of our army outside the city walls so that no untoward incident between our men and citizens would spoil our sojourn.

We rode through a succession of floral arches with words of welcome in Persian, *Khush Amdeed*, cunningly woven of roses, jasmines and marigolds. From the balconies women in veils showered rose-petals on us. These Hindvis certainly knew the art of flattery! The fragrance of flowers mingled strongly with the sharp smell of asafoetida and garlic which pervaded Lahori Bazaar. We passed a large mosque built, we were told, by one of the begums of Emperor Shah Jahan and named after her: Masjid Fatehpuri.

We turned into a broad street called Chandni Chowk. It had a water channel running in the centre and was lined with trees on either side. When we passed by the jewellers' quarters, known as Jauhari Bazaar, we were presented with a trayload of precious stones. Next we passed a newly built mosque. This, we were told, had been erected by Nawab Roshan-ud-Daulah, the keeper of Mohammed Shah's treasury. Although it was small, its marble and gold spoke eloquently of the wealth of the treasury keeper. (We later learnt that Roshan-ud-Daulah was a notorious bribe-taker. As in Iran, so in Hindustan money-makers were also the builders of mosques).

Immediately following the mosque was the city kotwali, with its jail and execution yard. And next to the kotwali was the flower-sellers' market, Phool-ki-Mandi. Here there were many patterns off floral decorations; the balconies on the opposite sides of the bazaar were linked with strings of garlands, making the bazaar appear like a tunnel of flowers. At the gate of the next bazaar, Dariba, silversmiths presented us with salvers inlaid with precious stones. Some of them were allowed to touch our stirrups before they flung palmful of coins in our name to beggars who abounded in the city. Near the entrance to the fort was Urdu Bazaar, the soldiers' encampment. This had been vacated by the Mughal for our Qazilbash bodyguards.

As we entered the fort, Mughal guns fired a salute in our honour. We were pleased with the reception given to us. By beat of the drum we had it proclaimed that Delhi was under our protection and that as long as the citizens conducted themselves with propriety they could go about their business without fear. We presented robes of honour to Lutfullah Khan, Governor of Delhi, and to the Kotwal, Haji Faulad Khan. We complimented them on the excellent arrangements made by them.

Several places around the Diwan-i-Khas had been prepared for our stay. Here we received princes of the Mughal household and accepted tributes from them. We presented them with robes of honour.

In the evening we watched a display of fireworks on the bank of the river Jamna. It was followed by dancing and singing. Although we felt that our recent victory called for celebration, we did not deem it wise to indulge ourselves in the company of strangers. However, to please our host, Mohammed Shah, we took

a goblet of wine from his hands and accepted a girl, said to be the
most beautiful of her sex in Delhi. Without as much as looking at
her we told her to await our pleasure in our dreamchamber.

Mohammed Shah drank so much wine that he forgot himself
and the guest he was entertaining. He tied bells to his ankles and
joined the nautch girls. He could dance as well as they—with the
same sauciness in his eyes, the same delicacy of movement in his
hands and the same nimbleness of feet. When one of the *omarah*
applauded his performance and said that His Majesty had more to
him than any dancing girl in Hindustan, Mohammed Shah grinned
like an ape and suddenly took out his member from the folds of its
privacy. 'No dancing girl has this!' he boasted as he waved it about.
'A hundred gold coins for anyone who can produce a bigger one.'
We smiled at this foolish exhibition. Encouraged by our smile he
doubled his wager: 'And two hundred for anyone, Turk or Iranian,
who can put it to better use!'

No one deigned to take up his challenge. The foolish man was
emboldened to direct a barbed shaft at us. He quoted Saadi:

> . . .*O little mother of ancient days:*
> *Thou hast cunningly dyed thy hair but consider*
> *That thy bent back will never be straight!*

He turned to his cronies with a meaningful smile. The besotted
sycophants applauded: '*Wah! Wah!*' We knew the allusion was to
us for we had not had the time to dye our beard and its roots
showed the same grey as the hair on our head. The double-faced
Saadath Khan, who only a few hours earlier had been kissing the
ground before our feet, took up the refrain with another quotation:

> *I have heard that in these days a decrepit aged man*
> *Took fancy in his grey head to get a spouse*
> *A beautiful lass, Jewel by name.*
> *And when he had concealed the jewel casket from other men*
> *He tried to perform the feat customary at weddings*
> *But in the first onslaught, the man's organ fell asleep.*
> *He spanned the bow but failed to hit the target.*

We wanted to slap Saadath Khan there and then but decided

to postpone his punishment to another day. However, we did not want these besotted men to get away with the notion that we were not aware of the direction in which they had aimed their poisoned darts. As soon as their laughter subsided, we replied:

A nice face and a gown of gold brocade
A haw of rose, aloes, paint and scent
All these a woman's beauty aid,
But man, his testicles are his real ornament.

They applauded us at the top of their voices: '*Marhaba! Subhan Allah!*'

We dismissed the *mehfil* and retired to the bed prepared for us. No sooner had we reclined on our couch than the slave girl made her bow, took off our shoes and began to massage our feet. After the tiresome journey of many days the sensation was most pleasurable. We placed our legs in her lap and let her press our legs as well. We noticed that she was young and beautiful. 'Girl, what is your name?' we asked.

'Your slave is known as Noor Bai. Can your slave have the honour of presenting a goblet of wine to Your Majesty?'

She looked up at us. What eyes Allah had given her! Larger darker and more limpid than those of a Persian gazelle; and how she could speak with them! She poured wine from a silver decanter into a gold goblet and offered it to us with both her hands. We took it but, as was our wont, put it aside on a table. We never took wine, water or a morsel of food from a stranger's hands. Noor Bai did not press us to drink. 'Do I please Your Majesty?' she asked, digging her forefinger into her cheek and wagging her head.

'Your face is very pleasing to us. Of the rest we have as yet no knowledge,' we replied.

She sensed what we meant. She placed our feet on a footstool and stood up. She unbuckled her trousers and let them drop at her feet. Then she took off her chemise and flung it on the carpet. Overcome by bashfulness she covered her face with both her hands, thus exposing herself completely to our gaze. We had never seen a girl fashioned as she: dark as cinnamon; bosom bursting with wanton impudence, waist so slender that we could enclose it within the palms of our hands. She was small but her buttocks were as large as the melons of Herat.

'Noor Bai, how old are you? Have you known a man before?' we asked her.

She pretended to be shocked. 'How could anyone dare to offer Your Majesty something soiled by another? I was raised for your pleasure. No other man has touched, or ever will touch my body after it has been honoured by Your Majesty.'

She was a child in years but adept in the art of seductive speech. We asked her to draw close to us. We ran our hands over her face and body; firm and smooth as polished walnut without a trace of hair on her limbs, armpits or privates. She had rubbed her body with aromatic oil and exuded the fragrance of jasmine. It occurred to us that our hosts had some design in sending so young and wanton a girl to our bedchamber.

Fifty summers spent in hardship and strife reduces a man's appetite for women. But we were determined to prove to our hosts that the men of Persia are as potent in the harem as they are powerful on the field of battle. We had a snow-white sheet spread over our couch. We ordered Noor Bai to minister to us till our passions were fully roused. She had been well-groomed.

The look of childish curiosity on her face changed to alarm when she saw what we were to present to her. We were gentle with her. She cried in pain and the bedsheet received ample testimony of her virginity and our manliness.

When we had finished, we loaded her naked body with gold ornaments studded with precious stones. We told her she was the most comely woman we had taken to couch. She wiped away her tears and smiled. But when we expressed our wish to take her into our harem, she began to cry again. 'If Your Majesty stays in Delhi, your slave will serve you till her last breath, but if Your Majesty takes me away from Delhi, she will take poison and kill herself,' she said very stubbornly.

We had heard that the people of Delhi loved their city as bees love flowers. But we could not believe that the child of a courtesan would prefer to live in a Delhi brothel rather than in our palace in Iran!

However, we did not wish to converse with the girl nor make her unhappy. We told her to be in attendance on us during our sojourn in her city. Perhaps she would change her mind. Or we, ours.

The next day being Friday we ordered the *khutba* to be read in our name in all the mosques of the city. This would make it as clear as the sun that we had come to Delhi only to restore order in the country of Islam.

In the afternoon we sent for Saadath Khan. He came accompanied by his sons and a cavalcade of retainers. Because he, along with Asaf Jah Nizam-ul-Mulk, had addressed the letters of invitation to us to come to Hindustan and told us of the enormous wealth collected in the vaults of the Red Fort, he presumed a degree of familiarity with us. He also wanted to impress his entourage with his own importance. We felt that we should strip him of his delusions. We said nothing about his behaviour on the night before but reminded him that we had come to Delhi on the assurance that if we saved the empire from the Maratha infidels, they would meet the expenses for the expedition. We told him that his behaviour since our arrival in Delhi gave us the impression that he did not mean to honour his undertaking.

Hazrat Ali Murtaza has rightly said: 'Often a word pierces like a sword and the tongue can have a sharper point than the lance.' So it was with the tongue of anger that we spoke words of admonition. 'Saadath Khan, the army of the defenders of Islam has not been compensated for its sacrifice,' we said bluntly. 'Not one cowrie shell of the four crores promised has so far been given. If an earnest of this sum is not paid by tomorrow sundown, we will make our displeasure known.'

This remonstrance failed to impress its seal on the wax of Saadath's brain. 'What is money to the conquerer of the world!' he said jauntily as he turned to his entourage for approval. 'What is money!' he repeated. 'We will lay down our lives for the Great Nadir!'

His followers applauded his audacity. Our temper rose. 'Come here, Saadath Khan!' we commanded. The silly grin disappeared from his face: his knees shook as he approached us. As he bowed to us we grabbed him by his left ear and pulled him up. 'We do not like this kind of clever talk! We do not like men who break their word!'

Saadath's face first turned red, then yellow. He began to stutter. We boxed his ear and slapped him on his face. As he reeled back we gave him a kick in his belly. 'Get out of our presence!' we roared. 'If we do not get what is due to our army by tomorrow we will have you flogged in front of the kotwali in Chandni Chowk.'

Saadath Khan had to be carried away from our presence. The chastisement proved too much for him. That very night he plunged a dagger in his heart and ended his miserable existence.

The people of Delhi are both ungrateful and cowardly. Instead of thanking us for the trouble we had taken by coming hundreds of miles over mountains, through ravines and desert waste to save them from the infidels, they had the audacity to insinuate that it was not the love of Islam but the love of gold that had brought us to their country.

We were informed that the natives had created a tumult at the Royal Mosque when the Imam was declaiming the *khutba* in our name. Our officers brought reports that our Qazilbash bodyguards had been spat upon in the streets; women had thrown refuse on their heads as they passed below their houses. Grocers and butchers were demanding higher prices from our Iranian soldiers than from their own people. The citizens of Delhi did not appreciate that it was for their safety that we had kept the bulk of our army outside the city. Seeing that there were only a few hundred Iranians in the walled enclosure of Shahjahanabad, the citizens had the effrontery to raise their cowardly eyebrows at us. Thus did they invite the angel of death to visit their city.

On Saturday, 10 March 1739, the sun entered Aries. It was also the holy day of Id-uz-Zuha, commemorating Hazrat Ibrahim's offering of his son, Yusuf, to Allah. Our bodyguards took a few stray bulls and heifers loitering in the streets to offer as sacrifice. The Hindus, who regard all bovine species of animals sacred, were incensed. They refused to sell rice to our men. We ordered our soldiers to buy instead of rice, flour from Muslim dealers. It was then that the perfidy of the Muslims of Delhi was brought to our notice; they trebled the price of wheat flour. Once more we controlled our temper. Had not Hazart Ali Murtaza said: 'Anger is a species of madness'? We fixed the price of wheat at ten seers to the silver rupee and ordered grain depots to be thrown open.

In the afternoon we received reports that our men who had gone to buy provisions at a grain market called Paharganj, a musket shot to the west of Ajmeri Gate, had been assaulted. It was not our habit to lend ear to rumour. We sent a party of seven of our bodyguards to verify the facts. Only three of the seven were able to return; these three bore evidence of violence on their persons. They told us that the leaders of the rabble were two Pathans, Niaz Khan and Sheh Sawar Khan.

These thugs had surrounded a party of our musketeers and burnt them alive. We were told that a large number of our soldiers had been killed and an armed mob led by the villain Niaz Khan was heading towards the Red Fort to try and lay their impious hands upon our person. We went up on the ramparts above Lahori Gate which commanded a view of Urdu Bazaar and Chandni Chowk. We heard sounds of gunfire. We saw a sea of spears, swords and matchlocks flooding Chandni Chowk and the bazaars right up to the Jamia Masjid and surging towards the fort.

Our bodyguards posted in the Urdu Bazaar were valiantly holding their own against this ocean of madness. We sent instructions that they should evacuate Urdu Bazaar and retreat to the sandbank between the river and the eastern wall of the fort. We had a cannon mounted on the Lahori and Delhi Gates which faced west and south and ordered grape to be fired into the rabble. We sent word to the commanders of our troops at Shalimar to send reinforcements immediately and be prepared to march into the city the next morning.

The night was made hideous with the howling of the mob and the roar of cannon. Our peace of mind was further disturbed by the fact that Mohammed Shah made no attempt to apologize for the conduct of his subjects. We received a report that it was being openly said in the bazaars that we had been poisoned by Noor Bai and were on our deathbed. When the Mughal's chamberlain came to call on us we could read in his visage that he had come to see for himself whether mischief had been done to our person. Our mind was made up. We did not allow memories of the earlier evening to sweeten the bitterness that now flooded our soul. We hastened to our bedchamber. We sent for the decanter of wine which had been sent to us earlier and ordered Noor Bai to be brought to our presence.

Noor Bai came swaying her hips and smiling as saucily as the night before. Her eyes did not betray treachery. But as soon as she saw the anger on our face she took fright. She clasped our feet and asked: 'Has your slave been guilty of some misdemeanour?'

If she was a liar she must have been the world's best liar under sixteen years of age. 'Who gave you this decanter of wine?' we demanded. She looked innocently puzzled. 'No one, Your Majesty. It was lying here. I thought it was Your Majesty's favourite wine from Shiraz. Has it upset Your Majesty?' We picked up the decanter, filled a goblet and held it out for her. 'Drink!' we commanded.

A look of fear came in her eyes. She took the goblet from our hands. 'I have never touched wine to my lips.'

'Drink! Or we'll force it down your throat.'

Noor Bai dipped a finger in the goblet and put it on her tongue. She puckered her face in distaste. Then she shut her nostrils with the fingers of one hand and with the other tilted the goblet into her mouth. She brought up some of it and was convulsed by a fit of coughing. Her face became a deep red, she held her throat as if she was choking. 'Your Majesty drinks this poison for pleasure?' she asked us through her tears.

We were not sure whether this wine was the same as the one that had been left in our bedchamber the night before. But since neither we nor Noor Bai had suffered any ill-effect from taking it, we were assured that it had not been tinctured. We asked Noor Bai to draw closer to us. We cupped her face in our hands and looked into her tear-stained eyes.

'Noor Bai, if anyone says anything about us to you or asks you to do something to us, you must tell us. You will have our protection and we will load you with as much gold as you weigh.' She slipped down on the ground and kissed our feet. We placed a necklace of rubies around her neck and dismissed her. We deputed a spy to watch her movements for some days.

On Sunday, we rose earlier than was our practice. We said our *fajar* prayer in Aurangzeb's Pearl Mosque and had a light repast. The commanders of our garrisons had come into the city and awaited our orders. We told them to take positions in front of Lahori Gate.

As the sun rose, Delhi's rabble reassembled in the streets. We saw that the breezes of mischief had roused the populace like a stormy wind rouses the seas to turbulence. We thought that our presence would becalm their senses.

When the sun had risen above the walls of the Red Fort we

rode with our escorts into Chandni Chowk. What we saw there brought tears to our eyes. Many of our faithful comrades lay dead about the streets. Their bodies had been horribly mutilated. The double-faced wretches, who only two days earlier had welcomed us with flowers and tributes of precious metal and stones, now yelled abuse at us. The flower-sellers of Phool-ki-Mandi, who had showered rose-petals over us, now pelted us with clods of mud and stones. We dismounted at Roshan-ud-Daulah's mosque and took our seat on the balcony.

Filth and stones were hurled on us from the balconies of neighbouring houses. Then somebody fired a gun. The bullet whizzed past us and hit our fly-whisk-bearer. The poor man fell on us; his blood poured over our tunic; he expired in our arms with a cry of anguish: '*Ya Allah!*'

We laid our faithful servant on the floor. Our cup of patience was full to the brim. We drew our sword. 'As long as this sword is out of the scabbard the life of every citizen of this wretched city is forfeit. Spare no one,' we ordered.

We saw yet another aspect of the character of the people of Hindustan. They were cunning in the way they had invited us to come to their help. They were double-faced in the way they continued to protest their loyalty to their monarch and to us till they were sure who was going to be victorious. We had seen how timid they were in the field of battle and how abject in the hour of defeat. We had suffered their florid speeches in which they concealed insinuations under a sugar-coating of flattery. We saw how violent they could be when they came in large numbers upon a few unsuspecting soldiers. And now that the angel of death hovered over them they were as supine as a flock of sheep. Our soldiers slew them by the score till their hands were tired.

We left Roshan-ud-Daulah's mosque to return to the Red Fort. While passing the gateway of Dariba we ordered our men to level every home in that accursed street inhabited by the infidels. Our soldiers slew every man, woman and child in Dariba and then set fire to the bazaar. The only parts of Shahjahanabad we spared were the bazaars around Jamia Masjid and Delhi Gate, because Nawab Sarbuland Khan came and pleaded with us that no one from these localities had joined the rioters.

In the afternoon Mohammed Shah craved permission to

present himself. The fire of our anger had by then been dowsed in the river of blood. We allowed him to kiss our feet. He knew the art of stringing words.

'Not a soul has been spared by your avenging sword,' he whined. 'If it be Your Majesty's wish to carry on the work of destruction further, infuse life in the dead and renew the slaughter.'

We had no idea how many had been slaughtered except that for six hours thousands of our brave soldiers had done nothing else but kill. We put our sword back into the scabbard and ordered that our pleasure be announced by beat of the drum.

We did not wish to expose our eyes to the results of the carnage and ordered that the streets be cleansed of blood and corpses. It was a strange coincidence that this day happened to be Holi when infidels celebrate the advent of spring by dowsing each other with red water, the colour of blood! The infidels burnt their dead as was their custom and thus sent them to hell as was their desert. The Muslims buried their slain along the sandbanks of the river. Those that had no one to burn or bury them were disposed of by kites, crows, cats, dogs and jackals that abound in this city.

Although we allowed the sweet breeze of forgiveness to blow over the accursed city, we did not want its citizens to believe that their crimes had been atoned for. We sent our men to enter the homes of the *omarah* and rich merchants and take everything they could find.

Those who remonstrated were brought before us. We had them flogged in front of their kinsmen. The floors of their homes were dug up and their women stripped naked. Many unable to face themselves after the chastisement they had received, ended their miserable existence with their own hands. Gold and silver and precious stones flowed into our treasury as the waters of the Oxus flow into the sea. We sent the good news to Iran with the proclamation that no taxes would be levied on our Iranian subjects for the next three years. For rightly has Hazrat Ali Murtaza said: 'The better part of generosity is speedy giving!'

After all this we found we were out of countenance with ourselves. We dismissed our attendants and told them we wanted to be alone. We sat for many hours taking counsel with ourselves. We had conquered the four kingdoms prophesied for us in our dreams. With the spear of Islam we had pierced the heart of the land of infidels and sent thousands of idolaters to hell; we had served Allah and His Prophet (peace upon Him).

We had amassed wealth and lit the lamp of prosperity in millions of Iranian homes; our sons and their sons up to seven generations could eat their fill and not finish the harvest we had reaped with our sword. The people of Asia stood in awe of our name. All men were eager to follow our banner to wherever we chose to take it. We had the fairest of women in our harem: Caucasians, Turks, Iranis, Arabs, Afghans and Hindvis. Our loins had yielded a host of sturdy sons and comely daughters. We had everything a man could ask for. And yet a strange melancholy pervaded our being.

Noor Bai was ever in our mind. We went over the night she had spent with us. We could not believe she could have wanted to harm us or even let herself be used as an instrument of another's mischievous design. We were not even sure whether any mischief had in fact been contemplated. But our ears had been filled with venomous rumour with Noor Bai's name mixed in it. We clapped our hands and asked the attendant to bring the girl to our presence

Noor Bai washed our feet with her tears. She lay on the carpet and between sobs asked us many times to tell her why we had ever suspected her. We had no reason; so we did not deign to reply. We only gazed at her prostrate form—a waist that curved like a bow and buttocks that would delight those who desired to take their pleasure in them. Our appreciation of her did not kindle any desire in our loins. Besides, by now we knew that although we could command her body, we could not rule her heart.

Once again, to atone for the suspicion we had harboured against her, we slipped a pair of gold bangles on her wrist and told her to leave. She refused to go. She sat with her head between our knees, peering into our face. 'Your Majesty is angry with the world,' she remarked, truthfully reading our disposition. 'It is all the people you have had killed. That was not a good thing to do.'

We were amazed by her boldness. We stroked her head and were suddenly overcome with revulsion against ourselves. We covered our face with our hands to hide the tears that welled up in our eyes, but we could not hold back a sob that convulsed our chest. Noor Bai became bolder and without seeking our permission made herself comfortable on our lap. The unmanly spasm of weakness passed. We gently removed Noor Bai from our middle and asked her to leave us alone. Before she left she made us promise that we would send for Hakeem Alavi Khan of Ballimaran. 'He will apply leeches and remove the angry blood that courses through Your Majesty's frame,' she said.

The next day we sent for Hakeem Alavi Khan who, we were told, had the healing powers of Jesus (upon Whom be peace). He was bent under the weight of years and his long white beard; he walked with the aid of a stick. He had the audacity that old men gain when they know they have not very long to live. He began reprimanding us. 'If you do not learn to control your temper, your temper will control you,' he said.

We agreed we were quick to temper. 'Not only quick to anger, Your Majesty,' retorted the hakeem, 'but dangerously ill-tempered; anger is a species of madness. If not checked, it becomes incurable.' His words were more bitter than his medicines. But after the braying of sycophants and flatterers, this man's blunt speech sounded like the music of the lute. It was from his tongue that we heard of the havoc that had been caused in the city. We tried to explain to him that it was the people of Delhi who had first laid hands on our soldiers and we had but given them freedom to retaliate.

'*La haul valla quwwat!*' exclaimed the old hakeem. 'Retaliate against women and children! Kill innocent people! Is that the kind of justice that prevails in your country?'

We did not take offence but let him speak on. Thereafter we sent for Hakeem Alavi Khan more to hear what he had to say than for his prescriptions. While he had the temerity to bring our shortcomings to our notice, he also gave us aphrodisiacs compounded of crushed pearls and Yemen honey. For although we were in robust health, we felt that the thirty-three ladies in our harem and now the young and ardent Noor Bai might strain our constitution.

We cannot recall whether it was the advice of Hakeem Alavi Khan or the ministrations of Noor Bai that changed our mind. We passed no sentences of death for fifteen days. We began to laugh and joke with our companions. We asked Qazmaruddin Khan, who was Chancellor of the Mughal Exchequer, if it was true that he had 850 women in his harem. When he admitted that it was so, we remarked, 'You should take another hundred-and-fifty and become a *mim-bashi* (commander of one thousand).' People laughed and laughed till tears came into their eyes. The joke was repeated to us many times by many flatterers.

We left the Mughal to his own counsel in the hope that he would have the good sense to make *peshkash* of his own accord. But Mohammed Shah's skull was stuffed with cunning instead of commonsense. He tried to match our patience with guile. He had it conveyed to us that our two households should be linked by a marriage alliance. We gave our consent in the belief that he wanted an excuse to pay his dues in the from of dowry. Consequently our well-beloved son, Prince Nasrulla Mirza, the second fruit of our loins, was betrothed to the daughter of Yezdan Baksh, son of Kam Baksh, son of Emperor Aurangzeb.

On such occasions it is customary among the people of Hindustan to indulge in jest. Women of the Mughal seraglio who were very proud of their lineage asked our son to name his ancestors up to seven forefathers. Prince Nasrulla Mirza became speechless with embarrassment; he knew of the days when all our worldly wealth consisted of a camel and a flock of sheep. His tongue remained locked between his teeth. We intervened on his behalf: 'Son, tell them that you are the son of Nadir Shah, the son of the sword, the grandson of the sword; and so on to seventy instead of seven generations. 'The women responded with '*Ash! Ash! Marhaba!*'

All this was happening only fifteen days after the terrible punishment we had meted out to the citizens of Delhi but they seemed eager to forget it and join the marriage celebrations. The walls of the Red Fort were lit with oil-lamps and there was a grand display of fireworks. There was much drinking and nautch. The *nikah* took place on 26 March 1739 followed by *dawat-i-valima* (a grand feast of consummation). The Mughal made presents to us and our officers. Perhaps he hoped that having given one of his kinswomen to our son he could settle his account with a few trinkets. We decided to teach him a lesson that an Iranian could as easily outwit an Indian in wile as he could outmatch him on the field of battle.

We were informed that there were two very precious things in the possession of the Mughal royal family. One was the *takhi-i-taoos* (the Peacock Throne) made of solid gold, inset with diamonds, rubies and emeralds. It was valued at nine crore rupees. The other was the diamond *Koh-i-Noor* (the Mountain of Light), said to be larger than a pigeon's egg and worth all the world's income for seven days. We ordered a search of the palace vaults but neither the throne nor the diamond could be found.

We questioned Mohammed Shah. He told us that the throne had been broken up nineteen years earlier and that he had never seen the *Koh-i-Noor*. Saadath Khan had however told us that the *Koh-i-Noor* was in the possession of Mohammed Shah. Instead of wearing it on his arm, as was the custom of his predecessors, he hid it in the folds of his turban. We planned a stratagem by which we would acquire this diamond without betraying our desire to have it.

We assembled a darbar where all the Indian *omarah* and our Iranian generals were present. First we explained to Mohammed Shah the duties of a king. Then we escorted him to the marble seat of his ancestors and beckoned to one of our servants to bring a crown we had ordered to be prepared for the occasion. We removed Mohammed Shah's turban and placed the crown on his head.

'May Allah grant you prosperity and long life!' we said. The courtiers applauded. We noticed that Mohammed Shah's eyes hovered round the turban which now lay between us. The speech he made in response seemed as much addressed to us as to his headgear. He said he looked upon us as his elder brother. That made our task easier. As he sat down we rose to our feet and said that we were given to understand that in Hindustan it was customary for men who pledged fraternal friendship towards each other to exchange turbans. We removed the crown from his head and placed our turban in its stead. We bowed our head for him to do likewise. The poor fellow did as he was told. He gave us the *Koh-i-Noor* with his own hands. We embraced him and dismissed the court.

The diamond was indeed in the folds of his turban. It was the size of a hawk's egg and so brilliant that it seemed to have captured soul of the sun in its breast. We made no secret of having acquired it and wore it on our right arm.

By the end of April the sun's rays had become like tongues of flame from the fires of *gehennum*. Our body was covered with prickly heat and despite Hakeem Alavi Khan's sherbets we lost appetite for food and female company. 'Delhi is not the place for you,' said the old hakeem to us. 'Ameen,' we replied. 'A day in Isphahan is worth a lifetime in your country.'

We spoke truly, for though we had heard so much in praise of Delhi there was little that pleased us about it. We did not like the people or their manners; we did not like their food or their wines. Their watermelons were without flavour and produced wind in our stomach. The mango which had been lauded so much we found too sweet for our taste; besides it soiled our hands and beard. And Delhi's climate produced only laziness, prickly heat and bad temper.

We ordered that all that had been taken from the city should be loaded on elephants, camels and asses and preparations made for our return to Iran. We made arrangements for the administration of the country. We attached the four subahs beyond the Indus to our empire but the rest we left to Mohammed Shah and Nizam-ul-Mulk. The king was simple and pleasure-loving; the minister cunning and ambitious. If the arrangement did not work, we would have the right to annex the country.

On Saturday, 5 May 1739, we left the capital city of the Mughals. There were only two people with whom we left some of our heart. One was the sharp-tongued Hakeem Alavi Khan and the other the saucy Noor Bai. An Emperor my command anything within his empire except an honest man and a woman's heart. We could have forced both to accompany us but we knew that the old man would not be able to make the journey and Noor Bai would have cried all the time. We realized that we could take her body with us, but her heart would remain behind in Delhi. And what is a woman's body worth if her heart not be in it!

We loaded the hakeem with presents and gave Noor Bai her weight in gold and bade them and the city of Delhi farewell.

Bhagmati

Bhagmati has just left. I suspect she was not happy with the previous night's love-making. But what am I to do? I am old now. I feel morose. The phone rings. The Tughlak Road police station on the line. 'Am I speaking to Budh Singh's employer?'

'Well, sort of, he is chowkidar of the entire block, I pay him a little extra to keep an eye on my flat. What's the matter? Has he been run over; accident-*shaksidant*?'

'No, he has been molesting women.'

I can believe anything about Budh Singh, but not molesting women. There must be some mistake. If the poor fellow has named me as his employer, I must not let him down. I drive to the police station.

Budh Singh is sitting on the floor of the verandah chained to a policeman who is seated on a chair chewing a betel-leaf. Neither of them take the slightest notice of me. I bend down and ask Budh Singh to tell me what happened. He glowers at me without saying anything. I plead with him to tell me what transpired so I can get him out on bail. 'He's mad,' says the policeman spitting betel phlegm on the floor. Budh Singh slowly turns his head, fixes the constable with a baleful look and mutters: 'You mad! Your mother mad; your sister mad. Who are you to call me mad? *Bahinchod!*'

'I told you he is mad,' says the constable calmly chewing the cud. 'No use talking to him. Go inside and speak to the inspector sahib.'

I go in to the reporting room, tell them what I have come for. The sub-inspector offers me a seat then tells me that Budh Singh has been arrested for 'eve-teasing'. I protest. I tell him that Budh Singh is a man of impeccable character, has never shown any interest in women and so on. But at times something happens to him. I point to my head.

The sub-inspector nods and tells me of Budh's eve-teasing. He was apparently walking along the corridors of Connaught Circus mumbling to himself ('Prayer,' I interject, 'he prays all the time') when he suddenly grabbed a young woman's bosom, pressed it and said *bhawn, bhawn*. Before she could recover from the shock, he grabbed the other bosom and likewise pressed it with a *bhawn, bhawn*. 'Ah yes, poor man! You know he was once a truck-driver in the army; he must have thought they were bulb horns,' I explain. The sub-inspector is more understanding than the women in Connaught Circus. Apparently Budh Singh pressed many other female bulb horns. There was a hue and cry and some students beat him up. That wasn't the end. There was a woman banana-seller with her basket full of bananas sitting on the pavement. Budh Singh examined them and asked the price. He thought they were overpriced and offered to sell his own at a much cheaper rate. And showed it to the banana-seller. The lady did not appreciate the gesture and told Budh Singh to offer it to his mother. What could Budh Singh do? He grabbed the banana-seller's bosoms with both his hands and said *bhawn, bhawn*. Then the police got him. 'He must have been thinking of his trucking days,' I explain again. 'It comes over him once in a while.' The sub-inspector is most kind. They've already beaten Budh Singh. 'That's enough punishment for pressing four bosoms and showing his penis. He did not fuck anyone's mother, did he?' he says. 'But don't let him do it again.'

Meer Taqi Meer

I do not know which I was more, a lover or a poet. Both love and poetry consumed me. An affair of the heart brought me into disrepute; my poetry earned me a name which resounded all over Hindustan. Love brought me anguish; poetry a feeling of ecstasy. What neither love nor poetry brought me was money. Whatever I earned was by stringing garlands of words. Living amongst people who could not tell the difference between a finely cut diamond and a bead of glass, it was more the whims of my patrons than the excellence of my craftsmanship that determined what I had to eat. My father, the saintly Meer Mohammed Ali, once said to me, 'Son, I worry over your future. A fire has been lit in your heart. I fear for what it will do to you.' I was only nine years old and laughed at his words. He had the wisdom of age; he wept because he knew that the fire of love would both make me and destroy me.

One evening after he had said his afternoon prayer, he said to me, '*Beta*, the world changes very fast and there is very little time to catch up with it. The road of life is also very uneven; you must watch your steps. Whatever time you have, devote it to knowing yourself.' I was only ten years old and had plenty of time to do whatever I liked. Also I did not think there was very much about myself that I did not know.

We lived in a hermitage on the outskirts of Akbarabad (Agra). Besides my father's children from his two wives, there was *Chacha* Amanullah who lived with us and like my father spent most of his waking hours in prayer and meditation. When they were not praying or meditating they argued about love. My father said if you love God you love everything created by God. *Chacha* put it the other way round: If you love God's creatures you love God. I could not understand how two old men could go on talking for hours on end about the same thing day after day. It was only later that I understood the kind of love which was on *Chacha* Amanullah's mind. I used to wonder sometimes why when he talked so much about loving God's creatures, he never raised his eyes from the ground when women were around. Then one evening he was taking in the air in an Agra bazaar when he happened to exchange glances with a beautiful boy and fell madly in love with him. After this incident he lost his appetite for food and his peace of mind. A few days later he died pining away for the love of that lad.

Love meant something quite different to my father. Once he told me: 'Son, make love your only companion. It is love that maintains the universe. All that you see in the world is a different manifestation of love. Fire is the heat of love, earth its foundation, air its restlessness, night its dream-state, day its wakefulness.' At the time his words made no sense to me. However, all unknowing, the quest of love was enjoined upon me from my infancy and became the guiding star of my life. Unfortunately it was neither the kind of love that consumed *Chacha* Amanullah nor the sort my father spoke of that became my abiding passion but the type that envelopes a man when he loses his head and his heart to one woman.

My father married twice. From his first wife, the sister of the well-known poet Aarzoo of Delhi, he had a son, Hafiz Mohammed. My mother, who was his second wife, bore him three children of whom I was the eldest. My step-brother had no love for his father, his step-mother or her children. Most of all he hated me. My father was well aware of this and thought it best to divide whatever he owned between us in his lifetime. One summer afternoon, when the sun was at is zenith and hot winds blew, he went to Agra to see some ailing disciple. When he returned, he had a heat stroke. He smelled the breeze of paradise in his nostrils and sent for Hafiz Mohammed and me. He spoke to us: 'Sons, I am a fakeer. I have no money, land or property. All I have are some three hundred books. I also owe about three hundred rupees to creditors. Before I shut my eyes to the world I would like to divide my books and debts equally between you.' At this my step-brother replied, '*Abba Jan,* you know perfectly well that I am the scholar of the family and the only one who can profit from the study of books. What will Taqi do with them except make kites of their pages and fly them?' My father was very upset with him but being close to death only admonished him weakly, 'Hafiz Mohammed, mark my words! The flame of learning will never illumine your home but that of Taqi.' He turned to me and said, '*Beta,* do not bury my body till you have paid off my creditors. Do not worry. Money will come to you.'

With the name of Allah on his lips my father took leave of the world. As news of his death reached Agra, people began to collect at our hospice to pay their last homage to him. Among them were some Hindu shopkeepers who offered me money. I declined to take it from them but when one of my father's Muslim disciples put a bag with five hundred rupees in my lap, I accepted it. I paid off my father's creditors and buried his body next to the grave of *Chacha* Amanullah. At the age of eleven I was left alone in the world to look after my widowed mother, younger brother and sister. Besides the hundred rupees that remained with me after I had paid for the burial expenses and creditors my only wealth consisted of the words of wisdom bequeathed to me by my father.

Chacha Amanullah had taught me Farsee and Urdu as well as the technique of composing poetry. I used this little knowledge to coach the children of rich families. Some evenings I would go to *mushairas* and hear the famous poets of Delhi and Agra recite their compositions. I found most of them were commonplace rhymesters without a single new thought in their poems. Such poets, particularly a songster named Masood who was a great favourite at *mushairas,* roused my contempt. Masood was a handsome, roguish looking fellow who could make up for the execrable quality of his verses by singing them in a dulcet voice. No sooner would a *mushaira* start than the audience would clamour for 'Parwana' (moth), the pseudonym which he used. (I always referred to him as Patanga which is the pejorative for a moth). Women loved him. At every gathering I saw maidservants bring slips of paper from their mistresses seated behind the purdah with requests for songs composed by him. These songs were usually about the moth's love for the flame in which it burnt itself. It amazed me how a theme as old as Moses and Abraham could rouse people's emotions. What irritated me about Parwana was that even on this hackneyed theme he could not produce a single new variation. I confess that it was envy of this worthless moth that first impelled me to try my hand at composing poetry.

While the others in my household slept I would sit beside an oil-lamp and compose verses. They poured out of me like the waters of the Tasneem. Although I was too shy to recite them in public I showed them to some poets whose work I thought was above mediocre. They expressed surprise that one so young could have such facility with words; some suspected I had stolen someone else's writing. 'If these verses are really yours, the days of Parwana will soon come to an end,' said one. 'He will have to leap into a flame,' said another. 'He is a mere *tuk-baaz* (rhymester) with the voice of a castrated male.' The story went round that a twelve-year-old *chhokra* had the audacity to use insulting words about the reigning monarch of Agra's *mehfils*. In due course Parwana got to hear of what I had said. 'Who is this son of Meer Taqi?' he roared. 'I will teach him a lesson he will never forget.' Some families known to him dispensed with my services. Not satisfied with this, he decided to humiliate me in public.

At a *mushaira* in the haveli of Agra's richest Nawab, Rais Mian, whose begum was said to be enamoured of Parwana, somebody whispered in his ears that I was present in the crowd. I could see his eyes scanning the audience while his informant directed his gaze towards me. He nodded his head and said in a voice loud enough for everyone to hear: 'Now watch the tamasha.' After a poet had finished his recitation, his cronies began to shout, 'Parwana Sahib, Parwana Sahib!' He raised both his hands asking for people to be quiet. 'Gentlemen, I am grateful to you for your appreciation of my poor talents. I am your slave, ever ready to comply with your commands. But this evening, before your humble servant opens his mouth, I pray silence for the rising star of Hindustan. Parwana is a mere *patanga* before him. It is no fault of yours that you have not heard of his name because the world has yet to hear his *kalaam*. He is still wet behind his ears but regards himself as the *ustad* of *ustads*.' His voice was loaded with sarcasm. His cronies sniggered with pleasure. He turned to one of them and asked loudly, 'What did you say is this *launda's* (urchin's) name? Ah, yes, Meer. Full name, Meer Taqi Meer. Let the candle be placed before his august visage.'

I was taken aback. I had never opened my mouth in a *mehfil* nor had I brought any of my compositions with me. The candle was placed in front of me and hundreds of eyes were fixed on me. Sweat broke out on my forehead and my hands began to tremble. I shut my eyes and thought of my father. I prayed, '*Ya Allah!* Thou art my help and my refuge.' I could not think of what to say except a couplet I had composed on the *shama-parwana* (flame-moth) theme only to prove that it could be handled in ways other than by this hack trying to humiliate me. 'Parwana Sahib,' I said with all the humility I could command, 'before I recite my composition, I crave permission to present you a gift which I beg of you to accept.' Then in a clear voice I recited:

The flame it saw,
But thereafter nothing besides the curving, leaping tongues
of fire.

By the time its eyes were on the flame,
The moth was in the fire.

None of them had seen this aspect of love—love that thinks of nothing except to be consumed by its beloved. As the words sank in the minds of the audience it exploded —'*Marhaba! Subhan Allah!* How beautifully put!' Emboldened by the appreciation, I sought permission to recite a poem on love that I had composed the night before and which was still fresh in my mind:

It is love and only love whichever way you look;
Love is stacked from the earth below to the sky above;
Love is the beloved, love is the lover too,
In short, love itself is in love with love.
Without love none can their goal attain,

Love is desire, love its ultimate aim.
Love is anguish, love the antidote of love's pain.
O wise man, what know you what love is?
Without love the order of the Universe would be broken
God is love, truly have the poets spoken.

The audience was moved by my recitation. Every line was applauded with *Wah! Wah! Wah! Mukarrar!* I had to repeat the lines over and over again. Many people came and showered silver coins on me. A maidservant handed me a gold ashrafi with a note asking me to make a copy of the poem in my own hand and deliver it personally at the haveli the next morning. The note was from the mistress of the house. This was the beginning of my career as a poet and a lover.

I got no sleep that night. The applause I had received ran in my ears. I had humbled that charlatan Parwana and he would never again be able to show his face in a *mehfil* where I was present. But who was this lady who had asked for my poem? My head was in a whirl. Despite the sleepless night, in the morning I felt fresh and triumphant. I told my mother what had happened and handed over the gold ashrafi and silver coins showered on me. 'All this is due to your Abba,' she said. 'He is watching over you. He will see that you become the most famous poet of Hindustan.'

I made a fair copy of my poem, hurried back to Nawab Rais Mian's haveli and had myself announced. Nawab Rais was out exercising his horses. After a while a maidservant came to escort me into the women's apartments. 'You are only a little boy; you don't even have hair on your upper lip,' she said to me saucily. 'No one will object to your presence in the zenana.' I found myself in a heavily curtained, dark room from with a few bolsters laid on a Persian carpet along the wall. Some moments later Begum Sahiba entered the room. I bowed and made my salutation and with both hands presented the parchment on which I had written my poem. 'I am greatly honoured by your appreciation of my humble talent,' I said. She protested. 'It is I who should feel honoured by your presence. When you become the most famous poet of Hindustan you may remember this creature who was the first to appraise your greatness.'

Her words were celestial music in my ears. I dared to raise my eyes to see her. She was seated on the carpet reclining on a bolster. Since her eyes were fixed on me, I could not look at her for too long. She was a short, stocky woman about thirty years of age. She was fair, round-faced with raven-black hair long enough for her to sit on. The only other things I noticed about her were her taut bosom and big rounded buttocks which almost burst out of her tight-fitting pyjamas. Her steady gaze unnerved me; it felt as if she was eating me up with her eyes. It was quite some time before she asked me to be seated and ordered her maidservants to serve me refreshments. Even while I was partaking of the repast placed before me, I felt her eyes hovering over me. She invited me to the *bismillah* ceremony of her younger son. She asked me if I would condescend to see some of her verses and advise her how to improve them. She offered me the post of tutor to her children. I felt like a bird on whom a silken net was about to fall. I was happy but also somewhat apprehensive. My days of penury were over but my days of freedom seemed to be coming to an end.

When I told my mother about the meeting she shared both my joy and my apprehension. 'I have heard a lot of things about this Begum Sahiba. She comes from a poor family and was given away to Nawab Rais when she was barely sixteen and he over fifty and the father of many children through his first begum. They say that her second son is not her husband's but is of that poet fellow Parwana whom she had taken on as an *ustad* for some time. Nawab Rais is getting old and is often away in Delhi.' After a pause she added, '*Beta*, you are old enough now to get married. I will look for a nice girl for you.' Although I was only fifteen years old, I understood what disturbed her mind. She thought it would be a good idea if she called on Begum Sahiba to thank her and at the same time seek her advice about a suitable wife for me.

Begum Sahiba was very gracious to my mother. She gave her a silk dress and flattered her for having a son who would soon become the brightest star in the firmament. When my mother broached the subject of finding a wife for me, she replied without a pause, 'Leave it to me. I have just the right girl for him. Would you like to see her?' My mother protested, 'Begum Sahiba, if you approve of her what is there for us to see or say? May your choice be blessed!'

The next day Begum Sahiba teasingly told me that she had found a wife for me. 'She is not a *houri*; only a simple-minded girl, chaste as white marble. With a wife like her not a breath of scandal will ever pass your home. Her parents are not rich but we will look after the marriage expenses and provide her with a suitable dowry. You will not regret my choice.'

The father of the girl the Begum Sahiba had chosen for me was a distant relation of the begum and was employed as a caretaker in one of the Nawab's orchards. It was only after I had married this girl, Saleema, that the Begum Sahiba's designs became clear to me. My wife was indeed no *houri*: she was as thin as a bamboo rod; I could grasp her waist between my hands. Her breasts were hardly perceptible. Her front teeth stuck out even when her mouth was shut; when she spoke you could see her gums as well. She had no choice except to be chaste as white marble; but her being my wife tempted me to take the path of infidelity.

Begum Sahiba was a designing, masterful woman who had her way in everything. In old Nawab Rais she had the husband she wanted; with the singing rhymester who passed for a poet, she had the part-time lover she wanted. Her taste for poetry was determined by the applause a poet received and not its real worth. Since Meer Taqi's star was in the ascendant, she was determined to be his patron and his mistress. She found Taqi a wife he could ignore.

I will not divulge the name of the Begum Sahiba. Of all the crimes listed in the Holy shariat, the worst is to betray a woman who has willingly given herself to you. I will only reveal the name I gave her because of her fair, round face: Qamarunnissa—like the full moon. She was flattered by the comparison. She had a thousand years of womanhood in her: she knew how to seduce; having seduced, how to give the man of her choice the illusion that no one else in the world mattered to her. She as willingly surrendered her soul as she surrendered her body to her lovers. For the time she was my mistress she made me feel as if I was the only God she knew and every sentence I wrote was like a *sura* of the Quran. She became at once my mother, mistress, nurse and companion. She could not bear to be parted from me for a moment, unable to tolerate my having any other friends save those she approved of. She swore eternal fidelity to me in this life and for lives to come. I often felt handcuffed and shackled by her and wanted to break loose; at the same time I felt the long silken tresses with which she bound me were plaited by God to fulfil man's eternal quest for his beloved. When she discarded me like a pair of worn-out slippers, and turned her attention to yet another rhymester whose only qualification was that after I left for Delhi he became the favourite butterfly in the mehfil of Agra, I was shattered. This woman made me and destroyed me. That in brief is the life story of Meer Taqi Meer, the poet and the lover.

ॐ

I have already narrated how I came to be invited to Nawab Rais's haveli and was appointed tutor to his sons. Begum Sahiba was always present during the lessons. While I taught the boys, her eyes rested on me. After the lessons were over, she insisted on my reciting whatever I had written the previous night. She praised every line and when I recited the *qita* she would exclaim *Subhan Allah*! then take the paper on which I had written the verse out of my hands and press it against her bosom. She would give me her own compositions. They were poor poetry but quite clearly addressed to me. I praised them, made suggestions on how to improve the rhyme and metre and at times took the paper from her hand and pressed it against my forehead. She gave me my midday meal. When I returned home in the evening, I would find she had sent biryani and other delicacies for the family. Thus she made me feel the most important man in the Mughal empire. Later in the night when I took my skin-and-bone wife to bed I would fantasize about the Begum's broad hips heaving upwards to receive me.

Once Begun Sahiba made up her mind to get something she spun a web of intrigue that ensnared everyone concerned: she was the master puppeteer with all the strings in her fingers; they the puppets to act out her commands. From our exchange of verses she had assured herself that I was a willing victim. She then turned her wiles on her husband. She persuaded him that for his future he should visit Delhi and find out what truth there was in the rumours that the Persian Nadir Shah was planning to invade India. At the same time she asked him to persuade Nawab Samsamuddaulah, the royal paymaster, who was the most powerful man in Delhi, to present me to the emperor. Who would suspect this strategy: if she desired me why would she want to send me away from Agra? Her husband not only agreed to both her proposals but also pressed me to stay in his haveli while he was away so that there was a reliable man to look after his household and his sons' education was not interrupted.

Soon after Nawab Rais left for Delhi with his retinue of

horsemen the living arrangements in the haveli were reorganized. The boys were shifted to their father's bedchamber and their room was given to me. Between the two rooms was Begum Sahiba's own retiring-room.

She did not believe in wasting precious moments which she knew would not last long. Her duplicity was as astounding as her audacity. In the morning she bade a tearful farewell to her old husband; in the afternoon she busied herself with having the hair shaved off her legs, armpits and privates and her body massaged with perfumed oil. I discovered all this an hour after the evening repast when the children were asleep and the servants had retired to their quarters. She came to me as if she was coming to the bed of her husband awaiting her. Like people long married we did not waste time exchanging words of love. (In any case words that lovers exchange before they engage in love-making had been exchanged in the poems that we had passed to each other and in the dialogue our eyes had carried on since the day they had first met). Without bothering to blow out the lamp, she shed her clothes, stripped mine off my body and put her arms around me. We drank honey out of each other's mouths till we could drink no more. She pushed me quietly on the bed and spread herself over me. Her thighs were moist as if with the dew on a rose-bud on a summer morning. She pressed her face into mine till my teeth hurt. After a while she began to moan, and with a shudder that shook her entire frame, collapsed, drenched in sweat. Such ecstasy I had never known; nor can I put it into words.

When she tried to get up I held her down by her buttocks and did not let her move. She was of riper years and richer experience; I was younger and had more lust. She gave me a smile of approval and as a gesture of subservience turned over to let me play the master. I bit her all over her face and neck and bosom and with my tongue ravished her ears. This time she climaxed many times before I spent myself. We rested for half-an-hour and resumed the game of love. So it went on throughout the night. I do not know when it ended or when she slipped out of my room to retire to her chamber. When I woke my eyelids seemed as if they had been stuck together with glue. Instead of feeling tired I felt more refreshed. Instead of feeling guilty of having betrayed her husband's trust or of having been unfaithful to my wife, I felt that Allah had blessed this union of minds and bodies; it was not profane but divine love.

I went down to the courtyard and found Begum Sahiba seated on a *moorha* with two maidservants massaging her feet. The floor was littered with the Nawab's pouter pigeons billing and cooing. As I made my *adaab* she smiled and said: 'I trust our poet-friend had a restful night,' and ordered one of her maids to serve me breakfast. She read out a letter her husband had sent her from Sikandra where he had camped for the night and informed me that she had sent a tray of dry fruit to my wife.

She planned our lives as it suited her. The money she gave me to teach her sons was more than my wife and mother had ever seen. 'Aren't my sons also your sons?' she asked my wife. 'You will be putting us in an eternal debt of gratitude if you allow your husband to teach them. What am I offering in return except a pittance, barely enough to chew betel-leaf!' Through money and gifts she kept my wife and mother happy. To her husband she wrote that she had prevailed upon me not to take on any other work except teaching the children.

With me she was very truthful. She lied to the rest of the world but never to me. She told me of her marriage to Rais Mian who had already had children of his own. All he needed was someone to look after him and his affairs. This she did and left him with plenty of time to exercise his horses and train his pigeons. Once every few months, when roused by diink, he had sex with her. To restore his self-esteem she pretended to be worn out by his passionate love-making. She even confessed her liaison with Parwana and what trouble she had had to abort the foetus she had conceived from him. There was nothing left unsaid between us. Such was the intimacy she created that I felt guilty when I approached my wife. The Begum Sahiba persuaded me that while it was necessary for our relationship for her to keep up a pretence of loving her husband there was no need for me to consort with my wife. And because the poor thing was too modest to make demands on me she did not protest. She believed that all my energies were consumed in writing poetry and teaching.

I spent many blissful days in the Begum's company. It was in her tightly-clad, firm body that I learnt the true meaning of life. We spent long hours fulfilling the yearnings of our hearts and bodies, hoping thereby that our hunger for each other would be forever satiated. But that was not to be: each time we were left to ourselves it seemed like the first time. We would pass our nights lying naked in each other's arms, but no sooner came the dawn, than, like a newly-wedded bride, she would coyly cover her face. I was overcome with the desire to find out the mystery that lay behind her veil. The more I saw of her the more my passion for her body grew. Her beauty shone like a pearl in limpid water. Whenever the moonlight of her radiance spread, real moonlight appeared no better than a spider's wed:

> A simmering fire burns our hearts away;
> We sink and my heart in depth of agony lies;
> As with the dawn the taper of the lamp
> Laps up the last drops of oil and dies.

I became indifferent to the world, my mother, my wife and child. My relatives set their faces against me for neglecting my family; but what greater joy than to be tormented for the sake of love!

Nawab Rais returned from Delhi after a month. By then I had come to assume that he meant nothing to her and she would contrive to send him away on some other mission. I was taken aback by the show of affection she put up to welcome him and the formality with which she addressed me in his presence. She dressed herself in her best silks, darkened her eyes with kohl, reddened her lips with *missi* and showed great eagerness to be left alone with him. No sooner had we partaken of the midday meal than she announced, 'After his arduous journey Nawab Sahib needs to rest.' She followed her old man into their private apartment. I was left alone, holding my pen.

I could not sort out the confusion in my mind. After the intimacies we had enjoyed it seemed scarcely possible that either of us could bear anyone else's touch. I could not understand the shameless wantonness she displayed in wanting to be with her husband. Even more upsetting to me was her appearance after she came out of her room later in the afternoon: her hair was dishevelled and kohl was spattered on her cheeks. It was as if she wanted everyone to know what she had been up to. While I sulked she made solicitous enquiries about my comfort. In the presence of her husband she told me that she had sent a note to my wife that I had been detained in the haveli on important business. 'My husband will tell you of what transpired between him and Nawab Samsamuddaulah,' she said. Her husband said: 'Yes, I have to return to Delhi as soon as I can as there are rumours afloat of a Persian invasion. If they are true we have to gird our swords to our loins; if they are not true I will be back home within the month. Meanwhile you will stay here and look after the ladies.' The Begum Sahiba pleaded: 'Please! Please! I swear by the hair on your head if you do not accede to our entreaties, we will never speak to you again.' Though I was very angry I was left with little choice and agreed to stay. That evening a large number of Agra citizens came to call on Nawab Rais to enquire about his health and get news of Delhi. He was very discreet in his replies and quickly changed the subject: 'Don't bother about what they say in Delhi; you must stay to share our dry bread and dal and listen to Taqi Sahib. If you have not heard Meer Sahib's *kalaam* you have heard nothing.'

After a lavish feast, a *mushaira* got going. I listened to the rhymed *tuk-baazi* rubbish without comment. A slip of paper was handed to me by a servant. I recognized Begum Sahiba's handwriting—'Let your *kalaam* be worthy of your humble maidservant.' The candle was placed in front of me. From behind the screen I felt her eyes fixed on me and her ears awaiting what I had to say:

> How dowhearted was Meer at night!
> Whatever came to his lips became a cry for help.
> When he started on the path of love, he was like fire;
> Now it's ended, he is a heap of ashes on a pyre.

The *mushaira* went on till late into the night with repeated requests for my *kalaam*. While it lasted I felt flushed with the wine of applause; when it ended, and I was alone on my charpoy on the roof with a myriad stars looking down on my wretchedness, my liver churned up angry vapours. Below the roof on which I lay, the woman who had made herself a part of my person was welcoming another man between her parted thighs. She had made me a stranger to my wife without any intention of changing her relationship with her own husband. I felt deserted and betrayed.

561

Nawab Rais decided to return to the capital. I accompanied him as far Delhi Gate. That day, instead of returning to the haveli I went back to my family.

In the afternoon I took my wife to bed and savagely ravished her as I had not done since the first time I had deflowered her. The poor woman suffered my mauling with gratitude. She saw it as proof that I liked her. (That afternoon she conceived my second child, another son). In the evening the Begum Sahiba's servants arrived with a trayful of food and fruit. The maidservant, Naseema, in whom the Begum Sahiba confided her secrets slipped a note in my hand. It began with a couplet I had composed: 'For a long time no letter or message has been sent. A rite of faithfulness has been ended.' It continued that without me her world was desolate and if I did not return by the next morning, she would take poison and her death would be on my head. My anger vanished. I was full of remorse. I told Naseema I would present myself the next morning.

I went to the haveli like a criminal to a court of justice appealing for forgiveness. Without looking at me the Begum Sahiba remarked sarcastically: 'Meer Sahib treats us like beggars. When it pleases him he throws a few crumbs of his favour in our begging bowl.' I made no reply. I spent some hours taking the boys through their lessons. She sat gazing dolefully at me without saying a word. I had my afternoon meal and retired to my room. There I found a note on my pillow, again a couplet I had recited to her:

> *Life is somewhat like a line drawing,*
> *Appearances a kind of trust,*
> *This period of grace we call age;*
> *Examine it carefully!*
> *It is a kind of waiting.*

I awaited her all afternoon. She did not come. In the evening when I found her alone in the courtyard I asked her in a dry tone if I had her permission to return. She replied: 'Don't bother to come to my funeral,' covered her face with her dupatta and ran inside.

I was not used to playing the role of villain in a melodrama. I wished Nawab Rais had taken me with him to Delhi and I would be free of this woman who made me feel like a fly stuck in a pot of honey. More was yet to come. No sooner did I retire after the evening meal, than she came into my room, regardless of the servants who were rinsing the utensils, bolted the door from the inside and came towards me. Before I could stop her she fell at my feet and began to cry. The wife of Agra's richest Nawab crying at the feet of a poor teacher and poet! 'You are angry with me,' she said through her tears. 'Punish me any way you like. Beat me, treat me like a prostitute, do whatever you like but don't be angry with me!' I forced her up on my charpoy and wiped away her tears with my hands. She drew her breasts out of her chemise and pressed my head towards them. 'Bite them as hard as you can till you draw blood.' I kissed them tenderly. Then I kissed her eyes and lips. When I entered her she entreated, 'Let us run away to some place and get married; I hate that husband of mine. I don't want him to touch me ever again.' I smiled and asked, 'What about your children? And the scandal?' She looked intently into my eyes: 'I will give up everyone and everything to be with you and serve you. Promise you will marry me.' I promised. Soon I was about to climax and tried to withdraw; she held me tightly between her legs and cried hoarsely: 'Don't! Come what may this night I am yours.'

When the first bout was over, I asked her timidly whether she had extended her favours to her husband. 'What kind of woman do you take me to be?' she demanded angrily. 'When I am in love with you can I offer my body to another? I knew it upset you to see me so solicitous about the old man. But one has to keep up appearances with the world, doesn't one? Were you unfaithful to me with your wife?' I lied by putting the question back to her, 'You think that is possible?'

We slipped back into the game of love. Everything ever written about in books on sex and much that is written nowhere we practiced on each other. We had our own private language: she was Qamar to me; I Jaan (life) to her. We gave our genitals pet names: mine was Raja babu, hers Bahoo rani. When she was unclean she described it as a visitation of a gossiping crone she did not like. We made it a point that every coupling was a complete success. If I was hasty she patiently rekindled my lust. If she felt exhausted by what was permitted she would generously offer other avenues for my pleasure. Could any man have known a woman better? Or a woman a man? I composed the following lines:

Passions have made mortals of us men
If men were not slaves of passion
They would have been Gods, each one.

Thus the days went by. And the nights. Whenever we were left by ourselves we told each other of our past. I had very little to say about myself but she kept nothing back from me. She told me how she had fallen for that useless fellow Patanga because of the way he sang only to discover that he was a philanderer and betrayed her trust by boasting about his conquest. There was nothing that we did not know about each other. A man can get away with his affairs with women, but a woman known to be promiscuous can be ruined for ever. That this woman should lay herself bare before me convinced me that there would never be another man in her life. How little I knew of womankind.

It was not long before tongues began to wag. However, it seemed that the Begum Sahiba was not concerned about anything so long as the scandal did not get to the ears of her husband. Her servants knew that the slightest slip of the tongue about their mistress would bring ruin on their families. So they made it a point to tell Nawab Rais how, when he was away, the Begum Sahiba hardly ate anything and spent hours praying for his return. The old man would become most solicitous. Such is man's vanity! However, the haveli was not Agra. Whenever I went out in the bazaar, people who knew me would talk in words which had two meanings: 'Meer Bhai, what power you have in your pen! It can tear hearts as well as pyjamas.' Or slap me on the back and say, 'Meer Taqi, how fortune smiles on you!' One evening, when I was visiting my family, my mother took me aside and spoke in a voice full of alarm. '*Beta* Taqi, there are as many stories as there are tongues. No one can lock up people's mouths. Everyone in Agra is talking about you and the Begum Sahiba. I don't believe any of it; but if such tales are carried to her husband, do you think nothing of having all of us murdered! I beg of you to stop going to the haveli. Make any excuse you can. Say your old mother is dying. Say anything you like.'

I told the Begum Sahiba what my mother had said. For once she became pensive. Then she said: 'People have such dirty minds!'

Thereafter there was less ardour in her passion. And she began to tell me how important it was for me to gain recognition in the Mughal court. A month later she read out a letter from her husband saying that he had arranged for my presentation at the exalted Fort Palace as well as a patron and I should proceed post-haste to Delhi. She said: 'My life will become desolate; but when I see your star shine brightly over Hindustan, I will say this man was my lover, I his beloved.'

When the day of my departure came she wrapped several gold ashrafis in a green silken scarf and put her lips close to my ear to whisper: '*Fallahu Khairun Haafiza wa huwa arhumurrahimeen*—Allah is the best protector, He is compassionate and merciful.' She tied the scarf round my arm and added in plain Hindustani: 'Allah be with you wherever you go; may He preserve you from harm, and bring you name and fame.' However her prayer did not include this sentiment—'May Allah bring you back to me.'

Before leaving I composed a few lines which I left with her as a keepsake of our love:

> *You came here of your own accord and are lost in yourself;*
> *I know not what you search for, or who.*
> *If I want anyone it is you, if I want to see anyone it is you.*
> *You are the desire of my heart and my eyes' prayer.*

ॐ

I wasn't sure whether Begum Sahiba was more grieved or more relieved to see me leave Agra. I was not even sure of my own feelings. At first I felt like a bird let out of a cage and wanted to sing with the joy that freedom brought me. Then I missed the golden cage in which she had imprisoned me for more than two years, sang love songs to me, fed me and taken care of me. Was I in love with her? I did not know. Perhaps it was her love for me that made me feel worthwhile and fall in love with myself. Whatever it was, before I had passed Mathura which was our third halt, I found myself thinking more of my Qamarunnisa than of my aged mother, my younger brother to whom I had entrusted the care of the family, my wife or even my two-year-old son, Kalloo.

These were disturbed times. Gangs of Jats, Gujars, Marathas and Rohillas roamed over the country to prey upon hapless travellers. Even the royal road from Agra to Delhi was not safe from their depredations. I said to myself, 'O Meer, why complain of thorns at the start of the journey, it is still a long way to Delhi.' I had attached myself to a caravan which had armed horsemen and matchlockmen to guard our front and rear. We travelled only during the day and halted at night in fortified sarais. At Ghiaspur I took leave of my travelling companions to pay homage to the tombs of Hazrat Nizamuddin Auliya and Khwaja Ameer Khusrau whose works had inspired me. I stayed two days and nights in an Arab sarai close to the mausoleum of Emperor Humayun. It was from its marble tower that I had my first look at the city of the Mughals which was to be my home for many years to come.

I approached the city by the Delhi Gate. Nawab Rais had sent word to the havildar guarding the gate to let me in. The havildar detached one of his sentries to escort me to the house where Nawab Rais was staying. The Nawab Sahib was exceedingly kind to me—a man who after having eaten his salt had betrayed his trust by becoming his wife's lover. I told him how much the Begum Sahiba, the children and the household missed him. If nothing else she had taught me how to lie with a straight face.

Through Nawab Rais's influence I was able to rent a couple of rooms in a bazaar close to Fatehpuri Masjid. It was a mean-looking hovel but it was the best I could afford with the money in my purse. I called it the 'boaster's grave' and wrote a description of it in my diary: 'There are fissures and cracks in the walls, dust dropping from everywhere; in one corner a mole, a mouse peering out of another hole; bandicoots share my home, ever present is the mosquitoes' drone; spiders' webs hang from the walls; at night the crickets' grating call; edges crumbling, shutters tumbling, stones edging out of their places. Beams and rafters with soot-black faces. This was poor Meer's bower; there he spent hour after hour.'

A few days later Nawab Rais presented me to Mohammed Wasit, the nephew of the great Nawab Samsamuddaulah who was the power behind the Mughal throne. He promised to help after I had proved my worth at a *mushaira* which was due to take place soon and where his uncle was expected to be the guest of honour.

The *mushaira* was arranged on the roof-top of a mansion in

Faiz Bazaar called Daryaganj. It was the night of the full moon which always reminded me of my Qamar. On the floor were carpets covered with snow-white sheets with jasmine and rose-petals scattered on them and bolsters placed along the sides; *surahis* (pitchers) of sherbet were lined on the parapets; a soft breeze blowing across the Jamna mingled with the fragrance of khas, rose and jasmine. Only the nobility of the town had been invited. Over a dozen poets of repute were present including the most famous—Sirajuddin Ali Khan 'Aarzoo', the brother of my step-mother. Most people had heard my name but none had seen my face or heard my voice. I was very nervous and kept rubbing my palms against my shirt to keep them dry. I did not know which of my compositions I should recite before such an august assemblage.

The nawabs of the courts began to arrive. As their names were announced we rose from our seats to salaam them. The last to arrive was Nawab Samsamuddaulah. Everyone made a low bow to greet him. He acknowledged our greetings and asked us to be seated. After a while, the host announced that it was Nawab Samsamuddaulah's pleasure that the poets and guests should be allowed to wet their moustaches before the proceedings began. The announcement was greeted with applause. It was the first time in my life that besides sherbet wine was served at a *mushaira*. Goblets went round and soon everyone was in high spirits. I had tasted wine before but never of such excellence—made from Kandahar grapes and chilled in snow brought down from the Himalayas. I had a poor liver for liquor. I realized that if I made a fool of myself at my first public appearance I would become the laughing stock of the city and decided to refill my goblet only after I had recited my piece.

The *mushaira* began with recitations of the Delhi poets. Their compositions were on worn-out themes of moth and flame, bulbul and the rose, Laila and Majnun. Not one new idea, not one new turn of phrase. Nevertheless they were dutifully applauded. At long last the candle was placed in front of me. The host announced my name. He said that although I was young in years, I had become a household name in Agra and was appearing for the first time in Delhi. I acknowledged the compliments he paid and said that I had planned to recite an old poem on love which had been acclaimed in Agra but seeing the mood of the audience sought permission to recite one which I had composed in my mind while the wine-flask was going round. (To be truthful, I had composed it one night in Agra when Qamar had passed wine from her mouth into mine as she lay above me). *'Irshad! Irshad!'* they cried. I recited my poem on drunkenness:

> *Friends forgive me! you can see I am somewhat drunk,*
> *If you must, an empty cup let it be,*
> *For I am somewhat drunk.*
> *As the flask goes round, give me just a sip—*
> *Not full to the top, just enough to wet my lip;*
> *For I am somewhat drunk.*
> *If I use rude words, it is all due to drink,*
> *You too may call me names and whatever else you think,*
> *For I am somewhat drunk.*
> *Either hold me in turn as you hold a cup of wine*
> *Or a little way come with me, let your company be mine,*
> *For I am somewhat drunk.*
> *What can I do, if I try to walk I stumble,*
> *Be not cross with me, please do not grumble;*
> *For I am somewhat drunk.*
> *The Friday prayer is always there, it will not run away,*
> *I will come along with you if for a while you'll stay*
> *For I am somewhat drunk.*
> *Meer can be as touchy as hell when it is his whim*
> *He is made of fragile glass, take no liberty with him;*
> *For he is somewhat drunk.*

The audience was enthralled. One nobleman after another embraced me, pressed money into my hands. I was taken to be presented to Nawab Samsamuddaulah. He allowed me to kiss his hand and spoke very graciously to me. *'Beta,* I was one of your father's disciples. Seeing you here in Delhi I presume he has departed from the world. I owe a lot to him and will repay his debt to you. Present yourself at our residence in the morning and we will see what we can do for you.'

I kissed his hand again and took my seat. I had my goblet refilled several times and drank the chilled wine as if it was water.

My head was full of noises. I did not hear what the other poets had to say. Before the repast was served, I slipped out of the house. The world forgives a drunkard. I stepped out into a moonlit Delhi. Drunk with Kandahari wine everything looked beautiful: the streets bathed in silver, a deep blue sky with a few stars twinkling. I was a little unsteady on my feet put had no difficulty in finding my way from Faiz Bazaar to Jamia Masjid and through the prostitutes' street, Chawri Bazaar, to the eunuchs' quarters, Hauz Qazi. I kept thinking about my Qamar and how happy the two of us would have been and how we could have celebrated my victory over the other poets. I stopped by a paan-shop. I pushed my way through a ring of clients and ordered, 'Roll me the best paan you have.' The paanwalla regarded me for a while before replying: 'Meer Sahib, I'll make you one the like of which you have never tasted before. Perhaps you will compose a *qaseedah* on my paan and include my name in it.' I was pleased to know he recognized me. 'How did you know me?' I asked. He smiled. 'Who in Delhi has not heard of Meer's *kalaam*. It is on everyone's lips.'

From his brass copper bowl he pulled out a bundle of maghaee leaves, selected the smoothest, smeared lime and catechu paste on them, added scented betel-nut and tobacco and then a powder of crushed pearls and powdered gold. He folded the leaf, stuck a clove needle in it and wrapped it in gold leaf. 'In Delhi we call this *palang tor* (bed crusher). You try it out and if what I am saying is not true, my name is not Hari Ram Chaurasia, the best paan-maker of Shahjahanabad.'

I did not like his talking like this to me in front of other people. I gave him a silver rupee and proceeded on my way towards Lal Kuan. I put the paan in my mouth. It was strong stuff and brought out the sweat all over my body. I then noticed that one of the fellows I had seen at the paanwalla's was following me. I turned round and accosted him: 'Sir, have you any business with me?'

He addressed me very courteously: 'Meer Sahib, a night like this is made for love, not for walking through deserted streets. I can take you to the most beautiful girl in Delhi, no less than a princess of royal blood and barely sixteen years old. If she does not give you the time of your life, my name is not Chappan Mian.'

I do not know if it was the wine, the paan or the thoughts of my moon-faced Qamar that made me throw away the cloak of caution and follow the pimp through a dark, narrow lane branching off Lal Kuan. He slapped on a mean-looking door. A woman's voice demanded: 'Who is it at this hour?'

'Open, I have a customer.'

An old woman unlatched the door and let us in. She salaamed me and said: 'Sir it is very late but I will wake up my daughter and get her ready to welcome you. *Huzoor* may give this poor hag something to buy paan.' I gave her one of the gold ashrafis presented to me earlier in the evening. She was obviously pleased with my bounty but being an experienced woman, turned the coin in her fingers and said, 'I had bigger expectations from a gentleman of your rank.' I gave her another gold coin. She paid off the pimp and took me indoors.

Lamps were lit. She placed a tray of dry fruit before me which I waved away. Some minutes later a girl she called *beti* (daughter) entered the room rubbing the sleep out of her eyes. She was certainly young and beautiful—just as my Qamar had probably been at that age: fair and round-faced but somewhat shy. 'Be gentle with her, she is only a child,' said the old woman as she left the room.

I gave the girl a gold ashrafi. 'This is for you. Don't tell your old woman or the pimp.' She took it, put her head in my lap and began to sob. I stroked her long hair, then bare back. I slipped my hand in her *garara* and stroked her rounded buttocks. My sex was roused. She undid the cord of my pyjamas. I laid her on the bed and entered her. Was I being unfaithful to Qamar? No. In this little girl I recreated her and relived the times we had lain together. Drink and the paan loaded with aphrodisiac made me stay in for an hour. She climaxed over and over again and was drenched in sweat by the time I spent myself in her.

She washed herself and then with a wet rag wiped my middle. Then she sat down beside me: 'That Chappan fellow says you are a famous poet,' she said. 'Give this maidservant a couplet as a gift.' I was not in a mood to compose poetry but did not want to hurt the girl's feelings. 'Give me a piece of paper, pen and ink and I'll scribble something for you.' She tore out a page from a notebook and gave me a reed pen and held an earthen inkpot in her hand. After thinking for a while I wrote:

The season of clouds, a flask of wine too.
Roses in the rose garden, as well as you.

When I got to my home in Fatehpuri, the dawn was about to break. My head throbbed with pain, my mouth was parched. It was when I was changing my clothes that I noticed that all the gold and silver coins I had received were gone. Who could it have been except the sixteen-year-old girl passing for a Mughal princess! Meer, better look after your terrain, this is no ordinary habitation! This is Delhi!

I was in ill-humour when I presented myself before Nawab Samsamuddaulah. So it seemed was the Nawab Sahib. His nephew Mohammed Wasit pleaded with him to fix an allowance for me. The Nawab Sahib regarded me with his bloodshot eyes and said: 'Yes, we heard him last night. He is a deserving case. Besides we are beholden to his late father. Let him be paid one rupee a day. Next!'

Before the next supplicant could open his mouth, I presented a parchment before him and said: 'Nawab Sahib may be pleased to put his order in writing.' Though young in years, I knew the ways of civil servants who never did anything without demanding proof in writing.

My simple request put the Nawab Sahib out of composure. He snapped in Farsee, *'Waqt-e-Qalaam Daan ne'st*—this is not the time of the pen-and-inkholder.' I stood my ground. 'Sir, I do not understand the way you have framed your sentence,' I said. 'If your honour had said, "This is not the time for signing," or that "the pen-and-ink-bearer is not on duty," I would have understood. But to say that "pen-and-inkholder have no time" sounds extremely odd. It is not an animate object and therefore does not have proper or improper times; it can be brought at your honour's command.'

The Nawab Sahib's face lightened up with a smile. 'Meer Taqi, you are a saucy lad. We will gladly put our promise on paper.' With his own blessed hands he wrote out my allowance, signed and stamped it with his signet ring.

'Go and prosper. Let your *kalaam* be worthy of your father and bring you name and fame.'

❧

571

How wonderful life was in the Delhi of those days! People thronged to my home to solicit my opinion on their compositions. Wherever I went people recognized me and praised me; there was not a *mushaira* in the city where I was not the star performer. Friday prayers at the Jamia Masjid were a treat by themselves. Although I could hardly call myself a Mussalman and saw no great difference between Believers and Idolaters, I made it a point to join the Friday prayer because of the adulation I received from the congregation after the prayer was over. The people of Delhi loved me; I loved them and their city.

Alas! The days of happiness were not to last for ever. It was reported that the Persian, Nadir Shah, had occupied Afghanistan and was on the banks of the Indus. While preparations were being made to meet the invader panic started growing in Delhi. Rich merchants began to leave the city. I received several letters from my wife, begging me to return to Agra. She also wrote that the Begum Sahiba had stopped sending food or gifts and had employed another tutor for her sons. People coming from Agra told me that the Begum Sahiba to whom I had sold my soul was emamoured of her son's *ustad* and was showering gifts on his family. I did not believe these tales and decided to call on Nawab Rais, who happened to be in Delhi on a short visit before returning to Agra to raise troops to fight the Iranians. He was full of praise for the man appointed as my successor; he was not much of a poet, he said, but a good teacher and his sons were devoted to him. He had become like a member of their household and during Nawab Sahib's absence from Agra stayed in his haveli.

My mind was more disturbed by what was happening in Agra than by the Persian invasion. However, I stayed on in Delhi for as long as it was safe because Delhi provided me sustenance. I said to myself if a woman can be so perfidious it is best to consider her dead and forget about her rather than lose sleep over her. But the more I tried to wipe her from my mind, the more painfully she kept coming back to me. A heart on fire needs a stream of tears to put it out; a drop or two only makes it burn more fiercely. And the betrayal by a woman whom my words had made divine and with whom I had exchanged my body and my soul soured me against humanity. I became short-tempered, quarrelsome and morose.

By the autumn of 1737 Nadir Shah had advanced into the Punjab plains. The Mughal army went out of Delhi to check his progress. Amongst the commanders was Nawab Samsamuddaulah. I prayed for a Mughal victory and the safe return of my patron.

One day in the spring of AD 1738 the two hosts clashed at Karnal. Allah granted victory to the Persians; the Mughals were routed. Amongst the thousands who attained martyrdom was Nawab Samsamuddaulah, royal paymaster, patron and protector of Meer Taqi Meer. No panegyric I write in his praise could do justice to his greatness and magnanimity. He was like a rain-cloud of generosity above my head. May Allah rest his noble soul in peace! I was left with no one to shield me from the darts of envious pen-pushers. Neither was there anyone before whom I could spread the apron of my poverty. I was left poor, weak, helpless and alone. 'It is in the nature of lighting to strike; it has struck your nest O Meer!'

No sooner did I hear of the disaster at Karnal, than I hired a horse and took the road to Agra. There was no need to join any caravan as the entire route was one long caravan of people fleeing from Delhi to neighbouring towns and villages. On the way more than the Iranians we feared our own countrymen—Marathas, Jats and Gujars who robbed and killed any man they could lay their hands on and raped any woman who fell into their clutches. It took me five days to reach Agra. By then Nadir's horde was busy pillaging and looting Delhi. I said to myself: 'No matter, a city can be rebuilt and repopulated, but no power on earth can put together a heart that has been shattered.'

Agra was the city of my heart's ruination. I returned to see with my own eyes the debris that remained. Friend, it is my business to cry, how long will you keep wiping tears from my eyes! I recalled how our liaison had progressed and how we were carried away by our infatuation like paper-boats cast on a powerful stream. Love is an affliction which spares no one, neither the old nor the young, neither married nor single. How in my infatuation I had strewn flowers of homage at her feet; how a woman, who I had at first not thought particularly beautiful, had become the most beautiful, had become the most beautiful in the world to me after she became my beloved. In a *mehfil* of fair women, she had shone like the full moon amidst a galaxy of stars; her smile was like a rose-bud burgeoning into full bloom; her tresses lent their fragrance to the morning breeze; all this she became to me because she was cast in the mould of my desire. That this woman should have proved false to me and taken on another lover was beyond my comprehension.

But I still desired her. And now that I was back in Agra the raging fire of passion which I believed to have been reduced to ashes was once again fanned into a flame.

I returned home empty handed but was warmly welcomed by my family and saw my second-born for the first time. With some anguish I learnt that barely a month after I had left Agra, the Begum Sahiba had turned cool towards my family (so the rumours had been true!) and on their last visit to the haveli had refused to see them on the pretext of being unwell. My step-brother who enjoyed hurting me told me with some relish how her affair with the new teacher she had hired for her children was commonly talked about. His words pierced my heart like arrows.

Next morning I went to pay my respects to Nawab Rais. Far from raising troops to fight the Iranians, he denounced the Mughals for not having made terms with Nadir, who he was reliably told was an upright and just man, a devout Mussalman who would uproot idolatry from Hindustan. He took me inside to the zenana where the scene was exactly as I had left it except that instead of me there was this other teacher teaching the boys with the Begum Sahiba sitting on her *moorha* watching them. The boys greeted me very warmly, as did the teacher. But I could discern the look of triumph on his ugly face.

The Begum Sahiba had put on weight. The sparkle that had lit her eyes whenever she saw me was gone. She was as deferential towards me as she would have been to a stranger; her heart as cold as an extinguished oil-lamp. 'Meer Sahib, we hear Delhi resounds with your name. It is a matter of great pride for the people of Agra,' she said. How composed this woman was in the presence of three men, all of whom she had bedded! My face was flushed with anger and recrimination. I wanted to run out screaming and tell everyone in Agra that this woman had not only been unfaithful to her husband but also to her lover. They would have stoned her to death, not once but thrice. However, I did not open my mouth but

574

made some excuse and took my leave. And the people of Agra. Far from being proud of me, they turned their faces against me. Men who had used the dust of my father's feet as collyrium for their eyes averted their gaze from me. My voice was like the echo of a caravan bell in the wilderness. After six months of this humiliation I decided to quit Agra.

I arrived back in Delhi in the middle of summer. Strangely, though I had left Agra bitter at the betrayal by a woman who had sworn to be my companion in lives to come, and was plotting ways to avenge myself, I could not get her out of my mind. I sought her everywhere among the ruins of Delhi. Like the cup of a narcissus I carried the begging bowl of my eyes asking for alms of her sight. At every dawning of the day like the morning breeze I went knocking at every door of every street. I became like the flame of a candle flickering in a gusty morning wind. I burnt inside, melted, diminished and came close to death. A strange madness came over me. Physicians told me that insanity ran in my family and that it had now erupted in my blood and could only be cured by being bled out. They cauterized me, stuck leeches on my body and locked me up in a dark, dingy cell as if I was a raving lunatic. The Hakeem Sahib who came to see me was astonished at my condition. 'What can I prescribe for a man who is stricken with the pangs of love!' he said. The only one who showed any sympathy for me was a distant relative, an old woman who brought me changes of clothes and food and words of comfort. Allah bless her!

I despaired and said to myself, 'Better be enchained, locked up, even die in a dungeon than be enmeshed in the net of love and longing.' I wrote a couplet of despair.

> *'The eye hath ruined me,' the heart complained.*
> *'The heart has lost me,' the eye replied.*
> *I know not which told the truth, which lied*
> *Between the two, it was Meer who died.*

I wanted to write my last will and testament with words of warning to myself : 'Friend Meer, do everything your heart desires but never let it fall in love; love spares neither lover nor beloved.'

At long last they let me out of the cell in which they had confined me for many weeks. I loitered about the streets and bylanes. Whichever way I turned my eyes I saw signs of devastation caused by Nadir's vandals. Not a house had been spared. The Qila-i-Mualla had been stripped of its precious stones and furnishings. Princes of royal blood had been reduced to beggary; some had to go without food for days. Who was I to complain! In despair I went looking for the dingy hovel where I had spent a night in the arms of the girl passing for a princess. Not one house in the land had been spared. No one I asked knew what had become of the old woman and the girl. Perhaps the old woman was dead and the girl taken as a slave by some Irani-soldier.

What misfortunes had visited my beloved city! Sikhs, Marathas, thieves, pickpockets, mendicants, rulers—all preyed on us. Happy was he who had no wealth; poverty was the only wealth. Seeing things in that light, I was the wealthiest of the wealthy and at the same time the poorest of the poor.

One day sauntering through the city I came to buildings recently destroyed. I had known the locality well but I could not recognize the houses because little was left of them. Nothing was known of their inmates. If I asked for someone by name, they replied: 'He is not here any more.' If I asked for their whereabouts, the reply was the same or 'I know nothing about where they have gone.' Entire rows of houses had been razed to the ground—as far as the eye could see it was one vast scene of desolation. The bazaars had gone and with them the swains who had frequented them. Where would I look for beauty now! Where had fled all my pleasure-loving companions of yesterday? Comely youths and aged men of wisdom—all had vanished. I recalled a verse composed by someone:

Once through this ruined city did I pass
I espied a lonely bird on a bough and asked
'What knowest thou of this wilderness?'
It replied : 'I can sum it up in two words:
'Alas! Alas!'

అ

In the wilderness that the Delhi despoiled by Nadir Shah became, I was left with hardly anyone I could turn to for help. In despair I sought the company of Sirajuddin Ali Khan 'Aarzoo', who before my coming, was Delhi's most celebrated poet. At first he seemed well-disposed towards me and even helped me to find patrons. It was on his advice that I gave up writing in Farsee and instead concentrated on composing poetry in the language spoken by the common people, the kind who thronged the broad steps of Jamia Masjid. This brought me popular acclaim. Then suddenly and for no reason known to me Aarzoo turned against me. I thought perhaps my step-brother had written to him about my affair with the wife of my benefactor. Or maybe he thought that because my mother was Shia, I had leanings towards the Shiites (Aarzoo was a bigoted Sunni). But I was neither Shia nor Sunni, neither Muslim nor Hindu. About my faith I wrote:

> *I have gone beyond the temple and the mosque,*
> *I have made my heart my sanctuary;*
> *On this thorn-strewn path end*
> *All my wanderings and my journey.*

Like other Muslims I went to the mosque every Friday. Like Hindus I had drawn castemarks on my forehead. I worshipped in temples of idolatry and had ages ago abandoned Islam. However, the most likely cause of Aarzoo's anger was my growing popularity. He saw the crown worn by the Sultan-ul-Shoara (King of Poets) slipping off his head and being placed on mine. Envy slays friendships quicker than the sword. Aarzoo's hostility cost me many patrons and made life more difficult for me. As I had no regular income, I owed money to Banias, vegetable-sellers, milkmen and the like.

But as I've written earlier why should Meer mourn his own fate when loud cries of lamentation rise from every quarter of the city extending from the marble palaces of the exalted Red Fort to the humblest hovel in Paharganj! The accursed Nadir Shah had left behind him in Delhi thousands of widows to beat their breasts over their dead husbands and forced thousands of orphans to go begging in the streets. Of the bandobast the less said the better. We had one king, Mohammed Shah, and three rulers: Chief Minister Nawab Safdar Jang on one side, the Paymaster-General Nawab Imadul Mulk, and Nawab Intizammuddaulah on the other. The

Emperor's writ did not run even in his own harem; it was his Hindu wife who had once been a dancing girl and her adviser, Nawab Javed Khan, who issued orders on his behalf. Javed Khan was a *khwaja sara* (eunuch) in charge of the royal harem, and despite his shortcoming was reputed to be the paramour of the Hindu empress. Why should Meer complain? Javed may have been deprived of his manhood in one way but he proved his manliness by ignoring my detractors and spreading the umbrella of his bounty over my head. I was assured of at least one meal a day and a change of clothes when those I had on were tattered.

For a while fortune favoured Nawab Safdar Jang. When Mohammed Shah died he put the emperor's twenty-one-year-old son, Ahmed Shah, on the Mughal throne. Ahmed Shah preferred the company of nubile damsels and his wine-cup more than the business of State which he left to his mother and her confidant, Javed Khan.

Javed did not like Safdar Jang had joined Nawabs Imadul Mulk and Intizammuddaulah to plan his overthrow. A few months after Safdar Jang had become Chief Minister an attempt was made on his life. At Nigambodh Ghat in the vicinity of which he had his mansion a fusillade of gunfire was opened on him. Safdar Jang escaped by falling off his horse but many of his retainers were killed. Safdar Jang suspected Javed Khan of being the brain behind the conspiracy and plotted his destruction. He feigned friendship towards Javed and invited him for a morning repast along with Raja Suraj Mal Jat of Bharatpur. After the repast he took Javed aside and one of his retainers stabbed him in the back. His head was struck off his body and thrown on the sands of the Jamna. The empress went into mourning. I was deprived of yet another patron.

A regular war started between the soldiers of Safdar Jang and the empress's retainers. Every day they clashed, bullets flew, swords flashed and blood flowed in the gutters. They hired Rohillas, Jats, Marathas and Sikhs to fight for them. These hirelings fought for their paymasters by day and robbed the poor by night. The people of the city did not feel safe even in their own homes and pleaded with the empress to give them sanctuary. She acquiesced in their request and thousands of families moved into the open space of Sahibabad gardens alongside Chandni Chowk. Mercifully the monsoons were gentle and not many people died of exposure.

Ultimately Nawab Safdar Jang gave in. He was a Shia but there were few Shias even amongst his Muslim troops. After trying to win over the Jats and Marathas (who proved to be most untrustworthy), he quit in disgust. He spent his time erecting his final resting place on the road between Raisina and the Qutub and looking after his estates in Avadh.

The rule of Ahmed Shah came to an end while he was still living in the Fort Palace. The Marathas under Holkar after plundering Delhi's suburbs installed Mohammad Azizuddin, the great-grandson of Emperor Aurangzeb, as the new emperor. He was crowned on 5 June 1754 and assumed the title of Emperor Alamgir II. This self-styled conqueror of the Universe ruled an empire no longer than the enclosed space between the walls of the Red Fort.

Why labour the tragic tale of the King of Cities? Delhi was never the same after the Iranians had slain its soul. Kings, noblemen and their hirelings came like flocks of vultures to peck at its corpse. I stayed on in Delhi because there was nowhere else I could go except Agra. But one woman's perfidy had made me turn my face against that city forever. Through all these killings and massacres she did not send me even one letter enquiring about my health or safety. It is best to forget that such people exist. My wife and children—by now I had two sons and a daughter—joined me in Delhi. We lived in extreme poverty. I earned very little besides name and fame. I taught my children and found that all three were more inclined towards writing poetry than doing anything that might bring us money.

In the winter of 1758, Nadir's successor, the Afghan, Ahmad Shah Abdali, staked his claim to the empire of the Mughals. The Afghans marched through the Punjab without anyone daring to stop them and occupied Delhi. Abdali promised us security of life and property. But night had scarcely fallen when the outrages began. Fires were started in the city, houses were looted and burnt down. Afghan ruffians broke down doors, tied up those found inside, burnt them alive or cut off their heads. There was bloodshed and destruction everywhere. People were stripped of their clothes to wander naked in the streets. For many days no one had anything to eat. The cry of the oppressed rose to the heavens. Abdali who styled himself *Dur-i-Dauraan* (a Pearl among Pearls) and a pillar of the faith, was as rapacious as a hungry lion and remained unmoved by the plight of his fellow Muslims. People in their thousands fled from Delhi into the upon country where many died of hunger or exposure to the elements. I, who was poor, became poorer. My house, which stood on the main road, was levelled to the ground.

In my constant search for patrons, I turned from the Muslim nawabs who no longer helped me to the Hindu nobility. Raja Jugal Kishore and Raja Nagar Mal were fond of poetry and sent their compositions to me for correction.

In the winter of AD 1759 events took a turn for the worse: Nawab Imadul Mulk once again soiled his dirty hands by spilling the blood of Alamgir II. Mirza Abdullah Ali Gauhar, the late emperor's eldest son, fled to Avadh and proclaimed himself Shah Alam II (he was the seventeenth in the line of Babar). As for me my hardships in Delhi were too much for me to bear. I put my trust in the countryside than live in a capital that was little better than a wilderness laid waste every six months.

I moved to Bharatpur ruled by Suraj Mal Jat. When I was there the Maratha armies marched northwestwards to meet Abdali and his Afghans who had once again descended on Hindustan. On 17 January 1761 we received the news that two days earlier the Marathas had been decimated on the field of Panipat. Those who had managed to escape the Afghans' swords were set upon by gangs of Gujars and Jats and robbed of everything including their lives. I decided to stay on in Bharatpur until the Afghans departed and peace was restored in Delhi.

Six months later I ventured to return home. I quote from my diary written in the summer of 1761:

'I am back in my beloved city. The scene of desolation fills my eyes with tears. At every step my distress and agitation increases. I cannot recognize houses or landmarks I once knew well. Of the former inhabitants, there is no trace. Everywhere there is a terrible emptiness. All at once I find myself in the quarter where I once resided. I recall the life I used to live: meeting friends in the evenings, reciting poetry, making love, spending sleepless nights pining for beautiful women and writing verses on their long tresses which held me captive. That was life! What is there left of it? Nothing. Not a soul with whom I can pass a few pleasant moments in conversation! I come away from the lane and stand on the deserted road, gaping in stunned silence at the scene of devastation. I make a vow that as long as I live, I will never come this way again. Delhi is a city where dust drifts in deserted lanes; in days gone by in this very city a man could fill his lap with gold.

'Raja Nagar Mal has withdrawn his bounty. So what! I will no longer have to correct verses which are beyond correction. I have been left with nothing. I go out begging, knocking at the doors of noblemen. Because of my fame as a poet I manage to live—as a dog or a cat might live.

'I pray that Delhi will never again see the accursed Afghans. Abdali's troopers have more loot than they can carry on the camels and elephants they have captured. They have told their king that if he wishes to stay in Hindustan he will have to do so by himself. Wisely, Abdali has given in. He has made arrangements for the administration of the territories he ravaged and is on his way back to Afghanistan. Allah be thanked for small mercies!

The Afghans had become so arrogant and proud that Allah decided to teach them a lesson by having them humiliated at the hands of the Sikhs who were the lowest and the worst elements of society. A force of some forty to fifty thousand Sikhs blocked the passage of the retreating Afghans and fought them with a courage rarely seen in battle.

'Everyone knows that though severely wounded a Sikh will not turn his back on the enemy. Their bands move rapidly, surround straggling groups of Afghans and put them to the sword. No sooner the sun sets, than they descend on the Afghans from all directions and disappear in the morning. They make life hell for the Afghans. These Sikhs grow their hair and beards long and have a fierce aspect. Sometimes they let their long hair down before they fall on the Afghans and make them fly in terror. They fill the nights with their weird cries. Their footmen fight Afghan horsemen and their swords hack through Afghan saddles. In short, these Sikhs humiliated the Afghans in a manner never seen or heard of before. The Afghans lost the will to fight and the best they could do was to flee for their lives and to leave the governance of the State in the hands of a Hindu.

'The Sikh armies pressed on toppling crowns and thrones on their way, and chased the Afghans right upto the Attock river. Then they returned to the Punjab, slew the Hindu governor of Lahore appointed by Abdali, and became rulers of the Punjab. Now they have turned their bloodshot eyes on Delhi. What worse fate could befall a beautiful city than that it become the abode of savages!'

꒰ꔷ

Heavy as a rain-bearing cloud I wandered from one place to another. Delhi no longer could provide the food to keep me and my family alive. Once again I sought refuge in Bharatpur. My fame preceded me and people came from the south, east and west in the hope of getting a glimpse of me.

However, fame and words of praise do not fill an empty stomach. I know I have only one life to live, a hundred aspirations and a thousand desires to fulfil. I feel the weight of years on me and have become more and more like the flame of a candle flickering in a strong wind.

After the Persians, Afghans and the Marathas, came the Jats. I was still in Bharatpur when the Jat Raja Suraj Mal plundered Agra and Delhi. There was nothing left in Delhi for anyone to plunder but letters from my friends said that *jaatgardi* (Jat lawlessness) was worse than the Nadir Shahi of the Iranians. The only hope left for Delhi was Nawab Najibuddaulah who kept both the Jats and the Sikhs at bay. That hope died with Najibuddaulah's death. The Marathas whom Abdali had routed at Panipat only four years earlier again became powerful. It seemed that either they or the Sikhs, both accursed races, would become the rulers of Delhi. Allah preserve us from such a calamity!

For ten long years I went from one city to another like a homeless wanderer. When Shah Alam II returned to Delhi I also decided to return and resume my quest for fame and fortune. I pinned my hopes on Mirza Najaf Khan, the Chief Wazir, who being Iranian was Shiite, a faith with which, because of my mother, I had a close affinity. Mirza was a veritable *Zulfiqaruddaulah*—master of the sword. He had freed Agra from the Jats and had beaten back Sikh brigands and Rohilla freebooters. Even the Marathas were afraid of measuring swords with him. Would Allah keep his sabre ever victorious?

That, as it turned out, was not Allah's will. In April 1782 Mirza

Najaf Khan died and was buried in a garden facing the mausoleum of Nawab Safdar Jang. The bloodstained dagger of destruction was once again pulled out of its scabbard. Najaf Khan's nephew, Mirza Shafi, wrested power from the hands of Mirza Afrasiab, the dead ruler's adopted son. In September 1783 Mirza Shafi was murdered by an assassin hired by Afrasiab. And a few months later Afrasiab was slain by the brother of Mirza Shafi. Not a day passed without someone murdering someone else. No one was safe.

Hunger and insecurity drove me from my beloved city to Lucknow. Here Nawab Asafuddaulah received me kindly and fixed a stipend for the upkeep of my family. However, the Lucknowis, who prided themselves on their etiquette and polished speech, displayed neither towards me. At the first *mehfil* which I attended, they looked disdainfully at my large turban, my loose-fitting clothes and asked me where on earth I had come from. When the candle was placed before me I gave them a befitting reply:

> You men of these eastern regions
> Knowing my beggarly state you mock me;
> You snigger amongst yourselves and ask me
> Where on earth can you have come from?
> Let me tell you!
> There once was a fair city,
> Among cities of the world the first in fame;
> It hath been ruined and laid desolate,
> To that city I belong, Delhi is its name.

The Lucknowis do not understand me and I do not understand them. How can I tell my tale in their strange land? I speak a language they cannot comprehend. They do not know that every word of Meer has a meaning beyond meaning. The language I speak is best understood by the common folk of Delhi. O Meer, why bother to speak to this assembly of the dead? Tears flow like rivers from my weeping eyes; my heart like Delhi lies in ruins. The fresh bloom of the rose gives me no joy; its piercing thorn no pain. Within my heart I know that I must return to Delhi where I passed

583

my life intoxicated with love which I drank with the rose-red wine of my heart's blood. With a sigh I recall a couplet I had composed: 'Already you bewail your blistered feet; it is a long way to Delhi, my friend!'

The news from Delhi brings tears to everyone's eyes. Neither Nadir Shah nor Abdali, neither the Marathas, nor the Jats, nor the Sikhs caused so much havoc as is reported to have been caused by the ill-begotten Ghulam Qadir, the grandson of Najibuddaulah, and his ruffianly gangs of Rohillas. This villain insulted and deposed Shah Alam II before putting out his eyes. May Allah burn his carcass in the fires of *gehennum*! Only Allah knows how long murder and looting will go on in Delhi! They will have to revive the dead to find victims and bring back some loot to be able to loot again. Delhi is said to have become like a living skeleton.

Burnt in flames till every building was reduced to ashes
How fair a city was the heart that love put to the fire!

ᴣᴀ·

There is some good news. The Marathas have inflicted severe defeat on the Rohillas. Ghulam Qadir has been captured alive, tortured and beheaded. Not a tear is shed for him. I am at peace with myself because at long last one villain who desecrated my beloved city has been punished. Will Delhi ever return to its days of glory? Only Allah knows.

I have now seen eighty-eight summers and winters on this wretched earth. The light in my eyes has dimmed; in three years I have lost four members of my family—my sons, daughter and my wife. I can neither read nor write and have no one left to look after me. Fain would I have mingled my dust in the scented dust of Delhi, but even that last wish is denied to me. Fate brought me to Lucknow into a *mehfil* where the *saqi* serves wine to everyone else but puts poison in my goblet. Here Meer will find no resting place; he must go like running water flowing through the gardens of the world.

Why do people tell frightening tales of the road of death when there are so many going along the same way to keep one company? I have no fear of dying. I had two loves in my life, Begum

Qamarunnissa and Delhi. One destroyed me, the other was destroyed for me. I have nothing more to live for. For my two loves I compose the following lines:

> *As I opened my eyes after my death*
> *My only wish was to once again see your face;*
> *It was in my heart you had your habitation*
> *Where will I find eyes to see this plundered place?*

Bhagmati

Bhagmati is to spend the evening with me. She will expect me to take her. If I do not show enthusiasm she will say I am growing indifferent or worse, impotent. I must have a good excuse for abstaining: high fever, a broken arm or a fractured penis. But all I have is wind in my stomach. Anyone who suffers from wind knows that until expelled, it will not allow the flame of lust to be kindled.

A long time ago when this trouble first started I made a list of wind-producing items. It included many of my favourite foods: raw onions, mangoes, cheekoos, ice-cream, cakes . . . I got over the problem that faced me by making a slight change in my love schedule. I ate them after and not before. With the years I had to add other items to the 'after-not-before' list: rice, lentils, potatoes, fried foods. The list continued to grow till it included just about everything edible. Nevertheless by the evening my belly would be full of air. I gave up lunch and moved the trysting hour from the evening to the afternoon. It worked well for some time. But it takes two to make a tryst and Bhagmati is not a nooner. So whenever I was sure Bhagmati would visit me I restricted my breakfast to black coffee and Vitamin B tablets—the closest thing I've discovered to an aphrodisiac.

Today all I have had since the morning are two mugs of black coffee and a capsule of Vitamin B Complex. Still there is a balloon full of wind in my stomach and no lust in my loins. I do not desire sex; instead I pray for a long, satisfying fart. I have tried hopping round the room on one leg, lying on my back with knees pressed against my paunch, massaging my belly. All to no avail. Verily hath Shaikh Saadi said:

> O Sage! the stomach is the prison house of wind,
> The sagacious contain it not in captivity,
> If wind torment the belly, release it, fart;
> For the wind in the stomach is like a stone on the heart.

O Sage of Shiraz! The wind doth truly torment me like a stone on my heart! How shall I release it?

Farting is one of the three great joys of life. First, sex; second, oil rubbed in a scalp full of dandruff; third, a long, satisfying fart. With the onset of middle age I have reversed the order of merit; farting now tops my list of life's pleasures.

The king of farts is the Trumpet—known to our ancestors as Uttam Paadam—its noise rendered as *phadakaam*. It is an act of will, it is proclamatory, it is masculine. It has much sound, little smell. The louder, the less odorous. My friend, the bald, beady-eyed photographer who has done considerable research on the subject is an exponent of the Trumpet. He is of the considered opinion that the Trumpet can only be produced by people who restrict their diet to fresh fruits and non-fibrous vegetables grown above the ground. Such food is *sattvik* (pure). (Poultry, fish and meat, though nourishing, are of the secondary *rajas* category. Spices, stale foods like pickles, preserves and chutneys; vegetables which grow underground like potatoes, radishes, carrots and garlic, or are attached to the earth like onions, cabbages, turnips and cauliflowers are definitely *tamas*). My photographer friend demonstrated the Trumpet by consuming a succulent watermelon on an empty stomach. An hour later he was airborne like a jet plane.

Second in the order of farts is the Shehnai—our ancestors also give it a secondary status Madhyamaa—and its sound is rendered as *thain, thain*. I prefer to compare it to the shehnai, a wind instrument made famous by the maestro Ustad Bismillah Khan of Varanasi. Like the Trumpet, the Shehnai is also an act of will and may be produced by a simple shift in position or gentle pressure on the paunch. It differs from the Trumpet in its softer tone and longer duration. The opening notes of a Scottish bagpipe sound very much like it—*pheenh*.

The third variety is the Scraper which makes a sound like the squelch of uncured leather or the rustling of old parchment. It is in fact not one but a succession of little farts—*pirt, pirt, pirt, pirt*. The Scraper is a by-product of eating too much of *tamasik* food. It is also a phenomenon of rectal muscles softened by age.

The fourth is the Tabla. It proclaims itself with a single *phut* like is a tap on a bongo drum. The Tabla is its own master as it escapes without the host's consent causing him or her deep embarrassment if they happen to be in company.

The fifth is the noiseless stink bomb, the Phuskin. Since it is unspoken it is best-suited to be planted on a neighbour as a secret gift—*gupta daan*. The donor can assume a 'not-I' look on his face or hold his nostrils and turn towards someone else with an accusing look. But he must heed the Japanese saying: 'He who talks is the one who farted.' If you have let off a stinking *gupta daan*, let others guess the identity of the benefactor.

Nations have different attitudes towards farting. The Europeans and Americans are quite shameless about it. It is a part of their Greek inheritance. Niarchos (1st century AD) extolled the virtues of farting any time wind built up in the belly:

> *If blocked, a fart can kill a man;*
> *If let escape, a fart can sing*
> *Health-giving songs; farts kill and save.*
> *A fart is a powerful king.*

Niarchos knew the difference between a noiseless stink bomb and the audible varieties of wind-breaking. To wit:

> *Does Henry sigh, or does he fart?*
> *His breath is strong from either part.*

Exhortations to the fart are also found in contemporary English literature:

> *Men of letters 'ere we part*
> *Tell me why you never fart?*
> *Never fart? Dear Miss Bright,*
> *I do not need to fart, I write.*

Although white races eat bland *rajas* food which does not produce much wind, when they have it, they release it in company with total unconcern for propriety. This is particularly revolting in the case of the wine-drinkers making a *gupta daan*: wind produced by wine is singularly stenchful. The ultimate in white people's vulgarity was a Frenchman who displayed his fart-power on stage. He had a slit made in the back of his trousers and for a small wager would blow out a candle placed three feet away from his posterior.

If the Whites are disgusting, the Indians are not much better. Indians have a very poor sense of humour and treat farting as a topic of jest. Since they eat highly spiced *tamasik* foods, they are the world's champion farters and have much occasion to laugh at each other. Once a Minister of Cabinet recording a talk for the External Services of All India Radio let out a Trumpet. The talk had to be re-recorded. However, when the time came, by mistake the original recording was put on the air. It gave an Indian the unique distinction of having his fart heard around the world. The Guinness Book of Records, please note.

For an unrelenting attitude towards farting the palm must be given to the Persians and the Arabs. There is a tale told on a young Iranian who broke wind in a *mehfil*. He was so overcome with remorse that he left the town. After many years in self-imposed exile he returned home hoping that his small misdemeanour would have been forgotten. Naming himself, he asked some boys to direct him to his old home. 'You mean the home of so-and-so the farter?' demanded the urchins. The poor man went back into exile.

The first prize for courtesy extended to farters goes to Sufi Abdul Rahman Hatam Ibn Unwan Al-Assam of Balkh, known for reasons of his noble attitude to farting as Hatam the Deaf. It is said that while he was explaining a matter of some theological import to an old woman, the lady farted. The saintly Sufi raised his voice and said, 'Speak louder, I am hard of hearing.' And for the fifteen long years that the woman continued to live, Hatam pretended to be hard of hearing and suffered people shouting in his ears. Hatam the Deaf is the patron saint of embarrassed farters.

I wonder if Bhagmati will accept this learned thesis on wind-breaking in lieu of the real thing.

1857

Alice Aldwell

I can never forgive myself for persuading my hubby to move to Delhi. 'What's wrong with Calcutta? We are quite happy here,' he used to say.

There wasn't anything wrong with Cal but there were many reasons why I did not want to go on living there. For one the place was full of Eurasians and if you didn't cut yourself off completely from them, English gentry began to suspect you were one of them. Mind you I have nothing personal against Eurasians! I know some fine gentlemen who have a bit of the tar-brush in them. Being half-caste is not their fault, is it? but I simply had to get away from them. Mum had lived in Cal so long that she had forgotten where she had come from back Home. She had also picked up that awful *chichi* of the half-castes. For another I had married a pucca English gentleman: Alexander Aldwell Esquire of Her Majesty's Post and Telegraph Services. Although yours sincerely was only a sweet eighteen and he going into his fifties when she went up the altar with him, he was, as I said before, of pucca English stock—sixteen annas to the sicca rupee! I didn't want him to mix with the riff-raff of Cal.

Alec gave me two girls in the first two years of our marriage. Then he went *phut* just like that, *phut*. At fifty-five he was retired from service. I hoped he would take us back to Ole Blighty. But he refused to leave Cal. 'Livin' is cheaper here,' he said. 'Back home we won't have an ayah or *chhokra*.' In any case he hadn't saved up anything so we did not have money to pay the ole P. & O. our passage money. We had to move into cheaper digs in the Eurasian quarters between Chowringhee and the native bazaar. I tried to have as little to do with our neighbours as possible! But Alec took to them like a duck takes to water. He started drinking toddy with Eurasians and going to their homes. I pleaded with him: 'Alec, I don't want my girls to grow up in India, I want to send them to a good school at Home. If you can't afford it on your pension, let's go up country where they are short of sahibs. I am sure you could get some kind of job. With your salary plus the pension we would give the girls what they deserve. We can save up and then join them in England. Meanwhile we could mix with the right kind of people.' If I said this once, I said it a hundred times. You think that Mister Alexander Aldwell would listen! In through one ear, out of the other! 'Who'll give me a job at my age?' he would say and go out of the house as fast as he could.

I got fed up. Without telling Alec I went to see Mr George Atkins who had been his boss. Mr Atkins was real nice. Only forty and a bachelor. He listened to me and said he'd like time to think it over. He asked me to dine with him at the Calcutta Club. Real swanky it was! Gentlemen in tails, ladies in long dresses! Bearers, *khidmatgars*, *abdars* and what have you! And Mr Atkins so gallant! He said he was mighty proud to be seen with anyone as pretty as yours sincerely. I gave him a friendly peck on his nose. After dining and dancing he drove me back in his buggy. I gave him a real mouthful of a goodnight kiss.

A few days later, Mr Atkins invited me to dine with him at his bungalow. So romantic it was! Candle-light and champagne and all that kind of thing. English ham, cheddar cheese and everything of the best from Calcutta's poshest store—the Hall of All Nations. I knew what he wanted. And I knew what I wanted. After supper we got down to business: I gave him a real nice time. As I said, my hubby had gone *phut*. I was only twenty-six and hadn't known a man for more than a year.

George Atkins did not know the first thing about making love—I mean full twenty shillings to the pound worth of love. No sooner he put his thing in, he was finished. He worked himself up for a second bout. This time he was very rough; he bit my breasts, dug his nails into my poor bottom and rammed away as hard as he could. As he was about to come, I screamed, 'You are killin' me darlin'!' He lunged away and with a great 'whoa' spent himself. I pretended I had come and was exhausted. He looked like St George who had slain his first dragon. He turned very gentle: 'Did I hurt you, dear? Do forgive me.' Hurt me? My foot! I replied in my most tired voice, 'No, darling, you did not hurt me. You just did me in. It was wonderful. Thank you, thank you, thank you.' George Atkins looked as if his salary had been doubled and he had scored a century at a cricket match. He lay beside me tapping his chest as if it were full of gold medals. I began to play with his nipples till they became hard. I kissed his paunch and stuck my nose in his navel. I could see his member was a sorry state of dejection. I ran my fingers in his fuzzy red pubic hair and gently played with his whatnot. It began to stir like a snake in a snake charmer's basket. Then I applied my tongue to it till it was fully revived. It was quite a size. I came over him and took him between my thighs. I wanted him to have a night he would remember as long as he lived. 'I expect it's the Indian in you which makes you such a superb lover,' he said crossing his arms behind my back. I didn't like that and told him so. 'No Georgie dearie,' I told him, 'there is nothing Indian about yours sincerely. I am as pucca as you: one hundred per cent British and proud of it. Now promise me one thing. You must get Alec a job some place up country. God promise?' I kissed him and wiggled my middle on him. I looked directly into his eyes and asked: 'Do I have your word?' He tried to look away, but I held his head in my hands. 'Promise! I'll make it worth your while,' I assured him. 'I will do my best,' he replied. That was enough. I glued my mouth to his, ran my tongue in his mouth and worked on him till both of us were like two animals: biting, clawing, drawing blood. We almost killed each other in the final act. This time it was, as they say in an attorney's office, 'Signed, sealed and delivered.' His *syce* drove me home at 3 a.m.

The next morning I nagged Alec and made him call on Mr Atkins. (I told him that I had spoken to someone who had spoken to Mr Atkins). My only fear was that Atkins might want to keep me in Cal. But you know what men are! Within a week he fixed Alec with a job in Delhi. I went to his bungalow to thank him. This time there were no candles, no champagne, no supper. He just fucked me.

That's how we came to be in Delhi in the spring of 1856. We rented a large double-storeyed house in Daryaganj where most of the European civilians lived. Our bungalow had a spacious compound and quarters for our ayahs, *khansama, masalchi, abdars, bhishties, syce, jamadars* and other servants. It was like a fortress with high walls and a massive iron gate. On the eastern side of our bungalow was the city wall with the river Jamna running below it.

In November I had my third child, another girl. We had her christened at St James Church in Kashmiri Gate. I chose the name for her: Georgina. (I sent Mr Atkins a card announcing the birth and the name of our girl). Fifteen days later we had a party to celebrate Georgina's arrival. Just about everyone who was anyone in Delhi was invited. More than fifty ladies and gentlemen responded. The Resident, Mr Theophilus Metcalfe, who was the *burra* sahib dropped in for a few minutes. Mr Beresford, the manager of the bank in the main bazaar, Chandni Chowk, and his wife came with their children. Captain Douglas, commander of the guard at the Red Fort came with Mr Simon Fraser, the Commissioner. Because of the baby I could not drink or dance. Everyone else had a wonderful time.

We did not ask any natives. Nevertheless many sent us presents. Amongst them was a lovely brocade piece from Begum Zeenat Mahal, the favourite wife of the old king Bahadur Shah.

Mr Metcalfe took me aside and asked me for a favour. He said that he wanted someone to keep in touch with the harems of the nawabs to know what their begums were saying. I do not know how he guessed that I could understand Hindustani. Since he spoke to me personally, I promised to do anything I could after I had weaned my baby.

Winters in Delhi are very pleasant. By December it is cold enough to have a log fire. There is frost on the ground in the mornings; the days are bright and warm. I made my place real comfy and kept an open house for Europeans. Captain Douglas and his young subalterns became regular visitors. I served them hot rum punch with cloves and nutmeg which they loved. On Christmas eve, we went to the carol service at St James Church. Next morning, our verandah was full of baskets of fruit and flowers sent by my husband's native subordinates for the *bara din*. In the afternoon, Mr Metcalfe was at home to the European community. We toasted her Majesty the Queen on the lawns of his mansion beyond Kashmiri Gate. That evening we had a few bachelors join us round our Christmas tree. Everyone got very drunk: Alec was quite blotto and had to be put to bed. The men flirted with me—mind you nothing very serious! Just a lot of Christmassy kissin' and cuddlin'.

On Boxing Day Alec went out with Captain Douglas for shikar. They brought back two blackbucks, four geese and almost fifty partridges. We sent legs of venison and a brace of partridges to our friends.

We organized a grand feast on New year's eve. Mr Metcalfe again did us the honour of a short visit. Once more he took me aside and reminded me of my promise to find out what the native women were saying. He sounded very eager about it. I assured him I would get down to the job.

The real fun began after Mr Metcalfe had left. Alec passed out and had to be put to bed. One of the subalterns almost raped me within a yard of where Alec was lying drunk. That stupid, besotted husband of mine kept egging him on, 'Take the bloody bitch . . go on . . .' Such was life in Delhi.

After the season's festivities were over I sent letters of thanks to the wives of the natives who had sent us gifts on Georgina's birth and the *bara din*. Some begums came to call and protested that letters were not necessary between members of the same family. ('I a member of a native family! Really!') Natives are given to this kind of exaggeration. I was 'sister' to everyone. Their children called me *mausi*. Fawning and flattering you to your face but always ready with a dagger to plunge in your back!

ॐ

It was some time in the April of 1857. I remember it had turned very, very warm. We had *bhishties* splashing water on the khas curtains we hung on the doors. No one dared to stir out in the afternoon. Even the nights were unpleasant. We slept on our roof and had a relay of pankhawallas to fan us throughout the night. One day Begum Zeenat Mahal sent us a trayload of watermelons and mangoes from her estate in Talkatora. I gave a handsome tip to the bearers and informed Mr Metcalfe about it. He sent me word that I should join the party of European ladies who had also received baskets of fruit and who were calling on Zeenat Mahal to thank her.

I took my two older girls with me in the phaeton sent by Mr Beresford, the banker. Captain Douglas received us at Lahore Gate. It was a memsahibs' afternoon. There was old Mrs Flemming, wife of Sergeant Flemming and her daughter, Mrs Scully, and a few others. Captain Douglas passed us on to Basant Ali khan, a fat eunuch who was the head of the harem guard. He escorted us through the Meena Bazaar and endless corridors with rooms on either side occupied by the *salateen* members of the royal household. A scruffier, smellier lot would be hard to find anywhere in the world. Their quarters were worse than those of my servants; the women were more poorly dressed than my ayahs. We were conducted to the queen's reception room which overlooked the river.

We were seated on divans overlaid with Persian carpets and bolsters covered with brocade to rest our backs. Carpets in the heat of summer! But there are natives for you! Every visitor had two women standing behind her waving huge fans. They sprinkled us with rose and kewra water. A female herald announced: 'Her Majesty, the Queen of Hindustan, Empress of the Universe, diadem of the age.' Natives love high-sounding titles. In came the queen. She certainly was a beauty! Large almond-shaped eyes, olive complexion and jet black hair. She was exquisitely dressed in her native chemise and *garara* with a gossamer-thin dupatta flung over her head. We stood up to greet her. She shook each of us by the hand, said 'good-afternoon' in English and patted my children on their cheeks. My girls curtsied to her. Trays of fruit and sweetmeats were passed around. She pressed us to taste them. Although she knew a little English, she spoke in Persian or Hindustani. Most of us had picked up a few words in Hindustani, so we got along quite well. When we ran out of words we giggled or laughed.

There was much coming and going of begums and their daughters all very curious to see the memsahibs and talk to them. Men were not allowed in the zenana apartments but Prince Jawan Bakht, the queen's only son, a sallow-skinned youth of sixteen who had recently married his cousin, was allowed in with his wife.

The queen had presents for all of us. We also had presents for her and her daughter-in-law. My girls received a silk chemise, a salwar and a gold bangle each. In return I gave the queen a bottle of Yardley's lavender water and her daughter-in-law, a lady's watch. They were very happy with the gifts.

The party broke up into small groups. I joined a group with Jawan Bakht and his wife. The boy had not been taught how to behave in the company of ladies. He kept chewing betel-leaf and spitting the horrible, bloody phlegm into a silver spittoon which a eunuch carried everywhere he went. And like common natives he kept scratching his privates. He also had the nasty habit of whispering in the ears of his cronies. At times he made remarks in Persian which he thought we could not understand. Since I had tried to speak to him he directed his evil eyes and tongue towards me. He recited a couplet in Persian to his wife:

Expect not faithfulness from nightingales
Who sing every moment to another rose.

The silly girl covered her face with her hands and went into fits of laughter. As his eyes were fixed on me, I suspected the couplet was about me. While his mother was talking to some of the ladies, he again said in Persian: 'An arrow in the side of a young damsel is better than an old man.' His wife re-doubled her laughter. This only encouraged the lout to go on:

When she saw something in her husband's hand
Something limp, hanging like the lower lip of a hungry man . . .
My ministrations will rouse one asleep but not a corpse.

I was really *gussa*. 'What is this *buk buk* your husband is saying?' I demanded of his wife. Jawan Bakht tried to be very clever. It did not occur to the fool that I could understand Persian. 'Aldwell memsahib, this is poetry in praise of youth and beauty,' he replied with a smirk on his face. 'You have no cause to be angry. Regarding an angry woman, the same poet, the peerless Saadi, has said . . .' And he quoted in Persian:

A woman who rises unsatisfied from her bed

Will quarrel and contend with her man;
An old man who cannot rise without the aid of a stick
How can his own stick rise?

'I know exactly what it means,' I cut him short in Persian. 'You should be ashamed of yourself. Shall I tell your mother what you have been saying?' You should have seen the fellow's face! Yellow as a dry banana-leaf. And squirming like a worm on the hook. His mother turned to me and asked: 'What are you two quarrelling about?' 'You ask your son, Your Majesty,' I replied.

I left Jawan Bakht's group and went across the room to speak to one of the girls who had been trying to catch my eye. She wanted to try out the words of English she had learnt. Jawan Bakht also quickly turned away and began to talk to Mrs Scully. I don't know what he said to her but she suddenly stood up and spoke to Mrs Flemming: 'Mother do you hear what this young rascal is saying? He says that he will soon have the English under his feet, after that he will kill all Hindus.' Mrs Flemming was old and very blunt.

'Did you say that, Jawan Bakht?' she demanded angrily.

The queen looked very angrily at her son. Jawan Bakht grinned like a monkey with red teeth. 'I was only joking,' he replied.

'What kind of jokes have you been learning lately?' asked Mrs Flemming. 'First you are rude to a lady (meaning me) and then to the English race! If there is any trouble in Hindustan, you will be the first to have your head taken off your shoulders.'

'*La haul valla quwwat!*' chanted the maidservants. Queen Zeenat Mahal's face was flushed with embarrassment. Everyone knew that she had been knocking at the doors of the sahibs wanting them to proclaim Jawan Bakht as the next king of Delhi. And there he was pouring cold water on her hopes, 'What kind of ill-mannered talk is this? You must apologize at once,' she said very firmly.

'*Amma Jan!*' whined the lout, 'I was only saying that there are rumours afioat that the Persians are going to invade Hindustan. And like Nadir Shah a hundred years ago, they will massacre the infidels. *Amma Jan*, you know very well that I would give my life to protect the lives of the European ladies of Delhi.'

That just proved what I had been saying about these

natives—blatant liars from head to foot! Anyway, I had something for Mr Metcalfe.

The reception came to an end. Zeenat Mahal sent for the tray of betel leaves and gave us one each with her own hands. I can't stand betel any more than other Europeans, but court etiquette required us to accept. So we stuffed the leaves in our mouths, salaamed the queen and left.

I told my hubby about the party in the palace. He was not surprised. He said he had overheard natives talking of a Persian or a Russian invasion and even seen posters on the walls of the Jamia Masjid saying that the invasion would take place that summer. He said that these rumours had been going on since the day Lord Canning had become Viceroy. When walking up to take the oath of office His Lordship's foot had caught in the carpet and he had stumbled. The natives were saying that this was a sign from Allah that Canning's government would likewise stumble and fall. Alec said that most natives believed that British rule would end on the hundredth anniversary of the Battle of Plassey, which was to be some time in June. 'All these bloody niggers can do is yak yak,' he assured me. 'Let them try and we will stick a greased pole up their dirty black bums.' Alec had been using that kind of language ever since he had gone *phut*.

Alec called on Mr Metcalfe and told him what I had picked up at the palace and what he had heard in the bazaar. Mr Metcalfe thanked Alec and asked him to request me to keep in touch with the ladies of the harem of Mirza Abdullah, one of the many grandsons of the king.

Mirza Abdullah lived in Daryaganj. He was a follower of a fellow called Hassan Askari who lived in the street behind our house. This Hassan Askari was known to have the king's ear. The king's daughter who had died two years ago had been his mistress. Mirza Abdullah's sister had called on me many times. I really had no intention of returning her calls. But after what Mr Metcalfe had said to my hubby I felt I should do my bit for the Old Country.

One afternoon I dropped in at Mirza Abdullah's house. My, how flattered these natives are when a European lady calls on them! And how flustered! The women were so excited and out of breath that they could hardly talk. And they were all very eager to tell me of the rumours about invasions and risings. 'You can't stop tongues from wagging, can you?'' said Mirza's senior begum. 'There are as many rumours as there are people.' I asked her about Hassan Askari. 'He's a man of Allah,' replied the begum. 'But he is not of our faith. He is a Shia and we are Sunnis. We have nothing to do with him.'

I knew this was a lie. The tailor who did odd jobs for me also worked for Mirza Abdullah's family. He had told me that he often saw Hassan Askari in Mirza Sahib's house. As I said before, you can never trust natives. They learn to lie from the day they learn to speak. They think it's more clever to tell a lie than to tell the truth.

Alec went to report on my visit to Mirza Abdullah's house to Mr Metcalfe. When he returned he told me of mysterious fires in the cantonments and strange people running about with chappaties. That the wily blacks were plotting against us we were sure, but we did not realize how soon these double-faced traitors would stab us in the back. How well I recall the day it happened!

Our usual practice before we retired was to spend the evening on the roof-top (unless there was a dust-storm blowing) where we had our sundowner and our dinner. Then as I've said, we'd have the *bhishties* sprinkle water and servants lay out the beds. At first I had mine alongside Alec's. But when he had eaten hot curry, he used to get very windy and make things unpleasant. So I had his bed removed to a distance so that we were not disturbed by his farting. On the roof-top the nights were cool and the early morning breeze very pleasant.

The betrayal began one morning in the month of Ramadan when Muslims fast from sunrise to sunset. I remember being woken by the muezzin's call for prayer. It was still very dark but I could not sleep because there were many mosques in Daryaganj and one muezzin followed another. Our Muslim servants were making a racket cooking and gobbling their day's meal. Just as the dawn appeared above the jungle across the river, a cannon was fired from the Royal Mosque. The explosion woke Alec and the children. The *khansama* brought up our *chota hazri*.

My girls were soon romping about on the roof, taking their time over their tumblers of milk. Alec and I were having our tea when we saw a fat Bania come with his brass jug and squat down near the wall: these natives can never resist a wall. Alec always had a catapult and a trayful of pebbles brought up with his morning tea. Before the Bania could relieve himself, Alec sent a pebble flying towards him. It hit the brass jug, *ping*. The Bania quickly stood up to adjust his dhoti. 'Bugger off you black bastard!' yelled Alec. And so the poor fellow did. We had a big laugh. Then along came a man carrying a wicker cage with a partridge in it. Another partridge ran a few yards behind calling *teetur, teetur, teetur*. Alec raised his *bundook*—he always had his *bundook* by his bedside to shoot geese or duck coming overhead from the river—aimed it at the partridge and said, 'Bang! I'd like to get that fat one; make a nice partridge pie, what!', He used to aim his *bundook* at the partridge every morning and say the same thing. The day had begun like any other day.

The sun came up bloody red and bloody hot. With the sun came the flies. Alec and the children went downstairs. I was near the staircase when I noticed a cloud of dust on the other side of the river. I stopped to see what it was: It was a party of horsemen galloping over the boat bridge, firing their carbines. 'Alec, Alec,' I shouted, 'Come up and see!' By the time Alec came back to the roof-top the horsemen had disappeared behind the fort. But another party followed. This lot rode along the wall towards Daryaganj. They saw us standing on the roof and yelled, '*Maar dalo saley firangi ko*—kill the bloody foreigners.' They were in the Company's uniforms.

We ran downstairs and had the gates of our bungalow shut.

The Last Emperor

There is a saying that when a sinner goes on fast Allah makes the day longer. So it seemed to us during the month of Ramadan of the year 1273 of our Prophet (Allah's blessings on Him), corresponding to May 1857 of the era of Jesus the Healer (on Whom be peace). We did our best to observe the injunctions of Islam; but the flesh is weak and often bends the will to its satisfaction. And that year the holy month of fasting fell during the mango season. The best time to enjoy mangoes is between mid-morning and the afternoon. This was forbidden. So be it. If Allah wished to test our faith, we who are King would abjure the fruit which is king among the fruits of our land.

Of late it had been our habit to rise a watch before sunrise and sit on the balcony overlooking the river. We had issued instructions that no one was to disturb us till we had said our *fajar* prayer. This gave us three to four hours to be alone with ourselves. We used these hours for contemplation. We liked to sit wrapped in darkness and in silence; we liked to watch the light of the waning moon reflected in the Jamna; on moonless nights we liked to gaze into the black heaven with its myriad stars; we liked seeing the silvery brilliance of the morning star fade into the paling sky. We liked to see the sun come up noisily with the screaming of koels. The cool morning breeze never failed to rouse the melancholic muse of poetry in our breast. Sometimes we would light the taper and pen a couplet or two; at other moments we would allow the lines of a ghazal to turn into song in our mind. And there were mornings when we scanned lines sent to us by Zauq or Mirza Ghalib or one of the other poets of our city.

We cherished these hours of peace and repose because we felt closer to our Maker then than at any other time; they prepared us for the unpleasant realities that pressed upon us during the day. When the world is itself draped in the mantle of night, the mirror of the mind is like the sky in which thoughts twinkle like stars; it is the best time to commune with one's inner self and realize how insignificant one is even though he calls himself King of Kings and Emperor of Hindustan.

After these hours of solitude we repaired to Moti Masjid built by our illustrious ancestor, Alamgir Aurangzeb (may Allah rest his soul in Paradise). In the snow-cool atmosphere of this marble mosque we paid homage to our Maker (who gave silver to the stars and the moon, the fire and light to the sun) and His Messenger (Allah's blessings upon Him).

In the holy month of Ramadan this routine was somewhat altered. Kitchen fires were lit in the early hours so that people could feed before dawn appeared over the eastern horizon. During Ramadan we spent these early hours on a couch in the Diwan-i-Khas telling the beads of our rosary and repeating the ninety-nine names of Allah. Our morning meal was brought to us. We ate it alone. Our beloved Queen Zeenat Mahal, sent us a betel-leaf rolled by her own hands. We chewed betel, smoked our hookah and watched the stream of the Jamna change its hues under the ordinance of the heavens. As the cannon roared over Lahori Gate to proclaim the beginning of the fast, our hookah-bearer removed the pipe from our presence.

୨୦

To the best of our recollection this is exactly what took place on the morning of Monday, 11 May 1857, the 16th of Ramadan. The night before, our royal consort Begum Zeenat Mahal and we had spent some time strolling on the balcony. She made some remark on the reflection of the moon in the river for the moon was full and the sky clear. And when we complained of the oppressiveness of the weather, she replied that it took the searing heat of the desert winds to give mangoes their delicious flavour, the jasmine and the maulsari their fragrance. She untied from her hair a chaplet made of these flowers and presented it to us as proof. We inhaled their perfume and when we held it back for her she said: 'Keep it beside your pillow. It will remind Your Majesty of your servant Zeenat.' Since knowledge of women is forbidden during Ramadan we had accepted this floral token. Its fragrance had filled our dreams; when we woke, the morning star and the morning breeze both reminded us of our beloved.

On the 11th of May we were a little late in our ablutions and prayers—nevertheless we beheld the dawn come over the Jamna. We saw the fires lit by the melon-growers across the river grow pale under the light of the rising sun and our soldiers change guard on the boat-bridge. We had a light meal of partridge *pilaf,* followed by a couple of Tsamar Bahisht (paradise) mangoes which had just come in season. We also drank a tumbler full of ice-cooled milk spiked with saffron. This was followed by the usual betel-leaf and a few pulls at the hookah. After *fajar* prayer we returned to the Diwan-i-Khas. The royal physician, Hakeem Ahsanullah Khan, was ushered into our presence and permitted to feel our pulse. By the grace of the Almighty who alone determines the humours of the mortal frame, he pronounced us in good health. Then our slaves, the eunuch Basant Ali Khan and Vakil Ghulam Abbas, presented the accounts of the royal household. Our expenses were, as always, more than our income. We refused to look into them and waved the men away. We turned our back on the crowd of petitioners that had assembled and began to gaze at the scene along the Jamna.

The sun had risen. Dhobis were pounding their washing on slabs of stone while their women were spreading out washed garments on the sandbank to dry. Their children played in the sand. A line of labourers carrying baskets of melons was crossing the boat-bridge. It was like any other summer morning.

Suddenly there was tumult. We saw horsemen galloping across the boat-bridge firing their carbines in the air. The sentries on the bridge did not arrest their progress. The men galloped across the sand towards us and drew rein beneath the palace walls. *'Dohai! Dohai!'* they screamed. 'Listen to our *faryad!'* Some shouted slogans: *'Badshah Salamat zindabad!'* We looked down over the parapet. The men wore uniforms of the East India Company. As soon as they saw us, they saluted and repeated: 'Long live the Emperor of Hindustan!' One shouted at the top of his voice: 'We have murdered the *firangis* in Meerut. The *nasara* (Christians) want to destroy our faith. We will rid the country of these vile infidels. We will make you Emperor of Hindustan!' Then they all shouted together: 'Long live the dynasty of the Mughals!'

'La haul valla quwwat illah bi-illah hil ali yul aleem! No fear, no power save Allah who is powerful and mighty!' we exclaimed. 'Who are these men?' we demanded of the eunuch Basant Ali Khan. He did not reply. He had a smirk on his black, bloated face. 'Inform Captain Douglas at once and see that they are not let inside the city,' we ordered.

Basant Ali Khan bowed and withdrew. Something in his manner told us that he was in no haste to carry out our command. We sent another messenger to the Captain. The soldiers from Meerut moved along the wall towards the harem apartments and began to yell: 'Long live the *Malika-i-Hind!'* More horsemen came galloping across the boat-bridge.

Captain Douglas who was officer-in-charge of the palace guards made his obeisance. He wanted to go down to speak to the men. We forbade him from endangering his life. We went to the balcony. We stood beside him to see that no one harmed him. 'What do you want?' he demanded of the men. 'What right do you have to disturb His Majesty in this way? Return to your regiments at once or you will be severely punished.' The men below stopped shouting and rode away to join their comrades assembled under the windows of our harem. Captain Douglas took leave to apprehend the mutinous gang.

We waited. We saw troops of soldiers wearing the uniform of the Company marching over the bridge. Mr Simon Fraser, who also lived in the fort, sent a messenger begging for a loan of palanquins to bring their ladies to the safety of our harem and permission to mount cannon on the gates of the fort. We ordered that these requests be complied with at once. But as fate would have it, the 'man' to whom we entrusted the execution of these orders was the eunuch Basant Ali Khan.

We waited. Messengers brought news of disturbances from different parts of the city. We pondered. Could we, whilst the fires of confusion were burning low, put them out by sprinkling on them the waters of stratagem? We issued orders that the mutineers should not be allowed to enter the city. We advised the sahibs going out of the city to remonstrate with them. No one paid heed to what we said.

An hour later we heard that the mutineers had been let into the city and had killed some Europeans in Daryaganj. Then we heard that the family of the manager of the bank who lived in Begum Samru's palace in Chandni Chowk had also been murdered. We became very concerned about the safety of the Europeans in the fort and enquired whether their ladies had been brought into our harem. It was then that we learnt that poor Captain Douglas, Mr Fraser and their ladies had been slain in their apartments.

Someone opened the gates of the fort to let in the mutineers. We were surrounded by a mob of soldiers which included many of our palace guards. They acclaimed us as their true monarch and the Emperor of Hindustan. 'Who calls us Emperor?' we protested. 'We are a fakeer prolonging our days on this wretched earth. We have no strength in our arms; our feeble voice is not heard beyond the walls of this fort.' But they would not listen. We were like a paper-boat set afloat on a mountain torrent.

All through that morning and afternoon soldiers kept streaming into our palace uninvited and unannounced. They did not bother with court etiquette. They pushed aside our servants, marched into the Diwan-i-Khas meant for special audience, grabbed our hands, kissed them and so extracted our blessings. Some presented us with silver coins; most of them only soiled our fingers with their lips.

It seemed like a dream compounded of episodes good and bad. And as sometimes happens we were violently roused from our dreams by an explosion which sounded like a thousand claps of thunder. The walls of our palace shook as in an earthquake. A few minutes later we were informed that English soldiers had set a torch to the powder magazine in Kashmiri Gate; several hundred of our subjects had been killed by the explosion. The whole city was in tumult.

Alice Aldwell *alias* Ayesha Bano Begum

I have never trusted the word of an Indian and I have been proved right every time. But as I said that afternoon we had no choice. I told my husband: 'Alec, let's not put all our eggs in one basket. You go with the others. I'll take the girls to Mirza Abdullah.' Alec agreed.

I dressed my girls in the native costumes that Begum Zeenat Mahal had given them. I borrowed a clean pair of salwar-kameez from my ayah and put on her dirty burqa. I sent for two palanquins. I put the two older girls in one and took the baby with me. One of our servants agreed to come with us. The flaps of the palanquins were lowered as they are when native women of rank travel in them.

Mirza Abdullah was, as I said before, grandson of the king. He lived in Urdu Bazaar close to the Royal Mosque. He had received many favours from my husband. His wife and sister had often called on me. 'You are our sister,' they used to say and called my children *betis*.

The crowd let us pass. We got to Urdu Bazaar without anyone questioning us. The ladies of the Mirza's household received us very kindly. His sister kissed my children and said that as long as she was alive she would not allow a single hair on their heads to be touched. I assured them that as soon as the trouble was over my husband would compensate them for their hospitality.

Urdu Bazaar was a Mohammedan locality. It had some

bookstores and an assortment of shops—butchers, dyers, kite-makers, sweetmeat-vendors, betel-leaf-sellers. Behind these shops were the mansions of the rich nawabs. Although the approach to Mirza Abdullah's house was through a narrow lane, with a foul-smelling drain running alongside, the inside was very airy, with a large courtyard and verandahs. In the centre of the courtyard was a big peepal tree with boxes for Mirza's flocks of pouter pigeons. The verandahs were lined with potted palm and jasmine. On one side of the courtyard were the women's apartments where lived the Mirza's wives, mother, sister and a host of other female relatives and maidservants.

Mirza Abdullah was a bird fancier. On the roof of his house he had a loft where he kept his champion birds. He used to fly them round every afternoon directing them with a scarf and a whistle. He also owned partridges and fighting quails. Like other princes of royal blood, the Mirza had never grown up to be a man. Although he was in his thirties, he had never done a stroke of work. He lived on the allowance he received from the king. He was always in debt to the local Banias; his womenfolk were forever pawning their jewellery. None of this prevented him from taking more wives and going to brothels. He spent his afternoons challenging his neighbours at kite-flying or enticing their pigeons. In the evenings he took out his quails and partridges to fight other nawabs' quails and partridges. And if there was anything going on in the city, Mirza Abdullah was sure to be there.

Mirza Abdullah came home after dark. He was talking at the top of his voice. I could tell from his tone that he was boasting. He suddenly quietened down as someone told him of my presence in his house. He came into the zenana and greeted me with a familiarity he had never dared to assume before. 'Good-evening, memsahib,' he said in English, 'or rather, seeing the way Madam and her children are dressed, I should say As-Salaam-Valai-kum.'

The natives have a saying: a poor man's wife is everyone's sister-in-law. They think nothing of sleeping with their brothers' wives. I was certainly a poor sister-in-law to them. I accepted the pleasantry and replied very polite-like: 'Valai-kum-As-Salaam. Nawab Sahib, it is very noble of you to allow us the shelter of your home for a few days. Allah will reward you for your kindness.'

'It is a great honour to have you here,' he continued in his bantering tone, scratching his privates. 'But I would advise you to be in some place safer than Urdu Bazaar which is entirely Mohammedan,' he said. 'You know how Muslims feel about the *firangi* and the *nasara!*'

I could hardly believe he would use the word *firangi* for us and *nasara* for Indian Christians! There was no telling with these fellows.

'But now you look a true Mussalmanni,' he went on. 'For your own safety all of you should learn the creed of Islam. I will send a maulvi to teach you. He will also escort you to my other house in Nai Sarak. You can leave your valuables here for safekeeping. Your slave will present himself tomorrow to see that you are comfortable.'

I decided to fall in with anything by which I could save my children's lives. When the maulvi came, I told him that my mother was a Kashmiri Mussalmanni and that though I had been given away in marriage to a sahib, I had remained a Muslim. He had us repeat: '*La Illaha Lillillah, Mohammed Rasool Illah*—there is one God and Mohammed is His Messenger.' He gave us Muslim names. From Alice I became Ayesha. The elder, Mary, became Maryam. The second, Fiona, became Fatima. Georgina became Jahanara. The maulvi was very pleased at having made three converts.

I left a bundle of silver rupees in safekeeping with Mirza Abdullah and took my leave of the women and set out for the nawab's other house. I took the girls in my palanquin. We were challenged many times but a word from the bearded maulvi was enough to let us through. We arrived at a haveli off Nai Sarak. The maulvi spoke to the caretaker who let us in.

With half an eye I could see that Mirza Abdullah used this place for his fun and games. The caretaker was a *hijda*. The room he showed us into had a wall-to-wall carpet covered over with white sheets. Bolsters were scattered about on it. There were large mirrors on the wall and a chandelier hanging from the roof. There was a dark anteroom with charpoys which was made over to us. The girls were worn out and fell asleep at once. I spent the night sitting beside them.

The next morning I sent my servant to Mirza Abdullah for the money I had left with him. He came back an hour later and said that Mirza Sahib denied having received anything from me.

Furthermore he wanted us to get out of his house by the afternoon. The *hijda* promised to intercede on our behalf if I did as he told me. I agreed. I did not care what happened to me as long as my girls were safe.

In the afternoon the *hijda* came to help get me ready for the Nawab Sahib. He put henna paste on my palms and the soles of my feet. While the paste was drying he got *bhishties* to fill the bathtubs and poured cupfuls of rose-water in them. In the bathroom he undressed me. He ran his calloused hands over my body. He made me lie on the floor and spread out my thighs to shave my pubis. He inserted his dirty finger in me and made lewd gestures. While bathing me he squeezed my breasts. After drying my body with a dirty towel he rubbed gallnut powder on my privates: natives believe it tightens the muscles. To make sure that the powder had the desired result he made me lie down and applied his tongue. What the *hijdas* lack in the real stuff they make up for by doing lots of other things. This fellow worked himself into a frenzy. He stripped himself and thrust his stinking misshapen middle into my face screaming hoarsely, 'Kiss it, kiss it.' That was too much. I pushed him away. He slapped me. 'If you breathe a word to the Mirza,' he threatened, 'I'll slit the throats of your girls.'

He dressed me in embroidered silk. He put lamp black in my eyes and made me chew a foul-tasting, aromatic betel-leaf.

Confusion and shame together describe what I passed through that afternoon. I narrate what happened to me so that the world knows how rotten, villainous, treacherous, degraded and lecherous these Indians are! The entire nation deserves to be put against a wall and their carcasses thrown to pye-dogs!

Mirza Abdullah arrived with two of his cronies: their hair was oiled, eyes black with antimony, ears stuffed with swabs of scented cotton, mouths drooling the bloody phlegm of betel-leaf-juice. They wore thin muslin shirts and baggy pyjamas.

'*Wah! Wah*! Memsahib! How this dress becomes you,' shouted Mirza Abdullah as he introduced me to his friends. 'They are like my real brothers; nay, dearer to me than my real brothers!'

'You have shot a tasty piece of shikar,' said one of them.

'She looks ripe and experienced.'

Even in the circumstances in which I was that remark stung

me.

'It's been my heart's greatest desire to make love to a white woman,' remarked the other. 'Mirza Sahib, I have to thank you for fulfilling my life's ambition.'

'You can only half thank me because only half of your desire will be fulfilled,' replied Mirza Abdullah. 'Alice alias Ayesha Begum is only half a memsahib; the other half is Kashmiri. No doubt you've disported yourself in many a Kashmiri vale!' The men roared with laughter and slapped each other's hands. This half-caste business I did not like at all.

Mirza Abdullah took me by the hand and made me recline on his bolster. The others sat facing us. The *hijda* brought a pitcher and poured out some evil-smelling liquid in four silver goblets. When he held out one to me, I shook my head. 'It is an unpardonable crime to drink during Ramadan,' I said.

'*Wah! Wah!*' exploded Mirza Abdullah. 'Yesterday's Mussalmanni reads us sermons on Islam. Ayesha *bi,* during *jihad* everything is forgiven.' He gulped down the stuff in his goblet and repeated, 'During a *jihad* everything is allowed. Everything; you understand?' I understood. The men emptied their goblets; the *hijda* refilled them. Mirza Abdullah put a tumbler to my lips and commanded: 'Drink! Or I'll force it down your throat.' I knew what the blackguards meant to do to me. I decided I would be able to take it more easily if I were drunk. I took a sip and then gulped it down. It was spiced brandy; it burnt its way down my gullet into my belly.

'*Shabash,*' they cried in a chorus. 'Now the *mehfil* can get going.'

My goblet was refilled. The brandy loosened their tongues. One recited a poem of Saadi. Mirza Abdullah replied with lines from some court poets called Zauq and Ghalib. The third fellow quoted lines composed by the old king Bahadur Shah. Then they talked of the glories of Mughal rule and the wickedness of the English. 'As soon as the Company forces surrender,' said Mirza Abdullah, 'we will castrate all the *firangis* and take their women in our harems.' They laughed loudly at this joke.

Mirza Abdullah put his hand on my knee. He began to stroke and pinch my thighs. He touched my breasts and began to play with my nipples. His friends got up and asked: 'Have we Your Highness's permission to retire to the next room?' Abdulla'

609

nodded. They tottered out leaving the two of us reclining on the same bolster.

For some time Mirza Abdullah continued playing with my nipples. His other hand slipped round my waist. He undid the knot in the cord of his pyjama-trousers, took my hand and placed it on his middle. He was in a state of agitation. I picked up the goblet and drained it of its liquid fire. Now I did not care what anyone did to me. I thought it wiser to take the lead myself. I lay back and directed Mirza Abdullah into my person. A drunk man takes an age to come. At long last, when it seemed he was working himself up to a climax, Abdullah hollered out to his friends to see what he was doing. He dug his teeth into my cheeks as he shot his seed. As soon as he got up, his friends stripped me of the little clothing left on me and assaulted me. I was like a piece of white meat fought over by two brown dogs: snarling, biting, clawing, shoving. So it went all through the long, long, sultry night. By the time one had finished, another had worked himself into a frenzy. And there was that *hijda* poking his fingers or tongue or whatever else he had. I was drenched with sweat and almost dead with exhaustion. By morning Abdullah and his friends were drained of all the poisonous semen in their vile bodies. They stumbled out singing and yelling obscenities. Only the *hijda* remained. He went on till the cannon announced the beginning of the day of abstinence. How much had passed between two risings of the sun!

I was woken up by Georgina's crying: 'Mummy, mummy, wake up!' The girls were in a state of shock. They had never before seen me like that—naked and bruised.

The only people who remained true to their salt were my servant Ali Ahmed and his wife. He realized what I had been through. At his own cost Ali Ahmed hired two palanquins and took us to his hovel. Very soon a large crowd collected. I heard voices shouting: 'Hand over that *firangi* woman.' Ali Ahmed's wife went out very boldly and scolded them: 'I am a Qureish of the tribe of the Prophet. The woman and the children whom I shelter in my home are Muslims. You will first have to kill me and my husband before you can touch them. Is there anyone here who wants to have the blood of the Prophet on his hands? Come on, it is the holy month of Ramadan,' she challenged. The crowd melted away.

I did not want to endanger the lives of these poor folk. I asked

Ali Ahmed to take a letter to the king and Queen Zeenat Mahal begging for help. I told them that I was born of a Muslim mother and had along with my two daughters recited the creed of Islam. I signed my name Ayesha Aldwell. I got no reply.

I wrote to many nawabs. Either they did not reply or sent notes regretting their inability to help. When all the rich and influential deserted us a poor man who owed us nothing came to our help. This was a tailor whose name I had never bothered to ask. He had stitched my daughters' frocks and got very fond of them. He came one morning with his cousin who was a sepoy. Although this cousin had gone over to the rebels he swore on the Quran that he would not let anyone harm us. We spent a day and night with the tailor's family. At sunset when the Muslims were at prayer we slipped out of the bazaar. The tailor and his sepoy cousin escorted our palanquins to the fort. We were taken over by the guards and produced before the king's son, Mirza Mughal. I then discovered that Mirza had intercepted the letters I had written to the king and Begum Zeenat Mahal. He ordered the guards to put us in the same underground dungeon as the other Europeans but to treat us as Muslims and not as *badzat nasara* (low-caste Christians).

On Wednesday, 13 May 1857, the family was re-united. Alec forgave me for what I had been through. He swore: 'I will split that bloody bastard Mirza Abdullah's bum in two.' But the English ladies were cold towards me. The favours that the guards showed towards us because I was a Mussalmanni made them angry. They were given coarse chappaties, I was served meat-curry. Sometimes the guards would ask me and my children to eat with them.

The heat and the stench in the dungeon was terrible. There was no latrine and we had to relieve ourselves in a dark corner and with our own hands throw the slop out through a hole in the wall. And the insults we had to suffer! Every day crowds came to see us as if we were animals in a zoo and screamed the vilest abuse at us. One day Jawan Bakht came in and addressed me as *bhabi*. 'Mirza Abdullah is like my own brother,' he said with a smirk. 'So you become my *bhabi*, don't you.'

Then came Saturday, the 16th of May.

I knew something dreadful was going to happen. There were no chappaties for breakfast. 'You'll get plenty where you are going,' the sentries said. They reassured me that I need have no fear about myself or my children. A dozen sepoys came into the cell and ordered all the other men, women and children to march out. My girls ran to Alec and clung to his knees. The sepoys tore them away from their father and thrust them towards me. 'Don't let them take daddy,' they cried. I pleaded with the sepoys but they took no notice of me. Poor Alec was pushed along with the others. They bolted the door leaving my daughters, myself and an old Mussalmanni who had been caught helping Europeans in the dungeon.

I heard people shouting. Then a shot. Then children and women screaming. Then it became still. Absolutely still.

I am ashamed to confess that my first thoughts were: 'Now there is no one left to turn up their noses at me. Only Mirza Abdullah and his pals will talk about me. As soon as this is over, I will get Alec's pension. I will take my girls to England and start life again with no one making nasty talk about where I came from and who I was!' Then I cried a lot.

Bahadur Shah Zafar

Later in the afternoon some forty Europeans, men and women (there were possibly some children among them), their hands tied with ropes, were brought in our presence. A huge mob followed; the guards had difficulty in keeping it back. '*Dohai! Dohai!*' they screamed. 'They've killed our men, we want justice. Hang these foreigners or hand them over to us.' The people wanted to avenge the lives lost in the explosion of the powder magazine. The white race had done many wrongs to us and our forefathers; but we refused to sanction vengeance on people who had nothing to do with the setting of fire to the powder magazine. We ordered the prisoners to be taken in our protective custody and lodged in an underground cellar of our harem.

The mob became very abusive; some men shouted slogans derogatory to our royal status. We ordered our Chamberlain to terminate the audience. He shouted '*Takhlia*' and dropped the red curtain. The tumult continued for some time before saner people were able to persuade the hot-heads to bow to the wishes to their Emperor: '*Khalq Khuda ki, mulk Badshah ka, hukum Jahan Panah ka*—People belong to God, the country to the King, obey the law of One who gives shelter to the world,' they shouted as they departed. We ordered that food from the royal kitchen be sent to the European prisoners.

We said our afternoon *maghreb* prayer in Moti Masjid. We noticed that many strangers had lined themselves up behind us. We held our peace because we were in the house of God. But our mind was very disturbed; we were unable to ask Allah for guidance. When we came out of the mosque these people again began to shout slogans demanding the blood of the *firangi*. Some had the audacity to ask us to hand over the prisoners to them. Once again we refused to accede to their demands. We expressed our sympathy to those who had lost relatives in the explosion and advised them to submit to the will of God and bury their dead.

In the evening we learnt that the *khutba* had been read in our name in the Jamia Masjid. Our courtiers flattered us by extolling the greatness of our royal forefathers and our virtues. Thus did destiny launch our kite in tumultuous clouds without handing us the string with which we could control its movements.

We allowed ourselves to be seated on the silver throne which had been stacked away in the basement for over thirteen years. On this silver chair had sat our ancestors: Taimur and Babar; Humayun, Akbar, Jahangir, Shah Jahan, Alamgir Aurangzeb I, Bahadur Shah the First, Jahandar Shah Farrukhsiyar, Mohammed Shah, Alamgir II, Shah Alam and our revered father Akbar Shah the Second. We received homage from our subjects till the cannon boomed to announce the setting of the sun and we terminated the proceedings.

The crowd did not disperse. Many men spread their sheets on the stone and marble floors of our halls of audience to spend the night. Their horses filled their bellies with the flowers of our garden. Only the palaces alongside the river were left to us.

We asked to be left alone with our thoughts. We reclined on our couch in the Diwan-i-Khas and let our eyes rest on the ceiling. We remembered the days when it was encrusted with silver and gold leaf. Now even the plaster had peeled off in many places. We saw the marble columns and the empty sockets which once had been studded with ruby, amethyst, lapis lazuli and cornelian. Our gaze fell on the faded lettering proclaiming the glory of the days of our illustrious ancestor Shah Jahan: *Gar Firdaus bar roo-e-zaminast; Hameenasto, hameenasto, hameenast*—If on earth there be a place of bliss, it is this, it is this, it is this. A deep sigh rose from our breast; our eyes were dimmed with tears.

✿

We were thus lost in our thoughts when our attention was drawn by a polite cough. The chief lady-in-waiting bowed and said that her mistress, our Queen Zeenat Mahal, begged the privilege of our company to break the fast.

We dragged our weary feet towards our harem. Eunuchs and female heralds proclaimed our advent as we proceeded from one room to another. This time the very words we had been hearing for twenty-two years since we had been king seemed to have acquired a new meaning: 'Sirajuddin Khan, Mohammed Abu Zafar Bahadur Shah Ghazi, Shadow of God on Earth, Emperor of Hindustan.' We came to Begum Zeenat Mahal's apartment. The food was already laid on an embroidered table-cloth. Garlands of jasmine and maulsari hung from the chandeliers; cobs of kewra stood in vases in the corner. As we entered, maidservants bowed and backed out of the room. We took our seat on the carpet and rested our weary back on a bolster.

Begum Zeenat Mahal made her entrance. She was dressed as she was on the day seventeen years ago when we had brought her as a bride to our harem: in gold brocade with a white spider-web dupatta to cover the glossy black of her hooded-cobra curls. In it she wore the emerald-and-pearl clasp we had given her Her large gazelle eyes sparkled with desire. She glided so gracefully towards us that although there were no bells on her feet our ears heard their musical tinkle. It seemed as if invisible hands had turned the knobs of lamps and made their tapers burn brighter. As Saadi said: 'A vision appeared in the night and by its appearance the darkness was illumined.' The tongue of eloquence could not describe her beauty.

'Has your slave permission to greet the Emperor of Hindustan?' She bowed low and salaamed us three times.

'*Subhan Allah!*' we exclaimed, taking in her beauty through our eyes. *Subhan Allah!* was all we had been able to say when we had first cast our eyes on her. She was then sixteen and we sixty-five. The seventeen summers that had ripened her beauty had also increased our appetite for her. We would rather have laid our head on her fleshy lap and let her run her fingers in our grey hair than eat the delicacies she had prepared for us. She must have read our mind. She asked us if we found the arrangements to our satisfaction. We quoted Saadi: 'I am hungry and opposite to a table of food; I am like a lusty youth at the door of a *hamaam* full of females.' This brought the colour of pomegranates to her cheeks.

We noticed that Zeenat Mahal had prepared our favourite dishes: venison kababs and nauratan chutney made of nine condiments; roast wings of peacocks and quails; kulfi covered with gold leaf and garnished with slices of mango. She helped us wash our hands. She picked the food with her own fingers and placed it in our mouth. We could not recall when last she had shown such tenderness towards us. When the meal was finished she rolled a betel-leaf, mixing lime and catechu paste with scented tobacoo, and placed it in our mouth.

While we were chewing the leaf, she asked us boldly whether she could have the privilege of sharing our couch for the night. We were a little taken aback. But it was not for nothing that it was said of our Mughal ancestors that they could take women till the last day of their lives. Though little else remained of our inheritance no one could deprive us of our ancestral blood. At the age of seventy we had run a nilgai across a boulder-strewn hillside and sliced its head off with our sword.

Allah had given our lions the same strength as He had bestowed on our arms. It was not the years but the holy law that set our head and heart at variance with each other. She read the conflict in our eyes. She assured us that the shariat provided for dispensation in times of stress, and since we had launched on a holy war, a little indiscretion would be forgiven us. In her sweet coquettish voice she recited Hafiz:

> *Do not sit one moment without your love or wine*
> *For these are days of celebration, roses and jasmine.*

So fragrant was the smell of her mouth, so great the warmth of invitation of her soft, fleshy hips that despite our eighty-two years, and the tumult of the long day, we banished fatigue from our limbs. We replied in the words of the very poet whose lines she had recited:

> *O how many vows of repentance are undone*
> *By the smile of wine and the tresses of a girl?*

We took a large spoonful of the aphrodisiac that Hakeem Ahsanullah had prepared for us. A little later we took our begum with the same passion with which we had consummated our first union. When we had finished our business, we again quoted Hafiz to convince her that we did not regret what we had accomplished:

> I do not restrain desire
> Until my desire is satisfied
> Or until my body touches hers,
> Or my soul from my body goes.
> When I am dead, open my tomb,
> You will see my heart on fire
> And my shroud in smoke.

Thus like young lovers we lay in each other's arms with nothing save the hairs of our bodies between us. We were roused from our slumbers by the firing of cannon. Zeenat Mahal opened her large almond-shaped eyes and was overcome with shyness. She quickly dressed and asked: 'Who is firing guns at this hour of the night?' She began to count the reports. 'One, two, three . . . twenty-one,' she said finally. 'A salute to the Emperor of Hindustan. Permit your maidservant to be the first to pay Your Majesty homage.' She bowed, salaamed thrice and glided out of the room.

We took our pen and put the final touches to a poem we had been composing for some weeks:

> *In love it's not the loss of peace*
> *Or patience that I mourn.*
> *Love's sorrow has become my friend*
> *When other friends I have forsworn.*

'Tis a thousand wonders that even now
The cup-bearer brings not jug and wine,
Knowing the days of pleasure, the rounds of mirth
Not forever last upon this earth.

Of myself nothing did I know
But others' good and bad I knew
Then fell my eye upon my evil deeds
Remained none so evil in my view.

With the dazzling glory of the Sun
Today, after many days, she came.
All calm and patience did I lose
Not all her shyness did her restrain.

O Zafar! know him not as a man
However clever, wise, benign
Who in pleasure's pursuit forgets his God
In anger's passion wrath divine.

So was the candle of our hope lit in the gale of fortune. So did we launch our frail and ageing bark upon the stormy seas of Hindustan.

ঌ

In youth the slumber that follows the night of love is oblivious of the progress of the sun. What use is it to the days that are past? We were roused by a gong striking the midnight hour. We rose from our beloved's couch with the weight of our years heavy in our limbs. We went to the mosque, performed our ablutions and said the *isha* prayer craving Allah's forgiveness for transgressing the rules of Ramadan.

We continued to sit in the mosque for some time. The moon was directly over our head. The marble courtyard was as cold as the snows of the Himalayas. We recalled that it was in the third week of Ramadan that the Almighty had summoned our Prophet (on Whom be peace) and charged him with His divine mission. We recited sura 96, the first that Allah transmitted to the world:

Recite: In the name of your Lord who created,
Created man from a clot.
Recite: And your Lord is most generous,
Who taught by the pen,
Taught man what he does not know.
No, but man is rebellious
Because he sees himself grown rich.
Indeed the return is to your lord.

We had a strange feeling that Allah heard our prayer and forgave us. We left the mosque with a lighter heart and were able to get a few hours of restful sleep.

We were up before any of our servants had risen and went to the octagonal tower to spend some moments with ourselves. It was then that the enormity of the events that had taken place the day earlier came crowding into our mind. Had we acted rightly? Were we master of our destiny? Or a mere puppet in the hands of some wilful puppeteer?

We penned the following lines:

We are caught in the whirligig of time
Gone are sleep and life of ease
Death is certain, that we know
At dawn or dusk our life may cease.

The mirror of our mind was not clear. We were King only by title. We lived in a palace which was once said to be the most beautiful in the world; it was now a palace only in name. And even that was to be denied to our sons. We had been informed that on our demise (would that Allah send for us soon!) our family would be asked to quit the Red Fort. The *firangi* had given us only a drop out of the ocean of fortune that our great ancestors had bequeathed to us; we accepted that drop and called it a tribute. What other word can one use for what is owed to an emperor? But the *firangi* insisted it was a pension. An emperor a pensioner of his subjects!

One after another the great kingdoms of Hindustan (at one time all vassals of our great ancestors) were swallowed up by the *firangi*. He spared neither friend nor foe. Only a few months ago the great house of Oudh which had befriended the *firangi* was by the *firangi* deprived of its dominion. And before Oudh there were Nagpur and Jhansi and Satara and Tanjore and Murshidabad and Karnatak.

The holy book says: 'God does not love the oppressors.' No one could oppress the poor as did the *firangi* because he even interfered with matters of faith. For him religion made no distinction between clean and unclean flesh. He was allowed to eat both cows and pigs. But what right had he to order our Hindu and Muslim soldiers to put cartridges smeared with the fat of cows and pigs in their mouths? Did we need more to prove that he meant to despoil both Islam and Hinduism and make everyone Christian? His padres vilified the name of our Holy Prophet and the sacred Quran. What did a man live for except his faith and the honour of his name? What lived after a man died but his name? We put our trust in God. It is rightly said: 'What fear of the waves of the sea has he whose pilot is Noah!'

Then there was the vexing question of our succession. Our beloved Zeenat Mahal was anxious that Mirza Jawan Bakht, born of the conjunction of our groins, should be nominated in preference to the elder Mirza Dara Bakht. The Governor-General refused to take our advice. Allah in His divine wisdom took Shah Rukh then Mirza Dara Bakht as well. It was after we had lost these two sons that we gave in to Zeenat Mahal's pressure and forwarded the claim of Mirza Jawan Bakht. Once again the Governor-General brushed aside our advice and recognized another of our many sons, Mirza Fakhroo.

Fakhroo was bribed to sign an agreement whereby he would give up the Red Fort for a small pension. Then Allah sent for Mirza Fakhroo as well. After Allah deprived us of three of our sons, the *firangi* proclaimed his intention of depriving our successors of the fort and palace—and our successors, whoever it would be, of even the title of His Majesty. 'O Zafar, this rule is but for thy lifetime; after thee there will be no heir nor name to the kingdom for anyone to rule.' So eager was the *firangi* to shorten our sojourn on earth that once when we were ill he posted his own guard at the palace gates. We were constrained to write to the President. 'Honourable Sir, are we not to be accorded the privilege of dying in peace? Do you suspect our corpse will rise up in arms against you?'

Saadi had so rightly said: 'Ten dervishes may sleep under the same blanket but no country can hold two kings.' We have the same saying in Hindustani: 'A country can no more have two rulers than a scabbard hold two swords.' It had to be us or the *firangi*. This was clear to us.

We summoned a council of princes, noblemen and representatives of the sepoys. We advised them to reorganize the administration and draw up plans to expel the foreigners from our domains. The Council chose our elder son, Mirza Mughal, to be supreme Commander. Mirza Abu Bakr who was most eager to draw his sword was made a colonel.

After business was finished we sent for Hassan Askari. Askari was a dervish who, as it is said, had 'deeply plunged his head in the cowl of meditation and had been immersed in an ocean of vision.' He was possessed of eyes that could peer into the future. He lived in Daryaganj in the house of our lately departed daughter, Nawab Begum. While we awaited the dervish we ordered the daily papers to be read to us. The *Delhi Urdu News, Siraj-ul-Akhbar and Sadik-ul-Akhbar* had eyewitness accounts of the explosion of the arsenal at Kashmiri Gate with the names of the hundreds of martyrs who had fallen in the attempt to capture it. We asked if the English newspaper, *Delhi Gazette*, had written anything on the subject. Our newspaper reader informed us that there was no issue of the Gazette as its English staff had been slain and only one man, an American who had accepted Islam, had been spared. We heard all this without making any observation and dismissed the newspaper reader.

Hassan Askari was ushered in. We rose to receive him. He was a man of God. He had also petitioned Allah to take twenty years of his life and add them to ours. We seated him beside us on our couch and asked him what he felt about the storm that was blowing over our city. The dervish hoarded his words as a miser hoards gold. He shut his eyes and began telling the beads of his rosary. After a few minutes he raised his face to the ceiling, brushed his beard with both his hands and exclaimed: 'Shukr Allah! Shukr Allah!' We became impatient and implored him: 'Dervish Sahib, you who read the future in the book of destiny, tell us what fate has in store for us.'

The dervish pointed to the sky and replied, 'Only Allah knows the future. I am dust under the feet of the faithful. Occasionally I have glimpses into the mirror of time.;

He fell silent again and resumed telling his beads. We entreated him again: 'In the name of Allah, look into the mirror of the future and loosen your tongue. Do not torture this poor man any more.'

At last the dervish spoke: 'Your Majesty may recall my dream of the flood engulfing everything save the throne of the Mughals.' 'Indeed we do!'

'At the time we had interpreted it as presaging the invasion of Hindustan by the Persians or the Russians. Now we know that the flood has risen from within Hindustan itself. It will drown the enemies of Your Majesty's dynasty. Only the peacock throne will be borne above the floods.' (Although the peacock throne had been taken away by Nadir Shah over a hundred years ago, our people continued to speak of the wooden stool covered with silver leaf which was now our throne as the peacock throne.)

'*Ameen! Ameen!*' We exclaimed. 'Allah will surely fulfil the prophecy of those beloved to Him!'

We asked him of the prospect of the Persian army coming to our aid in the crusade against the *firangi*. He assured us that the armies of Islam were ever eager to measure swords with the Nazarene. The dervish told us of the birth of triplets to a Hindu woman in Hauz Qazi. The girls spoke immediately on birth. The first said: 'The coming year will be one of great calamities.' The second said: 'Those who will live will see.' The third said: 'If Hindus burn Holi in the present season they will escape all their evils. God alone is omniscient.' The Hindus, said dervish Askari, were burning Holi fires now instead of the usual time at the end of winter.

We thanked Hassan Askari and requested him to continue praying for us. We pressed a gold mohur in his hand, and before he could protest, walked away to our harem.

༝

We were anxious to tell Zeenat of what the dervish had told us. She dismissed her visitors and maidservants. 'The dervish Hassan Askari was here,' we said. We paused to heighten her sense of expectancy.

'And he told Your Majesty of his dream of the flood. And the Hindus lighting Holi fires. And the three girls who began talking as soon as they were born. Your slave should also be given a gold mohur for predicting the end of the Nazarene and the restoration of the Mughal dynasty,' Zeenat said.

How quickly news travelled round the palace! As if the walls had ears and the breeze tongues! Zeenat noticed the surprise in our eyes. 'Your Majesty, I have my own way of finding out what is written in the book of kismet,' she said, tapping her forehead. 'This is what the great Hafiz has forecast.' She opened a *divan* of Hafiz to a page she had marked with a silk tassel and read:

> *In green heaven's fields I saw the sickle of the new moon*
> *Remembered by sowing and by harvest,*
> *And said: O Kismet, you sleep and the sun blossoms*
> *The reply: Do not be as hopeless as the past.*

She repeated the last line: 'Do not be as hopeless as the past.' It pleased us to see her happy and we kissed her cheeks. She blushed. 'What, in broad daylight! Has Your Majesty no shame?'

'You speak of shame? Shame is my renown,' we replied quoting Hafiz.

During the first two days following the uprising we really felt as if we were Emperor of Hindustan and the *firangi* had taken his caravan out of our domains. But by the third day the veil of illusion that had clouded our vision was lifted. Our son Mirza Mughal had usurped all the functions of a ruler. People went to him for orders. Even our personal servants like the eunuch Basant Ali Khan paid court to the prince.

Prince Mirza Mughal incited the rabble of the city against the Europeans we had taken into protective custody. We argued with him and warned him against lending an ear to 'men' like Basant Ali Khan. But it was to no avail. Three days later—we believe it was Saturday the 16th of May—they dragged the prisoners out of the dungeon and slit the throats of thirty-nine of them including women and children as if they were sheep being sacrificed on Bakr-Id. The royal fountain in front of our palace was full of the blood and corpses of these innocent people. We sought refuge in our harem. Zeenat Mahal buried her head in our lap and wept like a child. We could not silence the shrieks of the victims from assailing our ears. And at night the howling of jackals on the riverbank sounded like women wailing at a funeral.

When we reprimanded Mirza Mughal and that impudent, emasculated Basant Ali Khan, they had the audacity to ask us whether we were on the side of the *jihadis* or the infidels. They insinuated that Begum Zeenat Mahal's father and our physician, Ahsanullah Khan, were in the pay of the *firangi*.

We listened to these calumnies with the expression of one whose ears register no sound. But thereafter our heart was divided. Sometimes we hoped for a speedy victory and the restoration of our empire; at others we wished that the sahibs would make peace with us, recognize us and our heirs as kings of Hindustan and administer the country in our name. In either case we prayed for peace so that we could spend the remaining years of our life in prayer and quiet meditation in some secluded hermitage.

On the evening of Sunday, the 24th of May, the new moon was sighted. Our eyes could not discern it because of the dust in the air but Zeenat Mahal pointed to the red sky above the setting sun and assured us that it was there, shining like a silver poniard. The next day we rode on our favourite elephant Maula Baksh through the bazaars and joined our subjects for the afternoon prayer at the Royal Mosque. On our way back we showered coins on the crowds of beggars that milled about the feet of our elephant. By the time we approached Lahori Gate the sun had set. The walls of our palace were lit with oil-lamps. We turned round and saw the whole city including the Jamia Masjid twinkling with lights. Rockets shot their way into the sky and exploded in multicoloured stars. Cannon fired a twenty-one gun salute in our honour.

Id-ul-Fitr has always been a day of rejoicing. The knot of restraint which binds the faithful during the month of Ramadan is loosened. We shut the eye of censure to let people enjoy themselves. But our sons did not know how to take their pleasure without causing hurt to others. At midnight we were roused by the *darogha* who begged us to help him restrain one who had broken into the house of a rich Hindu merchant of Dariba. Another was picked up naked and drunk in the *hijda* quarters of Lal Kaun. A third was embroiled in a fracas in a house of ill-fame in Daryaganj run by a princess of royal blood. So low had the house of Taimur and Babar fallen!

Next morning we sent for our boys and let the tongue of reprimand lash their ears. They heard with their heads bowed. From their bloodshot eyes and waxen complexions we could see that their silence was more occasioned by ill-humour of the body than repentance of the heart.

The men who had taken over the reins of government were like novices on unbroken horses. They knew how to squander but not how to earn. They could not be bothered with accounts and let the treasury become empty. There were so many who wanted to fight in the jihad. But no one bothered to train them. They were sent into battle armed with pick-axes, spears and knives against trained men armed with muskets. Five days after Id-ul-Fitr there was an engagement across the river at Ghaziabad. Victory went to the *firangi*; martyrdom to our Ghazis. The same story was repeated a few days later at Badli-ki-Sarai on the Grand Trunk Road.

Dervish Hassan Askari told us that these reverses were Allah's warning to us to be better prepared. Our astrologers also predicted that the *firangi's* rule would end on the 23rd of June which was the hundredth anniversary of the Battle of Plassey. Our Ghazis went out in their thousands and fell upon the enemy who had massed his troops outside the city wall at Sabzi Mandi. Once again Allah granted our Ghazis the *houris* of paradise but gave the *firangi* and his Sikh and Gorkha hirelings the pleasure of victory.

The reverses at Sabzi Mandi plunged the city in gloom. People lost faith in their commanders. Everyone accused everyone else of treachery and being in the pay of the firangi. The hot winds blowing from the desert tried people's patience. Suddenly merchants began to hide their wares. There was no grain or fodder in the market. The poor were driven to desperation. Many turned to thieving and robbery. We did not know what the outcome would be. Then a strange man appeared in Delhi.

Nihal Singh

All my life I had been hearing of Dilli. When I was a child Mai told me of Aurangzeb, King of Dilli, who had cut off the head of our

Guru. She called him Auranga and spat whenever she used his name. I also learnt to *thoo* on Auranga's name. When I was older, Bapu told me of the exploits of our ancestors who looted Dilli and brought back saddles full of gold and silver. And of Sardar Baghel Singh who built a gurdwara on the very spot where our Guru had been martyred. When I joined the Punjab police, my friends said, 'If you haven't seen Dilli you have seen nothing.' In Dilli, they said, you could get everything; young whores with small mango-shaped bosoms, boys with rounded pumpkin bottoms; and if you did not have money to pay for a woman or a boy, you could have a *hijda* for a couple of pice—and he (she or it) could give you more fun than either. I prayed that something would take me to Dilli.

The Guru who knows the secrets of our hearts answered my prayer. One day when I was home on leave two men came to our village. One went round beating a drum asking everyone to assemble under the big peepul tree. The other fellow then told us that the Mussalmans had risen against Jan Company and put back a Mughal on the throne in Dilli. This Mughal was the grandson of the grandson of the same Auranga who had murdered our Guru. He said if we joined the army of Jan Company and captured Dilli all the gold and silver we could find would be ours. I asked the man to write an *arzi* to the police station asking for more leave, touched the feet of my Mai and Bapu and took the road to Dilli.

There were two others boys from my village with me; Lehna and Natha. How hot it was! As if the whole world had been put inside a tandoor. The dust blew into our eyes and nostrils and turned our black beards to khaki. We said to ourselves 'What is heat to Sikh Lions?' and rode through the burning afternoons. We washed ourselves at wells along the road, rested a little under the shades of neem trees and were off again. In two days we reached Ambala.

A big bald sahib with a face as red as a monkey's bottom came to inspect us. He had already a hundred Sikhs given by the Raja of Jind with him. He picked another hundred from villages on his route. I was in my police uniform and had my own horse, so he took me. He also took Lehna and Natha. Then he spoke to us in Poorabia language. I did not understand everything he said except that we were to fight Mussalmans and that our Guru had told Auranga that the sahibs would come from the side of the rising sun and with the help of the Sikhs overthrow his dynasty. Neither my Mai or my Bapu had told me of this prophecy. However I said to myself, what the sahib says must be true because the sahibs are wise people. One morning at parade this sahib whose name I found out later was Hodson, walked down the line poking his finger into the boys' chests and bellies and feeling their arms. He did the same to me. He looked me up and down from my turban to my shoes. I was taller and bigger than all the boys on the line.

'What is your name?' he asked.

'Nihal Singh.'

'Nihal Singha,' he says exactly like a pucca Punjabi, 'Nihal Singha, you will be my orderly.' Hodson Sahib was like that. He never asked anyone anything. He just gave orders.

The boys were burnt up with jealousy. They slapped me on my back and said *Shabash! Vadhaaee!* (congratulations!). But when my back was turned they called me the sahib's *chamcha* (spoon). I did not care. I liked Hodson Sahib. Hodson Sahib liked me. And even though my wage was no more than that of the other *sowars*, even Sardar Man Singh who was our subedar always addressed me politely as Bhai Nihal Singhji.

We were given new uniforms; red turbans, khaki-shirts, red cummerbunds and khaki breeches: red-khaki, red-khaki. Other sahibs began to call us flamingoes. We were given a new matchlock which could fire very rapidly and had a long knife at its nozzle. We also carried lances.

After a few days drilling we were on the royal road to Dilli. At Karnal *gora* companies came down from the hills to join us. The *goras* could not stand the sun and the hot winds. So we rode by night and spent the days sleeping under shades of trees. We went through Gharaunda, Samalkha, Raee. These towns had turned against Jan Company. They did not dare to make the slightest *choon* before us. We reached the outskirts of Dilli in the pitch dark of the night. We were directed to our tents. The sahibs' bandobast was very good.

We had ridden twenty miles through a very hot and still night. The men were tired and fell asleep without taking off their cummerbunds or boots. I was excited and could not shut my eyes. There were twelve men snoring and farting in the tent. So I came out, washed myself and found a flat stone to lie on. I loosened my long hair and let the breeze cool me while I gazed at the sky full of bright stars. I must have dozed off because when I opened my eyes the stars were less bright and the sky had turned grey. My heart grew bigger and bigger till it was as big as the world I beheld. I recalled the words Guru Nanak spoke to his disciple: 'Look, bother Mardana, the miracle of the Lord!'

'*Wah! Bhai Wah!*' I exclaimed to myself. 'The great Guru has certainly raised a wonderful city.' On my left from where the sun was coming up there was a river as broad as the Sutlej. It went behind the grey wall of the city. This wall was very high and very long. It ran from the river bank right across to the sunset side as far as I could see and was lost behind clusters of trees. It had many bastions and many gates. Behind this grey wall I could see another red wall of a big fort. And domes and minarets and tops of houses. I could not see any signs of battle; not even a sign of anyone living.

❧

As the red rim of the sun comes over the river, a cannon fires—*badham*. Thousands of pigeons fly and crows *kan kan*. I see hundreds of vultures sitting on tree-tops and clustered on carrion like bees on a beehive. Then I notice half-eaten corpses dangling from the branches. Vomit comes to my throat. I go inside my tent and stretch myself besides my companions. I am very tired.

The bugle calls. We are up. I get myself a mug of tea and look round to see how our camp is laid. We are on a high ridge of red rocks. On top of the Ridge is a big house which the cook says belongs to a Maratha named Hindu Rao. It is beyond the reach of enemy guns so the sahib officers occupy this house. *Gora Paltans* are encamped on the higher parts of the ridge which are also beyond range. We blacks are closer to the city wall. There are Pathans, Biloches and Punjabi Mussalmans. 'What are these Mussalmans doing here?' I ask the cook. 'They will fight the Hindus on the rebel side,' he says. 'And these Gorkhas?' I ask him. 'They will fight anyone the sahib tells them to fight,' he replies. 'A Gorkha's skull is made of iron and its inside is stuffed with cowdung. If the sahib says shoot your father, he will shoot his father and mother.' It is wonderful how the sahibs keep us natives separated from each other. The Guru has given them great wisdom.

Also courage. As Hodson Sahib says, 'One white man is as good as ten blacks.'

It is high noon. Sun right above our heads. I am snoring peacefully under the shade of a neem tree when somebody shakes me violently. 'Oi, Nihalia, haven't you heard the bugle? Do you want to be murdered in your sleep?' I jump up and wrap my turban round my head. Who do I see? Sahibs peering through their telescopes. I look the way they are looking. What do I see? From the extreme right end of the city called Sabzi Mandi enemy cavalry is riding out towards us. Behind the cavalry are troopers on foot. They are in uniforms of the Jan Company. While I am still looking they start letting off fireworks from the city wall as if somebody is getting married. *Bhanh, bhanh* says the cannon; *shanh, shanh* go cannon balls. They crash on the ridge knocking down our tents and killing our horses. You have to admit these villains have good aim. They also know lots of tricks. Just as we get into our saddles, their drums begin to beat and they charge into our flank yelling '*Har Har Mahadev . . . Ali, Ali, Ali.*' Hodson Sahib draws his sword and yells '*Hamla!*' We ride full gallop to meet them. As soon as we are within range they fire their muskets at us, wheel, and ride away. While we are counting our dead and wounded their snipers start shooting at our sahibs. One fellow yells at me: 'O Sardarji, why are you selling your life to the *firangi sooer*? Come over to our side. You'll get more rupees.'

They kill many of our men. We kill some of theirs too. But they do not get any of our boys alive; we capture about thirty of them.

We search their dead and find plenty of gold and silver coins in their belts. We hack off the ears and fingers of those who have rings.

Hodson Sahib lines up the captives under a tree. He orders them to go down on their knees. He loads his carbine and aims it at an old grey beard. 'How long have you eaten the salt of the Company?' he asks.

The grey beard clasps his hand and pleads: '*Kasoor hua* (I've been at fault). Forgive us!'

Others do the same, '*Huzoor*, forgive us,' they whine. 'Take all we have, but don't kill us.' They take off their belts and empty out coins, rings and other trinkets.

Hodson Sahib doesn't even look at the things. 'What regiment were you?' he asks the grey beard.

'The 26th. We served the sahib in many battles. We will fight for you again whenever you send us.' He grabs Hodson Sahib's foot. Hodson Sahib kicks him with the other foot. 'Who is your commander?'

'Mirza Mughal . . . Sahib, don't kill us. We will tell you all we know.'

'How many are you?'

They vie with each other in giving names of their regiments. There are 10,000 or more on the other side. Hodson Sahib knows all he wants to know. He cocks his carbine, jams it into the old man's chest and fires. 'Take this you *namak haram!*' The grey beard rolls over with a loud cry, '*Ya Allah!*'

'Hack off the heads of these namak harams and feed their carcasses to the jackals,' he orders.

The prisoners become like living corpses. We take off their belts. Our sweepers pull off their uniforms and boots. We march them naked down the ridge. We line them and tell them to kneel with their heads bent. They whine, urinate, defecate. We hack off their heads with our *kirpans*. It is like slaughtering goats for the Guru's kitchen. Only a man's neck is thicker than a goat's and cannot always be severed at one *jhatka* (stroke).

Hodson Sahib gives us an extra ration of rum.

❧

Two of our *risallah* had been badly wounded. I went to see them in the camp-hospital. They were lying under a keekar tree; there was no room inside for natives. The doctors were busy looking after *goras*, many of whom had cholera, dysentery or shivering fever. Some had just melted like wax under the heat of the sun. I sat with the boys and pressed their legs. Hodson Sahib brought a doctor who threw a packet of ointment on the ground and said: 'Spread this on your injuries and report back for duty in two days.'

In the afternoon I went to see Hodson Sahib. He was in his tent writing something. 'Sahib must be very tired. Shall I take off Sahib's boots?' He did not open his mouth but turned in his chair. I sat on the ground, unstrapped his *putties* and massaged his legs. He stopped writing and turned to me.

'Good fighting today, eh?'

'Sahib, they have killed a lot of our men,' I replied.

The Sahib looked at his paper. 'Seventeen dead, twenty-five injured, twenty horses dead or destroyed.'

I had seen many more than seventeen dead. I understood. The Sahib was only counting the *goras*. 'It takes more than an army of jackals to fight the English,' he said. 'This was their big *hamla*. We have broken their backs,' he explained: 'Today is the 23rd day of June. It is the hundredth anniversary of the Battle of Plassey when the English defeated the Mussalmans. They believed that after hundred years, it would be their turn to win. It takes more than a pack of jackals to beat the *sahiblog*,' he said again.

I pulled off his boots. 'The English are very *bahadur*,' I said as I pressed his feet.

'The best fighters in the world.'

I nodded my head. 'Sikhs are also very *bahadur*. One Sikh is qual to 1,25,000 others.'

Hodson Sahib didn't like that. He ran his hand over his bald head and asked 'What happened at Mudki and Pherushahr and Sabraon and Multan and Chillianwala and Gujarat?'

'Sahib, the Sikh army was betrayed by its officers.'

'That is what the defeated always say—we were let down by our commanders.'

Hodson Sahib had a very short temper; I did not want to get him *gussa* by arguing with him. I said in my mind: 'If the Sikhs were led by good generals instead of traitors, they would have marched up to your London town and fucked your mothers.'

I took off his socks and rubbed the soles of his feet. He shut his eyes and began to *ghurr ghurr* like a cat. After a while he said, '*Theek hai*. You can go.'

I saluted and left.

Next morning when I went to see how the boys who had been wounded were doing, I did not find them under the keekar tree. I went to the hospital. They were not there either. A sweeper told me that they had died at night and their bodies had been taken away to be cremated.

❧

These Dilliwallas would not let us breathe. At midnight when we were fast asleep they would start firing their cannon at us. On the hottest afternoon when we were dozing under the shades of trees they would creep up like thieves and go *thah thah* with their carbines. They sent emissaries to our camp. To the Mussalmans they sent Mussalmans with the Quran and begged them to *jihad* against the pig-eating *firangi*. To us Sikhs they sent Brahmins carrying Ganges water in brass-pots asking us to murder the cow-eating *maleechas*. They offered us hundred rupees for every *gora's* head and service with more pay. We remained true to our salt. We took the money they brought. Then we strung them up on neem trees.

The sahibs also employed spies. The chief was a one-eyed man called Rajab Ali. He came to our camp whenever he wanted and went back to the city. They said he had the ear of the king. And he did a lot of *phus phus* in Hodson Sahib's ear and took money from him.

The blacks liked Hodson Sahib but the *goras* did not care for him. I saw this when a *paltan* called the Guides arrived from Peshawar. Hodson Sahib had often talked of the times *'Jab ham Guides me tha . . .'* From the way he spoke, the Guides must have been the greatest warriors in the world. I didn't know why he left them. Only once he mentioned some 'hanky panky'. However as the Guides marched in and saw Hodson Sahib, the black men broke their ranks and ran up to embrace him. What a sight it was! Pathans, Biloches, Sikhs all embracing Hodson Sahib! The sahibs looked away as if they did not know him.

One day a *gora* asked me who I was.

'Hodson's Horse,' I replied coming to attention. He laughed, turned to the other *goras* and said, 'Hodson's arse.' They all laughed. I did not understand what made the sahibs laugh.

Even the *Jangi Lat* Wilson Sahib did not like Hodson Sahib. He would not allow him to attack Dilli till he got more troops. And Hodson Sahib's temper got worse as hot winds became hotter and dust-storms began to blow every afternoon.

One day early in July there was a storm the like of which I had never seen. Brown dust roasted by the sun was flung in fistfuls into our eyes and nostrils! After an hour the same dust turned cool. The day turned into night. The sky exploded with lightning and thunder. Then came the rain sweeping the dust and everything else before it. I ran out of the tent shouting to my friends: 'Oi, Lehnia! The rains! Oi Nathia! You opium eater come out, the skies have burst!'

We threw off our turbans and uniforms and came out in our under-shorts. We let down our long hair and danced and sang. 'Oi, if we only had a *mashooka* today we'd make the soles of her feet count the stars.'

The *goras* asked the natives what had happened to us. The Pathans shook their heads and smiled. The Dogras sniggered. 'Sahib, these Sikhs have long hair. The heat gets them and they go crazy.' We yelled back at them, 'Oi, your mothers and sisters also have long hair. They must feel the heat. Send them to us, we will cool the heat between their thighs.' That shut them up.

At dusk the trees were covered with fireflies. We caught them and stuck them in our beards till our beards sparkled. And we danced the bhangra.

It rained all through the night. It beat on our tent like a roar, sometimes like a faint echo from far away. No one could get much sleep.

I rose at dawn. The sky was full of grey and black clouds. Everything looked washed and green. I heard a peacock call *paon paon*. There were three—one cock and two hens on the parapet of Hindu Rao's mansion. The cock raised its tail and made it into a fan full of green-blue eyes. I put my head inside the tent and yelled: 'Get up you opium eaters! A peacock's dancing!'

'Let the peacock sleep with its mother,' replied Lehna gruffly as he turned over. Two men came out to see the wondrous sight.

A peacock dancing on a house-top with black clouds rolling behind is a sight worth a hundred thousand rupees. What beauty the Guru has given this bird! The peacock arched its 'neck backwards as proud as a young prince vaunting his manliness. It took two steps forward, two steps backwards. Its brown under-wings panted like an impatient lover out of breath. Its feathers quivered with delight.

Thah.

Down came the peacock tumbling over the wall.

Thah Thah.

The two peahens also tumbled down to the ground.

632

'*Hoi*, we've got all three!' cried the *goras*.

I sat down on the wet ground and wept. These were the peacock-killing mother-fuckers we were fighting for! What do these white *bunderlogs* know of the rains? Their women do not have black hair to remind them of dark monsoon skies. Nor do they have large-rounded bosoms which would remind them of billowing white clouds. Their girls do not know how to make swings on mango trees and sing songs to the monsoon. Have you ever heard *goralog* sing? I heard them in their church at Ambala: the mems screaming *hee, hee, hoo, hoo*; men braying *bhaw bhaw* like donkeys. How could they appreciate the ragas of rain and the dancing of peacocks? When all the world around was green and beautiful these *goras* thought only of killing. When I got up to give Hodson Sahib his morning mug of chai he said, 'Now is the time to strike! Get the men ready for battle.'

❧

Heavy cannon are hauled out by elephants. Camels and oxen are yoked to lighter guns. The ground is slippery. So we go barefoot. Only Hodson Sahib is on horseback. The rain slows down to a drizzle. The rocky ridge is all right, but near Sabzi Mandi we are knee-deep in slush. An elephant slithers and falls on its side with a great splash. Its mahout leaps clear but the cannon rolls over and its nozzle is stuck in the ground. The elephant manages to get on its feet and meekly raises one of its front legs to let the mahout clamber up. It takes twenty men to get the cannon back on its wheels. A slithering elephant is funny enough, a slithering camel is even funnier. It tries to sit on its bottom and gets its long legs entangled. The camel gets very *gussa* if you laugh at him.

We push on through the drizzle—slithering and falling as we go. It takes us two hours to cover a mile-and-a-half to get to Sabzi Mandi. We get there without attracting the enemy's attention. He is enjoying the first day of the monsoon drinking *bhang* with his *mashooka*.

The rain stops. Patches of blue appear in the sky. Soon the sky over Dilli city is full of mutlicoloured kites. They battle in the air and as one has its string snapped it wafts down in majestic sweeps. We hear boys yelling '*Vo kata*'. I see men waving scarves and whistling while flocks of black, white and brown pigeons wheel in the sky. From some house in Sabzi Mandi comes the jingle of dancers' bells and the beating of tabla drums. It seems as if everyone in Dilli has given himself up to merry-making.

'*Bhoom, bhoom, bhoom*' echo our cannon far away near Kashmiri Gate. Kites are quickly pulled down. Pigeons return to their lofts. Sound of singing and dancing dies out. '*Bhoom, bhoom, bhoom,*' reply the rebels' guns from the bastions near Kashmiri Gate and Mori Gate. Our trick has worked. While guns are hurling abuse at each other around Kashmiri and Mori Gate, we surround an area of Sabzi Mandi including a bazaar and a garden with a big house in its centre. The bugle sounds: '*Hamla!*' Our cannon fires into the bazaar. Then we go in on the double—shooting at any face that appears at a window, bayonetting anyone—male, female or child that comes in our way. Only from the big house in the garden is our fire returned. We take cover behind the trees. Every time any one of our party tries to get closer, he is shot. We bring up our cannon. The first ball makes a hole in a wall; the second, another. A part of the ceiling comes crashing down. We fire a volley into the house, fix bayonets and charge. There is no one to face us. We do not take chances. We surround the house and tiptoe in single file. I lead one party through a big room and up a broad staircase. And what do I see? I'll give you a thousand chances and you will not be able to guess right. A woman! There she stands on the top of the stairs with eyes bright as stars and a diamond glistening in her nose. And what do you think she is doing? Waving her sword at me.

'Oi, Nathia!' I shout to Natha Singh who is following me. 'Look what I've found!'

Natha Singh comes alongside and stares at the woman. '*Balley, balley!*' he exclaims. He shouts to the others. The staircase is full of Sikh soldiers armed with muskets and here is this woman waving an old talwar at us. She is no yesterday's chicken either. At least forty, flabby and pale as these city women are. Her white hair is dyed red with henna. Her teeth stained with betel. Her big bosom sags beneath her thin muslin shirt.

'*Bibi*, do you use that to pick your teeth?' asks Natha pointing to her sword. Then he goes up boldly and takes the sword out of her hand. '*Bibi*, why do you want to kill us with this?' he asks. 'It is easier to do so with your eyes.'

'Don't jest with her; she is the age of your mother,' I tell Natha.

'*Bhai*, I am a renowned motherfucker,' replies Natha.

We have a hearty laugh.

Hodson Sahib rides up and we stop laughing. Natha drags the woman down the stairs and flings her at the feet of the Sahib's horse. The woman stands up and asks: 'Do you want to shoot me?' Not a tremor in her voice.

Hodson Sahib is taken aback. '*Aurat!*' he exclaims.

He guesses what she does for living. 'Are you a prostitute? What were you doing in this house?'

'I am a *jihadin*,' she explains. 'I was helping my brothers to fight the *badzat nasara*.'

Hodson Sahib knows Hindustani well enough to know what *badzat nasara* means. To please the Sahib I stick my bayonet behind the woman's back and warn her. 'If you don't keep a rein on your tongue, you'll see the other end of this bayonet come out of your navel.'

The shameless wretch doesn't even shudder.

'Nihal Singh, take her to the camp for questioning. Then you can send her to the paradise she is so anxious to go to.'

We march the woman in front of us. If she slows down, I give her a smack on her buttocks; once I slip my finger in her tail. We have a lot of fun on the way.

'*Bhai*, tonight we'll polish our weapons,' says Natha.

'Good woman! You cool our hot carbines and we'll cool a bullet in your body,' says Lehna.

The woman doesn't say a word. She doesn't even bother to look at us.

I take her to the Sahib's tent. He has just put off his helmet and unbuckled his sword. Without saying a word, Hodson Sahib turns round and slaps her hard across her face. He is not very big but he is very strong. The woman reels and falls on the floor. She begins to cry. 'If you want to kill me, kill me. Why do you torture me?' she whines.

Hodson Sahib sits down in his chair. He takes out his notebook and pencil from his desk. 'Name?'

'Anwar Bai.'

'Where do you live?'

'Chawri Bazaar.'

'Who is commanding your troops?'

'Bakht Khan, the Bareilly General who took over two days ago.'

'Who made a *namak haram* subedar into a General?' demands the Sahib angrily. 'How many soldiers are there in Sabzi Mandi?'

'I do not know. I was sent there today to keep guard. Normally I stay in the women's barracks.'

'Women's barracks?'

'*Ji huzoor*! There are some women *jihadins*. Some like me are with the soldiers; others work in the hospital, or cook food for the troops.'

'What were you doing in that house?'

'I have already told the Sahib, I was with the guard. I gave up the profession two months ago when I joined the *jihad*. I hope Allah will forgive my sins.'

Hodson Sahib becomes very *gussa*. 'You call murder of innocent women and children a holy war?'

The women does not reply. Hodson Sahib roars. 'Speak! Is this how you bloody Mussalmans fight a bloody *jihad*?'

This woman is not only without shame, she is also without fear. You know what she says in reply? 'Sahib, I have seen your people thrust their swords into women's bellies. With my own eyes I have seen children tossed in the air and spiked on bayonets.'

Hodson Sahib goes red in the face. I have never seen him in such a rage before. He cannot even speak. The woman goes on as if she did not care what anyone did to her: 'And Sahib, now with your own hands you are going to spill the blood of a woman.'

She's a cunning whore. She wants to find out what the Sahib intends to do to her. Sahib remains silent for some time. He becomes cool again. He says to me: 'When a woman bears arms she has no right to expect to be treated any different from any other soldier. Take her away. I do not wish to hear anything more about her.'

I grab the woman by the arm and take her out.

The sun is about to set. It will soon be dark. I will have her first as I am the Sahib's orderly. Then I will have some sleep and let the others take their turns. Then I will have her a second time; then a third time. In the early hours, I will take her to the dump and shoot

636

her. We have a saying: first quench your thirst, then spit in the well.

I bring the woman to our tent. The men are munching their chappaties. They resume their bawdy jests: '*Makhan pher*! What about it! Will you let us or shall we take you to the police lock-up?'

'Oi, oi, let her be, she is an old *buddhi* . . . .'

'I bet her oven is still warm. We can bake our loaves before putting it out.'

'Oi, she's a whore. She must have run an army kitchen on her oven . . . I bet many regiments have passed between her thighs.'

'Nihalia,' says one of the youngsters, 'you scrub your weapon in her first, then we can also get rid of our surplus of semen.'

The woman pretends to be deaf. She turns to me and says, 'Sardarji, if I have your permission, I would like to say my evening prayer. Then you can do what you like with me.' She says this as coolly as if she were asking me to cook her an aubergine.

There is a chorus of approval. 'Nihalia, let her pray to her Allah. If it lightens her heart, she will lighten ours.'

'All right,' I reply. 'But make it quick—*phuta phut.*' I join the others over our ration of rum.

The whore spreads her dupatta on the muddy ground and sits down on her knees with her face towards the setting sun. The diamond in her nose sparkles.

'Who's going to get her nose-ring?' asks Natha.

No one answers. 'She's also got gold in her ears and on her arms,' says Lehna. 'Let Nihal Singh sell them and we can share the money.'

The whore stands up. Her eyes are closed, her lips keep moving. She bends down. Through her muslin shirt I can see her breasts hanging down like over-ripe marrows.

She goes down on her knees, presses her forehead on the ground a few times. Then she sits back on her heels and holds the palms of her hands in front of her as if she is reading a book. Her face glows. We stop making jokes about her. Her eyes fill with tears; they run down her cheeks and on to her muslin shirt. We stop talking. Her lips stop moving. She runs the palms of her hands across her tear-stained face. She turns her face first to the right and then to the left. I know Mussalmans do this to bless people on either side; we are on her right side. She takes out a rosary from her shirt-pocket and tells the beads. By now it is almost dark. She puts the rosary round her neck and stands up. 'Sardar Sahib, I am ready.'

No one answers. No one even looks up at her. After a while I say, 'Come inside.' She walks into the tent. I throw down the flap of the tent behind me. 'Sit down.' I thrust three chappaties and the lentils into her hands. 'Eat.'

'Sardarji, why do you take this trouble if you are going to shoot me?' she asks casually.

'Eat! We will talk afterwards.'

She eats a few morsels. I give her my water bottle. She drinks a lot of water. It is quite dark now. I pick up my carbine and order her to get out of the other end of the tent; the nozzle of my gun almost touches her spine.

Sentries challenge me. I give the pass word and explain, 'A prisoner to be shot.' We pass the dump heap; the stench is horrible. The woman covers her nostrils with her dupatta. We come within musket shot of Sabzi Mandi where we captured her. 'Can you find your way from here?'

She turns round and faces me. 'May Allah keep you . . . May Allah give you and your children long life . . . May Allah . . . .'

I put my carbine on the ground and touch her feet. 'Forgive us for the way we treated you . . . forgive us for the hard words we used . . . you are like our mother.'

'Allah is the forgiver of all sins. If Allah can forgive mine, He will surely forgive yours.'

She is lost in the dark. I hear the *shap, shap* on her slippers in the mud. Then nothing. I hear a rebel sentry challenge someone.

I raise my carbine to the sky and fire a shot.

Bahadur Shah Zafar

Bakht Khan was as big and as black as a rain-cloud. His eyes flashed like lightning; his speech was coarse like thunder. He came to Delhi just about the time everyone was praying for rain. Bakht Khan knew nothing of court etiquette. But as soon as he made his obeisance and thrust a couple of rupees into our hands we knew that Allah had answered our prayer. We presented him with a robe of honour. When he reappeared we addressed him as General Bakht Khan.

'*Badshah Salamat,*' he replied in the rustic accent of Bihar. 'I am no *jurnail-vurnail.* I am only a subedar. But I have ten thousand Ghazis with me. And we ask for nothing more than the honour to shed our blood for Your Majesty.'

It had been reported to us that Bakht Khan had been acclaimed by our troops and citizens, both Muslim and Hindu. 'Bakht Khan, we make you General and Commander-in-Chief of our forces,' we said to him. 'May Allah crown your sword with victory!'

'*Arre Bhai, Badshah,*' he said without decorum. 'Your name is Japhar, isn't it? Japhar means victory, doesn't it? You will be Japhar. Anyone can take any bet with me,' he said putting out his hand in challenge.

With Bakht Khan came the monsoon. A short spring came to the autumn of our garden. For a while we let Bakht Khan take over affairs of war. We spent our days in the monsoon pavilions, Sawan-Bhadon, that we had raised in Hayat Baksh Garden behind Moti Masjid. Between these two pavilions was a large reservoir in the centre of which was another stone pavilion which looked as if it were afloat on the water. We had a small boat to take our guests to it. Our subjects named it after us, Zafar Mahal. Here we used to hold symposia of poets, entertained our friends with song and dance. That year we organized a small *mushaira* in honour of Taj Mahal Begum, younger sister of Zeenat, whom she had persuaded to join our harem. With Zeenat's consent we did honour to her virgin sister and had her share our couch for several nights.

For some days we did not hear the sound of guns; only the growling of black clouds, the pitter-patter of raindrops and the jingle of dancers' bells beating time to tabla drums. We spent the mornings flying our pigeons.

Then came the Flower-Sellers' festival. We took our beloved Zeenat Mahal and Mirza Jawan Bakht with us to pay homage to the tomb of Qutubuddin Bakhtiyar Kaki at Mehrauli.

We rode on our favourite elephant Maula Baksh out of Lahori Gate and down Chandni Chowk. We alighted at Ballimaran to pay our respects to our spiritual mentor, Kale Khan Sahib. At the mosque of Begum Fatehpuri we turned left to Lal Kuan where Asad Quli Khan (Zeenat Mahal's father) presented *nazar* and a basket of mangoes. We passed on through the prostitutes' quarters in Qazi-ka-Hauz. These ladies sprinkled flowers on us from their balconies.

We went out of the city through Ajmeri Gate. We went past the village of Paharganj and Raisina. At the observatory of Raja Man Singh known as Jantar Mantar, the gardeners of Talkatora orchards, which we had gifted to Zeenat Mahal, presented us with another basket of mangoes. We made a brief halt at the mausoleum of Safdar Jang to inspect the mosque and the *madrasa*. Our next halt was at Yusuf Sarai where we sampled the mangoes presented to us and took our siesta. When we rose the noon was well advanced and the southern horizon was heavily overcast with rain-clouds. Our mahout quickened the pace of Maula Baksh.

When we arrived at Mehrauli it began to rain. We were welcomed by the citizens who had been awaiting our arrival for many hours. They formed a procession led by parties of singers and dancers. We proceeded slowly through Mehrauli's narrow streets. People showered us with flowers, the heavens showered us with rain. When we arrived at our residence, Jahaz Mahal, fireworks were let off. The waters of Shamsi Talab already pocked by the falling rain burned bright crimson and blue and gold as cracker after cracker exploded in the sky and its embers came streaming down into the pool. *Wallah!* What a beautiful world it was! We slept to the sound of the rain beating on our roof and the gurgle of running water.

❧

Next morning the sky was clear. We said our *fajar* prayer at the Auliya Masjid. This little mosque has been hallowed by Khwaja Muinuddin Chisthi of Ajmer, Fariduddin Ganj-i-Shakar of Pak Pattan and innumerable other saints who had performed *chillas* (forty days of prayer and fasting) in its cells. After the morning prayer we went to the tomb of Qutubuddin Sahib Bakhtiyar Kaki and said a *fateha* at the graves of many of our kinsmen who were buried in the precincts.

Begum Zeenat who was with us was not allowed near the tomb of the saint. She presented a canopy made of roses and jasmines which was hung over the tomb. Then we watched divers leap eighty feet into a well in the courtyard and rewarded them suitably. We spent the rest of the day riding through the innumerable ruins that surrounded Mehrauli. First we went to the Qutub Minar and the Quwwat-ul-Islam mosque. We said *fatehas* over the tombs of Alauddin Khilji, Altamash and Imam Zamin. Then we rode past the house of Metcalfe Sahib to the mosque of Kamali the poet. The tomb of Emperor Balban was in a state of neglect. We ordered its repair.

We spent the evening in Jahaz Mahal. On the other side of the Shamsi Talab there were umbrella-shaped pavilions. We ordered a party of shehnai players to perform in them. The notes of the shehnai floated softly over the waters raising ripples as they came towards us. With the slow movement of the *alap*, clouds in the sky began to take bulbous shapes. As the melody went into the next movement, the *gat*, a gentle breeze began to blow. The clouds began to roll over faster as if keeping pace with the tabla. What improvization! We heard thunder and lightning and the hissing of the wind. And behold the sky was overcast! It became dark, lamps were lit. And as the shehnai moved into its finale in fast tempo, it began to pour. It is truly said that a great master can move the heavens to shed tears and the tapers to light themselves and burn in anguish and ecstasy! We heard the Raga Megh Malhar (melody of the rains) and then Deepak (melody of the lamps). And we were like one in a daze.

Thus we spent three days free of care. We visited monuments, listened to music and watched Kathak dancers. Sometimes we simply rested our head on a bolster and gazed at the clouds.

When we returned to Delhi, the state of affairs was, to use Saadi's expression, entangled like the hair of Negroes. The enemy had received reinforcements and siege trains. Our army was short of everything: powder, arms, provisions. Mirza Mughal and Bakht Khan aimed barbed shafts of speech at each other. There were many incidents between the citizens and the soldiers. The citizens taunted the soldiers for their cowardliness, soldiers taunted the merchants for trading with the enemy. Most of our soldiers were Muslims; most merchants, Hindu. And Bakr-Id was approaching. Mirza Mughal and some of the Muslim *omarah* were in favour of taking away the Hindu's property, because the Hindus favoured the *firangi*.

Bakht Khan was against this policy. We lent our support to him. We forbade the slaughter of cows and ourselves set an

641

example by sacrificing a camel. Bakr-Id passed off peacefully.

Two days after the festival the hand of Satan touched the powder magazine. Vast quantities of gunpowder was lost. Many people were killed and their houses destroyed. The *firgani* took full advantage of this misfortune. He circulated forged letters insinuating that our trusted adviser Hakeem Ahsanullah and our Queen Consort Zeenat Mahal had a hand in the explosion of the magazine. The mob set fire to Ahsanullah's house. We sent our bodyguard to rescue him and his family. The rabble had the temerity to force its way into the Diwan-i-Khas and make vile accusations of treachery against us. Our firmness saved the situation. We swore that if anyone was found in possession of the hakeem's property we would have his belly ripped open.

> *Mine enemies assembled in force on all sides*
> *O Ali! All powerful, for God's sake!*
> *Thou hast sent an unseen army to my aid*
> *It is from Thee I supplicate victory in my prayers.*

Foul vapours of suspicion continued to float over Delhi. We came to the conclusion that fate itself had loaded the dice against us and we could not win. Delhi was doomed. Prudence dictated that we should try to salvage whatever we could. We sent a secret emissary to Wilson Sahib, commander of the enemy troops, that if our life and those of Zeenat Mahal and our children were guaranteed and our pension restored to us, we would continue to have the city gates thrown open to his troops. He did not have the courtesy to send us a reply.

We waited for the last grain of sand to run down the hour-glass. It took only seven days to do so. On 14 September the *firangi* and his allies, Pathans, Punjabi Mussalmans, Sikhs, Dogras and Gorkhas launched their attack on Delhi. The entire northern side of the wall from Kabul Gate to the river was subjected to incessant bombardment. Cannon balls fell in the Red Fort. Homes of some of the *salateen* were wrecked.

General Bakht Khan fought back valiantly. He was everywhere; at Sabzi Mandi in the morning, at Mori Gate in the afternoon, at Kashmiri Gate in the evening. After sunset he came to the palace to report. The enemy forced his way into the city. The citizens fought them in every street. Even women and children hurled stones on the heads of the assailants. Although age had made our bones brittle we mounted our Arab horse Hamdam and went out to encourage our troops. But Allah willed that we would be taught a lesson in humility.

On 21 September Bakht Khan told us that Delhi was lost. He asked us to accompany him towards Oudh so that we could continue the battle. We asked him to forgive us; our eighty-two years weighed heavily on our frame. As the venerable Saadi had said: 'We thought proper to sit down in the mansion of retirement, fold up the skirt of association, wash our tablet of heedless saying and no more indulge in senseless prattle.'

People began to leave the city. We also decided to go. At first we thought of going to Mehrauli where we could be closer to the sacred dust of Khwaja Qutubuddin Bakhtiyar Kaki. But Mirza Elahi Baksh (father-in-law of our late heir apparent Mirza Fakhroo) advised us to seek shelter in the mausoleum of our ancestor Emperor Humayun. Mehrauli, he told us, could not be defended; the mausoleum on the other hand was like a fortress and we would be in a position to negotiate with the sahib. We accepted his advice.

The hand of fate struck the drum of departure. Our heart was heavy. We bade farewell to Maula Baksh and Hamdam who had been our companions from the days of our youth. We released all the pigeons in our pigeon lofts and told them to spread the news of our wretchedness. Our palanquins took the Agra Road. Our harem, *salateen* and servants followed in our train. All along the route we passed hundreds of people on bullock carts, *ekkas*, mules and on foot. When we arrived at Arab-ki-Sarai we saw that the gardens around the mausoleum were crammed with people. All our sons, grandsons, nephews and nieces along with their families and relatives were there. That night we rested our weary head at the foot of the grave of our ancestor Emperor Humayun.

Early next morning while people lay like corpses in their shrouds (the nights had turned chilly) we threaded our way to the tomb of Nizamuddin Auliya. No heralds proclaimed the advent of the Badshah Ghazi, the Shadow of God on Earth, the Emperor of Hindustan. After prayer we sat at the foot of Auliya's tomb and told the beads of our rosary. We said the *fateha* at the tombs of our father, Akbar Shah II, our brother, Mirza Jahangir, Begum Jahanara and the poet Ameer Khusrau. It occurred to us that we too would be soon sleeping among them. We recited the prayer of the dervish: 'O Lord, have mercy upon the wicked, because Thou hast already had mercy upon good men by creating them good.' We returned to the mausoleum fully prepared for the fate Allah had ordained for us.

Nihal Singh

Thereafter it rained every day. The Jamna rose and the flood swept away the boat-bridge. This was lucky for us as the rebels used to get most of their men and supplies from across the river. There was not too much fighting during the rains—an occasional skirmish in Qudsia Garden or the guns barking at each other.

The rain stopped as suddenly as it had started. More *goras* joined our camp. They brought big guns and gunpowder sticks. Two Sahibs, Nicholson and Taylor who were said to be great fighters, came to lead the attack on Dilli. Banias who came to sell us provisions told us that in the city the price of 'red pepper' was going up and the price of 'black pepper' going down day by bay. That one-eyed Rajab Ali started coming every day and doing a lot of whispering in Hodson Sahib's ear. One evening as I was massaging the Sahib's feet I asked him: 'Sahib, what does this one-eyed man *phus phus* in your ear?' At first Hodson Sahib looked very *gussa* and said, 'So you try to listen?' I replied, 'No Sahib. If I listened in I would not be asking you.' Then Hodson Sahib told me: 'The old badshah says if we spare his life and give him his pension he will throw open the gates of Dilli.'

'And what do you say?' I asked.

'I say, first throw open the gate, then we will talk.'

Hearing this kind of talk I thought the *hamla* would begin any day. But nothing happened. More than two thousand *goras* were in hospital; every day a few died vomiting or shitting blood. Other *goras* complained of not getting enough rum and made pictures on the walls of Hindu Rao's mansion showing officers drinking and fucking. How could such people go into battle! Wilson Sahib Bahadur kept saying 'Tomorrow . . . tomorrow.' And that fellow

Bakht Khan, subedar or General or whatever he was, kept attacking our camp, killing our men and our horses.

❧

Whatever else you may say of the *goras*, when it comes to fighting they fight like no other race on earth. Nicholson Sahib, for example, is as big as the demon Ravan with a beard as long as our Gurus' (some fools called themselves Nikalsainis, even said he was one of our Gurus reborn). He is so strong that with one blow he could fell on ox. Our own Hodson Sahib, who though he has no hair on his head or chin nor is as big as Nicholson, is as brave as a lion. Nicholson and Hodson Sahib become very restless. 'What kind of *Jangi Lat* is this Wilson Sahib Bahadur when all he can says is "Tomorrow, tomorrow"?' they ask. The two of them go to Wilson Sahib and say, 'We must start the battle now.' Just at the time the one-eyed Rajab Ali brings information that Bakht Khan is taking a large army to Najafgarh and Rohtak to attack *gora paltans* coming from the Punjab. So Wilson Sahib Bahadur says to Nicholson, 'If you are so anxious to fight, go to Najafgarh.' To Hodson Sahib he says: 'If you are also eager to fight, you go to Rohtak.'

Next evening we ride out to Rohtak. We are five hundred *sowars* and ten *gora* officers. We ride through the night and halt a mile short of Rohtak in the early hours of the morning. We have our chai and feed our horses. When the sun comes up, we are ready for battle. Half-an-hour later, the town gates open and out pours a stream of horsemen armed with muskets and swords. They charge towards us.

Hodson Sahib orders us to retreat. We gallop back half-a-mile. The fellows think we are running away. They chase us yelling 'Ali, Ali.' When they are almost on us Hodson Sahib gives the command: 'Turn about and at them.' We wheel round. We unsling our carbines and fire a volley. Fifty of them topple down. Then we charge them with our lances. They break ranks and scatter. Only a handful are manful enough to face us. I see with my own eyes how my Sahib really loves fighting. He draws his *talwar*, gallops up to one of the fellow and challenges him to single-handed combat. The fellow slashes, lunges and backs away. The Sahib parries his blows. 'Try again—is this all you've learnt about swordsmanship?' shouts my Sahib. When the other has had his try, my Sahib strikes one blow that cuts the fellow in two halves. Then he takes on another. Then a third one. 'Wah! Wah! Hodson Sahib. *Wah! Wah!* You are one in a hundred thousand!

We slay over three hundred of the enemy for the loss of only two.

By the evening we are back on the Ridge. So is Nicholson Sahib. He gave that Bareilly General, Bakht Khan, such a thrashing at Najafgarh that he ran back whimpering like a dog with its tail between its legs.

Now Wilson Sahib Bahadur has no excuse to say 'Tomorrow.' The *gora paltan* from the Punjab marches in with all the guns we need. They are hauled into position and start firing. Within a few hours the city wall looks as if it has had an attack of small-pox. It has to be blown up before we can launch the big attack. This is left to our Mazhabi Sikhs. What courage the great Guru has given these poor Mazhabis! They go out one night with bags of gunpowder. Just as they are nearing the wall, rebel snipers spot them. Its too late to run back so one fellow charges forward with the bag in his arms. *Thah!* He falls. Two others run up, pick up the charge and carry it a few steps forward. *Thah! Thah!* Both are killed. A fourth Mazhabi runs up, picks up the bundle and takes it still closer to the wall. In this way forty brave sons of the Guru lay down their lives. But it is the ambrosial hour of the dawn and the great Guru blesses their task with success. The charge is placed beneath the wall and fired: *Bharam!* The loudest *bharam* you can have ever heard! The earth trembles. A section of the wall comes crashing down The breach is wide enough to let five pairs of oxen with ploughs pass through.

The sahibs do not tell us when we are to launch the big *hamla*. They *git mit* with each other. If any one of us blacks comes near them, they use bad words like *belady* or *daym* or *foken* and stop talking. They are getting very short tempered.

It is the first week in the month of Assu (September). Early one morning our batteries open up: *puttack, puttack*. Stones fly like fluffs of cotton from a carder's bow. It goes on all day and continues till midnight. At midnight we are roused and told that the big *hamla* is to take place before sunrise.

Our army is divided into five columns which will start the

attack at the same time all along the city wall stretching from the river to Sabzi Mandi. We get a double ration of rum. We are promised six months' additional wage if we take Dilli.

The night is as black as a Negro's face. When I stretch my arm, I cannot see my hand. No one is allowed to speak. We take off our shoes and stealthily move to our positions. We are facing Kashmiri Gate. As the grey dawn appears, cannon begin to roar. The rebels seem to have sensed our moves. They let go at us. It is like the end of a tamasha with both sides firing away with everything they have. This goes on for about one hour. Then the guns fall silent. What an awful silence! Sweat pours down my forehead. I gulp down my rum. Then a huge explosion. Stones fly into the air. A pillar of dust and smoke rises from Kashmiri Gate. The gate has been blown up. Our subedar, Man Singh, draws his kirpan and yells: *'Boley so Nihal.'* We draw our kirpans and yell back: *'Sat Sri Akal.'* We rush forward into Dilli city.

Rebel drums begin to beat—*dug-a-dug-dug, dug-a-dug-dug.* They let loose a hail of bullets at us and meet us boldly shouting: *'Ali, Ali, Ali'* or *'Har Har Mahadev.'* Who said they had no fight left in them! But we have more guns, more carbines, more men. So we press on over the bodies of the dead and dying. We leap over the earthworks. That one-eyed bastard Rajab Ali had lied about the rebels when he said they would lay down their arms. They come on us like a swarm of hornets without any care for their lives. Their women and children yell filthy abuse at us. They call us the *firangi's* bootlickers and hurl rocks on our heads. (If that whore—what was her name?—is caught again it will be the end of my life).

The battle rages through the morning and into the afternoon. By the evening we have taken the bazaars stretching from the Kashmiri to the Mori Gate. We are tired and thirsty. In Kashmiri Gate there are many liquor shops. We break in and drink whatever we can find. The *goras* get drunk. All night they sing ho, ho, in praise of a bottle of rum. We ransack houses, take gold and coins from the dead. We drive cows and buffaloes tethered in homes out of the city wall for safe-keeping with our Mazhabis. Wilson Sahib Bahadur is very *gussa* and has all the remaining liquor spilt into the moat and orders anyone found looting to be shot. Who is to shoot whom? Sahibs say they will appoint prize agents to divide the loot. We say *achcha*.

Next morning the battle is resumed. We have to fight our way into every street and every lane. Everywhere we see women in veils and little boys helping the rebels. The *goras* say the rebels killed their memsahibs and children, so they kill every woman or child that comes their way.

It takes four days of fighting in the bazaars before the gates of the Red Fort are thrown open to us. We march in through Lahori Gate with our bands playing. There is no one in the Red Fort except a blind woman and an old cripple. *Goras* make sport of them with their bayonets; one plunges his weapon from the front, another from the behind to see if they can meet in the middle of their victim's body. They have a good laugh.

The British flag is hoisted. We present arms. The *goras* sing a song praying for long life to their Queen. A salute of twenty-one guns is fired in Her Majesty's honour. The *goras* are housed in the palace. We are ordered to encamp in the open beyond the moat.

ॐ

The next day we drive the rebels out of Chandni Chowk and the bazaars surrounding the great mosque Jamia Masjid. There are no singing girls in Chawri Bazaar, no whores in Qazi-ka-Hauz, no *hijdas* in Lal Kuan. But we get plenty of gold and silver, cows and buffaloes. We blow up many old palaces and set fire to many streets. The goras want to blow up the Royal Mosque, but Wilson Sahib Bahadur says: 'No, it will anger the Pathans, Biloches and Punjabi Mussalmans on our side.' The sahibs are wise.

The mosque is allotted to the Sikh *risallahs*. The space under the domes is for the men! To the long verandahs on the sides we tether our horses. There are two cisterns in the middle of the vast courtyard. One we use to bathe ourselves; the other to bathe our horses.

I climb up a minaret to have a look at Dilli. I feel like a king looking down on his kingdom. Palaces, houses, mosques and bazaars, smoke rising from many places which we set on fire. I look towards the south. What do I see? A stream of humanity pouring out of the city gates. I am still wondering where all these people are making for when I hear *thah*. A chip of the parapet flies into my beard. Some bastard is trying to kill me. The shot is from the direction of Chawri Bazaar. Now what would a chap be doing in the whores' quarter when all the whores have fled? I am not frightened. I don't take cover. I open my trouser buttons and show him what I have.

That evening I tell Hodson, 'Sahib, they are taking away everything. We will get nothing but our big thumbs.' He runs his hand over his bald head and thinks over the matter. Then he goes to Wilson Sahib Bahadur and gets permission to attack the city from the southern end.

Two days later, Hodson's Horse rides round the city walls. We have a great game of tent pegging. Only it is not blocks of wood we stick our lances into, but people trying to run away from us. Those who escape our lances we shoot with our carbines. We re-enter the city through Dilli Gate, ride through Daryaganj and up the steps of the Jamia Masjid. After the great ride and the grand shikar of humans we wash our lances in the mosque-cistern. The water becomes so red that even the horses refuse to come hear it.

Bahadur Shah Zafar

We waited for two days. On the third morning a *gora* with a posse of fifty Sikh cavalry arrived at the gates. Their emissary was Rajab Ali, the one-eyed sycophant who had so often prostrated himself before us and begged the privilege of kissing our feet. He informed us that Mirza Elahi Baksh had promised Wilson Sahib Bahadur, the commander of the English army, to have us arrested. A Major Hodson had been authorized to execute the warrant. Our ears refused to believe that Hakeem Ahsanullah had also gone over to the enemy and was making an inventory of our properties. It is rightly said the smoother the skin of the serpent the more venom it has in its fangs.

We had no words left for anyone. The loathsome, one-eyed bastard, Rajab Ali, assured us that if we went with him our lives would be spared. What was our life worth at eighty-two? But we had to think of Zeenat Mahal and Jawan Bakht. Then there was our elder son, Mirza Mughal. He urged us to spit in the face of Rajab Ali. 'We will make kababs of this *gora* and his bearded *Sikhra boorchas!*' he boasted.

We listened to the contentious debate for an hour. We did not speak our mind but sent for Begum Zeenat Mahal and our son Jawan Bakht. We took them with us and descended the steps of the mausoleum. Mirza Mughal and his soldiers continued to shout. We became deaf to all advice save what Allah gave us. We told Mirza Mughal and our other sons to see how the sahibs treated us and then decide on their own course of action. We embraced them, little realizing that this would be the last time for us to be doing so. We bade farewell to our relatives and servants. They kissed our hands and wept.

Our palanquins were borne out of the gate of the mausoleum to where our captors awaited us. Before stepping out we recited the Throne verse ten times, ten times the Messenger Believes, and then times Say He Is God. We raised our hands to the heavens and intoned: 'Allah! We commit Thy Servant Bahadur Shah Zafar to Thee. Watch over us.' We approached the sahib in command of the Sikh cavalry and enquired whether he was Hodson Sahib Bahadur. He nodded his head. We asked him if he would be good enough to repeat the assurance that our life and those of our Queen and son would be spared. He nodded his head again. We presented the famous Zulfiqar given by the Persian conqueror Nadir Shah to our ancestors to the sahib. Our son presented his sword. We were ordered into our palanquins. We were prisoners of the *firangi*.

৯৯

It look us a whole day to get back to Delhi. We could hear the shouting of the crowd and many times our palanquins were halted. By the afternoon the tumult died down. When we finally entered Delhi Darwaza it was *Shahr-i-Khamoshan* (a silent city). We could hear no sounds except those made by the horses of the escorting cavalry. At Lahori Gate Hodson Sahib handed us over to a troop of *goras*.

In the past whenever we entered the fort, cannon were fired to announce our arrival and the band played at the Naqqar Khana. This time all we heard was our name mispronounced 'Baddur Sha' as one *gora* soldier passed us on to the next. Our palanquins were borne through the Meena Bazaar. We were lodged in the subterranean rooms where a few months earlier we had given shelter to the Europeans families before they were butchered by the mob. The doors were bolted from the outside and an armed guard placed at the gate. We were cut off from the world, from everything save evil tidings.

The bow of fate loosened a hundred poisoned shafts into our body. As a limb numbed by poverty of blood feels not the prick of the thorn so was our mind numbed against sorrow.

Nihal Singh

It took seven days flushing out rebels from the hideouts before we could say Dilli had become the property of Jan Company. All that was left were empty houses and corpses. And dogs, cats and rats to eat them. After a few days the Hindus were allowed to return and open their shops. Mussalmans who tried to pass off as Hindus paid with their lives. We made them take off their clothes. We poked their cocks with our bayonets and asked: 'How did this fellow get his top chopped off?' The blood would drain out of their faces and they would start urinating. We knew they had come back for buried silver or gold. So we would march them to their homes, take whatever we could find and turn them over to the sahib judge. He would ask them a few questions and order them to be hanged. They would be brought to the kotwali in the centre of Chandni Chowk where our Guru had been executed by Auranga. A dozen gallows had been erected. In the evening after having had their dinner the sahibs would ride up to the place. *Khidmatgars* would lay out chairs and sofas for them and *abdars* would fill their glasses with brandy and port and light their cheroots. And the tamasha would begin. In batches of six the wretches would be hauled up, their hands tied behind them, and nooses would be put round their necks. The sahibs would give the signal by clenching their fists with their thumbs pointing down and the planks would be pulled away. The sahibs would lay bets on which one would last longest. It was easy to tell who would die first—the one who struggled most, strangled himself quickest. Their eyes would pop out, blood pour out of their nostrils. Some died quickly; others had to have their legs stretched to finish them off. The sahibs enjoyed themselves laughing and joking, drinking and gambling.

ఇ

Hodson Sahib never wastes his time on this kind of tamasha. His mind is on bigger game. One day he goes to Wilson Sahib Bahadur and says, 'Let me go and capture the King of Dilli.' The *Jangi Lat* replies. '*Achcha*, but I don't want to loose any more *goras*.' Hodson Sahib says, 'I will take my Sikhs.' He then tells me, 'Nihal Singha, pick up fifty of your bravest boys and be ready in the morning for the big shikar.'

It is the 21st of September. The weather has changed. The nights are getting cool and the dew falls like the drizzle of rain. I pick fifty boys including Natha and Lehna and tell them to sleep round the pulpit of the mosque. I rouse them while it is still dark. We swallow a couple of chappaties and drink a mug of tea. We get into our uniforms and ride down the steps of the mosque. Hodson Sahib arrives with two Mussalmans riding behind him. One is that same one-eyed Rajab Ali. The other is dressed like a nawab: big fur cap and a coat of gold kinkob. My Sahib addressees him politely as 'Mirza Sahib'. (I later discover his name was Mirza Elahi Baksh and that he was the father-in-law of the king's eldest son who had died some time ago).

The Mirza says something in the ear of Hodson Sahib and takes his leave. We proceed clip, clop clip, clop through Faiz Bazaar and out of Dilli Gate. Hodson Sahib rides in front holding his unsheathed sabre on his shoulder. The one-eyed Rajab Ali follows behind him. I am behind the one-eyed fellow leading my fifty *sowars*. We carry our lances in our hands; our loaded carbines are slung behind our backs. We have two kirpans each—one attached to the saddle and the other to our belts. By the time the sun rises we are on the royal road to Agra. On either side of the road are many ancient ruins. They are full of people. The men are armed with guns and swords. But no one dares come near us or say a word.

The one-eyed Rajab Ali rides up alongside the Sahib and tells him about the buildings. Hodson Sahib is not interested, but this fellow keeps talking. 'That, Sahib, is a Buddhist pillar on top of the palace of Firoze Shah,' he says. I ask you what can a Buddhist pillar be doing on top of a Mussalman king's palace? We pass very high walls of an ancient fort. The one-eyed chap says: 'This, sir, is the

Purana Qila—the old fort—said to have been first built by the Aryans and was known as Indraprastha. Inside there is a mosque of Sher Shah Suri and the library of Emperor Humayun.' Who is to tell the Sahib that there cannot be a mosque inside a Hindu fort! I keep quiet as Hodson Sahib is paying no attention to the one-eyed *tuttoo*. By the time the sun is a spear high we arrive at the gate of a very large building with very high walls. All we can see of the inside is a huge white marble dome. This the one-eyed fellow says is the tomb of Humayun Badshah. The old king and his family are hiding inside.

The one-eyed fellow continues to babble. 'And this, Sahib Bahadur, is the tomb of Isa Khan and beyond that where the crowd is was once known as Arab-ki-Sarai. Beyond that you can see the red dome of the tomb of Abdul Rahim Khan-i-Khanan, one of the great ministers of Emperor Akbar. And these buildings behind you belong to the mausoleum of His Holiness Shaikh Nizamuddin Auliya. Many kings and queens and princes of royal blood have their graves close to the tomb of the saint.'

Hodson Sahib becomes very impatient. 'Yes, yes, Rajab Ali, another time you can tell me all about these ruddy monuments! We have more important work on hand. So get on with it *juldi*—I haven't the whole day to waste!'

Hodson Sahib and the one-eyed fellow dismount. I also dismount to take the reins of their horses. The one-eyed fellow slaps the big gate with the palm of his hand. 'Who's there?' demands a voice from the other side.

'Maulvi Rajab Ali, emissary of the Company Bahadur. I have an urgent message for His Majesty.'

After a while a small door in a corner of the gate opens. A sentry sticks out his head and sings: 'His Majesty Bahadur Shah Ghazi, Emperor of Hindustan, King of Kings, Shadow of God on Earth, commands the presence of Maulvi Rajab Ali Vakil of the Company Bahadur. Maulvi Rajab Ali may enter.'

'*Wah bhai wah!*' I say to myself. 'You hide like a rat in a hole but call yourself King of Kings!'

Rajab Ali disappears inside the little door which is shut behind him.

Hodson Sahib spits on the ground. He begins to pace up and down in front of the gate. He does not speak a word to anyone or even bother to look up at the crowd that is looking down at us from the walls. So many people and not a *choon*! The silence of thousands of people frightens me. All I can hear is horses champing at their bits, neighing, farting and urinating. And crows cawing. Then I hear voices of men quarrelling with each other. And a loud call: '*Narai Taqbir*!' And a roar of hundreds of voices yelling, '*Allah-o-Akbar*.'

More yelling: '*Mar dalo firangi ko* (kill the *firangi*).'

What can fifty Sikhs and one *gora* do against thousands? They will make mincemeat of us. But *wah, wah* Hodson Sahib! No one can be like you! He continues to pace up and down pretending he hasn't heard a sound.

Another hour. My mouth is dry; my tunic is wet with cold sweat. Voices on the other side come nearer and nearer. Hodson Sahib remounts. I tie the one-eyed fellow's horse to a tree and get into my own saddle. Hodson Sahib takes his pistol out of the holster and cocks it. I clutch my lance. Slowly the huge gates draw backwards. Three palanquins, one behind the other and a mob of wild looking men flourishing swords and carbines. Some women wailing surround the palanquins. They see Hodson Sahib and his Sikh *sowars* and turn to stone. The one-eyed Rajab Ali comes up to the Sahib and waggles his head. He goes back to the second palanquin and says something to someone. An old man steps out. He is tall, very thin and bent with age. He has a white, trimmed beard. He wears a big fur cap and a long fur-lined coat trailing down to his feet. He hobbles up to Sahib, looks up and asks: 'Have I the honour of addressing Hodson Sahib Bahadur?'

'Yes, I am Major Hodson. You Bahadur Shah?'

'That is the name by which this unfortunate man is known. Hodson Sahib Bahadur, do I have your word that our life, the life of our Queen Zeenat Mahal and that of our son Prince Jawan Bakht will be spared?'

'Yes, Wilson Sahib Bahadur, the *Jungi Lat* has promised you your lives.' There is a murmur in the crowd.

Hodson Sahib holds up his pistol and shouts at the top of his voice, 'Listen you people! If anyone of you make an attempt to interfere, I will shoot the three people in these palanquins like dogs. Understand!'

What audacity! The crowd shrinks back. The old king ungirds

his sword and holds it aloft with his shaking hands. Hodson Sahib dismounts, takes the sword and hands it to me. What a sword! Green jade and gold handle studded with precious stones! Then the *badshah's* son, a young chap named Jawan Bakht, steps out from the last palanquin and also hands his sword to the Sahib who passes it on to me. Another beauty! Gold, diamonds and rubies! Hodson Sahib orders the three palanquins to be brought out. Fifty *sowars* in front, then one palanquin, then my Sahib and I. Behind us the huge mob. We don't look back lest they think we are frightened of being shot in our backs. I have shivers going up and down my spine and more cold sweat on my body. But Hodson Sahib! Not a trace of fear on his red face! We pass along the battlements of the old fort with the crowd still trudging behind us. Thousands of rebel sepoys come out of the old Indraprastha fort. We ignore them and go along at the pace set by the palanquin-bearers. Another half-a-kos and the crowd begins to drop off. And we are taking with us as prisoner the Emperor of Hindustan, his queen and their son. It is miracle of the great Guru!

Instead of going through Delhi Gate we turn sharp left towards the side where the sun is setting and ride past Turkman and Ajmeri Gate. Then we turn right into Kabuli Gate to enter the city. Hodson Sahib wants everyone in Dilli to know that we have their King, Queen and the son as our prisoners. But the streets are deserted. Only dogs tearing up corpses pause to look up. Vultures shuffle away a few paces to let us pass. In front of the kotwali, six corpses are still dangling from the scaffolds with crows pecking on them. As we pass the gurdwara where our ninth Guru was martyred by Auranga, we unsheathe our *kirpans* and dip them in salute. I raise the Sikh battle cry *'Boley So Nihal!'* The *sowars* shout back *'Sat Sri Akal.'*

It is still daylight when we draw up outside the Red Fort. 'Who is there?' demands a *gora* sentry.

'Major Hodson to deliver up prisoners Bahadur Shah, ex-King of Delhi, his wife Zeenat Mahal and their son Jawan Bakht.'

The gate opens. Hodson Sahib and the one-eyed Rajab Ali go in with the palanquins.

We ride back to Jamia Masjid.

We slaughter twenty goats. And while they are roasting we drink a lot of rum. We get very drunk and begin to sing. Lehna starts off with a song about a little old man who wanted to copulate with a she-camel. Lehna knows a lot of songs about this *buddha baba*. But my kismet! The Sahib's *syce* comes and says I am wanted in the Red Fort. I am very high on rum but I follow him.

I ride to the Sahib's quarter. When I enter the Sahib is examining the two swords he has been given that morning. Under the light of the lantern the stones in the handle sparkle like stars. What craftsmanship! The Sahib tells me that one bears the name of Emperor Jahangir and the other of the Persian invader Nadir Shah. He is not very happy. 'That's all I got from Wilson Sahib Bahadur,' he says. 'Not even a *shabash*. I wish I had killed the old *badshah* and his puppy.'

'Sahib, if you had given me the slightest hint, I would have severed their heads from their bodies.'

'I know,' I know,' he replies impatiently. 'I would have done it myself. But the white man's word has to be honoured. Now it will be different. I have permission to get the king's other sons and nephews. They are the *badmashes* who murdered the memsahibs and their little *babalogs*. Wilson Sahib says, "Do what you like but don't let me be bothered with them." Tell Subedar Man Singh to be ready with a hundred *sowars* at the same time tomorrow. This may be dangerous work. There'll be plenty of rum when this is over.'

❧

Next morning I had great trouble getting the men ready in time. Subedar Man Singh had to shout at them. But Hodson Sahib arrived with another *gora*, Macdowell Sahib, and the one-eyed Rajab Ali. We were in our saddles lined up in front of the mosque. The two sahibs rode in front with Rajab Ali and myself directly behind them. (I was on his blind side so we did not even have to exchange glances). Behind us were our two subedars and then the hundred Sikh *sowars* with the ends of their turbans fluttering in the morning breeze and their spears glittering in the light of the morning sun. Rajab Ali didn't try his *buk buk* about the ancient buildings of Dilli on me.

We arrived at the northern gate of Humayun's mausoleum. And as soon as we arrived, a crowd began to collect around us.

Some came from Arab-ki-Sarai, next door, some from Nizamuddin. The roofs and walls of buildings were soon full of people. Many men were armed with carbines.

৯

Once more Rajab Ali goes in. Once more we hear yells of *'Allah-o-Akbar'*. We can hear them coming nearer and nearer the gate. Slowly the gates open. A cart appears, drawn by two humped oxen, with three men sitting huddled on it and the one-eyed Rajab Ali standing by the wheel. Behind the cart a mob of sullen-faced, evil-looking men armed with carbines and swords. The sahibs mount their horses and ride up to the cart. Hodson Sahib commands: 'Rajab Ali, identify the three prisoners.'

Rajab Ali puts his hand on one: 'Mirza Mughal Bahadur.'

The man steps out of the cart and with trembling hands offers his sword. Macdowell Sahib takes his sword.

'Mirza Abu Bakr,' says Rajab Ali putting his hand on another. This man also steps out and hands his sword to Macdowell Sahib.

'Mirza Khizr Sultan.'

The third man follows the example of the other two. All three go back and huddle on the ox cart. The crowd watches the scene. You can see some people are getting very agitated. The *burr-burr* of anger becomes a roar. As the cart moves forward, the mob surges behind it.

Hodson Sahib turns round his horse, draws his sword and holds it aloft. 'Halt,' he orders. The mob halts and falls silent. Hodson Sahib orders fifty *sowars* to go ahead with the cart. He and Macdowell Sahib ride up to the mob. The mob withdraws step by step till it is back in the mausoleum gate. Hodson Sahib shouts at the top of his voice, 'Lay down your arms.'

Another miracle of the Guru! They throw down their swords and muskets on the ground. It takes us two hours to collect them and load them on carts. Never in my life have I known hours like these! And never in my life have I known a man like Hodson Sahib Bahadur! He, as I am always saying, is one of a hundred thousand!

We ride at a smart canter to catch up with our party. There are gangs of armed men all along the road. The gangs become bigger and bigger as we approach the city. We plough our way through and join our party escorting the prisoners. All round us and upto the city walls is this armed mob shouting *'Allah-o-Akbar'* and brandishing swords at us. I pray to my Guru and promise to offer one rupee four annas at the Chandni Chowk gurdwara if my life is spared. The Guru hears my prayer. Hodson Sahib gallops up to the cart carrying the prisoners and orders it to halt. The *burr-burr* dies down. We are passing through a gate about half-a-mile from the city. On our right is the grey-black ruin of a Mussalman palace with that Buddhist column the one-eyed Rajab Ali was talking about; for the rest it is just a sea of heads, naked sabres and carbines. The sun is about to set. Hodson Sahib raises his hands and turns about in his saddle to speak to everyone. 'These three men in our custody are murderers. These butchers have the blood of many innocent women and children on their hands. You will now witness the justice of the Company Bahadur. Stand back, see, and remember.'

The crowd falls back. Our *sowars* form a ring around the ox cart. 'Get down all three of you and take off your clothes,' orders Hodson Sahib.

The three men obey. Their faces are yellow. Their hands tremble as they remove their shirts. 'Everything,' orders Hodson Sahib again.

Their knees shake as they slip down their pantaloon-type pyjamas. These Mussalmans not only cut the ends of their cocks, they also shave their pubic hair. I have never seen sadder looking penises hanging their circumcized heads as if in shame!

'You Abu Bakr, step out in front,' orders Hodson Sahib.

A heavily built man of about thirty-five comes up a few faltering steps. He covers his nakedness with his hands.

'Nihal Singh, take that thing off this man's arm,' he orders pointing to a charm tied round Abu Bakr's arm.

I wrench off the amulet and put it in my pocket.

'Hand me your carbine.'

I give my carbine to the Sahib.

'Sahib, *mat maro*—don't kill,' wails Abu Bakr, clasping his hands in prayer.

Hodson Sahib aims at his chest. *Thah*. Abu Bakr cries *'Hai Allah'* and collapses in a pool of blood.

The crowd is struck dumb with terror. Not one person moves.

The other two prisoners are more dead than alive when Hodson Sahib shoots them through their heads.

We have three naked corpses sprawled in the dust; blood gushing from their wounds, saliva oozing from their gaping mouths, eyes turning to grey marbles. The thousands of armed men who watched the executions look as dead as the three lying at our feet.

Subedar Man Singh raises his kirpan and shouts: '*Jo Boley So Nihal.*' We draw our kirpans and reply: '*Sat Sri Akal.*'

The corpses are loaded on the cart. We resume our ride back to the city. The crowd melts before us as the mist melts before the rays of the sun. We ride through Daryaganj. At Chandni Chowk we wheel left till we come to our gurdwara. We throw the three corpses on the steps of the gurdwara. We return to the Jamia Masjid to drink rum and eat goat's meat. Lehna sings of the little old man who wanted to copulate with a she-camel.

Next morning I go to congratulate my Sahib for his great courage. I enter his room and salute. He is writing a letter (he writes a letter to his memsahib every day). 'Well, Nihal Singh!' he says as if nothing had happened. When I don't reply he asks, 'What do you want?'

'Sahib, I came to pay my respects and congratulate you for your great *bahaduri.*'

He nods his head and goes on writing, as if I am not there. I stand where I am not knowing what to do next. Then I ask: 'Does Sahib require me for anything.'

He puts his letter inside an envelope, seals it and hands it to me. '*Dak.*'

I take the letter. Suddenly he looks a little happier. 'Ask Subedar Man Singh to tell the *sowars* that the Sahib is very *khush*. Give them as much rum as they like. No more work for some time.' After a pause he asks: 'What are they saying in the camp?'

'Sahib, each time your name is uttered people say' '*Wah! Wah!*'

He is pleased. Then I ask him of a story I had heard just before I left Jamia Masjid. 'Sahib, is it true that the heads of the three men you shot were cut off and presented to the old king? What did he say?'

Hodson Sahib's expression changes. He looks me in the eye. 'Nihal Singh, where did you pick up that gossip?'

'Sahib . . . People are saying . . . .'

'Listen,' he cuts me short. 'The sahibs are a civilized people; they are not like the natives of Hindustan. They do not cut off people's heads and present them on trays to their relatives. The Company Bahadur is just—strong but just. Understand!'

'*Jee huzoor*,' I reply. I salute the Sahib and return to Jamia Masjid.

Bahadur Shah Zafar

A messenger was let into our dungeon to break the news of the deaths of our kinsmen and supporters. Our two sons, Mirza Mughal had Mirza Khizr, and grandson Mirza Abu Bakr were shot dead. We made no protest but only sent a petition that whatever was recovered by the sale of our property be expended on giving a proper burial to the dead. The bodies of Mirza Mughal, Abu Bakr and Khizr Sultan were interred in the mausoleum of Emperor Humayun. The nawabs of Jhajjar and Farrukhnagar who were hanged were buried in their family graveyards adjoining the tomb of Hazrat Qutubuddin Bakhtiyar Kaki a Mehrauli. The Raja Bahadur of Ballabhgarh, who was also hanged, being a Hindu was cremated at Nigambodh Ghat on the Jamna. Of the fate of our other sons and nephews and grandsons who were also executed we could not get any details save that their bodies were buried either at Nizamuddin or at Mehrauli. Amongst the thousands shot or hanged by the sahibs was our friend and poet Shaikh Imam Baksh 'Sabhai' and his two sons. No one knows what they did with their bodies.

An autumnal gale had blown through the garden that was once our kingdom. It uprooted every tree. We lost our peace of mind. We lost the will to live. As a captive bird beats its wings against the bars of its cage, we banged our head against the walls of our dungeon and lamented our fate. There was a time when the world seemed like a flower garden where the afternoon sun warmed the buds to unlock their treasure chest. The same world now exuded the stench of a hundred thousand rotting corpses. Here was a city bathed in the day by the sun, by the moon by night; here was a city in which lived women as beauteous as the *houris* of paradise! Who despoiled this city? Where has he taken away the loot? This was Delhi, the queen of all the cities of the world, now a ruined desolation. 'O Zafar, what calamity has come to pass? Or is it that thy own youth hath fled?'

It would take an ink-well full of tears to write of the way we were treated. At all hours people peered through the windows to gaze at us as if we were some kind of animal. The gates of our dungeon would be suddenly thrown open for parties of sahibs. Our womenfolk hid their faces against the wall. We had to stand up and salaam every white man and woman. They taunted us: 'You wanted to become Emperor of India, did you?' Sometimes a young *gora* imitated the bleating of a goat. '*Buddha* man where are your young wives?' he would ask. And all of them would laugh. We accepted the insults as the will of Allah.

Our request for pen and paper was refused. We saved pieces of charcoal from our hookah and used the walls of our dungeon as our slate. We spent our time in prayer and in composing poetry.

In our younger days we had composed a verse on a lover's complaint at being imprisoned and tormented by his beloved. These lines which had become very popular ran somewhat as follows:

> *Why should our beloved jailer not torment us?*
> *May God not place anyone in anyone else's mercy.*

How appropriate were these lines when the jailer was not the beloved but an enemy!

The worth of the white man's plighted word was soon made clear to us. He called us savages because our troops had killed white women and children. People who knew swore that we had done our best to prevent these killings. The sahibs refused to believe us. For the three dozen of their own killed they slew more than a thousand times three dozen. Despite solemn assurances conveyed to us by Rajab Ali, that one-eyed product of evil seed, that bootlicking bastard, we were put up for trial. The sahibs were our accusers, our attorneys and our judges. They lined up men who had eaten our salt—Hakeem Ahsanullah, the dervish Hassan Askari, Rajab Ali, Ghulam Abbas, Mukund Lal—to repeat parrot-wise what they had been told to say.

It grieves us to record that amongst those who turned their

tongues against us was the half-caste Ayesha Aldwell. We had
risked our own life to save the life of this woman and her three
daughters. This Ayesha's mother had taken a *gora* husband.
Ayesha had been brought up as a Mussalmanni. But as she
inherited a lighter skin from her father and from him learnt to *git
mit* in English she passed off as a white woman and married on old
gora. We could not save her husband. But as she recited verses from
the holy Quran and made her daughters repeat the *kalima*, we were
able to intercede on her behalf. We had hoped she would testify to
all that we had done for her. She proved false to both faiths, the
Muslim and the Christian. May Allah punish her!

Allah was our only witness. No mortal dared to open his
mouth in our favour. They pronounced us guilty on all charges
levelled against us. We were sentenced to be exiled from the land
our ancestors had conquered and ruled for three hundred years.
We would rather they had sentenced us to die and let our bones
mingle in the sacred dust of Delhi.

Fourteen begums and our son Jawan Bakht agreed to share the
misfortune of our exile. Later many of them changed their minds
and on one pretext or another deserted us before we crossed the
boundaries of Hindustan. Our beloved Zeenat Mahal stayed by our
side. She remained our companion in the camel-litter of misery and
our comrade in the closet of affection. We were reminded of the
words our Holy Prophet used for his wife Khadijah: 'When I was
poor she enriched me; when all the world abandoned me, she
comforted me; when I was called a liar, she believed in me.'

On our journey we composed the following lines:

> My beloved tormented me so much
> We were forced to leave our native land;
> As drops wax from the burning taper
> So as we quit the circle of life
> Fell tears from our eyes.
> The gardener forbade us sporting in his garden,
> With laughter we came,
> With wailing we parted.

Bhagmati

Bhagmati is very disappointed with me. 'All these Punjabis came to Delhi without a penny in their pockets. And look at them now! They own the whole city. They have made palaces for themselves. They live on tandoori chicken and drink whisky. They take their fat wives out to eat the Delhi air in imported motor cars. And look at you! The same little flat, the same *rhat-khatee* old motor, every part of which makes a noise except its horn. Why, even those fellows who came from your village only a few years ago own half of New Delhi and live like *crorepatis*. What do you get out of killing flies on paper all day long? You haven't bought me a sari or a bangle for many years.'

When Bhagmati is in this nagging mood, it is best to say nothing. But sometimes even my silence provokes her to go on and on. 'Why don't you say something? Why don't you do something? You are just getting old sitting and farting in your armchair all day long.'

That stings. I explode. 'Shut up! You get your fucking and get paid for it. What more do you want?'

'Not much of that either these days,' she retorts looking into my eyes. 'As for the payment, even that Budhoo Singh outside asks me everytime I leave—"What did he give you for your paan-beedi?" That's all I can buy from the money you give me. It's no use getting angry with me. Truth hurts but I am saying it for your own good. I say do some *dhanda* like contracting business, exporting readymade garments. You will make a lot more money than scribbling pieces for newspapers and taking memsahibs to see the Qutub Minar.'

There is some truth in what she says. But how can I at my age start a new *dhanda* of which I know nothing. And where will I find the money to do so? I relapse into silence: silence and sulking are the best defences against this kind of onslaught.

I pick up a book and pretend to read. I wish she would go away and leave me alone. I am beginning to tire of Bhagmati as I am of Delhi. One of these days when I have enough money I will buy myself a one-way air ticket to London or New York and slip out of Delhi at midnight without telling Bhagmati.

She takes the book out of my hand and sits down on the floor in front of me. She places her hands on my knees and continues, 'You are becoming irritable these days. You get *gussa* with me whenever I say anything to you. You never used to lose your temper with me. What is happening to you?'

A sigh of resignation escapes my lips. I don't reply because I know what she is saying is right. She begins to press my legs with both her hands. It is very pleasant and sensuous. I know I have lost the battle. Where will I find another woman like Bhagmati who will abase herself to soothe my temper? She puts my legs in her lap and rubs the soles of my feet. She is a skilled masseuse. She knows I am beginning to enjoy a good massage more than sex. Sometimes I can't get roused till she has rubbed oil in my scalp and vigorously massaged the dandruff itch out of it with her stubby, sturdy fingers. Next to my scalp it is my feet which respond to her ministrations. If I don't fall off to sleep I end up by sleeping with the masseuse. My frayed nerves are soothed. My temper dissolves. I no longer want to buy myself an air ticket to go abroad to get away from Bhagmati and Delhi. I told you—once you are in their clutches there is no escape.

The Builders

We had two colour prints on the walls of our *deorhi* which was both the entrance to our home and waiting-room for male visitors. One above the wooden platform on which my father sat reclining on a bolster was of Queen Victoria. On the wall facing the Queen was Guru Nanak. Every morning after my mother had said her morning prayers, while churning the earthen pitcher of buttermilk, she would light two joss-sticks and stick one each in the frames of the pictures and make obeisances to them: first to the Guru, then to the Empress. And every evening, after he had recited his evening prayer and the invocation, my father would stand in front of the Queen with the palms of his hands joined together and say loudly: 'Lord, bless our *Malika*! Long may she rule over us! And bless us, her subjects! May we forever remain loyal and contented!'

When Queen Victoria died in 1901, we had a non-stop reading of the Holy Granth lasting two days and nights and prayed that her soul find a resting place beside the lotus feet of our Guru. When her son, Edward, was crowned king we sent plates of sweets to families with whom we maintained *bhai chaara* (fraternal relationship). Nine years later when Emperor Edward died, we again had a non-stop reading of the Granth. And a few days later when George V was proclaimed Emperor of Hindustan we celebrated the occasion by sending our sweets. Our family was as devoted to the Gurus as it was faithful to our English rulers whose salt it ate.

When the ship bearing King George and Queen Mary docked in Bombay on 2 December 1911 my father and I reached Delhi by train. He wanted to have the *darshan* of our rulers and explore possibilities of getting building contracts. He had been in the building business for some years. He had bored tunnels and laid the railtrack between Kalka and the summer capital, Simla, but was lately of the opinion that there was more money in building houses than in drilling holes in mountains. He forced me to give up studies before I could take the final school-leaving examination. 'Education is for making money,' he said. 'For making money all you need to know is how to add, subtract, multiply, calculate simple and compound interest. You have learnt all that. The rest is *aaltoo faltoo* (dispensable rubbish).' When I protested that I wanted to learn how to speak English like Englishmen, he lost his temper and called me a *bharooah* (pimp) which was his favourite term of abuse. When he realized he had hurt my feelings, he added very gently that English gentlemen did not like Indians who spoke English like them and much preferred Indians who spoke *tutti-phutti* (broken) English.

It did not take much to make my father lose his temper and lay about with his walking-stick. When he decided that at fourteen I had learnt all there was to learn, I had to leave school and join his contracting business. When I was seventeen, he decided I was old enough to get married and chose a thirteen-year-old girl from a neighbouring village to be my wife. Before she was eighteen (and I twenty-two) she had borne me two sons. Then my father decided that I should leave my wife and sons in the village and accompany him to Delhi to seek our fortunes.

I had never seen a city as grand as Delhi. At the time it looked bigger and grander because more than five hundred rajas and maharajas were encamped there with their retinues. Also hundreds of thousands of common people from distant provinces had come to see Their Majesties. It took us three days to find accommodation. We rented two rooms on the first floor of an old building behind a bioscope close to Dufferin Bridge under which passed trains running between Delhi and Punjab, Delhi and Rajputana, Delhi and Central India.

We bought charpoys, tables and chairs before we went to see the preparations for the darbar. A city of 40,000 tents called Kingsway Camp had gone up on the northern side of the city stretching over twenty-five square miles from the river Jamna in the east to the Shalimar Gardens and beyond in the west. All day long there were rehearsals with regimental bands marching up and down; caparisoned elephants being made to kneel and raise their trunks in salute; maharajas and their sons being lined up and told how to bow before the King and Queen. Every minute of the programme was gone over many times with the Viceroy, Lord Hardinge, his Vicereine and their Chief Adviser, Malcolm Hailey, riding around on horseback checking everything in detail. They said that over 90,000 rats had been killed in the previous month to make sure that nothing disturbed the proceedings of the darbar.

On the morning of 2 December 1911 the alarm clock which regulated my father's life went off at 4 a.m. It was bitterly cold. My teeth chattered while I washed my face in ice-cold water. After a quick repast of stale chappaties left over from thee previous evening gulped down with tumblers of steaming-hot, over-sweetened tea, we set out in the pitch dark. We had to cross over Dufferin Bridge well before Their Majesties train was to pass under it on its way to Delhi railway station as the railtrack passing through Delhi including the bridge was later to be cordoned off by the police as a precaution against the designs of evildoers.

We had to walk almost three miles with crowds milling around us before we reached our destination. The roads near Kingsway Camp were brightly lit. By the time the streetlights were switched off we were in our places. A very bright sun came up on the huge open square. At one end of the square was a platform covered with a red carpet with two 'thrones' placed under a canopy. On all the other sides of the square were rows of chairs at different levels. There must have been over 3,00,000 people in these enclosures. I asked myself where in India you could see such an orderly, well-behaved crowd except in Delhi! White soldiers were directing people to their allotted seats; no one dared to question them. No shouting. No squabbling. And military bands playing all the time; as one brass band ended, bagpipes began to whine; when they ended another roll of drums and the clash of cymbals.

Suddenly the bands fell silent. From the distance we heard the thunder of cannon firing a twenty-one gun salute. Their Majesties had arrived at Delhi railway station.

An hour or so later we heard the roar of crowds from the city side come nearer and nearer towards us and sensed that the royal procession was on its way. A long line of elephants came lumbering down with bells clanging. Then came regimental bands followed by infantry, cavalry, more bands and more elephants. I trained my eye on every passing *howdah* to see if I could recognize Their Majesties from pictures I had seen. After all the elephants had gone by, I asked my father, 'Where are the King and the Queen?' He had also failed to spot them. 'That's the *Laat Sahib*,' he said pointing to a tall man on horseback. 'And that small gentleman riding on the white horse alongside Lord Hardinge is the King,' said a man sitting next to my father. I was disappointed. He should have been seated on an elephant. Besides the tall Viceroy, the king looked like pink dwarf with a beard. I am sure few people realized that the king had ridden past them till they saw him and his queen walk up to their thrones. Then everyone stood up as massed bands struck up the National Anthem 'God Save The King'.

From where we sat we could not hear any of the speeches Though the white soldiers would frighten Indians into staying in their places, no power on earth can stop Indians from talking all the time. *Yeh dekh! Voh dekh!* (See this! See that!)—everyone kept telling everyone else. All at once there was an uproar. A *shamiana* was on fire and people began to run. Tommies hollered at the top of their voices: 'Sit down, sit down.' No one cared; everyone valued his life above everything else. My father and I ran with the crowd and were out of the camp in a few minutes. We did not pause for breath till we were back in our apartment.

I had read about the disloyal activities of mischief makers in Bengal and Maharashtra. Perhaps they were behind this conflagration. In the bazaars people were making wild guesses about who started it, how many had been killed, how narrowly Their Majesties had escaped. And the heads that would roll because of the fiasco. Surely the wrath of the *sarkar* would fall on the city and it would order parts of it to be burnt down! It was only in the evening that we learnt from special bulletins issued by the local papers that the fire had been caused by a short circuit and had been put out immediately without any loss of life. The bulletins also mentioned two momentous decisions taken by the government: the partition of Bengal made six years ago was to be revoked and the capital of India would be shifted from Calcutta to Delhi.

The partition of Bengal by Lord Curzon in 1905 had angered Hindus who felt that it was designed to further divide Hindus and Muslims and create a Muslim state in East Bengal. Young Bengali Hindus and Maharashtrians and some misguided Sikhs viewed to undo the partition and destroy British rule. In Bengal bombs were thrown at English officers and some were murdered. In Gujarat an attempt was made on the life of Lord Minto who had succeeded Curzon as Viceroy. A Punjabi boy studying in London shot and killed Wylie. The English being wise realized that the partition of Bengal had caused too much heart-burning and decided to revoke it in the hope that it would put an end to terrorism. For a while it did. But it also created an impression that the English could be frightened with bombs and pistols. Indian nationalists said it was wrong to think that the white race was superior to the brown. If a yellow race of dwarfs like the Japanese could defeat the mighty empire of the white Tsars of Russia surely a nation of hundred-and-fifty million Indians could make mincemeat of the handful of Englishmen in India! They said if all Indians were to stand alongside and urinate in a tank there would be enough urine to drown the English population of India.

The transfer of the capital to Delhi was widely welcomed—the only exceptions were Europeans with businesses in Calcutta. They suspected that Lord Hardinge was behind the move and started a campaign to have him dismissed. They said that the letters H.M.G. no longer stood for 'His Majesty's Government' but for 'Hardinge must Go'. Their efforts came to nothing. Delhi had always been the capital of Hindustan. It was closer to the heart of the country. Before Hardinge there were Viceroys who had given clear hints that they regarded Delhi as India's most important city. In 1877 it was in Delhi that Lord Lytton had read the proclamation recognizing Queen Victoria as Empress of Hindustan. Likewise in 1903 it was in Delhi that Lord Curzon had held the darbar in honour of the coronation of King Edward VII.

Having made the proclamation there was no question of the king going back on it. Three days after inaugurating the darbar Their Majesties Laid the foundation stone of the new capital at Kingsway Camp. The next day they left for Nepal to shoot tigers before returning to England.

My father was a man of foresight and had a knack of making

669

money. He was also very tight-fisted and haggled over the prices of peanuts, onions and potatoes. 'Money saved is money earned,' he often said. 'Put a rupee in the bank today and let it accumulate compound interest—*sood dar sood*. Sitting in the bank without doing anything in a hundred years that one rupee will become one lakh rupees.' Although he could not speak English he could get round English officials and get them to do what he wanted. Whenever he went to call on them he wore his big white turban, a black coat and a gold-brocaded sash running from his left shoulder to his waist. He bought the best fruit available in the market and presented them to the sahibs saying they were from his orchard. We had no orchard. The only fruit that grew in our native village, Hadali, were date-palms. He told me, 'Never try to give sahibs cash or jewellery; they will abuse you and will kick you out. But fruit is *daali*—an acceptable gift.' He was open-handed with his tips to the sahibs' chaprassies and clerks. 'This is not *baksheesh*,' he explained to me later, 'but sound investment.' It was true. The sahibs' orders in his favour were never lost in officials' files but immediately attended to.

As soon as the darbar tents were struck, plans for building the new capital were taken in hand. Malcom Hailey was made Commissioner and put in charge of the capital project. My father had met Hailey when he had visited our district town, Shahpur. He took me along when he went to pay his respects to the Commissioner. We bought oranges, apples and Kandahari pomegranates then available in Fatehpuri Bazaar and had several baskets nicely wrapped in pink tissue-paper and silver thread. One basket was presented to the sahib's personal assistant and the contents of another distributed amongst the orderlies. It was the personal assistant who reminded Hailey that my father had met him earlier and brought the pick of fruit from his orchard. Hailey who must have known that there were no fruit grown around Shahpur nevertheless graciously accepted them. He asked my father in Punjabi if there was anything he could do for him. My father introduced me to him 'as your own son,' and mentioned the experience we had in building. Hailey put down our names and address on a piece of paper and said, 'You will hear from me if anything comes up.'

Since we had nothing to do except wait for Hailey's letter my father decided to call on other officials—bank managers, property owners and heads of Delhi's leading families. 'You never know when one of them may prove useful. One must keep up with everyone who matters,' he said very wisely. We also saw the Red Fort and the Royal Mosque and went round Sikh gurdwaras. These last were poorly maintained as there were not many Sikhs in Delhi and none of them very rich. Even on Sunday evenings the congregation at Sees Ganj did not exceed a hundred men and women. Everyone we introduced ourselves to as newcomers asked us if we had seen the Qutub Minar. They said it was the highest tower in the world and from its top storey you could see the countryside with its ruins for miles around. 'One day we will hire a tonga and go to the Qutub,' my father said to me. By then I had started having dreams of my own. I replied, 'I will go to the Qutub driving my own motor car.' At the time no more than a dozen of the richest Indian families of Delhi owned cars. I could see my father was pleased with my ambition and self-assurance. Nevertheless, he laughed and snubbed me: '*Bharooah!* learn to earn before you talk of buying a motor car. You know how much one costs?'

He let me buy a bicycle—a beautiful, dark-green Raleigh made in England. It did not take me long to learn to ride it. The Raleigh cycle was to be my Rolls-Royce and my Daimler for the next fifteen years.

Give it to the English, when they say they will do something for you, you can be sure it will be done. A month after we had called on Hailey, we got a note asking us to report at his office.

There were a lot of English officers present. He simply introduced us to the Chief Engineer of the Central Public Works Department (CPWD). Without bothering to reply to our greetings, the Chief Engineer said: 'You can start with roads and clerks' quarters. I'll see your work first and then we can think of other things. See the Superintending Engineer tomorrow morning.'

My father went straight to the CPWD office to find out who was who. From a clerk my father got the names and addresses of every one who worked there from the SE down to his chaprassies. On the way back we stopped at the telegraph office. I drafted a telegram to my younger brother who was looking after our property in the village to send a few reliable men who could organize labour and keep accounts.

The next morning before going to the office of the SE we called at his residence with the usual baskets of fruit 'from our orchards'. We gave handsome tips to his chaprassies. The SE did not see us; his chief orderly told us that the sahib never received Indians in his home. To this day I do not know whether the fruit ever reached him or was eaten up by his chaprassies.

We went onto the CPWD office. A few minutes later the SE drove up and sent for us. It was easier than I expected. He gave us a map of the roads to be laid round the temporary Secretariat building on Alipur Road. No tenders were invited. We were asked to submit in two days an estimate of the cost and the time it would take us to complete the work. We spent the afternoon working out the costs of hiring labour, stone, cement, sand and transportation. It came to a couple of lakhs of rupees. The next day my father handed over the estimate to the overseer with a thousand rupee note for him. The following day the overseer came to see us. He had scaled down our estimates very marginally, still leaving us a handsome margin of profit. My father gave him another thousand rupee note and a bottle of Scotch. They embraced each other to cement an on-going business partnership. That became the pattern of our working life. Every Indian who had anything to do with our building contracts was given his cut in advance. Most Anglo-Indian officials also expected money or whisky. English officials who knew what was going on never accepted anything beyond baskets of fruit with a bottle or two of whisky thrown in on *bara din*.

It did not take me long to catch on to the business. We sent agents to hire Baagree labourers from Rajputana. This was not difficult as that desert land always suffered from drought and famines. They were happy to get half-a-rupee per day (less for women) and break stones, dig, mix mortar and cement from sunrise to sunset. Every evening they trooped back to their hovels with their women singing all the way. We who made money spent our time counting it and were miserable if other contractors were making more than us.

In April 1912 Edwin Lutyens, the architect approved by the king, and a team of town builders came to Delhi to inspect the site of the new capital. They went by horseback around Kingsway

Camp, the Ridge and along the river Jamna from above Majnoon Ka Tilla to Okhla. They went over the area several times again on elephants before deciding that Kingsway would not do because it was low-lying, too close to the river and swampy. They spent another fifteen days riding around villages between Paharganj and Mehrauli and from the Jamna behind Purana Qila to the Ridge before deciding that the most suitable site for the new city would be round village Malcha and that the Viceregal palace and the Secretariats should be built on Raisina Hill. Lord Hardinge who had earlier chosen the Kingsway Camp site agreed with them. It did not bother them that Their Majesties had laid the foundation stone at Kingsway. There was nothing sacred about the site, they said. The same foundation stone could be re-laid elsewhere.

And so it was. Hailey sent for my father (by now my father had become his most reliable contractor) and told him that he was to remove the foundation stone from Kingsway to its new site at Malcha. Not a word of this was to be breathed to anyone. He drove in his own car to the tomb of Safdar Jang and then took us on foot to a spot near Malcha where the stone was to be replanted. There was a barbed wire fence round the spot with a couple of armed policemen on guard.

Taking out the foundation stone and planting it in its new site was the first job my father entrusted to me to do all on my own. I was thrilled. First, I had a pit dug for the stone. Then I hired a bullock cart and selected half-a-dozen labourers for the job. We were given four policemen as our escort. Finally, one evening in May I rode my bicycle alongside the bullock cart loaded with labourers and policemen and reached Kingsway Camp an hour after sunset. I had the stone dug out and placed on a bed of straw spread in the cart. I covered it up with tarpaulin. We then proceeded on our journey led by a man carrying a petromax lamp. I walked with the rest of the party behind the car. We looked like a funeral procession. It was a long distance to traverse as we had to skirt round the city. We reached Malcha after midnight. It took us another hour to fix the stone in the pit with mortar. I gave the labourers a rupee each as a reward. By the time I reached home it was daylight. My father interrupted his morning prayer to ask me how it had gone. I gave him the details. When I told hm I had given the labourers an extra rupee each, he called me a *bharooah*.

673

We were now making enough money to live in better quarters. (However, as we were used to going out in the open to relieve ourselves we found going to a dirty, smelly lavatory very constipating).

We did not get any contracts for the building of the temporary Secretariat which was almost entirely taken over by the CPWD and decided to move out to the site where the new city was destined to come up. With the labourers and the building materials available to us, it didn't take us a month to put up a couple of rooms, kitchen and courtyard. This was close to an old flour mill. Following our example other Sikh contractors also built shacks alongside ours on what later came to be known as the Old Mill Road. Although we came from different parts of the Punjab and belonged to different castes, we soon became like members of one family.

Lutyens prepared a plan of the layout of the new city and where he meant to locate the Viceregal palace and the Secretariats. I heard that in his original plan Lutyens had wanted to dam the Jamna behind Humayun's tomb and make a huge ornamental lake extending from the Red Fort to Purana Qila with a lakeside drive and waterways running through the city. This was not approved because of the enormous cost. Lutyens also wanted to drive a road from the Viceregal palace to the Jamia Masjid piercing the old Mughal city wall and the bazaars. This was also turned down. The rest was approved by the Viceroy as well as King George whom Lutyens met on his return to England. Lutyens got an old colleague, Herbert Baker, to share the work with him. In addition to the general layout of the city, Lutyens assigned to himself the Viceregal palace and the War Memorial Arch; Baker designed the Secretariats and the Parliament. The rest of the work was equally divided between them. They had known each other for many years. Baker had chosen Lutyens to be his co-architect for buildings in South Africa. Lutyens was returning the compliment by choosing Baker as his partner in the building of New Delhi. Everyone thought they were good friends. But envy of Lutyens's genius and popularity with royalty and the Vicereine soured Baker's mind.

Lutyens was a man of vision. Although neither he nor Baker had too great an opinion of our old palaces, mosques and temples, they agreed to give an Indian touch to their designs. What impressed me most about Lutyens was that even before roads were laid, he ordered trees to be planted along the proposed routes. A huge nursery was set up to raise the right kind of saplings. Lutyens wanted slow-growing but massive, long-living trees like banyans, neems and tamarinds. The official horticulturist imported some exotic trees like the Sausage and the African Tulip tree from East Africa. Lutyens talked of designing a city which would meet the needs of its citizens for two hundred years and forecast that one day the English would leave India and let Indians manage their own affairs. I am not sure whether he was like some crazy Englishmen who sided with Indian nationalists, but his wife was known to do so. It was rumoured that she had run away to Madras and was having an affair with a Hindu boy who had been proclaimed a messiah. All I can say is that though I saw Lutyens many times in his office and bungalow I never saw his wife. Also, the English didn't like talking about Mrs Lutyens.

Our first summer in Delhi made us decide that we would make our home there. It was less hot than our desert village and the rainy season was very pleasant. Above all, we were making more money than we had dreamed of. By the autumn we had added more rooms to our home, hired a gardener and a couple of servants. My mother, wife and sons joined us. So did many other families from our village whom we employed as clerks, labour managers and storekeepers. Thereafter we only went back to the village to attend the marriages of relations or the funerals of people we knew.

Exactly a year after the royal darbar there was another. This time it was in honour of the Viceroy and Vicereine formally taking up residence in Delhi. Elaborate arrangements were made for their reception at Delhi railway station and the Red Fort. As in the year before, there were many rehearsals and great precautions were taken to see that no untoward incident marred the solemnity of the occasion. Hailey who was in charge of the arrangements apprehended mischief and had Cleveland of the DID inspect every home and shop that lay on the route to make sure there were no terrorists lurking about. Armed policemen were posted on the roof-tops of Chandni Chowk. I felt that these precautions were overdone because till then I had not met a single Dilliwalla who had anything to say against the English.

As on the royal darbar so on the day of the Viceregal darbar we got up at 4 a.m. This was quite unnecessary as the Viceroy and

Vicereine were not due to arrive till the afternoon. But such was the excitement and anxiety to find a place from where we could watch the procession that we were eager to get there well ahead of time. The morning of 23 December 1912 was cold and clear without a cloud in the blue sky. By the time the sun came up every flower and blade of grass was washed clean by the dew. It was as perfect a start to a day as I had seen since I had come to Delhi.

We set out from the house at 11 a.m. We hired four tongas to take us, our servants, our clerks and their families. Hundreds of labourers and their women kept pace with us as crowds on the road made the going very slow. We dismissed the tongas at Ajmeri Gate and walked through the prostitutes' Chawri Bazaar, Nai Sarak and were in front of the Clock Tower a little after noon. Crowds had already started collecting there. We went down Chandni Chowk to Gurdwara Sees Ganj. The caretakers had been instructed to let in only Sikhs on that day. So we had a balcony facing the Fountain on the other side of Chandni Chowk all to ourselves.

The firing of cannon informed us of the arrival of the Viceregal train. At the railway station, the Hardinges were received by some maharajas; at the municipal buildings an address of welcome was presented to them on behalf of the citizens of Delhi. As the police band which led the procession marched past below us, we knew that the reception at the municipality was over and the Hardinges were on their way. The police band was followed by Highlanders playing bagpipes, Sikh cavalry and other troops. I could not see very far towards the Clock Tower but I saw the line of elephants slowly lumbering towards us. There were over a dozen of them. The viceroy and the Vicereine were on the eighth, the biggest in India, called Gajumat, which had been loaned to him for the occasion by the Raja of Faridkot.

Suddenly the procession came to a halt. A lot of people started yelling at the top of their voices. I am sure I heard a loud bang but I was not sure if it was a cracker or a bomb. The four elephants in the front row stopped some yards away from us. I saw men running away from Chandni Chowk into the side-streets. Those on the roof-tops had disappeared. Some men running down the street on the Clock Tower side were shouting: '*Bhago, bhago* (run,run).' Other words I caught were 'bomb' and '*maar dala* (killed).' Had somebody thrown a bomb at the Viceroy's elephant and killed the

Viceroy, his Vicereine and their attendants?

We were stunned. We did not know which way to turn. If the Viceroy had been killed we knew what would follow. Just a few yards on the left side of the gurdwara separated by a police station was the Sunehri Masjid. It was from this mosque that Nadir Shah had ordered the massacre of the citizens of Delhi because someone had fired on him. The sahibs were slow to anger but once their temper was roused their wrath could be terrible. After suppressing the Sepoy Mutiny in 1857, they had hanged hundreds of people in this very Chandni Chowk and blown up a whole bazaar with its shops and mansions in front of the Royal Mosque. We shut the gates of the gurdwara and collected round the Granth Sahib to listen to recitations of the Guru's words. The city awaited its fate.

We waited till it was dark before we slipped out of the gurdwara. There were no tongas or *ekkas* available and we had to walk home in the dark through deserted streets. My father kept muttering, *Wah Guru! Wah Guru!* all the way.

I could not get much sleep that night. What would happen if the Viceroy had been killed? Would they still go ahead with building a new Delhi? After this experience would the English ever trust any Indian?

It was from the morning paper that we learnt the truth of what had transpired. A bomb had been hurled from the roof of a bank building. It had killed the Viceroy's umbrella-bearer, and grievously wounded the Viceroy who had been immediately taken to hospital by car. The Viceroy's personal servant had also been injured. The Vicereine and another servant on the same elephant were unhurt. The ceremony at the Red Fort had taken place nonetheless with Mr Fleetwood Wilson reading the proclamation on behalf of the Viceroy.

Lord Hardinge who till then had thought of little else but the new city lost interest in the project. It took him a long time to recover from his injuries. He became impatient with Lutyens's grandiose plans and began to turn to Herbert Baker for advice. The Vicereine who did her best to keep up her husband's enthusiasm took Lutyens's side. Then she fell ill and had to be taken back to England for a major operation. She died soon after surgery. By then the papers were full of rumours of a war breaking out in Europe. Who would think of building a city while fighting a war? If

England lost there would be no New Delhi.

In August 1914 England declared war on Germany. Lord Hardinge read the proclamation on behalf of India. Malcolm Hailey sent for my father. His note said that he should bring me with him. He was very friendly and very clear in his message. 'Sujan Singh (that being father's name) you know India is at war with Germany. We will need a lot of fighting men to go to the front. You come from a region which has some of the best soldiers in the country. You go back to Hadali and recruit men for the army. You will be well rewarded.'

My father assured Hailey that he would do his very best and pray to God that England be victorious.

We divided the work between us. I looked after the business in Delhi. My father toured villages in district Shahpur. He did not have much difficulty in raising recruits as there were lots of young lads with nothing to do. They were mostly Baluch Muslims with relations serving in the army. He also managed to persuade some Sikhs to enlist. From our tiny hamlet, Hadali, with barely two hundred families living in it, he raised four hundred and thirty-seven men for war. He sent me their names so that I could show them to Hailey. I had no problem getting more contracts on very favourable terms. Hailey also promised to let us buy as much land in New Delhi as we could afford as the government wanted private people to share the burden of building the new city by opening shops, restaurants, hotels and cinemas.

While the war was on, no major construction work could be undertaken. The Viceroy devoted his energies towards winning the war. He travelled all over India and the Middle East. His mind was also distracted by tragedies that occurred in his family. After his wife's death, his elder son was mortally wounded in a battle in France. Three of his ADCS were killed within a few months.

The war that the British had expected to win in a few months dragged on and on. they were not as invincible as we had come to believe. Although thousands of our men were fighting on their side, we Indians being what we are, we secretly enjoyed the reverses suffered by them. Whenever the topic of war came up, someone or the other would always quote an Urdu poet: 'The English are victorious but it is the Germans who capture territory.'

Lord Hardinge was persuaded to stay on for another six

months after his tenure as Viceroy was over. Lord Chelmsford who succeeded him as Viceroy showed even less interest in the capital project than his predecessor had in his later days. It was also known that Lutyens and Baker had fallen out and did not speak to each other. It was difficult to believe that two of the best-known architects of the world could get so worked up over trivial matters like the comparative levels of the Viceregal palace and the Secretariats and the incline of the road running through the Secretariats to the palace. Lutyens wanted the palace to be on a higher level and the gradient of the road at such an angle that the palace could be seen from a long distance. Baker wanted both buildings to be on the same level with the road rising gently so that the palace came into view when you were halfway up the incline. The matter was put to Hardinge who sided with Baker. It was again put to Chelmsford who took the easier line of agreeing with his predecessor. To me (I was taking private tution in English), it seemed a good example of making a mountain of a mole hill. All that Lutyens wanted was a foot-and-a-half change in the angle of the approach road. They called it 'the battle of the gradient'. It was also an example of building castles in the air as even the foundations of the buildings had not been dug.

The longer the war dragged on the more restive Indian politicians became. They were Banias and lawyers who had not raised their little fingers to help our fighting men but were the loudest in demanding more self-government which would give them greater privileges. Chelmsford being a weak man gave in. He wrote to his government in London that more power should be entrusted to Indians. A thirty-eight-year-old Jew, Edwin Montagu, came to India in November 1917 to study the situation. He stayed nearly six months. Between the two they prepared an elaborate scheme of reforms which came to be known as dyarchy. In the provinces more departments would be administered by elected members; in the centre three of the Viceroy's six councillors would be Indians. The princes were to have a chamber of their own. All this was to await the successful termination of the war.

The war suddenly came to an end in November 1918. It was the time to reap the harvest of rewards promised to us. We did better than we had hoped for. We were granted large tracts of land in the canal colonies of the Punjab. I was given the choice of plots

I wanted to buy in New Delhi. When tenders were invited for the main buildings, I bagged the South Block of the Secretariat, the War Memorial Arch and many clerks' quarters. My father, who was by now an older and a mellower man, was honoured with the title of Sardar Sahib. While he was still alive, I became virtually the head of the family. I let my younger brother look after our lands and properties in the Punjab and devoted myself wholly to building work and making money to realize my ambition of having my own car to drive to the Qutub Minar.

The end of four years of war did not bring peace to India. We had more peace during the war and more turmoil when the war ended. I saw some of it with my own eyes because I had been made an honorary magistrate and was often summoned by the Deputy Commissioner to be present with the police when there was trouble in the city.

A new leader appeared on the scene, Gandhi. He even got Muslims to join Hindus in anti-government agitations. At this time there was a lot of misery caused by an influenza epidemic which killed millions of people and famine caused by a succession of poor harvests. On top of all this Gandhi demanded that since the war was over, the government must give up powers it had assumed for the prosecution of the war. Even more mischievous was his supporting Muslims in their demand that the victorious British keep their hands off the Turkish empire of the Caliph. What did Turkey or the Caliphate mean to Hindus or Sikhs who together formed over eighty per cent of the population of India? But the trick worked. I saw Hindus and Muslims drinking water from the same water booths, marching through the bazaars arm in arm chanting *Hindu-Muslim Bhai-bhai*—Hindus and Muslims are brothers. Muslims invited a Hindu, Shradhanand, to address their Friday congregation in the Royal Mosque. The government quite rightly forbade Gandhi from entering Delhi. The fellow then tried to go to the Punjab where trouble was brewing in many towns and cities including Lahore and Amritsar. This encouraged the Amir of Afghanistan, Shah Amanullah, to plan on invading India. The government dealt with the situation with an iron hand. For three weeks I was on duty almost the entire day and night helping the police disperse agitated mobs. In Amritasar General Dyer fired on an illegal assembly at Jallianwala Bagh killing over three hundred and fifty people and wounding over a thousand. The province was placed under martial law. Mischiefmakers were flogged in public, their properties were confiscated and their leaders exiled. As for Amanullah, before he could mount an invasion, he was toppled from his throne. The years 1919 and 1920 were certainly very bad years for India. But they were the beginning of the realization of my dreams.

Nothing deterred the government from going ahead with building the new city. A narrow gauge rail-line was laid from village Badarpur, twenty miles south of Delhi, ending in what is today Connaught Circus. It was named the Imperial Delhi Railway. It was meant to transport red gravel, sandstone and rubble to the building site. Two huge sheds were raised under which stone-cutting machine were installed; thousands of stone-cutters were hired to chisel stone and marble to required shapes. Over 50,000 men and women from Bangardesh were employed as labourers. My own staff consisted of over fifty *munshis* and accountants and a labour force of over 3000. While politicians did their *buk buk* in their legislatures, often criticizing the capital project as a criminal waste of money, we went ahead raising a new city the like of which India had not known.

By the winter of 1920 the situation had taken a turn for the better. I had my family (by then consisting of my wife, three sons and a daughter) living with me in Delhi though my father had decided to go back and live on the land with my younger brother. Although I could afford to buy a car I was uncertain of my father's reaction—he was dead-set against such wasteful extravagance. Instead I bought a four-wheeled victoria and a horse to take my children to school in Daryaganj and then take me round the different building sites. I seldom got back before 10 p.m. Sometimes after a day's work I would go and visit my friends where I would take a whisky or two and listen to *mujras* preformed by prostitutes from Chawri Bazaar. I would never have dared to do this if my father had been living with me in Delhi.

I built myself a double-storeyed house on Janter Manter Road where half-a-dozen other Sikh contractors had also built their houses. Although I was earning more than them, they spent more on themselves than I. One of them who had got the contract for the supply of stone and marble built himself a palatial mansion of stone and marble bigger than any private residence in Delhi. Another whose father had been a dacoit and was not doing half as well as I, acquired two cars.

One summer I received a telegram from my brother saying that father had been taken ill and I should come over as soon as I could. At the time they were living in Mian Channun where my brother was running a cotton ginning factory and had over two hundred squares of land. He had persuaded the railway authorities to name the nearest railway station after my father as Kot Sujan Singh. I arrived in Mian Channun just in time. It almost seemed as if my father had been waiting to see me before taking his leave from the world. No sooner I went to his bedside, he began to question me about the business. He was short of breath but refused to listen to the doctor who kept insisting he should not strain himself. He broke down and cried that he was leaving my brother and I an uncleared debt of one lakh rupees. We assured him that if that bothered him either of us could wipe it out within one minute by writing a cheque in favour of his creditors as between us we had assets of about one hundred lakhs. 'That may be so,' he replied amid gasps, 'but before leaving the world a person should balance his account by repaying every loan he has taken.' He began to cry because he was very weak. We cried because he was crying. Then he asked everyone save me, my mother and brother to leave the room. 'I want you two brothers to make me a promise in the presence of your mother that you will stick together and share everything no matter what profits or losses the other incurs.' We brothers embraced each other and bowed over his chest to let him put his arms over us. Being a man of the world he added, 'And if you ever decide to partition the family property you will do it amicably without anyone in the world knowing about it. If you have any dispute, you will accept your mother's verdict without question.' My mother who had been pressing his feet all this time broke down and began to wail. 'Don't talk of leaving me. The doctors say you will be all right. The great Guru will give you good health.'

The doctors gave him different medicines but the Guru closed his account book. Half-an-hour later he sat up and looked around as if he wanted something. He opened his mouth very wide as if he was yawning and with a gasp sank back on his pillow and stopped breathing. My mother closed his eyes with her hands and wailed the lament for the dead: 'My light is the name of the one Lord; its oil is sorrow.'

The news quickly spread to the town. Within an hour it seemed as if the entire population of Sikhs, Hindus and Muslims had come to share our grief. Professional women mourners came in groups beating their breasts and singing litanies in praise of the departed. That afternoon his cortege decorated with coloured strips of paper and balloons was led by the town band followed by over 2000 mourners. Mothers made their children walk under the bier so that they could live as long as he. In our family it was customary not to mourn the death of an old person but celebrate it as release from the world's bondage. My father was sixty-five when he died.

I stayed with my brother for the ten days of mourning and then returned to Delhi with my wife and children. A few months later my wife bore our last child, a son. And a few months after that I bought a secondhand car, an Oldsmobile, from an English engineer who was due to return to England in a few weeks. Since he had helped me secure contracts, I gave him the price of a new car for his old one. He more than compensated me by passing all my inflated bills.

I did not know how to drive. I hired a Muslim chauffeur who had a teaching licence to teach me as he drove me to work. I stuck to my resolve that I would drive myself to the Qutub Minar in my own car.

It took me a month to learn how to drive. Being an honorary magistrate I got a driving licence without having to pass a driving test. The great day came. I told my family that we would have a picnic at the Qutub Minar the following Sunday. My wife made great preparations and filled baskets of parathas stuffed with potatoes and fruits. There was enough to feed twenty people. When I took the wheel, we were nearly a dozen in the car. The driver cranked the handle (there were no self-starters those days) and the automobile throbbed into life. My wife and children and maidservant crammed into the rear seat. My head clerk and chauffeur were in the front with me. Four servants, (two on either side) stood on the footboards of the car. We started off with a loud cry of *Sat Sri Akal*. One servant standing beside me blew the bulb horn all the way. We passed by Safdar Jang tomb and hundreds of other ancient buildings strewn about the wilderness near Yusuf Sarai and Hauz Khas. And suddenly the Qutub Minar came into view and everyone shouted, 'Look, there's the Qutub Minar!'

While the servants spread durries in the gardens and laid out the food, we went up the Minar, climbed all its steps and looked down at the ruins lying below us. I came down and walked round the mosque and tried to embrace the Iron Pillar standing in its midst. I did not know much history, the names of the builders or the things based on the place. My elder son told us about the first Muslim city of Delhi, of Qutubuddin, Altamash and Alauddin. I was pleased he had learnt so much in so short a time at school.

We ate our potato-stuffed parathas. The children went round looking at the monuments. I lay on my back on the durri gazing at the Minar which seemed to sway as wisps of clouds blew past it. I wondered how much the contractors had made out of the job. It was obvious they had stolen a lot of stone and marble from older buildings. Did they pass it off as new? Did they have to bribe architects and overseers to get their bills passed? How was it that without cement or concrete they had been able to make buildings last a thousand years? Would the buildings I was making last five hundred years? Would anyone know I had made them? Or would they only be known as the handiwork of Lutyens and Baker and the Viceroys in whose times they were begun or ended. Somehow these thoughts did not depress me because for me it was a day on which one of my ambitions had been fulfilled. I had driven to the Qutub in my own car. Soon I would be able to buy a new car every year. I was well on the way to becoming a rich man, a millionaire. What more could anyone aspire to in Life?

In January 1921, the king's uncle, the Duke of Connaught, came to visit New Delhi. At this time Delhi did not look like an inhabited city. All it had were a few bungalows along broad avenues lined by young trees. The Viceregal palace, the two Secretariats and the War Memorial Arch were well behind schedule. Nevertheless the Viceroy was anxious to commemorate the Duke's visit in some permanent way. So he was asked to lay the foundation stone of the new legislative building which included the Princes Chamber and was to be located close to the Secretariat. It was also announced that new Delhi's main shopping centre half-a-mile northwards of the Secretariat would be named Connaught Place. At the time there was only a circular road without a single building. I was among the contractors presented by the Viceroy to the Duke. The Viceroy had been informed that I had bought more land in the future city centre than anyone else. So he told the Duke in front of me, 'This man is going to build the first shopping arcade, cinemas and restaurants in the shopping centre to be named after Your Grace.' Till then I had no idea what I was going to do with the land. There were not enough people in New Delhi for it to have shops or restaurants. But I knew that so broad a hint dropped by no less a person than the Viceroy was a command which had to be obeyed. As if to encourage me, at the king's next birthday I was given the title of Sardar Sahib.

A few words about the contractors' families. We came from different parts of the Punjab and had not heard of each other till we met in Delhi. I was the only one of them who had been to school and had picked up some English; the others were a rustic lot and few could even write their names in any language. It made no difference. We were Sikhs and began to look upon each other as members of one clan. There were a few Sikh engineers and overseers as well. Although they kept their distance from us and extracted their percentages for passing our bills, they felt a part of us. In times of tension (such as times when Hindu-Muslim riots broke out in the city) we guarded each other's homes. If any of our boys got into trouble with the police we exerted joint pressure to get him out. One afternoon when an eighteen-year-old daughter of a Sikh engineer eloped with her Muslim music teacher, her father alerted the community. We posted our men on every road going out of Delhi and on all platforms of the railway station. Before nightfall the couple were nabbed in a car heading for the Jamna bridge. The girl was handed over to her father to be dealt with as he deemed fit. The Muslim boy was given a thrashing he would not easily forget. To forestall his reporting the incident to the police and claiming the girl had been converted to Islam and had married him as well as getting his fellow Muslims to take up his cause, we told him that we had already lodged a report charging him with abduction and rape. The fellow decided to get out of Delhi as fast as he could.

Sudden wealth creates its own problems. We were far too busy making money to be able to keep our eyes on how our sons spent it. We also derived some pleasure from spoiling our boys. When I say we, I really mean the others, because I was very strict with my sons. While others gave their sons cars to drive about in, I gave my two elder boys bicycles. As a result while my sons went through school and college, theirs went to the bottle and the prostitutes of Chawri Bazaar. The eldest son of one who was a most devout Sikh acquired a veritable harem of women from different parts of India and sired dozens of children through them. Another who had five sons was lucky in having one who was sober who helped him with his building contracts. The others just had a good time going for shikar, having nautch parties and getting drunk. One of them became the most notorious whoremonger of Delhi. He used to boast that he had three different women every day and before he died he would fuck every prostitute in the city. Nobody knew how far he got in achieving his ambition but one night after he had finished with his third assignment for the day he got into a brawl with some Muslims at a paanwalla's shop. One man struck him with an ice pick which pierced his chin upto his mouth. He grabbed his assailant by the scruff of his hair (he was very strongly built) and marched him to the police station. Then he went to the emergency ward of a hospital and had his wound stitched and bandaged. Having done this he walked to his home which was four miles from the hospital. Before going to bed he felt blood oozing out of the bandage and went to the bathroom to wash it off. As he bent into a tub full of water he collapsed into it. His servant found him dead with his head in a tub full of blood. His father did not shed a tear. When I went to condole with him he said without any emotion: 'He died a dog's death. He asked for it.'

My lifestyle changed. I began to wear European clothes. On formal occasions I wore a black frock-coat, grey striped trousers and spats on my shoes. I was amongst the select few Indians allowed membership in the Gymkhana Club. I never learnt to dance and sensed that Englishmen did not like Indians dancing with their women unless they brought their wives to dance with them. My wife, despite my attempts to get her to learn English from an Anglo-Indian woman, failed to pick up more than a few words and would even confuse 'good-morning' with 'good-bye'. As for dancing, she would have sunk into the ballroom floor if asked to fox-trot. I went to the Gymkhana Club once every week to keep up appearances. I offered drinks to English members who cared to accept them. They seldom returned the hospitality. For relaxation I sought the company of Indians. I felt more at home with my Muslim and Hindu friends than with Sikhs. A Muslim engineer had Delhi's most famous singer as his mistress. I found her a flat to live in and was often invited to listen to her singing. Another Hindu friend had the prettiest Muslim girl as his concubine. We often met in her apartment for drinks and a chat. As far as possible I avoided going to parties in the prostitutes' quarter.

Lord Chelmsford was succeeded by a sixty-year-old, Lord Reading, as Viceroy. He had no *picchha* (breeding) being the son of a fruit-seller and a deck-hand on a ship. Being a Jew, he had brains. Also being a Jew he wanted to prove he was more British than the English. When he arrived in India in 1921 there was an agitation amongst the Sikhs to liberate their gurdwaras from hereditary priests. Gandhi and his Congresswallas were also demanding self-rule and the Muslim Moplahs of Malabar had risen against Hindu money-lenders. Reading first invited Gandhi over for a cup of tea to be able to size him up. A few months later he jailed him as well as the two Nehurs, Motilal and his son, Jawaharlal. All of them had called for a boycott of the visit of the Prince of Wales. (Incidentally, with the Prince came the last Viceroy of India, Lord Mountabatten, who became engaged to Edwina Ashley at a party given by Reading). He sent the army to Malabar to crush the Moplahs. Reading was that kind of man: he only befriended Indian politicians to know their minds. However, he couldn't do much to stem the Congress tide. The party swept the polls in the 1923 elections and Motilal Nehru became its main spokesman in the Central Assembly.

Reading was more interested in Indian politics than in the building of New Delhi. Nevertheless, it was during his tenure that the city began to take shape. The Viceregal palace was completed and only needed furniture and fittings. The two Secretariats were in the last stages of completion; so were a large number of bungalows and clerks' quarters. I had built a block of shops with apartments above them and was well on the way to giving New Delhi its first cinema house, restaurants and department stores.

A sense of urgency was given to the building operations with the arrival of the new Viceroy, the forty-five-year-old Lord Irwin. Since he had only one arm, he was known amongst Indians as the *tunda laat*. Being very religious minded, he was also known as the padre. We were told that all the work on the Viceregal palace and the two Secretariats had to be completed by a certain date as the new Viceroy intended to inaugurate the new city. Work went on round the clock in three shifts.

With the Viceroy being so friendly with nationalist leaders we felt that Englishmen and Indians would work hand-in-hand as partners. The real trouble was that the nationalists were split into many factions: some were willing to cooperate with the English; others wanted to drive them out of India, by force if necessary. I was witness to one such attempt.

One morning in April 1929, having obtained a pass, I was seated in the visitors' gallery of the Central Assembly. It promised to be a very lively debate as the Congress party was to open up with all its guns against the passage of the Public Safety Bill introduced earlier by the government to combat terrorism. I was looking down into the hall to see if I could recognize any of the members from their pictures I had seen in the papers. I did not take any notice of the others in the gallery except two young men who took seats on my right. They wore no coat or tie and looked like boys from college. The debate was not as exciting as I had expected. There were a lot of long-winded orations which I could not hear distinctly. I had brought a newspaper with me and began to scan its headlines. Suddenly I heard a loud explosion. I looked up and saw the two young men who had been sitting next to me firing shots at the members. Smoke was rising from the hall and everyone was running towards the doors or taking shelter behind the benches. The visitors' gallery was empty; only I remained seated where I was with the boys shooting into the pit of the assembly. They took no notice of me. I saw one of the boys slapping his gun with his hand. It had jammed or run out of ammunition. Then policemen with pistols in their hands surrounded us. 'Hands up,' ordered an Anglo-Indian sergeant. We put up our hands. The boys smiled at me before handing over their weapons. Since I was an honorary magistrate the policemen recognized me and escorted me out of the building.

What those boys wanted to achieve by killing legislators was beyond me. I knew they would hang for it. (They did for the murder of an Anglo-Indian sergeant committed earlier. Bhagat Singh, Sukh Dev and Rajguru were hanged on 23 March 1931). What I found more appalling was the attitude of the Congress leaders who talked of non-violence in one breath and condoned political killings in the other. Even padre Irwin was disappointed at their reaction. In a statement he said, 'To condemn a crime in one breath and in the next to seek excuse for it by laying blame on those against whom it is directed, is no true condemnation.'

I was out of step with the times. I believed that British rule was good for India; we Indians never had nor ever would be able to run an administration which was just and fair to all communities. But there was no one who seemed to agree with my views. My old mother who had at one time lit incense in front of a picture of Queen Victoria now spent her time praying and spinning her *charkha* and once gave me a bundle of yarn she had spun to be presented to Gandhi. Two of my elder sons when they went to buy material for their school uniform came back with *khadi* (handspun, hand-woven cloth) because Gandhi had proclaimed a boycott of British fabrics. I knew that behind my back my Sikh employees called me a *jholi chook* (one who stretched his apron for alms). Many a time when I was on duty with the police to prevent a riot, the mob yelled *todi-baccha* (son of a toady) and beat their breasts shouting *hai, hai*. I persisted in my belief that the English would stay in India as rulers in my lifetime. I had eaten their salt and was not going to betray them.

Lord Irwin did his best to accommodate the nationalists. At his instance a commission headed by Sir John Simon which included Attlee visited India in 1923. The nationalists organized massive demonstrations against the commission wherever it went. Irwin arranged for Round table Conferences in London to discuss giving India Dominion Status. The nationalists boycotted the first one and sent only Gandhi to the second. They launched one civil disobedience movement after another bringing the country to near anarchy. They talked of *satyagraha* (truthfulness) and *ahimsa* (nonviolence) but gloated over bombings and political murders. The worst example of this was the way they treated a god-fearing man like Irwin. The date for the inauguration of New Delhi had been fixed. Lady Dorothy, the Vicereine, had sent for Lutyens to help her choose the right kind of furnishings, curtains and decor for the Viceregal palace and the kind of flowers to plant in the Mughal gardens. All was ready by the end of August 1931. On 23 December 1931 the Irwins came by train for the inaugural ceremony. I was amongst the dignitaries chosen to receive them on the ceremonial platform of New Delhi railway station. As the train slowed down on its approach to the station, a bomb planted on the track went off. Fortunately it missed the Viceroy's carriage and blew up the one behind it. The Viceroy and the Vicereine looked completely unperturbed and went through the ceremony as if nothing had happened. Ironically it was this Viceroy, Lord Irwin, who had given his heart to India and who chose the words inscribed on the Jaipur column facing his residence:

> *In thought faith*
> *In word wisdom*
> *In deed courage*
> *In life sevice*
> *—So may India be great.*

My rewards came in the form of titles—Sardar Bahadur, then C.B.E., then a knighthood and nomination to the Council of States. I am not sure what Indian nationalists said about them behind my back, but after every award, they turned up in their hundreds to felicitate me with garlands. By now I was regarded as the main builder of New Delhi and often referred to as owner of half of the new city (which was untrue). I was by then living in a large double-storeyed house on Queensway which I had named as I had my earlier house on Jantar Mantar Road, Baikunth (paradise). Top nationalist leaders readily accepted my hospitality. There were times when Sapru, Jayakar and C.Rajagopalachari stayed with me. Gandhi who stayed in Birla House across the road from my new house on the one side and Jinnah who had a house on the other would walk over to discuss political problems while strolling in my rose-garden.

※

Now that I am an old man and have seen all there is worth seeing in life and India being ruled by Indians, the new generation asks me tauntingly, 'What did you get out of a lifetime of licking the boots of the British?'

I am not a man of great learning nor have I read many history books. What I say in reply comes from the heart based on what I have seen with my own eyes, experienced of my own countrymen and the few Englishmen I have known. I have seen the city I helped to build and which Lutyens designed for two centuries ruined in twenty years. We built magnificent buildings which will last for many centuries; they build shapeless, multi-storeyed offices and jerry-houses wherever there is open space and have smothered hundreds of ancient monuments behind bazaars and markets. We laid wide roads; they make narrow lanes on which two cars cannot pass each other. We planted slow-growing, long-living trees which will give shade to our great-grandchildren and their great-grandchildren. They plant quick-growing gul mohars and laburnums which blossom for a fortnight or two and yield neither fruit nor shade. All they want is something to show in the shortest possible time. They have no sense of the past or the future. As for licking British boots, I tell them that if I was given the choice of being born in any period of Indian history I liked, I would not choose the Hindu or the Muslim—not even the short period of Sikh dominance in the north—but the British. I would re-live my days as a builder-contractor under the British Raj.

'Have you no pride in being an Indian?' they sneer. 'Have you no sense of shame praising alien rulers who exploited and humiliated us for over a hundred years? Have you forgotten what they they did to your forefathers after the First War of Independence of 1857? Have you in your generosity forgiven them the massacre of innocents at Jallianwala Bagh in 1919? And the hangings, tortures and imprisonment of thousands upon thousands of freedom fighters?'

'No, I have not forgotten any of this,' I reply as calmly as I can. 'Nor have I forgotten what Indians have done to each other. I can show some of their handiwork in Delhi. Ever seen the Quwwat-ul-Islam next to the Qutub Minar? Twenty-seven Jain and Hindu temples demolished to build one large mosque! Faces and limbs of gods and goddessses hacked off. Tell me of one place of worship, Hindu, Muslim or Sikh which the English destroyed?

Remember Babar raising pyramids of Rajput skulls, the general massacres of citizens ordered by Taimur, Nadir Shah and Abdali! No one was spared, neither the aged nor the new born, nor their mothers. Tell me of a single instance of a massacre ordered by the English. Not even after the massacre of their women and children in Delhi, Lucknow and Cawnpore after your so-called First War of Independence did they touch your women or children. They hanged a few people, levelled some bazaars to the ground. That was all.'

'That was not all,' they yell back at me. 'They treated us like dogs—worse than dogs because they are dog-worshippers. they called us niggers, had their "Europeans only" clubs, "For Europeans and Anglo-Indians only" compartments in railway trains. There was one law for the white man, another for the black.'

I shout back at them: 'There was no justice in India till the British came. There will be no justice in India after their impact has worn off. They gave you freedom to do your *buk buk* against them and only took action when you preached violence. Can you think of another race besides the British who would have put up with your Gandhis and Nehrus preaching sedition against them? If they had ben Germans, French, Russians, Italians, Chinese or Japanese, they would have strung up your Congresswallas on the branches of the nearest trees.'

'If they had tried that their lease would have ben shorter. Our freedom fighters would have booted them out during one or the other of the world wars when they were neck deep in trouble in Europe.'

'Freedom fighters my foot!' I shout back. 'Hired yellers of slogans who spent more comfortable times in jails than in their own hovels. And now want to be compensated with life pensions. Don't talk to me about freedom fighters. They make me sick.'

'You have been brainwashed,' they tell me. They tell me of the great progress India has made since the British were thrown out—'More advance in ten years of independence than in a hundred years of British rule. We produce all the food we need because of the dams and canals we have built. We produce the best textiles in the world; we produce our own cars, aeroplanes, tanks and guns; we can make nuclear bombs, send satellites into space, pick up nodules from the ocean bed; the Indian tri-colour flies in the wastes of Antarctica. Don't you feel a sense of pride in your country's achievements?'

'Indeed I do. Also a sense of foreboding. We are amongst the poorest of the poor, the most ignorant of ignoramuses of the world. We breed like rabbits. Soon we will be more than we can feed, clothe, or shelter. Then we will resume fighting each other like dogs on a dung heap. We are also the corruptest of the corrupt. Everyone from the Prime Minister down to the poorest-paid police constable has his price. And we are more prone to violence than the most violent races of the world. What we saw in the summer and autumn of 1947 when we slew each other like goats unveiled our real nature. You will see much worse in the years to come. Hindus, Muslims, Christians, Sikhs, Buddhists will go on killing each other in greater numbers. Your Ganghi and his *ahimsa* are as dead as . . . . as dead as . . . . Whatever the dead bird is called.'

'Dodo.'

'That's right! Dead as the dodo.'

'So are people like you. The last of your tribe will go with you. India is a great nation, that is the truth. And you may or may not know that our national motto is truth will forever be triumphant—*Satyamev Jayate.*

Bhagmati

Bhagmati's great passion other than me (as I like to think) is mangoes. It's been a good year for mangoes but a bad one for the monsoons. That often happens in Delhi. The first crop of mangoes start coming in from Tamil Nadu some time in April. Fat, pulpy stuff without any character. In May the much-fancied Alfonsos from Maharashtra make their appearance in Delhi's markets. Delicious but murderously expensive. More so since Delhi's foreign community cultivated a taste for mangoes. I only get to taste Alfonsos when some industrialist or minister of government sends me a crate. I send a few to my neighbours in the hope they will return the gift when mangoes from Uttar Pradesh start coming in. These days I have to scout around for more and more mangoes for the way Bhagmati tucks in I wouldn't get to eat any. Without as much as a by your leave she will eat three or four at a time, suck their kernels with great relish till there's nothing left on them. She ends her feasting with a loud belch, washes her hands and face—then proceeds to tie up whatever fruit remains on the table in the folds of her sari to take home. 'I know you haven't paid for them,' she tells me. 'My poor family hasn't tasted a mango this season,' she says as she leaves.

Nothing in the world of fruit compares with Dussehris, Langdas and Ratauls from the orchards of Uttar Pradesh. Of the nearly thousand varieties of mangoes, these are the three I relish the most. Unfortunately they also happen to be Bhagmati's favourites. During the mango season her visits are more frequent. When she comes she makes a meal of my mangoes and takes away what she can't eat. She says they are good for her digestion, the best thing to take for constipation. She is not bothered about putting on weight.

As I said we've had a poor monsoon. In the first week of June I heard the monsoon bird calling. Rain should have followed within a few days. There is news of heavy downpours in other parts of India. The Bombay and Calcutta streets are under water, and floods are devastating Assam. But not a drop in Delhi through June and July. A few miserable showers in August. The bloody songbird of the clouds, the meghapapeeha, hasn't been heard of for the last three months. 'There will be famine,' prophesies Bhagmati tucking into her fifth Langda, 'people will die of hunger in the streets of Delhi.' Then she adds philosophically, 'No matter. People are always dying in this wretched city. If it is not hunger, then it is by cholera, plague, small-pox, murder, suicide. Or old age.'

The Dispossessed

What brought us to New Delhi can be briefly recounted. We lived in a hamlet in the midst of a vast desert. On our east ran the river Jhelum; in the north was a line of barren hills which yielded nothing except rock salt. The rest was sand dunes as far as the eye could see. Hadali had about two hundred families of which at least a hundred-and-sixty were Mussalman and the remaining Hindu or Sikh. Mussalmans owned the deserts and strings of camels. They grew a few blades of wheat and some vegetables near their wells or gathered dates from date-palm trees that grew in the waste. They sent their sons to the army or the police. These sons sent home their earnings, and when they retired, came back to settle in Hadali. We Hindus and Sikhs were tradesmen and money-lenders. We lent money to the Mussalmans. And when they did not return our money with the interest we made them pay it off by serving us. We bought rock salt from the Range and had these fellows take it on their camels to distant cities like Lahore, Amritsar, Ludhiana and Jalandhar. We sold the salt and brought back tea, sugar, spices and silks to sell in our desert villages.

We Hindus and Sikhs lived in brick-built houses and had buffaloes in our courtyards. The Mussalmans lived in mud-huts and looked after our cattle in exchange for a pot of milk a day. We looked down upon them because they were poor. They looked down upon us because we were few and not as big-built as they. Even their women were taller and stronger than our men. they could pull up large full buckets from the well as if they were thimbles. They could carry four pitchers full of water, two on the head and one under each armpit without the least bother. And their men were over six feet tall and made as of whipcord. We were scared of them.

I will tell you of the incident which compelled us to leave Hadali. It took place sometime in the last week of August 1947.

For some months we had been hearing stories of Mussalmans killing Hindus and Sikhs in Rawalpindi and Lahore. We heard that Hindus and Sikhs were fleeing eastwards where there were not many Mussalmans. Then we heard that the Mussalmans had got a country of their own called Pakistan and Hadali was in Pakistan. Some of our elders suggested leaving Hadali and joininig other Hindus and Sikhs who were going to Hindustan. But we had money owing to us, we had our brick-houses and buffaloes in our courtyards. So we decided to stay on till we got our money back and had sold our properties.

I, Ram Rakha, was then sixteen years old. I had a sister, Lachmi, a year younger than I. She had been betrothed to a second cousin since she was born. (This was not uncommon amongst us! Pregnant women often agreed to betroth their children to be born if they were of different sex). My parents felt that it was unwise to keep a fifteen-year-old unmarried girl in the house. The date of marriage was fixed. As was the custom in our village, *bhaaji* (sweets) were sent to most families in the village including those of the Mussalmans. A fortnight before the day fixed for the wedding, the groom's father needing money to feed his guests asked one of his debtors to pay up. And when the fellow said he hadn't any money, the groom's father filed a suit against him. No one had done this before.

The Mussalmans returned our *bhaaji*. This too had never happened before.

We went ahead with the preparations for the wedding. According to custom, my sister spent the last week before her wedding indoors wearing the same dirty clothes. On the seventh day woman of the family bathed her, dyed her palms with henna and slipped ivory bracelets on her arms. They sang songs to the beat of the drum. In the evening Lachmi and her girl-friends went out together to relieve themselves. They were sitting on their haunches defecating and babbling away, when a gang of young Mussalmans surrounded them. The girls were so frightened that they could not even scream for help. The thugs had no difficulty in recognizing Lachmi. A lad picked her up, threw her across his saddle and rode off into the desert.

My father was like one possessed of the Devil. He screamed and tore his hair. He went about the village lanes calling the Mussalmans sons of pigs. He ran thirteen miles over the sand dunes to a police station and lodged a report. He gave wads of rupee notes to the inspector. Next day, he came back with the police with warrants of arrest against the boys he suspected of being Lachmi's abductors. Two days later we went to a magistrate's court. The accused were brought in handcuffs. The rascals twisted their moustaches and made lewd gestures at us. One of them said loudly, 'Let me get back to Hadali and if I don't split the bottoms of all these *kafirs*, my name isn't Turrabaz Khan.'

Their lawyer said that my father's complaint was false as my sister had of her own accord gone away with the boy she loved. He asked Turrabaz Khan to stand up. Then Lachmi was produced. She was wearing a burqa so she could not meet our eyes. 'Yes,' she said, 'I love Turrabaz Kkan and went to him of my own will. I have become a Mussalman and have married him. I do not wish to return to my parents' home.'

The inspector and the police were Mussalmans. The accused and their lawyer were Mussalmans. Our lawyer was a Mussalman. (All the Hindu lawyers had fled to India). The magistrate was also a Mussalman. He dismissed my father's complaint and ordered the accused to be released forthwith. They went out of the courtroom jumping for joy.

We begged for protection. The magistrate sent for the Mussalmans and said, 'You've got what you wanted. Leave the miserable *kafirs* alone.' The inspector took more money from us to escort us back to Hadali. Constables were posted outside our homes for our safety. They also took money from us.

How could we continue to live in Hadali with one of our own flesh and blood being ravished a few doors away? Our womenfolk said they felt unsafe; when they came back from the well, the Mussalmans would wait for them and expose themselves. We complained to the policemen but they did nothing. One evening when a dust-storm was blowing we packed our utensils and quilts, loaded them on our buffaloes and cleared out of Hadali.

We travelled all night and day with hot sand blowing in our faces. We came to Sargodha and found the encampment where thousands of Hindus and Sikhs were waiting to go to India. Our buffaloes were taken away. For many days we lived on stale bread and pickles. Then soldiers came and put us in their trucks. They drove us to Lahore. We passed long lines of people on foot and in bullock carts. Those going our way were Sikhs and Hindus. Those coming from the opposite direction were Mussalmans. We saw many Sikhs lying dead on the road with their long hair scattered about and their bearded faces covered with flies. We crossed the Indo-Pakistan border. There were many more corpses along the road. From the shape of their penises I could tell they were Mussalmans. There were lots of women and children among the dead.

We were sent to a camp in Kurukshetra where more than 70,000 refugees were living in tents. For many days we did nothing except stand in lines for rations and talk to everyone we met. My mother cried all the time calling my sister's name. Then officers came and told us that we must go and look for work. 'What kind of work?' my father asked them. 'We were money-lenders. We have no money to lend.' However he sent a postcard to a Sikh whom he had known as a boy in Hadali. This Sikh was said to have made a lot of money as a building-contractor and had been living in Delhi for many years. Two days later we got his reply asking us to come over. We took the train to Delhi.

In the train my father talked of the days when he and this Sikh had played together on the sand dunes around Hadali. The closer we got to Delhi, the more my father's childhood memories came back to him. I was sure that as soon as they met, my father and the Sikh would fall into each other's arms.

We had to walk six miles from the railway station carrying our utensils and quilts on our heads. With great difficulty we found the Sikh's house. My father asked us to wait at the gate while he went in to find out. He had hardly gone ten paces when an enormous dog charged at him. My father ran back. The dog ripped off a piece of his shirt before he was able to get back to us. A man in khaki uniform came out of the house and demanded angrily what we wanted. My father asked very humbly whether this was the house of so-and-so. 'Yes,' growled the man, 'state your business.' My father showed him the Sikh's letter. 'Wait here,' ordered the man in khaki. The dog stood baring its teeth at us.

The man came back, shooed away the dog and beckoned us to follow him. We picked up our belongings and followed the man. It was a large, two-storeyed house with a big garden. The Sikh and his wife were in the verandah having tea.

'So you've come, Sain Ditta' said the Sikh sipping his tea. My father put down the load on his head and touched the Sikh's feet. My mother slumped on the floor, laid her head on the Sikh lady's knees and began to wail. 'What will you make by wailing? What's happened has happened,' said the lady and told the man in uniform to take us to the kitchen and give us something to eat.

We were told to make ourselves comfortable in a garage. Half of the garage was used to store trunks and crates. The other half was to be our home. We slept on the floor like people who have had a death in the family.

This is how we began our new life in New Delhi.

ॐ

My parents were quicker in getting used to the new surroundings than I. My father was given the job of night-watchman. He had to walk round the house all night with a hurricane lantern in one hand, a stave in the other and yell *'Khabardar ho'* at every corner. He made friends with the big dog which had torn his shirt. The dog kept him company. My father learnt to answer to *'Oi'* and say *'jee'* to the Sikh who had once been his best friend. My mother swept the floors and pressed the feet of the Sikh's wife.

What hurt me very much was the way my parents changed towards me—their only remaining child. I knew the reason. They had spent all their money. My mother's gold bangles and ear-rings had to be sold as my father's wages were not enough to feed the three of us. If I asked for another chappati, my mother would ask, 'Have you a belly or a well?' My father started calling me *mushtanda* (lout). One day both turned on me and told me to go out and look for work. So I was thrown out into the strange world of this strange city.

Where was I to start? My father told me to go to peoples' houses and ask if they wanted a servant. Delhi was full of Punjabi refugees looking for work. Every house I went to had a man at the gate who asked me my business. When I told him, he would order me to move on. I got to know Delhi, both the old city and the new; the big buildings where big officials went to work in their big motor cars and clerks on their bicycles. I got to know all the bazaars and what was sold where. But I found no work. My father got very harsh with me. My mother had to shield me from his temper. I began to come back after dark and slip into the garage when my father was doing his rounds. My mother would then give me food and press my legs till I fell asleep.

I often dreamt of Hadali with its stretch of treeless expanse and the sands on which I used to play on moonlit nights. I dreamt of the tall Mussalman women with pitchers on their heads, the black points of their nipples showing beneath their wet muslin shirts and the joy of being crushed between their legs. Sometimes the dreams turned into nightmares. I saw the Mussalman men menace me with their penises the size of randy donkeys'. I would start moaning. My mother would shake me up, take me in her arms and rock me back to sleep.

My father stopped talking to me. My mother tried to make up for his behaviour. She would ask me what I had seen. 'Why don't you take your mother with you some time?' she would say.

One Tuesday she took permission of her mistress to come with me. I showed her the government Secretariats and the Parliament House. She gasped with wonder as if she was a little girl. She asked me all sorts of questions; I made up all sorts of answers. She made me feel very important. She took my hand when she got nervous of buses and motor cars; she made me feel like a strong, grown-up man. I took her to the Birla temple. She prayed to Shiva and Parbati and Ganesh; to Vishnu and Lakshmi; to Kṛishna and Radha, and then to Rama and Sita and all the other gods and goddesses. She prayed for Lachmi. She waved a copper paisa round my head and gave it to the pandit. She asked him to smear my forehead with sacred ash and bless me so I could get a job.

From the Birla temple we went to the Hanuman temple. There was a large crowd and lots of stalls of sweetmeats, toys, balloons and bangles. Here too my mother gave a paisa to the pandit and prayed to Hanumanji to get me a job. We went round the stalls. She gave me some paise to buy her glass bangles and slip them on her arms.

By the time we left the temple, the sun had set and the sky was like a grey giant about to go to bed. The trees in Connaught Circus were full of chattering mynahs and parakeets. Once more my mother took my hand. We watched well-dressed ladies and gentlemen buying things and driving away in their beautiful motor cars. By the time we got home, it was dark. My father was out with his stave and lantern yelling '*Khabardar ho.*' Although she was very tired, she warmed the food for me. When I lay down, she took my head in her lap and rubbed oil in my scalp. The last words she said before I fell asleep were: 'Surely, one of the gods will hear my prayer and get you a job!'

The gods heard my mother's prayer and the very next morning I got a job. Where do you think I found it? In a house just across the road. That is a story by itself.

The house in which we lived faced a roundabout from which many roads branched off. Across one road was the house of Jinnah Sahib who made Pakistan. Before running away to Pakistan, this cow-eating Jinnah sold the house to a rich Hindu who made it the headquarters of the Cow Protection Society. On the other side across the road facing our garage was an even bigger house belonging to Seth Birla, nephew of the man who had built the temple. This Birla was said to be the richest man in India. There was always a crowd at his gate and lots of policemen. At first I thought that these people were looking for jobs like I was and that there would be no point in my joining them. And I was frightened of policemen. I had heard songs and speeches coming over the loudspeaker and was told that Mahatma Gandhi lived there and anyone could go in to have his *darshan.*

The next morning I went to have Gandhiji's *darshan.* Nobody stopped me. There were many people including white sahibs and memsahibs sitting on the lawn. In the front there was a platform with a microphone. I sat down in a corner. A party of young men came and sat near me.

A few minutes later the Mahatma arrived leaning on a woman's shoulder. Everyone stood up. Some people shouted, '*Mahatama Ghandhi ki jai*'. The young men sitting near me shouted, '*Bharat Mata ki jai* (Long live Mother India).' Mahatma Gandhi sat down on the platform and shut his eyes. A party of men and women began to chant:

> *Raghupati Raghav Raja Ram*
> *Patitpavan Sita Ram.*

I had never heard this song before. It sounded very nice. Then they sang:

> *Ishwar Allah Terey Nam*
> *Sab Ko Sammati Day Bhagwan.*

That also sounded nice. A young man sitting near me muttered: 'Not *Ishwar Allah* but *Mohammed Allah Terey Nam.*'

When the hymn ended, a bearded Mussalman came and sat beside the Mahatma. He opened a book and drew the microphone towards his beard. He began to intone something. The young men beside me began to shout: 'Shut up. . . . the Mussalmans have ravished our mothers and sisters . . . . we will not allow the Quran to be read in our country anymore.' They jumped up and began yelling, '*Bharat Mata ki jai.*'

The Mahatma drew the microphone towards him and in a toothless, frog-croaking voice said, 'Brothers and sisters, I will continue to respect all religions. If you do not agree with me, do not come to my prayer meetings. If you cause interruption, I will pray alone. Go back to your homes and ponder if it is right that our independence should end in this way, in the killing of brother by brother.' He stood up, said namaskar and went away.

Before I knew what was happening , the police surrounded us. I was pushed along and forced to get into a van along with the other boys. They continued to shout '*Bharat Mata ki jai,*' till there was no one to hear them.

The officer-in-charge who was sitting with the driver turned back and said, '*Mahatma Buddhoo* (stupid) *ki jai!*' The young men laughed. The constables and the van-driver also laughed. 'Sub-inspector sahib, don't take us too far,' said one of the young men.

'Wherever you like! But please do not go back to Birla House,' he said joining the palms of his hands, 'otherwise they will slit my throat.'

'Just let us off near the Birla temple; we have no more programmes for the day,' the young man assured him.

We were dropped at the Birla temple. It was then that one of the boys noticed me '*Arre*! Who are you? What troop are you?' he asked. 'I know no *troop-shoop*,' I replied and explained that I was a refugee and had been arrested by mistake. They had a big laugh. 'Why don't you join us?' another boy asked, 'Or are you one of the Old Man's Mussalman-loving disciples?' I told them that my sister had been abducted in Pakistan; how could I be a Mussalman-lover? 'You are a big, strong Punjabi,' said a fellow who appeared to be their leader. 'You should be like a true Kshatriya fighting for the Hindu dharma.' He patted me on my back and felt my muscles. No one had ever called me big and strong before.

They asked me what I did. I told them I did nothing. 'Then come and join the Sangha,' said their leader. 'You can work in the office and eat in our canteen.' I did not know anything about this Sangha but I went along with them. I signed a piece of paper and was given a number (only the leader knew the names of the boys, the rest of us were known by numbers). I was to dust the office furniture and sit outside the door to see that no one who did not know the password for the day came in. I was given a uniform and five rupees as an advance against my salary.

This Sangha which I joined had a long Sankrit name. Every time I said *Rashtureeya*, the boys laughed. Every time I said *Savayam*, they laughed. So I simply called the Sangha by its English initials—RSS.

I gave the five rupee note to my mother. She was very happy. She made some *halva*, gave some to the Sikh and his lady and their servants. She even gave a palmful to the dog. My father stopped taunting me.

I used to leave home early in the morning and dust the furniture. Then I got into my uniform and lined up with the boys. Our leader hoisted the saffron flag of the Sangha. We saluted it by holding our hands across our chests. This was followed by an hour of drill and wrestling. We were taught how to fight with sticks. They told us we would soon have guns and be taught to shoot. In the afternoon we had lectures on Hindu dharma and history. They told us of the greatness of Aryavrata, the land of the Aryans. They told us how the Mussalmans had come and destroyed our temples and massacred millions of innocent Hindus, abducted and raped Hindu women; how thousands of these noble Hindu women had burnt themselves on funeral pyres rather than be dishonoured by the Mussalmans. They exhorted us to fight for our dharma, cleanse Bharat of the unclean *maleechas*, Mussalmans as well as Christians, who were also foreigners and ate our sacred cow-mother.

What right had the Mussalmans to be in Delhi or anywhere else in India when they had driven us, Hindus and Sikhs, out of their Pakistan? Why could we not take away their women and property as they had taken ours and send them packing to Pakistan or *gehennum*? Such questions were put to us every day.

One day the chief sent for me. 'Are you number 840?' I came to attention and saluted. 'Is it correct that your sister was abducted in Pakisan?' I replied, *'Jee haan.'* 'Are you going to do nothing about it? How long will you keep sitting with one hand on the other?' I did not know what he wanted me to do. I replied, 'Sir, 840 can make a present of his life. He has nothing else to offer.' The chief smiled. 'We Hindus only know how to give our lives, not how to take the lives of others! It must change. Are you prepared to lead an attack on the Muslims of Delhi? Remember what they have done to your sister!'

Blood rushed into my face. I again sprang to attention, saluted and said, 'Number 840 is ready to lay—ready for any sacrifice.'

The chief had a paper in front of him. he read out some numbers. 'These boys will be with you. When you are ready for action, you will report to me. I shall see that the police do not come in your way.'

I saluted and left the room.

The real problem was to find out who was Muslim and who was not. As soon as the Mussalmans of Delhi heard what had happened in Karnal and Ambala and Amritsar and Jalandhar, they burnt their red fez caps and furry Jinnah topees and started wearing Gandhi caps instead. They shaved off their beards, gave up wearing sherwani coats, loose pyjamas and learnt to tie dhotis round their waists. Their woman stopped wearing burqas when they went out and started to put red dots on their foreheads and say namaste. The only way we could tell if the fellow was a Mussalman was to see if his penis was circumcised. How could we stop everyone and say, 'Show me your cock?' We could not go into action without careful planning and preparation. We began by marking Muslim homes and shops with swastikas. Muslim goondas got to know of this and put swastika marks on Hindu shops and homes. We changed our plans and decided to attack a few well-known stores owned by Muslims and watch the results. There was a big one in Connaught Circus in the centre of New Delhi. The chief approved of the plan and suggested a date for its execution.

As the day came closer I began to get nervous. I wanted all the Mussalmans to be dead but I was frightened of killing one. I wanted to run away from Delhi. There was no one I could talk to about the things going on in my mind. If I confided in my mother she was sure to kick up a fuss and tell my father or the Sikh lady.

The evening before we were to go into action I went home early. My mother was in the garage shelling peas for the Sikh's kitchen and talking to the dog which was often with her. I lay down on my mattress. '*Vey Shambia!*' (his name was Simba), you have not seen my Lachmi, have you? Well, if these evil Mussalmans had not taken her, she would have been here with us. You would have seen her married. You would have seen the fireworks and heard the bands. But her kismet!' She slapped her forehead with both her hands and began to cry: '*Hai Lachmi! Hai beti*! Where are you! May the accursed Mussalmans who took you go to hell.' The dog came to her, sniffed in her ears and began to whine. My mother put her arms round its neck and hugged it. This was too much for me. 'Why do you cry mother?' I asked her. 'I will teach these Mussalmans a lesson for what they have done to our Lachmi.' After that I could not back out, could I?

I slept very poorly but was up before dawn when the jeep came to pick me up. The other boys were already at the headquarters. We said a short prayer, had tea and biscuits and were driven to Connaught Circus. I posted the boys at positions I had selected earlier and showed them the exact spot where the jeep would await us after we had done the job. We compared the time on the watches that had been given to us and I told them to look out for my signal. I had a sharp-pointed steel rod tucked inside the sleeve of my shirt.

I strolled along leisurely in the inner colonnade of the Circus. I saw shop-owners arrive, mumble prayers and unlock their shops. The Muslim store we had selected was still shut but four attendants were waiting outside. I passed by them. Despite their Gandhi caps, I could tell from their speech that they were Muslims. I had hardly gone a few paces when I saw a car mount the pavement opposite the store and pull up under a tree. One of the boys who recognized the owner dropped a small cane he was carrying to indicate 'this is our man'. I took my position behind a pillar in the colonnade. The man put up the window-panes, locked the car, tried the handles and then sauntered across the road. He was a paunchy man, about forty years old. He was dressed like a fashionable Delhiwalla: muslin kurta with gold embroidery down the middle; white, baggy trousers stiff with starch. He carried a silver betel-leaf-case in one hand, a tin of cigarettes and a matchbox in the other. A half-smoked cigarette dangled from his lower lip. He walked like a pregnant woman. The boys emerged from their places: three from one side, three from the other. I awaited my quarry. As he crossed the road and stepped into the colonnade, I came up behind him. The attendants bowed and said: '*As-Salaam-Valai-Kum.*' He nodded his head. He handed over his betel-case to one of the attendants and put his hand into his pocket to get the keys. I drew the steel rod from my sleeve and lunged it in the middle of his back. '*Hai Allah!*' he screamed as he fell back on me. His eyes were wide with terror. I pulled out the rod and let him drop to the pavement. I blew my whistle. The boys fell upon the attendants. '*Bachao* (help); police; *mat maro* (don't kill),' they screamed. No one came to their help. Within a matter of seconds five Mussalmans lay on the pavement in puddles of blood, groaning and writhing. We smashed the plate glass of the store-windows and rushed in. It was a shoe-store with other kinds of leather goods: bags, belts and wallets. I picked two large suitcases and stuffed them with whatever I could lay my hands on. I cleaned up the owner's table which had a small radio set, a silver calendar and some fountain pens. By then many other people—chowkidars, peons, students were in the store taking whatever they could find. We took our haul to the jeep. By that time the whole of Connaught Circus was in turmoil. Hindus and Sikhs began attacking Muslims and looting their shops. Police vans went around in circles, constables ran about blowing their whistles. We had no difficulty in getting away.

My hands and knees shook as if I had fever. My heart thumped against my chest—*dhug, dhug, dhug*. I could not talk. When we reached the headquarters I lay down on a charpoy. They gave me a mug of tea and two aspirin tablets. I put a cushion on my face to blot out the scene I had enacted. It was of no use. I saw the whites of the eyes of that Mussalman I had murdered. My ear-drum resounded with the scream, *'Hai Allah.'* It went on and on and on till I was exhausted. I was not able to stand on my feet till the afternoon. Then I had a bath and felt better. I examined the things I had stolen. I put aside some things to take home and put the rest back in the other suitcase. I took the things to Sadar Bazaar. Since many Muslim shops had been looted I could not get very much. Nevertheless I came back with more than a hundred-and-fifty rupees. The radio alone fetched me a hundred.

On my way home I bought a flashlight for my father and a coloured muslin dupatta for my mother. I also bought some fruit and a small tin of clarified butter. I waited till it was dark so that no one in the Sikh's house would see me come in with my big, new suitcase. I went straight into the garage. My mother was baking chappaties on an earthen stove.

I told my mother that I had spent my month's wages to get these things. I spread the dupatta on her shoulder. She hugged me and cried. She heard my father's footsteps and ran out to get him. She was so excited that all she could say was *'Vekh, vekh* (See, see).' I took the lantern from my father's hand and gave him the flashlight. He was like a child with a new toy. He pressed the button and played the beam on the walls of the garage. They tried out the shoes, patted the wallets and the suitcase. They were very happy.

I could not sleep. I was afraid of shutting my eyes. I was frightened of the ghost of the man I had killed. He kept on crying, *'Hai Allah'* in my ears. I waited for the crunch of my father's footsteps on the gravel and his cry, *'Khabardar ho!'* to reassure me that I was safe. I began to shiver and moan. I pretended I was having a nightmare. My mother woke up and asked me what was wrong. I moaned louder. She came over and took my head in her lap. I put my arms round her waist and feigned sleep. She rubbed my back. After a while she lay down beside me. My shivering stopped. I felt warm and safe and unafraid. I tightened my arms round her bosom, put my right leg over her and drew her closer to me. Then I fell asleep.

৯

The morning after the killing I complain that my bowels are loose and stay at home for the next five days. In any case I could not have gone out because riots have broken out in different parts of the city. The Muslims are being flushed out, their properties are being looted, their shops and businesses are being taken over and their homes occupied. They are fleeing in the hundreds of thousands to Pakistan. Those that remain are herded into the Purana Qila and the big mosques. The first battle for Delhi has been won. But much more remains to be done. We have to fight these Mussalman-loving Hindus like Gandhi and Nehru, drive out the remaining Muslims to Pakistan and wipe out all traces of Islam from our Bharatvarsha.

Gandhi is our enemy number one. He says: 'Get out of the mosques and Muslims' homes.' I want to ask him: 'Oi Old Man, if we get out of their mosques and homes, where are we to live? On the pavements? It does not behove you who lives in Seth Birla's palace to talk like this.'

Nehru is our enemy number two. He calls us *goondas*. I want to ask him: 'Oi Pandit, where was your police and your army when Mussalman *goondas* were slitting our throats?'

Sardar Patel is our friend. 'They are not thieves and dacoits but love their country,' he says. Only to please Gandhi and Nehru he adds that we are 'misguided'. The police are also our friends And why not? Most of the new police are refugees from the Punjab. They know the truth about the Mussalmans and are not beguiled by the Gandhi-Nehru *bakvas*.

One day the Sangha chief says to me, 'We must know what this Gandhi fellow is up to. Number 840 you will attend the Old Man's meetings and report what he says and who comes to see him.'

I am given money to buy a white Gandhi cap, a thick, handspun khaddar shirt and trousers and a woollen shawl. I start going to Birla House in the early hours. I take down the names of people who come to the meeting. I make note of all the *buk buk* I hear about Hindus and Mussalmans being brothers.

I learn to imitate Gandhi's voice. When I report what I have heard I use the same toothless, gummy Gujarati-Hindi: 'I am waiting for the direction of the inner voice . . . straining my ear to catch the whispering of the inner voice and waiting for its command.' Everyone roars with laughter. I can also imitate his gestures. I sit cross-legged, wrap the shawl over my head and continue: 'I am in a furnace. There is a raging fire all around. We are trampling humanity underfoot . . . I am groping for light.' I strike a match to show how. 'I can as yet only catch faint rays of it.' I bring the match close to my nose. 'When I see in full blaze the *dosti* (friendship) of Delhi then it will really become *dili* (rooted) in the heart.' They double over their bellies. The boys rename me Gandhiji Maharaj. They say that if the Old Fellow had been a member of our Sangha he would not have got a more appropriate number than mine; 840 is twice 420 which is the section of the penal code defining fraud—and Gandhi is a double fraud.

The Sangha chief tells us that we should gird up our loins because soon war will break out between India and Pakistan. We must finish Pakistan once and for all and plant the saffron flag of Hindu dharma on the Khyber Pass.

Our chief is right. Pakistani tribesmen invade Kashmir. Every day we expect India to declare war on Pakistan. But Gandhi goes on croaking about peace and love. As if that is not bad enough he says India owes pakistan a lot of money and must pay up at once.

Gandhi fasts every Monday. That day he also keeps his mouth shut. Instead he grins at everyone who comes to see him and scribbles notes on bits of paper.

Monday morning, January 1948. It is very cold and since it is the Old Man's day of silence, instead of going to Birla House, I stay snugly wrapped in my quilt till the sun is up. Then I bask in the sunshine and feel good. I have a mug of tea and a stale chappati, then saunter across to Birla House. Old Gandhi is in the garden soaking in the sun and scribbling something. His secretary, Dr Susheila Nayar, is seated on the grass by his chair taking charge of scraps of paper he hands to her. I like Susheilaji. She is fair and buxom, her hair is curly and she has dimples in her cheeks. Although she is much older than me, I would like to make love to her. She reads something the Old Fellow has written, jumps up as if a wasp has stung her on her big buttocks. She runs and tells her brother, her brother tells someone else who tells someone else till everyone knows about it. A meeting is summoned and Susheilaji reads out a statement on behalf of the Old Man. Tomorrow, when he opens his mouth, he will begin a fast to death.

I can't remember everything that was said but it was about two kinds of fasting! You may fast if you are fat; or you may fast if you have done wrong to someone and want to punish yourself. The Old Man wants to fast because we have done wrong to the Mussalmans. He says he's been feeling impotent of late. He's been brooding over it for three days and knows that if he fasts he will become potent again. He says, 'No man, if he is pure, has anything more precious to give than his life. I hope and pray that I have that purity in me to justify the step. God sent this fast. He alone will end it, if and when He wills.' Whatever he says about God, it is clear he doesn't want to die. He says if there is a re-union of hearts between Hindus, Sikhs and Mussalmans he may change his mind and start eating again.

I take a taxi to the headquarters.

They have heard the news over the radio. 'Let the Old Man die; Hindu dharma is eternal,' says the chief. 'But we must watch the situation very carefully.' 'You,' he says pointing to me, 'you must remain on duty at Birla House and report everything immediately. Take a taxi if you have to.' (Thank you for that! Six to seven rupees for me for the next few days, I calculate). 'We must organize demonstrations to counteract the mischief of these Gandhi followers.'

I get back to Birla House.

The crowd is bigger than ever. The regulars strut about looking very important; besides them there are lots of others including whites and some Negroes as well. Though it is still Monday, Gandhi is yakking away. I push through the crowd and get nearer him. Lots of chaps scribbling in their notebooks. Lots of questions to flatter the Old Man to show how concerned they are.

His son, Dev Das, is also there and the two go at each other. The son calls the father impotent. The father calls the son's thinking impotent and superficial, then tells him to mind his own business. You can see the father and son don't like each other. Gandhi does not like any of his three sons.

'I claim that God has inspired this fast,' repeats the old humbug many times to many people. 'No human agency has ever been known to thwart nor will it ever thwart Divine Will.'

I do not think this is worth reporting so I go home to get a good night's sleep.

Next morning there are more policemen and soldiers about Birla House than ever before. And more newspaper chaps. And Nehru and Patel and Maulana Azad and Sheikh Abdullah of Kashmir. I gather they are planning demonstrations in Gandhi's favour. I rush to the headquarters, make my report and am back in Birla House.

There is a prayer meeting at 11.30 a.m. It begins with the Old Man's (and my) favourite hymn:

He who feels the pain of others
Is truly a man of God.

Susheilaji sings something in English. I don't like the way she imitates white women's *whoo, whoo, whoo*. Then comes the hymn about God being both Ishwar and Allah. The Old Man speaks into the microphone. He tells the Muslims he is fasting for them. He tells the Kaskmiris he is fasting for Kashmir. And he tells God he is fasting because God told him to fast. Even now he is on lime and orange-juice.

In the evening our chief sends three busloads of refugees to Birla House. They march up from one end of the road chanting '*Khoon ka badla khoon sey lengey* (We will avenge blood with blood).' Nehru looks up but says nothing. They chant: '*Gandhi Buddha murdabad* (Death to Old Gandhi).' Nehru becomes like one possessed of the jinn. He rushes towards them flailing his arms. 'Who dares to say Gandhi *murdabad*?' he demands. 'Let him who dares repeat those words in my presence. He will have to kill me first.' He vents him temper, glowering at everyone. Then he drives off in his Iimousine, followed by a jeepload of armed policemen.

I slip into Gandhi's room. He is lying on a charpoy, wrapped up in a shawl with only his bald head and face showing under the light of the table-lamp. The room is full of people. He asks, 'What are they shouting about?' Susheilaji replies, 'Gandhi *murdabad*!' and brushes a tear off her cheek.

Gandhi says, 'Ram, Ram, Ram' and hides his face under his shawl. So passes another day.

The next morning the Old Man is brought out on a charpoy so

that the crowd can see him. The crowd shouts, '*Mahatma Gandhi ki jai.*' He joins the palms of his hands and bares his gums. He doesn't look like a man who has not eaten anything for two days.

The entire government of India is now on the lawns of Birla House. Pandit Nehru and his ministers sit on chairs round a table. They decide to give Pakistan thirty-five crore rupees so it can buy guns and bullets to kill Hindus. They go to Gandhi and say: 'We have done what you wanted us to do, now will you give up your fast?' He shakes his head and replies, 'No, not yet. I want much more. My sole guide, even dictator, is God, the infallible and omnipotent.'

ॐ

The Ganga has begun to flow in the opposite direction—upstream from the sea towards its source in the mountains. That is the only way I can describe what is happening. Three days ago we were driving the Muslims out of Delhi and everyone was with us. Now the Muslims are coming back to Delhi and everyone seems to be against us. People who looted Muslims' shops come to Birla House to give up their loot; men bring women they abducted to Birla House and ask them (the women) to forgive them in front of Gandhi. Men who spilled Muslim blood cut their own hands and with their own blood sign petitions asking Gandhi to give up his fast. Everyone is going Gandhi-mad. An old sahib, who has been editor of an English paper, starts to fast and says if Gandhi dies, he will also die. How can anyone fight this kind of madness?

The chief wants me to be at Birla House all the time because something big is to happen. He has given me his residence telephone number so I can ring him at night. As soon as the sun goes down it turns very cold. I curl up on a sofa in the verandah. I have my pullover and coat, warm socks and a shawl over me; yet I shiver so much that I cannot keep my teeth from chattering. The Old Man rises at 3.30 a.m. The sky is black and full of stars. Lights are switched on. Hymns are followed by silent meditation. The old fellow gets to work. I can see him under the light of his table-lamp picking up one letter after another and mumbling something which a fellow takes down on a piece of paper. This goes on for some hours. Then the Old Man has his Bengali lesson. What is the point of learning a new language if he really means to die? By then the sun is up and the sunshine streams into the verandah. I stop shivering.I try to get a little sleep. But there is so much jabbering around me that I have to get up. The doctors are examining the Old Man. They give him orange-juice and waggle their heads. The Old Man joins the palms of his hands and sends them away. You take it from me it is all a put-up show, a tamasha.

The Old Man is his own doctor. He takes no medicines or injections or anything. 'The name of Rama is my nature cure,' he says. It is taken down on paper by a dozen scribes. It is, as I said before, a put-up tamasha.

Hymns, recitations from the Ramayana, the Gita, the Quran and the Granth go on all day. And all day there is a continuous stream of people with the sorrows of the world on their long-drawn, stupid faces. Nehru is in tears. He says if Gandhi dies, India's soul will die with him. Maulana Azad is in tears (later in the day he blabbers to 1,00,000 people for one hour. He loves his own voice).

In the evening the Lord Sahib Viceroy Mountbatten, his Lady Sahiba and Missy Baba come to Birla House. The Old Man makes some joke about his fast bringing the mountain to Mohammed. The tall handsome Maharaja of Patiala comes and says he saved thousands of Muslims. The Old Man does not believe him. The Nawab of Malerkotla comes and says he saved the lives of thousands of Sikhs and Hindus by threatening to kill ten Muslims for each Sikh or Hindu killed. The Old Man believes him.

Everyone in Delhi has turned a Mussalman-lover. A procession of 1,00,000 come to Birla House chanting:

Hindu, Muslim; Sikh, Isaee
Bharat mein hain bhai-bhai.

They yell, '*Mahatma Gandhi ki jai.*' Hotels, cafes, shops close down. It is like a big holiday. I tell you it is Delhi's biggest tamasha of all time.

On the sixth day of his fast, the Old Man complains he can't piddle. I would like to ask him: 'What happened to all the orange and lime-juice you drank?' He babbles as if only half-awake. The radio says he is dying. Thousands turn up as if their real fathers were dying. They tell him that they have been fasting with him—their fathers, mothers, wives and children too. They submit petitions saying they will not molest Muslims; they will get out of mosques and Muslims' homes, even welcome Muslims returning from Pakistan.

They bring Muslims from wherever they can find them, put garlands round their necks and parade with them in the streets. They force tea and lemonades and sweets done the Muslims' throats. They form Peace Committees. The chief says if everyone is going mad, we should also pretend to be mad. The RSS puts its name down on the Peace Committee. The Old Fox is only waiting for this. As soon as he hears that the RSS has joined the Peace Committee he agrees to give up his fast.

It is Sunday, 18 January. It is also the birthday of Guru Gobind Singh, the last of the Sikhs' ten Gurus. The Mussalmans had killed his father, his sons, thousands of his followers and then murdered him. We had planned to celebrate the day by driving every remaining Muslim out of Delhi. Our chief had said, 'Once we start it, the Sikhs are sure to join us.' But as I said, the Ganga is flowing the wrong way. There are hundreds of thousands of Sikhs at Gurdwara Rikabganj where the Guru's father's body was cremated a hundred-and-seventy-two years ago. Amongst them are hundreds of Mussalmans paying homage to the Sikh's holy book. The Old Fox says it is an auspicious day and since he's got what he wanted he is going to break his fast. At 12.45 a.m. he takes a glass of orange-juice from the hands of the goatee-bearded Maulana Azad, says 'Ram, Ram' and drinks it up. The hypocrite! So the work we have done over the months, the blood we have spilled is undone by the Old Man in six days!

You can see how he enjoys his victory! Nehru comes running to congratulate him. He replies: 'Live long and continue to be the *Jawahar* (jewel) of India.' He has the sahib editor rung up to give up his fast because the battle has been won. In the afternoon, Mussalman women draped in their tent-like burqas arrive in shoals and say, 'We've been fasting with you.' The old fellow grins. 'Oh, have you? Let me see your faces. No woman veils her face before her father. I am your Bapu.' The burqa flaps are thrown back. The old lecher has a good look at the sallow-faced Mussalmannis . 'This shows what real love can do,' he says, very pleased with himself.

He rubs more salt in our wounds. He tells us Hindus and Sikhs to read the Quran.

In the afternoon the sky clouds over and it begins to rain. The gods in heaven shed tears at the fate of Bharat.

કે

I don't remember who started it but the boys are saying that the gods desire human sacrifice before they will restore dharma to its rightful place. The chief says that such honour is reserved for a Karmayogi who the Gita says must act without expectation of reward. What reward can anyone expect for such sacrifice except the gallows? However none of the Delhi boys is considered good enough for the task. One tried and failed.

It is two days after Gandhi has given up his fast. The prayer meeting is over. The Old Fox is at his usual *buk buk* about loving everyone including those who hate you and poke your mothers and sisters. There is a loud *puttaakha*. It must be the fart of a passing motor car, I say to myself. But there is smoke and Gandhi *chelas* running about as if Hanumanji has set fire to their tails. 'Listen! Listen everybody!' screams Gandhi. 'If we panic like this over nothing, what shall be our plight if something really happens?'

No one listens to the Old Man. They run as fast they can. I run too, out of Birla House, get into a taxi and tell the driver to take me *phuta phut* to the headquarters. When I tell them about what happened, all the chief says is '*Buss*, that's all?'

He orders that all the papers in the office should be burnt immediately and he orders me to return to Birla House and not budge until summoned. 'More is yet to come. Victory to the Hindu dharma,' he intones.

કે

Gandhi talks a lot about his 'inner voice' and God telling him everything. But he does not know anything about the explosion. He thinks it was the police at target practice. As a matter of fact it was one of our boys aiming at a target which happened to be the Old Man himself. He is a Hindu refugee from the Punjab. His name is Madan Lal Pahwa. The police had thrown him out of a mosque in which he had been staying since he had come out of Pakistan. Pahwa threw a bomb. He had another with him when a policeman caught him.

The next day Gandhi says that Pahwa probably looks upon him (Gandhi) as an enemy of Hinduism and himself as an instrument sent by God for his removal. He requests the police not to harass Pahwa but to convert him to 'right thinking'. I want to tell the Old Fellow there is no 'perhaps' about it. He *is* the enemy number one of the Hindus.

ও

Gandhi wants to be different from everyone else. On 26 January everyone goes to see the great parade. Gandhi says he does not like parades and stays in Birla House. I take the day off and take my parents to see it. It is a wonderful tamasha! Thousands of soldiers come down the slope between the Secretariat left-righting; hundreds of tanks, guns, armoured cars follow and rumble through India Gate. They salute Nehru. Nehru salutes them. Airplanes streak across leaving trails of coloured smoke in the sky. Then Nehru tells us that India is the land of Gandhi; India does not believe in tanks, guns, armoured cars or airplanes but in *ahimsa*.

Gandhi does not like a military tamasha because he has his own special kind of tamasha. The next day he announces he is going to the tomb of Qutubuddin Bakhtiyar Kaki near the Qutub Minar in Mehrauli. It is this Kaki fellow's death anniversary. Kaki had come to India some 600 years ago and converted many Hindus to Islam. Hindu refugees from Multan drove away the Mussalmans and settled in Mehrauli. They broke the marble screen around Kaki's grave. But when they hear Gandhi is coming they line the road and shout 'Hindu-Muslim bhai-bhai' and serve tea to the Muslims. I am so angry that I want to yell: 'Bastards! Have you forgotten how your mothers were raped in Multan?'

Gandhi bows to Kaki's tomb. The Mussalmans ask him, 'Repeat our *fateha*.' Gandhi raises his hands, recites: 'In the name of Allah, The Beneficent, The Merciful.' That makes him a Mussalman, does it not? If a Hindu were to kill him he would be reducing the population of the enemies of Hinduism by one.

Gandhi asks the Muslims to forgive the Hindus and Sikhs for breaking the marble screen. He tells them he has heard some very good news. One-hundred-and-thirty Hindus and Sikhs have been massacred by Mussalmans at Parachinar near Peshawar in Pakistan. He says it is good news because the Hindus and Sikhs showed 'non-violent courage.' I say *shabash*! Do you need any more evidence of Gandhi being our greatest enemy?

A man who has escaped a massacre of Hindus and Sikhs at Gujarat railway station tells the Old Fellow: 'You have done enough harm. You have ruined us utterly. You ought now to leave us at once and retire to the Himalayas.'

'I cannot retire at anybody's orders,' replies the Old Man. 'I have put myself under God's sole command.'

'No,' insists the refugee. 'It is through us that God speaks to you. Our minds are crazed with grief.'

'My grief is not less than yours,' replies the great hypocrite.

How could you put sense into the skull of a man who keeps saying, 'I am right, everyone else is wrong. Muslims are right, Hindus and Sikhs in the wrong.' It is Friday. The date, the 30th of January. The day, the month and the year (1948) are printed on my mind like my name Ram Rakha is tattooed on my right arm.

I am sleeping on the sofa I have been using for the last many days. It feels like the coldest night of the year. The lights are switched on at 3 a.m. I get up. I slap my arms across my chest, jump up and down to get the ice out of my limbs. I go and defecate in the dry water drain outside the house. I wash my bottom at a hydrant in the garden and rinse my hands with mud. I tuck them under my armpits to prevent them from freezing. I go to see what the Old Man is up to. I say namaskar. He looks through his glasses and smiles at me. He drinks a glass of hot water spiked with honey and lime-juice. Then another glass of orange-juice. He tells people that he will live to be a hundred-and-twenty-six. That's all he knows of God's ways.

Before the sky turns grey he goes through his routine of hymns, recitation from holy books and meditation. With the sun come the crowds. It is a regular mela. Morning turns to afternoon. The crowd becomes bigger. Sardar Patel arrives with his daughter Maniben. He has a scowl on his face. She is pale, thin as a stick and looks as if she has never known a man or how to laugh. They spend a long time arguing about something with the Old Man. Gandhi who is never late is ten minutes behind time.

When the Old Man comes out for his afternoon meeting he seems very happy. And why not! He has one arm resting on one girl, the other on another. Both girls are young and pretty. He jokes with them. His jokes are very silly. One girl gives him a carrot. 'So you are giving me cattle-food!' says he. Everyone laughs.

He pulls out his watch from the fold of his dhoti. 'I am late by ten minutes. I hate being late. I like to be at the prayer punctually at the stroke of five,' he says.

I edge up closer to him. I like being close to him because I get into the pictures in the newspapers and show them to my mother. People stand up to greet him. Someone shouts '*Bolo, bolo*'; others respond '*Mahatma Gandhi ki jai*'. The Old Man grins and says namaskar.

And then everything happens so quickly that I have to go over it again and again to make sure I really saw it happen. A stout, young fellow muscles his way through the crowd, pushes aside a girl who tries to stop him, bends down as if to touch Gandhi's feet, draws a revolver from the fold of his dhoti and before anyone can guess what he is up to pumps three bullets into the Old Man, *thah, thah, thah.*

Gandhi's hands remain joined as if he is bidding namaskar to the world. He says, Ram, Ram. Then he crumples down in a pool of his own blood.

A fit of madness comes over me. I jump on the man and bring him down. I tear the hair off his scalp; I bash his head on the ground and call him all kinds of names: mother-fucker, dog, bastard, son of a pig. A policeman grips me by the neck, pushes me aside and grabs the fellow. There is a lot of confusion. I jostle my way out of the crowd and run away. I start crying—running and crying, crying and running. I sit down on the pavement and slap my forehead with my hands and yell *hai, hai, hai.* A crowd of people gather round me. They ask me very kindly: 'Son, why are you crying?' I look up at them through my tears and reply: 'My Bapu is dead.' They make clucking sounds of sympathy. One says, 'You must be brave. You must stand by your mother. You must carry on whatever work your Bapu was doing.' Then he becomes more serious and asks, 'How did your Bapu die? Was he very ill?'

'No, he wasn't ill at all, I killed him with my own hands, I killed him.' Then I slap my forehead and yell, *'Hai, hai,* I murdered my Bapu.'

Bhagmati

Budh Singh is very angry with Gandhi and his *dhoti-topee* gang as he describes the Mahatma's followers. They want the British out of India. Budh Singh wants them to stay. He is setting up a British Retention League. He has invited H.M. the King of England to become its chief patron. He has nominated me as honorary treasurer and designated my apartment as the headquarters of BRL. He has started a signature campaign and proposes to send a scroll of a million Indian names protesting the transfer of power from the King to the *dhoti-topeewallas*.

So far he has only succeeded in persuading Bhagmati. She can't write so he's made her affix her thumb impression against which he has inscribed her name, sex and profession. Bhagmati—Sex: neutral *Hijda*; Profession: prostitute. Proudly he displays the scroll to me and asks me to be the second signatory. I try to reason with him. I tell him all the events he wants changed took place a long time ago and there is nothing he can do about them. He looks at me as though I am mad so I decide to adopt his line of thinking and try and deflect him using an argument he will understand. I say: 'The British themselves want to leave India. Didn't you read in the papers that they will give Muslims their Pakistan and go away on the 15th of August?'

'That is all *buk buk*,' he retorts with disdain. 'This Lord Mountbatten is a Gandhi *chela*. I have written to Buckingham Palace about his mischief.'

'He is related to the king. His nephew is married to the king's daughter.'

'It is the traitor within who brings down the castle.'

'Don't you want India to be free?'

Budh Singh hasn't given the problem much thought. He mumbles in his beard: 'What freedom? Freedom for what? Loot, kill. Everyone talks freedom, freedom—don't know what freedom means.'

The doorbell saves me from Budh Singh. 'Let me think over it,' I say and go to open the door. It is my friend the Sikh journalist. Before he can explain the aims and objects of the British Retention League to my visitor, I gently push Budh Singh out. 'Another time, after I've had time to think. One should not decide such important matters in a hurry.'

The Sikh journalist is a joker. He tells me an old joke as if it were the latest one. 'When Rama, Sita and Lakshmana were leaving Ayodhya for their fourteen year exile, the citizens came to see them off. At the city gate Ramachandraji begged them to return to their homes: "Ladies and gentlemen, thus far but no further." The citizens obeyed his orders and went back. Fourteen years later when the exiles returned to Ayodhya they met a party sitting outside the city gates. "You did not give us permission to return to our homes," they said. "You only allowed the men and women to go back. We are neither because we are *hijdas*." Sri Ramchandraji was so overcome by their devotion that he blessed them: "In the year 1947 I grant you *hijdas* the empire of Hindustan."'

He bursts into loud laughter, 'Ha, ha, ha.' I join him, 'Hi, hi, hi.'

The doorbell rings again. It is Bhagmati. 'What is the big joke?' she asks me.

'You tell her,' replies my journalist friend, looking at his watch 'I must go to the Coffee House at 11 a.m.' And breezes out of the apartment.

'What was he saying?' demands Bhagmati as she flops on the sofa. How can I tell her?

આ

After the rains come months of dew and mists. Every dawn when I set out for a game of tennis I have to wipe dew off the windscreen of my car. The duster turns soggy and black with soot. One morning I return home to see Budh Singh sitting on his haunches with his head between his knees. He looks up. His eyes are bloodshot. He glowers at me with murderous intent. 'What is the matter, Budh Singh?' I ask him in as kindly a tone as I can manage.

'My eyes have come,' he mumbles wiping them with the back of his hand.

'You should see a doctor.'

He takes no notice of my suggestion and puts his head back between his knees.

I go into my apartment. My cook is lying on the carpet and groaning. 'What is the matter?' I ask him.

'My body is breaking.'

I ring up the doctor. His home-clinic is in the neighbouring block. He comes over, takes one look at Budh Singh and pronounces, 'Conjunctivitis, everyone in Delhi is getting it.' He prescribes on ointment.

Then he asks the cook to open his mouth and say 'aah'. The cook opens his mouth and says 'Aah'. The doctor turns up his eyelids and peers into his eyes. He sticks a thermometer in his mouth. Temperature: 102 degrees. He asks him if he is having loose motions or vomiting. 'No,' replies the cook. 'My body is breaking.'

The doctor turns to me and says, 'It is not hepatitis or cholera; lots of it around in Delhi. It is probably malaria or dengue-fly fever or perhaps viral fever. Everyone in Delhi is down with something or the other. I'll have to examine samples of his blood, urine and faeces to make sure.'

He prescribes analgesic tablets for the cook, malaria preventive pills for me. I fork out one-hundred-and-fifty rupees for the visit. I go to the chemist, get the prescriptions and hand medicines to Budh Singh and the cook. I tell them to stay in their quarters. 'These diseases are very catching. Don't come back till you are well.'

I have the apartment all to myself. It would be nice if Bhagmati were to come over. We could have some nice conjunctivitis together. Probably the bitch has already contracted one or the other ailment from her diseased patrons.

After a cold shower, I make myself a mug of Ginseng tea and get down to the newspapers. First, I pick up *The Hindustan Times*—Delhi's worst paper with the largest circulation. I start with page four which is largely devoted to obituaries and in memoriams. In Delhi all demises are sad and untimely. When their time is up, Delhiwallas do not simply die, they go up to their heavenly abode with reassurances from the Gita that death is no more than a changing of garments: the body (which wears garments) perishes, but the soul does not as it is eternal. So good care is taken that their earthly remains are consumed by fire at Nigambodh Ghat or at other crematorium. Delhi's dead consume a sizeable forest of timber every day as they proceed on their onward journey. The only takers for the electric crematorium which costs less than a quarter of the expense of disposal by wood are the dead of the anglicized rich or the unclaimed bodies of beggars. The right bank of the Jamna from the Tibetan colony at Majnoon ka Tilla to Raj Ghat where Gandhi was cremated has been consecrated to viharas, temples, burning ghats, the electric crematorium and memorials for the famous: Nehru, Shastri, Charan Singh, Sanjay Gandhi, Indira Gandhi and the original Gandhi, Father of the Nation. The Jamna riverside has become the launching pad for the journey into the unknown.

Back to page four. A boxed item says Nigambodh Ghat has been inundated by the flood waters of the Jamna. People should take their loved ones elsewhere. Perhaps for the first time, the electric crematorium will be earning dividends. I have nothing much to do. So I decide to take a look before joining my cronies at the Coffee House, I go by Purana Qila to the Ring Road. I leave the regional Headquarters of the World Health Organization (WHO) on my left, the prime cause of Delhi's ill-health, the filtration plant, on my right. Its four chimneys belch smoke all round the clock and provide WHO brochures their best illustrations for environmental pollution. They shower Delhi with soot. Its filtered water gives Delhiwallas Delhi belly, hepatitis, cholera, dysentery and other intestinal disorders. From the top of the overbridge I catch a glimpse of the Jamna licking the lower road of the old iron bridge and rolling its muddy waters past Gandhi's *samadhi* and the Velodrome. At the roundabout near the bridge is a police barrier: the bridge is closed to vehicular traffic. I turn round and drive into the electric crematorium. Sweepers are busy sweeping the road and the hall. Three corpses of beggars are put on a wheel-borrow behind the building to await disposal when bookings have been taken care of. The clerk in the office looks at his wrist-watch and asks me, 'Has the body arrived? There are three bookings for the morning. I've fixed them an hour apart.'

I tell him, I am not a mourner, just a *tamashbeen* (a sightseer). He gives me a dirty look and says acidly, 'If you like this kind of tamasha, take my job.'

I get out of the crematorium just in time. Coming in from the other side is a hearse laden with wreaths followed by a long cavalcade of cars with military markings. Old soldiers also die.

The Coffee House is crowded. My journalist friend and our political adviser have their faces covered with their newspapers as if they are not on talking terms with each other. I join them, they put down their papers. 'Say brother, where have you been all these days?'

I tell them of the number of relations and friends down with viral fever and conjunctivitis. And my servants.

'You are lucky you haven't got AIDS,' says the Sikh journalist. 'Knowing what you are upto with all these foreign cunts, you'll be the first Delhiwalla to get it.'

'Thanks,' I reply, 'you look out for yourself. It's sods like you who get AIDS. Straight sex does no harm to anyone.'

'Do you have anything else besides sex on your minds?' reprimands the politician. 'Here in Delhi people are dying like flies and all you can think of is sodomy and fucking foreign women. Are you one bit concerned about the future of your city?'

'No,' we reply in a duet. 'As far as I am concerned it can go to hell,' I add. 'It is no longer the Delhi I grew up in and loved. You Punjabis who invaded us in 1947 have buggered it out of shape.'

'Be more serious,' he advises me. 'We had no choice in 1947 except coming to Delhi. It is the others coming in every day who are creating the problems. Do you know 70,000 pour into Delhi every year from all over India? As if Delhi is the nation's orphanage. Where are they to be found homes, schools, hospitals? Do you know thirteen lakh Delhiwallas shit in the open because there are no lavatories for them?'

'You start a movement restricting shitting to once a week,' suggests the journalist, 'I promise to put it on the wire service.'

'It's no use talking to fellows like you—absolute waste of precious time,' says the politician getting up. 'Mark my words,

Delhi is a dying city. The more it has of people like you, the sooner it will die. For this prophecy, you pay for my coffee,' he says as he strides off.

૨ล

Life has gone by faster than I thought possible. When was it that I found Bhagmati lying on the road under the noonday sun? How many times had we lain together? Countless. And in between while she had plied her trade, I coupled with scores of women from countries known only to the Secretariat of the United Nations. Today I can recall only a few names and faces. I am not ashamed of what I did but can do no more. Bhagmati does not seem to mind my diminishing appetite for her. Her visits have become rarer and rarer. From dropping in once in two or three months when she needed money, for the last three or four years she has visited me only on Diwali. She no longer talks of her *hijda* husband (perhaps he is dead) or of sex but of Ramji and of Hindu temples and Muslim dargahs she visits. (Despite the years she consorted with me she has never displayed more than a cursory interest in Sikhism; she has certainly never bothered to go inside a Sikh gurdwara). She says she would like to spend her remaining years on the banks of the Ganga at Hardwar or Varanasi. At times she also talks of going on Haj (or is it Umra?) to Mecca and Medina. 'If only I could tear myself away from the lanes and bazaars of Delhi,' she says. 'But I think I will die in Delhi. Sometimes she adds, 'I hope you will take my ashes and throw them in the Ganga.' At others she says, 'Buy a two-yard plot of land near the mausoleum of Hazrat Nizamuddin for my grave.' I tell her that I am likely to go before her and she should throw my body into the Jamna. Both of us know that we may not hear of the other's demise till months after it has taken place.

Budh Singh has turned very hostile. After the incident of 'eve-teasing', he sank into deep melancholia. I took him to the mental ward of the Medical Institute. The doctor gave him some electric shocks which upset him very much. He was more upset at the doctor's suggestion that I should have him admitted to an asylum in Agra or Ranchi. Budh Singh snapped out of his melancholia and turned aggressive. He called the doctor *bahinchod* and nearly hit me when I restrained him from hitting the doctor. He sits in front of my apartment and growls at me every time I come in or go out. He has made friends with the Bhai of the gurdwara behind my apartment and the two have devised ways of torturing me. The Bhai switches on his microphone at full blast at four in the morning and starts chanting prayers with the loudspeakers turned towards my bedroom. When I remonstrate with him, he tells me to mind my own business. Once when I reported him to the police, he told the sub-inspector that it was the wish of the *sangat* (congregation) and who was I to object? His only *sangat* was, and is, Budh Singh. When the sub-inspector left , the Bhai warned me that the next time I reported him to the police he would get Sant Bhindranwale's followers to put me on the right path. Budh Singh yelled: *Sant Jarnail Singh Bhindranwale zindabad!'*

My cook-bearer went on his annual leave and never came back. I have to fend for myself. Living alone is not so hard as I thought it would be. Between and electric kettle and toaster I make tea, boil eggs and eat toasted sandwiches. The Bhai's loudspeaker wakes me up at 4 a.m. I make myself a mug of tea and go into my study where the Bhai's unmelodious voice cannot pursue me. I switch on the BBC news at 4.30 a.m. Thereafter I can choose between the Bible Society's Service in Hindi or the morning service from the Golden Temple in Amritsar. I usually opt for the Golden Temple because I am familiar with the morning hymnal. Perhaps suppressed religiosity is rearing its head. Perhaps I will make my peace with the Great Guru as the time of confrontation with Truth draws near.

As the light comes on I go for a walk in Lodhi Gardens. Most of the walkers here know each other. Some deign to answer my namaskar. Back in my apartment I make myself another mug of tea and a couple of pieces of toast. I read the papers while the sweeper woman sweeps the floor. Then I do not know what to do. I cannot afford to run my rickety old car more than a couple of miles a day; but I have to drive it a little to keep the battery going. At times I run it to the Coffee House. It is not much fun to hear people say: 'This old man has been coming here for over fifty years.' I spend my afternoons at the India International Centre library of which I fortunately took a life membership in my more affluent days. Sometimes someone asks me to join him over a cup of tea. There is always some lecture, cinema show or dance-recital which I can attend free of charge. So pass the long evenings. On my way back to my apartment I buy chop suey or seekh kabab from a take-away joint in Khan Market. The only thing I really look forward to is whisky (now, alas, Indian stuff) which I sip listening to old tapes of ghazals of Mehdi Hassan or Iqbal Bano or Farida Khanum. I sleep badly. I am beset by nightmares. What will happen if I am taken ill? There is not one to look after me. It would be nice if I went one night in my sleep and next morning the sweeper girl found me dead in my bed. She could take everything she wanted from my flat: transistor radio, cassette player, watches, clocks, ball-point pens, cash and deposit them in her home before she came back and screamed that the old man was dead and would somebody do something about him. It wouldn't be too bad if a thug broke into my flat and did me in. It would save a lot of people a lot of trouble. And save me all the bother of finding a bed in hospital and paying doctor's bills.

Days go by. I am less and less awake when I get out of bed and drag myself to my study. One morning I kicked the stool on which I keep my electric kettle. I was lucky—only a few drops of boiling water fell on my foot. At times I doze off listening to the *keertan* from the Golden Temple. It is becoming a bore. I listen to it because at that hour there is nothing better to tune into. Ever since that fellow Bhindranwale started spouting hateful wards against Hindus from the precincts of the Golden Temple, something seems to have gone out of the *keertan*. The Bhai and Budh Singh call him a saint. I feel a lesser Sikh because I think he is a *bhoot* (incarnation of Satan).

On the first of June 1984 the morning service from the Golden Temple is somewhat erratic. I am not sure whether the tabla drums have been put too close to the microphone or it is something else. The beat sounds like gunfire. Papers say that the army has been ordered to get Bhindrawale dead or alive; perhaps it is trying to frighten him to surrender. Mrs Gandhi has been assuring the Sikhs that she will never order the army into the Temple. Sensible woman! She knows that mounting an invasion on the Temple will turn it into a bloody battlefield. No Sikh will ever forgive her.

I read newspapers more carefully. And listen to the morning services more intently. The 3rd of June is the anniversary of the martyrdom of the builder of the temple. Thousands of pilgrims have come from distant villages to bathe in the sacred pool.

I can hear the hubbub of their voices behind the *keertan*. And the crying of babies roused from their slumbers. And their mothers bribing them with their breasts to keep silent. Roars of *Wah Gurus!* during the invocation include women's voices. Foolish people! What are they doing in the Temple with Bhindranwale's men and the army trading shots! Curfew has been imposed on the city. Punjab has been handed over to the army and sealed off from the rest of the world. On the morning of the 5th of June I hear gunfire more clearly than the *keertan*. The next morning there is silence. Papers carry triumphant headlines: 'Tanks of the Indian army blast Bhindranwale's stronghold.' The BBC says well over a thousand including Bhindranwale have been killed. The bullet-ridden corpses of women and infants-in-arms float in the sacred pool. What made Indira Gandhi do such a stupid thing?

A deep depression enters my soul. I ask myself over and over again, am I Sikh? I am certainly not the Bhindranwale brand nor the gurdwara Bhai brand. Bhindranwale was loonier than Budh Singh. I cannot remember when I last went to a gurdwara. I have not prayed in fifty years.

On the morning of the 6th of June I go to the gurdwara behind my apartment. There is quite a crowd. Many are in tears. Their tears bring tears to my eyes. I am one of them. At the end of the service, the Bhai makes a short, fiery speech. 'We Sikhs never forget or forgive. Remember what we did to the Afghans and to Massa Ranghar? We desecrated their mosques and cut off Massa's head. That's what some son of the Guru will do to these demons. You wait and see,' he says. Great boasters, these Sikhs! They live in the past and refuse to understand that in a civilized society you don't desecrate mosques or cut off people's heads.

The Bhai and most Sikhs seen on the road have taken to wearing black turbans. After a few days I also have a couple of my turbans dyed black. Yes, I am one of them.

Budh Singh has turned more rabid. Everytime a Hindu passes by my apartment he yells: '*Sant Bhindranwale zindabad.*' They laugh at him. If he is too absorbed in himself, they provoke him: 'O son of Bhindranwale! Let's have the slogan again!'

So passes the hot summer. And the torrid months of rains and clouds we call the monsoon. September gives way to October. And comes the autumn season of festivals.

◆

It is the last day of October. I am in low spirits. No reason whatsoever. Slept soundly. Long relieving fart while peeing. Pee no longer a powerful jet but an intermittent spray. Enlarged prostate. To be expected when you are seventy. A mug of hot Ginseng and bowels as clean as the inside of a gun barrel. News no worse than other days. Weather has changed for the better—neither too warm nor too cool. Fragrant madhumalati and hibiscus about the windows in full flower. Two chorizzias on the lawn covered in pink and white. Moonbeam hedge along the face like a green wall speckled with stars as in the milky way. Dew on the grass sparkling like diamonds in the early sun. What more can Allah do to assure me that He is up there in His heavenly abode and pleased with His handiwork?

My spirits refuse to lift. Read the headlines of papers and toss them in the grate. Stretch my legs on a *moorha* and doze off. Dream of Bhagmati. Since she has become a once-a-year visitor she makes up by often coming into my dreams. We haven't had sex for the last ten years but in my dreams she is still very bawdy and very lusty. I wake up with a start. Bell rings non-stop; thumping on the door. Bhagmati? I run up and upon the door. It's Budh Singh. Eyes madder than ever; nostrils flared. He yells in my face sending a spray of spit from his beard to mine: 'Indira Gandhi shot dead! Long live Sant Jarnail Singhji Bhindranwale!'

Budh Singh is becoming impossible. I try to shut the door. He sticks out one foot and prevents me from doing so. 'You think Budh Singh mad? You think Budh Singh lie? Listen to radio BBC.' He turns about and marches off swinging his arms and yelling: '*Khalistan zindabad! Indira Gandhi Murdabad! Sant Bhindranwale amar rahey.*' I switch on my transistor. All India Radio Stations merrily play film music, programmes for farmers, youth of the land. Half-an-hour later I get the BBC. Indira Gandhi has been shot by her Sikh bodyguard and has been rushed to the All India Medical Institute. There will be no official statement on her condition till President Zail Singh and her son Rajiv Gandhi return to Delhi.

Indira is unlikely to survive the volley of stengun fire and pistol shots pumped into her frail body etc. etc.

I sit in my chair. Head between hands. Dazed. Look blankly from bookshelves to ceiling, ceiling to bookshelves. The bell rings again. I tiptoe to the door and peer through the Judas Hole. Not Budh Singh but the Bhai of the neighbouring gurdwara. I open the door. He dips his hand in a bowl he is carrying and takes out a palmful of flour pudding. *'Pershad,'* he says, 'the desecration of the Golden Temple has been avenged. The Sikh *Panth* has won a victory. Indira *kutti* (bitch) is dead.'

Without replying I slam the door in his face and return to my chair. Celebrating the murder of a frail, little woman! What have the Sikhs come down to? If only the stupid woman had owned up her mistake, gone to the Temple and said, 'My Sikh brothers and sisters I am sorry, I made a big mistake, forgive me,' they would have forgiven her. But to get one demented monk and his gang of armed goons she let the army slay a thousand innocent pilgrims: grey-beards, blackbeards, no beards, women and babies-in-arms. Blasted the Akal Takht, seat of Sikh spiritual and temporal authority. Let the army loot cash, utensils and burn down the archives. In short, to kill a rat, she pulled down the house. One crime is followed by another. One lie by a bigger lie. The entire country pays the price for these blunders and lies.

I fiddle with my transistor switching from All India Radio to the BBC, to the Voice of America to Radio Germany to Radio Moscow. AIR says she is still alive. The BBC and the Voice of America say she is dead. Moscow simply quotes Delhi. Hours pass. Not a soul on the lawn in front. Not a soul on the road facing the gurdwara. A few buses run by without their usual hooting, a few cyclists hurry homewards bent double over their handlebars as if facing a strong wind. An eerie quiet spreads like a pestilent fog.

The shadows lengthen. The newspaper boy shoves *The Evening News* under my door. Banner headlines: 'Indira Gandhi Shot by Her own Sikh Guards.' One of them has been killed; the other badly wounded. At the All India Medical Institute, teams of surgeons are taking out bullets and pumping in blood into Indira Gandhi's body and trying desperately to save her. Stale news. By then most foreign radio stations are saying she died on the operating table. What now?

The bell rings. Followed by slapping on the door. I peep
through the Judas hole. Some fat old woman I cannot recognize in
the dim hallway light. She bangs on the door with her fist. I open
the door. It is Bhagmati. Sparse hair daubed with henna. No teeth.
Squashed mouth. Hair-bristle about her chin. Is this the same
Bhagmati I had lusted after most of my lustful years? 'Hai Laam!
Hai Laam!' She says with her toothless mouth. She holds her ears
with her hands, sticks out her yellow tongue, 'Toba! Toba! what I
have seen with my own eyes, may no one ever behold! They are
killing every Sikh they see on the road, burning their taxis, trucks,
scooters. Connaught Place is on fire. They are looting every Sikh
shop, office, hotel. And you are sitting here waiting for them to
come and kill you! Hain? I am going to take you to Lal Kuan.
Nobody will bend a hair on a *hijda's* head. *Chalo*,' she orders.

'Patience!' I tell her as I open the door to let her in. 'If they are
killing every Sikh they find, how do you think we will get to Lal
Kuan? It is best to stay where you are. The police is bound to stop
it in time.'

'Police?' she asks contemptuously. 'Those *bahinchods* are with
the mobs. "We give you thirty-six hours to finish every Sikh in the
city," they tell them.' She sinks down on the sofa, covers her face
with her hands and is convulsed with sobs. It is my turn to comfort
her. I put my hand on her shoulder, 'It can't be all that bad. This is
a civilized country,' I tell her.

She looks up with her tear-stained eyes. 'You want to see it
with your own eyes? Come up on the roof and look.' She takes my
hand and heaves herself up from the sofa. We climb up the four
storeys of my apartment building and go on the roof. She points
northwards towards Connaught Circus. The sky is aglow: not with
electric lights but with flames. In the dusk I can see clouds of smoke
rising from different points. I look around in other directions. There
are bonfires and smoke on many roads. 'Sikhs' taxis and trucks,'
Bhagmati informs me. The evening breeze wafts across the voice
of crowds roaring in unison, 'Indira Gandhi zindabad (Long live
Indira Gandhi). Sikh hatyaron ko khatam karo (finish the murderous
Sikhs).' A mob is moving up the road towards my apartment.
Bhagmati panics. 'Chalo, chalo,' she screams. 'I'll cut your hair and
beard quickly. Then we can get out safely. All they can burn will
be your books. They are of no use to Dilliwallas.'

'Don't be silly,' I snap, 'Nobody is going to cut my hair or beard.' I follow her down the dark staircase back into my apartment. There is no time to unscrew my nameplate; I get an iron rod, stick it in the space behind the door and the plate and wrench it off. It breaks into two. 'Now no one will know who lives here.'

'You are a stupid Sikh!' she exclaims angrily. 'They will ask your neighbours. Do as I tell you. Let me cut your hair and beard and we can go to some hotel or something.'

'No,' I yell back stubbornly. 'Let them do their worst. I'll kill one or two before they get me.'

'And me. You stupid, old *buddha bewakoof*! Will you ever get sense in your head?' I am not used to being abused by Bhagmati. My temper rises. Our argument is silenced by the mob yelling somewhere behind my back garden. We slip out into the dark garden and watch through the thick hibiscus hedge. The mob is composed of about fifty young boys armed with iron rods. Some have canisters of petrol in their hands. They surround the gurdwara and storm in. They drag out the Bhai and beat him up with their fists and rods. He cries at the top of his voice: '*Bachao! Bachao!* Police!' They shout back: '*Bhindrawale key bacchey* (son of Bhindranwale)! Ask your father to save you now.' They bring out the Granth, its canopy, carpets and durries, heap them up in a pile and sprinkle petrol on it. One puts a match to it and the heap bursts into flame. The Bhai's hair is scattered over his bloodied face but he pleads, 'Do what you like to me but don't dishonour the holy book. *Rab da vaasta* (for God's sake).'

'Let the bastard go with his holy book,' shouts someone. They pour petrol over his hair , splash it on his beard and push him on the flaming pile. He shrinks and crumples into a flaming corpse. They yell triumphantly: '*Indira Gandhi amar rahey* (Indira Gandhi is immortal).'

My knees buckle under me and I sit down on the wet grass. I cannot hold my bladder. Bhagmati sits down beside me and massages my back. After a while she helps me stand up and whispers in my ears, 'Let's go indoors before they spot us.' I stay rooted to the ground and peer through the bush. I see a fellow reading something from a paper in his hand. He points to garages owned by Sikh mechanics. The mob moves to the garages. Cars lined outside for repairs are set on fire. Garage doors smashed open. People watch them from their balconies. Someone pleads, 'These cars belong to Hindus; the Sikh mechanics have fled. If you set fire to the garages, the whole building will catch fire. We are only Hindus, Muslims and Christians here. Why don't you go to the taxi-stand?'

That makes sense to the mob. It makes its way past the Bhai's funeral pyre towards the cab-rank. I can hear the exchange of abuse. The cab-drivers are defiant. I stagger to the other side of the garden with Bhagmati tugging at my arms and pleading with me to get back into the room. Six unarmed cabbies face an armed mob which has grown to over two hundred. Abuse changes to hurling of stones. A posse of armed constabulary watch the unequal combat without moving from their places. Stones smash into the cab-drivers kiosk and the window-panes of the cabs. The fellows nevertheless keep the mob at bay. A shot rings out and a driver crumples down beside his cab. The other five run away as fast as they can. Armed police form a ring round the cabs, take out wallets, transistors, cassette players. Then they let the mob set them on fire. The policemen direct the mob to sikh shops in the market. They move away from my apartment. Bhagmati tells me to change my trousers. I feel ashamed of myself.

Pins and needles down my legs. Bhagmati stares vacantly at the wall without saying a word. I get out my last bottle of Scotch (which I had kept for an emergency) and pour out a stiff one. 'The best thing in times of trouble,' I announce to her.

'And nothing for your old *buddhia* woman?' asks Bhagmati. 'I have never touched the stuff; but today give me poison or give me wine.' I pour her a generous portion and mix it with Campa Cola to sweeten its taste. She gulps it down as if it were a glass of buttermilk. A glow spreads over her wrinkled, toothless face. 'More,' she orders.

'Not so fast, you'll get sick.'

I help myself to a second, a third. She eyes me banefully while she shakes her empty glass. I take a fourth and give her another smaller one. 'Don't gulp it down; learn to drink like a lady.'

'Lady be buggered!' she replies. She is her old self. 'What's happened to that mad Sikh you had? What was his name? Buddhoo or something like that.'

'Budh Singh. He was around this morning. Raving like a

734

lunatic. If these fellows lay their hands on him, they will make a seekh kabab of him. If he comes round, we must lock him up in a room.'

I empty a packet of cheese crackers on a plate and put it before her. 'This is all I have at home,' I tell her. She picks up one and feels its texture. 'How can I eat wooden biscuits? I have no teeth.' She soaks one in her scotch and cola till it turns soggy and pops it in her mouth. She eats up the entire packet without bothering to find out if there is anything left for me. In any case I have no appetite for food. I tell her to sleep in my bed while I sleep on the sofa. She accepts my offer and waddles into the bedroom. A few minutes later I hear her belch, snore and break wind.

I switch on my radio and tune it to foreign stations. All give detailed news about Indira Gandhi's assassination at the hands of her own Sikh bodyguards. And very briefly talk of anti-Sikh violence. Only Radio Pakistan talks of hundreds of Sikhs massacred and hundreds of gurdwaras burnt in Delhi. The telephone rings: 'Is that you?' it asks. 'Yes.' The caller proceeds to abuse me. 'Bloody bastard you murdered your mother.' I hit back. 'Bloody mother-fucker, bastard yourself. You murdered your Bapu Gandhi, who are you to *buk buk*?'

The abuse upsets me. The telephone rings again. This time it is someone very polite. 'Don't drink water out of your tap. It's been poisoned by the Sikhs.' He puts down his receiver.

A few minutes later another ring. 'Trainloads of dead Hindus massacred by Sikhs in Punjab have arrived in Delhi. Hindus will avenge these killings.' Again the receiver is put down before I can say a word.

I sit and wait for the phone to ring again. It is dead. At midnight there is another hubbub. Slogans, yelling, people running from somewhere to somewhere. Everyone is awake. Another truckload of boys arrives. They burn another couple of cars and disappear. People peer through their windows to see the conflagration. Policemen armed with rifles stop by for a few minutes and then walk away.

Fatigue overtakes me and I doze off in my chair. I am woken up by the sound of shouting coming from the side of the gurdwara. I get up with a start and run out into the garden to see what is going on. It is early dawn but everyone seems to be on their balconies and at their windows looking at the gurdwara. Bhagmati comes heaving herself along as fast as she can and shouting at me.

'Get inside,' she screams. I ignore her and peep through the hedge.

I see Budh Singh in the gurdwara courtyard beside the smouldering ashes of the Granth and the Bhai. He has a *kirpan* in one hand and is whirling about like a dancing dervish, yelling abuse at a gang of young men armed with steel rods who have surrounded him. 'You *madarchods,* you *bahinchods,* may your seed be destroyed! You burn our holy book. May your Vedas and Shastras be burnt!'

The young gangsters play a cat and mouse game with him. They take turns prodding Budh Singh in the back with their rods. The old fellow is getting tired. He can't fight so many men. As he pauses for breath, an iron rod crashes on his shoulder and brings him down. His kirpan falls out of his hand. One fellow picks it up and pokes it in his bottom. Two lads pounce on him and pin his arms behind his back. One takes out a pair of scissors and begins to clip off budh Singh's beard. Budh Singh spits in his face. The fellow slaps him on the face, catches him by his long hair and cuts off a hunk. They've had their fun. They get down to serious business. A boy gets a car tyre, fills its inside rim with petrol and lights it. It is a fiery garland. Two boys hold it over Budh Singh and slowly bring it down over his head to his shoulders. Budh Singh screams in agony as he crumples down to the ground. The boys laugh and give him the Sikh call of victory: '*Boley So Nihal! Sat Sri Akal.*